IN THE
SHADOWS
OF GODS

IN THE
SHADOWS
OF GODS

Adam Kristos Radley

an apocalyptic novel

LIBERTY HILL PUBLISHING

Liberty Hill Publishing
2301 Lucien Way #415
Maitland, FL 32751
407.339.4217
www.libertyhillpublishing.com

Paperback ISBN-13: 978-1-66283-659-6
Ebook ISBN-13: 978-1-66283-660-2

Dedication

To all the teachers who carefully and diligently execute the duties and responsibilities of an educator of our youth, you are few and far between.

Table of Contents

Preface

All books are religious. Not all books are eternal, and not all books are true. This book will never be a bestseller. It is something of an experiment in literature. It does not fit neatly into any one genre. I suspect it is too deep for atheists, and too down-to-Earth for Christians. So, who will read it? For those wanting a feelgood story where nothing bad happens, that's not real, and you will not find it here. For those wanting a gritty, action-packed survival story where characters continue breathing for as long as possible, at all costs, and for no reason, that story would be as pointless as the lives of the characters; you too will be disappointed. It is my hope that you find this book both entertaining and edifying. I have read many of the contemporary books involving similar subject matter, and I have been disappointed with all of them. This is my attempt to write a relevant novel in the way I believe it should be written. I doubt it will succeed.

While an author should never tell a reader how to read his work, I believe it is permissible, and perhaps even necessary, to tell you how not to read it. This story will require fortitude and endurance on the part of the reader. It is not a children's book. This work is, at times, dark, violent, and profane—even lamentable—but it is not nihilistic. If you find it to be depressing, you are reading it incorrectly. This is a story of faith, hope, love, growth, and redemption—wrapped inside a warning.

The characters, while based on real people, are entirely fictional. Likewise, the setting, while based on real places, is an invention. Any resemblance between the characters of this story and real people is entirely coincidental. That being said, much of the dialogue, including most of the dialogue from students and professors, consists of direct quotes, from real persons, which I personally heard with my own ears as a student. Many of the character descriptions are likewise derived from real individuals; however, they are not caricatures or portraits of particular individuals, but rather amalgamations of qualities and characteristics of real people.

There are graphic scenes of violence which some may find distasteful. Before you complain or condemn the work, I would encourage you to reread two of the oldest and most foundational texts in the Western Canon: *The Iliad* and *The Bible*. If either of these works were produced on screen with any proper adherence to the text, I bet you wouldn't allow your children to see the films.

One final note on the language used in this book: I believe one should strive to speak with clarity, brevity, veracity, and beauty, to the best of one's ability. Therefore, as a general rule, profanity, obscenity, and expletives should be avoided to the greatest extent possible; however, in real life, people talk this way, and to deny that would be to lie. The first rule of writing is: always tell the truth. I believe the reader would notice the lack of realistic language, and the unrealistic dialogue would serve to distract more than to clarify. Furthermore, it is a silly and childish weakness to be overcome by mere words which one does not approve of, but alas, most of our current society cannot muster the fortitude to tolerate language they deem offensive. Finding myself in such a position, wherein I must choose to either offend half my audience with the use of profanity or another half with the use of unrealistic dialogue, I have chosen to take the middle road, using only expletives that can be found in the text of the King James Bible and describing the rest as "curses," so I will doubtless offend both halves in the process. Nevertheless, if you have the heart, Dear Reader, read on.

Introduction

Americans, in our modern age, have become accustomed to unprecedented luxury and ease. The least among us have access to plenty of food, medical care, transportation, and shelter. At no time in history, anywhere in the world, has this been true before. The least wealthy Americans now have cellphones, internet access, on-demand entertainment, heating, and air conditioning. We have become so detached from the reality of our ancestors that we can no longer even comprehend the fact that only a few generations ago, not even the richest men in the world, not even kings or emperors, had these things. Poverty, true poverty, is rapidly becoming extinct, and with it, our perspective on the natural state of humanity is shifting. We now seem to think that everything from healthcare, food, and shelter, to education, money, and status is owed to us, and that we have a right to expect to live a happy and healthy life to the age of eighty-five, at least. We expect to have a home, food, rest, entertainment, respect of our fellow citizens, and a long retirement wherein we will travel the world on cruise ships and play golf. This delusional state of our collective mind is afforded to us by one thing and one thing only—technology.

For most of human history, ninety-eight to ninety-nine percent of humanity consisted of sustenance farmers. They lived every day trying to put food on their table, keep rain off their heads, heat their homes, avoid disease, and put away enough preparations to survive the winter until the planting season. Every day was a struggle for survival. There was very little choice in diets or lifestyles. You ate what you could grow, gather, catch, and kill, or you starved to death. Nature was trying to kill you every second of every day. Animals were either resources or dangers, and often both. The weather itself was often a merciless enemy. Injury and disease were ever-present threats. The most effective medicines available were teas and ointments made from plants, tree bark, and mushrooms found in the environment. These were discovered over time through trial and error. People died from ailments rendered benign by modern medicine, if not eradicated completely, and they died from the treatments for them too. Those who were mentally or physically deficient seldom survived the cruelty of natural selection.

Not only was disease a daily and mundane phenomenon killing people in horrible, painful ways, plagues were a common occurrence. They swept through societies quite regularly, sometimes wiping out a quarter of the population or more. Bodies would pile up in the streets and rot, being torn apart by rats and scavengers before they could be burned or buried, and every child would grow up seeing this. Along with the ever-present threat of disease for which there was no treatment, women often died in childbirth, and men often died in the perpetual wars that were a routine part of life.

In 1800, parents had an average of just over seven children. They would bury four of them. Forty-six percent of children died before the age of five. The worst thing that can happen to any parent was virtually guaranteed for every parent. The average life expectancy was thirty years. You killed your animals every year so you could eat, you buried your children, you buried your parents, you buried your spouse, and you got married again so that you had someone to help you survive a little longer. And when thieves or enemy forces came to rape, pillage, and burn, you were likely on your own, and you had to be ready to kill them too. You confronted death all around you on a daily basis.

That was in the United States. In more impoverished countries, the life expectancy was even lower, and the infant mortality rate higher. Before Europeans brought their technology to the Americas, the natives of the entire hemisphere existed in a stone age culture of hunting, foraging, and raiding one another for food, supplies, slaves, and sacrificial victims. They had no written language, metal tools, domesticated animals—apart from the odd dogs and turkeys—nor even a wheel. They killed animals by poisoning, strangling, bludgeoning, sticking them with spears and arrow shafts and chasing them until they bled out, or driving them off cliffs or into pits to break their legs. They died in their twenties, and more of their children died than survived to adolescence. This was the norm around the world for thousands of years. As Thomas Hobbes stated, the natural state of man's life was "solitary, poor, nasty, brutish, and short." The default was war of every man against everything, all the time.

Strange as it may seem, the worse life was, the more people held on to religion to give them hope in a world of endless tragedy and a reason to carry on amidst the brutal struggle of life. Naturally, therefore, as people became wealthier, they began to abandon their religions and traditions, and as scientific discovery and technological advancement provided longer lifespans and greater quality of life, science and technology took the place of faith for an increasing number of people. Scientific theories such as Darwin's and political theories such as that of Marx assaulted traditional religion from all sides, and by 1882, Friedrich Nietzsche declared that God was dead, and we had killed Him. What he meant was that the idea of an all-powerful, all-knowing, and all-loving creator was no longer taken seriously by most intellectuals. This was a cataclysmic paradigm shift in the history of humanity, greater than the rise and fall of every empire before it. Religion was universal for all of human history; something would have to take its place.

As science, innovation, and industry stepped into the void, politicians and philosophers began appealing to science, reason, and progress rather than religion. People grew wealthier, and with luxury, came decadence. People no longer respected the traditions and accrued wisdom of their forebears but believed themselves to be enlightened with a new and superior knowledge of reality. With decadence, came resentment. History was reexamined and rewritten to conform to the contrived scientistic claims that humanity was on an inevitable progression toward a perfect world free of inequality. With resentment, came revolutionary politics that divided the people into opposing classes. Everything old was bad. Everything new was good. By the end of the twentieth century, over 100 million unarmed civilians were murdered at the hands of their own governments in the name of "science" and "progress." Some estimates range as high as 262 million. In trying to evolve beyond their traditions, they had inadvertently devolved back to a pre-Christian morality in which the identity of the collective superseded that of the individual and genocide was a standard practice.

"The Science" demanded that utopia be made reality, so they had to rewrite the past to attribute every evil to opponents of their vision rather than to their own contrived schemes. They tore down statues of people they deemed to be out of line with the anointed vision. They banned books, defaced art, silenced and ridiculed those that did not conform to their vision. They ignored facts and emphasized opinions. They cherry-picked data and deemed activists experts. Nature was egalitarian and just, they taught, and only social constructs had degraded it. By the twentieth century, History was dead, and politics had killed it.

The technology that divorced Westerners from the tragic reality of life had implanted a new morality, in which the highest virtue was harmlessness. People no longer wanted to see death outside of their television screens, and with the technology afforded by science and the efficient supply chains afforded by free market economics, they no longer had to. The dirty jobs of building, destroying, cleaning, butchering animals, fighting wars, maintaining law and order, combating disease, and disposing of corpses had all been outsourced away from the general population. "Animal rights" groups abounded. "Environmental justice" activists abounded. Standards were lowered in every sector to allow for less capable people to have greater self-esteem as they pursued status without risk or sacrifice. People had become fat, docile, and ignorant, reducing their ambitions to food, rest, and entertainment. As they stared at their screens in the comfort of their climate-controlled rooms, their connection with the true nature of the world eroded away, and the world collapsed around them.

A decade into the twenty-first century, Stephen Hawking declared that philosophy was dead, and science had killed it. A decade later, science was dead, and the decadence and resentment had killed it. Scientific questions that had been settled before the advent of written language, were coming under attack. Not even the most obvious truths could be agreed upon. When we killed it all, it seemed the hate was all we had left. "If you want a picture of the future," Orwell said, "imagine a boot stamping on a human face forever." The intellectual class no longer believed in God or reason or even objective reality. Only subjective reality remained. People took refuge in comforting lies like "Age is just a number," and "Gender is a social construct," and "You can be healthy at any size," and "You can be anything you want in life," and "If you don't succeed, it's because you're oppressed," and "Everyone is equal," and "America's best days are ahead of her." They held on to their delusions and sought to force others to affirm them. Truth was seen as harmful, and harmlessness was the chief virtue, so lies were given preference. And in a nation founded by citizens taking up arms and killing the soldiers and officials of the most powerful empire in the world so they could survive on their own as free men, even the churches preached to their dwindling audience that peace and harmony and tolerance were sacrosanct ends to which all other considerations came second. Christianity was reduced to niceness.

Masculinity was seen as harmful, and harm was the only wrong. They wanted people to be harmless, so the men became harmless and acted like women. The women tried to fill the void and act like men, growing more resentful as they failed. The population had been declining for decades as the relationship between the sexes became more complicated. People became too scared of hypothetical futures, too self-centered, or too disinterested to reproduce. Most people didn't try to act like anything more than animals, seeking nothing but pleasure and the avoidance of pain. They stuffed their guts with sugar and fat and sunk into their chairs and couches to watch football games and titillating, uninspired, emotional displays between the pandering and propagandistic commercial breaks desperately trying to convince them to buy more junk. The love of money was the root of all American culture.

In their arrogance, even the military had begun to morph into social experimentation, betting on their technological advantages to preclude the need for strong, hardened fighters, since wars were now waged with keyboards and joysticks from air-conditioned rooms thousands of miles away from their unknowing victims. As the masses grew more lazy, ignorant, and impotent, the elite political and intellectual classes grew more powerful and more controlling. And rather than evolving into genetically superior superhumans, humanity came to resemble a collection of farm animals. All of this was afforded by the technology, which resulted from science, which resulted from philosophy, which resulted from universities, which resulted from the church. But while the society became more detached from the reality of nature, the reality of nature never changed.

Meanwhile, America's enemies stoked the flames that were consuming the West, and not every country bowed down to this new self-indulgent god or practiced the virtue of harmlessness. In fact, as they saw the American decline happening before them, they distanced themselves from every cultural malaise that they recognized as having caused the decay of this once great civilization, and they began to turn their societies in the other direction. As the West crumbled, the East prepared for the fall.

This is the story of what happened next.

Dramatis Personae

The Rawlings Family

- **Kent** – Father of three, 53 years old, truck driver for a factory in Columbus, Indiana

- **Faye** – Mother of three, 50 years old, former art teacher

- **Keith** – Eldest son, 24 years old, Marine veteran recently returned, full-time student

- **Joe** – Youngest son, 22 years old, HVAC technician

- **Lynn** – Daughter, 19 years old, full-time student

The Faulkners

- **Tim** – Father of seven, 37 years old, software engineer, homesteader

- **Emma** – Mother of seven, 36 years old, homesteader, midwife, herbalist

DRAMATIS PERSONAE

The McCormicks

- **Malik** – Husband, 38 years old, optometrist

- **Jordan** – Wife, 33 years old, retail store manager

The Jorgensons

- **Eric** – Father of Rachel Owens, grandfather of Abigail Owens, 61 years old, Preacher

- **Lydia** – Wife, mother of Rachel Owens, 60 years old, retired teacher, gardener

- **Rachel Owens** – Daughter, widow, Abigail's mother, Faye's friend, teacher, 40 years old

- **Abigail Owens**– Daughter of Rachel, Lynn's friend, 18 years old

The Packards

- **Fred** – Retired government contractor and musician, 66 years old

- **Donna** – Retired teacher, 66 years old

Bruce Galloway – "Cyclops," Kent's friend and coworker, 52 years old

Ben Jameson – Plumber, 50 years old, hobby farmer

Mark Jameson – Ben's son, 12 years old

Jack Winters – Father of four, Marine veteran, 49 years old, Dan Tyler's cousin

Dan Tyler – Father of three, Army Veteran, 44 years old, Jack Winters' cousin

Matthew Tyler – Dan Tyler's son, 19 years old

Brad Nielson – Father of two, 48 years old, carpenter

Jim Baker – Farmer, 52 years old

Ernie Jacobs – Farmer, 68 years old

Bill Campbell – Farmer, 78 years old

Jeremiah Davis – Machinist, 45 years old

Scott Adams – Water treatment plant worker, 36 years old, survivalist-prepper

Derek Gillian – Career criminal and drug addict, 29 years old, cousin of the Rawlings family

Noah Rosenbaum – Jewish doctor, 41 years old

Mary Goldstein – Jewish Professor, 59 years old

Joshua Jackson – Emma Faulkner's brother, 42 years old

Dale Daniels – Kent Rawlings' brother-in-law, 60 years old

Beverly Daniels – Kent Rawlings' sister, 56 years old

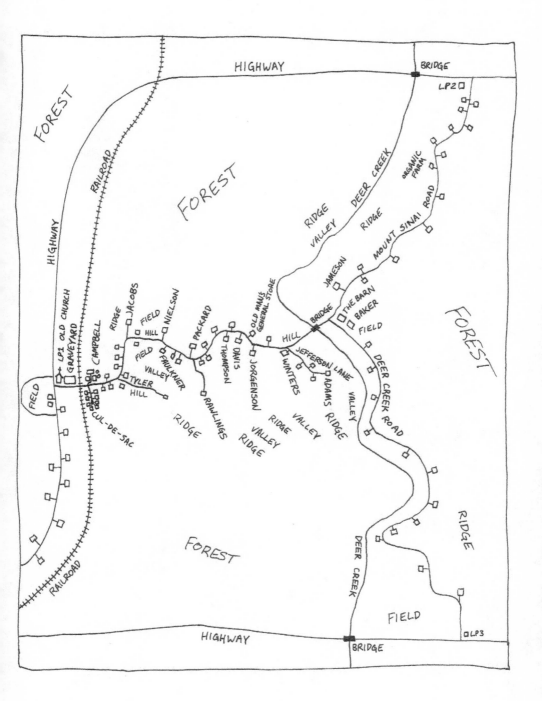

Prologue

O bserve.
It was a cold, wet January day in southern Indiana. Keith Rawlings parked his truck in the shadow of the football stadium, grabbed his backpack, and locked the doors as he made his way to the bus stop. The girls walked across the salt-covered asphalt, staring down at their phones, with earbuds in their ears, oblivious to the cars swerving around them. Most wore the standard winter uniform of leggings and crop-top sweaters and four-hundred-dollar boots as they made their way to the awning. The boys—very few of them could be called men, despite being older than their great-grandfathers were when they went to war to stop the spread of global tyranny—likewise bobbed their heads to the beat of hip-hop tunes pouring into their ears through their wireless earbuds. Below their coats, most wore sweatpants and slides as if they had just managed to get out of bed and hadn't had time to dress before their 10:30 classes. Some, like the girls, wore the fashionable designer boots with shoestrings which they never tied, and they dragged their feet along the pavement, through the salt and sludge of melted ice as their peers, arriving late, slammed on their brakes to avoid hitting the pedestrians in their hurry to find a parking space.

Near the bus stop, a group of missionaries stood with large cardboard boxes, handing out pocket Bibles to the students who walked by. Many ignored the do-gooders, while

1

others took the Bibles they were handed and promptly threw them into the trash receptacles around which plastic cups and piles of garbage were strewn, rolling around the sidewalk in the wind. The students stepped over the litter or kicked it aside as they huddled into the pavilion. Keith took a Bible he was handed and slid it into his back pocket before picking up the trash skidding into the grass and stuffing it into the trash can.

As he waited, he watched the five buses wrapped in advertisements sitting on the other side of the parking lot. Two of them displayed a young child's cartoonish crayon depiction of the Earth and said: "Do your part to save the planet" and "Go green." They lined up along the sidewalk in front of the stadium, sitting idly as the exhaust poured from their tailpipes. Over one-hundred students were now waiting for a bus. Keith stood, watching, as another bus pulled into the parking lot, dropped off a handful of students beside the awnings, and pulled around to join the other busses in line, burning fuel and waiting. Finally, one of the six stationary buses lurched forward and turned toward the awnings, pulling around and coming to a halt beside the mass of students before opening its doors. Keith waited as the students crowded on, pushing their way in front of him, never looking up from their phones. Something like a quarter of the students pushed their way onto the bus before the driver announced that the bus was full and shut the doors. As the bus drove away, Keith stood and looked back at the other five buses idling in front of the stadium. He glanced around at the renewed hundredfold students piling up at the bus stop, and he began walking.

It was two miles to his classroom, but he could make the short hike in under twenty minutes on foot, so he would still be in his seat before the start of class. It was his first semester at the university, and ever since he had joined the United States Marine Corps, he had devoted his energy to educating himself in preparation for an academic career. Like many other students, he began working toward his degree at the local community college where he could acquire his general education credits in the smaller classrooms before transferring his credits to the university. He had finished two semesters at the college and had two more to go before completing the requirements, but he decided to begin on some of his more advanced university courses in the hope that this mixed schedule would be more manageable. Despite having received top marks in his classes so far, he had little confidence in his intellect and thought it best to give himself all the help he could get. He expected the university to be challenging and rewarding—a step into a world of intellectual rigor and the pursuit of excellence.

As he strode along the sidewalk, he admired the campus's limestone architecture and sculptures surrounded by huge trees with small bronze placards at their bases identifying the types of trees they were and when they were planted. Fat, fluffy squirrels scurried around and rifled through the mulch around the trees, and as Keith walked within inches of the creatures, they did not run from him but either ignored his presence or came closer, apparently hoping he would drop a bit of food for them.

Striding past the tennis courts and soccer fields and the plate glass windows of the newer buildings, he examined the old stone castles of the centuries-old campus with wonder. They were the closest things to a proper castle he had ever seen, and his imagination ran wild with fantastic visions of grandeur. Students walked along the sidewalks, alone and in groups of twos and threes, some talking, most staring down at devices in their hands. Keith stepped around students scrawling messages in colorful chalk on the sidewalks. There were tables set up on street corners where activists handed out pamphlets and shouted slogans from atop limestone retaining walls, recruiting allies in their cause. Over their sweatshirts they wore t-shirts displaying party symbols and campaign slogans, and they held up signs and banners with phrases like "Save the planet" and "The earth is on fire."

Keith observed the students he passed as he made his way toward the building indicated on his schedule. He could tell the ROTC cadets and his fellow military veterans by their backpacks, haircuts, and their civilian attire. They walked upright, in straight lines, wasting no time as they maneuvered through campus toward their destinations. Apart from the handful of burkas and saris and the several conservatively dressed foreign students, most others wore ripped up jeans or sweatpants and coats unzipped to reveal hundred-dollar designer t-shirts displaying slogans like "Fuck Capitalists" and "Eat the rich." Their backpacks were decorated with pins of red stars, ancient pagan gender symbols, strips of rainbow-colored ribbons, political party signs and slogans, and stickers which read "I voted." On almost every lamp post, bulletin board, and window, were flyers with symbols of hammers and sickles, black fists, equal signs, and advertisements for invited speakers as well as new classes which would fulfill the diversity requirement for every degree path.

Keith walked up the steps and pushed open the heavy oak doors of his building. Following the room numbers as he walked through the hallway, he saw the walls were arrayed in flyers and posters, and students lay on the floors, staring at their phones with their earbuds in. Keith tiptoed his way through the web of legs and Birkenstocks stretching across the floor from both sides of the hallway. "Excuse me," he said as he tried to avoid stepping on anyone. The students continued to stare down at their phones, not acknowledging his presence. Keith found the classroom and opened the door, and as he made his way to a desk in the front row, the students who were lying about the hall outside the door got up and followed him in. They filled the seats from back to front, never speaking or looking up from their phones.

Keith pulled out his notebook and pens and looked around the room at the faces staring down at the screens in their laps. Beside him was a girl with a buzzed head, tattooed neck, lip piercings and a nose ring, with large gauges in her ears. She pulled out a laptop covered in stickers and looked over at him with a glare. Keith turned away from her and looked around the room. Nearly half of the students had dyed hair and nose rings. Most wore glasses, some with brightly colored plastic frames, some with wire rims of various thickness. Keith took a drink from his water bottle and put it back in his bag as he waited for the professor.

Finally, the door swung open, and the professor walked in, seven minutes late. She wore circular glasses, white plastic shoes, ripped up jeans, and a black, pinstriped tuxedo vest over a flannel shirt. She placed her coat and scarf upon the desk and removed her hat to reveal a bright purple crew cut. She sighed and mumbled curses under her breath, already in a bad mood as she pulled down the projector screen and began typing on the computer keyboard.

Keith glanced around at the other students once again. Most of them had removed their earbuds by now, although some continued to listen to music, and most were still looking at their phones, scrolling through social media, shopping online, or watching videos on their laptops. When the professor had finished clicking around on the computer, she looked up with a labored smile.

"Hello, everyone. And welcome to English 317. I'm Dr. Shepherd. I've been a professor of English for twenty-two years. I'm the Dean of the English department, and I've published eighteen books and fifty-four peer-reviewed academic papers. I'm uber excited to be teaching this class, but first, why don't we go around the room and introduce ourselves. Maybe tell us the name you'd like us to call you and a couple things about yourself—what year you are, I assume you're all English majors, but maybe what your focus is, or if you're doing any other majors, you know, stuff like that."

The students introduced themselves as the teacher marked their names down on her roster. When they had finished, she said, "Okay, that's great. Now, we're going to talk about English and stuff, but first, I thought we'd watch a couple of videos. Can we put the phones away, please? I don't want anyone recording me. Everything that happens in this room stays in this room. Okay? Okay. Thank you. Now, as I'm sure you know, it's an election year, and I can't express to you how important it is for you to exercise your right to vote. Now, some of you might not feel like you know much about politics or which party to vote for, and that's fine. The important thing is for you to vote. Don't worry about learning all the names or policies or any of that. You don't need to listen to..." she raised her fingers in a gesture of air quotes, "both sides—as if there is such a thing." She lowered her hands. "You just need to vote for the party that you feel holds your values and is the most progressive. Okay? So, we're going to watch a couple of videos that might help you decide which party to vote for if you're a good person, and then, we'll move on with the class. I know this isn't technically what we're supposed to be doing in here, but I feel very strongly about this, and it's important, so—yeah—if you don't like it, well, I have tenure," she laughed.

She played the videos, both campaign ads for the same party, and when the videos were done playing, she said, "So, now you know all you really need to know. You have no excuses. Get out and vote and make your voices heard." She closed the window on the screen and pulled up another with the course syllabus. "Now, has anyone bought the books for this class already?"

Keith raised his hand.

"Okay, so, most of you haven't. Well, that's good, because I am making some changes to the syllabus, so don't buy your books yet, if you haven't. I know we're supposed to be talking about, like, Shakespeare and Milton and whatever. Blah, blah, blah." She rolled her eyes. "But those are a bunch of dead, old, white men, and I wouldn't be properly teaching English if I didn't introduce you to some more diverse voices that you may not be familiar with. I feel like that old stuff is too hard and boring and full of outdated views anyway. So, um, I hope nobody's disappointed, but we're going to make, like, a compromise. I'm going to teach everything you need to know about that old stuff by having you read some essays deconstructing Shakespeare and the rest of them, and then, we'll move on to some more exciting stuff. Sound good?"

It did not sound good to Keith. He was disappointed, but he didn't want to sound stupid during his first day in class, so he kept it to himself. This was the dean of the English department, after all.

"Professor?" said a girl with wire-rimmed glasses and a sweater she had cut apart. The modified sweater now had a plunging-v neckline, and the bottom had been cut off to expose half her ribcage down to her sheer leggings. "Are we, like, going to talk about, like, dismantling the patriarchy and, like, the male gaze?"

"Great question. Yes, that is a crucial part of understanding Shakespeare and Milton and any work of literature. Obviously, they had a lot of views that I feel like, are, like, really problematic. So, we will definitely be covering that in this course, along with literary criticism that shows how every sword in Shakespeare is a phallic symbol." The professor raised her eyebrows up and down with a grin. "So, stay tuned."

Keith had three classes that day: English, American History, and Science—and all of them were like the first. Regardless of the course's subject matter, the professors always found an opportunity to inject their political views and criticism of the country Keith had devoted four years of his life to serving. They all showed videos to encourage the students to vote. They passed out voter registration forms and offered extra credit for turning in the completed forms.

In Keith's history class, the professor said the course would cover slavery, the oppression of women, racism in America, critical theory, and the ongoing civil rights movement, which would bring them to the present day. When one of the students blurted out, "Eat the rich," the professor raised his left fist and smiled as he repeated the slogan. This tenured professor had been at the university for twenty-six years and received an annual salary of over $181,000, which was publicly available information. That figure, however, did not include the revenue from his books, which he required his students to purchase for his graduate courses, nor the speaking fees he collected from seminars and conferences around the world. In his first class, after going over the syllabus, the professor led a discussion on what history was, how to conduct research, which sources to use, and which to avoid. He explained that the arc of history bends toward justice. "Bias is good," he said. "The truth," he informed them, "is liberal." And he told them they could only use sources less than twenty years old and that were published by respected universities, because everything older than twenty years had been debunked as racist, and everything outside the control of competent university professors is propaganda for oppressors. Finally, he told them that they would be using critical theory to deconstruct the U.S. Constitution, and he would not tolerate anyone advocating for or defending the originalist interpretation of the Constitution because it was written by "slave-holding white bigots."

In Keith's science course, the professor informed them that his course would cover how humans were the same as any other animals, only more destructive to the planet. He described how the earth was a perfect system, precisely calibrated for life, but had arrived entirely by chance, which is why it was paramount that they do everything necessary to stop the greedy capitalists from destroying the planet. He explained how science refuted religion, which was merely a construct for keeping the ignorant masses under the control of the powerful. And finally, he declared the need for human population control in order to save the purposeless, randomly formed planet from the disease that was humanity. He offered extra credit to students who attended environmental and anti-religious protests. The world would end in their lifetimes, he told them, unless they demand radical change.

Keith walked back to his truck, feeling deflated. The university was not what he had imagined. The professors dressed like high school students and cursed like drunken sailors as they berated and belittled every view they did not endorse, attacking and smearing the thinkers with whom they disagreed. The classes at the community college were not a great improvement, but at least at the community college, the professors presented themselves as professionals. He looked at his schedule as the truck warmed up. He had philosophy and psychology the next day. What great nuggets of wisdom would he learn there? Putting the truck into gear, he turned on some music and drowned out his thoughts as he pulled out of the parking lot.

Keith decided to pick up some more feed for the animals before heading home. It was out of the way, but he was running low, and there were other items he wanted besides. Every time he went to a store, he purchased extra items such as salt, rice, beans, and ammunition. He felt better having a decent stockpile of the supplies he couldn't produce himself. He pulled into the parking lot and shut off the truck, locking the doors behind him as he quickly went to grab a cart. He wanted to be in and out in as little time as possible.

In the parking lot of the farm and home store, Keith took in the sight of the bustling shoppers climbing out of beat-up, old minivans and dented cars and rusted pickups. They carried children on their shoulders or held their hands as they crossed the cracked and cratered pavement. There, a forty-year-old man with three kids and an abusive wife, in the process of a divorce. There, a pregnant nineteen-year-old who prays to God every morning, noon, and night to send her a good husband. There, a thirty-five-year-old man still living with his parents as he tries to save up money, working overtime at the grocery store. There, a twenty-eight-year-old woman living in a trailer with four children from three different fathers. There, a fifty-eight-year-old man pulling an oxygen tank and dying of lung cancer after forty years of smoking cigarettes to stay awake while he delivered truck-loads of products to keep the country running and provide for his family. All the humanity in its flawed and broken state, trying to make it through. They nodded and said 'hey' to one another as they passed, held doors for strangers, helped to lend a hand where they could, and kept on keeping on, hoping for a brighter day—these humble sinners.

Country music played over the speakers in the farm and home store—at least, what passed for country music nowadays—apart from the overplayed accent with which it was sung, it was indistinguishable from pop. The smell of coffee and popcorn filled the air inside as people walked through the aisles with their dogs. People here wore boots and jeans or canvas pants. Some wore overalls. There were Amish ladies in dresses and bonnets pushing carts through the feed section, and men and women examining tools with holstered pistols hanging on their belts.

In the chainsaw section, Keith looked at the new machines aligned on a rack along the wall. Back when tools were made to be used, the saws were far more powerful and easily maintained. These new saws were underpowered and made more complicated to meet government-imposed emission standards. Keith's small, thirty-year-old chainsaw was still far more reliable and more powerful than the bigger, heavier, new saws being sold today. Where before, one could remove the cover over the air filter with the turning of a single latch, now all the saws had several screws bolting the cover down so that it would take much longer to check and clean the filter. It was almost as if the tools were being made to prevent people from using them, and that through increasing regulations, they were trying to dissuade people from cutting their own firewood, thereby training out the self-reliant mindset from the people. Decades ago, a man could take apart and fix every device he owned; now, that was all but impossible, even for the most skilled. The high-tech gadgets were deliberately designed to fail within a few years, if not months, to keep people buying more, to keep them dependent on the supply chains. Eight of ten products in most stores were made in China; it was becoming increasingly rare to see the words "Made in USA" anywhere, and even those were usually of poor construction now.

Keith loaded a few fifty-pound feed bags onto his cart and made his way to the gun counter in the back where a group of shoppers were filling out forms and talking. He looked at the rifles and shotguns lining the rack and examined the pistols in the glass case before taking a few boxes of shotgun shells and a box of arrows. Through the store's speakers, came the radio news announcement: China had invaded Taiwan. The U.S. threatened sanctions. On his way to the checkout counter, Keith picked up some bleach, vinegar, salt, oil, beans, rice, and batteries. In less than thirty minutes, he was checked out, loaded up, and on his way back to the house.

He drove along the bypass and glanced at a group of runners jogging along the sidewalk, past an old, stone building with large plate glass windows looking out toward the football stadium. What used to be a church was now just another administrative building bought up by the university. The congregation moved away, the building was sold, the stained-glass windows were removed and replaced with generic panes of tinted glass, and the cross atop the building was cut off and tossed in with the rubbish, to be scrapped out and recycled. Now, all that remained of that symbol so emblematic of the town of his childhood was a stone building with a huge, jagged piece of hastily cut iron protruding from the peak of the roof.

Keith's head was swimming with conflict. Perhaps, he had made a mistake in going to school. He couldn't push the thoughts from his mind, and he wasn't in the mood for music. As he sat in traffic on the bypass, he changed the radio station. At the sound of a news report, he stopped and listened. There were riots erupting all over the country. Crime was skyrocketing. Buildings were being burned and looted.

Politicians endorsed the violence. District attorneys refused to prosecute. Police were resigning in record numbers.

As Keith turned onto Mount Sinai Road, he waved at the man and two boys picking up litter around the graveyard. He didn't know their names, but he regularly saw them trying to clean up trash tossed out of passing cars on the sides of the road. Most Americans no longer cared about their environment; they lived for instant pleasure, happy to let others clean up after them. Of course, the cities were the most polluted—no one cared about keeping their neighborhoods clean and beautiful there, and no one cared about passing on a better world to their children anymore. Indeed, most people in cities were no longer having children; they wanted to get rich quickly, experience as much pleasure as possible, and sacrifice nothing in the pursuit. Americans thought of little more than food, rest, and entertainment. In the cities, you could feel the pollution. But the air was tainted with more than smog.

The suicide rate was rising every year, and people either pretended not to understand why or pretended not to notice. It wasn't polite to talk about it. They worshipped science as an omniscient deity, and science told them they were nothing more than randomly constructed chemistry sets inside piles of meat. They kept themselves distracted with noise, because when they were alone, the unavoidable question hung over them like an anvil: why go on with the drudgery of life when all there was to live for was the pursuit of pleasure and the avoidance of pain? All they had was their desire for wealth, status, and power, but it was never enough. Americans' modern view of meaning was not enough to live for, and when they didn't get everything they expected to be handed in life, a growing number of them quit. There were no more great causes to fight for, so they invented imaginary antagonists; but nothing seemed to be worth sacrificing for—success was implicitly defined as dying with the most toys while condemning the greed of anyone who had more than them. When the going got tough, Americans either complained or simply gave up.

Keith drove past the barns and cornfields, the horse pastures and cattle fences, and pulled into the long gravel driveway that led to the Rawlings house. Beneath the canopy of trees overhanging the driveway, chickens darted in front of the truck as they flocked to the porch in hopes of getting some grain or food scraps. As the reporter on the radio announced record unemployment and record inflation, Keith shut off the truck and got out.

The delightful scent of woodsmoke saturated the air as it poured from the chimney and swirled in the frosty breeze. Chickens gathered around him, clucking and following him as he took the feed to the steel trash cans behind the house. When he had topped off the feed supply, Keith took a scoop of grain and tossed it on the ground for the expectant chickens. Taking his other bags from the truck, he walked to the house, stepped over the chicken gate on the porch, and opened the door.

Keith Rawlings was the eldest son of Kent and Faye Rawlings. Since returning home from his service with Hawaii's Third Marine Regiment, he had lived with his parents while he attended school. It seemed absurd to move away when the school was only a few minutes' drive from the home of his birth, and his parents were insistent that he stay with them while he saved money for a house. In the United States, there had developed an expectation that kids would move out around the age of eighteen, but in most countries and cultures around the world, multiple generations of families lived together in the same house, maintaining stronger familial bonds. While it was seen as backward and outdated by those who left their families behind to seek their fortunes in the cities, the people of the soil retained deeper roots which kept them connected to their heritage and traditions. When they moved away to start their own families, it was usually within walking distance of the house in which they grew up. This system of homestead culture, passing on land to progeny, and expanding family-owned property allowed for larger tracts of land to be shared by extended families for farming, hunting, and living a more self-reliant lifestyle entirely foreign to a growing number of modern Americans.

Keith's younger brother Joe, likewise, occupied the house, having recently finished trade school and now working as a heating, ventilation, and air conditioning technician. As he multiplied his savings and searched for a nearby house, he enjoyed the benefits of home-cooked meals shared around the family's dining table and the support system of close relatives who shared labor to one another's mutual benefit. Every year, the family members would join in wood cutting parties to supply heat for the home and for the houses of relations who were unable to provide for themselves. They would bale hay, mow lawns, reroof houses, plant, weed, and harvest garden crops, trade canned goods, service vehicles, and help with processing wild game or the butchering of animals. They had family gatherings, meetings around campfires, and regular Bible studies. Even this culture, however, was slowly eroding away as the influence of the prevailing modern culture seeped into their lives. While Keith was away, the Rawlings family, for the first time since he could remember, had stopped planting a garden, and not until he returned, did they take it up again.

The woodstove radiated warmth throughout the house. Kent and Faye sat in their overstuffed chairs, watching the news, commenting on the weather forecast and how disgusted they were with the political climate as they sipped from glasses of iced tea. Keith set his bags on the kitchen countertop and glanced at the screen as Kent looked over his shoulder.

"So, how was your first day of classes?" Kent asked. "Did you learn anything?"

"Oh yeah," Keith sighed. "All kinds of stuff I never knew I needed."

"Well, good. I'm proud of you," Kent nodded. He turned his attention back to the television screen as the station went to commercial break. "Maybe I'll go back to school one of these days. I'd kind of like to have a degree of some kind. You can't put a price on education."

Keith chuckled. "That's what the administrators say, anyway."

"Did you eat yet?" Faye set her glass on a small bookshelf covered in junk mail and bills. "We had pizza. There's some left in the fridge."

"Thanks," Keith replied. He removed the contents of the plastic bags, stuffed the bags in the cabinet under the sink, and began taking the items to the pantry and various cupboards around the house. At the sound of crunching gravel, he looked out the window to see his brother's company van rolling down the driveway.

Joe entered the house, looking tired.

"There's pizza in the fridge for you," Faye called.

"I already ate," said Joe, closing his bedroom door behind him.

When the news program returned, the reporter described how a man had been sentenced to ten years in prison after pulling a gun on a mob of protestors who had pulled him from his truck and beat him with chains and bats on the highway. No charges were filed against the attackers. Keith shook his head. His country believed in nothing, not even their own Constitution. America was rotting. Rotting from the inside out. And beneath the façade of wealth and power, worms were feeding on the decay.

"Oh, Lynn's here!" Faye exclaimed in jubilation as she watched her daughter's car through the window.

Keith stepped outside and packed a tin of tobacco in his fingers, watching the light of the gray sky shimmering off the surface of the small pond. He pulled the chicken gate out of the way as Lynn neared the steps.

"You at least need to trim that beard," Lynn said. "You look homeless. It's gross."

"Thanks." Keith put a pinch of tobacco in his lip.

"Just doin' my job," Lynn replied. "And you ought to quit that. When you get cancer, they'll have to cut your face off. Granted, it might improve your looks, but it's really not worth it."

Keith laughed. "I'll keep that in mind."

"So, how was your first day?"

"Taxing."

"Yeah, well, don't worry. It gets worse." Lynn had already completed two semesters at the university.

The door opened. "Lynn!" Faye was all smiles as she hugged her daughter. "Want some pizza?"

"I'm just here to pick up some supplies for class, and then I have to get back to the dorm. I've got food there."

"Come on in."

As the door shut behind him, Keith walked up the long, muddy driveway, watching the squirrels scurrying away through the leaves and up the large hickory trees on either side. He examined his small fruit trees with their scarred bark and broken twigs ravaged by the deer. One of the farmers' huge new tractors hummed past on the road, followed closely by a tiny, cartoonish-looking car squeaking its cute, little horn at the farmer. The old pickup trucks that hauled families, feed, and firewood along this road were gradually being replaced by cars like this one, built to carry a maximum load of two people and a single bag of groceries. The small farms were being replaced by massive industrial farming empires. It was cheaper to buy mass-produced food grown by farmers with computer-programmed precision machines plowing, planting, spraying, and harvesting thousands of acres every year, and the small-time farms simply couldn't compete. They were selling off their livestock, selling off their land, giving up the business, and dying out. There were a stubborn few that still held on to the old ways here, but they wouldn't last long. The old farmland was being subdivided, developed, and modernized, and instead of the homesteads and small cattle farms, they were seeing an increasing number of houses without American flags flying in the yard, with toy cars in the driveway, displaying bizarre bumper stickers, with residents who had never touched a weapon, who needed warnings for content that could disturb their emotional wellbeing and mental health, and who didn't know where their food came from but were ready to change the world.

Keith spat a stream of black juice onto a patch of dirty, gray snow. The red sun was sinking behind the hills. America was changing, and despite what the proselytizers for progress, science, efficient production, and cheap goods at all costs said, anyone who had any sense could sense that it was not all for the better.

PART I
PLANS

Chapter One

"Go! Go! Go!" Joe shouted anxiously at the television screen, spilling popcorn on the floor as he jumped from his chair. The football player on the screen was closing in on the end-zone. The team was down twenty-four to twenty-eight with a minute remaining in the fourth quarter. As if by Divine Providence, the other team's quarterback threw a pass to his wide receiver, but the ball sailed directly over his shoulder and into the hands of the safety behind him.

The safety now sprinted past the other players with almost superhuman speed to the exuberant shouting of the announcer, "He's at the fifty! The forty! They're almost on him! The thirty!"

"Come on!" Joe screamed.

The announcer yelled, "He's going..." The screen went black.

"What!" Joe bellowed. "No!" He kicked over a glass of iced tea as he frantically grabbed for the remote.

"What did you do?" Kent shouted.

Joe pressed the buttons on the remote. "I didn't do anything! Oh, what... Did you put new batteries in the remote? I told you to..."

"I did! I just bought those batteries a couple days ago."

"Well, this stupid thing isn't working!"

"Did the TV come unplugged? See if it's plugged in."

"It is!" Joe dropped the remote on the floor. He looked back at Kent. "Why..."

"Wait a minute." Kent flipped the light switch beside him. "The power must have gone out."

Joe began walking quickly to the basement. "Lynn, how many times have I told you not to plug so many things in at once! Probably overloaded the circuit."

"That's not going to help," Kent announced.

"Worth a try." Joe opened the breaker box and began flipping switches. "Anything?" he shouted.

"Nothing," Kent answered. "You know, that's not really a problem nowadays. Circuits don't get overloaded anymore. More likely a tree fell on the power lines or something."

Joe emerged from the stairway, grumbling, "Of all the days... Really? It had to happen during the Super Bowl? Unbelievable. Can you get it on your phone?"

Kent pressed the power button on his phone. "It must have died. I forgot to charge it last night. Where's yours?"

"I told you. I can't find it."

"Oh yeah. Well, where did you have it last?"

Joe sat down in his chair again. "I don't remember."

"Well, you'd better find it before tomorrow. You don't want to be driving on those roads right now without a way to communicate." Kent leaned back in his chair and closed his eyes.

"No kidding." Joe sighed loudly, "This is just great. Now what do we do?"

Lynn slumped down the stairs pulling the headphones from her ears, "Hey, did the power go out?"

February 3

The shot rang out through the woods. Keith flipped the safety back on and leaned the old Winchester against a snow-covered oak tree. The coyote kicked and writhed in the snow at his feet as blood seeped from a hole in its head. There was no need for another shot; the old .22 had done its job. It was merely nerves firing off at random.

Keith took a canteen from an insulated pouch on his bag and sipped some cold water. At five feet nine inches, he was the tallest of the siblings. His gray-blue eyes squinted out from his reddened, wind-burnt face. He was a lean one-hundred-eighty pounds, powerfully built, with broad shoulders. Since he had returned from service in the Marine Corps, he had let his beard grow out, and the reddish-brown wreath collected icicles as he breathed now. He was the first-born son, twenty-four years old, and living with his parents once more as he went to school. Like most of his generation, he didn't know what he was going to school for, so he spent much of his time in the woods, collecting his thoughts.

The forest sparkled against the gray sky. It was beautiful. Frigid, but beautiful. With the temperature at seven degrees below zero, he normally wouldn't venture far from the woodstove, but he had to check the traps. The law required it, but more than that, he couldn't stand the thought of an animal being stuck in a trap in this freezing cold. He hated unnecessary cruelty. Nature was cruel enough; he understood that better than most Americans, but that didn't mean he had to add to the suffering. The coyote lay still now. Keith put his canteen back in his backpack and took the coyote's paw out of the trap. After loading it on the sled and resetting his trap, he grabbed the rifle and made his way back.

Joe met him in the small field behind the house, where Keith had set up a waxed canvas tent as a trapping cabin. "You got one?"

"Yeah, unfortunately." Keith stopped and pulled out his knife.

"Why unfortunately?" Joe asked.

Keith put a slit in the skin between the muscle and tendon of the coyote's back legs. "Because now, the real work begins," he grumbled. "How was work?"

"Uneventful."

"Well, that's good, I guess." After slipping the hooks of the gambrel through the slits in the coyote's skin, he hoisted the animal off the ground and tied off the rope. "Hey, can you start a fire in that stove, there?"

"Sure." Joe ducked inside the flap of the tent and went to work breaking up sticks for kindling.

"So, who won the game?" Keith ran the edge of his blade in a circle around the coyote's back legs, just beneath the holes he had made for the gambrel hooks.

Joe snorted, "Would you believe the power went out?"

"Yeah, I noticed that." Keith slid the knife down the inside of each of the hind legs.

"It's some kind of sick joke," Joe spouted. He lit his tinder and continued breaking sticks into pieces.

"Well, it's been an exceptionally hard winter this year," said Keith. "I don't remember the last time we had so much snow or so many power outages."

"It's been takin' 'em a lot longer to fix it too," Joe said. "Those guys have been dealing with trees falling over the lines all over the state. They're working around the clock. They're making good money right now, but I'm sure glad I'm not one of 'em."

"Me too." Keith shook his head. "Way too cold for that nonsense. And they're trying to help out other states too. That's rough."

"You don't mind a bit though, do you?"

"About the power outages? Not really." Keith pulled the coyote skin down toward the head, intermittently running his knife over connective tissue to release tension on the hide.

Joe fed a couple more sticks into the stove as he stared into the flames. "Admit it." He looked up and out the open flap of the canvas tent. "You like it when this kind of thing happens. Makes you feel like you're surviving. Like you had a good reason to hoard all this crap and practice for your role in the *Jeremiah Johnson* remake."

"I don't know about that..."

"Oh, come on. You got the beard, the guns, the knives, the tools. All you need is a horse and a coon-skin hat."

He had the hide down around the dog's face now. His fingers were long since numb, and he was beginning to shiver. He pulled slowly and carefully ran his knife in circles around the circumference of the animal's snout. "Nah, I don't want a horse. Too much work, too much money, and besides, I don't trust them."

"And the hat?"

Keith made one last cut, and the hide came off, leaving the coyote's carcass swinging on the gambrel. He held the skin up and smiled. "What do you think I'm doing with this?"

Lynn sat by the window, reading a book. She loved nothing more than to curl up in an overstuffed chair beside the wood stove with a gothic novel. She could read for hours. The books fed her imagination which manifested itself in the art adorning the walls of the Rawlings home as well as those of several friends and family members and even the local high school. She was very much like her mother in many ways, but along with the book-loving, artistic side of her, she displayed several traits from her father as well. She was confident, perhaps overconfident, socially adept, and athletic, enjoying a quick jog through the woods nearly every day to maintain her fitness outside of the softball season. Today, however, was far too cold for a run, and she was content to do nothing more than read and nibble on chocolate. Besides, without power, there was nothing else to do. The only thing she wished for now, was an end to the raucous cacophony emanating from the living room.

Kent snored so loudly he could be heard from outside. When he wasn't at work, he could generally be found in his chair; and it never took him more than a few minutes in front of the television, whether it was on or not, to slip out of consciousness. He had worked at a factory for the past twenty-eight years, and the years had not been kind. He was old, he was always tired, he had a headache nearly every day, and an incessant ringing in his ears. A man of simple tastes, he was a devout believer, an avid consumer of the news, and a sports enthusiast who watched more to reminisce about the glory days than anything else, though he could hardly stay awake long enough to see an entire game. He had missed the end of the super bowl last night, but truth be told, he had missed most of the middle as well. After hearing nothing but Super Bowl highlights from his coworkers at the factory all day, he came home exhausted as usual, so he wasn't losing any sleep over the power outage.

Faye pulled meat, cheese, and mayonnaise out of the refrigerator and then shut the door quickly. Most power outages didn't last this long. She decided that it was best to use what was in the refrigerator first. There was no telling how long the power would be out, and Indiana weather was anything but predictable. She was a stay-at-home mom of three, and even though her youngest was now a sophomore in college, housekeeping was undeniably a full-time job. She had taken a few part-time jobs here and there, teaching art at a small private school over the years, but she never stayed on long. A family emergency or something always seemed to get in the way, and in truth, she wasn't all that committed to a career in teaching. Along with nearly everything else, she was terrified of public speaking – even in front of first graders. Fear governed her entire life, so she needed to use up the food in the refrigerator before it became contaminated with bacteria and her entire family died from food poisoning.

Joe walked through the front door, shaking off the cold. He brought with him a split piece of firewood from the stack on the front porch. In this bitter cold, they burned through firewood incredibly quickly. The vents on the wood stove were kept wide open, and the stove would have to be refilled nearly every hour. Burning this amount of wood meant that the ashes had to be scooped out every day. This task was performed first thing every morning, since it required the stove be empty or nearly empty to get to the ashes sitting on the bottom, and by the time Kent and Joe woke up to go to work in the morning, the fire had burned out, leaving nothing but ashes and a house with temperatures in the thirties. In subzero weather such as today's, it took all day to get the warmest room in the house up to seventy degrees; by then, it was time to go to bed and wake up chilled to the bone all over again. Joe opened the door to the wood stove, slid the log in, shut the door again, and stood beside it for a couple of minutes, clenching and relaxing his hands repeatedly.

Faye stepped into the room and handed him a sandwich on a plate. "Here, eat this." She set another on the table beside Lynn who was too immersed in her book to look up.

"Thanks," Joe said, taking the sandwich. "It's cold out there."

"No kidding. I told you not to go out there. You guys are going to get sick. Is Keith still out there?"

"Yeah. He's in his tent though."

Faye went to the window and peered out at the snow-covered landscape. "I don't care. None of you guys should be outside. It's too cold. Call him and tell him to come inside."

"I don't have my phone," Joe asserted, taking a bite of the sandwich. He grimaced and swallowed as if in pain and then set the plate on the table. "Mom, I told you I don't like mayonnaise."

Just then, the front door opened, and Keith stepped inside, his hands covered in blood and fat. He leaned the old rifle in a corner of the wall.

Faye looked up and exclaimed, "There you are! What were you doing out there?"

Walking directly to the bathroom to wash his hands, Keith began, "Well, I..."

"Did you kill something?" Faye interrupted.

"A coyote."

"Why?" she gasped. "Did you get attacked?"

"No..."

"So, you just killed an innocent animal? Why would you do that?" Faye demanded.

Joe chuckled a bit, dipping out of the room to make himself a sandwich.

"First of all," Keith began. "The coyotes have no other predators and are overpopulated. When they are allowed to go unchecked, they kill off the game animals, our chickens, and people's pets. Small children aren't safe to go outside, and eventually the coyotes run out of food and die slow, painful deaths of starvation. Secondly, I need the practice of running traps for food and pelts if we ever need to resort to that."

Lynn snickered and looked up from her book as Keith entered the room.

"And thirdly," he glanced over at Lynn. "I'm gonna eat that sucker."

"Gross," Lynn interjected, looking disgusted.

Faye raised her voice, "No, you're not! You'll get some kind of parasite!"

They were interrupted by a loud yawn from the living room. Evidently, Kent had awakened from his third nap of the day. "Is there anything to eat around here?"

It was getting dark. The power had been out for more than twenty hours. Faye was lighting candles and putting them around the house. Keith took a head lamp and went outside to grab a couple more pieces of firewood. The wood was frozen together. He took an axe from beside the wood pile and knocked a couple of logs loose. With the firewood cradled in his left arm, he stopped and looked at the thermometer hanging on the wall beside the door. Negative three degrees. It was warming up. There was no telling what the weather would be like tomorrow. Even the meteorologists seemed to get it wrong more often than they got it right. He laughed to himself. Scientists couldn't tell you for sure whether it was going to rain or not tomorrow, but they knew beyond a shadow of a doubt what the weather would be like ten years from now. Well, it certainly wouldn't get above freezing tomorrow. He opened the door, set the firewood beside the stove, and took a trash bag from under the sink.

"What are you doing?" Faye asked, setting a candle on the counter.

Keith began pulling packages out of the freezer and filling the trash bag. "We have over three hundred pounds of meat and vegetables in the freezers. That stuff is going to start thawing out soon. We don't know how long it will be before the power comes back on. We have to get it outside."

Faye nodded, "You're right." She grabbed three more trash bags from under the sink and handed one to Joe and Lynn sitting in the next room. "Okay, guys, start getting the stuff out of the freezer downstairs."

Keith filled his bag and took it out the back door. He set the bag inside one of the empty trash cans. It was not uncommon for raccoons to come up onto the deck in search of food. He went back to start filling another bag.

Joe and Lynn came up the steps from the basement, toting trash bags full of frozen meat. After each of them had made a couple of trips, they finally had both of the freezers completely empty and all the frozen food secured in steel trash cans on the back deck.

Joe went to his room and fell onto his bed with a sigh. He grimaced and ran his hand under the comforter beneath his back. Removing his cellphone, he held it up and looked at it. "Huh. That's where it was."

Keith pushed down on each of the trash can lids and secured them with bungee cords. Satisfied that the family's food supply was safe, he shut the door behind him quickly and went to fuel the wood stove one last time before heading to bed.

Faye bustled about the house locking all the doors, blowing out the candles and making sure the refrigerator door was shut. Lynn finished the chapter she was reading, placed a bookmark between the pages, and took the candle with her as she approached the staircase. Just then, the lights came on.

February 5

0932

With a budget of two-hundred dollars, Faye had to plan her grocery shopping meticulously. She was short and stocky at five feet tall and a weight it was not polite to ask about. Her frizzy brown hair was always in her face and found its way into everything she cooked, scrunchies taking too much effort to use. At fifty years old, she didn't care how she looked. She usually wore baggy sweatpants and t-shirts with what appeared to be the cheapest and ugliest pair of orthopedic shoes she could find. Unfortunately, she couldn't find any at the second-hand stores where she got most of her clothes. Her life was dictated by price tags. She knew her death would be as well.

Necessity of finding the lowest prices possible forced her to drive to the west side of town where she could usually find good deals on most of her usual purchases. She would pack coolers in the back seat of a car she inherited from her sister's estate and fill them with the most balanced diet she could afford. Milk, eggs, vegetables, butter, and cheese from one store. At another store, she would get bacon, coffee, flour and canned goods. Then, she would stop at the bread store and stock up on whatever she could get for under five dollars. With her careful planning, she was able to stretch the budget to fill two coolers and two large shopping bags with supplies that would last the family two weeks.

It hadn't always been this good. During the recession, she rarely made trips to any stores, and when she did, it was only to get a couple of highly valuable and very cheap sundries that they could not very well do without. She couldn't afford the fuel to get to the store, let alone the luxuries she was able to purchase now. The kids learned to grow their own vegetables and hunt for their meat. Ramen was a treat they looked forward to on special occasions. They had all worn hand-me-down clothes that their cousins had bought from thrift stores and outgrown. In the summers, they opened the windows; in the winters, they burned firewood. The lights had stayed off during the day and were only turned on when absolutely necessary at night. They had some family members who worked at local grocery stores and would bring them expired milk and baked goods, and not-yet-rotten produce that was supposed to go to the dumpsters. They could pick out the moldy parts from the bread, cut the rot off the fruit, only half of the milk was chunky, and if you used your imagination a little, the other half tasted like raspberries. It helped. The family had gone through a series of repossessed cars, all over twenty years old, two-to-three-hundred-thousand miles, slashes and cigarette burns in the upholstery, rust all over, mufflers falling off, reeking of cigarette smoke, vomit, and failure. They would drive them until they fell apart and sell them to the scrapyard for a couple hundred bucks. Combined with some cash from odd jobs and hocking things here and there, it would be enough to buy another repo that might last them another six months. But everywhere they went, they could be heard from miles away, as every clunker they drove seemed to have an exhaust leak that was exacerbated by their cratered driveway which hadn't seen new gravel in a decade. The mufflers always fell off, and Kent would find an old tractor muffler somewhere on his property that he could attach to the car with bailing wire. This was all but worthless and would just fall off again in a matter of weeks if not days. They held their heads low, and even ducked below the windows when cars pulled up beside them. Kent pretended not to notice, but he knew his family was embarrassed. He knew they were ashamed of their circumstances, and he knew there was nothing he could do about it.

But that was in the past now. Even then, they were better off than a lot of people, as Kent frequently reminded them. They were certainly better off than their parents had been at their age, and that was a fact. Some nights, Faye would have nightmares of being back on the farm in Illinois. No, they were alright. They never took welfare, they never sold the house, and they ate pretty well most of the time. The kids grew up with low self-esteem and not many friends, and they were made fun of frequently but never bullied like Faye had been. They had learned humility as well as some useful skills, and for better or worse, the kids had all sworn to themselves that they would never go back to that life again. Each one of the three found a way to go to college without a loan. The experience had shaped their personalities in different ways. Keith was obsessed with plans. He had a contingency plan for everything, or at least, that's what he said. He wanted to be prepared to survive any situation. Every decision he made started with his backup plan. He tried to be as well-rounded as possible, learning as many skills as he could, so that whatever the situation, he could quickly adapt to it. Joe decided to learn a trade that would pay well and would be in demand for the foreseeable future. He worked with his hands and didn't waste time on impractical trivia. He bought and sold things, making a profit with each trans-action. He was constantly working and constantly saving. Lynn followed her passion for art. If she was going to fail in life, she might as well fail at what she loved. She didn't need much anyway, and she could always hope to marry into money. Faye continued to live in fear of everything, staying tuned in to the television and radio for more threats to fear. Kent acted oblivious to it all and chose to believe that this life didn't matter; there wasn't anything he could do about it if it did.

Faye slammed on the brakes. The brake lights of the car in front of her startled her back into reality. It was more than three car-lengths ahead of her yet, but she saw red and reacted. She relaxed and looked around. At nine-thirty in the morning, there weren't many cars on the road, but she needed to be back by noon to avoid the traffic. If all went according to plan, she should be back around eleven or just a little after. She turned on the radio. Weird robot sounds reverberated through the speakers as some distorted voice seemed to make noises into a soup can from behind a box fan: "... ah, oh, ah, oh, ah, oh, ah, oh..."

"Wow. A modern art masterpiece," Faye said to herself. "Is that what they call pop music?" She changed the station and accelerated. A reporter's voice came in.

"Tensions rising as the U.S. continues negotiations with Iran. The president saying today, increased sanctions will be put on Iran until they agree to denuclearize. The Iranian president has vowed to defend Iran's sovereignty at all costs. Iranian officials are accusing the U.S. of genocide by cutting off foreign aid and placing sanctions on Iran. Protesters fill the streets of Tehran shouting 'Death to America' as Iran continues missile tests. Investigators continue looking into the mysterious sinking of the merchant vessel last week. The ship was carrying cargo to the U.A.E. but never arrived. Officials do not know what happened, but they say they have found the vessel. It is still unknown why no distress signal was transmitted. Meanwhile, the U.N. is still working to convince China and Russia to put sanctions on North Korea in the wake of increased nuclear tests. North Korea's president saying he will, quote, 'Bring eternal darkness to the enemies of a united Korea.' The Russian president says the U.N. has no influence over Russia and will not dictate what they may do. Chinese officials say they will agree to negotiations only when the U.S.

has lifted all tariffs on China's exports. North Korea's successful missile test last week has raised concerns that..."

Faye pulled into her usual spot in the parking lot and shut off the engine. She put the keys in her purse, put her hat and gloves on, and opened the door. It was still below freezing, but at least it was above zero. She took the two canvas shopping bags from the back seat, shut and locked the door, and went to get a cart.

0947

Kent pulled the truck around and backed the trailer up to the loading dock. He put it in park, killed the engine, and climbed out. He sauntered into the warehouse. His head was beginning to hurt. Pressure change. A storm was coming, or maybe it wasn't. The weatherman was wrong as often as he was right. It was pretty remarkable that he still had a job, really. Even more remarkable that people still listened to him. But Kent was one of those people, so what did that make him? As the truck was being loaded, he decided to go to the vending machine to get a Mountain Dew. Maybe the caffeine would help his headache. Maybe he had low blood sugar. Maybe he was dehydrated. Maybe he just liked Mountain Dew.

It was a waste of money, and he knew it. He was getting fat, and he knew that too. On the other hand, it just so happened that he had six quarters in his pocket, and a cold, delicious beverage would be great right now. He got his drink and sat down in a chair by the radio in the break room. He turned it on and received a blast of Mariachi music.

The warehouse erupted with cheers of approval: "Hey-hey!"

CHAPTER ONE

Kent turned down the volume, and from outside, he heard Luís yell, "¡Eso es lo que necesitas para calentar tus huesos! Professional!"

That didn't help his headache. He changed the station to a talk radio program. The show host was talking about a trade ship being sunk in the Persian Gulf. Kent twisted off the cap of his Mountain Dew and took a drink. He was fifty-three years old. His gray hair—always poorly cut, as he would not spend the money on a barber—was just beginning to turn white. He wore only the cheapest thrift store clothing, most of it more than two decades old, stained, ill-fitting, fraying at the cuffs, holes worn throughout. His round, weathered face was always clean-shaven—he thought men who wore beards were hiding something. He had finally consented to getting glasses, but since his prescription was out of date and he would have to pay to get a new one, he never wore them. At five-foot-ten-inches, he was nearly forty pounds overweight, owing to his natural aversion to exercise and his addiction to peanut butter, crackers, and soda.

Luís stuck his head through the doorway. "Hey, boss, what happened to the music?"

Kent looked up at him and said, "You listen to that same song every day."

"Not that song. That's a different song."

"Are you sure?"

"Pretty sure, boss."

"How can you tell? They all sound the same."

"Maybe so, but that's some good music."

"If you say so."

"It's okay, we can sing it for you." Luís went back outside and began singing. Several other voices soon joined in.

They were actually pretty good, Kent thought. He could hear feet shuffling as the workers showed off their dance moves in between loading pallets into the trailer and moving more into their places. Kent could not understand how these guys had so much energy. He knew many of them were working back-to-back shifts. Luís, who, six months ago, was Filipe, and a year before that, was named George, took as many shifts as the manager would allow him to. The Honduran forklift driver had told him about how he worked so he could wire money back to his family in Mexico. Like many of the other workers, he had been caught multiple times when the company was inspected; he would disappear for a few months and then, show up again as a new hire with a new name. Kent knew all about it because Luís told him all about it. Of course, everyone knew the money he sent was to pay the coyotes to traffic his family across the border, but he figured it wasn't any of his business anyway. The company could hire who they wanted, and no one could blame these guys for doing what they had to do to take care of their families.

He couldn't think about that too much though. All he needed to worry about was paying off the house. He was getting close. Barring any unforeseen catastrophes, they would have the house paid off by the end of the year. Once that was done, he could start saving. Maybe he could take Faye on a vacation somewhere. They hadn't had a vacation since their honeymoon. Perhaps he would take up golf or get a boat and spend his days on the lake, fishing. Only ten more years at this factory and he would retire. That was his plan. He turned the radio back up a little and took another gulp of Mountain Dew. The talk show host continued:

"And no one knew what they did with the money. Well, I guess now we do, don't we? We said, 'Hey, if you stop building nukes and scaring us, we'll give you all this money.' They said, 'okay,' they took the money, and who'd-a-thunk it? They built more nukes! And it sounds like that's not all they built, either. The CIA has photos of strange buildings that look like missile silos, we're hearing reports of submarines coming out of these areas, the whole world just got a lot more dangerous because we made a stupid decision. Well, I didn't, and you didn't, but someone did! And Russia hates our guts. And China looks like something out of George Orwell's nightmares. And both of them are working with North Korea. And the U.N. is saying, 'Please,

oh please, be nice to us. We'll give you money and goodies if you don't hurt us.' Folks, the world is a dangerous place, and we made it much more so, because we just won't learn. Appeasing crocodiles only means you'll be eaten later rather than sooner. But I don't want you to panic, folks. We're not done for yet, and when we come back from the break, I've got some good news that will cheer you right up. Stay right there."

Luís walked into the break room smiling. "You're good to go, boss."

Kent screwed the lid back on and stood up. He switched the station back to the Mariachi music and turned the volume up as he left the break room.

Luís laughed and began to dance. "Ha-ha-ha!"

Kent walked out to the truck as workers in the warehouse shouted, "Professional!"

"Hey, Kent!" someone shouted from across the parking lot.

Kent looked up. It was Cyclops. His real name was Bruce Galloway, and he was one of the most senior employees at the factory. He had been there almost as long as Kent had. Everyone called him "Cyclops" because he had lost an eye in a car accident in high school. Like most employees at the factory, he had back problems and bad joints and hobbled around hunched over as if he were straining under the load of some enormous weight slung over his shoulder. He was overweight, missing two teeth, and he smoked like a chimney. He limped across the street at a determined pace, watching where he stepped to avoid ice patches on the black top. "Hey, Kent, Ricky won't be here Saturday; you want to make double time?" He frowned and turned to peer into the warehouse. "Hey, Pedro! Turn that down!"

"John's not available?"

"He's already pulling a double shift that day. You're all we got." He took a drag on his cigarette and spat on the ground.

"Alright. Yeah, I can do it."

"Alright, thanks. Hey, you hear about that E-M-P stuff?"

"An EMT? Who?"

"No, E.M.P. Some kind of doomsday crap."

"I'll take E.L.O." Kent turned toward the spotter truck. "Don't bring me down, Bruce."

The cyclops waddled back, coughing out puffs of cigarette smoke into the frigid air.

Kent was already tired, but at least he had a Mountain Dew. He climbed into the truck and fired it up. It was now twenty degrees in Columbus.

0953

Joe's face and hands were numb. His fingers were stiff, but he had to make sure he didn't lose any of the intricate pieces of the disassembled heating unit. These new systems had so much technology built into them that when they stopped working, as they often did, it could take days for a professional service technician to diagnose the problem. Everything was electronic nowadays. Everything used computers. You almost needed a degree in computer science to fix a car anymore. He had to constantly take classes and study new systems to keep his certification up to date. Very few people could keep up with the advancing technology, so those who did were extremely valuable. He made sure he continued to be one of them. He was moving up the ladder quickly, and at twenty-two, he was already one of the most qualified employees in the company.

Joe was paid well for his labor, and he was saving up a considerable amount of money for a house. Most of his friends were struggling to make basic payments on their debts; Joe's struggle was in finding a house for which he could pay cash. He wasn't about to rent. The cheapest rent in the state was more than a mortgage payment, and renters were only throwing their money away. They never got any return on their investment. That wasn't the way for him. He needed to get ahead, not spin his wheels for twenty years trying to save up for a down payment. He knew he would have to put some work into it, but he didn't mind that. He enjoyed that sort of thing. He could get a cheap piece of property, build a barn on it, and sleep in there while he fixed up the house. It shouldn't take him more than five years, and he would have a house, a barn, a little bit of land, and no debt. At least, that was the plan.

Joe Rawlings was five-foot-three and one-hundred-forty pounds, the second largest of the Rawlings siblings. He kept his dirty blonde hair cut short, and since he couldn't grow a presentable beard, he shaved. He wore logging boots and jeans every day, so he was quite comfortable wearing them to work. Like the rest of the family, he had blue eyes, but no one knew where he got his straight nose. He was not as lean as Keith, but everyone agreed that he was the best-looking of the Rawlings siblings. His mother only wished he wouldn't chew tobacco.

The clanging of metal alerted him to the fact that he had dropped a screw into the induced draft fan housing. He cursed and spat. His hands were so frozen he couldn't feel the screw in his fingers. He would have to remove the entire housing a second time to get the screw out. The first time was to remove an unfortunate bird that had got itself trapped in the fan.

The people in the house had been without heat for a day and a half already. It was no small matter losing heat in temperatures like they had experienced last week. Every year, people across the country froze to death in the winters. The elderly and small children who had been left behind while a caretaker went to run errands were usually the first to die. Drunks and drug addicts would sometimes lose consciousness only to be found by the landlord weeks later, having succumbed to hypothermia in their sleep. The tenants depended on people like Joe to fix their heating system like they depended on the grocers to sell them food, the farmers to produce the food, the truckers to deliver it—like they depended on the oil workers to keep pumping the lifeblood of their economy through the veins of every state, county, city, and town—like they depended on the coal miners in places like Kentucky, West Virginia, southern Indiana and Ohio, the barges that brought their black payloads up the rivers, the trains that rolled on through the night and day along serpentine miles of steel track and wooden tie to deliver the coal to the power plants that allowed them to flip a switch and see. They depended on the ability to call a service technician whenever something went wrong with the system like they depended on the ability to call the police whenever something went wrong with the system. Their world was a web of connections, most of which they would never know existed. If ever a part of the web became damaged, they could be sure there was a plan in place to keep everything functioning properly.

Joe ducked down out of the blistering wind that howled through the morning air. He had been taking every bit of it for the past hour with no refuge from the icy gusts. He sat huddled behind the heating unit with his hands in his armpits for several minutes, trying to restore some sensation and dexterity to his fingers. He rocked back and forth slightly, spitting streams of black tobacco juice in front of him sporadically. He needed to be done soon. There were other people waiting on him too. As soon as he could feel his fingers, he got up and went about removing the housing once again.

1004

The smells of linseed oil, canvas, wood, and paint saturated the air as the sunlight shone through the giant windows of the studio. Lynn worked the tip of her brush delicately across the surface of the canvas before her. She stood on a short ladder to reach the top of the canvas. Of the Rawlings family, she was definitely the shortest. Now, at the age of nineteen, she had never reached five feet in height. Faye was happy to not be the shortest in the family, and Lynn didn't mind because she saved money on clothes by wearing children's sizes. The Rawlings were a mixture of Scotch-Irish and German, and it showed in their features. Descended from peasants and Irish slaves, generations of stunted growth from malnutrition continued to manifest in their genes. The Roman nose which was a trademark of their family on Kent's side was front and center on Lynn as well as Keith, somehow skipping Joe. Unlike her siblings, Lynn seemed to get the German hair. She sometimes donated the long, blonde locks for cancer patients. Like Keith, she had deteriorating eyesight due to reading so much. She wore glasses whenever she didn't feel like using contacts, but today, the glasses were gone. What she lacked vertically, she made up in academics, having been awarded a scholarship for an above 4.0 GPA which she insisted she had maintained since kindergarten.

At the aroma of coffee and sugar, she stopped and looked behind her. The professor was there, studying the image with admiration. "You have real talent, Lynn. I'm not kidding. You're going places with work like this."

"Thank you," Lynn responded with a satisfied smile.

"What are you planning to do when you graduate?" The professor took another sip of coffee and continued staring fixedly at the work.

"I'm not sure yet." Lynn hesitated. "I would like to go to an art school, but I don't know if I can or should."

"Well, you certainly can, and I would say you definitely should. What's standing in your way?"

"I'm just being indecisive, I guess. It's a big move, and I don't have the money, so I just keep working on my portfolio. Whatever happens, happens."

"Okay, look. I'm going to be completely candid with you. You know I would never lie about this. I don't care about anyone's feelings or anything like that. Most of these kids are going nowhere. They have no business being in the fine arts program. You've seen some of the stuff I'm talking about—they're atrocities. One student just poured a can of paint on the canvas and said he was the next Jackson Pollock. Another one turned in a blank canvas with dirt smudged on one corner and called it "postmodernist." I only pass them because if I fail them, they'll drop out and the school will lose that tuition money, which is bad news for me. You're nothing like that. I'm telling you; you have a future in this, and you should pursue it."

Lynn looked back at the canvas. It was pretty good, she thought.

"No, it's fantastic." The professor ran her fingers and her eyes over the surface of the canvas, following the lines without touching, without breathing on it. "It's spectacular. Your command of proportion, of lighting. The balance of colors and shades, tone, perspective. The emotion this evokes. It's phenomenal. You keep working on your portfolio, I'll help you with the logistics of getting into the school. The world needs this, Lynn. We're starving for good art; we've been without it so long, we forgot what it was."

Lynn and the professor gazed at the painting for another minute before a student called out, "Professor, can you, like, look at this. I feel like it's really good, but, like, I'm not sure... maybe it needs more spit."

"I hate my life," the professor mumbled, backing away from Lynn's painting. "No, I think you've used enough spit. Maybe it's time to try other media." She went to attend to the other student.

Lynn measured out more of her paint. She mixed a precise ratio of three colors on her palette, put down the squirrel-hair brush, and began applying infinitesimally thin layers of the mixture in areas of the portrait with her forefinger.

"Wow," Lynn heard the professor say from across the room. "That's, uh—really something."

"You like it?" the student's voice responded cheerfully.

"What is it?"

"It's postmodern."

"Oh yeah, now I see it. And what is the statement this, uh, work, is making?"

"It's a rejection of statements. Like, literally, a rejection of rules and, like, oppressive standards of aesthetics."

"I see." The professor stifled a cough. "What's that smell?"

Lynn applied a touch of Prussian blue to contrast with the yellow ochre. The depth of the shadows made her feel as if she were in the painting, as if the painting were the real world and she were looking out at the illusion from the eyes of the face in the portrait. She was nearly finished. Once it was dry, she would apply a varnish to the painting. In the meantime, she would begin her next project. That was her plan. She already had six pieces done this year. Hopefully, she would finish a dozen more by the end of the semester. She needed to mix more red.

1024

"I can't stop thinking that there was something I could have done," blubbered a student, crying into his sweatshirt. "If I had only known."

Several hands patted the twenty-three-year-old child's back as girls looked sympathetically with protruded bottom lips. TV shows had taught them that this was the appropriate response.

"What you're experiencing is called 'survivor's guilt,'" said the counselor. It's a common experience, but you need to understand that it's not your fault." The counselor made a pouty face from behind her circular glasses. "And all of you need to know that your professors care about you." The counselor choked back tears. "Everyone here loves you and accepts you for who you are. You can always talk to us when you're feeling sad."

The crying boy continued to pull the class's attention back to himself. "I just don't understand how this could happen," he moaned. "I should have been there for him."

Keith tried not to roll his eyes as the student recited generic movie lines to show how caring and sensitive he was. After only two weeks of the philosophy class, they had covered every known argument for and against the existence of an all-knowing, all-powerful, benevolent god in a universe full of evil, and compared to the arguments against, all the arguments for appeared ridiculous and absurd. Today, a grief counselor was called in to inform the class that one of their classmates had committed suicide the previous night.

"My office is just down the hall, and my door is always open. If you just want to talk, I'll stay here with you to help you through this difficult time."

"Thank you," said the professor. "In light of the circumstances, we're going to skip today's class. I encourage all of you to go and talk to the grief counselor. I do all the time, so there's nothing wrong with asking for a little help sorting out your feelings. So, uh, yeah. Class dismissed. The next time we meet, hopefully, it will be under better circumstances."

Keith slung his backpack over his shoulder and walked out the door as the boy in the sweatsuit blew his nose into a tissue and sobbed. Having no more classes scheduled for the day, Keith made his first stop at the urinal. He was very well hydrated. Then, he would head straight home.

Walking through the lobby, something stood out in the corner of his eye as he passed a newspaper stand. He took a paper. They were free, and they had a multitude of uses, one of which was gathering unreliable information which had a fifty-fifty chance of being corrected the next day. More importantly, they contained job postings. More important still, they absorbed grease rather well on a plate of fried fish, they could serve as acceptable emergency toilet paper, and they made excellent tinder for starting fires. This one had a picture of a submarine adorning its front page with the headline: PENTAGON CONSIDERS TROOP RECALL IN LIGHT OF SUNKEN SHIP FINDINGS. It was in the corner, at the bottom, right under the lead story titled: PLANS TO REDUCE YOUR CARBON FOOTPRINT.

"Hmm. That might be worth reading," Keith said to himself. He rolled up the paper and slid it into his backpack.

Exiting the doors, Keith was hit with a blast of gelid air. He strode quickly to his car in the parking lot. He unlocked the door, opened it, slung his bag into the passenger seat and shut himself in hastily. Starting the engine, he let it idle for a minute. The weather app on his phone said it was twenty-two degrees, which wouldn't have been too bad if not for the wind. It was days like this one that made him miss Hawaii. On the Big Island, it snowed on top of the mountains in the winter, but by the beach, it never fell below sixty degrees. He would sometimes sleep on the beach, listening to the waves. You could hear the crabs running over the rocks all night. Apart from all the homeless drug addicts and littered beaches, it was a beautiful place, to be sure. At the end of their years of active duty, many of the marines chose to stay out there, but Keith always felt sort-of trapped, almost claustrophobic on the islands. It wasn't home. Of course, Indiana winters weren't all that great either. You were dreaming of a white Christmas? You get a brown one. There's always a chance of a white Easter though.

He missed the Marine Corps. He still had dreams where he was back in uniform with the men. He had considered staying in, but as he saw the culture changing, heard speeches from the officers promoting "inclusivity" rather than combat effectiveness, and watched the politicization of the once great military, he knew that it wouldn't be the same. The Corps was no longer the Corps; like every other American institution, it was dying. Fat and apathetic, it was climbing into a warm bath, with a belly full of sugar, and slitting its own wrists. He wouldn't be there to watch it bleed out. The last Marines were gone.

Keith turned on some music and pulled out of the parking lot.

1030

Joe looked over his work. Everything was looking good. He flipped the power back on, and the system came humming to life. He threw his tools in his bag, locked the door, slid the key under the door mat, and turned to leave. Then, he heard the fan stop running. The blades hummed lower and lower until they came to a halt. He set his tool bag down, wiped the snot from his nose and upper lip with his sleeve, and stood in disbelief for a few seconds, thinking of what could cause the malfunction. He approached the unit, looking all around, there was no reason for it to shut off like that after he had it working. He checked the circuit board for error codes—no lights. Retrieving the key once more, he unlocked the door and flipped the light switch. Must have had a power outage. What a time to have it too, he thought. The people who lived there would have to wait a little longer before they could get heat. With any luck, they might have the power back on before they got home from work. He shut and locked the door again, returned the key beneath the mat, and walked back to the van with his tools.

The loss of power likely meant that everyone connected to the same substation was without power right now. This kind of thing happened all the time, and it was usually the result of a tree crossing the lines, or sometimes, a pole would break and fall to the ground. More often than not, the linemen could have the power back on in six hours or so, but if it was really bad, if there were multiple downed lines in different locations, it could take days. The linemen were stretched thin during bad storms, and energy companies would usually resort to outside help from journeymen in another district when situations like that arose. This one was probably just a tree falling on the lines again and shouldn't take too long to fix. There was a wind of about fifteen miles per hour or so, but it was a clear day. He was shivering, and his face and hands were numb again. He just wanted to get back in his van and warm up.

He unlocked the van and put his tools in the back before shutting the doors a little harder than necessary and settling in the driver's seat. Glad to be out of the wind, he put the key in the ignition and turned it. Stone-cold silent and dead. Nothing happened. He turned it again to no avail. "Seriously?" He breathed with exasperation. He was too cold, too tired to be angry. "I don't believe this," he muttered, pulling out his phone. The screen was black. He held the power button down. Nothing happened. "What is going on?" he said aloud. "This can't be happening." He rubbed his eyes. He needed to think. His mouth was dry. He could fix that. He took a long drink from a bottle of tea. He had charged his phone the night before. Maybe the cold drained the battery. He didn't know. There was a power outage, but that wouldn't affect his van or phone battery. Why would the van not start? The doors were all shut, the lights were off, he had the keys in his pocket when he was working on the heating unit.

Joe got out and retrieved his multimeter from the tool bag in the back. He popped the hood and looked at the battery terminals. Everything looked good. He checked the charge of the battery. Twelve volts. He could check that off the list of suspects. If he had an electrical problem, there was no way he was going to try to fix it now. He could barely keep his eyes open, and he was still shivering. He needed a bathroom as well. Looking around him, he saw no one. Everyone was at work or school at 10:35 on a Wednesday. He relieved himself behind the driver's side door, grabbed his bottle of tea, and began walking down the road in hopes of borrowing a neighbor's cell phone.

1030

Faye tore the check out and handed it to the cashier.

"Thank you," he said. He looked at it and began typing in numbers on his keyboard when the lights went out.

One of the shoppers gasped. Voices could be heard grumbling in the aisles, but nobody moved. It was as if everyone was waiting for something to happen. Nothing was happening. A voice called out from the back of the store, "Hello! What happened to the lights?" Suddenly, feet shuffling, a box hit the floor. A woman's voice: "My phone died!" A man's voice: "What happened to my phone?" Voices began erupting out of the darkness: "Mine's dead too!" "What just happened?" "What's going on!" The complaints grew louder, and the confusion began to morph into panic.

A door opened and closed, and a voice shouted, "Attention customers! May I have your attention, please. This is the store manager speaking. We seem to have had a power outage. Please take whatever items you have and proceed to the registers in an orderly fashion. We will get everyone checked out, and then, we will close the store until the problem is resolved. Thank you for your patience. If anyone has a flashlight, please help others find their way to the registers."

Faye didn't know what to do, but the cashier said, "We can do this later; you're good to go."

"Okay, thank you." She was truly grateful. Grateful that the store was so accommodating, and grateful that she was already checked out and not somewhere in the back of the store, trying to fumble around in the dark, surrounded by angry strangers. She pushed her cart to the sliding doors, but they didn't open. She felt stupid, and then scared, she didn't know how to get out, and she didn't want to ask for help when everyone was on edge. Looking around, she saw another glass door with a handle. She pulled her cart back with her through the portal and into the freezing air. Glad to be outside, away from the darkness and confinement, she pushed the cart to her car and took a deep breath. She pushed the unlock button on the key fob in her pocket and pulled the door handle. The door didn't budge. She pulled harder—maybe it was frozen. Taking the fob out of her pocket and holding it up to the door, she pushed the unlock button. She didn't hear anything. She tried again. Nothing. She yanked on the handle. It was locked. "Oh, come on!" she exclaimed. She took out her phone. The power button did nothing. She took her glove off and pressed it again. She held it down. Nothing was happening. Her vision was blurring. Tears welled up in her eyes as she started hyperventilating. Sucking in cold air. Light-headed. Knees buckling. She was having a panic attack.

1030

The car skipped over the train tracks. Keith was singing along to one of the best songs on his playlist. The guitar solo was coming up, the drums thundered through the speakers, and then, everything went silent. It took a couple of seconds for Keith to realize the radio's face had gone dark. It took him another couple of seconds to realize that he was no longer driving—he was merely coasting along the road. The engine was not running. He let the car roll nearly a quarter mile, slowing, slowing, until it finally rolled to a halt about fifty yards from the stop sign in front of him. He put the vehicle in park and tried to start it again. Nothing happened. One more time for good measure. Well, maybe someone could pick him up. He took out his cell phone. Holding the power button produced no effect. Apparently, it was dead. He pushed in the button to turn on his flashers and got out of the car. Walking up to the stop sign at the T-intersection, he began to see people getting out of their parked cars in the middle of the road. All the traffic had stopped.

He said nothing, though he was usually one to talk to himself. He just stared in wonder at the bizarre spectacle he was witnessing. People were talking to each other in the middle of the road, making hand gestures and looking around amidst a frozen river of cars and trucks and buses. He turned back. His flashers were not working. Driving was out. And it looked like there would be no help coming. He grabbed his backpack and began taking stock of the items he had in the car. He removed his schoolbooks and left them in the passenger seat. Lighters, tools, water, flashlight, anything worth its weight—into the bag it went. He had a special bag just for emergencies that stayed in the car all the time; he clipped it onto his school backpack. It was about ten miles' walk to get back home. He had hiked farther than that in the past. Double-checking all his supplies, he took a claw hammer from the trunk and slid it into his belt before locking the doors and slipping the keys into his coat pocket. There was nothing to do now but start walking.

Chapter Two

Day 1

Ten miles. He would walk through Bloomington. Third Street was the most direct way. It cut straight through the city, connecting East and West, but that meant going through downtown. If all the roads were jammed up with dead cars and scared people, he didn't want to be around them. The railroad would be a safer route. It would take him directly to Mount Sinai Road with far fewer travelers to cross paths with, probably. He turned right at the stop sign and began walking south on Curry Pike.

People were getting out of their cars. Some were looking under their hoods for something they could fix. One woman was crying as she continued trying to turn on her cell phone. She had two small children with her in booster seats in the back. Keith wanted to stop and help her, but what could he do? He slowed down a bit. Maybe... no. If she lived more than a couple of miles away, there was nothing he could do to help her. He was stranded too. It was too cold for those kids to be walking home. They were not dressed for the weather, and one of them looked to be only two. God help them. He turned away and walked on. Poor woman; his heart was telling him to turn back, to do something. He felt sick at the thought of leaving her there, but he had his own mother to... oh no. Where was she? He looked at his watch.

49

1041. Did she say she was going somewhere today? Yes. Or was that... He couldn't remember.

Keith picked up his pace and began talking to himself again. "If she's in Brown County, there's no way. No point in thinking about that then. Could she be getting groceries? Better check. It's out of the way. Take me an extra hour, at least. I have to. What's she going to do? I hope she's there and not... Well, I have to check them all if she's not. My watch still works." He looked down at his watch. Weird.

"Who you talking to?" a voice came from behind a car. "Is your phone working?"

Keith looked to his right but kept walking. "No. I was just talking to myself. Sorry."

The man who looked to be in his thirties took a step toward him and then, stopped. "Damnit." His hair hung down to his chest. He was wearing a hoodie three sizes too big for him and ripped jeans, likewise ill-fitting, sagging around his thighs. He took a puff on a cigarette and said, "What's in the bag?"

"Books," Keith replied, continuing at the same pace. "I'm coming back from school."

"Damn, dude. Alright. You ain't gotta be like that." He opened the door to the rusty, old minivan and flicked his cigarette butt toward Keith as he climbed in.

Keith left the man behind him and kept walking. "Leave it alone, dude," he mumbled under his breath. He heard the van door slam shut behind him with a curse from the man.

The stoplights were out. Two old farmers were looking at them and talking to each other. "I never seen nothin' like it," one man said.

"Yeah. Well, this damn technology they got in all this stuff nowadays is always actin' up. You can't rely on any of it," said the other.

"My wife convinced me to get this new truck just a couple weeks back. Last time I take her advice, I'll tell you that. My old truck never gave me no problems. Still runs good."

"I hear ya. Had mine for about a year now. Thought it'd be a good investment. Just a real good-lookin' piece of junk now. Hell if I know how to fix any of this stuff. All microchips and computers and whatnot."

"They sure don't make 'em like they used to, you know it?" The old man took a sip of coffee from a thermos.

"No, sir. They sure don't."

"How far are you from home?"

"Oh, it's pert' near twenty miles west."

"Well, hell, I'm only a couple miles that way myself. Come on over to the farm, and we'll see if my old pickup still runs. Ain't the first time we've had to walk home, is it?"

"No, sir, it ain't. Let me just grab my coffee, first."

The two men in their seventies began walking together down the road like two old friends. Neither seemed to be concerned with the breakdown of technology. They could probably remember what it was like before everyone had electricity, Keith thought. He'd heard there were a few houses in Monroe County that still didn't have electricity or indoor plumbing.

Keith turned east on State Road 48. He decided to cut across the parking lots and head south on Liberty Drive to see if Faye was there. Scanning the scene around him constantly, he listened to the sounds of this strange new environment. There were shouts of anger and frustration all around. People calling for help. Talking. The sound of voices had replaced the previously ever-present din of combustion engines and too-loud stereo systems blaring either hip-hop or pop-country music. It was far quieter though. Intermittent screams pleading for information. "What is happening!" Glass shattering. Keith turned. A man had smashed the windshield of his car and was continuing to beat it with a tire iron. He didn't say anything; he simply pounded away at his car, determined to punish it.

Faye could be anywhere around here. What would she be doing right now? He looked at his watch again. 1109. A rumble behind him. Truck driving by on 48. Needed a new muffler, by the sound of it. Wait. He turned around. It had already passed, whatever it was. He hadn't even thought about it, at first, but that was the sound of a truck. Driving. A woman ran out of a convenience store, looking around frantically. After a few seconds, she hung her head and went back inside. He could still hear it faintly. Half a mile away now, but there was a growl. Heading west. Interesting. It didn't make a difference to him now though. He turned back and picked up the pace.

He had heard that, right? Yes. Probably. Maybe. It could have been in his head. If he didn't find her at any of the stores, he would have to take Third Street back. Or would she have taken the bypass? There was no way to know and no way to check both. Not today. It would be dark in about six hours. And the temperature might drop again. That was bad enough, but... He heard a crash to his left. Shouting. He looked. He couldn't understand what was being yelled, but a man was running across a parking lot with a large bag in his arms. An overweight police officer ran out from behind a squad car, but after a few steps, he pulled out his pistol. The man had already run behind a building and disappeared. The officer holstered his weapon and tried to catch his breath as he walked into the building from which the man with the bag had run.

So, it begins, Keith thought. He needed to move quickly. There was no way he wanted to be out at night. He checked his watch again. 1115. If he didn't find Faye at one of the stores, or on the road home, he had to hope she was still at the house. If not, he would have to hope she had found someplace warm and safe to stay the night. He would go out looking again in the morning. If he couldn't find her then, he would have to just hope she could make her way home on her own. Plans are useless, he thought. Planning is essential. All he had now was hope. Stop thinking; you're overthinking again. Stay focused.

In a hardware store parking lot, a girl was walking frantically in circles around a group of cars. She was crying and pacing back and forth. She clearly couldn't decide what to do. He could almost read her mind, even from that distance. She stopped and looked up at him as he continued walking, and she began to sob. Fear. She was paralyzed by it. That could be me soon, Keith thought. "Don't think," he said aloud to himself, "Well, do think. But don't overthink. See, you're doing it again. Shut up and move." He looked at his watch. 1123. Poor girl. He thought about the woman in the car he left on Curry Pike. Two babies in the back seat. No. Don't think.

At 1130, he reached the parking lot of the first store. It was always the first store on her list, so it was the first on his. If she wasn't here, the next two stores were farther west, which would take him back farther from home. This store had already added nearly two-and-a-half miles to his trek. The other stores would take an additional mile-and-a-half of walking. Other than a few abandoned cars, the parking lot looked empty. Better make sure, he thought. He stepped carefully through the parking lot, staying away from the vehicles and avoiding patches of ice that had survived a recent application of rock salt. There, at the end. He saw it. That was her car. As he approached, he noticed a shopping cart handle on the driver's side. He reached the cart; it was full of bags of groceries. Keith looked inside the car, then circled around it. He scanned the parking lot again. Nothing. He tried the driver's door. Of course, it wouldn't open—he didn't have the key fob.

Keith approached the store's door cautiously but nearly ran into the glass before realizing that the automatic door wouldn't open. He felt like a fool. He was looking around for another entrance when a door to the side opened with a man sticking his head out.

"Keith?" the man said.

"Yes?" he asked hesitantly. Who was this stranger who knew his name?

"Please come in."

Keith followed the man into the store, and he immediately saw his mother sitting on the floor along with a few other people around the vestibule.

The man spoke quietly to Keith. "We had a power outage, so we got the customers checked out as quickly as possible. Took IOUs from everyone who didn't have cash or check, you know. Apparently, everyone's car is dead too. I found your mom sitting on the ground by her car about half an hour ago. Brought her inside, out of the cold. She's a bit shook up. I gave her a Gatorade and a chocolate bar. She seems to be doing a lot better now. I'm Tom, by the way. I'm the manager." He presented his hand to shake.

Keith shook his hand. "Thank you. I can't thank you enough." He looked at Faye. She had tears in her eyes, but she smiled at him. Keith pulled out his wallet and handed the man a twenty-dollar bill. "For the snacks," he said.

"Don't worry about it. On the house." Tom shook his head.

"No, please, I insist. You've done us a big favor. I don't know if this is worth anything anymore, but it's the least I can do. Take it."

"Alright," Tom took the bill. "But for that price, you should have some yourself." He pulled out a Gatorade bottle and a chocolate bar from a box on the floor beside him. "Here."

"Thanks." Keith put the supplies in his coat pocket. "We'll be able to walk back home. It's not that far."

"Oh, good. In that case, take one for the road." He handed him another bottle and candy bar.

"What about you? What will you do?"

Tom shrugged. "I'm the manager. I'll stay as long as I need to. I don't have anyone waiting for me at home. Hopefully, the power will come back. If not, maybe someone will come to pick these people up soon. They can stay the night here if need be. There's some pillows and blankets and stuff in some boxes back there. We'll be alright."

Faye got to her feet and hugged Keith.

Keith nodded to Tom. "Thank you again."

"Not a problem."

Faye turned and hugged Tom.

"Hey, that's alright," he said. "You two take care of yourselves."

"Likewise," Keith replied, shaking hands with Tom again. He looked at Faye. "Ready?"

She nodded.

As they turned to leave, Tom said, "Hey, if the power doesn't come back on by tomorrow, you guys are more than welcome to come back here and take what you want from the frozen and refrigerated sections. No charge. It'll have to be dumped otherwise."

"Thank you. We'll remember that," Keith said as he opened the door.

Faye went straight to her car. She tried the door again. Still locked. "What's wrong with this stupid thing? Can you fix it?"

"Definitely not," Keith replied.

"Where's your car?" she asked.

"Couple miles back that way."

"You walked here?"

"Yep."

"How did you know I would be here?"

"I didn't."

"How are we going to get back home?" Faye looked around.

"The old-fashioned way. Chevro-legs. I hope those are comfortable shoes."

"We can't walk that far!"

"Yes, we can. And we will."

"But what about the groceries?"

Keith thought for a second. I can take whatever can fit in my backpack. We'll have to leave the rest. Decide what you want most." He unslung his bag and unzipped it on the ground. He rearranged the tools in his bag and folded the newspaper in one of his coat pockets.

"Oh, man. I can't believe this." She looked at her full shopping cart and began going through it. "What a shame. What a waste."

Keith decided to eat the chocolate bar he'd been given. They were about to burn a lot of calories, he thought. He drank his Gatorade as Faye filled his backpack, stacking items meticulously. He looked at his watch. 1159. He was starting to get a little hungry. "Are you getting hungry?"

"No, I had a... Well, yes. I guess it is about time for lunch, huh?"

"Whatever doesn't fit in there we can eat as we go."

Faye finished packing her most desired items in the bag and zipped it shut. "Okay. There you go." She started eating some carrots from a bag. "And I'll carry this." She pointed to a canvas bag.

"Alright." Keith looked through what was still in the cart. Cheese? Oh, no way he was leaving that. He took it and looked at Faye who was frowning and looking in her bag.

"No. We need carrots. I should have put those in and maybe left out the... well... hmm. You have to have beta carotene. I read somewhere that..."

"Mom. Come on." Keith lifted his backpack. "Oh my... what did you put in here?"

"Is it too heavy? Don't hurt your back. I better put lettuce in there and take something else out."

"Lettuce?" Keith slung the bag over his shoulders. "Come on, let's go."

"Wait, but we can't leave..."

"Leave it." He looked at his watch.

"Keith, wait."

"Mom, it's a ten-mile hike back to the house. Now, I could make it in three hours, but with you, it's gonna be more like six. By that time, it'll be dark. Now, do you want to be walking around out here at night? I'm leaving." He turned and started walking.

"Okay, okay. I'm coming. Hang on." She grabbed the canvas bag and followed him. "Which way are you going to take?"

"I figure we'd better go north on this road until we hit the tracks and then, follow them home. Most people will probably stay on the roads."

"What if a train comes?"

"Are you serious?"

"Sorry." She bit into another carrot. "You never know."

"If we see a train moving on the tracks, we'll be ecstatic and celebrate as soon as we step aside to let it pass."

"Why would we celebrate a train?"

"Because that means that they may get all of this fixed before people start looting. You remember Katrina? Nightmare."

"Oh, don't be such an alarmist. They have plans for that."

"Ha! *I'm* the alarmist! That's funny."

Through the windows of some of the lifeless cars in the road and in the parking lots on either side, they could see people sitting in their driver's seats. Some people were apparently not sure what to do yet. Unwilling to leave their vehicles and walk what may be many miles in some cases, some people probably thought it best to wait for everything to come back to life. Maybe it would. Maybe the government would send people to help. Maybe even the National Guard would come to the rescue. They had plans for these scenarios, after all. There was some kind of malfunction, but it would probably be fixed soon. Maybe the best thing to do was to stay calm and wait.

They were not the only ones walking home by the looks of it. A woman was walking on the sidewalk with her arms crossed and her head down. She was crying, clearly not dressed for the weather, besides her wool coat, and she was walking in high heels. She stepped wrong and broke the heel off of her shoe, twisting her ankle and collapsing to the ground. She sat for a couple of seconds, silently, as if stunned, and then she began to sob uncontrollably.

Faye looked and gasped. She nudged Keith and quietly said, "We have to help her!"

Keith kept moving. "Somebody will. We can't. We're losing time."

Faye grabbed his coat sleeve. "Come on! How can you just leave her like that?"

Keith maintained his pace. "There's no time. Most of these people live in town. It's not too far for them to walk. We've got another nine miles to go. She'll be okay." He kept walking, but in the back of his mind, he thought he had just lied.

Faye's eyes began to water as she bit her lip and struggled to keep up.

A man approached them from ahead and asked, "Hey, do you guys know what's going on?"

"No," Keith said. "Probably, the best thing to do right now is get home and see if we get this all figured out tomorrow, you know?"

"You think we'll get this figured out?" The man looked around and back at them.

"Oh yeah. They have plans for this sort of thing. I wouldn't worry too much." They kept walking.

The man followed. "Where's home?"

"Not too far," Keith responded. "Are you going to be able to get back alright?"

Faye shifted the bag to her other shoulder and kept the man in her peripheral view. She moved to the other side of Keith, putting a little distance between her and the stranger.

The man looked at her. "I'm from out of town. I was on my way back from a business meeting." He stepped toward Faye. "Ma'am, can I help you carry that?"

"No," Faye got out.

"We're alright," Keith quickly replied. "Thank you, though. Hey, I'm sorry to hear you're away from home. You got cash? Maybe you could get a room for the night at the hotel just back that way. I'm sure by the morning everything will be worked out." They continued to walk.

The man continued to follow. "No. I don't have any cash on me. I normally use card, you know?"

"Yeah, me too."

"Where do you live?" The man asked.

Keith stopped and turned to look directly at the man. "We know how to get there, thank you. I hope you're able to make it back to your family soon. They're probably worried."

The man glanced up and down at Keith. The corner of his mouth twitched as he put his hands into the pockets of his leather jacket. He stepped back and said, "Alright. Thanks."

"Good luck," Keith said as the man turned to walk away. Keith watched him go for a few moments. The man adjusted the black beanie on his head, pulled up the hood of his sweatshirt, and pulled something out of the pocket of his jeans. Whatever it was, he popped it into his mouth and threw the wrapper on the ground. Once he was obscured by a building, Keith and Faye began walking again.

"What a creep," Faye said.

"Yeah. Maybe."

Faye looked back over her shoulder as she walked. "Do you think that guy was telling the truth?"

"I don't know. Can't afford to find out either."

Faye shuddered. "Ugh. Creep. Do you really think they'll have everything fixed by tomorrow?"

"I don't know."

"But do you think so?"

"No."

When they reached the tracks, Keith checked his watch. 1236. They followed the tracks east. Keith looked back at Faye. She was staring fixedly at the ground before her.

"Doin' alright?"

"Yep."

"Is that getting heavy?"

"I got it."

Once they reached the bridge over the interstate, Keith stopped for a couple of seconds to listen. He didn't want to be caught in the middle of a bridge with a train coming. Hadn't he seen that in a movie? He heard nothing. Nothing except the scuffing of shoes on the interstate below. A mumbling of voices now and then.

Faye stopped beside him. "What?"

"Shh." He heard something. Something else. A growl. Then, the voices below became excited and grew louder.

"Is that?" Faye started to say.

Keith ran up to the bridge to look out at the interstate as people below shouted. Yes! There was a car weaving through the halted traffic on the interstate below. It was old and rusty. It looked like a piece of junk barely holding together. Faye watched the car too. As it passed under the bridge, Keith noticed it was full of trash piled up in the seats, on the dashboard, in the rear window. The passenger side door was a different color than the rest of the car, and it was riding on a donut. But it was driving. People were waving at the car, trying to stop it. Some were even jumping out in its path. The driver swerved around them. All eyes were on the car. Keith looked at Faye who was taking in the spectacle. "We'd better move," he said. "While they're distracted. The fewer eyes on us the better."

They walked across the bridge as quickly and quietly as they could and reached the other side unnoticed as far as they could tell. The weight of the situation was growing on them. People were desperate. They wanted that car. They needed it. What were they willing to do to get it? The gray sky was growing darker.

Behind the theater, Faye stopped and set down her bag with a gasp. "I can't go any more. My hips and knees are killing me."

Keith turned and saw Faye looking around for a place to sit down. "Okay, we can take a bit of a break, but you can't sit down. In this cold, you'll start cramping up. Then, you won't be able to get going again."

"I'm already cramping up," Faye complained. "I'm too old to be doing this."

"Here." Keith pulled out his water bottle and the extra Gatorade Tom had given him. He drank a little of the water from the quart bottle, then poured the Gatorade in with the remaining water before pouring half of the mixture back into the Gatorade bottle. He handed her the bottle. "Small sips. Try to stretch a bit."

"I can't..." Faye began.

"You can." Keith looked at his watch. 1309. He scanned the scenery. It was eerily quiet.

Faye drank from the Gatorade bottle. She put the cap back on and froze in place, staring at something off in the distance.

"What?" Keith asked, looking at her.

"What's Lynn doing right now?" She looked back at Keith. "Where is Joe? Where is Kent? Where is everyone? Is this happening everywhere?" Her eyes welled up. She turned red.

"Hey! Stop!" Keith asserted quietly. "We can't do this. Stop it."

Faye was struggling to control her breathing. "What are we going to do?" She wiped the tears from her face.

Keith approached her. He picked up her bag and slung it over his shoulder. "We are going to walk home. Okay? And we will be going through campus pretty soon. And when we do, we will see if Lynn is there. We might find her. If not, she can handle herself. She'll make her way back. She's not going to stay in the dorms where there's no heat. Joe can handle himself. Dad can handle himself. You just worry about what you have to do. Alright? Now, let's go." He started walking.

Faye calmed down and, with a new sense of determination, began walking again. They crossed behind an apartment complex. Some voices, sounds of movement, someone shouting—a man apparently locked out of an apartment, begging to be let in. It was getting colder. At least, it felt that way. The man began screaming wildly, curses and pleas. Loud thuds. He must have been trying to break the door down. The wind picked up, and all at once, it began to snow. The screams continued, and by the time the noise was behind them, it had morphed into faint sobs and whimpering.

The railroad took them to Third Street, and they briefly stopped, looked both ways, and debated which way to go. They decided to stick to their original course. The road would have been a more direct route, and there were fewer people traveling on it than before, but they decided it was still too risky. There were too many opportunities to be turned around, redirected by roadblocks, or attacked. There was no law right now. No one could be trusted. They kept to the tracks where they would be less visible to desperate eyes. This would be a longer way, but it would probably be free of obstruction. On the other hand, they were about to come to The Hill. The Hill was what some people called low-income housing. People who didn't care for euphemisms called the place a dump infested with drug-addicts, drunks, and degenerates. Under normal circumstances, police sirens could be heard every night in this part of Bloomington. But these were not normal circumstances. No one would hear sirens tonight.

As they moved quietly along the rail line, the sounds of nature became increasingly prevalent. The wind howled between buildings and trees. Branches rattled against one another in the breeze. They almost sounded like millions of giant insects crawling on glass. The tinkling of windblown snowflakes striking the surfaces of trees, walls, rooftops, cars, their coats. It reminded Keith of the snap, crackle, pop of milk poured over puffed rice cereal. He used to love that stuff. Why do kids like Rice Crispies? It's like eating nothing, like those mealworms they feed to lizards and birds, like hollow shells that turn to dust under the slightest pressure. Floating in milk. You're eating nothing but spoonfuls of milk with dust floating in it. Dust full of air. Eat your fill, and you're hungry half an hour later. It's the sound more than the taste. They want to hear the snap, crackle, pop. Strange, the things one thinks about. A dog barked. *That* was something normal. One could always hear dogs. In the town or the country, the barking of dogs was ever-present. Keith had always wondered if they were talking to each other, the dogs. Did they understand each other? They were certainly barking at one another. Faye and Keith had decided to walk the tracks mostly out of a belief that it would not have much traffic, but they had not expected to be the only ones on the tracks. So far, they had not encountered anyone else. That was odd; even when people had cars, he would see people walking along the tracks sometimes. Now, it was a natural highway, but no one else was on it. When people had cars. Ha. He was thinking as if cars were a thing of the past—a relic of some bygone era. It had only been about three hours since he was driving himself. He checked his watch. 1342. Up ahead, he saw a shadow moving toward them. Apparently, he had spoken too soon. There was a fellow traveler making his way along the tracks.

"Are you talking to yourself?" Faye asked.

"Huh?" Keith looked back for a second. "Oh, yeah, I guess so. There's somebody coming this way."

"I see him. What should we do?" Faye said quietly, a little tension in her voice.

"Keep walking."

"What if he's up to no good?"

"We'll burn that bridge when we get to it," Keith responded. It was interesting; his mom had always been an anxious sort, but she was already sounding paranoid. It wasn't ill-founded, but it didn't take long for her to assume the worst in everyone. People had told Keith he was paranoid all the time though. They needed to be, he reasoned. Prejudice could save your life; naiveté could end it. What if this guy was crazy? What if this guy wanted to kill them and take their stuff? If he had just a crowbar or a hammer or even a rock. If everything were normal, if their cell phones worked, and if they were able to get them out, and if they were able call the police, and if they were able to tell the police where they were, they would be long dead before help arrived. Keith slipped his hand under his coat and ran his fingers over the hammer in his belt.

The man was dressed in a black trench coat. He watched them as he walked past. Shifty eyes. He looked at Keith. Keith looked at him. They nodded to one another, not saying a word. Keith kept walking but turned his head to watch the man walk away for a couple seconds. The man did the same. Their eyes met again. Keith smiled. It was kind of funny. The man smiled too and waved an acknowledgement back to them before continuing on his path. It was like something out of the old Louis L'Amour stories he used to read. Was this how people would interact from now on? Were they in the Wild West now?

A loud bang pulled him out of his head. It was followed by another. Keith scanned the horizon. Were they gunshots? Or the slamming of a screen door in the wind? He didn't see anything, and Faye didn't say anything. She had looked up at the noise, and again, began walking with her head down, her scarf up over her nose, protecting her face from the wind. She looked miserable but determined to make it. She had to see her family reunited. She held close to Keith and kept looking toward the sounds of shouting from behind the trees and buildings.

There were very few people walking around at present. They probably had the cold to thank for that. Most people just wanted to get to shelter. Out of the wind, away from the snow, they would wait out this power outage, or whatever it was, under some blankets. Many of them had gas stoves and candles or flashlights. Maybe they could make some hot soup and wait for the weather to break. That was one thing to be thankful for, Keith thought. They might be able to make it home without much hassle after all. They had to keep moving, though. People were used to power outages; those were normal. People were used to car problems, dead batteries or whatever. People were used to phones dying. These were annoyances that, even in the internet age, were not cause for alarm. But all of them at once? And not just for you, but for everyone around you too? As he thought about it, it was remarkable that everything seemed so calm.

If it weren't for the cold, everyone would be outside now. What would that be like? What would cause this? He had an idea. There were a couple of things Keith had read about that might do something like this. It would be impossible to know for sure which one it was, but if the effect was isolated, maybe help would come, and this would all be a great story to tell the kids one day. Like the Blizzard of '78. Or the Great Gulf Hurricane of 1900. Of course, this could be much bigger than that. Who knows? Maybe this would be like another Great Depression, shaping a whole generation into hoarders. He thought of the Amish. There were several Amish communities around the state. They wouldn't even notice. The only change for them would be that they would no longer have to worry about paying taxes. How many homesteaders and sustenance farmers didn't even know the Great Depression was happening at the time? It was just another day at the office for them. Life went on.

"How's your dad going to get home?" Faye asked. She had broached the subject once again. She had to be thinking of nothing else. Kent was thirty-seven miles away in Columbus. No one walked that far anymore. Except maybe thrill hikers. It would take him multiple days to walk that far back, if he could make it at all, and she would not know where he was or how he was doing the whole time.

"Somehow, I doubt he'll walk." Keith answered. "Too many cupcakes. And cookies. And pies. And Mountain Dews."

Faye chuckled a bit under her breath.

"And ho-hos and dingdongs and donuts."

Faye punched his shoulder. "He's not that fat."

"Well, it's not for lack of trying."

Faye snorted and rubbed her eyes.

"I'm sure he'll be fine. The power outage might not even be affecting them over there. We don't know. And if it is, he can at least make it to Grandma's house. He might stay there for a little bit."

"Oh yeah. That's true. That would be good. I wonder what she would be doing right now."

"She probably doesn't even notice. She hardly ever uses electricity."

"That's true. Doesn't want to waste money on unnecessary conveniences," Faye nodded sarcastically.

"Well, it hasn't been that long for Grandma. It was just the other day she was telling me how she remembers reading about Ben Franklin's experiment with the kite in the newspaper."

"No, she didn't."

"I swear she did. She also told me Thomas Edison stole her lightbulb design."

"You're making that up. You ought to be more respectful of your grandmother. She's got a lot of memories."

"Yeah, and what she don't remember, she makes up."

"She's forgotten more than either of us can ever hope to learn."

"Oh, I'm convinced of that."

Faye breathed another short laugh through her nose. "She can be pretty entertaining at times. But that's what they did back in her day. They didn't have TVs or computers or video games. They couldn't even afford a radio, so they sat around the fire, telling stories."

"Yeah, well, she'll feel right at home in this environment. Plus, you know, she's got a good stockpile of food and plenty of firewood. I'm sure that's the first place Dad would go, and it's the best place for him to be right now."

Faye still looked anxious. She looked down at the ground and said nothing.

Keith looked at her for a second. "What?"

Faye frowned. "I was just thinking about my dad."

Keith breathed and looked up ahead as he walked. Her family was in Illinois. Without transportation, there was no way they would ever see them again. "Oh, I know he's good. If this thing has reached that far, he's opening a k-ration tin with a bayonet right now." He was trying to lighten the mood. He looked back at Faye. It wasn't working.

Faye looked at the path in front of her, expressionless. "He's not so young now. He has a hard time getting around." She bit her lip. "And sometimes he forgets to eat..." She trailed off, looking up into the trees.

"One thing at a time," Keith offered. "Right now, we're going to find Lynn."

———————————————————

The university campus stood in stark contrast from the rest of Bloomington—a mixture of incongruous stone architecture. Most of the inhabitants here were from out of town, and they looked down their noses at the uneducated, uncultured rednecks that made up this part of the country. The intellectuals claimed that all cultures were equal, but clearly, some were more equal than others. These bitter clingers didn't vote the right way or listen to the right music or wear the right clothes or drive the right cars or eat the right foods. People like Faye and people like Keith. Antisocial people who knew where their food came from and knew where the university's power came from.

The campus was lit up night and day, using an enormous and continuous flow of electric power to maintain lighting, computers, heating, and cooling. All of this energy had been produced by burning coal, and every week, students drew cute, little messages in colored chalk on the sidewalks about saving the planet from fossil fuels. Dozens of them would meet inside buildings or outside on the lawns, depending on how nice the weather was, and they would demand somebody do something about the end of the world. The professors and administrators would praise their courage and commitment to change because their tuition went into the university's coffers, and it was invested into coal and oil operations among other revenue schemes, while the professors were paid to teach the students that the world would end in their lifetime if the energy sector was not destroyed. The university was buying up all the best real estate, expanding into new markets, and pushing out competing businesses throughout the region. Every year, they raised tuition rates and took more money from the state and federal governments so that the president of each college within the university could give himself a salary higher than the president of the United States was paid and receive accolades and praise for his speeches condemning wealth inequality and big energy companies. The only people who pointed this out were those deplorable, dirty, uncultured hillbillies who were morally and intellectually inferior and afraid of change. Now, the buildings were all dark and quiet.

The wind had died down. The snow had ceased to fall. The sun was beginning to shine through intermittent gaps in the clouds, and it felt much warmer now. With no way of knowing what the temperature was, Keith guessed it was close to thirty degrees. He looked at his watch again. 1537. They were making pretty good time. Better than he had expected.

Keith and Faye had turned south at the gym, leaving the tracks behind. Lynn's dorm was straight ahead. There was far more movement here than there had been a mile back. People walked up and down sidewalks, rode bicycles and skateboards through the streets. Who knows where they were going? Some of the students were talking to friends, and it looked as if they were organizing parties. Classes were cancelled; what else were they going to do? A man-bun on a skateboard rolled past the two with bottles of vodka in his hands. He disappeared behind a building, and a cheer arose from an unseen crowd of students. Lynn's dorm was directly in front of them, and as they neared the building, the skunk-like stench of cannabis smoke tainted the air. The strumming of guitar strings accompanied shouts and laughter. As Faye and Keith rounded the corner to reach the door, there appeared a group of what looked like about fifty students, standing, sitting, smoking, drinking, dancing, laughing, singing, and playing as other students brought out desks, chairs, and notebooks from the surrounding buildings and threw them onto a pile in the lawn.

Keith and Faye entered the building as quickly and inconspicuously as possible. "What are they doing?" Faye asked.

"No idea. I don't want to find out." Keith pulled a flashlight out of a pocket in his backpack. "Lead the way," he said as he handed Faye the flashlight. She depressed the button and illuminated the darkness before them as they navigated the dormitory hallways and stairwells. The flashlight worked.

Faye had been here several times to bring food and supplies to Lynn. She checked on her at least once a week. When she reached the door, she knocked and tried to open it. Locked. Keith set the bags on the floor beside the door and sat in the dark hallway. His back and shoulders ached in a way that brought back memories. He took out his water bottle and drank. Faye knocked again. She listened intently for movement of any kind behind the door. She knocked again. The door to the left of Lynn's opened.

A timid voice escaped the dark portal. "Mom?"

Faye shined the flashlight on the face of the speaker. "Lynn..." she choked on the name. She swallowed, composed herself, and lowered the light. "Sorry, I'm looking for my daughter Lynn. She lives in this room."

The girl sniffled. "Oh, I don't know her." She closed the door gently, and Faye could hear her crying from behind the door.

Keith breathed and didn't say a word as Faye sunk to the floor of the hallway. He didn't need to hear her say anything. He could feel it. She let the flashlight roll out of her hand onto the floor. Through the muffled sounds of the chaos outside the dorm, her irregular breathing whispered in the dark. The click of a button, and the light was gone. The two of them sat for several minutes in the blackness, the stillness; neither spoke. The only sound other than the din from the crowd outside was their breathing. And the soft hum from Faye's smothered sobs.

Keith pressed the light button on his digital watch. In the blue-green glow, the numbers 1551 appeared.

"What time is it?"

"Ten till four. We've got just over two hours until sunset."

"I don't know where her classes are. Do you think we should try to find her?"

"I think she's going to be somewhere warm and quiet. Maybe a friend's house with a gas stove or fireplace. They're probably playing board games, making chai tea lattes or whatever it is you people drink."

"Yeah," Faye sniffed. "That's what I would be doing right now, if I were her." She shook her head. "She's overconfident. She thinks she can do anything, but she's just so little."

Keith chuckled a bit at this, "We'll come back tomorrow and look for her. You can let her have a sleepover, can't you? How old is she now, anyway? Nineteen? When I was nineteen..."

"It's different for you. And anyway, I wasn't happy about you going off and joining the Marines either. You know how many nights I cried myself to sleep, wondering if you were going to come back?" Faye continued, "But she's not stupid like you. She's a lot smarter than I was." Her voice trailed off. "I wish I could do the things she can do." Then, Faye's voice changed pitch, and she said, "You're right. She can handle herself." The flashlight clicked back on, and Faye got to her feet. "Okay, let's go."

Keith got up, shouldered his backpack, and lifted the canvas shopping bag. "Wait for me."

When they opened the door, the pile of furniture and books was on fire. Students were dancing around the inferno, tossing things into the blaze. A bong was passed around. A girl with pink hair, wire-rimmed glasses, and a nose ring shouted, "Gaia's revenge!" A student with blonde dreadlocks and a misspelled word tattooed on his face shouted his approval, "It's what you fascists deserve! Ha!" He swilled from a vodka bottle and spat into the flames.

Onto the bonfire, the students flung books. History, philosophy, theology, biology, mathematics, literature. The flames licked at the pages, and smoke flowed up from the burnt offering. They mixed cheap vodka with juice from the fruit of the tomato vine and gulped it greedily. The blood-red liquid stained their mouths and hands as they wiped the drippings from their faces. A pregnant girl swallowed a cup of the sacrament, and taking a page torn from a Bible, she rolled a wad of green into a thick cylinder, ignited one end, and sucked in the incense as she tossed the book into the flames.

Keith and Faye tried not to be noticed as they crept past the students, but it was impossible.

"Look at the capitalists!" A green-haired girl shrieked. "Racists! Not-sees! Shills!"

A purple-haired kid in designer sunglasses laughed. "I don't know what any of those are!" He giggled. He took another drink.

As Keith and Faye rounded the corner of the dormitory, a bottle shattered against the stone wall beside Keith's head. They kept moving.

"What's in the bags? Are you, like, looting? Imperialists!" a blue-haired girl shrieked.

They continued walking until the group was out of sight; the screams followed them.

A voice screeched to no one in particular, "You thought you could, just like, rape Gaia and get away with it? You can't save the planet! You are the patriarchy! Colonizers! But Gaia took her revenge! Now you'll check your privilege! Hahahahahaha! Hahaha! Ha! Haha!" The entire crowd was laughing now. The echoes of their laughter and screams reverberated off the limestone walls of the campus buildings. "Gaia's revenge!"

With nearly one-hundred yards between them and the dormitory, Faye looked over her shoulder. "Higher education." She shook her head and sighed. "Is that the future of America?"

Keith checked his watch again. "I think about six hours ago, that became its past."

When they reached the railroad, they turned right and continued to follow the tracks east. "I don't want to leave Lynn out here with people like that," groaned Faye.

"I know," Keith said. "Don't worry, we'll find her tomorrow. With any luck, we'll reach Mount Sinai in a little over an hour."

They were out of water. The bags were getting heavy. It was definitely warming up. Water dripped from the glistening ice hanging on the tree branches. Keith was beginning to sweat. Normally, he would have stopped to cool down in weather like this. Sweating in freezing weather could be deadly, but with less than a mile to go before reaching the road, they decided to push on.

As they left the town behind them, the houses became gradually more dispersed. Apartments gave way to subdivisions; subdivisions turned into farmhouses. There was more grass, more trees. American flags flew in yards, sheds and barns were regular features of the scenery, and dogs ran around fenced-in areas, barking at the passing travelers. It was even quieter out here. Besides the dogs barking, the air was filled with the sounds of birds and the chatter of squirrels. The birds and squirrels shook pieces of ice from the branches. Ice particles crackled and plopped into the patches of snow and mud below. Out here, there were not only pickup trucks in driveways, but tractors as well, and as they neared Mount Sinai Road, horse trailers. They had seen some people carrying backpacks and duffel bags, riding bicycles or pulling wagons, heading toward town. Most people were probably trying to stock up on supplies right now; stockpiling was always the first thing people did in a natural disaster. It was warmer now, and after seven hours with no power, people were ready to go outside to collect some supplies, look around, and gather information.

Keith could see the graveyard up ahead, through the naked trees. A small grain silo and a weathered barn to the right of the tracks. They were almost there. Keith's watch said 1701 when they came to the road. A rumbling, sputtering, coughing engine growled as a rusty, old truck rattled down the road toward town.

"Why do you think some cars are still running?" Faye asked.

"I'm not sure, but I bet it has something to do with computers," Keith answered.

"Computers? What do you mean?"

"I don't know a lot about cars, but I know the newer vehicles are all computers and microchips and stuff. The old vehicles were much simpler. All mechanical. Whatever happened must have fried all the computers somehow."

"And that's why phones don't work either," Faye nodded contemplatively.

The sun was going down, the wind had picked up, and thick, dark clouds were rolling in. The temperature had to be in the mid-thirties. Keith looked at his watch again. 1721. Just as they reached the driveway, it began to rain.

"Oh! I better check the mail!" Faye hobbled to the mailbox as quickly as possible, opened and shut the little door, and hobbled back. "Nothing." She looked disappointed.

Keith snickered.

"I guess I should have known." She pulled her hood up and tried not to slip on the patches of frozen mud in the long driveway.

When they got to the house, Faye gingerly stepped around the slick, muddy patches in front of the steps, careful not to fall. They were both tired.

"Oh, I'm so happy to be back." Faye wiped the soles of her shoes on the welcome mat in front of the door. "I can't believe we walked that whole way." She opened the door and looked back at Keith. "Here, let me take that bag. Boy, we were lucky to get here just as the rain started." Carrying the bag through the doorway, she stopped in the glow of candlelight.

Lynn stood beside the woodstove, stirring a pot. "It's about time you guys showed up. Want some ramen?"

Chapter Three

Faye dropped her bag and wrapped her arms around Lynn as tears rolled down her cheeks. "We didn't know where you were. How did you get home?"

"How did you?" Lynn responded. "I'm not helpless, Mom."

"I know, but..."

"The power was out, and I had nothing better to do, so I walked here. It's only like four miles."

"But why didn't you stay in your room?"

"Uh, duh, because it was cold in there, and I was hungry. Now, get off me; my ramen's gonna burn." Lynn shook loose of Faye's grasp and took the pot off the wood stove.

Keith had put down the backpack and began filling his water bottle in the sink. At least that was still working. Keith sat down in a chair, sipping the cool water.

Faye sat down with a glass, clearly exhausted. Lynn put a bowl of ramen on the table in front of her. "Oh, thank you, Lynn."

"Sorry, you'll have to make your own," Lynn said to Keith before slurping up some noodles.

"That's fine." He wasn't hungry yet anyway.

As the light outside faded into black, the shadows grew long and dark and danced over the walls in the flickering candlelight. Faye clenched her teeth between spoonfuls of ramen and rubbed cramping muscles. They sat quietly around the table beside the woodstove for several minutes before Lynn said, "By the way, I fed your chickens. And the pigs."

"Oh, yeah," Faye said. "I forgot about them."

"Thanks," Keith responded. "I had forgotten too." He looked at Faye. "Let's just put the stuff in the fridge for now and deal with it tomorrow."

Once the groceries were put away, everyone took a flashlight to bed. Keith was coated in dried sweat, but he was too tired to shower, so he flopped down onto the bed without even bothering to undress.

Day 2

Outside, the chickens were cackling away. Time for breakfast. Keith awoke with a headache as he did every morning. It was just after dawn; sunlight was streaming through the window. He reached for his phone to check the time and stared at the black screen for a couple of seconds before muttering, "Oh, right." He let the phone slide out of his hand and fall to the floor. Taking a drink from his water bottle, he took a couple of pills and eased himself out of bed. The room was cold. He hadn't slept that well since the last time he hiked ten miles. "I'll have to do that more often," he said to himself. "Not."

Walking into the bathroom, he flipped the light switch. Nothing happened. He growled. The sunlight from the bathroom window was enough to brush his teeth and wash his face. After throwing on a jacket and shoes, he took food and water to the animals behind the house and checked his traps. Nothing today. When he had finished, he went back inside, slipped off his shoes and jacket and flipped the light switch only to hear a loud click.

"Ha ha," Lynn's voice came from the kitchen. She stuck her head around the corner. "Idiot."

Keith laughed for a second. Just then, they heard another loud click of a light switch followed by a dejected "Oh." They both burst out laughing. Faye began laughing too. They laughed for several seconds before Faye had to sit down, still sore from yesterday's walk.

Faye decided the first thing they needed was light. She hobbled around the house on her bruised feet and sore legs, removing any blinds, drapes, or obstructions of any kind from the windows. It was forty degrees outside, according to the thermometer on the deck, and the remaining snow was disappearing quickly. By noon, there would be nothing but mud on the ground wherever the sun shone.

Faye began pulling out the milk and yogurt she had bought the day before and quickly shut the refrigerator door again. Might as well use it now. It wouldn't last for long if the power didn't come back soon.

Sitting around the table with bowls of yogurt and cups of milk, they were about to eat when Faye asserted, "Stop!" Keith and Lynn looked at her. Faye reached for a hand on either side and bowed her head. "Dear God, thank you for our family. We ask that you please bring everyone home safely. Watch over Joe and Kent and my dad and sister and her family. Be with everyone who is trying to get back home." She paused. "Please bring the power back on. Amen." She squeezed their hands as tears welled up in her eyes.

Lynn took a sip of milk and looked at Keith. "How far did you walk yesterday?"

"From school, pretty much."

"Ha, that sucks. Where was Mom?"

Faye wiped her eyes and said, "I was still at the store."

"Whoa, you walked all the way from there?" Lynn looked incredulous.

"Yeah," Faye started to smile.

"Way to go, Mom. I would not have thought you could do that." Lynn held a fist up to Faye and bumped knuckles.

Faye was smiling now. She felt her status elevated; it was a pretty big achievement for her. Then, her face turned serious. "It was scary though. When we went through the campus, there were a bunch of psychotic kids drinking and burning stuff right beside the dorms! Was that going on when you were there?"

"What? No. People were starting to act kind of crazy, but nobody was burning stuff. They were just trying to, like, start parties. I don't believe you. The campus cops would never let that happen."

"What campus cops?" Keith said. "They're practically worthless when everything is normal. What do you think they're going to do without cars or any way to communicate with each other? What we saw was just a glimpse of Little Five weekend without the security." Keith had taken a temporary security job before leaving for the military, guarding an apartment complex during the "Little 500" bicycle race. The "Little Five" was a Bloomington tradition. There was even a movie made about it. It was an annual bicycle race, but no one cared about the race. Around the campus, it was one long week of binge-drinking and drug-addled house party chaos. Keith had seen several people who had nearly died from overdoses and alcohol poisoning just in the few days he worked that job.

"Well, that's probably true. But the cops, like, they have to have a backup plan for this kind of thing. They're not just, like, going to stop working."

"Why not? Everyone else did. What do you think they're going to do? They have no radios. No cars. Who's going to call them? The phones are all out. And they all have families too."

"Yeah, but, like, they're not just going to, like, go home right away. Like, they still have to..."

"Like, like, like, like, like!" Faye interjected. "Stop saying like! You sound like an idiot."

"She's not wrong," Keith concurred.

 Lynn raised her voice. "Okay, everyone talks like this at school!"

"Yeah, and they're all being swindled out of years of their lives and into five to six figure-debt for a piss-poor education! We didn't send you to college for you to get dumber!"

Keith and Lynn both stared at Faye. After a couple of seconds Keith said, "Where did that come from?"

"I'm sorry, I'm just a little stressed out right now." Faye finished the last of the yogurt in her bowl and took a drink of milk. "Does anyone else want coffee?" She left the room to fill a kettle with water.

Lynn took another gulp of milk and looked out the window. "I don't know why anyone would freak out over this. It's only been one day. It's a power outage. We have them all the time."

"And no doubt there are a lot of people who think that right now. But a power outage plus all the phones out and all the cars dead? We have not had that combination—not ever," Keith said seriously. "Whatever this is, it's not just a regular power outage. And most people are figuring that out."

Faye put the kettle of water on the stove and stood watching it. Thinking.

Lynn glanced at her and back at Keith. "Okay, but still, there's no reason for people to be freaking out over it. It's not the end of the world. We're all still alive, after all."

"I don't think you appreciate just how dependent our society is on electricity. We just walked for nearly six hours in sub-freezing temperatures yesterday. That store was about a twenty-minute drive before. Most people wouldn't even bother to dress properly for the weather because they would go from their heated house to their heated car to the heated store and back in a matter of minutes. If you sat outside in the temperatures we had yesterday, dressed the way most people we saw were, you'd be dead in three hours."

Lynn rolled her eyes. "Nobody's gonna stay outside for three hours."

"No, they won't. They'll try to get to shelter, but those that don't try to get home immediately will be stuck in public buildings with people they don't know, in need of supplies, and losing a dwindling supply of heat every time another person opens the door. No one is prepared for this."

"You sound excited, but I think you're going to be disappointed. This is probably just a local thing, and the government will have this all fixed within a few days. They have plans for this." Lynn took her bowl to the kitchen sink.

"We can only hope."

"Anyway, it's like forty degrees now, so people aren't going to be freezing to death." Lynn poured hot water over coffee grounds in a French press Keith had given her.

"That's another thing," Keith said. "What are we going to do about the freezers? If we put the food outside, it will thaw and freeze with the crazy temperature changes."

"You can get botulism that way," Faye said. "We can't risk that."

"Can't we pack it in salt?" Lynn asked. "Didn't they use to preserve food that way?"

"You know how much salt that would take?" Keith retorted. He shook his head. "There's only one thing I know we can do."

Day 3

Faye dug through the stacks of cookbooks and magazines she had collected since the early nineteen-nineties. "Ah come on, where is it?" The beam of her headlamp flashed over the surface of each publication, and every so often she would pause and look through one, muttering to herself. "Hmm. That sounds good. Ooh, I have to make that." Magazines and books were stored in cabinets, drawers, bookcases, and boxes in nearly every room of the house.

Lynn hauled loads of dusty, old mason jars from the basement as Keith washed them. There was a treasure trove of old jars in boxes in the basement. They had been given by family members as gifts, salvaged from cleaning out old houses, or saved after their contents were eaten. For many years, and even decades in some cases, they sat in boxes collecting dust in corners of the garage, in the basement, in a small shed outside. Many of them were utterly caked with gunk and looked to have housed vermin for some time. They smelled like rotting leaves, dust, and mold. One even had the skeleton of a mouse inside. Keith clenched his teeth and held his breath as he scrubbed the jars with soap and water, then bleach, then soap and water again.

"Ooh! Found it!" Faye entered the dining room with a copy of the *Ball Blue Book Guide to Preserving*. This was the Holy Bible of food preservation and could likely be found in the home of every farmer, gardener, homesteader, and doomsday prepper in the country. Faye sat down with the book and began looking through it. There were instructions for preserving nearly everything one could imagine, including things Faye had never even heard of. The family had three old pressure cookers somewhere in the garage. They used to can vegetables every summer, but for the last few years, Kent and Faye had lost the motivation. They were a little out of practice, but with the three of them, they might be able to save what they had in the freezers. Lynn found the pressure cookers, and with the last of the jars washed, they were in business.

They considered trying to can on the woodstove but decided against it when Faye warned that they would not be able to regulate temperature and pressure well enough that way. Keith agreed. Luckily, Kent had three old, salvaged propane grills lying around the place from cleaning up other people's junk. They were grimy, rusty, and looked like trash, but after setting them up on the back deck, Keith got one fired up. It would take a little longer than normal, but this would work, they thought.

Lynn cleared off the table in the center of the room and put down an old tablecloth. Keith began hauling up meat from the freezer and laying it out on the table. It was still mostly frozen, but it would thaw quickly near the woodstove. This was going to be an all-day operation, and by the time they got to the last of the food in the freezer, it would all be thawed out to the point that it wouldn't be safe to refreeze even if the power did come back. Faye told Keith and Lynn what to do, and the three of them worked in concert to preserve the food supply before it was lost.

By nightfall, they had canned forty-nine jars of meat and seven jars of vegetables. Keith had to move the grill inside the house and open some windows for ventilation after the shock of the cold air outside had broken two jars. They had run two pressure cookers simultaneously on the gas grill. After twelve hours of work, they were all exhausted. Jars just pulled from the canners sat lined up on the table, waiting to seal with the satisfying "pop." Lynn would carry them down to the basement when they were cool enough to touch; every time she took a batch down, she brought more food up from the freezer. Keith prepared the food with a butcher knife and a cutting board, cutting the meat and vegetables into chunks ready to go in the jars. Faye sterilized, packed, and put lids on the jars before arranging them in the pressure cooker. They had more jars, and there was more food to preserve, but it was getting dark, and they were too tired to do any more. They decided the rest could wait until tomorrow. It would be thawed but still plenty cold.

They could eat some more of the dairy products tonight before going to bed. As Faye was starting to make a sandwich, they heard the knocking of boots on the front porch. Everyone froze and watched the door. The doorknob turned, the door swung open, and looking at the room from the doorway, stood Joe.

Faye shrieked and sped toward him, seeming to forget how tired she was. She squeezed him with everything she had and cried tears of joy.

"It's hot in here," Joe said. "Is there anything to eat?"

Faye let go and wiped her eyes. "We were just about to make some sandwiches. Come on." She led the way to the kitchen.

Joe walked through the room, looking at the jars. "What are you guys canning?"

"Everything," Keith replied.

"Where were you?" Lynn asked.

Joe sat down on the couch in the cool living room and sighed. "Have I got a story for you."

Joe finished the last bite of his sandwich and gulped down the last of his cup of milk. He handed the plate and cup back to Faye, who took it to the kitchen and returned with a burning candle in her hand. Joe looked out the window at the black trees swaying in the night breeze. The glowing moonlight faded in and out between passing clouds.

"I was at a house, working on a system over in Whitehall. I had just gotten the thing running when everything went out. My phone was dead, the van wouldn't start, I had just locked myself out of the house, and it was about twenty degrees outside with a windchill of ten. No one was home, of course, and so I had to walk to find a phone to call somebody to pick me up. I knocked on several doors before someone answered, and she told me her phone was dead. I kept trying. No one had a phone that worked, so I walked all the way back to the office. By that time, it was afternoon. No one was there.

"There were abandoned cars all over the road and people walking around like they were lost. I walked past a sheriff's deputy who just kept trying to get someone to answer him on the radio. It was like he was in shock or something; he didn't know what to do, so he just kept calling into his radio and listening for a response. I realized that this was not just a power outage, and there was no one to call for help and no way to call them either. I was getting pretty hungry, so I went to a sandwich shop. The manager was still there, and he let me buy a couple sandwiches, chips, and drinks. I paid cash and took my food back to the office. I figured I should wait there to see if anyone showed up. After a while, my boss came in and asked me if I had seen anyone else. I told him I hadn't. He went out, got some food and drinks, and stayed in the shop the rest of the day. I slept on the floor of the office that night.

"In the morning, my boss told me he was going to go home and make sure his family was alright. He told me to do the same. I decided to walk down Third Street, thinking it would be the most direct route. The night before had been pretty quiet. I think everyone was, sort of, in a state of shock and confusion. Most people probably expected everything to go back to normal pretty quickly, but by the next day, everything was still dead. As I walked past the grocery stores, there were lines of people pouring in and coming out with shopping carts piled up with food and stuff. Everything was still mostly peaceful, but you could feel the tension building. As the day went on, the lines got longer, and people began to realize that the supplies were going fast and there wouldn't be much left by the time the people in the back got inside. Lines started turning into mobs as people tried to cut ahead of each other. By around noon, things started to get violent.

"I was coming up on a grocery store downtown when I really needed to go to the bathroom, so I decided to go inside. Everyone had a flashlight or headlamp and pushed through the dark, pulling things off the shelves. I had my pen light that I always keep in my pocket, and I squeezed my way through the shopping carts to get to the bathroom. People were running into each other and cussin' each other out. When I got out of the bathroom, there was a fight over the last pack of toilet paper. A guy tried to take it out of another guy's shopping cart, so the other guy shoved him. The dude punched the other guy, and I guess the guy pulled a knife on him, because he swung at him with something that slashed his face open, right down the middle. Well, the guy was laying on the floor, holding his face and screaming. No one would help him, and the guy that cut him had disappeared. People just kept moving and filling up shopping carts. So, I went over to him, opened up a box of maxi pads and told him to hold one on his face. I got him up and helped him to the hospital a block away."

Joe took out a can of chewing tobacco. "And, uh..." Staring at the floor, he shook his head. He put a pinch of tobacco in his lip. "I don't know. I guess I hadn't thought about it before, but I would have thought that, at least, the hospital would still have its backup generators. But it was pitch black in there, and there were nurses with headlamps and flashlights running around trying to help people, but—the smell. Already. The ventilators were all out, all the machines, the monitors, and the heat. I had called a nurse, but she told me to wait. And I guess they had been wheeling dead patients down to the morgue all night, because they were visibly exhausted. They started to just wheel them out into the hall with sheets over them. There was no more room in the morgue. There were screams and cries echoing through the halls as family members tried to get doctors. People who had come, expecting to see relatives recovering in comfort, found corpses instead. Finally, a doctor came and looked at the man holding a maxi pad to his face. He took a look at the wound and said, "At least I can fix this. Come with me." He took the man to another room, and I left."

Faye was holding a hand over her mouth. Keith and Lynn looked at one another and then back at Joe. No one said anything. The candlelight flickered and danced, throwing mesmerizing shadows around the room. Joe spat into an empty bottle and continued.

"Every grocery store, every gas station, every pharmacy, every hardware store. People were rushing them. Taking whatever they could. Looting. Even some clothing stores and restaurants. I went north on South College to get back on Third Street; the jewelry store had been robbed. The windows were all smashed in. When I got to Third Street, the police station appeared to be abandoned. Someone had spray painted one of the squad cars." He spat into his bottle again and looked up at Lynn. "What are they teaching you in that school?"

"Art and stuff. What do you mean?" Lynn looked puzzled.

Joe's eyebrows rose. "Well, the students must have been working on some kind of big modern art masterpiece or something, because when I walked through campus, there were kids pushing cars around and running back and forth with bags full of stuff."

"What? What kind of stuff? What were they doing with the cars?"

"I have no idea. It was weird though. They were just pushing cars into other cars. Some of them were looking at me like I kicked their dog, too. I don't know why. Anyway, I followed Third Street until I reached the gas station, and it was more people pushing shopping carts full of stuff around, the whole way." He spat in the bottle and raised his finger in the air. "Oh! But I did see people driving around. Not many, but every so often there would be a really old vehicle drive by, weaving through the dead cars on the road."

"Yeah, we saw that too!" Faye nodded.

"Well, I think I know why." Joe looked at all three of them with a grin. "And you know that old Ford sitting back there in the woods? Well, I bet I can get it to run."

Day 4

"Son of a whore!" Joe threw the wrench at a nearby tree and clasped his palm over his bleeding knuckles. He circled the truck and sat down at the base of the tree. The wrench lay beside him in the leaves. It didn't care. There was a gash in the tree bark beside his head, where the wrench had struck. The tree didn't care. And the truck didn't care. Nobody cared about his busted knuckles or his need to fix the truck. He didn't have the parts he needed. He didn't have the tools.

He didn't have any help. Joe stared at the wrench. "I guess that's everyone right now."

"Who you talkin' to?"

Joe flinched and turned to see Keith. "The wrench. What happened to canning?"

"It's going. Just got a batch in. Corn. I've got a while to wait. Thought I'd see what you were up to."

Joe put a pinch of tobacco in his lip. "Well, I'm not getting a whole lot done, honestly."

"Let me get a pinch," Keith said.

Joe tossed the can to his brother who started looking around the engine of the derelict truck hulk like he knew what he was looking for. "I don't have the tools I need," Joe said. "I need a socket set and some penetrating oil, but I don't know where Dad keeps anything in all that junk. Nothing's organized. I tried using some old motor oil and an adjustable." He looked at the blood dripping from his hand as he held it up. "That's what I get."

Keith tossed the tin back. "That's probably what Dad would do." He spat over his shoulder.

"Yeah." Joe wiped his hand on his shirt. "I bet he doesn't know where they are either."

"Probably not," Keith grinned. He wished he knew what he was looking at. He had never been any good with fixing cars. Kent tried to teach him, but it didn't take. Joe was always the mechanic, good with his hands. Joe and Kent got along a lot better. Mutual interests.

"Where do you think he is?" Joe's voice was low and somber. He picked up the wrench and brushed the dirt off.

Keith fidgeted with the fuses. "You know, I've thought about it, and I bet he's at Grandma's house right now."

"You think so? I think so too." Joe stood up, keeping his hand wrapped in a wad of his shirt.

"Yeah, you know, he's not gonna walk all the way from Columbus. And even if he wanted to, he wouldn't. He's not gonna just leave Grandma there. He can't take her with him, so he figures if something goes wrong, we would all meet up here. He doesn't have to worry about Mom then, you know?"

Joe nodded. "Yeah. That's what I was thinking." He stood beside Keith, peering under the hood of the truck and pulled a leaf out of the fan. "So, day four?"

"Day four," Keith affirmed, looking at his watch.

"That's a pretty long power outage. But it's happened before." Joe spat on the ground.

"Mmhmm." Keith nodded.

"But you don't think that's what it is." Joe looked at Keith.

Keith spat. "With cars and phones and backup generators out too? Do you?"

"Nope."

Lynn put her book down and went to check the grill. The timer had gone off, and the pressure was low enough that the weights on the steam vents were hardly moving now. Steam whistled softly from under the weights and shot up to the ceiling when she removed them. The hissing of the steam grew quieter until, after a couple of minutes, it was silent. Lynn twisted the lid off each canner, and a sweet-smelling steam billowed up from inside. She carefully extracted the jars, one at a time, with the jar lifter tongs, careful to keep them level until she set them on the table to cool and seal. Keith had showed her how to do it.

Canning was all about time and temperature. Everything had to be kept relatively consistent for the process to work. Normally, people would use either an electric or gas stove in their house, which could be easily and quickly adjusted, maintain a constant temperature, and be shut off to instantly stop adding heat to the cooker. Now, however, they did not have either of those options available, and the food would be spoiled in a day or two. The only thing they could think to do was to bring the old gas grill in the house, open the windows, and use the grill like a stove. They had lost two jars already from the sudden temperature changes of canning outside, so against Faye's better judgment, they were grilling in the house.

Faye packed freshly washed jars with green beans. Doing her best to keep the jars hot, she ladled boiling water over the beans, added salt, evacuated bubbles, wiped down the rims, and secured lids finger tight with bands. The lids they were using now were old ones, and the bands were rusty. It wasn't ideal, but none of it was. Some jars wouldn't seal, but they could try to do them again with another batch. If that didn't work, they knew what they were having for dinner.

Lynn lowered the jars into the bath, secured the lids on the pressure cookers, and the process started again. When the canner was hot enough, steam whistled through the vent, and Faye set the time on the stopwatch. Once ten minutes had passed, Lynn placed the weight over the steam vent and reset the timer. The two worked well together, taking turns restarting the grill and setting the timer. Lynn didn't mind. She could read her book by the woodstove as the pressure cookers worked away. Once she had the pressure gauge reading the right number, she opened her book and picked up where she left off.

Kent had slept in a chair downstairs the last night he was home. Faye couldn't fall asleep with the sound of his snoring, so he had let her take the bed. The last thing she told her husband was: "Go away." He had got up at 4:30 like he had every morning for the last thirty years, before anyone else was awake; he was out the door at 5:30 a.m. while Faye usually didn't wake up until 7:00. Faye sat down in front of the picture window with a drawing board, a pen, and paper. She hadn't written a letter in years, not since Keith was in boot camp. She needed to now, even if no one would ever read it.

Dear Kent,

Where are you? It was only last week I was fuming about how you were keeping me awake with your snoring. The house seems so silent now. Now, it's the quiet that keeps me up. I dreamt last night that you were on your way home, riding a bicycle. Ha ha! I woke up laughing at the thought of you on a bicycle again. Do you remember when we used to ride around town to get ice cream? We would go every weekend for several months when we were dating. That seems a lifetime ago. I can't imagine either of us trying to ride today. The ice cream has caught up with us. Ha ha! I guess you're in the same situation we are. What do you think is going on? Do you think life will ever go back to normal? Joe says he thinks he can fix the old, blue truck. He's been working on it all day. We canned most of the food in the freezers on the gas grill, so we'll be able to eat for a while. You don't need to worry about us. We're all doing fine, thank God. We'll have food when you get back, so hurry up. Are you walking? If so, walk faster! Ha ha! I walked from the other side of town! You should have seen me. Keith says it was ten miles. It felt like twenty. I wish you were here. I don't think I can go on much longer not knowing where you are. I need to know you're alright. We need you. Please come home.

Love,
Faye

Keith and Joe dug through piles of scrap boards, pieces of tin roof, coffee cans full of nails, screws, washers, nuts, and bolts. Some new, most used. Old tools that had been discarded by family members, co-workers, or total strangers often ended up here. Joe pulled a reciprocal saw out from a reclaimed shelf. "Well, that's worthless." He tossed it onto the concrete floor.

"Don't do that." Keith frowned.

"What? It's not like it's anything valuable."

"I know, but..."

"It's never going to work again." Joe was already pulling out another box.

"Well, you don't know that." Keith tried to sound hopeful.

Joe turned around. "No, I do know that." He picked up the saw and held it up for Keith to see. It had a cord that was spliced together in two places and wrapped with electrical tape. The trigger was gone, there was a hole in the side, exposing burned up wiring, and there was a broken piece of sawblade jammed in the blade clamp. "It's junk."

"Oh." Keith stared at the melted plastic and burnt wires.

"It was probably like this when he got it. I bet he thought he could fix it." Joe tossed it back on the ground. "He's like Fred G. Sanford. The 'G' stands for junk." Joe pulled out a rusty wad of chainsaw chains and threw them on the pile he was creating in the middle of the garage. "It's garbage. He likes it."

Keith shook his head. "Yeah, but it's not your garbage."

Joe pulled a drill out from under a piece of moldy carpet. "Actually, it is. This was my drill, I remember. I burned up the motor in it. I threw it in the trash about five years ago, and he must have dug it out." Joe tossed it over his shoulder onto the pile. "Like a racoon."

"Ah." Keith turned to looking through the shelves and drawers and boxes and bins and cans and piles. "Did you look in any of the toolboxes on the trucks and tractors around here?"

"Yeah," Joe said. "But I didn't see anything but rusted-shut pliers, roles of bailing wire, and mostly-empty pop bottles." He pulled out a black plastic case from under a fallen stack of drywall and opened it. "That's because it was right here. Ok, let's go."

Faye felt dumb, but she needed to get out of the dark house. She had been dealing with food for the last three days, and she needed to walk outside for a bit. At least the weather was nice compared to the week before. She ran her thumb over the stamp she stuck on her envelope and left the house. Up the long driveway, more dirt than gravel, she walked through the swaying trees. Poplars, oaks, beeches, maples, elms, hickory and sassafras cast long shadows across the driveway. Squirrels ran up and down trees around her. She wanted the air to smell like summer rain and fresh-cut grass. Instead, it smelled like mud and rotting leaves. Once she reached the top of the driveway, she looked around for signs of life. No one was on the road, and she didn't hear anything but a dog barking in the distance.

She opened the mailbox and read the address on her envelope before shutting it safely inside. She didn't expect the mail to be delivered, not really. But you never know. Maybe. She put her little red flag up and looked at it for a second before turning to walk back down the driveway.

"So, if you don't think it's a power outage, what do you think it is?" Keith handed a pair of pliers to Joe.

"You know, I was looking at my car over there." Joe reached into his pocket. "Check this out." He held up a fuse.

Keith took it and looked at it. "Blown?"

"Yeah, but look." Joe reached back into his pocket and pulled out a handful of fuses. "They're all blown."

Keith nodded and looked up at the sky. "Hmm."

"You don't seem surprised," Joe said. He took the battery out of the old truck and inspected it.

"I suspected. But there was no point in freaking people out. Besides, I could be wrong."

"I would say something caused a surge that fried the electrical system." Joe spat and set the battery on the ground. "But what would do that?"

"Electromagnetic pulse."

"Electromagnetic pulse," Joe repeated. "Yeah. I've seen small ones kill electronics, but I don't know how you could create one big enough to take out a car. And certainly not everyone's cars."

"There's a couple of ways. Maybe. It seems kind of speculative, from what I've read."

"What are you reading?"

"I've got reports from testing, but no one really knows for sure what would happen. It hasn't been tested on a large scale."

"Reports, huh?" Joe took the tobacco out of his lip and threw it on the ground. "Of course, you have reports. Government reports? Or..."

"Some. But even the government reports contradict each other. Like I said, I haven't found a whole lot of reliable information on it. But from what I've read, there's really two major ways to get an EMP big enough to take out the electrical grid. One is completely natural—a massive solar flare would send a wave of radiation that could knock out most electronics. It's happened before, but we weren't dependent on computers and cellphones back then."

"And the other one?" Joe took a drink from his water bottle.

"Nuclear blast. Way up in the atmosphere. Maybe several nukes. Some people say just one could do it."

"What do you think?"

"Do you remember what time it was when everything went out?"

"After ten, I think. Why?"

"Ten-thirty. Exactly. I know because I looked at my watch, and my watch still worked. Which makes sense. They say small, simple electronics are generally not affected by EMP."

"Small circuits wouldn't get interrupted by large electromagnetic waves." Joe nodded. "That's why watches and flashlights work. Of course that doesn't explain why radios would go out—unless... Well, I guess they're designed to be sensitive to electromagnetic waves, so maybe it does."

"Right. Well, I thought, ten-thirty in the morning? After the holidays, when everyone is at work or school. Early February? When the food supply is starting to run out and most of the country is freezing."

"You think this was planned."

Keith stood looking at the truck with a blank stare. "I don't know, but it's quite a coincidence if not. I mean, the worst possible time. Maximum damage. Ten-thirty on the dot. That doesn't look natural to me. That looks like a T.O.T."

"A what?"

"Time on target. A coordinated strike."

Joe rubbed his chin and looked up. "And what happens next?"

―――――――――

Faye took a batch of freshly sealed jars down to the basement in a banana box. She lined them up on the shelves. Her knees were hurting. She put the last jar in place and inspected the stockpile. How many did they have? She couldn't remember how many batches they had run. She started to count the jars... three, six, nine, twelve... Oh no.

Did she... What was she thinking? Faye hurried out the basement door as quickly as she could. She ignored the pain in her knees as she started speed-walking up the driveway. How could she be so stupid?

She didn't hear anything besides a dog barking off in the distance and a faint banging noise. The light was just beginning to fade as the sun sank behind the tree line, throwing orange light between gray-blue shadows. The air was tinged with woodsmoke. Not far off, a rooster crowed. Squirrels barked from hickory trees and darted across the driveway in front of her. A hawk screeched as it flew overhead.

She could see the mailbox. The red flag was still up. She looked down the road both ways as she walked. No one on the road. Reaching the mailbox, she opened the door to find her letter still inside. She breathed a sigh of relief. Taking the letter out, she closed the mailbox and put the flag down. That was careless, she thought. Why did she do that? Oh well, she got it. She laughed to herself at her blunder.

"Good afternoon," a voice said behind her.

Faye jumped and gasped a bit before turning. She hated it when people did that, but she looked at the face before her and smiled, stuffing the envelope in her back pocket under her jacket. "Hello."

A tall, young woman with blonde hair pulled back in a bun, wearing a long plaid dress and boots. She looked just like Olivia Walton, Faye thought. How strange. She smiled, showing white teeth and bright green eyes.

"I am so sorry to scare you," the woman said with a slight chuckle. "It's Faye, right?"

Chapter Four

Keith fed the animals and washed his hands before putting a pot on the woodstove. Joe scrubbed grease stains from his fingers. Lynn lit a candle and set it on the desk in the living room. The last of the jars were sealing on the dining room table. There were a couple that had failed to seal after going into the canner twice, so Keith dumped them in the pot, added a little seasoning, and sliced up the last of the bologna into the mix.

Joe walked into the room with a headlamp on. "What are you making?"

"Cowboy chili," Keith replied.

"Augh, good grief. I hoped I would never hear that again," Joe lamented.

In the recession, the family had not been able to buy much food. They had struggled to pay medical bills and the confiscatory taxes of the college town annex where money was extracted from families like theirs, living on thirty-thousand dollars a year, and redistributed to government officials and university administrators who decided their own salaries and required a minimum of six figures. As people in the area were losing jobs and being evicted from their homes, the government and the university broke ground on new multi-million-dollar projects such as roads and towers and stadiums, monuments to decadence, raising taxes and raising tuition respectively. The homeless piled up on the streets as the local government's zoning laws prevented developers from building enough housing for the town's inhabitants. Kent had resorted to selling heirloom shotguns just to get gas money to go to work. He had been fortunate to still have a job. He took a cut in pay and worked longer hours while many of the factory's employees were laid off. Faye was taking care of her dying sister, driving across the country in a desperate search for cancer treatments, leaving Kent and her children alone for days, and sometimes weeks, at a time. Kent would get back from work to find his kids wondering what they were going to eat. "Cowboy Chili" was what Kent called it when they filled a pot with every edible thing they could find in the house and mixed it all together. To the kids, it became sort of fun. Sometimes, cowboy chili was not half bad; sometimes, it was revolting.

"Don't worry. I don't make it like Dad," Keith said.

Lynn looked in the room, seemingly confused. She looked around. "Where's Mom?"

"I thought you said she went downstairs," Keith replied.

"She did, but I just looked, and she's not there." It was getting dark outside. Lynn went to the front door, and Joe followed. Lynn turned the doorknob, and as the door swung open, Faye stepped over the threshold, nearly running into her; they both shrieked and jumped back.

"Aaahh!"

Faye laughed as she came in, closing the door behind her.

"Where were you?" Lynn asked.

"Oh, I was just looking at the mailbox." Faye pulled the envelope out of her back pocket and walked to the stove. She opened the door, looked at the envelope, and tossed it into the fire.

"What was that?"

"Nothing. Just junk." Faye shut the door.

"That wasn't mail, was it?" Joe prodded.

"No. It's just trash," Faye looked at Joe seriously. "Do you know anyone named Emma Faulkner?"

"Sure. The Faulkners live just up the road. Why?"

"How well do you know them?"

Joe swallowed a spoonful of cowboy chili. With a furrowed brow, he looked at the stuff in his bowl and shrugged. "That's not bad."

Faye had covered all the windows that didn't have blinds with blankets and towels. The four sat around the table to eat in the light of a battery-powered lantern and scented candles. With everyone seated, she began: "So anyway, I was up by the road, and she just popped up from behind me and started talking to me. She knew who I was, but I didn't remember meeting her before, so I was a little cautious about what I told her."

"Well, that's good," Keith offered.

Faye continued: "She introduced herself and said that she knew you and asked if we were doing alright. I didn't want to give her any more information without knowing who she was, so I just said we were fine. She said she and her husband were trying to organize a community of our neighbors to make sure everyone knew they had help if they needed it. She talked about some of the crime they had seen in town, and they didn't want anyone here to feel desperate."

Lynn nodded and continued eating.

"Yeah, they're good people. I go fishing with Tim every so often. Good guy," Joe added.

Faye took a drink of water, shook her head and grinned. "She was dressed like someone from *Little House on the Prairie*."

"Yeah, well, she makes all her own clothes. They've got this homesteading thing going on."

"She didn't tell me that."

"And you didn't tell her about your jars of food in the basement or the animals outside either," Keith interjected.

"Right."

Joe went to the stove and ladled himself another bowl of cowboy chili. "Yeah, if anyone is going to survive the apocalypse, it's them. They have a pretty cool setup going on. I doubt they go to the store more than once a year." He turned around. "Ah, that's probably an exaggeration, but not by much."

Lynn raised her eyebrows. "That's probably why they want to make sure their neighbors don't get desperate. They have a lot to lose, and they'd be a prime target for thieves."

"So, like keeping your friends close and your enemies closer." Faye nodded.

"Probably the smartest thing to do right now," Lynn agreed.

Keith stood up. "Right. We have to assume, right now, that things are not going back to normal anytime soon. There is no law anymore. Just a lot of scared, cold, and hungry people trying to survive as best they can." He began pacing back and forth. He always had a hard time sitting still. "We can't trust anyone right now. From now on, nobody goes anywhere alone."

"Yeah, Mom," Lynn agreed. "Nobody knew where you were. We were about to go looking for you."

"Sorry."

"And we don't go anywhere unarmed," Keith said.

"I can't use a gun. They scare me." Faye shook her head.

"Then you can't leave the house," said Joe. "It's too much of a risk."

"I can shoot," Lynn said. "I'll stay with her." She turned to Faye. "But you really do need to stop being scared of everything."

"We're already a target here. People can hear the chickens from the road. They can see the fruit trees. They smell the smoke. When they run out of food, there's no telling what they might do." Keith took his bowl to the stove to refill it.

"Which is why we should be building a network of people we can trust," Lynn responded.

Joe interrupted. "You're right. We do need to do that. We have to know what other people are up to and be able to help each other out. The Faulkners have the right idea, and they're good people; I vouch for them. But Keith is also right. We can't trust anyone, and we all know there are some bad ones around here too. We can't afford to negotiate from a position of weakness. We help people out if we can. They help us too, hopefully. Keep the peace. We'll have a better chance if we all work together."

Keith sat down with his bowl. "We were born in the promised land. Bottle-fed milk and honey our entire lives. Now, we're about to see what life is normally like for humanity. We're all about to lose some weight. We'd better clean out the rest of the cowboy chili. There's no keeping left-overs anymore."

Day 5

Keith woke up cold. The temperature had fallen drastically during the night. As he pulled himself out of bed and took some pills for his headache, he heard the creak of the woodstove's hinges. He got dressed quickly and strapped a 1911 pistol on his belt before going downstairs.

The blankets and towels and blinds were all removed from the windows, allowing sunlight to flood into the dimly lit room. Joe was sitting in front of the woodstove, snapping sticks, and arranging them on the glowing coals inside, a pistol holstered at his hip as well. "Morning."

"Morning," Keith replied, going to the kitchen to fill the percolator with water. "Must have dropped thirty degrees last night."

"Thirty-two. Thermometer says it's eight degrees outside."

Keith put the percolator on the stove, grabbed his .22 rifle and trapping bag, and went outside to feed the animals and check his traps.

Lynn came down the stairs, hunched over, rubbing the sleep from her eyes. "Geez, it's cold."

As Joe blew the embers into flames, he heard the click of the bathroom light switch. Lynn growled and trudged back up the stairs. A few seconds later, she came back down with a flashlight. Smoke poured out of the open stove into the room, and Joe added wads of paper to the fire to quickly build up enough heat to carry the smoke up the chimney. When he had the fire going good and hot, he slid a couple of split logs on top and shut the doors. The sunlight glowed gray through the overcast sky but brightened the room just enough to see. Joe put a skillet on the stove and went to the refrigerator. He opened the door and saw that it was nearly empty now. Nothing but a few sauce packets and a couple of open jars. It was just a momentary lapse of memory that allowed him to think there would be bacon and eggs in there. He looked at a small basket on the floor next to the refrigerator. There was no bacon, but there were four eggs in the basket from yesterday.

When Keith got back, he held the stiff carcass of a squirrel in his hand. "Look at what I got," he said. "He was in a conibear."

"It's not bacon," Joe said. "But it's breakfast."

"I'll take that any day of the week." Keith set the squirrel by the stove to thaw out. He got a pot of water and a bucket and sat down by the stove to warm his hands and clean his catch. After about two minutes, he had the squirrel skinned and gutted. He rinsed the meat off, quartered it, and fried it in the skillet with salt, pepper, and garlic powder. As it was cooking, Keith went upstairs. He came back down with another pistol, a holster, and extra magazines which he set on the table beside Joe.

"What's this for?" Joe looked at it and back up at Keith.

"For you." Keith nodded.

Joe looked at the pistol hanging on Keith's belt and understood. "I see." It was a .45 like Keith's 1911.

Lynn walked in and looked at the squirrel cooking in the skillet. She made a displeased sound.

Joe took the 9mm off his belt and set it on the table. "Here, Lynn. You take this one." He picked up his brother's .45 and examined it.

"Thanks." Lynn took the pistol. She went to go get a belt.

Joe dropped the magazine out of the gun, pulled back the slide, and peered into the chamber. Satisfied, he reinserted the magazine and racked the slide.

"No safety on that. Remember," Keith warned.

"I know." Joe holstered the weapon and cracked eggs in the skillet.

Lynn came back in the room with the 9mm hanging from her belt. Joe made sure she knew how to load and unload, disassemble and reassemble, aim, and clean the gun. All the while, she assured both of them that she knew how to do it.

Then, Faye came down the stairs and looked at the three of them with guns at their sides. Her face contorted in fear and condemnation. "Oh, be careful."

"It's a good thing you said that, Mom. We were about to go play cowboys and Indians," Joe said with a smile.

"Sit down and have some breakfast, Mom." Lynn got some plates from the cabinet and set them around the table. "Your favorite. Squirrel and eggs." Lynn laughed.

"We should have some toast." Faye got up, went to the kitchen and arranged bread slices on a baking sheet to toast on the stovetop. She normally kept loaves of bread in the freezer when she got them on sale. Now, it would all go bad in a matter of days. They might as well toast it for breakfast.

Sitting down to eat, everyone had two or three pieces of toast, an egg, and some fried squirrel. The percolator bubbled away on the stove, and the room was quickly warming up. When they finished eating, everyone got a cup, and Lynn poured them some coffee.

"The food we have right now might last us a few months, if we ration. Of course, we have traps, and we can hunt and forage to make it last longer, but we shouldn't count on that. And we're nearly out of feed for the animals. At some point, we're going to have to make a trip into town." Keith took a sip of coffee.

No one said anything for a minute. Then, Joe said, "We're going to need parts too. Fuses, wiring, batteries, fuel, oil, belts, and a few other things. I've got a list."

"How bad can it be out there?" Lynn shrugged.

"Bad," Faye nodded seriously.

"And we still don't have a truck. And for some reason, there are a dozen parts stores on the other side of town but none on this side of town," Joe muttered.

"All the animal feed is on the other side of town too," Keith reminded him.

Faye put her hand on her head. "No, no, no. Just... Can't you just wait a little while? It might still..."

"We can wait," Keith said. "But not for long. And the longer we wait, the worse it's likely to get."

"Our best chance of getting through without trouble is probably when it's cold like this too. Most people will be hunkered down inside." Joe took a gulp of coffee.

"I'll go with you. I'm sure it'll be fine," Lynn said.

"No. Absolutely not." Faye glared at her. "You are not going anywhere." She looked back at Keith and Joe. "Can we just talk about this later? We still have to... What about the Faulkners? We haven't even talked to them yet. Maybe they have a truck or something."

"Yeah," Lynn voiced. "We have to talk to them. They're waiting on us to respond to their invitation. We can't be rude. We have to be diplomatic. I know about that stuff."

Joe sipped his coffee and set his mug down on a coaster. "I'm going to talk to them today."

"And who's going with you?" Faye asked. "I don't want to go."

Lynn interjected: "You need me to go. I'm the best when it comes to interpersonal communication."

Joe rolled his eyes. "I think I should take Keith."

"He's terrible at interpersonal communication," Lynn retorted.

"That's true," Joe looked at his brother. "But I think they'd like to meet him. He's just the kind of guy they would get along with." A wry smile stretched across his face.

Joe led Keith along the icy road. Woodsmoke mingled with the gray sky. Most houses on Mount Sinai Road had a chimney, and they all burned wood now. Fred Packard was splitting wood outside. His was a short driveway, and he and his wife Donna could usually be seen working outside, stacking wood, or doing something in their garden. They had a nice, clean garden that they kept free of weeds and in plain view of everyone who drove by, and they had an enormous stack of evenly cut and split firewood kept dry all year round by their enormous firewood shelter. Everything of theirs was better than yours, and they wanted you to know it. At least, that's what the Rawlings' thought. Fred stopped, glanced at Joe and Keith, and immediately grabbed another log as if he had not noticed them.

"At least we can count on one thing," Keith muttered to Joe. "Packard's still a turd." Keith looked back over his shoulder and caught Fred Packard's eye just before he looked back down and split another log.

They passed two driveways on their left, and one on their right. Up ahead, they could see the big, red tractor mailbox. Around this part of the world, green tractor mailboxes tended to get hit with pumpkins in October. Faye had learned that the hard way when she painted a green tractor on their mailbox many years ago. When they got to the Faulkners' driveway, Joe turned left as he passed the massive sugar maple tree. He nodded to the big, red tractor. "Now that's a nice mailbox." He looked back at Keith with a smile, his eyebrows raised, waiting for Keith's affirmation.

"Sure is," Keith agreed. "Too bad you didn't bring any Christmas cards to put in it."

"Right." Joe frowned and continued down the driveway.

There came a bark from the front porch of the yellow house with green trim. A golden retriever ran toward them. It jumped up on Joe and sniffed his face before doing the same to Keith. They both gave it a quick scratch behind the ears, the proper response to the greeting, and once the dog had decided they were now good friends, it ran back to the house and barked at the front door. Keith saw a shadow move from behind the blinds of a window, and as they stepped onto the front porch to knock, the door swung open.

A man in denim pants, leather boots, a thick, blue flannel, and suspenders stepped out and smiled. He was average height, a little shy of six feet. His black hair was cut just long enough to comb, and his oval face was freshly shaved, showing a full set of straight, white teeth and a pair of dimples when he smiled. "Hi, Joe. Doin' alright?" He reached out to Joe with a large hand and long fingers.

"Oh yeah, and you?" Joe grinned.

"Sure. This your brother?" He looked at Keith and held out his hand. "Hey. Tim Faulkner."

Keith shook his hand. "Keith Rawlings. Good to meet you."

"Jimmy didn't maul you too bad, did he?" Tim said, looking down at the dog wagging its tail and pacing around with excitement. "I guess he knows you well enough to call you friends, and that's good enough for me. Come on inside." Tim led the way into a room straight out of a Spaghetti Western. It was furnished with a woodstove, kerosene lanterns, an old upright piano, and what appeared to be a homemade table and chairs.

"You make these?" Keith asked.

"Yes, sir," He answered. He motioned with his hand. "Have a seat. They work alright."

They sat down. Keith looked around in wonder.

"Y'all want any coffee?" Tim offered eagerly.

"No, thank you," Keith was saying, just as Joe said: "Yes, please."

They looked at each other quizzically, and Tim looked back and forth at the two of them before looking into Keith's eyes with a pleading look, "It's fresh."

Keith shrugged, "Well, alright, sure, thank you."

Tim smiled and nodded and dipped out of the room for a second, returning with two steaming, handcrafted, ceramic mugs for them and one for himself, which he set down on stained oak coasters. "Here you go. Not quite strong enough to float a horseshoe, but it's hot." They thanked him, and as he sat down at the table opposite them, he took a sip of his coffee and smiled. "A bit chilly out there, isn't it?"

"A bit."

"Y'all got plenty of firewood, I hope?"

"Oh, yeah, we're alright."

"Good. Good." Tim took a sip of his coffee and looked up again as if he had just remembered something. "You'll have to excuse my wife. She's downstairs with the kids. They're in class at the moment. I don't want to interrupt their school, you know."

"Sure. That's great that your kids are still in school. I can't imagine what other people's kids are doing right now." Joe shook his head.

"God love 'em, I don't know either."

Joe smiled. "But it's just business as usual around here, huh?"

"Well, not quite for me, but for the kids, it is."

Keith took a sip of the coffee, swallowed, looked at the cup and then, up at Tim. "This is really good. What is it?"

"You like it?" Tim's face lit up. "Made it myself. It's not really coffee; it's chicory, grown right here."

Keith laughed. Joe laughed as well. Tim looked confusedly at both of them, and then, he began to laugh with them.

Keith stopped and took a drink of the fake coffee, looked into his mug again, and said, "This place is awesome."

"Thanks," Tim replied. "We like it. We've been working on it for several years now. So, anyway, we wanted to establish ties with some of our neighbors around here. Obviously, not everyone is going to be as prepared as we are. And we want to make sure that people don't, you know, get too desperate."

"Right," Joe said. "Mom told us about what your wife said to her. We figured you were trying to keep everyone from robbing each other, since, clearly, you have a lot of stuff that people would want right now."

"Well, yeah." Tim scratched his jaw and nodded. "That's certainly part of it. But of course, you know, we've got kids here, and we can't let things get too crazy."

Keith nodded. "Of course." He took a sip of faux coffee.

"Plus, it's just the right thing to do. You know, there's going to be a lot of people who don't know what they're going to eat or how they're going to stay warm. We can help."

"Sure. And by we, you mean..."

"Well, I talked to Fred Packard. He said they'd manage on their own."

Joe shifted in his chair. "Not surprising."

"But I talked to Brad Nielson over there and Ernie Jacobs just up the road. They're on board."

Joe leaned over to Keith and said, "That's the guy in the brown house across the road and the old farmer at the top of the ridge."

"And I was hoping you'd be the third."

Joe looked at Keith as he took another gulp of coffee. Keith was silent for a couple of seconds, looking out the window. "What are you proposing?"

Tim leaned back in his chair. "Well, I figured we can teach people how to grow food in the spring, help them out with heating their homes and cooking, maybe we can get the kids together to continue their schooling, and you know, set up a community here. So, no one would have to panic and resort to—bad choices. You know what I mean?"

"Yeah, makes sense." Joe nodded.

Tim looked at Joe, "I know Joe's a good guy. Honest, hard worker, lots of skills." He turned to Keith. "And you were in the military, right?"

"Right."

"And Joe tells me you're something of an outdoorsman. I know y'all grew a garden and cut firewood and all. I figure you can be pretty helpful. You like my coffee. My dog likes you. And I like you too."

Keith grinned.

"So, what do you say?" Tim smiled and gulped the last of his fake coffee.

Keith and Joe looked at each other and nodded. "Alright, we're in."

Chapter Five

Keith and Joe turned right onto the long gravel driveway. "I figured you'd like 'em," Joe said with a grin.

"And I like that coffee too. Nice of them to give us some," Keith said, looking down at a small bag of Tim's homemade chicory blend.

"How about those cookies?" Joe said, looking at the small parcel in his hands.

"Oh, man. Do you believe those don't have any ingredients from the store?"

"That's what she said, and I have no reason to doubt her."

"That place is amazing. I can't believe we never met before."

"*You* never met before, you mean." Joe took a can of tobacco out of his coat pocket. "I talk to them pretty regularly. I tried to introduce you before, but you didn't want to meet them. If you weren't so paranoid all the time, maybe you'd make some friends."

"I have friends."

"Could have fooled me." He put a pinch of tobacco in his lip. "Look, all I'm saying is you got to be more sociable. I have a pretty good network of people I know around here, and it's very valuable to me because I know whenever I need help with something, I can call somebody."

"Oh yeah?" Keith said, looking at him. "You're gonna call them, are you? I wish you would have told me about this phone you got working. I got some people I'd like to call too."

"Okay, okay. I take your point, but this is an abnormal situation."

"It's the situation we're in."

"True. And be that as it may, I've also got some people I know living on Mount Sinai. We could just walk over to their houses any time."

"Well, we ought to do that then. We can go talk to them first and see if they want to join us. Then, we'll work our way down the road, and see who else we can get on board. I'll leave all the talking to you."

They came to the front door of the house. Keith was about to open it, when suddenly, he stopped. He looked around.

"What's the matter?" Joe asked, reaching under his coat for the pistol.

Keith knocked on the door—shave and a haircut. He stopped and listened. He knocked—two bits. Then, he opened the door and stepped inside. "We're back," Keith raised his voice. No one answered.

As they walked through the house, the basement door opened. Joe stood looking through the doorway with his pistol drawn.

Lynn's head popped out from behind the door. Her eyes met the shadowy figure with a pistol in the dark room, and she shrieked, "Aaaah!" She slammed the basement door shut again.

"It's okay. It's just us," Joe said, putting the pistol away.

They heard heavy breathing. The door opened slowly again, and Lynn looked out from behind it. "I hate you guys." She shut the door behind her, shaking her head, and walked to the kitchen, holding a jar of canned venison.

"Did you not hear us just a few seconds ago?" Keith asked, unzipping his coat.

"Before I saw you backlit in front of the window, holding a gun? No."

"Sorry." Joe laid his jacket over a chair.

"Where's Mom?" Keith looked around again.

"She went upstairs to take a shower. I guess she didn't hear you either."

Joe went to the woodstove and sat down. "What are you making?"

"Lunch. I don't know." Lynn unscrewed the metal band on the jar.

Keith dug a couple of buckets out of the pantry. Rice and beans. He took a cast iron pot out and started filling it with water. "How about red beans and rice?"

"Normally, I'd say no, but that sounds fantastic right now," Joe said.

"I second that," Lynn agreed. "So, what happened?"

Just then, Faye ran down the stairs. "What happened? I heard somebody scream."

Joe was writing down a list of items to get from town.

Keith stirred some seasonings into his pot of rice, beans, and venison. "And then, Emma came in and gave us some cookies. Guess what. Made with acorn flour, preserved berries, homemade butter, eggs, and maple sugar—all from their property. They might have been the best cookies I ever had. Forget chocolate chip. These things were incredible."

"Well, let us try them."

"After you eat those, there's no way you're going to want beans and rice, I promise you."

"He's right." Joe nodded.

Once everyone had got a bowl, Joe tried a spoonful and looked puzzled. He dug around in his bowl with his spoon, examining the contents. "Beans, rice, and deer meat? That's it?"

"And some seasoning." Keith took a bite.

"You should have been a chef, dude. If you can make this garbage taste good..." He took another bite.

"It is good," Lynn said.

"Mmhmm." Faye nodded.

"Now you see why I keep a stockpile of beans and rice and seasonings."

"Yeah, yeah, yeah." Lynn brushed him off. "We get it. You're prepared for everything."

"You weren't prepared to run out of chicken feed though, were you?" Joe grinned.

"Nope." Keith admitted. "I guess if I had to, I could free range them completely, but they would run around all over the place and get eaten by foxes and coyotes and stuff. We might have to do that yet. In the meantime, we're going to need to get those parts, and we might as well try to get whatever feed we can get. Every day that goes by means less of a chance that it will be there."

"I've got some stuff I need too," Lynn said.

"Write it down." Faye glared at her.

"Does that mean you agree?" Joe asked.

Faye looked up at him. "I know we need stuff. We all need stuff, but how are we going to get it? You can't just walk into town. That's twenty miles, there and back. And there's nutcases all along the way. And how are you going to get the stuff back? You can't carry all that. What, are you going to push shopping carts? Don't be ridiculous!" Faye was shaking just a little and starting to turn red.

Joe put his spoon down and rubbed his jaw. "No. We weren't going to push shopping carts." He looked over at Keith and back at Faye. "Tim needs to make a trip into town too. And he's got a truck."

"That runs?" Faye asked.

"I wouldn't bring it up if it didn't." Joe affirmed. "It's a 1955 Chevy. In real good condition too. It was his granddad's truck. He's taken care of it."

"But it runs?"

"And drives. He showed us."

Keith nodded. "It's true."

Faye took a bite of beans and rice. She didn't say anything for a few seconds. "I wouldn't mind as much if you were in a truck, able to get away from dangerous situations quickly. And if you're going with someone else, that's better."

"I think so too," Keith said. "He's ready to go tomorrow morning. Hopefully, we can get there and back before anyone's really awake in town."

"Yes. Yes. That's good." Faye nodded thoughtfully.

"Well, make a list, and we'll get as much as we can." Keith took the percolator off the stove and poured some of the Faulkners' chicory coffee for everyone. They opened the small, brown, paper package containing Emma's cookies.

Faye and Lynn both took a bite and exclaimed, "Oh, wow!"

Day 6

No one showered anymore. The water was too cold. They still had water pressure, but the water heater went out with the power. When they "showered," as they still called it, what they were really doing was boiling a pot of water on a stove and taking it to a bathtub for a sponge bath. They all did this every other day. Keith and Joe had taken one the night before, so they were feeling as good as they could be right now. Keith brushed his teeth, washed his face, and got dressed. There were no alarm clocks now, except the rooster outside and the alarm on his watch. In the greenish glow, he read the numbers 0507.

Keith strapped on his pistol and went downstairs, flashlight in hand. He met Joe at the table by the woodstove. They checked their gear. Backpacks, extra flashlights, first aid kits, insulated water bottles, headlamps, hats, coats, gloves, boots, and weapons. They each took a fixed blade knife as well as a folder, and each took a rifle from the gun safe. Two copies of each list. No breakfast. No time. If everything went according to plan, they could be back within two hours. Lynn came down the stairs in her coat, some cargo pants, and wool socks, wearing Joe's compact pistol on her belt. She got a couple logs from the front porch to put on the smoldering coals in the woodstove. It was ten degrees outside.

"Lock the doors when we're gone. Don't open them until you hear us knock like this and announce ourselves." Keith knocked on the table—One-two. One-two—three.

"Ok. I got it." Lynn replicated the knock on the table.

"And if you had breakfast ready when we get back, that would be nice," Joe added.

"We should be back in about two hours," Keith said.

"What if you're not?"

"Wait. If we're not back by noon, check with Emma Faulkner to see if we're with them."

"And if you're not with them?"

"We will be." Joe opened the door.

Just then, Faye came down the stairs as quickly as she could. "Wait." Her eyes were red, and she was clearly trying to keep her voice under control. "Be careful."

"It's a good thing you said that," Joe began.

"I know, I know." She hugged them both. "Get back as soon as possible. Don't take any risks."

"We'll be back before you know it." Joe stepped outside.

Keith looked back at Lynn. "Remember."

Lynn nodded. "Don't worry. I got it." She gave her brothers a fist bump. "Now, hurry up, and don't forget to get my stuff." She shut the door. As Faye peered through the window, watching the flashlight beams moving away from the house, Lynn groaned. "I wish I could go. I'm getting cabin fever in here."

"There's only room for three, and it's not a job for someone who shops for clothes in the children's section," Faye said flatly.

In the darkness, the frozen, frost-covered leaves and grass crunched under their feet. They kept their voices down, kept the beams of their lights low to the ground and as dim as possible, partially shielded by their fingers. The icy tree branches crackled in the soft but biting wind. It had snowed in the night. Just a dusting, but it covered every surface in a thin, white powder which reflected the faint ambient light almost enough to see without flashlights. It was not enough, however, and they did not dare misstep on a patch of ice or a fallen limb right now. They could not afford injury or accident, and they wanted to remain as quiet as they could. They walked down the middle of the road and turned left at the giant sugar maple tree. As they neared the house, they could see just the faintest glow of a lantern from behind the shutters of a window. Approaching the steps, they gingerly crept onto the front porch to avoid making a sound.

A low growl reverberated from behind the door, and they heard a soft voice say, "Good boy, Jimmy. Go to bed." The door opened before they knocked, and Tim stepped out onto the porch, closing the door behind him quickly. "How you boys doing? Good?" When they answered in the affirmative, he wasted no time. "Ready to go, then?" He led the way to the barn behind the house, carrying a pump-action shotgun. The three climbed into the truck. "I see you guys are loaded for bear," Tim said.

"Yes, sir," Joe replied.

"Good. Me too." He pulled the truck out of the barn, got out, shut the barn doors and then, climbed back in before pulling out onto the road and turning on his headlights.

"When's the last time you were in town?" Keith asked him.

"Last week, when the power went out. There was nothing for me to do at work, so they let me go. Told me they'd call me when they needed me to come back in. Still waiting for that call." He chuckled. "I walked back when I realized I wasn't going to get the van to start either."

"So, this isn't what you normally drive?" Keith asked. Joe thought it was a stupid question.

"Oh, no. I don't take this thing out of the barn more than a few times a year. No, I normally drive the minivan to work. When you got seven kids, you have to make compromises, you know." He laughed.

They drove slowly. The roads were icy, and the truck was not a four-wheel-drive, so Tim decided to go through town to avoid the worst of the bad roads. The bypass was under construction, as usual. If there was an obstruction on the road in town, there would likely be a way to go around it without getting off the pavement. The yellow-orange glow of the headlights shone off the glittering ice and lit up dead hulks of cars, trucks, and vans along the way. Piles of garbage lined the road in some places, but Third Street was relatively clear, apart from a few cars and debris on the road.

As they drove through the campus, they could see a wall of cars to their right, lining the street. They were pressed bumper to bumper.

"Hmm. That's odd." Tim sounded a little anxious.

"That's what I saw them doing when I came through here," Joe said. "It almost looks like they're going to have a monster truck rally. Why do you think they did that?"

Keith stared out the passenger window. "It looks like some kind of barricade."

Tim slowed down as he passed a shopping cart in the road. "Why would they need a barricade? No one can drive. Or at least, very few can."

"No idea." Keith looked around as buildings passed from the illumination into the darkness, and he thought to himself. Through a window of the Wells Quadrangle, a castle-like building, Keith could see the flickering, orange glow of a fire. The string of cars stopped at Indiana Avenue. Now, there were remarkably few cars on the road. Far fewer than he had expected. Far fewer than he remembered passing on his walk through town, come to think of it. And something seemed different about the landscape, but in the darkness, he could not tell what it was.

They turned right on South College and left on East Kirkwood. "That's one thing we can be thankful for," Tim said as they drove past the graveyard and reached the other side of town. "Everything went down when people were at work. Not so many people on the road at the time."

"Yeah, that's true," Joe agreed. "That's one way to look at it."

"I'm a glass half-full kind of guy," Tim replied.

"I'm not," Keith said. "What's that up ahead?"

The headlights reflected off something in the road. Tim slowed down. In the headlights, they could see a white dog tearing at a large wad of fabric in the street. The ice appeared to have a dark, reddish tint around the pile; it faded into pink around the outer edge of a circle of paw prints beaten into the frost. The dog stopped and looked up at the truck. Its face, neck, and paws were stained pink. It stared for a couple of seconds before returning to the pile of what might have been clothing. No one said anything; Tim eased the truck around the obstruction and continued onward.

Their first stop was the auto parts store on the left. Tim pulled the truck into the parking lot, turned off the lights, and said, "I'll wait with the truck. You two, go ahead and get what you need. Better grab extras of everything while you're at it. And try to make it quick."

They got out. It was still dark outside, and in the store, it was black as pitch. The front door had been pried open, so they simply walked in. With their headlamps on, Keith and Joe combed through the shelves. There were a few boxes on the floor, and some things knocked off the shelves, but the store mostly just looked abandoned. They stuck together. In the darkness, they couldn't take the chance of mistaking a brother for a robber. It took them longer than they would have liked, but they found the supplies easily enough, took extras, and different sized parts, and some things that might come in handy later. When they left, Keith dropped a handful of hundred-dollar-bills on the counter before pushing the cart out the front door. Extra oil, oil fil-ters, gas cans, several batteries, coolant, brake fluid, brakes, tires, light bulbs, fuses, and more they loaded into the back of the pickup before heading to their next stop.

"If everything goes as smoothly as that, we'll be in busi-ness," Tim said, pulling out of the parking lot.

"Here's hoping."

When they pulled into the farm store, the light had started to creep up from behind the horizon, coloring the sky purple. Tim parked in a handicapped spot right in front of the doors. He shut off the lights and the engine before handing Joe a list and a one-hundred-dollar bill. With his headlamp, Joe read the list. He could not believe how short it was. Nails, bucksaw blades, rope, a couple of buckets, salt, and bleach.

"Are you sure this is all you need?"

"No, but we don't have much room, and y'all need to get your feed still. If they have any left. Get as much as you can. I can manage with what I got. Be quick now. Sun's comin' up."

The glass doors to the farm store were smashed in. Shards of glass littered the ground. Keith turned on his headlamp and stepped through the gaping hole in the glass door. They grabbed carts inside and pushed through the cave-like store as quickly and quietly as possible. The food was all gone. The bottled drinks were gone as well. There were racks knocked over and products scattered across the floor in several places, but they found salt, and there were a couple gallons of bleach. The rope was still there. There were several boxes of nails left. There was a stack of buckets, and a couple bucksaw blades were still there. They noticed all the axes and chainsaws were missing. The seeds were gone too, except for flowers and grass. Most of the canning equipment was gone. Keith took the last boxes of bands and lids and the last box of pint jars. He saw a copy of the *Ball Blue Book Guide to Preserving* lying on the floor and took it. It had been stepped on and kicked around; some of the pages were torn, but it was still intact. When they reached the animal feed aisle, the shelves were bare.

"I was afraid of this," Keith whispered as he pushed the cart through the aisle. When they reached the end of the aisle, they noticed there were a few bags left. Keith trained his headlamp on the labels. Llama feed. And to the left, catfish food. It would have to do. They loaded the bags onto their carts and pushed on.

They found most of the items on Lynn's list, but not all. Most of the traps were gone. Keith took the remaining two. A coon cuff and a conibear. The gun section was completely bare. All the firearms and ammunition had either been taken or locked away in the vault. The bows, arrows, broadheads, and all the knives were missing too. The lanterns were gone along with the lamp oil. All the batteries and flashlights had disappeared. The fishing rods, hooks, lures, line, and bait had all been taken. Even the mineral blocks were gone, but Keith found a bag of food plot seed behind a lawn chair.

Joe's cart rolled over something with a loud crunch. They stopped. A noise came from another aisle. A groan. They were not alone in the store. Joe took a step and unslung his rifle. His boot made another crunching noise as he did so, and they heard a startled yelp and running footsteps headed toward the entrance of the store and away. Whoever it was, he was gone now. They continued to listen for a moment. When they were met with silence, Keith and Joe looked down to see what they were stepping on. There were tiny purple dots all over the floor in this aisle. Keith looked around and found a torn bag of turnip seed on the bottom shelf. He grabbed it, twisted up the torn bag, taped it shut, and put it in his cart. They found a thermos and a couple of water jugs. Their carts were full. Joe wanted to look for boots and gloves before they left, and as they were nearing the boot section, they heard voices followed by the crash of broken glass from the front of the store. Keith and Joe immediately shut off their headlamps and kept silent. Keith looked around the corner and saw four flashlight beams sweeping around the store. He pulled the flashlight from his belt and unholstered his pistol. The lights passed the cash registers at the front and turned right. Keith waited until he could no longer see the beams; then, he holstered his pistol and flashlight and whispered, "Let's go."

They pushed the carts out as quickly as they could toward the light of dawn illuminating the entrance. Keith threw some hundred-dollar-bills on the checkout counter as they passed. They rolled their carts out to the truck, bumping over the glass and making far more noise than they would have liked.

Tim climbed out of the truck as soon as he saw them. He leaned his shotgun against the side of the truck as he helped them throw stuff into the bed. In half a minute, they were done. The brothers shoved the carts away, everyone climbed in, and they left.

Tim breathed relief as they pulled out of the parking lot. "I'm glad you boys got out as soon as you did. Some rough lookin' characters just went in there."

"We just missed them," Keith responded.

"Looks like you guys got a pretty good haul though."

"Real good," Joe replied. "Sorry it took so long."

"No worries, man. I saw one guy run out a little while before you, but I didn't hear any shooting, so I figured you were still doing okay."

The sun was fully up now, and they had one more stop to make. They decided it was best to get to the other side of town where there were fewer people before they stopped again. The townspeople were beginning to stir. They were coming out of the houses and apartment buildings, bundled up in coats and blankets, picking up sticks and leaves.

"I found the axes and chainsaws," Joe said.

Several men and a few women were carrying axes and hatchets and trying to cut down nearby trees. A man in glasses and a turtleneck, who had clearly never used a chainsaw before, was yanking on the pull cord with the bar pinched between his legs—probably a professor. A woman was pushing a shopping cart full of broken sticks down the sidewalk. The food had all been raided, but the pressing concern right now was heat. Most people in Bloomington proper would call themselves environmentalists, so naturally, most of them heated their homes with natural gas or electricity produced from burning coal, but those were no longer options, and the sub-freezing temperatures could kill in a matter of hours.

"Watch out!" Keith shouted.

Tim slammed on the brakes just as a tree crashed in front of them, smashing the windshield of a dead car on the other side of the road. The truck skidded a couple feet and slid within inches of the tree. A woman with an axe looked at them and began walking toward them. Third Street was blocked, and there was no way they were getting out to move the tree. "Hang on," Tim said as he put the truck in reverse. He backed up to Lincoln Street and went north. Fourth Street was blocked by a dead firetruck. He turned right on Kirkwood and drove past the library.

All along Kirkwood, there were trees wearing colorful, knitted sweaters with cute little things written on them like "peace" and "love." Now, they were being hacked down with axes, and hatchets, cut with hand saws and battery-powered chainsaws. A woman in a pink knit hat was furiously whacking a tree with a machete as the pink sweater lay wadded up in the storm drain at her feet. Trees lay across Grant Street as people cut off their branches for firewood. Children were helping to pick up sticks and put them in shopping carts and wheelbarrows. Across the street, they could see a tree still standing with no one trying to cut it down. At the base of the tree was the gray, frost-covered corpse of a woman hugging the trunk.

A man was trying to cut a log in the middle of Kirkwood to their left. Tim reluctantly took a right. People had noticed them. A crowd was forming in front of them, blocking the road. People were closing in around them on all sides now with axes. They wanted the truck.

"Do not slow down," Keith said. He rolled down the window and hung his rifle out. The people stopped, but they didn't move. He fired a shot in the air.

Tim accelerated.

"Keep going!" Keith fired another shot above the crowd, and they scattered before the truck hit them. He rolled the window up again quickly. It was bitter cold outside.

The roads were still icy, but Tim sped up to get through before they were blocked in. Someone in the crowd threw a brick at the truck. It nearly hit Keith's window but flew just past and landed on the feed bags in the back. Up ahead, there was another wall of cars lined up around the gate to campus. Tim turned left on Indiana Avenue. The road was clear now, since the cars had all apparently been used to build a wall around campus. Some of the trees on the outer edge of campus had been cut down.

"That's what looked different," Joe said.

"The trees?" Keith asked, nodding.

"Yeah."

At Seventh Street, the car wall ended. At Eighth Street, the sporadic cars sitting in the road began to reappear. There were people cutting down trees here too. Some hacked away at shrubs. Very few people had woodstoves in town. Some of the oldest houses might still have coal stoves in the basements, kept for the novelty. Some houses had gas fireplaces that could now be used to burn wood. But a lot of the houses appeared to have jerry-rigged stove pipes sticking out of windows where air conditioners might have been. They had already passed two burnt-up houses. And judging by the billows of smoke up ahead, there were more than those. Tim turned right on Tenth Street and took the truck past the library on campus.

At least some of the students were awake. There were groups walking around with pieces of paper and flashlights. In the distance, they could see a group walking into the clinic.

"They look like they're on a scavenger hunt," Joe said.

A group walked up the steps of the library. They stopped and watched the truck as it passed by them.

"What are they going into the library for?" Joe asked.

"Must be committed to learning," Tim chuckled to himself awkwardly. He was clearly rattled.

A student with long, purple hair hanging out of a hood shouted something in their direction.

"Definitely not," Keith said. "I wouldn't be surprised if they were going to burn it down." He looked at his watch. 0813. They were already taking longer than they had hoped.

"At least we're getting better traction now," Tim said. "That weight in the back makes a big difference."

When they got to the gas station, there were people standing outside, smoking in front of the doors. Free cigarettes, apparently. When they saw Keith, Joe, and Tim climb out of the truck with weapons, they scampered off toward the apartment complex across the street. Joe went inside as Keith stood by the door, watching both the store and the road behind Tim. Joe left the rest of the money on the gas station counter and took all the chewing tobacco they had left. The liquor was completely gone. That was too bad. It was another thing Tim said they should try to find. The food and drinks were all gone except for a few bottles of water and unsweetened tea.

Tim fished a hose, a hand crank pump, and some tools out from under the seat of the truck. From across the street, they could hear the sounds of shouting and trash cans being knocked over. It sounded as if there was a fight outside the apartments. Then, two loud pops, and someone screamed. Tim looked back at Keith. "Keith, you got me?" He said in a low voice.

Keith nodded and watched the apartments. Joe exited the store just as a loud growl emanated from the apartment complex across the street. An engine roared as a lifted, brown truck on oversized wheels burst through a pile of trash and sped toward them.

"Let's go!" Tim threw his tools in the bed of the pickup and hopped inside. As he started the engine, Keith and Joe jumped in. They raced out of the parking lot and down toward Mount Sinai Road.

Joe turned around to see the truck behind them. A man was hanging on the bumper guard, pounding on the hood.

The truck veered off to the side of the road and crushed the man against a telephone pole. The pole broke off and fell across the road as the man's mangled body slid off the front of the truck. "Did you see that?" Joe said to Keith. To their horror, the truck backed up, drove right over the fallen telephone pole, and continued to follow them.

Mount Sinai Road was just ahead of them. Tim looked in his rearview mirror and drove straight past it.

"You missed the..." Joe started to say. "Oh."

They crossed the railroad tracks. Tim thought about turning left toward Unionville, but that would take them back to town. "We can't outrun them on this ice!" Tim shouted.

The truck was gaining on them. It was only two car lengths behind now. Keith looked at the curve in the road ahead and pulled out his pistol.

The truck was just a couple feet from the rear bumper. A man leaned out the passenger window, holding what looked like a grappling hook on the end of a chain. "Get down!" Keith pushed Joe's head down, opened the rear window, and unloaded his magazine at the truck's windshield. Most of the rounds hit home, shattering the glass just as the truck hit the curve. The driver ducked and the truck flew off the road and into a ditch. Keith shut the window and reloaded his pistol.

Tim breathed a sigh of relief as he looked in the rearview mirror. "Nice shootin'," he yelled. "I thought we were in some serious trouble back there."

"Could you warn somebody before you blow out my eardrums!" Joe shouted, sitting back up in his seat.

"Sorry," Keith shouted, his ears also ringing. "Had to deal with some road pirates!"

"Freakin' road pirates," Joe laughed.

"Freakin' road pirates," Tim repeated, shaking his head. He turned right onto the north end of Mount Sinai Road and eased the old pickup toward home.

Mount Sinai Road was home to farmers, homesteaders, hillbillies, trailer trash, and hippies from end to end. The north end had more of the trailers and cabins though. They lived a mostly secluded life out here. It was quiet, except for the sounds of crowing roosters, barking dogs, a chainsaw or two, and gunshots which could be heard up and down the road every day. In this part of the country, there were more guns than people by an order of magnitude, at least. People moved out here to get away from neighbors, but over the past thirty years or so, enough people had had this same idea that the road was starting to look like an elongated, sub-urban cul-de-sac. Out here though, nearly every house had a woodpile outside. Most of them had small garden plots in the spring and summer. And some even made money from their hobby farms. There were signs beside mailboxes reading: "Firewood for sale", "Eggs for sale", and "Straw bales for sale." Some of them sold fruits and vegetables at the local farmers' market, some sold or traded them from their homes, and at least one or two of the families on Mount Sinai were professionals who sold their produce to gro-cery stores.

Tim looked around as he drove slowly, a smile creeping across his face. "You see what I see?"

"A lot of people who know how to survive," Joe offered.

"No." Tim shook his head. "An economy."

They pulled into the Rawlings' driveway, and all three of them had to relieve themselves beside trees. Tim helped the brothers unload the truck. They were all still shaking a little from the adrenalin as well as the cold.

"Got everything?" Tim asked, examining the remaining contents of the pickup.

"Yes, sir," Keith replied.

"Alright." Tim turned around and opened the truck door.

"You need any help with anything?" Joe asked.

"Not today, but tomorrow, maybe we can start talking to some more of our neighbors around here."

"We can do that." Joe took out a can of tobacco from the shopping bag.

"It's too bad we didn't get the gasoline," Tim said. "But considering what we saw today, I think we ought to be happy with what we did get."

"Yes, sir. We'll have to figure out a way to avoid going back into town. It ain't worth that." Keith shook his head.

"We can syphon a little gas from cars for now. I bet some of the farmers around here have fuel tanks though. They might be willing to trade fuel for something. But we'll worry about that tomorrow." Tim turned and started to climb into the truck, but suddenly, he stopped. He turned around and put out his hand to Keith. "Good shooting, Keith. I owe you for that."

Keith shook his hand. "Good driving. I think we owe you more."

"I owe both of you," Joe said. "Dip?" He held out a can.

"I'll pass. But thank you for getting my stuff and all." Tim shook Joe's hand and looked seriously at both of them. "Do not tell my wife about what happened out there. That stays between us."

"You got it."

Tim climbed in the truck and rolled on up the long driveway with a wave. Joe and Keith hauled their stuff up onto the porch and knocked on the door. One-two. One-two—three.

Chapter Six

Day 14

J oe had replaced most of the electrical system, the battery, the starter, all the fuses, and some of the wiring. He had got the engine to turn over, but the old truck still wouldn't run. He spent several hours every day looking over every piece of the truck, cleaning off rust, dirt, leaves and caked oil, trying to find something he had missed. Keith was of little help. He knew nothing about engines or electronics, so he spent most of his time cutting firewood nearby as Joe puzzled over the truck.

It had been two weeks since they had seen their father. He might have been the only one who could help with the old truck. The old man lived in this landfill most of his life. He had ideas for how to build all kinds of things with his free junk. He had collected scrap from the dumpsters at the factory, from relatives who were getting rid of trash, and from coworkers like Cyclops whom he talked to almost every day. They traded things like tools and vegetables. It was from Cyclops that Kent had got his free pigs. Potbellies. Some older couple had kept them as pets in their trailer, but they bred like rabbits, and when the couple could no longer take care of them, they called Cyclops to give them a new home. Cyclops told them he would take good care of them, and he immediately called Kent to tell him about his score of free sausage. He couldn't handle all seven of the pigs, so he gave two to Kent. Keith had been talking about raising pigs, so one day, Kent brought them home in a dog crate.

Keith had built two pens and two houses out of hog panels and rough-cut cedar fence posts, repurposed pallets, and old, scrap tin roofing. They didn't look half bad, and Kent was pleased with the price tag on his new hog farming operation. Potbelly pigs turned out to be a cheap and easy-to-raise addition to the homestead. They required very little food, and they ate most of the food scraps, half rotten veg-etables, and weeds that were thrown into their pens. They seemed content to walk around, digging up roots and taking naps whenever they weren't eating.

The Rawlings had been raising chickens for some time, and they too were fairly easy maintenance. Last spring, Keith began building a chicken coop out of scrap lumber and old fencing. He bought just a few of the pieces, but once the coop was done, it was nearly impregnable, and the chickens seemed to like it. Let out to hunt for grass and bugs every day, they didn't go too far away from their house, and they went back inside the pen every evening, waiting for Keith to close the gate. They hunted down spiders, worms, roaches, ants, ticks, grasshoppers, mice, frogs, snakes, and carrion with equally ravenous brutality, biting, tearing, clawing, and flinging their victims in the air, smashing them against rocks and rending them in pieces between their savage beaks before gulping them down their throats and turning them into eggs for the Rawlings' breakfast.

Keith paid rent with firewood, fruit trees, chickens and eggs, and the venison he harvested in the fall. He was good with animals, both raising them and butchering them, and he insisted on restocking the family's food supply when he returned from active duty. Keith had been muttering about plans and backup plans and building stockpiles ever since he came home. Kent and Faye sometimes wondered if some-thing had happened to him while he was gone, something that damaged his mind, but they couldn't get any clues out of him. He had been a planner and an outdoorsman before, but it seemed like he had just changed somehow and had become paranoid about imminent catastrophe. Joe and Lynn mocked him every chance they got, but it seemed that gradually, they all saw some wisdom in being better prepared. Over the first spring, Keith planted twenty fruit trees of different kinds. The property used to be an orchard, but the remaining orchard trees had not been maintained and had not produced fruit in many years. They had died off, one by one, and they were cut down and burned and never replaced until Keith returned.

In his tree stand, Keith read disaster novels, survival guides, books about edible and medicinal plants along with history, philosophy, and literature. He stocked the freezers with fish in the summer, venison and squirrels that fall, and began trapping in the winter once the deer season had ended. He fed the pigs and chickens twice a day, not including scraps. Last spring, Keith had convinced them to start gardening again. The grass, where the garden had been, had grown up to the point where you couldn't tell that a garden had ever been there, but they tilled it under and planted again. That year's harvest was a meager one, but Keith had saved some leftover seeds and some of the seeds of the heirloom fruits and vegetables they had harvested. He kept the seeds in an ammo can in the cool of the basement. There, they stayed, waiting for spring.

Until they could get the truck fixed, they would have to take small loads of firewood back by hand or drag them. The wheelbarrow was broken, and rather than waste time trying to fix it, Keith decided to use a sled. The firewood was running dangerously low, and right now, heat was everyone's top priority. In an hour, Keith could cut about half a cord of wood, known around this part of the world as a "rick." It was the standard measuring unit of firewood in southern Indiana; it was a staple product bought, sold, and traded in the backwoods, and the demand for it had just exploded in the last two weeks. Keith had orders lined up from neighbors all along Mount Sinai Road. He would cut a rick for the

Rawlings house and then, a rick to trade. Keith and Joe had signed on a dozen more houses in the last week; some of the neighbors required firewood as part of the bargain and would trade various other services for it.

Not everyone had a woodstove or fireplace on Mount Sinai, and Tim was working with some of the neighbors to build stoves out of steel drums and scrap metal. He was taking a lot of IOUs for the moment, and for that matter, so was Keith, but they wrote up paper contracts and shook hands on each deal with the assurance that they all knew where each other lived, and it wasn't likely that anyone would be going anywhere. A couple of people had old pickup trucks they had got running, and with nothing else to trade, they started a delivery service, taking shipments of firewood to people. Most of the neighbors had started using the barter system to trade for items they needed, but there were still a couple of people who were accepting cash as payment. It was a gamble, but they were betting on the country pulling through and continuing to use the almighty dollar. It was an investment—and one they hoped would make them rich when all was said and done. Most of the other neighbors were all too happy to give them the pieces of paper in exchange for food, clothing, medicine, and so forth. Still, there were already certain items that were becoming recognized as a viable currency in the new economy: liquor, tobacco, gold and silver to some extent, unopened packs of batteries, and ammunition. A few of the hunters on Mount Sinai reloaded their own ammunition, which made them potentially very wealthy men; for the foreseeable future, they sat on a stock-pile of liquid currency.

Next to old trucks and tractors, the most valuable thing on Mount Sinai Road was a generator which Jeremiah Davis used to power a welder and drill press and a few other tools to build woodstoves with Tim. If the country didn't go back to normal though, everyone knew that eventually, the fuel would run out; for that reason, the next most valuable things were horses. There were several people on Mount Sinai Road who kept horses, and without feed or law enforcement, they took to riding most of the day. They would ride up and down the roads, grazing their horses, armed with rifles. They traveled to the ends of the road, and sometimes, beyond, to see what was going on. They brought back news of what they saw, and they started to become something of an unofficial police force. There were some people on the road who were unhappy with their neighbors' self-appointed authority and didn't hide their displeasure.

Just about a quarter mile down the road from the Rawlings house, there lived a sheriff's deputy whom the horse riders would tell about stolen property and vandalism. The sheriff's deputy, Rick Thompson, was a friend of Joe, and while he did not want the responsibility of addressing his neighbors' grievances, he found himself being unceremoniously promoted to sheriff, it seemed. Tim had arranged a meeting of whoever wished to attend later in the day. It was expected that they would discuss things like law enforcement and trade among other things, perhaps they would have a vote and elect Rick Thompson to be sheriff. Maybe they would set up some sort of government. Tim had asked for Keith and Joe both to be there.

They still had a few hours until then, and Keith was determined to cut at least one more rick of wood. Ben Jameson was supposed to be picking up a load before the meeting. He and his son had started delivering firewood and payments to people with an old 1940s tractor and a wagon where his son would ride with a double-barrel shotgun. They hauled deliveries back and forth between customers and took a delivery fee for themselves. Firewood was getting to be very expensive. Those who could not cut their own paid a premium price for it, yet there were some who seemed to be getting theirs another way. It wasn't confirmed, but there were rumors going around about trespassers stealing from neighbors' woodpiles. It was not difficult to imagine who would be doing this. Some of the residents on Mount Sinai never traded for wood as far as anyone knew, and they were never seen cutting their own either. People had their suspicions, but no one was sure yet.

Keith shut off the saw and sat down on a log. The hills and valleys echoed with the sounds of chainsaws and the revving engine of a truck being resurrected. Keith tightened the chain, refilled the fuel and bar oil reservoirs, and began to sharpen the teeth. He heard Joe growl in frustration.

Joe spat on the ground and stood up. "Keith, can you give me a hand?"

Keith walked over to the truck and set his saw in the bed. "What do you need?"

"More hands. Here, hold these." Joe put some wires in Keith's left hand and a flashlight in the other. He reached back in a tight concavity behind the engine, trying to remove a bolt. "I'm almost convinced the engine's junk. It's not locked up, but it just won't fire. I might have to replace the whole thing, and I don't know if I could ever do it." He spat off to the side.

"It wouldn't be worth it, if you could," Keith replied. "There are enough vehicles going around here to keep things functioning well enough for now. But in, say, a year or so—we'll probably be out of fuel."

Joe wiped his nose with his coat sleeve. "A year."

"Well, who knows what could happen between now and then? But we're going to have to think about that possibility." The putt-putt-gurgle of an old tractor engine could be heard coming down the road. "And I imagine that's what we're going to discuss in this meeting. Here comes Ben Jameson."

"There it is." Joe pulled the bolt out and looked at it. "Nope. That's not it."

"Well, I better help them load this wood. Want to take a break from that?"

"Yeah. Let me just put this bolt back before I lose it."

The old tractor putted down the driveway and out into the field where it turned around. Ben's son Mark sat on the back of the wagon with his shotgun pointed up in the air, smiling. Keith met them in the field and directed them back into the woods where the firewood was ready to be loaded.

"Hey, Joe," Ben said, climbing off the tractor. "Keith." He nodded. "Everybody doin' alright?"

"Sure. Yourselves?" Joe responded.

"Well, to tell you the truth, my son is sick, but otherwise, we're okay."

Mark jumped off the wagon, "That's my brother. He's got a fever. He looks real bad."

"I'm sorry to hear that," Joe said.

Keith stared blankly at a tree for a few seconds, lost in thought. Then, he seemed to snap out of his trance, and he looked at Ben. "I've got some books on medicinal plants and things if you'd like to look at them, but I bet Emma Faulkner knows quite a bit about that sort of thing."

"Oh, I think it'll be alright. We've still got some medicine at the house, so I'm sure we can handle it." Ben nodded and squinted his eyes. "But it's probably good to think ahead, I guess. The medicine won't last forever."

"Right."

"Well, it sounds like something we ought to bring up at the meeting. You're going to be there, right?"

"Yeah, we plan to be." Joe took out a can of tobacco.

"You mind if I get a pinch?" Ben asked.

Joe immediately regretted taking the can out of his pocket. He hesitated. He couldn't think of a way to refuse without seeming rude, so he handed the tin over. "Sure." He knew he was going to have to quit before long anyway.

Ben took a pinch of tobacco and thanked him as he handed it back. "Where did you get the snuff?"

"When we went into town last week. There were still a couple cans left in a gas station." Joe put a pinch in his lip. "I doubt you can find any now."

"Yeah, I went into town five days ago, and I couldn't find any. Couldn't find much of anything useful really. Except a few tools." He spat on the ground. "Food's all gone, medicine's all gone, beer and tobacco's all gone. Plenty of clothes around though." He smiled.

"You didn't take the tractor in to town, did you?" Joe asked.

"Oh no. I went with Rick and Jeremiah. Jeremiah's got that old Dodge, you know. Still runs good."

"What was it like out there?" Joe said, glancing at Keith.

"Creepy. Like a zombie movie or something. Trash everywhere. People walking around. Some tried to take the truck. Saw a lot of dead people."

"Did you go through campus?" Keith asked.

"No way. We figured that would be a nightmare, so we stayed away from there. He converted the truck to four-wheel-drive."

"Has anyone else gone into town?"

"Yeah, at least a couple trips were made after I came back—you know, that I'm aware of. It's getting pretty hairy out there. We've been trying to tell people not to go. There's nothing to get anymore, anyway. You know that older couple in the white house across the road from me?"

"Yeah." Joe nodded.

"I seen them leave a couple days ago, and I never saw them come back."

Joe looked at the ground and shook his head.

"I mean, they could have gone to stay with a relative or something, but..." He coughed and spat a black stream off to the side. "Well, anyway, this firewood ain't gonna load itself, is it? What are you waiting for, Mark?"

The two started loading the wagon with help from Keith and Joe. Ben began handing logs to his son who aligned them on the floor of the wagon in a neat row. "Any luck with the truck?"

"No, it's always been a mess, so it's hard to know what all's wrong with it," Joe said, handing a log to Mark.

"Right, right. I've got one that fits that description myself. Whatever you do, don't leave your tools sitting out here though. People have been getting their stuff stolen around here."

"I heard about that. Have you had anything stolen?"

"No, not yet. At least, not that I've noticed. But I've talked to several people who have. I would keep an eye on the people in that purple house just down the road from you there," Ben said, nodding his head toward the place. "I've never seen them doing any work outside, but somehow, there's smoke coming out of the chimney."

"We'll keep it in mind. We've had problems with that house before, but I don't want to rush to conclusions."

"No, you're right. We'll have to talk about that this evening too. We're converting the wagon into a bus once we drop this load off. We're giving people from the other end of the road a ride to the meeting, for a small fee, of course."

After about ten minutes, they had the wagon filled with stacked wood. Ben paid them with five gallons of gasoline. He and Mark both shook hands with the brothers, and then, they putted the old tractor out through the field and up the long driveway.

"I'm coming too," Lynn said. "I'm tired of hanging around this house all day. I want to know what's going on." She had her backpack packed and ready to go on the table in front of her.

Keith looked at Faye. "Are you going to be alright here by yourself?"

"Yeah, I'll be fine. I'm going to lock all the doors as soon as you leave. Just stay together and be careful. What time are you going to be back?"

"Before dark, at least." Joe shrugged. "But I guess it depends on how much we have to talk about."

"It's going to be quite a bit, I imagine." Keith nodded. He looked at his watch. 1301. "I expect it'll take a couple hours, maybe three. We ought to be back by five. Just make sure you don't open the door unless you hear our special knock. Pretty much everybody on this road knows about the meeting, so it would be a good opportunity for a thief to rob somebody's house."

"Well, if they pick this house, they'll wish they hadn't." Faye ladled some stew from the pot on the stove into her bowl.

"Keep an eye on the animals especially. I'm not going to let the chickens out today," Keith said.

"Good. If I see anybody trying to steal chickens, I'll shoot at the ground in front of them or something. That ought to scare them off." Faye sat down at the table with her bowl of stew. "As soon as I'm done eating, I'm going to go sit in the other room by the window and read my book, so I'll be able to see anyone walking around back there."

Keith brought in a couple more logs and set them beside the woodstove. "Alright. We'll be back as soon as we can." He grabbed his water and his notebook and stepped outside.

After Joe and Lynn put their bowls in the sink and brought in more firewood, they joined Keith outside.

Faye swallowed a spoonful of the stew. Corn, beans, squash, and opossum stew. Keith had caught the opossum in a trap, so he cleaned it, scraped off the abundance of lard to the best of his ability, and simmered the carcass on the stove for a day and a half. He set the pot outside in the cold for a few hours to cool it, and when the fat had congealed at the top, he skimmed it off, removed the bones, and added the vegetables and seasoning to the meat and broth. Faye thought it was delicious. It tasted like a turkey pot pie, more or less. The chickens ate the crumbled bones and fat, and Keith took the skin and skull to the Faulkners' house, where one of the boys was learning to brain-tan hides. After all, opossum fur had long been prized in high-end ladies' fashion as some of the softest fur on the market. Nothing went to waste. Faye took another bite and smiled.

It was thirty-two degrees out now. Keith slung his rifle over his shoulder and looked up at the gray sky as he walked. He wondered if he would ever see contrails in the sky again. On the other hand, if the clouds ever cleared, he thought, they would be able to see stars in the night sky that hadn't been seen in over a century, perhaps.

"What are you looking at?" Lynn asked.

"Hmm?" Keith looked at Lynn. "Oh, I was just thinking about all the stars we might see now. Without all the ambient light."

Ben had offered to give them a ride, but they told him they would walk. It was only about a mile anyway, maybe a little more. They had considered meeting at the old church at the top of the road, but they quickly agreed that it was too far for some at the other end of the road and too exposed to the highway. So, they were meeting in Jim Baker's barn. It was nearly halfway between the two ends of Mount Sinai Road and close to the intersection with Deer Creek Road. Apparently, he had moved his equipment outside and set up chairs and tables. The barn was heated with a huge wood stove that he and Jeremiah Davis built together.

The three walked down the hill and across the bridge over Deer Creek. They could see people walking toward the barn from Deer Creek Road and people walking from the north end of Mount Sinai Road. They turned into the gravel driveway and stood outside the barn, looking around.

The others gathered in the driveway as well, and those who had met before shook hands. Those who had not met began introducing themselves. Some people no one seemed to recognize. They stood off to the side, beneath the trees, watching, but not speaking to anyone. Most were armed. Some were not. At least, not visibly.

"Hey, there's Rachel Owens. Let's go talk to her." Lynn began walking toward her.

"Lynn." Keith said firmly without shouting.

She turned around and looked at him.

"Stay together."

"Alright. Come on." She nodded toward the couple standing beside the corn field and waited for her brothers to catch up.

Standing in long dresses and thick winter coats, Rachel Owens and her mother Lydia Jorgenson watched the travelers trickle in in groups of twos and threes and, sometimes, individually. Standing with the women, was a tall man in simple denim pants, boots, and a denim coat. In his hand, he did not hold a weapon, but a leather-bound book. He looked stern and serious. The Jorgensons were friends of Faye from her time teaching at the private school. They were exceptionally religious people and were deeply involved with the school where both Lynn and Rachel's daughter had attended. Rachel and her daughter had moved back in with her parents after the death of her husband. Rachel's daughter was a friend of Lynn, and Lynn had spent many afternoons at the Jorgensons' quaint, blue house just a half-mile down the road from the Rawlings' place. Rachel and her mother could often be seen walking along the road and would sometimes meet Faye to talk about how their tomatoes were growing or what was happening at the private school.

Lynn caught the eye of Rachel as she approached, smiling. "Hi, Rachel. How have you all been?"

"Lynn! It's good to see you!" Rachel smiled. "Boys, how are you?"

Keith and Joe both smiled, nodded, and said they were well. The older couple stood behind Rachel, looking friendly but speaking softly to one another, probably about who these young men were and how they knew them.

Rachel nodded. "And how's your mom and dad?"

"They're doing as well as can be expected, you know," Lynn said, glancing over at her brothers. She received a slight nod back from Keith.

"Yeah, well, that's all you can hope for." Rachel looked behind her and said, "You've met my parents, right?"

"I have," Lynn replied. "But I don't think my brothers have."

"Well, this is Eric and Lydia Jorgenson, my parents."

CHAPTER SIX

The man stretched out his hand and greeted them with a deep voice, "Good to meet you."

The old woman shook their hands as well and said, "Your momma always brought us some of the best tomatoes and cucumbers! Oh, and that sweet corn! I hope y'all have as good a garden this year." She smiled.

"Well, we'll have no shortage of time this year, it seems. We always got overwhelmed with the weeds before," Keith replied.

"Happens to the best of us," Eric said with a grin.

"That's right. Those weeds sneak up on you every year." Lydia was nodding. "'Course, y'all always grew a great big garden. One of the biggest on Mount Sinai Road, I'd wager. I wouldn't have been able to keep up with that much work myself. We always just grow a small patch in the back yard, you know. Just a few things."

Rachel put her hand on Lynn's shoulder. "Hey, tell your mom to come over to the house some time. I would love to talk to her. We need to catch up."

"I'll do that." Lynn nodded. "Yeah, I think she would like to get out of the house for a while, you know? It would do her good to talk to somebody."

Rachel nodded and bent down to speak to her in a lowered voice. "Me too. And I'd like to send some of my rhubarb spread back with you to try."

"Oooh, I bet it's delicious."

From just up the road came the putt-putt-gurgling-growl of Ben Jameson's rusty, old tractor. It turned into the driveway with its wagon full of passengers. All eyes were on the tractor now, and the faces of those aboard. The tractor made a big circle in the driveway and came to a stop beside the cornfield. Ben shut the engine down, and when the gurgling stopped, Mark hopped out, put down a steel ladder, and began helping people climb out of the wagon. There were some waves and greetings and handshakes. The din of voices grew louder until a truck rumbled down the road from the north and into the driveway. Two pickups came from the south end of the road and delivered beds full of passengers. As the people poured out of the vehicles, a door to the barn opened. Joe turned around to see Tim walk toward him.

Tim smiled and shook his hand. "How's everybody doing?" He shook hands with Keith and Lynn and seemed quite pleased about something. "Pretty good turnout, huh?" He looked around.

"Yeah, I'd say so," Joe agreed.

Tim looked at his watch. "It's about time to start. I'm glad you guys are here. I've been working with Jim all day, trying to get everything set up. I think this could be a really good start to something."

The double barn doors opened, and Jim Baker stood in the doorway. He held up a large triangle and battered it with a crescent wrench. When all the talking stopped, he said, "May I have your attention, everybody?" With all eyes on him, he spoke. "My name is Jim Baker. This is my barn which we have set up for this meeting. There should be plenty of chairs inside for everybody, we got the woodstove going good and hot, and there's drinks on a table inside as well. So, please come on in, and make yourselves comfortable before we let out all the heat."

The people began filing in. Tim shook the hands of the Jorgensons, said he was glad to see them all, and led the way into the barn. Light streamed in through large, glass windows at the top. There were also several lanterns hanging from the walls and the ceiling. As the last of the guests trickled in, Jim Baker closed the doors behind them. It was still quite cool in the barn, but surprisingly warm compared to outside. The room was filled with collapsible chairs arranged in a semicircle with an aisle down the middle. On the side of the barn, where all the chairs were facing, was an empty space, and the aisle continued from the space to the opposite wall, where there were some fold-up tables with pitchers and cups. Several people gravitated toward the free drinks right away. The sound of voices began to grow louder once again.

Keith, Joe, and Lynn sat down next to the Jorgensons. To Joe's right, Rick Thompson sat down. He shook hands with him and exchanged greetings.

Jim went to the center of the semicircle and began to speak in his most stage-worthy voice. "I assume everybody has an idea of why we're all here," he began.

"Is that coffee I smell?" one of the old farmers asked with a grin.

Tim walked down the aisle and answered: "You're welcome to some of the coffee beside the stove, but I ask that you limit yourself to one cup please. As I'm sure you've all noticed, coffee is in short supply these days."

The old farmer smiled and hobbled toward the stove with a cup in hand.

As the chairs were filled, Jim Baker began again: "All of you have been asked by some of your neighbors for the past week or more if you would be interested in trying to build a bit of a community here on this road. I know I was approached by Tim Faulkner here, who explained his vision for the community going forward. I thought it sounded like something worth trying, and I figured, what else can we do but try? So, for anyone who hasn't heard what I'm talking about, I'd like to hand it over to Tim and let him explain it to you." He looked at Tim before he went to take a chair in the front.

The people had quieted down, but several were frowning, shifting in their seats, and murmuring to one another.

Tim stood up and spoke. "I don't want anyone to think I'm trying to take control of anybody's life. It's not like that. All I'm saying is, it's been two weeks since we've had power. We're all feeling the effects of the blackout—some more than others. And I'm suggesting that we try to work together to maintain some semblance of order and normalcy in this new situation. Otherwise, we will have a total breakdown of society, and I don't think anyone wants to see that. But we're here to discuss what we can do going forward, and we want to hear from everyone who has a suggestion or a question."

"What happened?" A woman's voice shouted out from the seats.

"We still don't know, for sure, what happened or how, but we've been discussing this for some time, and our best guess is that someone attacked us with some sort of electromagnetic pulse weapon. It's like a huge burst of radiation that fries all the circuits."

"But how?"

"Like I said, we don't know how. That's about all I can tell you, for now."

"What if whoever attacked us plans to invade?"

"We can't think about that right now. A lot of us don't even know how we're going to survive the winter, yet. We have to take this one step at a time and deal with the problems right in front of us first."

A man sat up in his seat and raised his voice. "You say you want to keep society from breaking down, but from where I'm sitting, it looks like it already has. I've had a lot of my property stolen from me in the last few days. Now, what am I supposed to do about that? We got thieves robbing people up and down this road, and there's a good chance they're in this barn right now." He looked around. The muttering voices grew louder, and a couple people shouted their agreement with the man.

"People are starving! And you're worried about protecting your property?" shouted a woman. "We need to collect all the food and supplies and distribute them evenly among the residents!"

Ernie Jacobs stood up. "I still remember a time when we went to war to kill people that believed in that garbage! If your dumb ass thought it was a good idea to buy jewelry, new cars, designer clothes, and fifty pairs of worthless shoes, then maybe you deserve to starve to death. And good riddance, you commie traitor! Anyone comes to my house, trying to redistribute my property, better not plan on leaving alive."

CHAPTER SIX

There were shouts and cheers of approval which drowned out the dissent. People in the barn applauded as the hippies expressed their fear and disgust.

Tim raised his hands for quiet. "Please! Quiet down!" A minute went by before the room was tranquil enough to hear him speak. "Well, I guess that's as good a place to start as any," Tim said. "We have to have the rule of law, first and foremost."

"Are you just going to let people die?" came another shout.

"Let's take a vote," Jim offered. "All in favor of stealing people's property and giving it to people who don't deserve it, say aye."

There were several "ayes" screamed throughout the barn. "All opposed."

The barn erupted in a thunderous "No!"

"The neighs have it," Jim announced. "See, lady? Nothing I can do. That's as democratic as it gets."

There was some laughter in the crowd.

"And it's a good thing too, because if you all voted in favor, we still wouldn't do it, because it's damn evil. Anyone who needs food or firewood can earn it by trading services to those who can pay them, and for the ones who are unable to work, get with some of the church leaders around here and we'll figure something out. The right to one's own labor is sacred, and if we violate that, we'll give up our freedoms as well as our souls. And what the hell would be the point of trying to survive, then?"

"We will have to make laws," Tim said. "And I think we should have a sheriff."

"And who's going to make the laws?" a man said. "And who's going to judge? And who's going to execute?"

"Who put you in charge?" came a shout.

"I'm not in charge, and I don't claim to be." Tim responded. "We're all free to live our lives as we please, so long as we don't infringe on the rights of others. I suggest we keep the same laws we've always had, and we elect the executives. As far as I'm concerned, the Constitution is still in effect."

One of the hippies stood up. "What if we don't like the laws? Why don't we take this opportunity to correct some of the societal injustices of our laws? Why should we value the American Constitution over other ones?"

There were some chuckles and groans among the seats.

Tim's brow furrowed; he shook his head. "Umm."

Jim Baker stood back up. "Which constitution would you rather live under?"

"I'm just saying, there are other cultures that we can learn from. We don't have to be bound to the same old system. Indigenous peoples like the Cherokee nations have a much more egalitarian society."

Jim blinked, looked at Tim, and then surveyed the people staring at the woman. "Okay, we'll take a vote. Raise your hand if you would rather adopt the Cherokee constitution."

No hands went up. Not even the hippies'.

"Alright, it's decided." Jim looked back at the hippie woman. "Thank you."

"All I'm saying is... we should think about... injustices and..."

"Thank you," Jim repeated. "Moving on. As far as an executive, I nominate Rick Thompson for sheriff. He was a deputy, he has experience in law enforcement, and we don't need a bunch of vigilantes acting as judge, jury, and executioner. Who agrees?"

There were a few hands and voices of approval rising, but Rick Thompson stood up. "I didn't put my hat in."

"You don't want the position?" Tim asked.

"No."

Murmurs rippled through the crowd.

"Very well. Who would like to be sheriff of Mount Sinai?"

A man in a long leather coat stood up and removed his hat. "My name is Jack Winters. I will be sheriff if you vote for me. I already have my deputies."

"And who the hell are you?" one man shouted.

"No! No police!" A woman yelled. "We couldn't trust the cops before. We definitely can't trust you!"

A man stood up, holding a pump-action shotgun. "I don't need law enforcement. I can enforce my own law." He racked the slide, and several hands went to their weapons. The man kept his shotgun pointed at the ceiling. He looked around and sat down.

"Please do not do that again," Tim said, looking sternly at the man. "Now, no one is asking anyone to disarm."

"I am," a hippie chimed in.

Tim looked in the direction of the woman. "She is. But no one else is asking you to disarm. You have the right to keep and bear arms, and that's not going to change. You have the right to defend yourself, your family, and your property, and that's not going to change either. All we're saying is, we need to have someone to settle disputes when they arise. Someone we all elect and agree to recognize."

A man stood up and said, "I vouch for Jack Winters. He's a good man, a family man, a Marine veteran, and a patriot. He raised his kids right, and he's got a level head. He cares about his community, and he's always ready and willing to help out his fellow man."

"Alright, thank you." Tim looked around the room. "Does anyone have a reason Jack Winters should not be appointed sheriff?"

"Yeah," a man said. "I don't like the way he and his kids are always riding their horses around with their guns out like we're all a bunch of peasants and we need to fear them."

At this, Jack looked at the man and responded: "Sir, that was not our intention at all. I apologize if it looked that way, but we were simply exercising the horses, and we didn't want to go anywhere unarmed because of the reports we've been hearing of the violence in town. I assure you; we do not believe ourselves superior to anyone. I merely want to help."

The other man shrugged in his seat.

"Alright, who votes for Jack Winters to be sheriff? Raise your hands."

A few hands went up, maybe a dozen out of the nearly one-hundred people there.

"Ok, well, raise your hand if you're opposed to Jack Winters acting as sheriff."

Three hands went up. Hippies. Everyone else was whispering to someone or looking around quietly.

"Well, let's name Jack Winters as the acting sheriff for now."

"You need to swear him in, at least," someone said.

Tim looked at Rick Thompson, "Can you swear him in?" When Rick nodded, Tim asked, "Does anyone have a Bible?"

Eric, the tall man sitting beside Rachel and Lydia, handed his book to Rick. "Here. Use mine," he said in his deep voice.

Jack Winters was sworn in in the center of the semicircle. He sat down. Rick returned the Bible and went to the back to get a drink.

"Property lines must be respected," Tim said. There was a shout of approval from most of the seats. "Those who steal the property of others, will be caught. They will be tried in front of the assembly and dealt with accordingly. Any objections?"

One of the hippies stood up. "That's easy for you to say, you have a lot of property already. Many of us have very little. I didn't steal anyone's stuff, but I'm just saying we should be understanding of those who might have been put in a desperate situation."

Another man stood up and responded: "We're all in a desperate situation. To steal someone's livestock, food, or heat right now is the same as murder. If anyone needs supplies that badly, let him work for it. Let him hire himself out and earn his bread like a man. Like the rest of us here. Then, we can all hold our heads up, and maybe we can get through this alive, but if anyone tries to rob me or sneaks around my house in the night, I've got something for you."

There was a roar of approval from the crowd again.

Eric stood up with his Bible. "For people who are truly unable to provide for themselves, I would like to start an assembly of church members. We can meet at my house for services if Mr. Baker does not wish to continue to lend us the use of his barn. Let those who are in exceptional need come to the church, and we will do all that we can together to provide for them." He sat back down.

Jim spoke up. "You may use my barn for now, but you'll have to supply your own firewood and your own oil or whatever you'll use for light."

"Thank you, sir." Eric nodded his appreciation.

"Now, I'd like to talk about something that should concern everyone." Tim stood up and began pacing in the semicircle. "Most of us are running low on supplies and we do not have access to the supply chain that was the economy any longer." The crowd went silent, and everyone looked intently at Tim. "It has been halted altogether. Some of us have made trips into town to gather supplies, and we have found mostly bare shelves for the past week, at least. Some things might still be available if one knows where to look, but I would caution against any further trips into town unless it's of the utmost necessity. I made a trip into town with Joe and Keith Rawlings last week." He looked at Keith. "Keith probably saved us from death on more than one occasion. Keith, would you describe what you saw in town?"

Keith stood up and relayed his account of driving through campus, the garbage piled in the roads, the raided stores, the townspeople cutting down all the trees for firewood, the burned down houses, the dead bodies, the mobs trying to surround them, and the pirates. The people listened fixedly, staring at Keith as he described the scene. Then, he said, "I think Mr. Faulkner is right. It's too dangerous to go into town anymore. The people have become desperate and are fighting to survive as best they can. There's no telling what they will do or not do to stay alive. Two weeks ago, we were snatched out of our comfortable lives and thrown back into the eighteenth century—only, we no longer remember how to survive in the eighteenth century. The rules have changed. There is no law, no government, no one protecting us but ourselves. The way of living that was possible before, no longer exists. The people in the towns and cities have never had to worry about where their food came from or how their homes were heated. They survived because they were allowed to. Now, those places are concrete deserts, and those people will eventually have to leave to find food and water. We have been forced to see the world for how it is. Nature is trying to kill us all, every minute of every day. We either survive, or we don't. The choice is ours, and no one cares which choice we make." He sat back down.

There was a silence in the room. Some of the hippies were wiping tears from their eyes. Then, another man stood up—Jeremiah Davis, the mechanic running the welding shop out of his garage. "I went into town just a couple days ago," he said. "I didn't go through campus, but I saw much of the same things Keith just described. We stayed on the outskirts of town, but what we saw was even worse than what he said. There were bodies in the streets. Several houses were burned to the ground. We saw people fighting over tools and cans of food. We saw what looked like gangs raiding houses, and we had to defend ourselves from attackers on the highway. We need to be able to fend for ourselves for the foreseeable future. And we should have a way to defend ourselves from outsiders."

There was murmuring. An anonymous voice could be heard saying it was ridiculous. "I agree," a man said. "So do I," said another. "We can't have gangs or looters coming to our houses," a woman said. "But how do we stop them?"

"If I may," Jack Winters said as he stood up. "I think we should start with blocking off the road from the highway with some of the dead cars. We can create a gate where we can go in and out if we need to, but we can block it with a car to prevent any vehicles coming in from the highways."

"Won't that look conspicuous?" a woman asked.

"Yes, but it's better than nothing. At least, in my opinion," Jack responded.

"I don't know," a man said. "That would just mean they would attack us from the woods instead of the road where we can see them."

"I don't think so," Jack said. "They will be attacking us for resources, not for sport. And they won't be able to carry any kind of supplies over this terrain. They will need trucks or, at least, some kind of carts to haul away anything. So, they will need the roads. They'll try to clear the obstacles before they take the woods."

"That is so long as they want to take things away," Keith said. "They may want to move here. Take the land and the houses along with the food."

The murmuring arose again.

"In that case," Jack said. "We'll be fighting for our lives."

The barn went silent again.

Tim stood up. "Who votes to barricade the roads at the highways?"

If the vote was not unanimous, it was nearly so. The barn was a sea of raised hands and voices of approval and affirmation.

"We'll start building the barricades first thing in the morning," Tim announced. "Sheriff Winters, your first task will be to oversee the construction. We'll need volunteers and permission to use some of the cars closest to the ends of the road. Please meet with Sheriff Winters afterward, if you've got a car we can use, or if you're willing to volunteer to help build the barricades."

A woman stood up and said, "Another thing that concerns a lot of us is feeding our livestock. I've been rationing feed, and I'm nearly out. How am I going to feed my animals?" There was an eruption of agreement.

"That's a major concern right now," Tim answered. "Keith and I and a few of the other homesteaders here can share some tips on feeding animals through the winter months, but I can tell you, it will not be easy. Anyone who wants to can stay behind after the meeting to talk about feeding livestock. We've been thinking about that, and we think we can set up a system that will work for people. For the long term, we'll need grain, and I'm hoping we can figure out an arrangement to plow the fields in the spring and grow our own, but we can discuss that at another time. Is there anything else?"

"Yes." An old man rose to his feet. "My wife is sick, and uh... well, I don't know what I can do..."

Keith had nearly forgotten. He was going to bring it up. What would they do for the sick and injured people? He had heard rumors that some on Mount Sinai had already died. Who knows how many had run out of life-extending medications or had lost the use of needed machines? He wondered how his grandparents were doing. Would they still be alive? Out of the corner of his eye, he saw Joe and Rick whispering to one another.

Tim asked if there were any nurses present. There were two in the barn. They said they would do everything they could to help the sick to the best of their ability, but they had no supply of medicine other than what they kept for themselves, and they would not perform surgeries on anyone. Tim said he would see about the medicine. They may be able to make a few things with plants, but it would never be as potent or effective as the drugs they had been accustomed to.

When Tim asked if there was anything else that should be discussed, the room remained quiet. "Well, I know everyone needs to be back before it gets dark, so let's end our discussion here, and we'll plan to meet again soon. Maybe in a week or two." He looked around the room. "If there's nothing further..."

"Before we leave," Eric stood up, clutching his Bible. "Let us pray."

The sky was still gray, the wind picking up again. The sun was sinking behind the trees. Keith, Joe, and Lynn crested the hill and saw Jack Winters' horses standing behind their split rail fence, watching them walk by. It was getting colder. Small, faint snowflakes were beginning to drift through the air as the roosters crowed, dogs barked, and a coyote howled from somewhere off in the distance. The ever-present tinge of woodsmoke tainted the air no matter which way the wind shifted.

"How did you get me roped into staying behind for an extra hour to talk about feeding livestock?" Lynn complained.

"Oh, come on, what else were you going to do? You're the one who wanted to get out of the house and talk to people. Besides, you said you wanted to meet Tim; well, now you have." Keith looked over his shoulder at Lynn. Then, he looked at Joe. "What were you whispering to Rick back there?"

"What?" Joe frowned quizzically.

"When that old man was talking about his sick wife, you were whispering something to Rick. He looked upset."

"Oh, yeah." Joe spat a stream of black tobacco juice onto the blacktop and sighed. "He was just telling me about his mother. She was on oxygen when the blackout happened. She ran out two days ago."

"Oh, no." Lynn stopped for a second. Her brothers did not. She caught back up with them. "But how is she... is she... still..."

"Nope." Joe spat again. "She died last night."

"What did he do with the body?" Keith asked.

"As far as I know, she's still layin' in bed in his house."

"Dude." Keith turned around and looked at Joe. "You can't let him stay in there with that."

"I know. I told him I would help him bury her tomorrow."

"That's good of you." Keith nodded. "I'll help too."

"I should tell Eric," Lynn said. "Someone should say something for her."

"I don't know if he would want that," Joe began. He thought for a second. "But maybe it's not a bad idea, just in case. Rick seemed to want to keep it private, but..."

"But he was probably just acting that way," Lynn added. "Dudes don't communicate their feelings well, and nobody really wants to be alone in a time like that. Even if they think they do. The worst that can happen is he'll say he doesn't want Eric there, and that'll be it. But I bet it's more likely he appreciates the thought behind bringing a minister to give her a funeral of some sort."

"Well, you're probably right," Joe said. "I'm going to go over there first thing in the morning. Best to get the body out of there soon, you know. That would be a nightmare to leave it in there for long."

"Right." Keith shook his head. "I'll go with you, and I'll help you bury her. He shouldn't have to do that."

"Well, since I never met him or his mother, I don't think I should be there," Lynn said. "But I want to go help with the barricades, then. Since you won't be there."

Keith slowed down but continued walking. He looked at Lynn like she had said something incredibly stupid. "Are you serious? You're not going up there alone. Remember, out here, there's only one law." He tapped the stock of his rifle.

"Come on. You too?" Lynn rolled her eyes, and her voice began to rise. "It's not enough I have to get it from Mom all day; I have to hear it from you too." She pulled up her coat to show the pistol on her belt. "I'm good, alright?"

Joe shushed her. "Keep your voice down."

"Look," Keith began. "It's time to get real. You're not even five feet tall. Now, a guy my size could do whatever he wanted to you, and all your friends put together couldn't do a thing about it if they were with you. And I'm not even the toughest guy on this road."

"You probably are," Joe put in.

"Ok, but I have the great equalizer," Lynn said. "I don't care how much you can lift or how fast you run or anything else. When I have one of these, *I'm* the toughest guy on this road."

"You barely know how to use that. You need to practice first."

"Well, you can teach me."

"Alright, I'll teach you. But who's going to take care of Mom?"

"Mom's going to have to take care of Mom. She's doing it right now, isn't she?"

They turned onto the gravel driveway. There were still patches of ice that never melted under the shadows of the canopy.

"We'll talk about it later," Keith said.

"Look." Joe pointed up ahead at something moving through the trees. "What is that?"

They all stopped and watched as something moved toward the house.

"Thieves," Joe whispered.

They stalked as quickly and quietly as they could down the driveway, keeping an eye out for others. The shapes moved slowly and methodically up ahead, oblivious to the three creeping up behind them. Keith and Joe had their rifles at the ready while Lynn drew her pistol. When they got within thirty yards of the shapes, they could see there were three. It looked like two people carrying a drunk. They were creeping along the tree line, looking at the house.

Keith aimed his rifle at the back of one's head, and he commanded in a loud, stern voice: "Stop where you are. Put your hands up and turn around slowly."

The three shapes stopped. They raised their hands in the air and turned around to look at the guns drawn on them.

Keith studied their faces, squinted, and lowered his rifle. "Dad?"

PART II
WINTER

Chapter Seven

The man collapsed to the ground.

Keith and Joe slung their rifles and rushed to lift him up.

"It's okay. These are my friends," he gasped in a labored voice. "Please, let them in."

They didn't argue with him. Keith and Joe hoisted him up between them and took him to the house. Keith knocked on the door. He looked over his shoulder at the two strangers for a couple seconds. The door opened, and they pushed in to get him on the couch. Faye was disoriented by the sudden rush of people through the front door. She stood back, processing the scene before her, wondering who these strangers entering her house were. Lynn shut the door behind them. Keith and Joe were breathing hard and told Lynn to get them some water. They laid the man back on the couch. Faye followed the commotion into the room. Keith asked the strangers to have a seat, motioning to the chairs in the room. They thanked him and sat down.

"Excuse me, what's going on?" Faye asked.

"He can't see. His eyes are swollen shut. He has some broken ribs, a torn muscle in his leg, and a head injury," said one of the strangers.

Lynn brought in three glasses of water. She handed one to Joe who held it up to his father's mouth, bidding him to take small sips. She gave one to each of the strangers, and they thanked her graciously.

Faye walked around to look at the man on the couch. He was dirty. His clothes were torn, and his grimy, discolored jaw was shrouded in stubble. His face was swollen and bruised. He lay breathing with difficulty. Then, she recognized him. She gasped, sunk to the floor, and cried.

Lynn rummaged through her parents' dresser and pulled out the least stained, ripped, and stretched clothing she could find. Even now, she was ashamed to show outsiders the contents of her parents' dresser. The world had gone to Hell, but as she looked through the ripped-up jeans, shirts, and socks, stained with paint, oil, and mustard, she couldn't help but feel disgust at how little her parents cared about their appearance. These clothes were all more than twenty years old, and the shirts had worn so thin that they could nearly be seen through. She collected a few items she thought would be a close enough fit and returned downstairs to show their guests the bathroom.

Keith and Joe had begun heating water in a stock pot on the woodstove for the strangers to bath with. Lynn placed towels, clothes, washcloths, and a lantern in the bathroom for them as the water was brought in a bucket and set in the bathtub. The strangers thanked them. Faye saw to it that Kent was bathed and dressed in clean clothes. As she removed his shoes and socks, she cried at the sight of his red, swollen feet and frostbit toes.

Keith, Joe, and Lynn sat around the dining room table eating opossum stew. When the strangers were done in the bathroom, they entered the dining room and sat down close to the woodstove. Joe got bowls and spoons for them and invited them to have some of the stew. They thanked them and accepted the invitation. They were eating when Faye walked into the room. She let them finish before asking them who they were, how they had met her husband, and how they got here.

They looked at each other, and the woman began to speak. "I'm Jordan. This is my husband Malik. We're from Cincinnati originally. We were driving back from a trip to St. Louis when it happened. We thought we would take the scenic route on the way back. We were in Nashville at the time. We didn't know what to do, so we got a room at a motel in town. We went to the local grocery store to get some supplies and came back with as many cans as we could carry, but after the first three days, the store had been emptied.

"At night, we stayed under a pile of blankets, towels, and coats in the motel. During the day, we would walk through the town and talk to the locals to see what we could learn. There was a building with a large firepit where the people gathered and brought wood to burn. We collected branches and trash every day and joined the group around the fire. After all the nearby deadwood was gone, we started cutting down trees in town. They began talking about the lack of supplies and trying to figure out how they were going to eat and stay warm. It didn't take long for people to start growing suspicious of one another. People were accused of hoarding supplies while others went hungry. We managed to mostly stay out of the tension, until one day, they took a vote and decided they needed to redistribute supplies to make sure everyone had an equal share. No one volunteered to give up supplies, so they formed a band of enforcers who would go from house to house to make sure everyone was being honest and not keeping more than the council said they could.

"About that same time, the owner of the motel told us we needed to pay him. We told him we had nothing to pay with. He said we would have to go get him supplies. We knew that it was time to go. The next day, we didn't bring the owner any supplies, and he sent the enforcers to collect. We woke up to the sound of screaming, and we saw the enforcers dragging a woman out of her house just a block away. They were heading our way. We packed the last of our meager supplies and left as quickly as we could. They saw us and ran after us. We hid in the bushes under the bridge, and as they searched for us, we heard what sounded like a lawnmower engine and then, a man's voice. He said something like, 'Hello there! How you doin'? Are ya playin' baseball?' The next thing we heard was the man being brutally beaten. We waited until after we heard the enforcers leave and everything was silent. We came out to see if the man was still alive. His head was bleeding, his eyes were swollen shut, he had been pepper-sprayed, beaten, and robbed. But he was still breathing. Malik picked him up and got him out of the road and into the woods.

"We tried to dress his wounds as best we could. We gave him some water and kept him warm while we tried to come up with a plan for what to do next. We didn't know where to go, and we only had three more cans of beans. We stayed there, shivering for a couple of hours, unsure of what to do, but then, the man began to make some noises. We told him what had happened and what we were doing. He said his name was Kent, and if we helped him get back home, we could stay at his house. By that time, it was beginning to get dark, and it was so cold we thought if we lay down out there, we would never get back up. So, we decided to walk through the night.

"Kent told us to feel for the moss on the trees and keep the side with the most moss facing to our right. That way we were able to continue heading west in the dark. We had to move slowly. Kent could hardly walk at all, and he couldn't see, so we mostly carried him or dragged him as much as we could without causing him to pass out from the pain of his broken ribs. In a way, the cold was helpful for Kent because it kept him numb.

"Whenever we crossed roads, we told Kent the names. He told us to keep going. The next morning, we shared the last of our beans with Kent. It wasn't enough, but we had to keep moving. Malik tried to catch a squirrel a couple of times, but we're from the city." Jordan looked at her husband who smiled weakly. They were both clearly exhausted and barely able to keep their heads up. Jordan continued: "We slept that morning for a few hours. It was the last time we slept or ate anything. That was two days ago. We reached the edge of a lake that night and tried to catch a fish with a piece of line and a hook we found caught in a tree branch, but I guess it was too cold. We didn't catch anything.

"Somewhere along the way, we lost our bags of clothes. They got soaked with water, and they were too heavy to carry, so we left them. We had to keep going. After two more days of climbing over hills and crossing creeks, we reached another road. We came to a T-intersection and read the sign to Kent. It said, "Mount Sinai Road." He told us this was his road and we would be safe here. So, from there, we followed the road, describing the houses we passed until he told us we had reached his driveway. We were walking to the house when you ran into us." Jordan smiled with a sigh, glanced at the siblings, at Faye, and then, she looked at Malik who nodded his affirmation.

Faye looked at the two, straight-faced. "You brought my husband back to me, and for that, I owe you. But you'll forgive me if I do not yet trust you. Kent said you may stay here. He seems to trust you, but he hasn't always been the best judge of character. Of course, I won't turn you away, but we were not expecting guests, so we'll have to make you a place here on the floor by the stove where you'll be warm."

"Thank you," the couple said.

"If you have any foolish ideas of robbing us or doing anything of the sort, I recommend you forget them. We're all armed, the doors will be locked, and we're all very light sleepers here."

Keith, Joe, and Lynn stared at their mother in disbelief. This was a side of her they had never seen before. Faye, in fact, had never been a light sleeper, and she had never been one to speak so directly to people outside her immediate family.

Malik and Jordan both assured her that they had no nefarious plans.

Faye and the siblings cleared a space and brought cushions, pillows, and blankets for their guests, laying out a nice sleeping arrangement for them on the floor—certainly nicer than anything they had experienced in the past two weeks. They left them a flashlight, reminded them where the bathroom was, told them to help themselves to the last of the stew, and took their candles and lanterns to bed.

Faye checked on Kent one last time. His breathing was shallow but steady now. He was asleep. She laid another of Keith's wool blankets over him, kissed his forehead, and left him to sleep on the couch.

Day 15

Keith awoke at dawn with the crowing of the rooster outside. He got dressed, brushed his teeth, and took his .22 rifle downstairs. Looking into the dining room in the faint light glowing through the windows, he could see Malik and Jordan still sleeping on the floor near the woodstove. The house was cold, but he decided to try and let the weary travelers sleep uninterrupted for as long as possible. The fire could wait a bit longer. He walked to the living room to find Kent still snoring on the couch. He was still alive. His face still looked like chewed bubblegum though.

Keith pulled on his boots, picked up his trapping bag, and slung his rifle as he stepped out onto the porch in the freezing morning air. The thermometer read eighteen degrees. Every morning, in the winter, when it was below freezing, it was necessary for Keith to heat water on the stove to melt the ice in the animals' water bowls. He would certainly need to do so today as well, but it could wait. His boots crunched through the snow as he dragged his sled behind him to check his traps. With a dozen traps set throughout the woods, the family could stay in meat all year round. More often than not, Keith returned from his daily check with at least one animal.

Approaching the first trap in his circuit, he found a raccoon with its front paw caught in the jaws of a foothold. The creature ran in circles, pulling at the anchor chain as Keith approached. It stopped, growled, and stared into Keith's eyes. Keith dispatched the animal, removed it from the trap, and placed the carcass on the sled. Once, the trap was reset, baited, and buried again, Keith sprayed it down with coyote urine and moved on to the next.

As he returned to the house, he stopped at the gambrel hanging from a tree branch. Today's catch was better than average with two raccoons. His fingers were already numb, but he needed to skin the animals before they became too stiff. With a daily supply of fresh meat from trapping, the family had been able to save their canned meat for leaner times. Everyone would prefer venison to raccoon and opossum, but Keith insisted, and succeeded in convincing everyone, that they needed to keep a supply of food in reserve and eat what was in season as much as possible. The colder months, being the natural season for meat, were the time to trap and eat what they caught. Animals had thicker coats in the winter which made for higher quality furs, but the cold also killed off parasites which never stopped being revolting when discovered in one's food. They didn't need any more meat at the moment, since they still had a frozen raccoon from yesterday preserved in a block of ice hanging from a tree branch. They had plenty of meat; what they did not have was feed for the animals. Keith knew that in two weeks or so, the supply of llama and fish food secured from last week's trip into town would be gone. When that happened, there would be no going into town for more. If they were going to feed their animals, they would need to find another way. Fortunately, Keith had thought of this years ago. One of the biggest reasons for raising pigs and chickens rather than other species was the fact that they were omnivorous. This meant that they could be relatively easily fed on unconventional food sources including insects, fruit, vegetables, roots; they could eat common wild plants and mushrooms in the spring and summer, seeds and nuts in the fall, and meat in the winter. It would be more labor intensive, less convenient, and less consistent, but it could be done. Since these raccoons were not needed for the pot, they would be fed to the animals. Keith skinned them out, quartered them, and put the meat, organs, and bones—everything but the head, skin, and intestines—in a stainless-steel stock pot to boil on the stove. The animals did not seem to like raw meat as much as cooked, and it was harder for them to digest besides.

Keith entered the house quietly and saw Joe building a fire in the stove. Their guests were still sleeping. Keith set down his rifle and filled the stock pot with water before putting it on the flat, cast-iron surface. Boiled raccoon did not have a pleasant smell, but it wasn't quite nauseating either. They would be burning some of the many scented candles that had accumulated over the years of Christmas, birthday, and Mother's Day presents for light anyway. By boiling the meat, Keith extracted every bit of nutrients possible from the animals, made the meat tender enough for the birds to easily pull it apart, and simultaneously, boiled the water he needed for pouring over frozen water bowls.

As the flames grew and enveloped the logs, Joe slid a couple more sticks on top and closed the doors gently. The iron hinges creaked. Joe met Keith in the kitchen as he was filling the percolator with water. "What are we going to do?" he whispered, looking at Keith.

"What do you mean?"

"I mean about them?" He nodded in the direction of the sleeping couple.

"I guess we're going to take them in," Keith shrugged.

"Do you think we can trust them?"

"I don't think we can trust anyone. Not completely."

"Right. That's what I'm saying. Remember, we're supposed to go to Rick's this morning."

"Oh yeah." Keith scooped coffee grounds into the percolator basket.

"If Lynn's going to get the preacher, and you and I are going to bury Rick's mother, then we'll be leaving them alone in the house with Dad, who's practically dead, and Mom, who's Mom."

"Yeah, I see what you're saying."

"What's to stop them from robbing the place?"

"Where would they go after they robbed us?" Keith put the percolator on the stove, looked at the still-sleeping couple, and returned to the kitchen.

Joe looked at the sleepers for a couple seconds, thinking. "I don't know. They could be lying about where they're from."

"They could be. I doubt it though. They wouldn't go through all the trouble to take Dad with them through the woods. It doesn't make any sense."

"Yeah, I know. It just seems weird to leave strangers we know nothing about in the house."

"Yeah, but it's not our house. It's Dad's house, and he invited them. If something goes wrong, we'll burn that bridge when we get to it."

Lynn entered the room with creaking footsteps, glancing at their guests on the floor and cringing at the noise she was making. It really couldn't be avoided; all the floors in the house creaked. Kent had enlisted the help of some relatives who were carpenters to build the house, and they spared every expense, including adequate flooring nails. It could be unbearably annoying to walk through the house if one was not in the mood to ignore these things. Once Lynn reached the peeling, linoleum-floored kitchen, the creaking intensified to the point where she simply stopped trying to avoid it. They would either wake up or keep sleeping. "What are you guys doing?" Lynn whispered. "What's for breakfast?"

"What are you making?" Keith said. "We've got coffee on the stove. Get some of the water-glassed eggs out, and we'll make something."

They had only collected one egg yesterday, so they would dip into the supply of eggs Keith had preserved for situations like this one. During the spring, when chickens lay the most eggs, the Rawlings would collect more eggs than they could possibly use. Keith would take the cleanest of these and preserve them in a jar of water mixed with pickling lime. This centuries-old method of egg preservation had kept fresh eggs edible for over a year for the Rawlings family before, and Keith had heard some people report having their eggs last up to two years with the method, although this seemed unnecessary to him. All they needed was for the eggs to last through the winter—one year, at most, from when they were collected; besides, the eggs gradually became more liquified the older they got, so by the time two years had passed, the eggs would have nothing like the consistency of fresh eggs, and that did not sound too appealing.

Lynn cracked eggs into a bowl and began whisking them with a fork. "What were you guys talking about?"

"The plan for today," Joe said. "You're still planning to get the preacher, right?"

"Yeah."

"Well, that means that we'll be leaving the house to Mom with these people in it." Joe raised his eyebrows as if to emphasize his point.

"So?"

Joe threw his hands up. "Alright. Whatever. Maybe you're right. Maybe it's nothing to worry about."

Lynn shrugged. "I'll get Eric while you guys are digging the hole. Are you going to take her up to the cemetery?"

"I don't know," Joe answered. "I haven't asked what he wants to do."

"The ground will be frozen." Lynn poured the eggs into a skillet she had put on the stove.

"I know." Joe looked out the window and rubbed his jaw.

"Better bring a pick." Keith poured a sample of coffee from the percolator into his mug.

Lynn went to see if Kent wanted some coffee. When she looked at the man rhythmically breathing shallow breaths on the couch, she could not tell if he was awake or asleep. His eyes were swollen shut. She hesitated for a second. "Dad? Do you want some coffee?" She waited for an answer but only heard a faint groan. He was probably still asleep, she thought, and she left him there to rest, returning to the kitchen to finish making breakfast.

The ceiling creaked. Faye was awake. The smells of breakfast and the sounds of talking, walking, and cooking had apparently awakened their guests who were yawning and rubbing their eyes. They were clearly still tired and visibly sore and stiff.

As Joe moved the scrambled eggs around the cast iron pan, Keith put together a sort of heavily seasoned racoon hash with potatoes they had canned. They were going to have a proper breakfast today. The new arrivals had probably not eaten a real meal since the power went out, and they were going to eat their fill today. Besides, gravedigging was hard work, and while they probably would not dig a full-six-foot-deep hole, the frozen ground would make it harder than normal. Then, there were the barricades that needed to be built. How many volunteers did Jack Winters manage to enlist? None of them knew. There would probably be some who decided to help out of sheer boredom, but Keith, Joe, and Lynn all thought they should go and check to see if they needed any additional help. Keith offered some coffee to Malik and Jordan, and they gladly accepted.

Faye walked into the room to see the two strangers groggily sipping coffee at the table. She walked past them without saying a word, and then poured herself a cup of coffee from the percolator. She shook the last few grains of powdered creamer into the coffee and silently cursed her luck and her lack of foresight for running out of this staple. Coffee without creamer? Horrible. At least they still had some sugar left. She tried to console herself in her mind.

"Good morning, Mom," Lynn said with a smile.

"Morning," Faye grumbled. She stirred the sugar and paltry sprinkling of creamer into the cup with a teaspoon, glancing up again at Jordan and Malik who were sitting at her great-grandmother's dining room table, quietly sipping from their mugs and whispering to one another as they looked around the room. "What did you say your last name was again?"

They looked at Faye. "McCormick," Jordan smiled. "Malik and Jordan McCormick."

Faye nodded, took a sip of her coffee and grimaced. Then, she raised her eyebrows as if suddenly remembering something. "I don't think we ever properly introduced ourselves. I'm Faye. Faye Rawlings." She shook hands with Malik and Jordan. Gesturing toward her children, she said, "This is my oldest son Keith. This is my youngest son Joseph. And this is my daughter Lynn." They all shook hands, smiling.

Lynn plated up the scrambled eggs and racoon hash. "Breakfast is ready."

Faye took a plate to Kent, but upon seeing him still asleep, she returned to the kitchen and set the plate on the counter.

Malik and Jordan thanked their hosts for the food but looked dubiously at the meat. Jordan looked up at Keith. "What did you call this?"

"Racoon hash."

"It's racoon?"

"Yes, ma'am."

"Is it good?"

"It's not my best cooking," Keith said, taking a bite. "But it's edible. If we had any bacon left, I'd give you some, but..." He shrugged and took another bite.

Malik shrugged and took a bite too. He chewed and swallowed. "It's not bad. If it was good enough for our ancestors, it's good enough for us."

"That's the way I look at it," Keith nodded.

Jordan smiled and took a bite. It wasn't very good, but they were hungry and couldn't afford to be picky now.

Faye returned to the room and sat down to eat. "So, what did you do before the world ended, if you don't mind me asking?"

"I managed a retail store in Cincinnati," Jordan said.

Faye nodded and took a sip of coffee. Everyone nodded as if to say, "Oh, that's nice." They looked at Malik.

"I was a doctor."

Their eyebrows raised as they glanced back and forth between one another.

"Really?" Keith inquired. "What kind of doctor?"

"Optometrist."

"Hmm." Keith took a bite of scrambled eggs and looked fixedly at the wall, deep in thought, as if watching a scene unfold before him.

Malik looked into Keith's blue eyes staring out from under the brim of his camouflage hat. He studied the face with its pursed lips framed by the reddish-brown beard on his wind-burnt cheeks. "Do you find that hard to believe?"

Jordan put her hand on her husband's and squeezed it.

At this question, the family members stopped chewing and looked at Malik.

Keith was pulled out of his thoughts and said, "What?"

"You seem to doubt that I could be a doctor." Malik responded.

Keith stared into Malik's dark, brown eyes. The man's dark lips surrounded by the black scruff of four days without shaving were pressed firmly together into a stern frown. "What makes you say that?"

The rest of the family members silently sipped coffee as they glanced back and forth between the two men.

"Malik," Jordan whispered, tightening her grip on his large hand.

"You said, 'Hmm,' like you didn't believe me, and then, you looked at the wall like you were thinking about what I actually was."

Keith took a sip of coffee and kept his eyes trained on Malik's. He put his mug back down on the coaster in front of him. "I was thinking that there are no doctors on Mount Sinai Road, and I was wondering what you could do without the use of the medical equipment you would normally have access to."

"I bet you don't have doctors around here. You don't have many black people living around here either, do you?"

"Not that I know of. Why?"

Jordan cleared her throat loudly, raising her hand to the barrette holding down her dark hair. She held her hand on her head and looked down at the table in front of her.

"Some people assume that black people can't be doctors."

"Who's assuming?" Keith said, never breaking eye contact. "I don't know what things are like in the big city where you come from, but out here, you won't find what you seem to be looking for. If it weren't for books and movies and the politicians trying to use it, I wouldn't have known that way of thinking ever existed. And if you had lived here, you wouldn't either."

"Malik, that's enough." Jordan let go of his hand and looked around at the family members. "Sorry, we're just really tired. We're your guests, and we really appreciate you letting us into your home and sharing your food with us." She looked back at Malik. "Don't we?"

Malik's eyes shifted to Jordan, and his tense body relaxed. "Yes, I apologize. You're very gracious. I didn't mean to be rude."

Keith nodded. "You don't need to apologize. I know I get a little grumpy when I'm tired, and I can imagine how exhausted you guys are."

"Yeah," Joe and Lynn both chimed in at once.

Keith looked around the room and then back at their guests. "We have a prior commitment that the three of us have to fulfill this morning, so once you've finished breakfast, you'll be able to get some rest without us making any noise. We should be back very soon, but in the meantime, make yourselves at home and get some sleep." He looked at Faye. "Right?"

Faye nodded. "Yeah."

———————————————

Rick Thompson opened the door without a word. His bloodshot eyes framed by dark circles and sallow cheeks suggested he had been drinking. The smell of his breath confirmed it. He turned with a quiet exhale and retreated back into the house, leaving the door open behind him. No one said a word as Keith and Joe followed him inside, their rifles slung over their shoulders. The house was littered with papers, clothes, bottles, and cans. Only a faint glow of sunlight seeped in through the gaps in the drapes. It sparkled off shards of broken glass. Joe's boot crunched as he stepped past the doorway.

"Watch your step," Rick mumbled in a barely audible whisper.

Keith and Joe turned on their flashlights. It looked as if every lightbulb in the house had been smashed on the floor, along with the television, radio, toaster, microwave, oven, and dozens of pictures. The refrigerator was lying on its face with the door handle broken off. There was a stale, musty, putrid smell in the air. Spoiled food was spilling out of trash bags on the floor. There were pools and trails of sludge leaking out of the bags. Joe tried to clear a path as he walked through the house. He pushed a trash bag to the side with his boot and nearly jumped back when mice scurried out from beneath it.

"Can we let a little light in here?" Keith asked as he moved to the towels covering the windows.

"I guess." Rick grumbled. "If you have to."

Keith pulled the towels back from the window, and light streamed in on the mess. Joe did likewise with another window as Rick shielded his eyes from the light and sunk onto the couch in front of the demolished television.

Joe got a glass from the kitchen, filled it with water, and brought it to Rick. "Here. Drink some water."

Rick took the glass and drank small sips.

Joe watched him carefully and kept his voice low. "I didn't ask you, but I sent for the preacher to come and say a few words. He should be here soon. Is that alright?"

Rick took a sip of water. He seemed to be thinking hard. He rested the glass on his knee and stared blankly at the floor. "Yeah. That would be alright."

Kent was shivering and breathing with difficulty. Sweat beaded on his swollen, red face. Faye swallowed her tears and dabbed Kent's forehead with a washcloth. She lay the back of her hand on his head. He was definitely running a fever, and a high one at that. Faye looked through the medicine they had. She wasn't sure there was anything that could help him. She didn't even know what was wrong with him. What wasn't wrong? He was malnourished, sleep deprived, bruised, and swollen. His ribs were broken, his skin was rotting off his feet, and he probably had a bacterial infection or parasites after drinking stagnant water. She didn't know what to do.

As she looked through the medicine, she found something for cold and flu and gave it to him. She went upstairs and got another blanket to put over him. Malik and Jordan were still sleeping on the floor beside the woodstove. Would Malik know how to help him? Probably not, she thought. If he did, he would have done so already. He knew the condition her husband was in better than she did, and he had done all he could already. Besides, he was hardly in good shape himself. None of them had had much food or sleep in recent days. She hesitated. She had to try. She put her hand on his shoulder and shook him gently. He didn't stir. Faye stood up and walked around the room. Kent didn't need an optometrist. She didn't know what he needed, but she knew it wasn't that. She walked back to the couch where Kent lay. He was groaning in pain.

Faye tucked the blanket in around Kent, placed a bucket beside the couch, and draped a wet rag over his eyes. She paced around the room for a minute or two and threw on her coat and boots. Faye had hardly been off the property in the last two weeks. She didn't know what it was like outside, and she didn't trust her children to give her a complete account of the dangers. Opening Kent's gun cabinet, she took an old single-shot .410 and stuffed a handful of shells into her pocket. She locked the cabinet, put the key in her pocket, and locked the bedroom door as well. She hobbled downstairs and out the front door as quickly as her knees would allow her.

There was still a layer of ice coating the leaves, and it crunched and crackled as she walked. She made sure to step on the leaves as much as possible to avoid the smooth surfaces of ice where she would likely slip. She stomped her way to the end of the driveway and turned left onto the road. The road was icy too, so she kept to the edge and stamped through the frosty leaves lining the ditch. Never slowing down, she rounded the bend, passed the huge sugar maple, and turned into the gravel driveway with the big, red tractor mailbox. She climbed onto the porch and rapped on the door.

Inside, a dog barked. Faye knocked again. She had once been bitten by a dog, but she didn't worry about that now. Faye was panting.

The barking stopped, the door opened a crack, and Emma Faulkner smiled as she recognized Faye. "Faye! How are you?" Her expression changed immediately. "Is everything alright?"

Faye tried to keep her breathing under control. Her face was red. "No. My husband is sick. He's burning up, and I don't know what to do. I thought maybe you would know."

"Okay, hang on." She turned and yelled to one of her children to watch the house while she was gone; she would be back as soon as she could. A girl's voice responded. Faye waited outside as Emma rifled through some things inside the house. A few seconds later, she stepped out in her boots and coat with a large satchel slung over her shoulder. "Let's go." Her long, quilted dress swished over the icy leaves as she walked beside Faye.

Emma asked what had happened and what other symptoms she had noticed. Faye told her as much as she could. Emma nodded as she listened.

When they reached the house, Faye led Emma to the couch where Kent was lying. Emma examined his ribs, looked at the cut on his head, and pulled out an old-fashioned thermometer from her bag. She put it under his tongue and watched seriously. After a minute or so, she pulled the thermometer out and stood up. "I need to get something." She pulled a knife and a small kettle out of her bag and ran out the front door.

Faye wiped the sweat off Kent's forehead and bit her lip. She held a cup of water up to his mouth and helped him to sip it. Then, she took the bucket outside and dumped it. When she came back, she set the bucket back down beside the couch as Kent coughed slightly and moaned. He held his ribs and gasped. Emma ran back in with her kettle and knife.

Faye went to help Emma and saw her pouring water into the kettle just before putting it on the stove. "What can I do to help?" She asked.

"He's going to need a lot of water," Emma said. She smashed up something inside the kettle and stirred it around with her knife.

Faye came back with a glass of water and again looked at Emma who had put the lid on her kettle and had begun breaking up small sticks and putting them on the fire inside the stove. "What are you making?" Faye asked.

"A dogwood bark decoction." Emma stuffed in more sticks, shut the doors, and opened the vents all the way. "I have some medicines with me, but he has a very high fever, and he needs something much stronger than anything I've brought with me." The water in the teapot was boiling now. "This will only take a few minutes. It won't cure the problem, but it should break the fever."

Faye stood staring, not sure about this. But what choice did she have? She didn't have any medicine for this. What he needed was a hospital, but that was no longer an option. So, she stood chewing on her bottom lip as she held the glass of water in her hand.

Emma went back into the room where Kent was dying. Faye followed closely behind. He was mumbling something to himself. It sounded as if he was praying, but his words made no sense to Emma or Faye. He rolled his head around on the pillow and muttered, "It's the pancakes. Mosquitos open dishwasher. I'm sorry, Mom. I don't like the flowers. No. Smokey go away. Kill 'em." He started crying.

Faye squeezed cool water out of the washcloth over his head.

Emma put her hand on Faye's shoulder. "Get as much ice as you can."

Faye hustled outside and began knocking chunks of ice off the tree branches into a bucket. She had barely anything bigger than a pencil eraser. She looked around and remembered the chickens' water bowls. She took her bucket to the pen and filled it with the large, broken pieces of ice that floated in the water. Closing the gate behind her, she toted the ice back to the house, sometimes carrying, sometimes dragging. When she got back inside, she took the bucket to the couch and started filling old plastic shopping bags with the chunks of ice and setting them around Kent's head.

Kent shook and whispered. "Tell Dad I'm coming." He rolled to his left side and vomited into the bucket.

Tears welled up in Faye's eyes. "Don't do that," she said. "Don't..." She shook her head and pressed the ice to Kent's temples.

Emma came back into the room with a cup of liquid and a spoon. "Get that water ready. And he's probably going to want something sweet in it. This stuff is nasty."

Faye poured a little of Keith's honey into the water and mixed it up with a spoon. She hurried back into the room as Emma took a spoonful of the liquid and put it into Kent's mouth.

She held his mouth closed with her hand and squeezed his nostrils shut. He swallowed, and as she removed her hand, he wretched and expelled the liquid back into her face. She wiped her face with her sleeve and got another spoonful ready. "He has to keep it down."

Faye whispered in his ear and stroked his head.

Emma forced another spoonful into Kent's mouth and made him swallow. His face was beet-red, and he let out a horrific groan. He gagged, but nothing came up.

Faye held the honey-water up to his mouth and he gulped it greedily.

Emma got another spoonful ready as Faye hurried to the kitchen to get more honey and water. When Faye returned, Emma dumped another spoonful of the decoction into Kent's mouth. He writhed a bit. Tears ran from the swollen creases around his eyes, but he swallowed. Faye held the honey-water up for him to drink. He gulped it down, and she got some more. After a couple of glasses of water, Kent lay still, and his breathing steadied.

It was only then that Faye noticed, out of the corner of her eye, two dark shapes sitting on the floor in the corner, their heads bowed, their lips moving silently. She turned back to look at Kent, and in the silence, they waited.

———————————

At the sound of the knock, Keith opened the door. Lynn stood in the doorway and nodded to him. Just behind her, stood the preacher Eric Jorgenson. He removed his hat and asked in a low voice, "May we come in?"

Rick said nothing. He continued to stare at the smashed television in front of him. He took another sip of water.

Keith looked back at him and then, to Eric and Lynn. "Thank you for coming. Come on in."

Lynn and Eric cautiously stepped around the shards of broken glass and piles of trash. Eric gripped his Bible tightly. Lynn pulled her scarf up over her face and covered her nose.

Eric moved around the couch to face Rick. He bent down, put his hand on Rick's shoulder and spoke softly, barely above a whisper, "I'm so sorry for your loss, brother. I know this is a difficult time. I'd like you to come to my house today, if you're willing, and share a simple meal with my family and me. We'd love to cook for you."

Tears welled up in Rick's eyes. He began to weep as Eric squeezed his shoulder a little harder. He reached up and grabbed Eric's hand. "Thank you."

Eric took his hand and clenched it as if to transfer his strength to Rick. "May we enter the room?"

Rick nodded and wiped his eyes. He stayed seated as Eric turned toward the bedroom.

Joe stood at the door which had remained shut. He opened it and stepped inside. Keith, Eric, and Lynn followed. Unlike the rest of the house, this room was clean and organized. On the bed, the body rested as if in a deep sleep.

Her cropped hair was thin and white. Her eyes were closed, and she lay beneath the blankets, as if she had just been tucked in for the night. Her skin was deathly pale in the halo of white light illuminating the room from the window. Her head was tilted to the side slightly as if she had fallen asleep looking out at the sky.

Eric bowed his head and whispered something. The siblings remained silent and respectful, watching the preacher out of the corners of their eyes. He raised his head and gave them a nod.

Keith pulled back the blanket. Frantic, haphazard movement erupted from the corpse. Keith and Joe jumped back as mice scurried from beneath the covers and down the sides of the bed. Lynn threw her hand to her mouth and choked. Evident through the rips in the bedclothes, the carcass was covered in oozing, open sores where the mice had gnawed at the cadaver. Lynn ran out of the room. A couple of the shameless, bloodstained mice continued to devour the decaying flesh.

Keith yanked the blankets off the bed and swatted the mice away from the body. They scuttled to the shadows of the closet, behind the furniture, and out the open bedroom door. Joe shook his head in disgust and looked around the room for a mouse to kick. Eric stood calm and poised with his eyes closed. Keith shook out the blankets and began wrapping them around the body. He looked at his brother. "Joe."

Joe stopped looking around the room and met his brother's eyes.

"Help me with this, would you?"

Joe said nothing as he went to rolling the body in the blankets. That done, Keith knelt beside the bed, and Joe helped to roll it over onto Keith's shoulder. Joe took hold of the legs as Eric moved to support the head and torso. The three of them lifted the bundle and walked it out of the room.

Rick did not stir as they carried the body past him. He may have glanced at them out of the corner of his eye, but he turned away and looked toward the window as they proceeded out the door.

Lynn came around the house to the enormous tulip poplar in the back yard, carrying the pick and shovel. As the men set the body down as gently as they could, Lynn held out the tools for them.

"Are you alright?" Joe asked.

"I'm okay," Lynn replied. Her face was red. She looked at the bundle on the ground.

Joe took the pick and swung. It struck the frozen dirt and bounced back with a ring. He tried again. He shook the shock out of his hands. He tried another spot, to no avail. Keith took the pick and tried. He struck the icy clay with a clang as a chip of ice flew back at him, striking him in the face just below his eye. He dropped the pick and put his hand over his face. The ground was frozen solid.

Eric stood silently, thinking.

"We might have to burn the body," Lynn said flatly.

Keith shook his head. "There's no way. We can't spare the fuel."

Joe spat on the ground and scratched his head. "I've got nothing. We can't just leave her sitting out for the critters to get to. Any ideas?"

No one said anything.

Joe spat on the ground again. "Maybe Tim would know."

Kent's clothes were soaked with sweat. Steam rose from his limp body. Emma pulled out a pocket watch. She checked his temperature again. "It's still too high, but it's coming down." She made him swallow two more spoonfuls of the decoction.

Faye breathed a little easier at the news. She now had a pitcher of the honey water at the ready and continued to refill the glass as he drank.

Malik and Jordan had been watching in the corner for the past hour. They had not spoken to Faye or Emma, nor had they been spoken to, so intently was everyone focused on the task of saving this dying man. Now, they got to their feet and approached Faye. "Is there anything we can do to help?" Jordan asked.

Faye appeared exhausted as she looked in their direction. She was emotionally drained, and her energy was waning. She tried to control her voice. "Only if you know how to fix my husband." Her eyes focused on Malik for a second, pleading with him.

Malik shook his head. "Sorry. I don't. Without equipment... And besides..." He shrugged sympathetically.

Faye nodded. She figured as much.

"Can we cook for you?" Jordan asked.

Faye thought for a second. She was going to say no, but she glanced at Emma and thought she should offer something to her. She owed her. "Sure." Faye nodded. "That would be nice. Thank you."

The two went to the kitchen and began looking through cabinets.

Emma took a bottle out of her bag and rubbed its greenish ointment on Kent's ribs and head. "This should help with the pain and prevent infection." When she was done, she set the bottle to the side, stood up, and looked at Faye. "I have to make more medicine." She took her knife and left the room.

Faye wiped the rivulets of perspiration off of Kent. The ice she had placed around his head was mostly water now; it soaked the pillow beneath his head. She went outside to collect more, and when she returned, she met a strange and delightful aroma. The McCormicks were frying something on the stove and working on what appeared to be a special and elaborate meal. Faye replaced the bags of ice for Kent and joined the McCormicks beside the woodstove. As she sat down at the table, Emma walked in, carrying her knife and teapot. Once she had refilled the pot with water, she stirred it and put it on the woodstove.

"You're doing a great job," Jordan smiled at her. "Where did you learn to do this?"

"My husband and I just decided we wanted to live a more self-sufficient lifestyle and live closer to the land. We learned as we went along."

"That's amazing." Jordan beamed and shook her head. "We're from the city, so you know, we were totally plugged in our whole lives. It's only now we see how dependent we were."

Emma shrugged and nodded. "We're all seeing that now."

"I'm Jordan, by the way. And this is my husband Malik." Jordan extended her hand to Emma. Malik stopped stirring and turned around.

Emma shook their hands. "Emma Faulkner. It's a pleasure to meet you. Faye tells me you rescued her husband in Nashville. And you walked all the way here through the woods?"

"We did."

"I call *that* amazing. And how very fortunate too. The Rawlings are some of the best people I've had the privilege to meet. You're blessed to get to know them."

"Yes, ma'am," Malik agreed. He caught Faye's glance and smiled.

"What are you making?" Faye asked.

"Eggplant parmesan," Jordan responded.

"We have eggplants?"

"We're using butternut squash. We found it in the basement. I hope that's okay."

"Yum," Emma said, checking her watch. She peaked under the lid of her tea kettle and saw it boiling away. Satisfied, she took it off the stove to let it cool and checked on Kent once again.

The preacher had taken Rick to his house while the siblings walked back up the road to find Tim. When they had reached Tim's house, they knocked on the door only to be told by one of the kids that he was building something on the road. They thanked the kid and started hiking, hoping that it was the nearest end of the road where they would find him.

At the southern end of Mount Sinai Road, there was a bustle around the old church as volunteers rolled cars into position. One of Jack Winters' deputies, his daughter, was sitting atop a horse, looking up and down the highway through her rifle scope. Cars were being pushed out of the cul-de-sac near the train tracks and into position at the intersection with the highway.

"Found him," Joe said.

Tim was talking to a man just outside the old church. With his shotgun slung over his shoulder, he pointed to the steeple and motioned out over the highway with a wave of his arm. As the siblings approached, the other man nodded in their direction, and Tim turned around to look at them. "Fellers." He smiled. "How's it going?"

"Not too well," Joe answered. "Can we talk to you for a minute?"

"Of course." Tim patted the man on the shoulder as he turned away. "To be continued." Tim turned back to Joe. He walked toward the cemetery with them. "What can I do for you?"

"We've run into a problem, and we could use some advice." Joe spat a black stream of tobacco juice onto the ice in front of him. "Rick Thompson's mother died. He's pretty tore up. We were going to bury her this morning, but we can't break the ground."

"Frozen." Tim shook his head.

"Right. We can't burn the body."

"No."

"And we certainly can't just leave it laying outside."

"Certainly not."

"What do you think we should do?"

"She's not the first." Tim rubbed his nose and scratched the scruff beginning to grow on his jaw. "We've buried two others so far. Ran out of their medicine."

"How did you do it?"

"Well, the first one, a guy used his tractor and buried his wife in this cemetery." Tim motioned to a freshly dug mound in the corner of the graveyard. "The other one was an old man who didn't have any family. No one wanted to spare the fuel to use a tractor, so we took his remains to the organic farm down the road. We got one of the preachers on this road to say a few words for him, and we buried him in the compost pile."

"Oh my..." Lynn blurted, putting her hand to her chin.

Tim glanced at her and back to Joe. "It doesn't freeze. The heat from the composting keeps it warm and loose."

Joe shook his head and spat again. "Man, that's..."

"You can't," Lynn said.

"It's not how any of us would like to do it, but we all get eaten by worms eventually, and besides, that's not his mother you're burying. It's an empty shell."

"I know, but..." Joe shook his head again. "There's got to be..."

"There's no other way right now. We can't waste the energy on trying to dig. We don't have the calories to burn, and if you work up a sweat out here, you'll get pneumonia, and we'll be burying your body next. We can't waste the fuel on burning a body, and you don't want to try to do it with just wood. It would be a mess. The fumes. And it would take more wood than you could gather in a day."

They stayed silent for a few seconds. Keith took a pinch of Joe's tobacco.

"You asked for my advice. That's my advice. I'll help you. We can take my truck."

"What do I tell Rick?" Joe looked at the rows of tombstones marking eight generations of his family and neighbors.

"Tell him the truth," Tim said firmly. "Or don't tell him at all."

They walked back to the barricade which was nearly finished now. As Tim told some of the volunteers that he was leaving, Joe made sure not to spit in front of anyone.

As they surveyed the barricade, all three noticed vultures perched atop the telephone polls on the other side of the highway, about a hundred yards to the west. Some were sunning themselves with their wings spread wide, facing north. More were coming in and alighting upon the roof of the large, red house that was home to some wealthy horse owners. Keith, Joe, and Lynn approached the line of dead cars blocking the road and looked out at the field to the north. Not far from the driveway of the big, red house, they could see a swarm of buzzards tearing at a dark mass on the ground. The corral gate was open. The horses were gone. A vulture swooped down into the mass of birds. There was a fight over the carcass, and as the creatures cleared away for just a second, the siblings could clearly see, that face down on the front lawn, was what used to be a man.

Tim returned with a backpack, and the four of them began the walk back to the Faulkner house to get the truck. "How are y'all doing on food?"

"We're good," Keith replied. "Why?"

"Were you able to save what you had in your freezer?"

"Yeah, we pretty much canned everything."

"Good. Good. A lot of people didn't." Tim took a drink from a steel canteen. "We might have some problems developing. I know of a few people who've run out of food already. Some of them are working for food, and I'm trying to work with people to teach them how to preserve. But some people are so far behind, and not everyone is interested in working for it. I know you heard about robberies."

"Yeah."

"I'm worried it's going to get bad. You haven't had any livestock go missing, have you?"

"I don't think so."

"Some have."

———————

Kent breathed rhythmically as he slept. After several hours of watching, taking temperature readings, and administering doses of medicine, Emma looked haggard, but Kent's temperature had returned to normal. Emma pulled the thermometer out of Kent's mouth and announced, "He should be fine now. He just needs to rest." Everyone breathed tired sighs of relief. Faye thanked her, hugged her, and tried to get her to take some food home with her.

"No, you need it. Thank you, though," Emma gave an exhausted smile. "I'm glad I was able to help. If you need anything, don't hesitate to ask." She left some ointments and tea for Faye to use, reiterated her pleasure at having met everyone, packed her bag, and left. She walked home as the sun was sinking behind the trees.

After talking to the owners of the farm, Tim had got permission to bury the body in the compost pile. As Keith and Joe stayed with the body and began working on digging the hole in the mound, Lynn had gone with Tim to get the preacher from his house. The preacher, his wife, and his daughter had all offered to help Rick clean his house after he ate with them, but he had refused. It was his mess, and he needed to clean it up himself. When Tim told Eric where they were going, Eric insisted on telling Rick. He put his hand on his shoulder and explained the situation with his deep, soothing voice. Rick merely nodded, said he understood, thanked his hosts for their kindness, and left to go clean up his house. He didn't want to be there for the burial.

Keith folded the compost over the bundle and buried it deep. The white sheets disappeared in the black muck. Wood ashes were dumped overtop and covered by straw, leaves, manure, and rotting animal remains.

Keith set down his shovel as the preacher recited his message: "Let the dead bury the dead. It is appointed unto all men once to die, and after that, the judgment. Out of dust you were taken, and unto the dust you shall return. Ashes to ashes. Dust to dust." He turned and climbed into the passenger seat of the pickup.

Tim started the engine. It was getting dark now.

Keith and Lynn climbed into the bed with their tools. Joe stood staring at the compost pile for a few more seconds. Then, he spat on the ground, laid his shovel in the bed of the truck, and pulled himself up onto the tailgate. "Well," he said with a sigh. "That's that."

Chapter Eight

Day 24

Reveille! Reveille! Reveille! 19,18, Kill! 17,16, Kill! 15,1 4,13,12,11,10,9,8,7,6,5,4,3,2,1, you are! Done, Sir! Kill, Kill, Kill 'em all! Fire! Face down on the concrete. Thud. Spiders. I just want to go home, Rawlings. Cease fire! Cease fire! Rawlings! You're dead! Mom, Dad, I love you. I'm sorry, Keith. She's gone. Sarah! Dogs barking. One-hundred-twenty degrees. Negative thirty degrees. Ten-thousand feet of elevation. Gas! Gas! Gas! Can't breathe. Can't see. Vomit. Help me, I'm bleeding. Boom. You're dead. Green star cluster. Mass Cas! They're all dead. What happened? Downed a gallon of bleach and jumped off the balcony. Hanged himself in the closet. Shot himself in the head. Drowned himself in the ocean. Fire! Cordite. Ears ringing. Perfume. What? Sarah! Darkness. Trees falling. Ashes in the wind. Walls of cars. Walls of corpses. White dog in the headlights. Pools of blood. Welcome home. Crows. Vultures. Sarah.

Keith woke up. The rooster was crowing. Sunlight seeped in through the window. He rubbed his eyes and reached for the headache medicine. Getting out of bed, he flipped the light switch. Why not? He got dressed in the faint ambient light from outside. He looked at the calendar on his wall. It still had reminders for tests and due dates for school projects in a few of its squares, but now, Keith crossed out the days with a red marker. He had begun this ritual just in the last week, starting with February 5, the day the power went out. He took the marker and drew a red X on February 28.

More than three weeks had passed since flipping the light switch had produced an effect. Heat had been the first priority since that day, but now, food was running low for many people, and those who had it either kept the fact to themselves or tried to trade it for work. Deer season had ended in Indiana nearly two months ago, but there were many who took to poaching to provide for their families. Jack Winters wouldn't try to stop them so long as they remained on their own property and didn't hurt anyone or steal livestock. But some *were* stealing livestock. At least, one person, anyway. One man had been shot already. Since he was on someone else's property, it was determined to be justified. No body had been found, but the property owner reported the shooting to Jack Winters who followed the blood trail into the woods until it stopped. One of Keith's hens was missing too. He couldn't be sure whether it was a thief or a predator, but everyone was on edge and distrustful of neighbors.

Firewood continued to be in high demand. The air was perpetually tinged with smoke emitted from the chimneys of every house and trailer on Mount Sinai Road. One of the trailers had burned down in the night with everyone inside. Two people in the past week had died from heart attacks while trying to cut wood. The traditional American diet consisting mostly of fat, salt, sugar, and carbohydrates, combined with the sedentary lifestyle afforded by modern technology, had produced three generations of increasingly unhealthy individuals kept alive long past their natural expiration dates by the abundance of drugs and medical procedures made available by the most effective and affordable healthcare system the world had ever known, but now, the healthcare system was nonexistent, and the life-extending drugs were running out. Several of the elderly residents of Mount Sinai had run out of their prescriptions and were quickly deteriorating. A couple of people, along with one of the nurses, had compiled a list of medications required by the residents and had gone into town to find them, but that was four days ago; they hadn't returned.

Keith went to the bathroom. When he flushed the toilet, the water gurgled down slightly, but the bowl did not refill. He pressed the lever again. Nothing happened. "Great," he murmured to himself. "Just what we needed." He decided he would worry about that later. He squirted some liquid soap into his hand and turned the knob on the faucet. As he spread the soap over his fingers, the faucet sputtered and spat out a couple drops of water, and then, nothing. He turned both knobs completely. There was no water. His heartrate rose as he thought. He turned the knobs back again and wiped the soap off onto his pants. He ran down-stairs and tried the sink in the other bathroom. Nothing.

Joe opened his bedroom door and came out into the hall, rubbing the sleep from his eyes. He went straight to the bathroom, and seeing Keith standing at the sink, he said, "Hurry up. I gotta go."

"Don't use the bathroom," Keith said. "There's no water."

"What?"

"There's no water. You'll have to go outside and fill a bucket."

Joe turned around and went outside, and after about a minute, came back in.

"What do you mean there's no water?"

"I mean just that. We have no water."

An emergency meeting was called with several of the neighbors. When Keith and Joe reached Jim Baker's barn, Tim was poring over a map with some of the men who had knowledge of the city's infrastructure. Mount Sinai Road was home to plumbers, pipe fitters, engineers, carpenters, foresters, property managers, electricians, farmers, truckers, linemen, and as Keith and Joe soon learned, a city water treatment plant worker whom no one had seemed to notice before. The council members had called on all of them to figure out what was going on and what they could do about it.

"I can't imagine anything else that would account for all this," one man said. "But this is worse than what I would have predicted."

"Well, I don't know what would happen in that situation. There was never a plan for this scenario." A short, pudgy man with a patchy brown beard and a knit hat crossed his arms and shook his head.

"Hold on." Jim Baker held up his hand. "Start from the beginning. Explain to me how this process works."

On one wall of the barn, they had erected a chalkboard, and the man picked up a piece of chalk and began drawing a diagram. His voice was a bit shaky, apparently a bit anxious in front of the group. His speech was punctuated with pauses and throat clearings. "The vast majority of the city's water comes from Monroe Reservoir. There are two wastewater treatment plants that process the water." He pointed to the map. "Here and here. They both operate basically the same, but your water comes through this one." He went back to drawing on the board. "The water is fed through the sand filters. That's all gravity fed. Then, it gets pumped into tanks for coagulation and flocculation. That's where they add aluminum potassium sulfate, also known as alum, to the water. It causes particles to stick together into clumps that they can then filter out. The water is pumped through the filters, into the clear well, where they add chemical to disinfect it. Either Chloride or Fluoride to kill the bacteria and stuff. Okay?"

"I'm with you so far. How is everything pumped?"

"Well, there's a lot of pumps all along the way. Huge pumps. And those pumps are usually pumping water right through the water mains to the pipes in every house and building connected to city water. But the demand is not constant, so to keep up with high demand, the pumps send water to the water towers when the demand is low, like at night, and when the demand is higher than what the pumps can easily meet, the water towers pick up the slack."

"And all those pumps run off of electricity," another man said.

"Well, yeah."

"So, what do they do when there's a power outage?" Jim asked.

"Well, they have backup generators, of course."

"Would those survive a pulse?" Jim pressed.

"I have no idea. I don't think anyone does."

Their eyes turned to the electrician and the lineman. The two men looked at each other and shrugged.

Tim scratched his chin. "You say the water gets pumped directly to the tap?"

"Yeah, for the most part."

"And the towers get refilled every night?"

"Well, that's how they're usually used."

"So, how could we have had water for this long if the pumps went out?"

"There are a lot of factors that affect the supply. For one, the demand for water is much lower in the winter, so we haven't been using as much. No one's watering the lawn or washing their cars." He raised his eyebrows as if to signal that they should laugh at his joke. No one seemed amused. "And, of course, the factories, schools, and businesses aren't using any water, so it would last much longer. Not to mention, you know, a lot of people are probably dead." He looked around and shrugged. "I mean, let's be honest." Meeting cold stares, the man coughed and went on. "That could give you a few days. Those water towers hold a lot. And who's to say if the generators went down or not? They might have survived and kept pumping, but eventually, they're going to run out of diesel."

The carpenter Brad Nielson raised his voice. "So, it was inevitable. Well, now what?"

The old farmer Ernie Jacobs shrugged, "I'm glad I don't use city water. I don't know what the rest of you will do, but, well, I guess you got the creek there. It was nice knowin' ya."

"What?" the lineman's face went red. "How can you say that?"

"Property rights."

There was a shift in the room. Several men stepped closer to the old farmer. Keith stepped in front of the farmer to save the old man from a pummeling. "Water rights." He looked at Jacobs and then back at the lineman.

"What?" the lineman demanded.

"Riparian rights. Common law. No one owns the water. Everyone has a right to it."

"Damn right," The lineman said seriously. The plumber and electrician voiced their approval.

Tim held up his hand in front of the lineman. "He's right." He looked back at Ernie Jacobs whose face had gone a couple shades paler. "Everyone has a right to the water. That's always been recognized under common law."

"Yeah, I know that." Jacobs swallowed. "I was just kiddin'."

"I agree," Jim said. "But doesn't Ernie have a right to his own pump? It *is* his."

"The pump is his, but the aquifer he's tapped into is not. It runs under a lot of properties. So, for the good of the community, and for your own good, I'm asking you to share the use of your pump with your neighbors. At least, for now, until we can work out a way to get everyone supplied with drinking water. I'll do the same." Tim's voice quivered just a bit. "I have a rain catchment system I built that supplies all the water I need, but you all know me by now, and you know that I also have a wife and seven kids. I don't want to see any more violence break out because people are desperate for drinking water."

Everyone fell silent.

Jim stood up. "We have the creek here. We have a few wells and ponds on this road. We'll share the water. We'll make sure we discuss it at the next meeting, but for the love of God, don't devolve into savages. We're not animals."

Tim put his hands in his pockets and looked around at the faces of the men. "We'll have to disinfect the water. I can show you how to do that. Jeremiah, Brad, Dave, I'll need your help, and anyone else who's able, to start building rain catchment systems for people. In the meantime, we have to work together to keep everyone supplied with water. Sneaking onto people's properties to get to their wells is a good way to get shot. We'll need a distribution system."

A young but confident voice announced, "I can handle that." It was Jack Winters' youngest son, all of fourteen years old.

"Good man," Jim said.

"I'll help you with the routes." An old trucker smiled and patted the kid on the back.

"We'll have another meeting this afternoon. Let's get to it." Tim clapped his hands together like a quarterback in a huddle. "Make sure to filter the water through some cloth and boil it for at least a minute before drinking. Spread the word."

The men filed out of the barn, talking to one another.

Tim caught Keith's glance and reached out to shake his hand. "Thanks," he said with a wink. "Common law. Very good." He put a hand on Joe's shoulder as well and looked at both of them. "You fellas are handy in a tight spot."

"That's all him," Joe said. "I don't know what he was talking about." He looked at his brother and grinned.

As the short man in the knit hat walked to the door, a hand alighted on his shoulder. It was Jim Baker's. The man turned to look at Jim.

"I don't think I've seen you before. Were you here at any of the other meetings?" Jim looked him in the eye and studied his face.

"No."

"Why not?"

The man gave an awkward grin. "I'm not much of a people person."

"Neither am I. Hell, I'm just a farmer. I didn't want to be caught up in this mess, but you seem to know quite a bit."

"I don't know anything." The man began to step back a bit.

Jim's grip tightened on his shoulder as he stared the man in the eye. "I think you know a lot more than you let on."

Tim, Keith, and Joe approached the two without saying a word.

"I don't know what you're talking about," the squat man objected.

"Have you been getting information from outside? Do you have a radio or something?"

"I'm not telling you."

"Fair enough." Jim squinted. "But I really think you should." His eyes scanned past the man who looked over his shoulder to see Tim, Keith, and Joe standing behind him. "I understand not trusting anyone right now," Jim continued. "But how long do you really expect to last on your own? You see what's going on here. Everyone's on edge. The safest bet is to keep everyone calm and working together, and to do that, we need to know what's coming. We can't afford any more surprises like the water running out when someone knows about it ahead of time. I'd really appreciate your help."

The man looked away at nothing in particular. "I don't want any trouble."

"None of us do," Tim said calmly. "That's why we're doing this. It's better if we get to know each other so we can keep some semblance of civility here. We all have families and property we want to protect. Let us introduce ourselves."

The men all made their introductions with the stranger and shook hands.

Finally, the man's shoulders relaxed a bit, and he said, "I'm Scott. Scott Adams."

"None of us is going to steal your property or tell anyone anything you don't want us to." Jim reassured him. "You have my word on that."

Scott looked around at the four faces nodding in agreement. "Fine." He adjusted the wool hat on his balding head. "I'll show you."

The sun had risen above the tree line. Keith's watch said it was just after ten. As the five men strode down the road, people were coming out of their houses, talking to their neighbors frantically. Seeing the men who were at least seen as problem solvers in their newly-formed community, they ran to them or shouted questions and demands: "What happened? My water is not working! What happened to the water?" One very unpleasant woman even screamed, "What did you do to the water! Did you shut off my water?"

Tim kept walking but assured them that they were working on the problem. He reminded them that they had potable water in their water heaters still, but once they went through that, they would have to collect water from the creek or some other source until they could figure something out. "Just make sure to filter it and boil it for at least a minute! We'll figure it out as soon as we can! Meeting this afternoon. Spread the word, please!"

When they reached the house, Scott told them to wait outside for a minute. They stood looking around, wondering what he could be doing and noted the tall antenna rising above the rooftop. They could hear some banging noises coming from inside the house. Some scuffling and scraping. Finally, he opened the door. He looked to each side warily and motioned for them to come in. They shrugged and followed him.

"Sorry about that," Scott said nervously. "Just had to tidy things up a bit." He cleared his throat again. "Right this way."

He led them through a narrow stairwell down to the basement. It was dimly lit by electric lanterns, and on the walls, they could see maps and charts and lists pinned to corkboard. There were stacks of boxes, ammo cans, fuel and water jugs, and batteries. Cases of water, MREs, and medical supplies were piled on steel shelving units. There was a large wooden table against one wall with a chair in front, and beneath a helmet and gasmask hanging on the wall, was an array of radios.

"Pretty rad, huh?"

"Yeah," came an awestruck response.

"You're not going to tell anyone about this, right?"

"Tell anyone about what?"

"Exactly."

"Do you have a license for that?" Jim motioned toward the large radio on the table.

"Yeah, of course not." Scott sat down in his chair and began fidgeting with knobs and buttons.

"You don't put much trust in the government, do you?" Joe said.

"Are you kidding? I work for the government. They're all idiots."

"What are we looking at here?" Tim asked, trying to get the conversation back on track.

Scott spun his office chair around and looked at them. "So, you've probably got some people on this road who use little HAM radios like these." He held up a couple of walkie talkies. "Well, actually, I know you do, because I can hear them. They're fun to play with, and they can give you some good signal for about a mile or two usually, but I doubt anyone around here has something like this." He patted a large box on the desk and turned a knob. A voice echoed through the speaker, and everyone listened. Music. A saxophone squealing and humming a melody to the rhythm of a snare and cymbals. Jazz.

"When's the last time you heard music?" Scott smiled. "Probably not since the blackout. I come down here and listen to this station sometimes when I'm feeling sad or anxious. It's nice, you know? Sort of soothing."

"Where's it coming from?" Tim asked.

"Europe. Apparently, whatever took out the United States didn't affect them."

"I saw cops trying to use their radios, but they didn't work," Joe said. "How is yours still working?"

"Well, it makes sense if your EMP theory is right," Scott said. "The only radios that would still work would be the ones that were protected by some sort of faraday cage. A metal shed, a footlocker, a steel trash can, even something like an ammo can would work as long as the radios inside were insulated from the metal. It just so happens that I store all of my gear that way, and I'm guessing some other people did too. Probably didn't even know they were protecting it from that."

"Wait a minute," Jim said. "Did you say the United States was taken out?"

"Yeah."

"You mean the whole country is down?"

"As far as I can tell, yes. I've been listening to some guys around the country, and they're all reporting similar situations. No electronics working anymore. Well, almost none."

"And you're able to listen to stations in other countries?" Joe prompted.

"Yeah."

"What have you learned about the cause of this? And the response? And... Well, what have you learned?" Jim pressed.

"Not a whole lot, honestly."

"What do you mean, not a whole lot? There's got to be all kinds of people talking about this!" Joe interjected.

Jim raised his voice. "Listen, damnit! Don't screw around with us right now. You have to have heard some news reports about this. It's the wealthiest, most powerful country in the world! There's nothing else to talk about! Tell us what you've heard!"

Scott's face reddened. He frowned and looked seriously at Jim. "Careful. You're in my house, and I don't owe you anything. I told you I would tell you what I know, and that's what I'm doing. So, you can just calm down and listen, or you can go figure it out on your own."

Jim swallowed and steadied himself. "You're right. I beg your pardon. I didn't mean to be rude, but are you sure?"

"I've listened to transmissions from radio operators all over the country. They're saying the same thing. There's no power, everything's in chaos, and there's been no coordinated response from government. A lot of people are trying to set up quasi-governments, but for the most part, it seems, it's every man for himself."

Keith looked at one of the maps on the wall. "You said you can listen to stations around the world. How much of the world do you think was affected?"

"Well, as far as I can tell, all of the US, including Alaska and Hawaii. Most of Canada too. It seems that just about the whole continent was taken out. I don't know how much of Mexico. Maybe all of it."

"But Europe is unaffected?" Jim asked.

"Seems that way. The rest of the world seems to be the same as ever, as far as I can tell."

"It can't have been an accident, then. It can't be natural." Tim shook his head.

"Unlikely."

"Who did it?" Joe asked.

"No clue. I can guess, but..."

"But if Europe is alright, they'll be coming to help us," Jim said. "What are they saying about us in Europe? Is the U.N. sending aid? What's NATO doing? You have to have heard people talking about the news."

"I've heard almost nothing about a mission to the United States. In fact, no one's even talking about us. It's like they don't even know anything's happened."

"What?"

"I heard a couple of transmissions from Europe talking to Americans, but after a day or so, they stopped."

"Censorship," Keith said to himself.

"But you've heard some news from Europe, right?" Jim continued, obviously flustered.

"Sure, but none of the news outlets are talking about us. It's like we don't exist."

Everyone was silent, but Jim paced around the room. "I can't believe that." He pounded his fist on the table. "At least the E.U. will send support."

"I wouldn't count on it." Keith shook his head while studying the map.

"What do you mean? They're our allies. Of course, they'll help us." Jim's voice cracked. "They need us."

"Not anymore," Keith said flatly.

"What are you talking about?"

"You don't pay much attention to geopolitics, do you?"

Jim raised a finger to Keith. "Don't get cute with me, boy."

"Go easy, Jim." Tim looked into Keith's eyes. "What *are* you talking about?"

Keith chuckled a little. A sad smile formed under his tired eyes. "We were the world's greatest superpower. After the second world war, we kept relative tranquility in the world by holding military installations in nearly every country on Earth and squashing conflicts as soon as they arose. We were part of multi-national coalitions designed to maintain peace, but we funded nearly all of them ourselves. Our allies, as you call them, flubbed their contractual obligations without consequence and relied on our benevolence to pick up the slack, and we dutifully did so. In this parasitic relationship, the European nations took the money they were supposed to contribute toward defense and instead used it to fund social projects like universal healthcare and mass immigration campaigns. Their militaries are a joke. I saw them. We were the only thing keeping them from being conquered by Russia. Same thing for the Asian and African countries. The only thing stopping China from colonizing them was us. Meanwhile, all the countries who depended on us for their very existence denounced us as backward, hardhearted capitalists who didn't care about the marginalized of humanity. They hate us, or at least, they have disdain for us, all the while depending on American funded defense and innovation for their survival. Now, if it's true that the entire United States has been reduced to eighteenth century technology, then we are no longer the world's premier superpower, we no longer have any influence, and they have no reason to come to our aid. They'll try to broker deals with the next most powerful countries, either China or Russia, or both. And they won't allow anyone to speak out against it for fear of retaliation from their new hosts. What choice do they really have? Even if they wanted to, they couldn't help us now."

There was silence in the room for several seconds.

"For what it's worth, I agree with that statement," Scott said. "I'll keep you posted if I learn anything new, but I'm getting tired now, so you can let yourselves out." He pulled out a cigarette and lit it before swiveling back around in his chair.

The four men said nothing but looked at each other quizzically.

"Just make sure you go out exactly the way you came in, and don't touch anything." He blew out a stream of smoke. "The house is booby-trapped. Have a nice day."

Malik and Jordan had rested for the first couple of days since they arrived, helping Faye around the house with small chores and preparing meals between long naps, but after recovering their strength, they soon grew restless and wanted to do more to contribute to the household. For the past four days, they had fed and watered the animals, eviscerated the carcasses of Keith's catches, and collected firewood for the household. They cooked raccoon and opossum with potatoes, wild onions, and corn. After spending so much time with them, Faye had grown to trust them, and she had, on two occasions, taken Lynn with her to trade canned goods with Lydia Jorgenson and Emma Faulkner, leaving Malik and Jordan to watch the house in her absence.

Kent had remained on the couch. His sight had returned, but he still was unable to walk. He hadn't spoken much, and the family members didn't want to excite him. He slept most of the day and tried to read his Bible when he was awake.

Keith and Joe routinely left the house just after dawn to talk with neighbors and work on projects with Tim Faulkner, Ben Jameson, Jack Winters, or Jeremiah Davis. Every house on Mount Sinai Road that needed one had a way to burn wood now, but modifications were still being made to improve the safety of their makeshift stoves and chimneys. Today, Keith and Joe had informed everyone that the water was out before hurrying to find out what was going on, skipping breakfast. Jordan, Malik, Faye, and Lynn were searching around the house for water and debating whether they should start collecting water from the ponds when Kent overheard the conversation and informed them that they had fifty gallons of water in the water heater in the garage. Just then, they heard the knock at the front door. Keith and Joe came in and set their rifles down. Everyone gathered around the table and looked at Keith and Joe.

"Well, the water's not coming back," Keith said.

Kent spoke up from the couch in the other room. "You know there's water in the water heater, right?"

Keith paused. "Yeah, but we still need to start planning to harvest water from other sources."

"What are we going to do?" Lynn asked.

"Get a stock pot and a clean t-shirt." Keith stepped outside and came back with a bucket of water.

Joe held the t-shirt over the stock pot, allowing it to droop in the middle. Keith poured the pond water through the fabric. They put the pot on the stove and waited for it to boil.

Joe sat in a chair beside the table, waiting and looking as if he were deep in contemplation. "Keith?" he asked finally.

"Huh?" Keith said, watching the water.

"There's no such thing as water rights, is there?"

"No."

"Well, I guess now there is, isn't there?"

"I guess so."

Nearly half an hour had passed before the water began to bubble. They watched the water boil for several minutes before taking it off and allowing it to cool. They had some half-gallon glass jars sitting around the house which they filled with the water. It still had a yellow tinge to it.

"It may not look good, it may not smell good, it probably won't taste good, but this is safe to drink," Keith poured a sample into a coffee cup and drank some. "Yep. It's pond water."

"Are you sure that's safe?" Faye asked.

"Completely." He looked at Faye staring skeptically at the yellowish water. "But if it makes you feel better, we can also add a little bleach to it."

"No, I don't want to drink bleach water."

"Ok, but if for some reason we aren't able to boil the water like this, there's a reason I stocked up on bleach. Eight drops per gallon. Sixteen if it's really dirty." He took another drink, and Joe and Lynn both filled cups and drank as well.

"It tastes different, but it's water," Lynn said. "It's really not bad at all."

Malik and Jordan both filled glasses and drank. Finally, Faye took a sip. She made a face but drank some more before taking some to Kent.

Keith refilled his water bottle, put it back in his backpack, and told everyone else to do the same. Then, he began gathering tools. "We're going to start building rain catchment systems all along this road, to keep everyone supplied with water," he said. "We could use all the help we can get. Malik, Jordan, you guys want to give us a hand?"

"Yeah, absolutely. We want to help," Malik said. Jordan nodded in agreement.

Keith slung his rifle over his shoulder. "Alright. But I can't ask you to leave the house unarmed."

A meeting had been called again, and this time, people from nearly every house showed up. They had told everyone that water would be supplied, so the neighbors had poured in on wagons, on truck beds, and on foot with bottles, jars, buckets, and jugs. The barn was standing room only, and the massive wood stove made from an old steel anhydrous tank was boiling cauldrons of water which were rotated out to cool and be distributed. A line had been formed with the stipulation that a representative from every household only take one gallon of water until everyone present had been provided. Of course, there were several people who disregarded this rule and had multiple people collect gallons of water. It wasn't difficult to see what was going on, but it was more important to keep everyone calm than to enforce the rules. The creek ran less than a quarter mile to the south of the barn, and members of the Winters family were using their horses to pull up water tanks on carts to the barn for boiling. There was a loud rumble as people talked to one another while they waited in line for water. Several people were talking to Tim Faulkner and Jim Baker asking about plans for rain catchment systems. Tim had brought his blueprints and was drawing a copy on the chalkboard.

Keith surveyed the space. With the combination of body heat and the industrial-size woodstove, the barn was exceptionally warm. Near the stove, it was downright sweltering. People were removing their coats and hats. By all appearances, no one was shaving anymore. Even before losing their tap water, hot water was too precious to waste on superficial trivialities. People were constantly scratching and rubbing themselves where the unfamiliar stubble asserted. Everyone was thinner now. Malik and Jordan looked rather uncomfortable. They kept a tight grip on their weapons.

Keith saw Eric, Lydia, and Rachel moving through the crowd toward him. They all smiled and shook hands with him. After extending their greetings, Keith looked at Malik and Jordan. "I'd like you to meet my friends Malik and Jordan McCormick."

"Hello, good to meet you." Eric shook their hands. "My name's Eric Jorgenson. This is my wife Lydia and my daughter Rachel." Rachel and Lydia smiled and shook hands with them as well. They exchanged pleasantries and were talking about how they were handling their water situation when Jim Baker's voice boomed throughout the barn.

"Let me have your attention, please! Quiet down, everyone! Excuse me, may I have your attention!"

The noise fell to a whisper as the crowd turned toward the sound of the shouting.

"Thank you. Now, as you've probably heard, we're developing a plan for collecting water. Some of us still have reliable water sources, but we're not going to deny anyone access to drinking water. Right now, we're disinfecting enough water from the creek to keep everyone supplied, and we will continue to do so until we have a better system in place. Several of the farmers have agreed to supply well water to the community as well, and we will be setting up a supply route to deliver to houses. Anyone is welcome to collect water from the creek, but if you want to have it delivered to you, you're going to have to put your name and address down on this list here." He held up a book for everyone to see. "And you will have to pay for the deliveries. Fuel, time, and energy are not free. Neither is equipment, for that matter. We will handle it in the same way we've been handling woodstoves and firewood."

There were a few objections raised to the idea of paying for water. Some of the hippies had apparently forgotten that they had always had to pay for water to be delivered.

Jim simply stated that they would have to work out barter arrangements with the people doing deliveries. He moved on. "There's no reason for anyone to panic, anyhow. I'm sure all of you have a water heater in your house, and that's still going to be full of forty to fifty gallons of clean water. That will give you enough of a buffer until we have a better supply lined out. Now, a lot of people are asking about the plans for the new system of harvesting rainwater. For that, I'm going to turn it over to Tim Faulkner."

"Can everyone see the board?" Tim asked.

"No!" several voices shouted.

"Well, you're welcome to stick around to get a look at it afterward, but for now, you'll just have to use your imagination." Tim pointed to a diagram on the board. "We're going to construct rain catchment systems all along the road. We'll need as many volunteers as we can get to help us, especially anyone with plumbing or construction experience. This is a blueprint of a system I built. There are many ways to build these things. Some of the gardeners here have already got systems like this. You can make these with barrels connected to your gutter system, and we encourage everyone to try to set up your own personal systems at home. Off a thousand square foot roof, a one-inch rain can give you six-hundred gallons. So, to harvest this water, we also need large-scale collecting systems. If anyone has a tank, we could sure use it."

Jim Baker interrupted. "We are *not* confiscating anyone's property though. No one is required to give up anything. It is completely voluntary, and you will be compensated for any materials you contribute to the project."

"That's right," Tim nodded. "Thanks, Jim. We want to utilize the runoff from rooftops, so we'll build the systems right beside houses close to the road."

Brad Nielson spoke up. "I know Jameson, myself, and a few of the other guys know our way around a blueprint. If you can get us the materials, we can build one of those every day."

"We'll get them to you," Tim said.

"But I can't do it for free. I have a family to provide for. I'll take firewood or canned goods as payment. Toilet paper would work too."

There was a chuckle from the crowd.

A woman who was clearly perturbed shouted. Keith thought she looked like one of the nurses. "I don't know what's funny. We have people dying left and right out here because they don't have access to healthcare. People are malnourished and freezing, and now, we're out of water. We've buried half a dozen people in the last week."

"We're all aware of that," Jim said. "We need to stay positive. This is no time to despair."

"I just want to stay focused on the problem at hand."

"I understand." Jim looked around at the crowd. "I have a feeling I know the answer to this, but are there any doctors here?"

Keith looked at Malik.

A man raised his hand. "I'm a doctor."

Jim looked surprised. "Really? What kind of doctor?"

"I'm a doctor of anthropology," he said proudly.

There were a couple of groans from the crowd.

Jim put his hand over his face and rubbed his temples. "Are there any *real* doctors here?"

Again, the crowd snickered.

"Neanderthals," the man said, shaking his head.

"I am." A deep voice cut through the flood of whispers. Keith looked to his right and saw Malik's stony face staring ahead, resolute.

"Who?"

Malik raised his hand. "I was an optometrist."

Everyone stopped and looked at Malik. Keith noticed Jordan looking around at the faces staring at her husband. Malik stood with his eyes fixed on Jim Baker.

"I don't know anything about optometry," Jim said. "Do you think you could do other stuff? I realize we don't have much equipment, but we could use someone with some knowledge of medicine and surgical practices."

"I'd need to consult some books to refresh my memory, but I might be able to help."

Jim looked at the nurse and nodded before looking at Tim. "We'll get you the books," he said, shifting his gaze back to Malik. "You've got plenty of patients."

Throughout the exchanges, the line continued to move as people received disinfected water in milk jugs and pickle jars. The barn was getting far too hot, and once they had collected their water and enough information for their satisfaction, they filtered out through the barn doors and made their way back to their houses. Tim continued to talk with several construction workers and hobby farmers who were making copies of the plans for the water catchment system. Some of the neighbors were coming to the group to ask how much they could get for sections of PVC and barrels and other materials. As the crowd gradually dispersed, the two nurses approached Malik and introduced themselves. They gave him a rundown on the sorts of cases they were dealing with and the problems they were having. He nodded and looked to be taking in as much information as he could. With the late afternoon sun approaching the treetops on the horizon, the neighbors resolved to get started on their projects first thing in the morning.

Keith, Joe, Malik, and Jordan were preparing to leave without collecting water, but they stopped to talk to Tim. Tim was visibly tired, but he turned to the four and smiled. After making introductions and shaking hands, they talked briefly about the plan for tomorrow, and Tim gathered his things to go home.

They walked back together. Most people walked now, unless they had horses or bicycles. It had been generally agreed upon that they needed to conserve the fuel as much as they possibly could.

At the Rawlings driveway, they began to part ways when Tim turned around to look at them with a bit of a forced smile. "We survive another day."

As they opened the door and entered, Faye ran to them, beaming with excitement. "Come and see! Come on!"

She waved them toward the living room, and they followed her through the dimly lit hallway. On the couch, Kent was sitting upright and alert. He had lost at least twenty pounds, but he looked healthy and vibrant. His eyes were gleaming through his still-discolored face as he watched them enter the room with a grin. "Hey, guys," he said. He looked at the weapons they carried. "What, are you coming back from a safari?"

They set their weapons down in various corners of the room.

"When are we going to eat? My bellybutton's pushing so hard against my backbone, I'm afraid it's gonna break it."

Faye laughed and wiped her eyes.

"How you feelin', old man?" Joe asked with a smile.

"Hungry. I hope a strong wind don't come. I'm liable to blow away."

"I imagine we can do something about that," Keith said.

"Well, let's do it." Kent tried to stand up. His face went red as his jaws clenched against the pain.

"Kent, don't get up. You're not ready..." Faye began to say.

"I've been stuck on this couch for a week with nothing to do," he said, sliding himself forward to try again. "I'm going to get up now." He began again.

Lynn and Faye rushed to help him.

"I can do it," he said. His face was turning purple now, the veins in his neck bulged, and spit ran out of the corner of his mouth as he growled with the strain. He sunk back into the couch and caught his breath. "This couch is too squishy." He looked around at them. "Alright, help me up."

Together, they made a meal with some of the canned venison, corn, potatoes, and green beans. It was the first time Kent had eaten anything other than broth since he had been back. They talked about what was going on in the community, what they thought had happened to the power, and what they planned to do in the next days and weeks. Kent insisted they make a pot of coffee for dessert, and as they sat around the table sipping coffee in the candlelight, Lynn asked the question that had been on everyone's minds.

"Dad? What took you so long to get here?"

The room was silent as all eyes focused on Kent's bruised face. He adjusted in his seat a bit, winced at the pain in his leg, and put a hand over his ribs. He sipped from his coffee cup and exhaled.

"Well, uh—I was at work, when, you know, my truck died. I couldn't get it to start, so I went inside to talk to the boss, but all the lights were out. There was all kinds of commotion as people were trying to figure out what to do. The managers were yelling at everyone to stay calm and make their way outside. They opened up all the doors so people could see the way out, and some of the office people brought flashlights. After a couple hours, the managers had accountability of everyone, and they told us all to go home. But my truck wouldn't start, and it looked like no one else could get their cars to start either. I couldn't get a ride, so I walked back to Mom's house. It took me all day to get there.

"Well, we hung out just like old times for the first couple days, but your uncle Cody started to get a little weird after a while. And I mean more than usual. You know how he is. Well, he ran out of cigarettes and started getting really grouchy. He'd pace around the house talking to himself and suddenly blow up on me or Mother. She'd start crying, and I became her emotional support animal or something.

"We ate all her canned soup after cleaning out the fridge. I figured I would just hunker down for a while until the power came back on, but after a week, Cody said he was going into town. He never came back. I started noticing Mom was getting sick. She couldn't stop coughing, and she began throwing up and—and—having other problems." Kent took another gulp of coffee and rubbed his forehead. "She would just stare at the wall for hours, and she seemed not to know where she was or what was going on around her. Eventually, she told me that she had run out of her pills. She hadn't been taking her medicine for several days.

"I got a list of all the medications she was on, and I decided to go into town to try and find them. I took my old bicycle out of the shed, aired up the tires and oiled the chain, and when I got Mom set up with food and water, I took off. I used to ride that bike to school all the time, but I wasn't old and fat back then. It took me a couple hours to get to the drugstore there on the corner, and I was huffin' and puffin' the whole way. When I got there, the windows had all been broken, and it looked like the place had been ransacked. I went through the window and found a man with a flashlight, sweeping up broken glass. He looked at me and continued sweeping like he didn't care that I was there. I asked him if he worked there. He told me he was the owner. I explained my situation and asked him if he would help me find the medicine. He took my list and went into the back room, and a few minutes later, he handed me a bag of drugs. I gave him money and thanked him, and then, I left him there, sweeping.

"I didn't stop to get anything else. I had to get back as quick as possible. By the time I got back, Mom was in very bad shape. She was barely breathing." Kent breathed deeply. His eyes watered. "It was too late. She died within a couple of hours." Kent wiped the tears from his eyes as he looked at his children. "Your grandmother went home."

Keith drank the last of his coffee and stared at the table in front of him. Everyone remained silent. Faye wiped her eyes with her sleeve.

Kent drained the last of his cup and continued. "She died in the night while I held her hand. She was getting cold and stiff, so I knew she was gone. I had to bury her, but the ground was so hard I had to thaw it out with a fire first. I spent the whole day digging the hole. I buried her under the maple tree you kids used to climb. I have no idea what happened to Cody. Who knows? Maybe he came back later. Maybe not. The house was empty, and I figured it was time to get back to Mount Sinai. I thought you guys would all be here. You guys are smart. You knew where to go. I thought about taking the bicycle, but the tires weren't holding air, and I wouldn't be able to take the supplies I needed even if they were. I was able to get Mom's old lawn mower to run, so I hooked up the little trailer, packed a bag with all the remaining food, a couple gallons of water, some blankets, and a tarp, and I loaded them into the trailer. I syphoned gas from Cody's truck into two gas cans and tied them down in the trailer as well. The next morning, I left a note for Cody saying where I was going, in case he came back, and I left.

"I took the highway. I figured I would go as far as I could with the fuel I had and would probably have to walk the rest of the way. I got all the way to Nashville when I came across these guys carrying baseball bats and duffel bags. They were walking down the road when they looked at me. They stopped me, and I started talking to them, and—well, they turned out to not be very friendly. That's really all I remember. I guess you've heard the rest." Kent looked at Malik and Jordan. "I couldn't have made it back without these guys."

Lynn poured Kent another cup of coffee.

"Thank you, Lynn." Kent wrapped his hands around the mug and breathed in the steam rising off the top.

Faye was crying quietly with her face buried in her hands. She looked up at Kent through tear-filled eyes.

"What's wrong?" Kent asked.

"Your mom..." Faye began.

Kent nodded. "She's in a better place than we are."

"I don't know if my dad is still alive." Faye began to sob.

CHAPTER EIGHT

In the flickering candlelight, Lynn hugged her mother. Malik and Jordan held hands and said nothing. Kent wiped his eyes once more, pursed his lips, and nodded empathetically. Joe put a reassuring hand on Faye's shoulder. Keith took another sip of coffee and sat, silently staring at the table, thinking.

Chapter Nine

Day 30

There were two kinds of rednecks from the economist's perspective. Both were poor by American standards. The first kind used his meager earnings to buy the cheapest possible items, which would soon break, become useless, and get tossed in a pile somewhere on his property, since he wasn't about to waste money on trash removal; he would then repeat this process several times and end up spending more than he would have for both one good item that wouldn't break and the cost of trash collection. And on top of spending more money, his property gradually came to resemble a junkyard, which depreciated its value and that of his neighbors' properties as well. The second type, seeing the first as a sucker who would never get ahead by living within his means while living paycheck to paycheck, chose to enjoy his life in the here and now, buying whatever he wanted with credit cards that would never be paid off in his lifetime. Kent was the first kind. He was one of the original residents on Mount Sinai, and his lifestyle was used by teachers as an example of what might happen to students if they didn't go to college.

Many years ago, Kent had begun collecting trash that was being thrown out at the factory. Among his collection of junk lawnmowers, rototillers, and farm implements, he had piles of tires, conveyors, scrap lumber, pallets, steel tanks,

55-gallon drums, and two enormous plastic water tanks sitting back in the woods. How he got them there, only he knew, but they had sat on his property, collecting dirt, leaves, and moss for the better part of two decades. Keith and Joe took the liberty of donating them to be used in the water project. Upon inspection of the tanks, they noticed that one had cracked and split down the middle, rendering it worthless, but the other, a 2,500-gallon beast, was still in excellent condition. With the help of Ben Jameson and Tim Faulkner, the tank was carefully loaded onto a trailer and transported to the next house over, which was much closer to the road. They cleaned it out and built one of the biggest water catchment systems on Mount Sinai.

To pay for the labor and materials, neighbors were starting small businesses to provide marketable goods to trade. All along Mount Sinai Road, signs made from plywood or plastic or scrap tin roofing with spray painted advertisements were being erected. They said things like "Soap for trade," "Jessica's Candles," "firewood," and "Susan's honey." One sign read "Barb's Maple Syrup." The next house over had a sign that read "Dorothy's Maple Syrup (better than Barb's)."

The economy was growing. Small water tanks could be seen outside many of the houses now. Keith and Joe had gathered several 55-gallon drums, cleaned them up, and traded them to neighbors for candles, soap, and syrup. Kent was able to walk around the house with the help of a cane Joe carved for him. He liked to remind everyone that while he may not have been a Rockefeller in the past, he was, by comparison, a Rockefeller now. His collection of junk made him one of the richest people around.

For the first week, Kent didn't leave the house. He was still recovering and had trouble walking, but he wanted to work, to provide for the family in some way. He felt that he was a burden on their limited resources, so he looked for any small jobs around the house that he could tackle. After fixing a broken wheelbarrow and repairing some old bicycles on the property, one of the first things he had noticed, as he walked around, was that the others were all dragging firewood from the surrounding woods on sleds. It was hardly the most efficient way, but they needed wood, and they didn't have time or energy to waste on new projects. Kent, enduring a prodigious degree of pain in his leg and ribs, collected wheels off of some nearby lawnmowers and rototillers, along with some scrap lumber, and he built a serviceable, albeit unsightly, wagon which greatly improved the speed with which firewood could be transported. He had a plan for every piece of trash on his property, and for his projects, he often pieced them together in ways that only he would think to do.

Kent limped toward the old Ford, leaning heavily on his cane and hugging his ribs with his free hand. His unkempt, shaggy, gray hair fell out from beneath his old, torn, orange stocking cap. Beneath his salt and pepper whiskers and wrinkled cheeks, the old man clenched his teeth. Gray daylight filtered through the smoky sky as crows cawed in the trees above and swooped down to scavenge from the piles of bones and viscera strewn about the field. Buzzards perched atop the telephone poles, casting ominous shadows across the long, dead grass and weeds of the field and down into the ravine. It was getting warmer. Thirty-three degrees, according to the thermometer on the porch.

Joe met his father out in the field and walked with him to the truck.

"So, what's it doing?" Kent asked.

"I got it to turn over, but it won't fire," Joe answered. "I got fuel, compression, timing, but no spark. I emptied the gas tank and refilled it. Changed the oil and topped off all the fluids, just to be doing something while I tried to think of what the problem was. I can't figure it out."

"Well, let's have a look." Kent peered under the open hood, touched a few components, and made a few noises as if checking off boxes in his head. "Try to start it."

Joe climbed into the driver's seat and turned the key. Apart from the squealing, nothing happened.

"Alright," Kent nodded after a few seconds. "Let me think." He hobbled around the truck, pushing sticks out of the way with his cane. "Where's your brother?"

Keith skinned out the opossum, removed the guts, put the scent glands into a jar, and took the carcass to Jordan to debone. They now had so much meat that they kept it hanging in bags outside. They boiled the meat they didn't plan to eat, shredded it up, fed it to their chickens, and traded it as chicken feed to local hobby farmers turned sustenance farmers. There were plenty of deer hunters, but for decades, no one had really hunted predators on Mount Sinai Road. There were so many predators here that, for years, they hardly ever saw turkeys on the property; there wasn't even a substantial population of rabbits, and pet cats and farm animals routinely went missing. If they wanted any chance of raising domesticated animals and having a healthy supply of game, they needed to tap into this long-neglected resource. Keith was not the only one who had recently started trapping either. There were several trappers on Mount Sinai now, who brought their furs to market. A couple of the neighbors knew how to brain tan hides. One of them was Tim Faulkner's eldest son. Tim Faulkner would trade canned goods or dehydrated foods for pelts, but he was the only one. His son would tan the hides and turn them into coats, hats, mittens, and pillows, but Keith suspected the Faulkners were taking pelts for trade more out of charity than anything else.

The demand for meat was high, but the demand for vegetables was higher. Many of the gardeners had put up cans of vegetables, but they sold them dearly. A can of corn or beans was worth three coyote pelts or six large raccoon pelts to the

Faulkners. With anyone else, it would cost ten squirrels, a box of shotgun or rifle ammunition, two new AA batteries, a fifth of liquor, or a days' skilled labor.

No one was trading animal feed, and Keith was scrounging to find food for the pigs. The chickens could free range during the day and eat meat scraps from Keith's trapping, but the pigs could not be left to wander. They would almost certainly roam onto someone else's property and be shot and butchered. He had been raking acorns out of the frozen leaves—most of them were already rotten or worm-eaten, but he threw them all in a bucket with whole cattails, wild onions, orchard grass, smilax, clover, and rotting tree bark filled with termites, grubs and beetles. It took a couple of hours every day just to gather enough forage to feed the pigs. Caring for five pigs was too much work without supply chains, even with help from Malik and Jordan, and people needed meat. Keith decided to butcher two of the pigs today and trade most of the meat. The tough pigskin would make good bags and boots, so he would process them just like a deer. No part of the pigs would be wasted.

Keith used soap and hot water from the stove to wash the opossum's blood and grease from his hands and knife. He honed the edge, sheathed his blade, and walked outside. Faye and Lynn watched through the window, sad to see their young pigs slaughtered, but the last four weeks had eroded much of their sentimentality. There were no vegetarians now. There were no environmentalists. And the word 'pet' was stricken from the lexicon. Animals were either useful or there was no justification to feed them. In the overfed and decadent United States, potbelly pigs had been kept as pets. In fact, that's what the Rawlings' hogs used to be before their previous owners could no longer care for them. Yet, in Asia, as Keith reminded them, these very animals were raised for meat, and good meat they were. They grew much slower than American meat hogs, but they also required much less food. Even so, the Indiana winter was hard foraging, and without a feed supply, the pigs could not be kept.

CHAPTER NINE

Keith opened the door to the pen and led the sacrificial animals out behind the house. He talked to them in a soothing voice as they snorted and grunted, rooting around in the leaves and wagging their tails joyfully. They rolled around in the snow and pushed each other with their noses playfully. Keith smiled. They were cute. He unholstered his pistol, shot them both once in the head, and drew his knife as they kicked and writhed in the reddening mud, rivulets of blood streaming from the holes in their skulls. Keith plunged his knife through their jugular veins until the point struck the vertebrae, he pulled the knife out releasing a dark crimson torrent spraying from their throats like a scarlet geyser. They flailed and splashed in the pool of steaming blood as Keith held them down to drain them.

When they stopped moving, Keith dragged them to the gambrels, hung them up, skinned them, and gutted them. He quartered the hogs, put the meat in coolers, and put the hearts and livers into a trash bag before taking them into the house. Using the innards, with some of the fat, they would stuff the intestines to make sausage. Even the feet would be cleaned and smoked to flavor soups. No one was going to give much for opossum and raccoon meat, but pork would be highly valuable for trade.

Keith had never cleaned out pig intestines before. The smell alone was enough to dissuade him from trying. Now, they had no running water, and to improperly clean food could mean worms. After squeezing out most of the excrement on the ground, he put the intestines in a sterilized bucket and brought them up to the back deck. He cleaned out an old funnel and tried pouring disinfected water into the intestine, but he didn't have enough hands to handle it all at once. Jordan, wanting to prove that she wasn't merely a city-dwelling retail manager, came to help him. She poured the water into the funnel as Keith held the intestines. The water filled the sack and Keith squeezed it through the length of the entrails with his fingers. The water came out a yellowish-brown color. It wreaked like the open maw of Hell.

Jordan held her breath and stepped away from the mess to take a breath. Keith dumped the bucket, trimmed off the fat that clung to the lining, and flung it over the rail. He took a breath and spat.

"You know, I've heard of people eating chitterlings," Jordan said. "I never had them myself."

"I have," Keith said. "Worst thing I ever ate."

"Yeah?" Jordan laughed. "That bad, huh?"

"Heinous." Keith shook his head. "Like giant rubber bands. Tasted exactly the way this smells."

Jordan laughed again. "I take it you won't be making any for dinner."

"Absolutely not. I thought I could make some good sausages out of these and trade whatever we didn't want to keep." Keith squeezed out more of the water. "But I'm starting to have second thoughts."

"Well, don't give up now. You've already come this far."

"If you can still eat this, I can still make it." He held the next intestine up for more water as she poured.

"I can do it," Jordan said as Keith squeezed out the brown water and dumped it.

"We'll never get all this gunk out with just water. We have to turn them inside out." Keith looked around and dropped the intestines back in the bucket. "I need some kind of a hook." He turned to go inside.

"Wash your hands first." Jordan poured warm water over Keith's slime-coated palms as he wrung them over the bucket. His hands were still slimy, but he shook the water off and wiped his palms on his pants as she opened the door for him.

Keith was searching around the house and looking through his toolbox when Malik entered the room with a notebook and ink pen. He had been sitting beside the window, reading over medical books and jotting down notes for hours every day.

"I can't take any more of this sitting and reading while you guys are doing real work," Malik said. "I want to help."

Keith looked at him. "Sure," he said. Then, his eyes went to the pen in Malik's hand. "Can I borrow that?"

Malik looked down at the pen. "Of course." He handed it to him and followed him outside onto the deck with Jordan.

Malik watched as Keith ran the ink pen through the intestines, bunching them up to his fist until the pocket clip came out the other end. He pulled the pen back through, snagging the end of the intestine and pulling it inside out. He pinched the intestine between his thumb and forefinger and pulled it through, collecting a fistful of pale, yellow slime at the end. It stank like Death and all his angels.

"Good Lord." Malik coughed and stepped away to gasp for breath.

Keith flung the filth off his hand into the leaves and did the same to the second. This done, Jordan poured warm water over the intestines into the bucket, and Keith swished them around vigorously in the water. He stood up, spat over the rail, and held the pen out for Malik. "Thank you."

Malik stared at the pen. "I'll get another." He turned and went back inside.

Lynn was painting alongside Faye as they waited for the stew to cook. In the Rawlings home, drawings and paintings and sculptures and cross-stitched images adorned the walls and shelves. There was an entire wall devoted to Lynn's paintings, and her bedroom was full of them, but the rest of the house was decorated with artwork Faye had done over the course of many years. There were portraits and landscapes and still-lives mostly inspired by friends and family and memories of her life on the farm in Illinois. They were full of pain and longing, but each one captured at least a spark of the beautiful, and they mesmerized anyone who walked through the house. But Faye had not created art in a long time. Life had got in the way, and she could never seem to find the time. She kept a scrapbook full of inspiring images and words that she had planned to incorporate in future works, if she could ever undertake another project, but the yellowing pages collected dust on a bookshelf.

Yet, nothing was stopping her now. They had three rick of firewood stacked beside the house, Keith made sure they had food in stock, and he and Jordan did most of the cooking while Lynn kept the house cleaner than it had been in years. Malik was wrapped up in his study when he wasn't visiting neighbors with one of the nurses, Kent and Joe were working on the truck, and she couldn't go to the store or anywhere else for that matter. Furthermore, she was depressed about her father and sister in Illinois, and nothing could bring her solace, and no one could give her comfort. That is, until Lynn suggested they start a painting together. Why not? There was nothing better for her to do. She had loved the idea of painting with her daughter, and if not now, when?

And they both had a passion for art. They would never be celebrated or recognized by the critics in coastal cities whose checkbooks dictated culture—most of whom were likely dead or dying now—but they too had dreams, and pondered the deep questions, and contemplated their place in the universe. Perhaps it was all for naught, and their world would never know art again—except those artifacts which could enhance one's ability to survive, add to the seconds one spent respirating in the atmosphere—but perhaps there was still a need for art, a desire for beauty along with truth and goodness.

Art used to have purpose, meaning. It used to be beautiful. Glimmers of light in a darkened world. In recent years, it was devoid of all that. Sculpture was haphazard, random shapes defecated onto the landscape. Music was provocative, bilious slurs put to discordant shrieks and robotic moans, with nothing but a beat to denote it as song. Painting was blank canvas and angry, flailing smatterings of shapes or colors strewn across surfaces, or dirt, debris, and bodily fluids smeared along a plane. Drama was enigmatic innuendo, venomous partisan screeds, and lackluster absurdity punctuated by flashing lights and shrill, shocking noises. Literature was slack-jawed libel, profane prevarication, and uninspired effluence, laden with expletive, excreted onto pages by pandering frauds and overzealous know-nothings who hid behind garbled grammatical confusion and newly-minted, intentionally unintelligible vocabulary. Rather than creativity, "art" had become, in a word, destruction. But "deconstruction" was the euphemism behind which it hid. Every meaningless masterpiece existed in defiance of the landfill as if to say, "Impart your own meaning here, for I have none to offer."

Lynn saw it, and she rejected it. Faye knew it was there too, but she had lost her will to revolt. Perhaps Lynn's fire could reignite those coals. Perhaps the embers had not been extinguished. If there was to be any hope for humanity, any future for generations yet unborn, the torch must be carried, and burning bright, to light the path forward and illuminate the trail behind. Someone would have to reclaim the language. The language we use to talk to God.

Lynn pulled a brush through viridian hue and ran it over the surface of the canvas. Faye pressed a sponge of red oxide through layers of titanium white and Prussian blue. She glanced at her daughter's contemplative face out of the corner of her eye. A tear rolled down her cheek, and she smiled.

From just outside the house, they could hear the thunderous roar of an engine. They both jumped as the rumble shook them out of their meditation. Lynn put down her palette and brush and ran to the window. Faye quickly joined her to look outside, and they saw the old Ford smoking and rattling as it rolled through the field and into the driveway.

"They did it!" Faye nearly shouted.

The driver's side door opened, and Kent slid out onto his cane and two feet, grimacing and hugging his side. He left the truck running and limped into the house with a haughty smile across his face.

Joe ran out in front of him and onto the deck as Faye opened the door. "I've been working on that thing for weeks, and I couldn't figure it out." Joe shook his head with a grin. "Points. Who knew?"

Kent stepped through the doorway. "Sometimes you just need a little redneck enginovation," he said with a smile.

"You mean ingenuity?" Faye prompted with a puzzled expression.

"That too," Kent said, taking a seat beside the woodstove. "That helps too."

The truck ran for a few minutes before Kent told Joe to kill the engine. After Keith and Jordan packaged the pig meat and put it outside in a cooler, the family gathered around the table. Malik and Jordan took seats with cups of pine needle tea.

Faye looked excited. "Now that we have a truck, we can go get my dad."

Everyone had been thinking this, but it was no small matter. The truck had not exactly proven itself to be reliable. Furthermore, it could only take three people in the cab.

"I'd love to go get your dad," Kent said with a sigh. "But we need to put some serious thought into this. We need a detailed plan."

"You're thinking about leaving?" Jordan asked with alarm.

"We have to talk about it," Kent replied. "That truck is running on six cylinders. Maybe we can get it tuned up to seven. Eight's a long shot. There are holes rusted out that you could throw a baseball through. The tires are good enough, but one of the wheels is the wrong size. We can fix that. I've got another wheel and tire. We just have to mount it. It gets something like five miles to the gallon, so we'll need to bring fuel. And it can only take two passengers. How many people are you wanting to bring back, Faye?"

"There's Dad and Aunt Ruth and my sister, her husband, and her son."

"Okay, so five people. That means we can either take two in the cab while the rest ride in the bed for at least three hours in freezing temperatures, or we'd have to make multiple trips."

Faye's face reddened. She collapsed into a chair and put a hand over her eyes, breathing forcefully.

"And that's assuming I travel by myself. A beat-up, old man on a six-hour-plus trip in a junky truck with no way to communicate to anyone if something goes wrong."

Faye rocked herself back and forth in the chair, not saying anything.

"So, if you really want to do this, I'll do it. I'll figure out a way to make it work, but I want you to understand what we're facing here."

Malik couldn't stay silent. "You can't take the risk. It's too dangerous. Please don't go."

"It's my family," Faye sobbed.

Kent looked at her and pulled out a chair. Lynn helped him to sit down as he clenched his teeth and leaned his cane against the table. "We can put a camper shell on the truck. We'll put cushions down in the bed."

"We have to all go together," Lynn said. "We're not splitting up again."

"I agree," Joe seconded.

"We'll bring blankets and an arsenal. Everyone must be armed to the teeth," Keith said. "Malik, Jordan, you'll have to watch the house. You keep your guns."

Jordan and Malik both shook their heads, pleading. "Don't."

"We'll need gas cans, tools, water, and a supply of food, just in case," Kent said. "I want to see what supplies we have. We need to make a list of all our tools and canned goods. Bring it all here so we can get a count."

They hauled up supplies from the basement. They emptied out the pantry. Keith brought down tools and equipment from his bedroom. Joe piled weapons and ammunition on the table. They laid out blankets, coats, boots, gloves, hats. Kent made a list of their stockpile.

After trading supplies to neighbors in need, they had a dozen jars of food left. Two jars of potatoes, two jars of tomatoes, one of corn, one of green beans, and six jars of venison. They had a five-pound bag of rice, four pounds of pinto beans, one pound of lentils, one pound of split peas, one box of pancake mix, a couple pounds of flour, six boxes of iodized salt, and one box of canning salt. They had two gallons of white vinegar, one gallon of apple cider vinegar, three pounds of honey, three pint jars of maple syrup. They were down to their last can of coffee, a fact that Kent lamented with a dramatic moan. Their spices were running out. Meat was not an issue, as long as the traps continued to produce, but they needed to can more of it if they were going to take any with them.

They had four gallons of bleach, ten bars of soap, including the three homemade bars they had acquired from trade. All the scented candles were gone, but they had a dozen unscented candles for which Keith had traded meat. They had a dozen AA batteries, nineteen AAA batteries, three D batteries, and one nine-volt, not including those in their flashlights and lanterns. They had a dozen fixed blade knives, not including kitchen knives and fillet knives, and they had eight folding knives. Three axes, two splitting mauls, five bucksaw blades, and three handsaws. They had three 12 gauge shotguns with 200 shells, two 20 gauge shotguns with 52 shells, one 28 gauge shotgun that was over a century old with ten shells, and a .410 with thirteen shells. Two .22 rifles with nearly 1,500 rounds. One 9mm pistol with 150 rounds. Two .45 ACP pistols with 584 rounds. One lever-action .44 magnum rifle with 457 rounds. One AR-15 with nine magazines and 2,055 rounds, one bolt-action .308 Winchester with 419 rounds, a .50 caliber muzzleloader with 115 bullets, 200 percussion caps, and two pounds of powder.

And they had three compound bows with a total of eighteen good arrows. Not bad—maybe average for this neck of the woods.

On the front porch, Joe brought a toolbox with all the tools they thought they would need to repair the truck in the event of anything short of a blown head gasket or transmission. He brought a spare battery, belts, bottles of transmission fluid, brake fluid, power steering fluid, oil, windshield washer fluid, bearings, and grease. They lined up two spare tires which Kent called "baloney skins." They syphoned gasoline from every car, truck, and lawnmower on the property, filling up all their gas cans, amounting to about 42 gallons.

It was after noon. They would divide up the supplies later, and Kent said they could start work on the truck tomorrow. He was too tired to start on it today, and he needed more time to think up a plan. He took to drawing diagrams and writing lists in his notebook while Keith went to trade pork and see how the water project was coming along.

They still traveled in pairs as much as possible. Joe went with him to discuss their plans with Tim, to see what was available for trade, and to provide Keith with some backup muscle. This much good pork rolling down the road would be a powerful temptation to anyone whose morals had been loosened by the laxative of hunger. They had weighed it before loading it into the homemade wagon. They had eighty-seven pounds of meat to trade, and that was not including the offal, which they still had to make into sausages, nor the meat they had kept for themselves.

Keith pulled the wagon along with his rifle slung over his shoulder. Out of the corner of his eye, he saw Joe turn, put a pinch of tobacco in his mouth, then slip the can back into his coat pocket, and continue walking, adjusting the shotgun slung over his right shoulder. Keith said nothing. He knew he was running low and was unwilling to let anyone know that he still had tobacco. He would have to quit eventually, but now was not the time to say anything to him about it. They slogged through the melting snow and icy mud up to the road. Overhead, crows cawed and flew away to distant treetops as the brothers came within shotgun range of them. They weren't about to waste a shotgun shell on a crow, but the crows were too wary to risk it. They were smart, far smarter than squirrels.

As they left the driveway and began walking on the road, they noticed Fred and Donna Packard in their front yard, raking leaves.

"Can you believe that?" Joe said. "The world ended a month ago, leaving their neighbors struggling to find enough raccoons to eat, and they're raking the leaves out of their yard like they want to maintain their property value or something."

Keith chuckled. "I don't know, man. They're weird."

They kept walking, and at the sound of the makeshift wagon rattling along over the pavement, with its squeaking wheels and rubbing tires, Fred Packard looked up at them. Joe waved at him, and he dropped his head and turned his back to them, continuing to rake his leaves. Joe shook his head and looked at Keith. Keith shrugged, Joe spat, and they kept walking.

Among the many awesome features of the Faulkner homestead, which was no more than ten acres, the Faulkners had a smokehouse. Tim had built the thing a few years ago, and the smoke rolled out of the chimney, night and day, during the winter. The Faulkners, of course, had their own livestock, which they butchered themselves and preserved in the killing season. One of the methods they used to keep their meat good all year round was the traditional practice of salt-curing and cold-smoking used by farmers, butchers, and homesteaders in this country and others for generations. After weeks of hanging in the smokehouse at a constant cool temperature with a steady flow of woodsmoke, the meat would be taken and hung in a cellar, which Tim hadn't shown them, but they could surmise he had somewhere near the house.

CHAPTER NINE

In the backyard, Tim's children were playing with their
dog Jimmy. They threw a ball around to one another in a
circle as Jimmy tackled them, licked their faces, and took
the ball. They laughed gleefully and wrestled the ball from
the dog. Jimmy wagged his tail and barked and ran circles
around them until the ball was thrown again. They screamed
and squealed and hugged the golden retriever and scratched
his furry belly and laughed as he kicked his leg and panted.
Then, Jimmy saw the brothers coming up the driveway. He
barked and leapt up to greet them, sprinting toward Keith
and Joe. The children followed him with their eyes and
waved at the two as Jimmy jumped up to lick their faces. Of
course, he remembered them. They were very good friends,
and once they scratched behind his ears and rubbed his neck,
he ran back to the children, wagging his tail.

"Are your parents home?" Joe shouted to the kids
with a smile.

"Momma's in the house," the oldest daughter replied.

When they knocked on the door, Emma answered. She
greeted them with a smile and told them that Tim was
working on the water project at the Jorgenson's house down
the road. She asked them about the wagon and the load they
were hauling, and they chatted about the pigs and what they
planned to do with the meat. Emma told them they could
leave the meat with her, and she would hang it in the smokehouse. They thanked her and left the wagon, expecting to
pick it up when they came back with Tim.

The brothers walked through the smoky, brisk air, back
down the road toward the Jorgenson house. They passed
the Packards again. This time, in the garden, aerating the
soil. The Packards' garden was always picturesque and surrounded by flowers and flowering shrubs. It was sickening.
And it was planted so close to the road that when they grew
squash or melons or cucumbers, the vines would creep out
across the ditch and onto the asphalt so that anyone driving
by couldn't help but notice. Some people would swerve
around the vines, not wanting to disturb such beautiful

plants in such a perfect garden. Some people would run the vines over. Maybe out of spite. Maybe out of principle.

They looked focused on their task. Fred picked up weeds and tossed them into a bucket while Donna hopped on a broad fork and levered it through the soil, uprooting the unwelcome vegetation. They didn't look at the Rawlings brothers walking by this time, but the brothers knew they were monitoring them in their periphery. Joe waved at them again and kept walking. It was the principle of the thing. Truthfully, Joe waved at almost everyone on this road, and a good deal of the people on most other roads as well. He was a people person, or at least, he tried to be.

They passed their driveway, the brown house with the big water catchment system, and the purple house where the pizza delivery guy lived—or at least, they thought he lived there, his car was parked there most nights before the blackout, but they hadn't seen anyone outside that house since the first week. They passed several signs advertising firewood and homemade groceries and sundries. One old man was cleaning out his garage, making a pile of all the things he wouldn't be needing now: power tools, a lawn-mower, a weed-eater, and various other articles of junk. One neighbor was trying to clean the leaves out of her gutters, apparently having problems with her rain barrel. They passed the big greenhouse where someone had told them a professor lived, and where they could always see blue flowers growing every summer. They passed a trailer on the right, where every day, men were working on a truck, and today was no exception.

Across the road from a man splitting wood, was the little, light blue house of the Jorgensons. In the front yard, Jack Winters was fitting two pipes together with the help of Tim Faulkner and two other men.

"Alright, that's got it," one of the men said.

"Good job," said Tim.

The door to the house opened, and Lydia Jorgenson came out with two glasses of tea in her hands. She was followed by

Rachel with two more glasses. The men graciously accepted the drinks and thanked the ladies.

Jack took a drink and shook his head. "Ma'am, this is some of the best sweet tea I ever had."

"Well, I wish I could make it every day," Lydia said with a smile. "But we do the best we can with what we have."

"Yes, ma'am," Jack replied. "I sure am gonna miss this." He looked at Keith and Joe walking into the driveway and tipped his hat to them.

Rachel looked at the two and smiled. "How you boys, doin'?"

"We're alright," Joe said. "Just thought we'd see if anyone needed help over here."

Eric stepped out of the house, carrying two jars of what looked like canned stew. "Well, you came just in time," he chuckled. Abigail followed behind him, and they handed a jar of stew to each of the men. "Thank you all. God bless you," Eric said.

This tank was not as big, maybe a 1,000-gallon tank by the look of it, Keith judged. "How many does that make?" he asked Tim.

"Five big ones. On this road, anyway." Tim took a drink of sweet tea. "I think Jim's working on one down on Deer Creek Road, and Jack and Ben built one up on Jefferson Lane there." Tim pointed just past the horse pasture of Jack Winters' property, to the fork in the Road where Jefferson Lane branched off from Mount Sinai Road.

Jack nodded. "We got some water tanks from some of the farmers and landscapers. There might be some more around here, but I don't know that anyone's too keen on giving them up right now."

"Which might be for the best," Tim said. "We may need to transport more water for crops later on in the year."

"Or fires," Jack added.

The sun was nearing the horizon. The two other workers finished their tea, handed the glasses back, and shook hands with Eric before excusing themselves. Tim and Jack thanked them for their help, shook hands with them, and stayed behind to talk. The Jorgensons went back inside, and Jack walked with Tim and the Rawlings brothers back up the road toward Tim's house.

"How's your old man?" Tim asked.

"He's good. He's doin' real well," Keith said. "Mom told us what your wife did for him. We owe you guys. We won't ever forget that."

"My wife will get even with you. Don't worry about that. I'm glad things worked out. It's a bad business."

"We butchered two pigs today. You want some meat?"

"No, we're good on meat, thank you."

"How about you, Jack? You need meat?"

"Not at the moment," Jack responded. "But when I do, I'll give you some business."

Keith looked back at Tim. "Well, we left it at your place. Your wife put it in the smokehouse for us. We owe you for that too."

"I'll put it on your tab," Tim chuckled.

"The economy is growing." Joe smiled, looking at the signs as they passed.

Tim nodded. "Yes, it is. If we can just hold it together for a few more months, I hope we'll have enough to keep going." Tim looked ahead in the distance contemplatively. "And then, who knows? Maybe we expand. Maybe we start to rebuild."

"How's security?" Keith looked at Jack.

"The blockades are all in place, but I know there's been some people coming in from outside. Friends, relatives, probably." Jack shook his head. "That's fine as long as people are putting them up in their own homes and taking the responsibility for feeding and sheltering them, you know. You can't ask people to just forget about their family members simply because they happen to live outside of our little bubble here."

Keith and Joe looked at each other, wondering if they should bring it up now. They were about to speak when Jack continued.

"But I'm concerned about some of the people we're letting in here. We don't know who they are. We don't know what kind of ideas they're bringing with them. There's a lot of desperate people out there. They weren't raised like you boys were. They don't know how to survive. And if they find out about this place and the resources we have here... I don't know. There's this one dude I've had my eye on. Goes in and out of the trailer between your two houses. The past few nights he's been walking up to the train tracks and sneaking out. I don't know where he goes, but I don't like it."

Keith and Joe both looked at each other again and went a little pale. They didn't have to say a word. They could tell what the other was thinking. They had a cousin they hadn't seen in years, who had been in and out of prison since he was a teenager. They didn't know what he was sentenced for, but gossip spread in the family. He had almost certainly been trafficking drugs, but there were rumors that he had been charged with everything from armed robbery to murder, and every time he got out of jail, he would wind up at his grandmother's trailer. They didn't know this for sure because they never saw him, but if it was true, there was no telling what he might do.

"Hmm. Speaking of leaving the bubble..." Keith began, partly to change the subject, but partly because they needed to tell them about their plans to drive to Illinois. "We, uh, we were thinking..." Maybe it wasn't the right time. He knew they would try to stop them from going. "Well, you know, Dad's doing a lot better now, and—he got the old truck running..."

Off in the distance, they could hear loud cracks echoing through the hills, then, a thunderous boom.

"What was that?" Tim asked.

Keith stopped and listened.

"Some kids playing with firecrackers, maybe," Joe offered. "Or somebody doing some target practice."

A shriek erupted from Jack Winters' jacket. He grabbed at his pocket before turning around and running back down the road toward his house.

Keith and Joe could hardly make out what the voice from Jack's radio had said, but they thought they recognized two words: 'church' and 'help.' They watched Jack run for half a second, and they turned back toward the sound of a bell ringing. More cracks and booms. Then, piercing the air, a scream. They took off running toward the old church.

Chapter Ten

As the gunfire continued, the roar of engines echoed through the valleys of Mount Sinai, reverberating off the hills. There was a grinding, shrieking screech of twisting metal and a loud crunch. Jack Winters rode past the three running men, toward the sound, at a full gallop. A bang, like the collision of two cars, and another revving of engines. The roar was getting louder. It was coming up the road toward them. They ran past the Rawlings driveway as a rusty, old car came speeding around the bend.

"Off the road!" Keith shouted. They jumped into the ditch, and the car swerved into view, screeching to a halt beside the Packards' driveway. It backed up perpendicular with the road, stopped, and was shut off.

Four men climbed out and surrounded the vehicle. They were dressed in black with what appeared to be police body armor. Two men ran toward the house and tried to break in the door. The man with a shotgun fired into the door latch. Keith leveled his .44 magnum rifle and aimed at one of the gunmen. Joe did the same with his shotgun. A muffled shot popped from behind the door, and one of the men fell backward, hit in the vest. He got up, and all four of the men poured fire into the house. Keith fired from behind a tree. The 250-grain nickel-plated hollow point struck the man in the hipbone. It shattered his right leg and tore out his left in a spray of blood, meat, and bone fragments. He crumpled to the ground. The man beside him, unsure of where the shot came from, hugged the wall, keeping away from the doors and windows of the house. Keith levered another round into the chamber. The two men in back kneeled behind the car, scanning the tree line to the left, searching for a shooter on the other side of the road. The driver climbed out, using the driver's side door for cover, and lobbed a flaming bottle through the window of the house. Keith took aim at the man hugging the wall of the Packard house. He fired and sent a bullet through the man's neck just above the collar bone. His head flipped back and bounced forward as he fell to the ground like a tree, leaving a pink mist drifting through the breeze toward Earth.

The driver saw where the shot came from and lobbed a Molotov cocktail over the roof of the car. Joe followed the object with his bead and fired a load of no. 4 birdshot. The bottle exploded in the air, sending a shower of flame and broken glass onto the car and the driver. The driver threw off his helmet and coat and rolled on the ground behind the vehicle. The other two men went to pat him down and smother the flames.

Keith took advantage of the distraction. "Stay here. Keep 'em pinned down," he said, and he took off through the woods around the backside of the house before anyone could respond.

Engines revved up the road to the west. The man shot through the pelvis was flailing on the ground now, trying to feel his legs with his hands. He screamed: "Help me! My legs! Oh God! John! Help me!"

"Shut up!" came a reply from behind the car. "He's in the ditch over there!" the driver yelled. The two men raised their heads and pointed their weapons toward Joe and Tim. Joe fired into the window, blowing out the glass. The men dropped back behind the car. "Move!" The driver yelled. He raised a pistol over the hood of the car and began firing wildly. The report of a rifle, and his face erupted in a flare of teeth, hair, blood, and brain matter. He folded over the hood and slid back onto the ground, leaving teeth and frothy globs of cream-colored gelatin streaking down the blood-spattered windshield.

Tim tried to hold his gun up, but it dropped in the leaves as he vomited.

A second shot from behind the house, and Joe could hear a body bounce off the rear door of the car. The man on the ground was mumbling and rolling his head around on the grass. The last man behind the car screamed a slew of curses as he moved behind the trunk and pointed his rifle in Keith's direction. Joe fired at the man's foot which was sticking out. He screamed and jumped up on one leg, spinning around. A round hit him in the back and knocked him out from behind the car. He spun and raised his gun in Keith's direction. Joe racked the slide and fired another turkey load into his face. He collapsed onto the ground. The mumbling man was silent now.

Keith shouted from behind the house, "Joe! Tim! I'm coming back toward you! Hold your fire, okay?"

The two men sat in the ditch behind the trees. Staring at the carnage before them, they said nothing.

"Joe!" Keith shouted again. "You hear me?"

Tim wiped his mouth and took a drink of water.

"Joe!"

"What?" Joe shook his head. "Yeah! I hear you! Come on!"

"You're not going to shoot me, right?"

"No, I won't!"

Keith stepped out from the woods in the Packards' back yard. He kept where Joe and Tim could clearly see him as he kicked the bodies and moved their weapons away from them. "Let's go! Stay with me!" he shouted back at Joe and Tim. They climbed out of the ditch and caught up with him as he jogged alongside the road.

There was screaming up ahead, more shots, and through the trees, they could see a black, lifted truck with steel armor bolted on the front and sides. It was in the Faulkners' driveway. Tim and Joe followed Keith's lead as he moved from tree to tree, keeping behind cover. Smoke billowed out of the open smokehouse doors as two men carried meat out and threw it in the bed of the truck. Hooked up to the truck, they had a horse trailer, and two men were bringing chickens in nets from the barn behind Tim's house. Inside the trailer, they could hear Tim's goats and pigs screaming in panic. The men opened the trailer door and threw the chickens inside. A squealing pig tried to escape as they did so, and one of the men kicked it with the heel of his boot and slammed the door. He moved around to the front of the truck and opened the driver's side door. "Let's go! It's getting dark!" he shouted.

One of the men was climbing the stairs of the front porch. "Just a minute! There might be some good stuff in here!" He tried the door. Locked. There was no light inside the windows. He pulled a crowbar from his belt and tried to pry it open.

Keith left Joe and Tim on the east side of the smokehouse. They waited for him to make his way through the brush to the north and take the first shot from the end of the driveway.

Keith was within thirty yards of the truck now. From behind the big maple tree, he took aim at the man on the porch. It was about a sixty-yard shot, and the light was fading. As he aimed, he noticed one of the men turn around, and he ducked behind the tree, out of sight.

The driver yelled at the man on the porch. "Hurry up!" He turned to a man climbing into the truck. "Go with him." He looked behind at the men tossing the last of the meat into the bed. "You two, go see what those guys are doing down there at the roadblock. It sounded like they were getting carried away."

The two men started past the smokehouse, down the hill. The man on the porch wrenched on the door and splintered the wood as he tore it open. He was in the house. Keith heard two thunderous booms from where Joe and Tim were positioned.

"What the..." The driver started, pulling a rifle from the truck. Keith didn't let him finish. He sent a bullet through the open window of the driver's door and into the driver's ear. The driver's helmet flew up two feet in the air with the top of his skull still inside. It bounced off the hood of the truck as he crumpled onto the ground. The man in the front yard turned and ran to the truck, spraying bullets toward the big maple tree. Keith fired, missed, and ducked behind the tree as he worked the lever. Out of the corner of his eye, he thought he saw a man running away from the house toward the east through the backyard. The truck began to roll forward, and the driver slammed the door shut.

Keith heard a crack from inside the house. He could hear a dog barking. Then, he heard a boom from behind the smokehouse.

The truck stopped suddenly and rolled back as the back tire ran into the body of the previous driver. The engine revved, and Keith could hear the crunching of bones. The truck rolled out to the end of the driveway, and as it came abreast of the big maple tree, the driver looked to his right and saw the flash of Keith's rifle muzzle. The truck revved and launched across the road, through the mailbox on the other side, and into a tree. The trailer doors swung open, and the animals began rushing out into the yard. The carcass lay on the horn, and Keith opened the door and pulled the body across the seat. The horn stopped blaring, and the tires quit spinning as a geyser of steam shot out of the smashed radiator.

Keith chambered another round and moved to the trailer where terrified chickens were flying past and squawking.

"I'm coming!" came a shout from the house. The man stepped out onto the porch with his back turned to the truck. In his right hand, he held a revolver, and in his left, he was dragging a woman by the hair. Emma. "This slut shot me!" He bellowed as he dragged her down the steps. Blood dripped from his jacket and ran down the leg of his jeans.

Emma flailed and clawed at him. He stumbled down the steps and struck her in the face with the butt of the revolver.

Tim ran out from behind the smokehouse with his gun raised. "Stop it!" he roared.

The man pointed the pistol at him.

Keith fired a round just over his head and shouted, "Drop the gun!"

The man turned around. "What?" He seemed delirious. Maybe from blood loss, maybe drugs. Maybe both. "What is this!"

Keith didn't dare take the shot in the twilight with Emma so close. The dog was barking inside. Just then, one of the children ran out of the house toward the man.

"No, baby!" Emma screamed, grabbing the gun in the man's hand. She hung on his arm as the little boy ran at him with a baseball bat.

The man kicked the boy in the head, sending the boy to the ground. He punched Emma once more in the face, and she collapsed at his feet. Keith fired and hit the man in the back. He stumbled forward, spun around, and fired his pistol at Keith who ducked behind the trailer.

The eldest daughter crawled out onto the deck with tears streaming down her face and blood running from her nose. Her hand was wrapped tightly around the barking dog's collar, and she let it go.

The golden retriever leapt off the porch and sprinted toward the man.

"Get him, Jimmy!" the girl screamed through her tears.

The man held his hands up to shield his face, and Jimmy jumped over Emma's body and sank his teeth into the man's right arm, yanking him to the ground. In less than three seconds, the dog shredded the sleeve of the man's coat, and blood poured from the mangled arm. The revolver was dropped in the grass, and the dog went for the man's neck. The man pulled out a knife with his left hand and jammed it into the dog's ribs until it lay still.

Keith was within thirty yards now, and as the man struggled to his feet, Keith fired, hitting him in the left shoulder and sending the knife sailing out of his hand. The bullet nearly tore his arm off. He stumbled around with the arm dangling by a strip of skin, white splinters of pulverized bone dropping from the spurting mess, blood running down his chest and legs. Then, he fell down with a dull thud. Keith walked up to the man and pressed his smoking muzzle against his eye. The body didn't move. He turned and opened the door to the truck and killed the engine. A shot rang out from up the road. A minute passed, and another was heard. Then, stillness. There was no gunfire now. It seemed to be over.

Tim was crying as he held his son in his lap and lay beside Emma in the grass. She was alive and conscious, but just barely. Her face was bleeding and swelling up. The boy had a knot on his head and a concussion, most likely.

The girl in the doorway of the house called out: "Papa? Are you okay, Papa? Are they dead?"

"No, baby, they're going to be okay. They're not dead."

"How's Jimmy?"

Tim choked on his tears. "I think Jimmy's gone, baby."

The girl cried as she ran to hug her parents.

Keith kicked the bodies as he walked along the driveway. Chickens clucked wildly from the excitement. There was no telling where the pigs and goats went. "Joe!" he yelled. He didn't hear a response. "Joe!" He shouldered his rifle. It was empty anyway. He pulled out his pistol and a flashlight from his backpack. The batteries were running low, but he was determined to get all he could out of them before throwing away such a valuable and nonrenewable resource. He found the bodies of the two meat thieves lying in the ditch. One was still breathing. His face was shredded from birdshot. His eyes were gone, as were his teeth. Foamy blood bubbled out of his mouth and nose and a dozen holes in his neck as he lay on his side, gurgling. If he was any other animal, Keith would put him out of his misery. He pointed the pistol at the man's head, but he didn't do it. He needed to find Joe.

Studying the leaves in the soggy ditch, Keith moved toward the south along the bank. He shined his flashlight in front of him. Then, he saw a body lying face down in the ditch. He nearly collapsed. It was Joe.

He holstered his pistol. He couldn't breathe. The lump in his throat was enough to choke him. His eyes welled up, and the mucus ran from his nose down his lip. "Joe?" He trembled. "It's me. Keith." His voice quivered and cracked.

"I know it's you. Get down. There's another one out there."

Keith was startled, but he dropped to the ground beside his brother, and shined the light on his face.

Joe shut his eyes and turned away from the light. "Turn that light off, idiot."

Keith killed the light and began breathing again. His heart was still racing, his ears ringing. He struggled to get his breathing under control. "Are you okay?" he asked finally.

"Yeah. You?"

"Yeah."

"A guy ran out of the barn when we started shooting. He looked like he was going to shoot at you, but then, he took off running. I think I winged him though. I shot, and he hit the ground. But then, he got back up and ran toward the woods over there."

"Alright." Keith's hand was still on Joe's back, patting him like a dog. He didn't even realize he was doing it until he stopped. He collected his thoughts.

"What do you think we should do?" Joe asked.

"Let's get out of this ditch. If we can't see him, he can't see us."

"What if he has night vision goggles or something?"

"He doesn't. Come on." Keith got up, and the two of them walked back to the Faulkners' front lawn.

A man came out with a lantern. He held it up and surveyed the carnage. From the glow of the flame, Keith could see it was Brad Nielson. He looked pitiably down at the dog, tiptoed around the blood and meat particles in the driveway, and announced himself to Tim. "Tim, it's Brad Nielson. Are you all alright?"

"Not really, Brad," came an exhausted response. Then, he added, "We're alive though."

Keith and Joe stepped out into the driveway. "It's Keith and Joe here."

"Boys." Tim choked. "My wife. My kids." He began to cry again. "Look what they've done."

"Let's get them inside," Joe said. "It's cold out here."

With Brad's help, they got Emma and the injured boy out of the yard and onto their beds in the house. The house was chilly, and Brad noticed that their fire had gone out. He went outside to get firewood and began building a fire in the woodstove. When he shut the doors to the woodstove, he said with an awkward smile, "There. That oughtta do it." The lantern glowed across his strange grin. "Is there anything more I can do for you?" he said to Tim.

The children came up the stairs and entered the room. They hugged their father silently, and he picked the youngest up and held him on his lap. He glared into Brad's face with a look of fury and contempt. "No, Brad. I don't need you to build my fire or light my lanterns or offer your sympathy. I needed a neighbor with a damn gun to stop those blood-thirsty savages from raiding my house and beating my wife and children right in front of him. Where were you then?" His voice was raised to the point of almost shouting. The children watched from behind the table.

Brad hung his head, unable to meet Tim's eyes. "I'm sorry, Tim. I—I—was just scared—I didn't know what to do—I..." His voice quivered. "I'm sorry." He turned and left, stumbling down the stairs. Keith watched through the window as he slumped back to his house across the road. The man held the lantern at his side, as if he didn't have the strength to lift it anymore. He tripped over the body of the dog and fell on his hands and knees into the bloody grass. He got up, whimpering, and crossed the road.

Tim squeezed the child who couldn't have been more than two, and he looked up at Keith and Joe. Behind him, the older children began whispering to each other and getting things to make tea for their mother and siblings. The four-year-old took cookies from a jar and wrapped them up in cloth napkins as carefully as Christmas presents.

Keith wiped the blood from his hands onto his pant leg. It was Emma's blood, and likely, some had come from her attacker. Her dress was drenched with it. "We'll go get the doctor," he said. As he turned for the door, Tim began to speak.

"I'm sorry. I shouldn't have said that to him. It wasn't his fault." Tim's lip began to quake. "I couldn't do it either. I didn't even fire the first shot." Tears rolled down his cheeks.

Keith looked at him. He went to pat his shoulder but saw the blood on his hand and stopped. "That's okay, Tim. You did good. We'll bring the doctor."

Joe followed Keith out the door, and they walked in the darkness, through the woods behind the houses, treading lightly in the shadows and the moonlight. They could see the faint glow of evanescent candlelight flickering between the gaps in the makeshift curtains of the windows of the Rawlings house as they followed a game trail through the brush. They emerged from the trees into the long gravel driveway and made their way to the front door.

At the first knock, there was a rush for the door, and Faye opened it with an anxious gasp as if she had not breathed since they left. Her face was red, her eyes moist, and she looked at the blood on their clothes and hands. "What happened? Are you hurt?" Kent stood behind her, and he set his shotgun down to lean against the wall.

"We're okay. It's not our blood." Keith set his rifle on the table. "It's Emma's. She's hurt." He grabbed a box of .44 magnum ammunition and began to reload his rifle. Then, he put another box in his backpack as Joe put shells in his coat pockets. "We could use your help, Malik. There might be a lot of people hurt."

CHAPTER TEN

"Okay," Malik said, beginning to pack a bag.

"Make sure you bring a light."

Faye put her hand over her mouth. "What happened?"

"I'll tell you later." He took out his water bottle and realized that he had not had any water in hours. Suddenly, he could feel how dry his mouth was. He gulped down what was in the bottle, refilled it with water from one of the jars, and drank that too. He poured water for Joe, who did the same. When they both had their bottles refilled, they put them back in their bags and started for the door.

Malik grabbed his bag and his shotgun and went to join the brothers. He kissed Jordan on his way out and said, "Okay, let's go."

"Not so fast," Jordan said. "I'm coming too. I can help."

Malik looked at her as if about to forbid it, but she stared him back in the face as if to say that it was no use; she would not be dissuaded.

"Don't go back out there! Why do you have to go?" Faye nearly shouted.

"If not us, who?" Keith replied.

"I'm coming too," Lynn said.

Keith shook his head. "Lynn, I am not lying when I say I need you to stay here and guard the house. There might be more out there." With that, they left.

Malik and Jordan followed the brothers along the game trail through the woods, back to the Faulkner house where Tim showed them to the patients. Keith and Joe left them there and went up the road to check on the others. There were lights glowing all along the southern mile of the road now—lanterns. Their yellow orbs of luminescence swayed through the darkness in strings and clusters across the hillside. Voices in the night—calls for help echoed through the valley.

The brothers hiked down the hill past Ernie Jacobs' farmhouse. The sulfurous stench of cordite still lingered in the air and mixed with the smoke and fumes of burning oil. In Ernie's long driveway, a smoking ruin of a truck with

241

shattered glass and blown-out tires was leaking fluids. A body lay in the ditch. Keith probed it with his rifle as he walked past the truck. Joe held his shotgun at the ready and swept the scene with the beam of his flashlight. The horse trailer was jackknifed behind the truck, its doors hanging open, creaking in the breeze. A body lay behind the trailer in a pool of steaming blood.

Ernie's door was open, and they could hear a scuttling in the house as they approached. Someone was crying inside.

"Ernie!" Keith shouted from outside the house. "It's Keith and Joe Rawlings. Is anyone hurt?"

A woman came to the door. It was one of the nurses. "Yes. Come in. Ernie's hurt bad. Follow me."

They followed her inside and saw Ernie lying on the bed, unconscious and covered in blood. His head was wrapped in bandages. His wife sat in a chair by his side, crying.

"He's got a broken arm and a gunshot wound to the head," the nurse said. "It just grazed him, but it knocked him out. He's still breathing, but he's bleeding pretty bad."

"Is there anything we can do to help?" Joe asked.

"I can stop the bleeding, but I don't feel comfortable trying to set the bone. Can you get Malik?"

"We'll bring him." Keith nodded. "He's working on the Faulkners right now, but we'll get him after we check on everyone else."

"Thank you."

The brothers turned to leave, but they were stopped by a voice, trembling with rage and excitement. "Boys." It was Mrs. Jacobs. She wiped the tears from her face. "He took one of them bastards with him."

"Yes, ma'am." Keith replied.

"We'll be back," Joe said as they left the house.

They walked up the hill toward the Tyler house, which stood at the junction of a quarter-mile-long, dead-end road branching off from Mount Sinai at a ninety-degree bend about a half mile from the highway. The Tylers were kin to the Winters family, and they too kept horses. Keith and

Joe thought they could remember hearing a lot of shooting coming from the bend at the top of the hill, and as they continued walking, they saw many more lanterns and flashlights gathered above them on the ridge. Halfway up the hill, they found a horse lying on the side of the road. Gritty, green sludge oozed from a hole in the horse's belly and the putrid steam tainted the air. The horse was dead, an effusion of blood running down the slope of the blacktop in a stream stemming from a hole near the creature's ear. Its stiffening limbs and neck were contorted in a grotesque pose of agony. The brothers hiked on.

There was shouting on the hilltop as people announced themselves and rushed to help their neighbors. Joe shouted to the Tylers who were trying to corral their horses back into the barn. "It's Joe and Keith Rawlings. Is Jack Winters here?" The horses were still running frantically through the grass.

"No!" came a response. "They need help up at the church! He's probably up there!" The man and two women were trying to calm a horse that was spinning around in panic. "Whoa!" The man shouted as the horse ran toward him, nearly knocking him down.

On the ground beside the house, two women were holding pressure on a child's stomach. The child was squirming beneath the women's hands. "It's alright, baby. Momma's here." A shaking voice said in the darkness. She looked at the brothers. "They shot him. They shot my baby."

Keith could see in the glow of the lantern on the ground beside them, their hands were coated with blood. "Get his shirt off," Keith said. He took off his backpack and knelt down beside them, pulling out a trauma kit and packaged rolls of gauze. He remained silent as he opened the package and handed the gauze to one of the women. She looked to be a teenager, probably the boy's sister. "Pack it into the hole," he said softly. "Finger over finger." He motioned to her how to do it. "That's it. Use it all." He pulled another roll from the package.

Joe was feeling sick. "What can I do?" he asked.

Keith looked back at him. "Run and get Malik as quick as you can."

Joe took off down the hill.

"Any exit wound?" Keith said softly.

The sister held pressure over the gauze as they gently rolled the boy's whimpering body over on its side. Keith gingerly wiped the blood away from the child's back but didn't see any holes. The flesh was a dark, greenish purple, and as they peeled the wet shirt up over his shoulders, Keith saw a lump protruding from the boy's shoulder blade. The skin around it was nearly black with contusion. The boy was quiet now.

"Keep him warm," Keith said. "The doctor's coming." He knew the child would die, but he pulled out a compression bandage and began to wrap it around the boy's waist, tight enough to hold the gauze in place but not tight enough to restrict his breathing.

They carried him inside on a blanket, laid him on the couch, and cut away the coat and shirt. With his head propped on a pillow, the mother knelt beside him, stroking his hair and singing to him softly as the sister draped blankets over his small body.

Keith went back outside to get the doctor. Lights were bouncing down the road. They rounded the corner at the base of the hill, and after a couple minutes, he heard footsteps running up the hill toward him. "Joe?" he shouted as the lights came nearer.

"It's us," came Joe's heavily breathing voice.

Malik reached the top of the hill first, followed by Jordan. "Where is he?" Malik panted, unslinging his duffel bag full of medical supplies.

"Inside." Keith led them into the house.

Joe waited on the porch, sipping water until Keith reemerged from the doorway.

"Let's go," Keith said. "We have to find Jack."

They took off jogging toward the old church, and both nearly tripped over a body lying in the road. Keith shined a light on the face. "Pirate," he said. They each grabbed a leg, dragged the corpse over to the ditch, and kept going.

As they crested the rise, the blackness of night was offset by a radiant orange blaze rising from the church. Neighbors were running buckets of water from the well at the farm across the train tracks. The flames spiraled from broken windows.

"It's Keith and Joe Rawlings," Keith shouted as they approached.

"Here!" came a voice from the well. "Grab buckets!" A woman was filling buckets of water as the men dropped them and took the refilled buckets to the church.

Keith and Joe began running buckets and flinging water into the flames.

For half an hour or more, they battled the fire until the church was saved. The choking stench of burnt carpet and insulation fumes dominated the air. With damp cloth masks, flashlights, and digging tools, several men picked through the smoldering debris, snuffing out any residual embers. They choked and spat as they walked around the scene.

As the two brothers looked for Jack Winters, they saw the blockade of cars had been smashed apart. A car had been dragged away from the blockade and shoved off the road by one of the trucks. It was lying upside down in the watery depression on the east side of the road with one side crushed in. Another of the cars had its rear end smashed and was spun around ninety degrees from its original position. There was broken glass and coolant all over the road, shimmering green in the beams of their flashlights. They shined lights on the faces of the bodies they encountered. How many were there? they wondered. They had passed four vehicles on the road up to the church.

"Where did they come from?" a woman's voice asked from a few feet away. They didn't know whose it was.

"Who knows?" Joe answered. "They look like some of the road pirates we ran into a few weeks back."

"Road pirates? Is that what you call them?"

"Well, that's what they are, isn't it?"

"I guess so," the voice said. "I think there were five vehicles."

"Six," a man's voice said. "Four of them drove past me down the road. One stopped on the other side of the train tracks. Five guys got out of that one to block off the road from the cul-de-sac. We shot two of them, and the other three got back in and took off. The other truck is behind Bill Campbell's barn over there."

"Two cars and four trucks. Probably thirty pirates," Keith said. "They came for the livestock."

"Pirates? Yeah, that's the right word for 'em, I reckon," the man said. "Who are you guys?"

"Joe and Keith Rawlings," Joe replied.

"Rawlings? You all live across from Fred and Donna Packard?"

"That's right."

"Did they go past you?"

"The other blocker car stopped at the Packards' place. They were trying to clear the houses on either side of the road when we engaged them," Keith said.

"You get any?"

"Yeah," Joe said.

"They shot up the Packards' house pretty good though. We haven't checked on them yet. We need to find all the wounded and take care of them. We've been looking for Jack Winters. Have you seen him?"

"I thought I heard him yelling back behind Bill Campbell's, but there was so much noise, I don't know," the woman said.

"We'll keep an eye out for him and tell him you're looking for him if we see him," the man said. "You know, I think the guy that lived in the old church got killed. I haven't seen him since the whole thing started."

"Well, we have enough wounded neighbors who are still alive to worry about," Keith said, walking away.

"What can we do to help?" The woman asked.

"We could use Ben Jameson's tractor and wagon right now," Keith replied.

"We'll find him," she said.

Keith and Joe continued walking across the tracks toward the old farmer's barn. Corpses lay all about the truck. One beside the grain bin. One beside the house. They kicked them as they walked by. Shining lights on the faces of the dead, they came across a teenager staring up blankly at the sky. His face was pale, and steaming blood saturated his coat. It was one of the deputies, Jack Winter's eldest son. The brothers closed their eyes and shook their heads as they walked on.

Behind the barn, they found a man sitting on the ground in front of a body. Jack Winters stared blankly as if in a trance. The brothers announced themselves as they approached. Jack was silent, and in the beam of Keith's flashlight, they saw blood running down the man's arm and pooling in the mud beside him. Then, the flashlight shone on the pale, lifeless face of the body in front of him, and Keith switched the light off. It was Jack's daughter. The brothers sat down on the ground beside Jack, silent for several minutes, listening to the sounds of animals being corralled in the distance, muffled voices calling for help, and Jack's slow, rhythmic breathing. Then, Jack began to speak.

"I had to shoot my horse," he said quietly. "He was gut shot." He paused for half a minute. "I was trying to get to my kids... I was too late... My daughter's dead... My son's lying just over there." He took a deep breath. "How do I tell their mother?"

"You raised them right, Jack," Joe said. "They saved a lot of lives."

"I know they did. Will you help me bury them?"

"Yes," Joe whispered. "They'll be buried as heroes."

Jack breathed deeply again. "Thank you." And he was silent for another minute.

"Jack, you're bleeding," Keith said.

"Oh—yeah. I think I got shot."

"We need to get you to the doctor. Let me help you," Keith said.

"What's the use? Who cares?"

"You still have a family that needs you, Jack. We all need you."

Down the road, they could hear the sound of Ben Jameson's tractor chugging along. Through the swaying, leafless tree branches, they could see the tractor and its wagon coming up the road and stopping periodically, followed by a procession of lanterns and flashlights as neighbors loaded the dead and wounded onto the wagon with a paramedic who crouched beneath the light of a lantern fastened to a post.

"Alright." Jack allowed Keith to look at the wound and bandage the arm. The fact that he was still conscious proved that a tourniquet was not needed.

Keith applied gauze to the buckshot holes in the arm and wrapped it tight with a pressure bandage as Joe hailed the tractor. "You'll need to have someone take the shot out of your arm," Keith said, helping the man to his feet.

They loaded the bodies into the wagon, leaving the pirates to rigidify on the ground. Jack refused to ride in the wagon; he walked beside it instead, with his hand on the side panel, all the way back to Jim Baker's barn where they set up a makeshift hospital ward. The wounded were unloaded and taken inside where a fire was being built in the stove and nurses were collecting cots and mattresses for their patients. Then, Ben turned the tractor around and delivered the dead to their families.

Keith and Joe helped carry Jack's children into the house. They said nothing to the family members as they did so. What was there to say? Keith had expected Mrs. Winters to scream at her husband for putting her children in danger. He thought she would collapse to the floor and cry or lash out with fists thrown at Jack and perhaps themselves. What she did when she opened the door was what he least expected. She clutched a chair for support, her white knuckles clenched around the wood, tears running silently down her face. She said nothing as Jack wrapped his arms around her. Her face was like stone as she stoically stared ahead, bearing the weight of death. Jack's two youngest children stood beside her in the oppressive silence. Jack hugged them, kissed them, and wiped the tears from his eyes. Keith and Joe laid the bodies on two couches in the living room. They looked at the family watching them, Mrs. Winters' cold eyes piercing through them. Keith tried to think of something to say. He couldn't. He bowed his head and stepped out of the house. Joe followed.

The brothers walked back up the road to the Tyler house. The horses were back in their barn, and men and women were pushing the truck out of the driveway and dragging the bodies of the pirates away from the house, piling them up in a ditch. Malik and Jordan were still inside when Keith knocked on the door.

Jordan answered with a finger to her lips. "He didn't make it," she said.

Keith nodded in understanding. Malik was packing up his supplies inside. They could hear the muffled sobs of the family members as Malik offered his condolences and came to the door.

"Ernie Jacobs needs you," Keith said as Malik exited the house.

"Take me to him."

They marched down the hill and up Ernie's driveway, past the truck and trailer to the front door. Upon knocking, they were shown in by Mrs. Jacobs. The nurse had left to attend to the patients in Jim Baker's barn. Mrs. Jacobs explained that Ernie was left there because there was nothing more the nurse could do for him and moving him would likely do more harm than good.

Malik studied the unconscious man lying in the bed. He looked at the bandaged head and examined the broken arm. Consulting his medical books for a couple of minutes, he asked Mrs. Jacobs if she had any alcohol. She went to the kitchen and came back with a bottle of bourbon from the liquor cabinet. She handed the bottle to him, and he pulled the cork and took a long drink.

"I thought you needed that to treat him," she objected.

"I do," he said. "I've never done this before, and I don't have the equipment to do it correctly. I have to set the bone. If I don't, he'll never be able to use the arm again. If I do it wrong, the bone won't fuse together properly, and it will break again." He took another pull from the bottle.

Mrs. Jacobs reached for the bourbon. He handed it to her, and she took a gulp as well.

"Lucky for him, he's unconscious," Malik said, running his fingers over the break in the arm. "Here goes." He took the arm in both hands and twisted the bone back into place, and he wrapped the arm in a cloth bandage. Then, he took two pieces of tin roofing and folded them around the bandaged arm, holding the splints in place while Jordan wrapped the makeshift cast with a long strip of cloth and tied it off tightly.

Malik looked at the gauze taped to Ernie's other arm. "Did the nurse give him an IV?"

"Yes," she answered.

He looked at the head again, listened to the man's breathing, and checked his pulse. "Well, there's nothing else I can do for him now. We'll have to wait until he wakes up."

"You think you did it right?" Mrs. Jacobs asked.

"I think so. It looks straight. Feels straight. But I'll check on him again when he's awake."

Mrs. Jacobs thanked him and gave him the bottle. He put it in his bag, slung his shotgun over his shoulder, and they left.

They drank from their water bottles and hiked up the hill to the east, back toward Jim Baker's barn in the valley. They were exhausted, and they hadn't eaten since morning. Keith glanced at his watch. It was morning now. It would be dawn in a couple of hours. Lightheaded and footsore, they continued on another two miles to the barn to care for the wounded and come up with a plan for what to do next. They wouldn't be able to sleep anyway. How could they? When so many people were dead and so many more would likely die from their wounds, no. No one would sleep now.

When they got to the barn, they found the building lit up with lanterns hanging from the rafters. People were scurrying about the place with towels and bandages. Keith and Joe stood in the corner, taking in the scene. There were neighbors coming in through the doors every few minutes, bringing small offerings of food and water, cleaning chemicals for the doctor's instruments, blankets, cots, pillows, and chairs for the injured and the nurses treating them. Eric and Lydia were distributing bowls of soup from a stock pot on the stove and helping some of the wounded to eat. Some had even brought changes of clothes to replace the torn, wet, bloodstained rags the patients wore. Even the hippies had come to help in whatever way they could, and they placed homemade scented candles around the barn to help cover the stench of blood and urine.

Keith and Joe scrubbed the blood from their hands with hot water and soap sitting on a washstand near the stove. Malik and Jordan were already at work, caring for patients. Some of the family members sat near their loved ones, praying, or talking to them in hushed tones. The neighbors left their contributions with Jim Baker or the preacher, and when they saw that they would only be in the way, many of them left.

Keith and Joe warmed themselves beside the woodstove for a few minutes and stepped outside. Jim was bringing in firewood. Ben Jameson was on the road, loading bodies into his wagon with several neighbors. Tim and Jack were at home. They would have to wait to discuss their next move. It was too soon. Keith's watch read 0513. The sun would be coming up before long. They needed to check in at the house, Keith said, and they began walking up the hill once again.

Joe put a pinch of tobacco in his mouth and offered some to Keith.

"You're running out," Keith said. "You keep it."

They walked for another minute in silence, and Keith could feel Joe thinking about something.

Joe spat. "Keith?"

"Yeah."

"It's not right to ask, but—have you done that before?"

"What?"

"You know what I'm talking about."

"Hmm." Keith understood. "That was the first time."

"I pissed myself," Joe said.

"Yeah. I did too."

They continued walking. The sky was clear now. They had never seen so many stars. They hardly needed flashlights to follow the road now. The moon and stars were brighter and more numerous than anyone had seen in well over a century.

"They were after the livestock," Joe said.

"Yeah."

"Well, I understand why they were at Tim's and Ernie's and the Tyler place, but what were they doing at Bill Campbell's farm? He doesn't have any livestock."

"Maybe they thought he did. They didn't seem to be that organized."

"Hmm. Maybe. You think they might have known something we don't?"

"I don't know," Keith replied. "But I have an idea of how they might have found out."

"Yeah, me too."

When they entered the house, Faye, Lynn, and Kent were all still awake. Kent answered the door with his shotgun. Faye and Lynn were sitting at the table working on a painting in the light of a single lantern.

"What's going on?" Kent asked, locking the door and setting his shotgun down.

The brothers explained the situation, leaving out as many details as possible. The family members listened in astonishment, though after hearing the shots, the engines, the shouting, and hours of the tractor going up and down the road in the night, they had started to expect as much.

Lynn got bowls and spoons and ladled some stew from the pot on the stove for them as they changed out of their bloody clothes and wet socks. They sat and ate and gulped down water, and after refilling their bottles, they went out again.

The stars were beginning to fade as the sky grew faintly tinged with red. At Tim Faulkner's house, they could see a light moving through the trees. They could hear the sounds of chickens clucking and the crunching of leaves. The brothers unslung their weapons and crept toward the disturbance. It appeared to be just one man messing around in the pen. Surely, it wasn't him, they thought. Could it be? Had they caught him in the act? They stepped lightly through the grass, toward the figure inside the fence behind the Faulkners' smokehouse. All around the man, the pigs, goats, and chickens swarmed with their noses to the ground.

"Put your hands in the air," Keith demanded.

The man dropped his flashlight on the ground and threw his hands up.

"Who are you?"

"Keith?" He turned around to look at them. "It's me. It's Brad Nielson. Quick! Shut the door! I finally got 'em all inside!"

The brothers lowered their weapons and closed the door to the fence. "What are you doing?"

"I was just trying to get the animals back in the pen," Brad said. "Just had to use a little food."

"What did you use?"

"Corn. I had a little saved up."

"You used your canned corn to get the animals back in the pen?" Joe said.

"Yeah. I had to. I cleaned off all the meat they took and hung it back in the smokehouse, by the way. So, you don't have to worry about that. It's still good."

"You're a good man, Brad." Joe noticed that the truck and trailer were gone along with all the bodies. Excepting the spent brass and blood-stained ground, the property was cleaned up like nothing had ever happened.

"It's the least I could do. I owe them. I owe you too. We all do, but me most of all. I'm sorry I wasn't there to help."

"Well, it's over now, anyway," Keith said. "We could use a carpenter's help on improving our security."

"Of course, I want to help."

"Alright. Let's go."

They left the Faulkners' property and headed back down the road once more in the dawn's vermillion flame. The wind had brought warmer temperatures, and the remaining ice and snow was quickly dissipating into mud. Already, squadrons of vultures were flying overhead. The crows swooped across the road in front of them as they walked. Rabbits darted into the brush, squirrels chattered in the trees, and a hawk eyed the men silently from a telephone pole as they passed. The woodsmoke hung in the air like a fog. According to one of the nurses, it had already killed two asthmatics on the road in the last few weeks. The disposable medical masks they had tried to use to protect them were utterly useless and did not avail them in the end.

They entered the barn and found Malik and Jordan sitting in chairs near the door. They looked indescribably fatigued. Someone had brought precious coffee to them and to the nurses and paramedic, and they sipped the elixir with relish, monitoring the stability of their patients as they did so. Keith approached the pair and asked how everything was going with them. Three of the dozen patients had already succumbed to their wounds, they informed him, and they expected a fourth to go any minute. Eric and Lydia Jorgenson were sitting beside the woman, reading from the Bible as she breathed sporadically in unconsciousness. Apparently, she had no family to stay with her, or if she did, they did not know where she was.

"Jack Winters came in about an hour ago," Malik said. "He looked terrible. Never said anything."

"Two of his kids were killed last night," Keith said.

At this, Brad put his hand to his mouth. His face went red, and his eyes began to water.

"God help them," Jordan said, shaking her head sorrowfully.

"He brought his own narcotic," Malik said. "Probably drank half a bottle of whiskey while I took the lead out of his arm."

"Where is he now?"

"I told him he needed to rest, but he got up and walked outside."

Keith nodded and looked at Joe standing beside him. Joe shook his head disapprovingly.

"You guys need anything from us?" Keith asked, looking back at Malik and Jordan.

"Other than a hospital, no."

"Thank you, guys, for what you're doing," Keith said. "It might not seem like it to you, but you're doing great. You're making a real difference."

"If you say so," Malik shrugged.

"You are." Keith turned to Joe and Brad. "Let's go."

Up the hill, they walked again, and when they came to Jack Winters' house, they saw the man himself, riding toward them on his son's horse and leading his daughter's behind him by the reins. His gaunt visage did not even acknowledge their presence as he rode by them on the lumbering horse. "Get the gate," he said flatly.

Joe hurried to open the gate to the corral, and the man led the horses inside. The left sleeve of his sheepskin coat was dark with drying blood. He slipped the reins of his daughter's horse over one of the Osage orange fence posts and climbed down from the horse he rode. The front door of the house opened, and his two remaining children came to the corral to help him.

"Put the saddles up, feed and brush the horses. And make sure they have clean water," he said.

"Yes, sir." The kids led the horses into the barn.

Jack watched them for a couple of seconds and turned to look at the three standing before him. His eyes hovered over Brad for a few seconds, and he turned his attention to the two brothers. "You get any sleep?"

"No," Joe said. "I don't think anyone slept last night."

Jack's cheek and lip twitched behind the gray-streaked stubble on his square jaw. "I don't think I'll sleep again," he said seriously. "Brad." He shifted his cruel gaze. "My horse is still lying on the hill just past Ernie Jacobs' place. The meat's still good. Get Jeremiah Davis to go with you in his truck. Cut it up and distribute it to anyone who needs meat."

"You sure, Jack?" Brad said hesitantly.

"Yes, damnit. It's no different than beef or venison. Just a little tougher. No sense in letting it go to waste." He breathed and put his hand to his wounded arm. "Will you do that for me, Brad?"

"Sure, Jack. I'll do it." Brad turned and began walking toward the machinist's house just up the road.

The three men watched him go for a few seconds, and Jack looked back at Keith and Joe. His eyes were full of hate and malice. His hands were shaking slightly. "Those mongrels weren't from around here," he said. "Someone told them about the livestock. They planned that attack. Someone told them where to go."

Joe glanced at his brother and back at Jack. "Last night, me and Keith was in a shootout with the pirates at Tim Faulkner's house. We got 'em all. But I saw one guy running out from behind Tim's barn after the shooting started. I shot at him, and I saw him hit the ground, but then, he got up and kept running. I think I hit him, but we never saw him again."

"Any idea who it was?"

"Yeah," Keith said. "We've got an idea. He didn't run toward the road or any of the vehicles. He went back in the woods behind that old trailer."

"That's right," Joe nodded.

"Let's find him," Jack said, snatching a coil of rope from a nearby fence post.

They hiked up the road to the Faulkner house and retraced Joe's steps to the ditch where he took the shot. The spent shell was lying in the leaves, where he had lain. They scanned the ground with weapons ready as they searched behind the barn. Keith picked up the plastic wad which had landed roughly thirty yards from the spent shell. They traced the imaginary line connecting the two points and stared intently at the leaves all around as they walked. Then, they found it. About ten yards past the wad, was a leaf flecked with blood. It lay in a trail of compressed and overturned leaves scattered by running feet. A couple yards from the first specks of blood was a divot in the leaf litter where a body had fallen, and more blood appeared on the leaves. They had a trail, and they followed the upturned leaves and specks of blood past a grimy, white trailer, along an old logging trail, back into the woods.

They scanned the surrounding trees as they went, alert, treading lightly, and listening for the slightest sound of movement. Nearly a quarter mile from the right-of-way clearing behind the trailer, they saw a derelict cabin made of rotting, moss-covered boards. The men halted, looked at one another, and listened. The sun was cresting the trees now, and the horizon had changed from red to orange to yellow. Birds chirped and flitted through the air, alighting on branches around the cabin. A woodpecker drummed away at a nearby tree. The flecks of blood sporadically speckling leaves had increased to steady droplets, and they led directly to the cabin. They saw no signs of human activity. There were beer cans and cigarette butts and trash scattered about the area, but they saw no signs of traps or anyone watching them.

They crept toward the cabin quietly, and as the brothers held their guns on the door, Jack slung his rifle across his back, took the rope from his shoulder, and tied it into a lasso.

He looked at the brothers and nodded, and then, he threw all his weight behind his boot and kicked the door in. The door burst open with a crash, and the occupant, who was sleeping on a cot inside, jumped up with a startled yelp as Jack dropped the noose over his head and yanked him to the floor by his neck. The man grabbed at the rope and flailed around in the dirt as Jack half dragged him out of the cabin. The choking man snatched a knife from off a chair by the door and tried to cut the rope, but Jack kicked his hand, sending the knife bouncing off the wall behind him. He crawled forward on his knees and one hand as Jack pulled him out into the mud and leaves in front of the cabin door.

Neither Keith nor Joe had seen him in years, but looking at the man now, they were sure this was their cousin Derek.

Jack pinned the criminal on the ground with his knee between his shoulder blades and loosened the rope just a bit, letting the man gasp for air as he untied the prisoner's boots and pulled them off his feet. With one hand, he pulled out the shoelaces and lashed the detainee's wrists together behind his back. Jack stood up and flicked the rope with his right hand. "Get up."

The prisoner pulled his knees under him and struggled to his feet. His pants sagged around his thighs. His unzipped coat revealed a t-shirt three sizes too large for his meager frame. He wore fake diamond earrings and had what appeared to be two teardrops tattooed beneath the corner of one eye. His coat was stained with blood, and insulation protruded from tiny holes in the sleeve. His bare hand was also wrapped with a strip of cloth saturated with blood.

"What were you doing last night?" Jack demanded.

The prisoner did not answer but gasped for air.

"Did you bring them here? Did you tell them to come here?"

The man didn't answer. He stared Jack in the face with a contemptuous grimace and spat at him.

"What were you doing at Faulkner's house last night?"

He refused to answer. Between breaths, he cursed them with the lyrics of every rap he ever listened to, and they dragged him along the logging trail, barefoot and struggling to hold his pants up enough to walk with his hands tied behind his back.

They marched him up the road in the sight of onlooking neighbors who stopped their work and watched the spectacle. People put down their splitting mauls, dropped the firewood they were carrying, and ceased cleaning up the wreckage left by the thieves, and a growing number of followers accumulated behind the men on their way up to the church. The cavalcade proceeded quietly with only whispers from the following crowd. The prisoner had abandoned his bravado; the ominous scene and the gravity of the moment were taking their toll on his bearing, and he began sniffling in futile attempts to stifle his fearful whimpers.

At the church, neighbors had dug out the charred body of the man who had lived there for the past five years. They wrapped the body in a sheet from inside the church. As most of the building remained unburnt, it seemed that the man had most likely died before the building ever caught fire, likely shot while trying to stop the breech of the blockade.

Ben Jameson and a few other neighbors had loaded the corpses of the attackers onto his wagon and brought them to the church, having no idea what else to do with them. Two of them, they had found, were still breathing—one who had apparently taken a load of birdshot to the face and a second who had probably received a 12-gauge slug in the vest, rupturing some internal organs. They loaded the two on the cart with all the rest and brought them to the church to decide what to do with them.

"They're not worth a bullet," one man said, using a clichéd movie line to try to mollify the deadly intent on the faces of the crowd.

"No, they aren't," Jack responded. "We can't afford to waste bullets, but we can reuse rope."

"Jack." The man put his hand up as if he could calm the storm inside this man.

Jack turned his malevolent stare at the man; his contemptuous, piercing eyes stopped him in his tracks. The man looked down, turned, and walked away from the crowd, shaking his head.

They hurled ropes over the crossarms of telephone poles on either side of the highway and unceremoniously hanged the three men for murder. Then, they piled the corpses of the pirates, stripped of their armor and gear, on the highway, in front of the reassembled blockade. And they left them there as a warning to outsiders, and they left the bodies of the hanged men to dangle from the beams, high above the landscape, swinging and spinning around the poles in the warm, wet southern wind.

Chapter Eleven

Day 31

Jack Winters said nothing as he stared at the bodies hanging above the highway. Without a word, he turned and walked away, back down the road toward home. The crowd was quiet. In ones and twos, they dispersed, with heads down and somber expressions.

The brothers walked back across the tracks and stopped at Bill Campbell's driveway. Several trees were marred and missing patches of bark where bullets had struck. One of the windows of the farmhouse was shattered, and the grain bins were riddled with holes. From the road, they noticed something peculiar in the morning sun. At the base of one of the bins was a small patch of yellow that stood out from the gray of concrete and galvanized steel and the brown of dead grass.

"What is that?" Joe said aloud.

Bill and his wife emerged from the barn with a piece of plywood, presumably to board up the broken window. They looked at the brothers who were coming toward them.

"Y'all okay?" Keith said as they approached.

"Yeah, we're alright," the old man replied.

Keith responded, "Can we help you with anything?"

"No, thank you. We can manage."

"We couldn't help but notice your grain bins took some shots. I think you're losing some product."

"What?" The old man set the board down and went to look at the grain bins. Keith and Joe followed him as he noticed the leaking holes and tried to hide them. From the holes in the metal, dried kernels of corn were dropping. "You're not supposed to see this."

"Relax. Your secret's safe with us. We're just wondering what it's doing here."

"The robbers didn't get the bin opened up, so I thought it was safe. I didn't think to check for bullet holes."

"Is that normal for farmers to have grain bins full of corn in late winter?"

"No. No, it's not. But the corn prices were so bad this season, that I would have just barely broke even if I had sold in December. So, I held out for good prices. I kept waiting all through December, and that turned into January without a change in prices. I kept holding out, and in February, it went up enough for me to finally sell it, but I only got one truck-load to market when everything went dark. That bin's been sitting three-quarters full since February Fifth."

"And you harvested in..."

"In November."

"How long can that corn keep?"

"Not that long without the fan blowing on it. I kept it a little drier than most. About eleven percent moisture. But that's because it sat in the bin so long, I was worried about mold, and I kept the fan running more than normal. Now, it's been sitting in there for over a month without the fan going. I don't know how much will be good by spring."

"Why don't you sell some of it?" Keith asked.

"I don't know that I want anyone to know about it being here. I know people are hungry, but I have to make sure I have something to plant in the spring. If I let on that there's several tons of corn up here, just sitting in the bins, then I'm likely to cause a run."

"I don't think that's going to happen. People aren't going to risk it after they see those thieves hanging up there." Keith shook his head. "No, they'll trade. And we're going to make sure we have the rule of law on this road. No one's going to ignore the sheriff now."

"I don't like having all my eggs in one basket," the old man said. "You'll forgive me if I'm not as trusting as I used to be."

"Look, we'll help you patch up the bin and keep people from seeing the corn. We can move half of it over to your other bin, if you like, so you know you'll have some set aside for planting."

The old man looked at the ground and put his hands in his pockets. "Can't do that."

"Why not?" Keith said.

The man looked around and muttered. "It's full."

"Full of what?"

The man spat on the ground, drew in a breath, and said in a low voice, "Corn."

Keith and Joe began to laugh. Their tired faces lit up with exhilaration and something like obscene joy at the absurdity of the situation.

"Shh! Keep your voices down," the old man said.

"I'm sorry," Keith said, shaking his head. "But you can't possibly plant all that corn. And you said, yourself, it's going bad. What if we could get those fans running again? We could save it before it spoils."

"You might be able to rig something to run the fans, but it won't be as efficient."

"Right, but it will be better than nothing. So, you could sell a lot of your corn for animal feed, and maybe we could get some help with putting together a system to keep the rest dry long enough to replant it."

"I don't know."

"What choice do you have? Are you really going to let all this mold and rot when people need animal feed and you could sell it to them?"

The old farmer looked at the grain bins for a minute, thinking. "I reckon you're right. It's no good to anyone if it spoils."

The brothers helped to cover the piles of corn which had spilled from the holes in the bin, and they put duct tape over the rags they stuffed into the holes. They again promised not to tell anyone about the corn without his permission, told him they would come back to help him with the fans, and they left.

As they walked down the road, Joe put his hand on his head as if trying to trap a thought inside. "Did we ever check on the Packards?"

"What?"

"Those guys that set up the roadblock at the Packards— they tried breaking into the house. It looked like one of 'em got shot through the door. They shot up the house, and we killed 'em all, but did we ever go back and see if the Packards were okay?"

"With all the trips we've made up and down the road, I don't remember."

"I don't think we did."

When Keith and Joe approached the door, they knocked and heard no reply. No one answered the door. The windows were still shattered, and the siding was riddled with bullet holes. The walls were scorched and smelled like creosote. Keith knocked again. He reached for the doorknob and found it to be locked. "That's weird," he said. "I swear I saw one of them shoot through the latch."

"You did," Joe confirmed.

"How's the door locked?"

"Hmm. I guess they must have fixed it. That means they're not dead. They can't be hurt too badly either." Joe smiled a little with his bloodshot eyes struggling to stay open. "Even now, they won't talk to us."

They turned to go.

When they got home, they were so exhausted they didn't even make it to their beds before they fell asleep. Almost as soon as they sat down in the chairs, their heads hit the table, and they slipped from consciousness.

Day 32

They buried thirteen of their neighbors the next day. The temperature had risen to the low fifties, and at the cemetery behind the scorched, old church, the bodies were interred within the all-receptive earth. More than a dozen neighbors helped with the burial. Eric Jorgenson delivered the funeral eulogy, and at Keith's request, "Taps" was played on a trumpet. They were not military members, but they had certainly fallen in battle, defending what was left of the nation. The veterans of the community agreed, and no one objected. Lynn and Faye had attended the funeral, and as the bodies were being buried, after the ceremony had ended, they requested photographs of the deceased from the family members. When they returned home, they would begin working on memorials for the dead, starting with Jack Winters' children.

The word "hero," like most other words in the vernacular, had been tossed about with abandon in modern culture, to the point that it no longer meant anything. It was used to describe scientists, doctors, nurses, teachers, journalists, police, military personnel, politicians, lawyers, even criminals who had done nothing but victimize their fellow citizens their entire lives. People who spoke truth to power, people who spoke power to truth, and people who merely acted in their own self-interest while lending credence to a political narrative by pandering for wealth and position. "Hero" had become a word that meant whatever one's feelings wanted it to mean, or whatever one's narrative needed it to mean at the time. People wanted status, so they played up their selflessness, downplayed their sins, wrote memoirs about their incredible achievements, and were lauded by sycophants who expected and received similar treatment for their own lackluster accomplishments. With the prosperity and security created by modern innovations, life had become boring.

It seemed, there were no longer challenges to overcome, no longer great evils to fight. Rather than making heroes irrelevant, however, this morass had produced an increasing need for them. Meek and incompetent Americans had turned to films and video games for adventure and heroic deeds, living vicariously through increasingly preposterous characters who repeatedly saved the universe from contrived, two-dimensional villains, while telling lowbrow jokes. Making superhero movies was among the most marketable and profitable industries in the world. The demand for heroes had far outstripped the supply, so the culture had produced counterfeits. This, however, had only cheapened the term, and it served to exacerbate the meaningless stagnation of intellect that had dominated the old world. The residents of Mount Sinai no longer had that problem. The neighbors they buried were the genuine article, heroes who had lived among them. They had been killed in a battle they didn't choose, defending the lives of their neighbors, and they were victorious, even in death. Their deaths quite probably saved the lives of everyone on Mount Sinai, and above the Mount Sinai cemetery, the American flag was raised in their honor.

After the funeral, Faye and Lynn walked back with Rachel, Lydia, and Abigail. The women, along with the children and elderly neighbors, returned to their homes, leaving the men to dig. Most of them would honor the tradition of taking gifts of food to the bereaved, and they went to prepare their small offerings. Some of the older men, and a few of the women, were going to join Jim Baker in the barn to discuss their plans to improve security. There were still wounded patients in the barn, but not many. Some had been stabilized and taken home; others were being placed in their graves now.

Jack stayed until the job was done. With his wounded arm, he was not able to shovel much, but he was too proud and too reverent to leave the job for others to do for him. The men hardly spoke a word as they performed their task. The sound of shovels striking clay was all they heard besides whispers for help with lowering a body or getting out of a hole. When the job was done, Jack took his shovel, put his rifle in the scabbard, untied his horse, and rode back home in silence.

Eric Jorgenson helped to bury the dead, and he stayed behind, watching Jack Winters ride slowly down the road to the east. He stopped the brothers as they were collecting their things to leave. "Keith, Joe, may I talk to you?"

"Yes, sir." Joe turned around, putting the lid back on his water bottle.

"How's Jack doing?" asked the preacher, leaning on his shovel.

"Not too well," Joe answered. "But what can we expect?"

"He'll pull through," Keith added. "He's tough. He just needs some time."

"Mmhmm," the preacher nodded. He glanced at the bodies swinging from the telephone poles in the background and back at the brothers. "And you?"

"There's nothing wrong with us," Keith said a bit harshly. "We didn't get shot, and we didn't bury our family. We have nothing to complain about."

"I'm glad to hear it. Were you able to get some sleep last night?"

"Yes, sir," Joe replied.

"Why do you ask?" Keith pressed.

"I'm just concerned about you is all." The preacher put a hand on each brother's shoulder. "You fellas experienced a hard thing. I want you to know you've got people who are thinking of you."

"Thanks," Joe said. "You don't need to worry about us."

Eric nodded. "Keith, I haven't seen you at the service on Sundays. The door is always open, you know. Everyone needs to be a part of something bigger than himself, and it helps to have some people to socialize with." Keith said nothing, but the preacher turned his attention to Joe. "Have you talked to Rick lately?"

"No, we've been so busy with everything else. I've been meaning to," Joe said. "Have you?"

"Haven't seen him since the day we buried his mother."

Joe knocked on the door to Rick's house. They waited for a few seconds, and he knocked again.

"Maybe he's not home." Keith shrugged. "Does he have any friends around here?"

"Yeah. I think he's friendly with a guy down at the other end of the road."

"Well, we'll come back and check again. Come on."

The brothers continued down the hill toward Jim Baker's barn, where they found a score of neighbors gathered around the chalkboard on the wall. They had gathered the weapons and body armor collected from the pirates and laid them out against one wall of the barn. They had been arguing about who should get the weapons and gear. Some said it should be distributed to those who do not have weapons. Others said it should be given to the victims of the marauders as reparations. After a lengthy discussion, it was finally agreed that any neighbors who were not wise enough to have their own weapons and ammunition before the blackout should not be rewarded for their foolishness nor trusted with free weapons and gear with which they have no experience. The equipment would go to the fighters who had saved the community and done the work of securing the gear in the first place. They could do what they wanted with it. Anyone who wanted a piece of the repossessed armaments would have to buy it from someone willing to sell. There was some grumbling, but the vote was taken, and it was decided this was the most just course.

"So, now that that's settled," one man said. "Can someone explain what happened? I wasn't there."

"I wasn't either," Jim said.

"I was," another man added. "But I only saw what happened at the church. There was six vehicles. Two cars and four trucks with horse trailers. They drove up the highway from the south. One of the trucks was hooked up to one of the blockade cars with chains, and they drug the car off the road. By that time, the Winters deputies were shooting at them. I think the guy in the old church was shooting at them too, but I couldn't tell. They shot up the old church and threw fire-bombs through the broken windows. Another truck rammed into the blockade car that was right behind the first one and shoved it out of the way while they unhooked the first truck from the first car. Then, they all poured through in a line. That's when I went and got my gun. By the time I got back, I could only see one car. It was blocking off the cul-de-sac from the main road, so that was where I started shooting. I know that one of the trucks went to Bill Campbell's place, just across the road from me, but I don't know what happened anywhere else. Maybe Keith and Joe could tell you more. I talked to them the other night. They saw what happened down at the other end."

The group turned their attention to the two brothers. Keith went to the chalkboard and began drawing a map of the southern mile of Mount Sinai Road. "There were six vehicles. A car on either end of the convoy for roadblocks." He drew rectangles on the map where the cars were. "You engaged the rear blocker. We took out the front blocker." He began drawing double rectangles in places on either side of his squiggly line, representing the trucks and trailers at each house. "The trucks came with horse trailers to steal livestock. They went to houses they had planned to hit in advance because one of the residents here informed them. He's dangling from a telephone pole now." Some of the listeners shook their heads, some nodded, but they continued to listen as Keith took the chalk and began drawing on the chalkboard again. "When the blocker stopped, it stopped right at the Packard's driveway. Five men got out. Two of them went to clear the Packard's house while the other three held security behind the car. Once they cleared the house, they would have returned and sent the other two to clear the other house across the road from the Packards, if they didn't use the same two, but they never got that first house cleared, because that's where we ran into them."

"How do you know what they would have done if they didn't do it?" someone asked.

"Because that's what I would have done," Keith replied. "These guys had trained. There were probably at least a couple military or law enforcement veterans among them. They planned the raid, they trained for it, and they executed the plan quickly and efficiently. They were good. Just not good enough."

"Why did they stop at Bill Campbell's place? He doesn't have livestock," a woman asked.

"They must have thought he did. Like I said, they weren't good enough." Keith replied.

"Not good enough? How did we stop them? We didn't have any training or coordination."

"They drove themselves right into an ambush where they were outnumbered and surrounded. No matter how well-trained you are, you're at a disadvantage in that situation."

Jim Baker cleared his throat and stepped up to the chalkboard beside Keith. "We need to make sure this doesn't happen again. We are running out of food. If they had succeeded in taking the livestock, we would be on the verge of starvation soon, and they almost did. We need to come up with a plan." Jim looked at Keith.

Keith squinted as he stared into Jim's serious eyes. "Defense in depth."

Jim nodded. "Alright, everyone, we're gonna need all hands on deck for this."

Day 33

Every one-hundred yards or so, the residents of Mount Sinai constructed a barricade of cars on the road. These barricades would not need to be monitored and opened to allow traffic to pass; they merely forced the flow of traffic to slow to a walking pace. It was not much of an inconvenience for the residents who either walked or rode bicycles and only moved loads of product in old trucks and tractors at tortoise speed. Each barricade required them to zigzag around three vehicles which jutted out into the road from the ditch on either side. It would be impossible to simply shove the cars out of the way for anything short of a tank or bulldozer, and only a Formula One car could weave through the hulks at more than ten miles per hour. The barricades would give them time to respond to threats coming from the road, keeping invaders funneled into a series of baffles where shooters could take them from either side.

They began at the intersection of the roads with the highways and worked their way back toward the center, building about a mile's worth of baffles for each end. Deer Creek Road was the least populated area and, therefore, the most vulnerable. It connected Mount Sinai Road to the southern highway, so if anyone came from Nashville or Bloomington, there was a good chance they would take Deer Creek. It would take several days, but they would reinforce the defenses even more at that end to make up for the lower number of defenders. Jim and a couple of neighbors on Deer Creek Road took charge of that, while Ben Jameson led the efforts on the north end of Mount Sinai. That left Keith and Joe to handle the south end of the road. They had hardly seen Tim since the night of the attack, and Jack Winters rode up and down the roads but didn't get down from his horse until he was back on his property; he didn't speak to anyone, nor anyone to him.

Keith planned to clean up the remains of the old church and turn the bell tower into a lookout post that would be collectively owned by the community. He would set up a basic firearms training course for any neighbors who wished to attend, and everyone would take turns on guard duty. Joe told him there were some problems with his plan. First, they needed to make sure no one owned the church before they decided to take possession of it.

"The owner died, remember?" Keith told him.

"Yeah, but what if he willed it to someone else or someone was only renting it to him? You need to bring it up at a meeting, at least."

"Well, yeah, of course."

"And you need to be careful not to sound like you're ordering people around. No one here has any real authority over anyone else, so there's no reason for anyone to do what you say if they don't want to."

"I know that. I haven't ordered anyone to do anything."

"So how are you going to get people to go to a training course or take on a guard duty?"

"These are just ideas that I'm presenting," Keith said. "People can agree or disagree with them. Everyone is free to make his own choices."

"So, it's all volunteer-based?"

"Maybe. We'll have to take a vote." Keith stepped around a car in one of the baffles, crouched, stood up, raised and lowered his rifle, looking across the road to the train tracks converging in the distance. "We should block off the tracks too," he said.

"Yeah?" Joe looked around. "Just in case somebody builds a steam engine to attack us?" He snorted and started to laugh.

"No, I was just thinking..." Keith began.

"I know. I'm kidding. I think you're right, but what are we gonna do when they come on foot through the woods like you said a couple weeks ago?"

Keith caught a whiff of something putrid. He looked around and noticed the bodies still hanging from the telephone poles. They were already beginning to stink. A crow perched on the shoulder of one of the corpses, pecked at its face, and flew off with a chunk of something in its beak. Keith looked back at his brother. "I've got an idea for that too."

Just then, they were startled by the sound of an engine firing up. It sounded like a tractor, and when the brothers moved toward the sound, they looked around the grain bin in front of Bill Campbell's driveway and saw an old, red tractor belching out an effusion of blue-gray smoke as Dan Tyler adjusted the throttle. The brothers closed the distance to the man and the tractor, both thinking he was stealing corn. Dan was looking down, intently, and unaware of their presence. As they approached the tractor, Bill Campbell stood up and looked at them with a grin.

"What do you know?" the old man yelled over the growling of the engine.

Dan turned around and met their stares. He nodded to them and idled the tractor down.

"Look-ye here," the old farmer shouted euphorically. He pointed to a massive belt running from the antique tractor to a wheel welded onto the shaft of the grain bin blower fan. The fan was whirring around as the belt turned it. Bill Campbell watched the spinning blades with delight. "I think it's gonna work."

Day 34

The following day was spent building more baffled barricades. They began at the crest of the hill between Ernie Jacobs' and Brad Nielson's houses. Out of the vehicles left by the pirates, only two of them were still worth fixing. The others were so shot up that nearly every component that made them automobiles would need to be replaced to make them function as anything other than overweight wagons. The two vehicles, one car and one truck, were taken to Jeremiah Davis to repair and be turned into community rental vehicles. The truck was probably the only one they would ever use, but they decided to fix up the car anyway, just in case. The non-repairable trucks were stripped of useable parts and incorporated into the system of barricades. The one between Nielson and Jacobs was number sixteen from the highway.

Brad Nielson had helped with the barricades every step of the way. He was the first one to arrive at the designated meeting place and the last one to leave when they quit for the day. When they had pushed the last of the cars into place, Brad took a drink from his thermos and looked around at the hayfield on the left and the cattle on the right. "It sure don't improve the scenery, does it?"

"No, it sure don't," Joe said.

"I hope it works." He looked over to the Faulkner homestead just south of the hayfield.

The cross standing above the little mound of dirt in the backyard marked the grave of Jimmy, the Faulkners' dog. Keith suspected that the grave was merely for the sake of the kids; Tim had probably composted the dog's body if he hadn't fed it to his chickens.

"One more?" Brad asked, screwing the lid back on his thermos.

"Yeah," Keith replied. "Let's get one between Tim's driveway and ours, and we'll go talk to Jim and the others about the next step."

"Alright. Sounds good."

Joe looked at his brother with a slight grin. "That's right in front of Packard's windows."

"Yep. It's a good spot."

They walked down the road until they came to a car in a driveway marked for them to take. One of the men climbed in, put the vehicle in neutral, and steered, as the others pushed the car into place. The man in the driver's seat, who was not yet eighteen years old, steered the vehicle wide to the right, then cut the wheel sharply to the left and steered the hulk into the ditch with a crash as the bumper slammed into the muddy bank. He got out, and the six of them moved to the next driveway to get another. As they lumbered forward, they were halted by a voice from behind them. They turned around to see a man walking toward them with a basket in his hand. It was Tim.

"Wait a minute, fellas," he said, striding toward them. "Here. I want you guys to have these." He handed everyone a small package. "You guys are doing great work. I'm sorry I haven't been helping you lately."

"You know you have nothing to be sorry for," Brad said. "I'm the one who should be sorry..."

Tim cut him off. "No, Brad, you're not. I shouldn't have said what I did. I was worked up and out of line. I'm sorry."

Brad's face reddened. He blinked several times and nodded.

"I know you got my animals back for me. I was getting up to do it myself when I saw you from my window. I really appreciate it." Tim reached out to shake hands. "You're a good man, Brad."

"Thank you."

Tim turned and walked back toward his house.

"Wait a minute, Tim," Brad Nielson called out. He jogged up beside the man and told him he had something for him. Tim waited on the road as Brad ran into his house and emerged a minute later with a beagle puppy in his arms. "I'm sorry about your dog, Tim. This one's just been weened."

"Brad," Tim said with a tremor in his voice. "You don't have to..."

"Please, take him," Brad nodded. "For the kids. I got others, and it's gonna be tough to take care of 'em all anyway."

"Okay." Tim took the pup and nodded to Brad. "Thank you, Brad." The men shook hands again, and Tim turned back toward his house.

Brad jogged back to the group standing beside the car. The men watched as Tim disappeared behind the big maple tree at the corner of his driveway.

There was a rustling of paper as one of the men opened the little package to look inside. "What is it?" He sniffed the contents. "Smells good."

Keith smelled the package in his hands and looked at the other. "Oh, you're in for something special."

Day 35

Opening the door to the barn, Keith and Joe were greeted by Jordan coming with her hands up to stop them. "We lost two more patients during the night." She looked back over her shoulder. "And another one is dying now. Keep your voices low." She was thin and gaunt. Her eyes told of the exhaustion she was enduring.

Malik left the cot where the woman lay and met them at the door. "She's the last one. Shot in the stomach. We stopped the bleeding, but she hasn't been able to eat or drink at all. We gave her an IV to keep her hydrated, but there's nothing I could do about the infection. She has minutes. Maybe an hour. It's already reached her heart."

Keith nodded his understanding. "Thank you. You did all you could. You guys look tired. Go get some sleep."

The couple gathered their things and left with a weak nod to the brothers. They left the barn behind and started up the hill back toward the Rawlings house.

Inside the barn, Eric Jorgenson sat with the dying woman and a relative who looked like her sister. She was pathetically thin and looked as if she had not eaten in weeks. He ladled the last of a container of soup into a bowl for the woman who watched her sister's labored breathing through her tears. Handing the woman the bowl of soup which consisted of little more than chunks of horse meat in broth, the preacher resumed reading from his Bible softly. The woman ate the soup slowly, continuing to wipe her eyes and nose as she did so.

Keith and Joe sat down on a couple of chairs against the wall of the barn, silently waiting for Jim Baker to show up. They watched the woman finish her horseflesh soup and set the bowl down on the floor. The preacher read louder as the dying woman's raspy breathing turned to hideous growls.

The preacher placed his hand on the dying woman's head and read: "Lay not up for yourselves treasures upon earth, where moth and rust doth corrupt, and where thieves break through and steal. But lay up for yourselves treasures in heaven, where neither moth nor rust doth corrupt, and where thieves do not break through nor steal."

The growls morphed into a rattling gurgle.

The preacher read: "For where your treasure is, there will your heart be also."

Just then, one of the nurses entered the barn from the door near the woodstove. The nurse whispered something in the preacher's ear. He stopped and listened. He looked at the woman lying on the cot. She was silent now. The preacher bowed his head and closed his eyes for a few seconds before looking up and nodding to the nurse. She stepped outside once more, and the preacher collected his supplies and followed her.

The brothers continued to silently watch the somber scene out of the corners of their eyes. The woman on the cot was still, lying with her eyes and mouth open, pale and gray. The preacher had left a Bible for the sister who sat beside the cot near the stove. She picked it up again and opened it to continue reading from where the preacher left off. In her quiet, trembling voice, she read to the woman lying on the cot. "Therefore, I say unto you, take no thought for your life, what ye shall eat, or what ye shall drink; nor yet for your body what ye shall put on. Is not the life more than meat, and the body than raiment? Behold the fowls of the air: for they sow not, neither do they reap, nor gather into barns; yet your heavenly Father feedeth them. Are ye not much better than they?"

The brothers listened as she continued to read aloud, pausing to wipe her eyes and nose or to take a deep breath and look at her sister.

"... For your heavenly Father knoweth that ye have need of all these things. But seek you first the kingdom of God, and his righteousness; and all these things shall be added unto you." The woman finished reading and held the book in her hands as she stared blankly at the wall for several seconds. She looked at the corpse on the cot beside her, and back at the wall in front of her. Her eyes were red and swollen, but she had run out of tears. Then, she shut the book in her hands, got up, and threw it into the woodstove. Shutting the door, she limped outside.

Keith looked at his watch. Jim should have been here by now, he thought. The brothers got up and left the barn. They looked around to see if the woman was still there, but she was gone.

Joe took out his can of tobacco and put a pinch in his lip. He busied himself with kicking rocks and spitting on the ground as they waited. Finally, they saw Jim walking down the hill toward them.

"Sorry I'm late," he said. "It took me longer than I had hoped to talk Scott into helping us."

"But he's going to do it?"

"He'll do it. He said to tell you that he thinks your plan is stupid, but he can't think of a better one. He agreed to loan us four radios. No extra batteries. I didn't want to push it too much, so I took the deal."

Keith nodded. "We'll make it work."

CHAPTER ELEVEN

Day 36

Two of the neighbors, an elderly gentleman, and his wife, had been consistently buying meat from Keith for the past couple weeks. They were too old to cut their own firewood, too old to hunt for themselves or do much of the physical labor required to survive in the new era. While Eric Jorgenson had offered to help anyone who was unable to provide for himself, the elderly couple were too proud to start taking charity, and besides, they all knew that no one was in a position to be able to give charity in the first place. Most of the families, like the Rawlings family, were eating two meals a day or less, and their sustenance consisted of watery soups cooked on the stovetop. So, the old man had cleaned out their garage and turned it into a small general store with a sign nailed above the garage door and another at the intersection of the road and his driveway. They bought goods from anyone willing to sell and sold them for a small profit. The system had filled the need for a middleman in their nascent economy. Now, vendors could bring their wares to the old couple for a guaranteed payout and pick out exactly what they wanted from the merchant's store. People no longer had to walk to individual houses and ask around for items to trade; they simply went to the sign that read "General Store" and picked from what was available. The merchants had shelves of canned goods, maple syrup, honey, soap, candles, clothing, shoes, a few dry goods, and toothpaste. Keith traded meat mostly, but when the store owner requested a shipment of anything else the family was willing to sell, he would usually bring it to him first.

Today, Keith was trading coyote meat. They were now in the last week of trapping season, or at least, what would have been the trapping season if there were any trapping regulations anymore. Keith had only been catching an average of one animal every three days lately, which meant he had done a good job of reducing the predator population, but it also meant that he would need to find a new source of feed for his chickens. He opened the door to the general store and greeted the old man who sat in a chair beside a small woodstove with a shotgun in his hands.

"Another coyote?" the old man said. "Go ahead and put him on the scale there and tell me what it says."

Keith did so and read the number to the man. "Twenty-two pounds."

"I'll give you ten pounds of corn for him," the old man said, getting out of his chair.

Keith looked around. "You got corn, huh?"

"That's right. It's dried corn. Good for animal feed. I can't hardly keep it in stock." The old man opened a deep freezer behind the table with the scale and pulled out a cloth bag. "What do you say?"

Keith smiled. "I'll take it." He handed over the bag of coyote meat, took the bag of corn from the old man, felt the weight and texture of the product, and shook the man's hand as he thanked him.

"I thank ye. Have a nice day," the old man said. "And if you have any fruit or vegetable seed you're willing to sell, I'll give you fifty pounds of corn for ten."

"Ten packets?" Keith asked.

"Hell no," the old man exclaimed. "Ten seeds."

"I'll keep it in mind." Keith turned and left. He had several packets of seeds in an ammo can in the basement, not including the bag of turnip seed he had acquired at the farm and home store on their run into town. With the corn, he would be able to maintain his animals much easier. He quickened his pace and met Joe at Rick Thompson's driveway. "No luck?" he asked, seeing Joe's contemplative frown.

"No." Joe shook his head. "There's no smoke coming from his chimney either. "You don't think he went away, do you?"

"Does he have family living around Bloomington?"

"I don't know. I think he might have."

"Could have. Seems like he would have told you first."

"Maybe he thought we would try to stop him. Isn't that why we haven't told anyone about our plans to go to Illinois?"

"Hmm." Keith nodded. "We'll check again later."

Kent had all the modifications complete. The truck was as ready as they were going to get it. All he had left to do was put the camper shell on it. Lynn had helped him throughout the process whenever Joe was gone. Kent would tell her what to do, and she would do it. They had the bed cleaned out and lined with cushions and blankets wherever there weren't tools and jugs of gasoline. The good tire was mounted, and the old one was secured to the bed for a spare. Kent did indeed get seven cylinders firing on the old truck. Eight wasn't in the cards, but seven would be sufficient.

Kent hailed his sons as they strode down the driveway toward him. "You're finally back. Took you long enough. Help me put this camper shell on here."

The siblings each took a side, hoisted the shell onto the bed, and secured it in place. Kent looked at the truck and shook his head as if answering a question in his mind. "I guess that's it."

"Did you tell anyone about what we're doing?" Lynn asked.

"Not yet," Joe answered.

"Why not?" Lynn pressed.

"Maybe it's better if we don't tell anyone."

"Well, you have to tell someone. Not only for them to know that you're gone, but because you need someone to let you out."

"And more importantly, to let us back in." Keith nodded in agreement.

Joe spat a stream of golden-brown tobacco juice into the snow in front of him. "Are you reconsidering trying to post sentries in the old church now?" He cocked his head to one side and raised an eyebrow as he looked at Keith.

"I'm not posting anyone anywhere. I'm not in charge."

"But you're the one making plans. What's your plan?"

"Gotta have a plan," Kent declared.

"I think we ought to tell Jim, at least, but we need to take the truck for a test run first." He looked at Kent. "Don't you think, Dad?"

"Yeah, I do. I think we need to drive at least a few miles to find out if there's any problems we don't know about. We can't burn too much gas, but we need to take it for a run."

"I agree," Joe said.

"But we shouldn't let anyone know who doesn't need to, and we have to make sure the defenses are in place before we leave." Keith spat in the mud. "We don't want to come back and find our little settlement under new management."

"It's getting cold out here," Kent said. "You can talk about it more inside."

"Let's see this painting you've been working on," Joe said as they mounted the steps on the front porch.

"It's finished," Lynn replied, opening the door. She led them to the painting which rested on an easel in the living room.

When they stepped in front of the painting, all three of them stopped in their tracks. Finally, after half a minute, Joe swallowed and said, "Lynn, that's incredible."

Day 37

A meeting was called to discuss and vote on security measures. Keith requested the use of Ben Jameson's tractor and wagon to transport the large painting along with the family members, minus Kent who stayed home, still in too much pain to ride over the cratered road in a tractor-drawn wagon, much less to walk the distance. Malik and Jordan rode with the family members, armed now with their choice of Keith and Joe's share of the weapons taken from the marauders. Malik planned to ride with Ben Jameson to make house calls to all the patients, both those wounded from last week's battle and those ailing from other afflictions.

With their earnings, Malik and Jordan were able to buy clothing from the general store, and they bought food and other goods to contribute to the family's supplies as well as saving a small stash for themselves. No one had discussed it yet, but there were several houses standing vacant, now that their occupants had died. It was not clear what should be done with them, but there were people wandering into the community, and many had been brought in from outside. The rule was that they were only to be admitted if they had a place to stay and permission to be there, and some of the houses were packed with family members and friends. More than a few drifters had wandered into the community, following the tracks, or roaming through the woods, and they had to be turned away—violently in some cases. Even so, some were camping around the perimeters, looking for ways to get in or rob people probably, and at night, their campfires flickered on the hillsides. They would need to find a way to repurpose the empty houses at some point, and the McCormicks were counting on moving into a place of their own when the chance arrived.

The Rawlings family, along with the McCormicks, were the first to arrive at the barn. When they unloaded the painting and all their things, Ben Jameson took the tractor back toward the north end of the road to collect a load of passengers for the meeting.

Joe helped Lynn to carry the painting inside, and they hung it on the wall opposite the chalkboard and map. It was covered with a sheet to protect it during transportation, and they left the sheet in place for the time being. Keith started a fire in the massive woodstove as Joe began to light the lanterns.

The east-end door of the barn opened, and in walked Jim Baker. He nodded to Keith and Joe. He greeted Malik and Jordan, and then, seeing Faye and Lynn for the first time, he introduced himself and shook their hands. He had just finished saying hello when the west-end door opened. Brad Nielson stepped inside. He tipped his hat to them as he entered, walking toward them with a smile. He didn't shut the door, and right behind him, Tim Faulkner crossed the threshold, followed by a retinue of children and Emma, her face still bruised and discolored. They smiled and greeted the others, and as the light in the barn grew brighter, the door opened once more. All eyes turned to the doorway as the sunlight streamed into the dim cavern. Through the golden halo, stepped Jack Winters, followed by his two sons and his wife. The room was quiet as they walked in.

They watched in silent anticipation. Together, Faye and Lynn pulled down the sheet which covered the painting. Mrs. Winters put a hand to her mouth and sunk into the chair beneath her. Her face went red, and tears welled in her eyes. As she let her hand fall away from her mouth, she got up and moved closer to the painting. A smile appeared upon her face as tears rolled silently down her cheeks. Jack's lip quivered as he stared at the painting. The kids hardly blinked. All present stared in astonishment at the memorial to the fallen.

Mrs. Winters decided that the painting should remain in the barn for all to see and remember the price that was paid for their community's survival. As the neighbors entered the barn, they noted Jack Winters' family. Not everyone knew who had been killed on that day, but as people talked, the word got around about the Winters kids, and they knew there were others who had lost family members that day as well. Over the past week, people had been dying in this barn, and everyone on the road knew someone who was now gone. As they entered the barn, eyes wandered, taking stock of who was left and in what condition. People came wrapped in bandages, families missing members. As they passed into the lantern light, young and old, they were arrested by the sight of the painting and gathered around to gaze in awe.

Jack Winters wiped his eyes and made his way to the front of the room and stood before the chalkboard, facing the crowd. He commanded the people's attention as he looked out into the throng with clenched fists. "Now you listen to me, damnit. We are not going to sit here and die like a bunch of sheep fearing for our lives. We're not going to rot away from despair and vanish into ruin. We're going to survive. We're going to rebuild. And we're going to leave a world for our children that's better than this—or else we'll die in the attempt, having expended every drop of sweat and blood we were given, with smiles on our faces and joy in our hearts, knowing we were not cowards who shrunk from hardship at the end."

The crowd, which was all attention, became a sea of nodding heads and affirming voices. Jack turned to Jim Baker. "Jim, I've been away for a while. Please bring me up to speed on what I missed."

Jim stepped in front of the chalkboard and looked at the map Keith had drawn. He began to point, and he stopped himself. "I've been helping with the project, but Keith is the one who came up with the plan for the defenses. He could explain it better than I could." Jim looked at Keith with a smile and a nod. "Keith?"

Keith stepped to the front of the room and began. "Alright, here's what we're doing."

Above the graveyard, the American flag flew in the breeze. Another was hung from Jim Baker's barn. Ernie Jacobs' barn had always been adorned with a flag above the doors on either end. Tim Faulkner, Dan Tyler, Jack Winters, and several others had always displayed the flag, but now, American flags and a few Gadsden flags were raised all along the road. They hung from the posts on front porches, were raised proudly from flag poles to wave in the breeze, and makeshift poles of wood and metal held the banners defiantly above the landscape. Some of the flags were homemade, quilted from fragments of clothing. They were not all uniform, but after the attack in early March, American flags of every shape, size, and material began to appear on Mount Sinai. No one would forget the events of that night and the sacrifices made by the fallen. After five weeks of living without power, without connection to the outside world, without the protection or order established by the government, few people believed life would ever return to normal. They were on their own. Their survival depended upon their ability to adapt and provide for themselves, and everyone knew that they would have had no chance of surviving if the livestock had been taken. Even the hippies flew flags now. They were all in this together.

Day 38

A cold front was coming through. The temperature had fallen back below twenty degrees, and it seemed to be getting colder by the hour. Keith and Joe stepped quietly through the woods. Along the hillside, they walked, scouting out the area. The ravine sloped down at more than a forty-five-degree grade. The ice-covered leaves crunched beneath their boots, trying to betray their steps and send them sliding down into the wash. Overhead, crows flew toward the houses five-hundred yards in front of them.

"It's a long hike to get through the woods from the highway," Joe said.

"Mmhmm."

"Over some pretty rough terrain."

"Yep."

"I don't think anyone would attack from the woods," Joe continued.

"Probably not," Keith replied, stepping over a log. "But we can't afford to gamble on probabilities."

"Hmm." Joe swept a smilax vine from his path. "I understand, but we also can't afford to waste materials, time, or energy."

"That's right."

Joe shook his head and pulled out his last can of tobacco. "Are you sure this will work?"

"Nope."

"Did you learn this in the military?" Joe put a pinch of tobacco in his lip.

"No." Keith pulled himself up around a young tree and climbed down into a depression hollowed out by a fallen oak's massive root system. He looked out over the ravine and the hillside across from his position behind the fallen tree's mass of displaced roots. "Hunting."

"Why can't you train people in some military tactics or whatever?" Joe spat on the roots of the tree.

"We don't have time or resources for that. And I don't have the patience. And it wouldn't work as well anyway."

"Oh, so you think you're smarter than the military?" Joe laughed.

"Yes." Keith stared up at the birds flying overhead. "Look at all these crows."

"Yeah. It sure is a lot. Where are they coming from?"

"Where are they going?" Keith climbed out of the hole and continued on in the direction the crows were flying.

They were coming up on the edge of Kent's property now, but just beyond, behind the houses on the other side of the ravine, the crows were amassing in the trees. The brothers carefully traversed the gulley and ascended the ridge.

"That's Jeremiah Davis up there," Joe said. "You don't ever see this side of the house, do you? But that's his shed over there, where he keeps some of his projects. And that's Rick's house right beside it. See that tree where we tried to dig?"

"I see it," Keith affirmed. "It's full of crows."

They continued up the hill toward the tree, and as Joe neared the huge tree, staring up as he approached, he tripped and fell to the ground. The crows scattered in an eruption of flapping wings and caws. Joe grabbed his shin and winced as he looked at what had tripped him. "That's Rick's ladder," he said, nodding toward the aluminum ladder lying in the leaves. "I know because I..." He caught the sight of Keith's face and followed his eyes to the tree branches above his head. With a shriek, Joe scrambled away from the dangling feet swaying in the breeze above his head. He threw his hand to his mouth and stifled the cries of horror that persisted unbidden from his throat as he saw the disfigured, eyeless face of the corpse suspended from the neck, ten feet above the ground.

They cut Rick Thompson's body down, and the stiff limbs bounced off the frozen clay beneath with a sickly thud. There were pink, ragged gashes in the icy flesh around his hollow eye sockets where the crows had pecked and torn at his face. Even in the cold, a disgusting odor surrounded the corpse. By the stains on his pants and shoes, they could see that his bowels had been evacuated as the life left his body. Excrement ran down his legs and froze to him—nature afforded no dignity in death. They found the key to his house on a string tied around his wrist. It was getting colder, and the light was beginning to fade. They would need to dispose of the body tomorrow, so they unlocked the house with the key and carried the stiff cadaver inside. As they laid the remains on the floor, they turned on their headlamps and looked around the house. It was nearly immaculate. All the trash had been removed along with the electronics which were broken when last they saw the place. It smelled of citrus-scented household cleaners, and every item in the house was organized like a hotel room. In the middle of the living room floor was a collection of items laid out neatly. All of Rick's firearms, including a 12-gauge shotgun, a bolt action

.22 rifle, an AR-15 rifle, a 9mm pistol, and a .357 magnum revolver, with several boxes of ammunition for each. Two pocket knives, a toolbox, flashlights, batteries, a radio, several sets of shirts, pants, and socks, two jackets, a coat, two pairs of boots, one pair of running shoes, two belts, three baseball caps, two stocking caps, and a pair of gloves, along with his police gear.

"He left this stuff for us," Keith said. "For the community." He shook his head as he stared at the collection of gear on the floor. "Didn't even waste a bullet on himself. He knew we'd need it."

"He was a good guy," Joe affirmed with watery eyes and red face. "He was a good friend. I should have been there for him." Joe rubbed his eyes with his coat sleeve.

Keith watched his brother, not knowing what to do. He couldn't recall ever seeing him cry before. "I don't think any of us could have done much for him," he finally said.

"You don't know that."

Keith stared into the darkness of the hallway. "We'll get Ben to bring his tractor tomorrow. Come on." He turned to leave.

"We're not putting him in that manure pile," Joe said flatly. "We're going to get the preacher, and we're going to bury him under that tree like we should have done with his mother."

"We tried, remember? The ground was..."

"I don't care. I'm doing it right this time. No matter what it takes."

Day 39

The next day, the brothers got the preacher with the help of their sister, and they dug through the ice which was only a few inches thick. The preacher said a few words, and they buried the body the better part of five feet deep in the cold, wet clay. With a large chunk of Mount Sinai's yellow sandstone, they marked the grave, and once the job was finished, Joe took out his tobacco tin. He ran his fingers around the moist, black plastic container, scraping out every solitary piece of the very last of his tobacco, and he put it in his lip. He pressed the lid back onto the can and tossed it onto the grave. "Well, that's the end of that."

PART III
SPRING

Chapter Twelve

Day 48

The pile of bodies, which had drawn so many swarms of crows and vultures, had slowly diminished in size as pieces were torn off and dragged away. Every night, the darkness was pierced by the shrieks, howls, and blood-chilling screams of coyotes and foxes, and the unsettling discord echoed throughout the hills and hollows and pierced the ears of every would-be sleeper on Mount Sinai. The scavengers glutted themselves, night and day, with the decaying flesh, and it was never allowed to escape the attention of the residents who were continually assaulted by the sight of the carrion birds by day, the noise of the predators by night, and the continual stench which greeted them with every gust of wind.

Once the corpses were reduced to little more than bones and sinew, the temperature rose for a week. It rained without stopping for six days, washing away every trace of blood and gore that, a week prior, had stained the land. The neighbors stayed inside for the most part, with their highest priority being avoiding pneumonia. But all the while, they prepared materials for the defenses, including old clothes and various pieces of junk they found lying around.

Now, the rain had stopped, and the ground was saturated. Standing water covered the fields and gathered in puddles throughout the woods. After a week of sitting inside, they were ready to get out and get to work. With baskets, carts, bags, and sleds, the neighbors pulled loads of clothing, logs, balls, string, tape, and various other items. Keith's plan was to build an army of scarecrows. Over the years, the Rawlings family had tried making several scarecrows in the hope of deterring deer, and of course, birds from raiding the crops. They seemed to have no effect on the animals, but whenever people drove by and saw them, it scared them half to death. Out of the corner of the eye, in low light, or while moving, the mind never ceased to see eerie human forms standing, watching them from the field. They had seen them hundreds of times, but the imposters continued to fool the senses. Every time.

The idea was that, like the baffle system of barricades on the road, the scarecrows would slow down and confuse foot-mobile invaders while allowing defenders time to pick them off. The invaders would be distracted by the scarecrows, and during the chaos, they would have a hard time differentiating between the human shapes of the scarecrows and those of the defenders shooting at them. It was a crazy plan, but no one could come up with a better one. Building many miles of wall around the community was impossible, and training a large defense force in military tactics and coordinating them into a combined effort was nearly impossible, not to mention expensive. There were quite a few hunters on Mount Sinai who could shoot, and many of them were already familiar with the use of decoys. Combined with the use of the radios and lookouts, they could quickly deploy their militia, like minutemen, to their prepared stations where they would, hopefully, be able to pick off attackers until either the defenders could be reinforced, or the attackers were spent.

Keith had no problem enlisting volunteers for guard duty. After the battle, after seeing the memorial and seeing their neighbors, after hearing the speeches and hearing what had happened on that night, the community was galvanized toward a common purpose. The promise of food in return for service sealed the deal, and Keith recorded the names of nearly fifty volunteers which he organized into a list before making duplicates to post on the wall of the barn, in the general store, and in each of the guard posts.

It turned out that no one had a claim to the old church, and it was agreed that they should use it as an observation post for the common defense. Once the rain had stopped, they began clearing the debris, and Brad Nielson checked the structural integrity of the building. It was still sound, but they reinforced it for good measure. On the north end of Mount Sinai Road, there was an old, abandoned fire station. It was unoccupied, save for the remains of a dead squatter they found inside. Once that was cleaned out, they had their second post. It was complete with a tower as well—a three-story structure used for training firefighters back when Americans had things like fire departments which people could call for help.

Ten miles south of the fire station, was the intersection of Deer Creek Road and the highway. There was no church down there, no fire station either. The idea of building a tower was floated, but it was soon realized that it would be far too costly. They needed to be able to see down the highway both ways, but there was nothing apart from open fields nearby for nearly five-hundred yards. And the nearest building to the road was a barn, which was still in use. The owner didn't want to have guards constantly going through his barn, and no one could blame him. Even if he did, it would have been a recipe for trouble. Instead, they eventually decided that the shale ridge was the place to post a lookout. It ran all the way from Mount Sinai Road to the highway, where it terminated in a cliff. The sheer wall of shale, where machines had cut to lay the highway, was still visible through the leaf litter and moss. Hidden inside the trees on the ridgetop, a small cabin could overlook the highway for at least a mile in one direction and several-hundred yards in the other without being seen by passersby.

CHAPTER TWELVE

Building a small cabin on the top of a ridgeline was simple enough once they gathered the materials for the project; there was only one problem: getting it up there. The ridges and valleys of southern Indiana were not easily traversed. Steep grades, thick brush, and slick, clay-covered shale patches hidden beneath wet leaves, all contributed to making the draws nearly impassable. Even bulldozers got hung up trying to maneuver through this terrain. The way people were able to build and live on these ridges was through the use of heavy machinery cutting down large swaths of timber and hacking through the very rock which formed them. With enough steel, diesel, and man-hours, the wild country had been tamed, at least enough to instantiate civilization. Now, the machines were gone, and those that remained were far too costly to operate. Bringing the land to heel was out of the question. Keith had often shot deer that ended up at the bottom of the ravines, and there was nothing to do in that situation but hoist the deer over his shoulders and hike it up the ridge. It could be done, but not many could do it, and with the amount of building materials they needed? He wasn't about to make all those trips himself. In the end, after scouting out the location for the post, it was clear they were going to have to cut a trail to get to it.

Day 50

In the wake of the hangings, theft had seemed to disappear. There was certainly no lack of motivation. The scarcity of supplies had only increased. Perhaps the thieves had had a change of heart. Perhaps they were afraid of getting caught. Perhaps they were dead. No one challenged Jack Winters' authority now. No one was unclear on what the consequences of stealing would be. Nearly everyone carried a weapon everywhere he went, and the practice had only grown more common after the attack. There was no doubt as to whether they would use them either.

No one knew for sure what had happened, but the little, purple house, two houses down from the Rawlings' driveway, was discovered to have three partially frozen bodies inside after several people had tried knocking on the door over the weeks and reported no smoke coming from the house—and a worsening smell surrounding it. The partially decomposed remains were found in a pile of liquor bottles and syringes. One on the couch, two on the floor, smeared with vomit. It looked like the degenerates had decided to party like it was the end of the world and either overdosed or got so intoxicated they froze to death in their stupor. Their bodies had been gnawed by mice. They were dragged out of the house, taken by wagon, and tossed into the manure pile at the organic farm to give back of their bodies what they had taken in life. No one felt the need to expend the precious energy to bury them, and they would not detract from the honor of the valiant dead by placing the corpses in the same cemetery with those who had died in battle. The cemetery was small and limited in space, and it had become consecrated ground, ransomed by blood.

Day 51

"Targets!"

Six rifles thundered in unison.

"Ceasefire! Ceasefire! Condition two! Muzzles down!" Keith scanned the line of shooters, making sure everyone had followed the commands.

Every weapon was put on safe, and the shooters pointed their muzzles at the dirt directly in front of them, keeping their eyes forward.

CHAPTER TWELVE

"With your weapons at the ready, face downrange, walk forward, and examine your targets."

The shooters stayed in line, closing the distance between themselves and their targets which were only twenty yards away. They had to start somewhere. In fact, they had already spent hours in the barn taking classes on weapons safety, shooting positions, nomenclature, and capabilities. Some of them were bored, but others, like Malik and Jordan, took notes and committed the knowledge to memory. They were determined to prove that they could hold their own with everyone else in the community. The students were taught to disassemble, clean, and reassemble their weapons, as well as how to respond to various misfire scenarios. For another couple of hours, the class practiced their aiming, breathing, and trigger control by dry-firing at small targets set inside the barn. They had performed these tasks for two days before firing the first round of live ammunition. This was now the third day of the class, and after reciting the weapons safety laws and the weapons conditions, they began firing, one shot at a time, to verify the zero of their sights. Then, live fire training commenced, beginning at twenty yards.

"I hit it!" Jordan said with a smile. She was quite pleased with herself. This was something they didn't get to do in the city. She knew twenty yards was not an impressive shot, but as she had learned from Keith and Joe, most deer in this part of the country were killed at a range of about fifteen yards, so it was an accomplishment nonetheless.

"Nicely done," Keith said. "Try to tighten this group up a little more. Aiming, breathing, trigger control." He patched the holes with black duct tape and moved to the next target.

There were twelve of them in all, and most of them had never fired a weapon before. The hippies, especially, realized they needed to purchase their own weapons and learn to use them. They turned out to be some of the most attentive students. No one was anti-gun now. Pacifism and tolerance were bourgeois luxuries now extinct.

After everyone had fired three shots at twenty yards, they moved back to forty. At forty yards, the groups began to open up for several of the shooters. They were still on paper, for the most part, but some of them could hardly be considered groups. Shooting at even forty yards was a feat that took dedicated practice to master. In the Marine Corps, Keith had trained to shoot offhand from the standing position at over two-hundred yards, but they dedicated countless hours and millions of dollars of other people's money to training.

"This is so much harder than it looks on TV," one of the hippies said.

"Yeah," said another. "I thought you could just pick up a gun and shoot whatever you wanted."

Keith snorted as he covered holes with duct tape. "That's because the people who make movies have never touched a weapon in their lives."

"They're probably all dead now," one of the students said absent-mindedly. "All the celebrities."

"It's amazing how much of what we thought we knew came from entertainment." Malik shook his head, looking at his target. "We thought we were knowledgeable. But the people we got our worldview from had no idea what they were talking about."

"They told us what they thought we'd pay to hear," Jordan replied.

Keith patched up the last target and looked over the shooters who stood rigidly facing their targets, only turning their heads to look at one another. "Alright. Shooters, face up-range. Return to the forty-yard line. Let's try again."

Day 52

The trail was cleared with axes, saws, machetes, and spades. To provide a sure path of rapid ingress and emergency egress, they carved out a muddy trail along the hillside with shovels and mattocks. It would take another week to complete the project, but the trail was clear enough now, that they could begin transporting materials up to the crest of the ridge. It was too steep and too uneven to use carts or sleds, so they resorted to carrying the materials by hand. Naturally, most of this labor was performed by the young men like Keith and Joe. The trail was over a mile long and connected to Deer Creek Road just behind their last barricade. At more than thirty feet above the road, and fifty yards to the northeast, the discreet dirt path provided a concealed, elevated position from which shooters could pick off invaders below. It would take an overwhelming number to take the ridge from just a couple of defenders.

With Brad Nielson and two other handymen working on the construction, the structure would take only two days to complete once the materials were in place. The portage of lumber and tin was exhausting work, especially on a restricted diet. The average resident of Mount Sinai had lost thirty pounds since the day of the blackout. They were beginning to look like third world refugees. The Rawlings family was better prepared than most of their neighbors, but after donating supplies to the church and helping their less prepared neighbors for the sake of maintaining the community, even they had begun rationing themselves to one meal per day.

Most of the people in the community hired themselves out to earn their food. There was no hope of trying to steal anything since everyone was armed all the time. Ernie Jacobs, who had recovered consciousness and was walking around once again, hired on two neighbors to feed and water his cattle and make sure they didn't get out of the fence. He, like most of the other farmers, usually paid in fuel. Many of the neighbors worked on splitting and stacking firewood for others who cut it. They would burn through far more firewood now than they had previously, not only because it was the only way they had to heat their homes, but it was the only way they had to cook food and disinfect water as well. They would continue to burn wood throughout the summer, and that meant that the sawyers would always be in business, as long as there were people in need of heat, and that meant as long as there were people. There were several men helping farmers cut and assemble rails and posts to replace their defunct electric fencing. Deliveries were made daily. Every functioning truck and tractor was used to pull loads of firewood, water, fence posts and livestock up and down the road.

Day 55

"How much corn is ten vegetable seeds worth?" Keith asked as he walked into the general store.

"I'd give you fifty pounds," the old man replied, getting out of his chair.

Keith took several plastic bags of vegetable seeds—ten seeds per bag—and dropped them on the table in front of the merchant. Tomatoes, yellow squash, zucchini, butternut squash, turnips, and beets. "There's your seed."

The old man stared with an open mouth for a second. "Where'd you get these?"

"I had 'em saved from last year. They're all good. Been stored cool, dry, and dark."

The merchant held the bags up to the light and examined them. "These are some of the most valuable things in the world right now." He counted the seeds in each bag and put them aside on the table as he went. "Well, you got enough here for four-hundred-fifty pounds of corn. Is that what you're trading for?"

"Yessir."

"There's fifty-pound bags in the chest, there. Help yourself. I'd help you load them, but I'm older than dirt, and I don't feel like it."

Keith carried the bags out to the community rental truck—the one left by the marauders—which he'd signed out from the motor pool, also known as Jeremiah Davis's driveway.

As Keith grabbed the last bag from the freezer, the old man followed him to the door, ready to shut it behind him. "Do you have any more seeds to sell?"

Keith smiled at him. "I might."

"Well, if you do, I want to buy them."

"I'll remember it." Keith paused as he stepped through the doorway. "Hey, have you seen Fred and Donna Packard come in here at all?"

"Packards? Oh yeah. They ride their bicycles down here from time to time and do some trading."

"Yeah? What do they trade for?"

"I don't see how that's any concern of yours."

"Well, what do they bring you to trade?"

"I don't reckon that's your concern either."

"Right, right. I should have known. Thanks anyway."

Day 56

The ground dried out, and the temperature was in the low fifties now. Ernie Jacobs asked Tim Faulkner to invite everyone in the community who wanted to join, to come to his house for a slaughter and barbeque. Having survived the winter, marauders, and everything else, Ernie wanted to have a party to celebrate. He would provide the cow, and everyone would get some beef. The idea was heartily supported. Finding the flags raised on their mailboxes, everyone found invitations to the feast, and at midday, Ben Jameson began dropping off loads of neighbors in the hayfield.

Ernie selected the animal, an older cow past calving. With the help of Keith and Tim Faulkner, and a couple of other homesteaders, the cow was butchered, and every piece was put to use. The beast was dispatched with a shot to the head and hung by a heavy gambrel made by Jeremiah Davis. They hoisted the carcass from a massive oak branch with a log chain hooked to a tractor, and the cow was bled from a slit in the neck. The homesteaders collected the draining blood in buckets to use for black pudding. The animal was skinned, and the organs were removed, all to be used for sausage. Once the carcass was cleaned, the head and hooves were removed, and the meat was carefully cut into pieces to be roasted over the fire. Neighbors came early to watch and help in whatever way they could.

As they poured into the field, many of the neighbors brought small contributions of food, spices, and drinks to add to the feast. They were not much, but with a few pounds of mixed beans, some smoked pork, and maple syrup, they filled a couple stock pots. Some, as payment for the meal, brought small bags of corn for Ernie's cows. Everyone brought his own plate, fork, knife, and cup. Those who had them brought lawn chairs as well, while those who did not sat on huge logs dragged out into the hayfield for the purpose. Around the bonfire, they sat and talked and watched the meat roasting on the fire. They savored the aroma, sipped pine needle tea from their cups, and reveled in the warm air and sunlight. Today, for the first time in a long time, they were thankful to be alive.

As the meat cooked over the fire, Eric Jorgenson stood in the center of the circle and asked for the crowd's attention. The din of voices fell to a whisper, and the preacher looked over the crowd. "Thank you. Today, we're celebrating the end of winter and the arrival of spring."

The crowd burst into cheers and whistles.

"First, we need to thank Ernie Jacobs for making this happen. Ernie." He looked at the old man who smiled from his lawn chair, arm tied up in a sling.

The crowd roared and applauded. Ernie stood up and waved at them. He said something, but his voice was too weak to be heard over the applause and shouting of the neighbors. When he sat back down, Eric continued.

"Thank you, Ernie. Secondly, we need to thank the cooks and the butchers who prepared this meal."

Once again, the crowd cheered and clapped, banging tin cups with utensils.

"We need to remember those who are no longer with us. We need to remember the ones outside this community who are not as fortunate as we are, the ones who can't be here to experience this great feast, and the ones who gave their lives defending this community."

The people were silent, somber, and nodding in agreement. A few tears were dabbed away with handkerchiefs.

"But most of all, we need to thank God. That's really why we're here. He got us through the winter. And by His grace, we'll get through the spring. So long as we remain strong and stay faithful to Him. Before we eat, let us pray." The preacher bowed his head.

Not all of the residents of Mount Sinai Road were religious believers. Indeed, most of them, if pressed on their beliefs, would admit the contrary. But there was no harm in praying. It was comforting to many of them, and if there was a God, some of them reasoned, it couldn't hurt to ask Him for a little help. They needed all the help they could get. They bowed their heads, closed their eyes, or simply kept silent while the preacher prayed.

"Our Father who art in Heaven. Hallowed be Thy name. We gather here today to thank you for your many blessings, and we ask you to continue to go with us into the planting season. Give us the strength to persevere through the challenges ahead. We know that this world is not our home, and we hope that what we do here, in this life, is honorable in your sight, so that one day, when we are called home, we may hear those words: 'Well done.' We ask you to bless this food to nourish our bodies, that we might better do your will. And Lord, as good as this food is, and as much as we appreciate it, we know that the ones who've gone on from this world are eating better than we are today. Please tell them to save some for us. We'll be there soon enough. In Jesus' name, Amen."

There was a loud "Amen!" shouted from the crowd, and the food was ready to be served. They cut slices of beef from the roasting legs and back of the cow. The ribs were cut and roasted separately, basted with a mixture of salt, garlic, ground chili peppers, and maple syrup. The meat was tougher and more strongly flavored than they would have previously purchased in grocery stores and butcher shops, but no one thought of complaining. It was genuine beef, not coyote or opossum or horse. Everyone lined up to collect a slice of meat and a scoop of barbequed beans, and soon, the nearly three-hundred people were happily eating some of the best food they had tasted in over a month.

After everyone had received a plate of food, the call for seconds was sounded. Many of the children were now playing games of tag and football and frisbee in the hayfield while their parents talked and got in line for more beef. Jim Baker took the opportunity to address the gathering which was larger than any previously assembled.

After gaining the crowd's attention by ringing a triangle, he began: "There's a lot more people here than we've seen at our meetings, so for those who don't know me, I'm Jim Baker. I own the barn we use for meetings down by the intersection of Mount Sinai and Deer Creek. I've also been working very closely with some of the community leaders who have taken initiative in community projects like the water catchment systems and the defenses. As all of you know, today, we're celebrating the end of winter and the beginning of the planting season. It is our good fortune to have several residents in this community with the wisdom and foresight to have stockpiled seeds for their gardens. There are seeds for sale for anyone who wishes to buy them, and I would say there are enough for every household to plant a small garden."

There was a cheer from the crowd.

"Now, I've been a farmer my entire life, so I know a little bit about growing crops, and I know we're all anxious to get some seed in the ground and start growing food. But I want to warn you, even though the astronomers would tell you that spring began on the Twenty-first of March, that means nothing to Mother Nature. For all intents and purposes, it's still winter here. We could still have a frost, so we need to wait a little longer before planting. For those of you who are wanting to plant a garden for the first time, there are a lot of experienced gardeners around here who would be happy to show you some of what they've learned. I recommend you take advantage of that knowledge. Growing plants is not as simple as putting a seed in the dirt and adding water.

"Another thing, we don't have access to commercial fertilizers and chemicals anymore. What you'll soon find out, if you simply plant seeds and expect them to grow, is that this ground doesn't want to grow your plants. It doesn't have the right nutrients. We're going to need to go back to the old ways, and that means collecting manure to fertilize the gardens. And that includes our own. We can't afford to be throwing away a resource as valuable as that. Some of us have already been doing this, but we all need to do it now. So, from now on, we're going to be starting a new system to collect manure from anyone who does not intend to use it. For everyone who sells us crap, we'll pay in produce."

There was a chuckle from the crowd.

Jim paused to take a sip of pine needle tea. As the laughter subsided, he set his cup back down and continued. "We'll have Ben or somebody come through to pick up the buckets every day."

Ben Jameson stood up and shouted, "Not me! You get your own crap!"

There was another burst of laughter from the crowd. Jim waited for them to quiet down again. "Well, we'll figure it out. Somebody will get it anyway. And for those who are looking for work, speaking for myself here, the farmers are going to need help with the tilling, planting, fertilizing, and weeding of the fields, so you can look forward to that." He paused and took another drink. "I think that about does it for the planting. The other thing, some of you might not have known, is that we're also celebrating the completion of our defense system today."

There was another round of applause.

"You've all seen the barricade system we have in place, but a couple of days ago, we also completed our third lookout post. Now, every intersection with the highway is covered by a watch."

The crowd applauded once more.

"We have radios for each of the lookout positions as well as for the barn which will function as our sort of command center, or whatever, as well as the hospital area. Now, of course, we don't have an unlimited supply of battery power for the radios, so the radios will remain shut off until one of the alarms is sounded. Each radio position has been equipped with its own alarm bell that will be sounded whenever the sentry sees invaders or needs to communicate over the radio. The bells should be audible from anywhere along the road, and it will signal everyone to repeat the alarm, turn on their radios, and get prepared to defend themselves. We've also been making quite a bit of progress with the scarecrow army, but that's going to be up to individual property owners what you want to do with that. We're going to need to run some drills to make sure everything works out, but you should all feel much more confident in our security here."

The crowd applauded again, and Jim asked if anyone else had any announcements. Tim Faulkner stood up.

"Oh, that's right. I forgot," Jim said, nodding to Tim.

"Many of you know my wife Emma. She's homeschooled our children for the past several years, and she's teamed up with a couple of the teachers to start classes beginning next week. If anyone wants to send their kids to continue school, you can talk to her or one of the teachers about the schedule and what they'll need to bring."

There was another cheer from the crowd. Tim sat back down, and Jim said he had nothing else to announce, so he went to get a second helping of beef. Several neighbors who had been practicing together took out instruments from the cases they had brought, and setting up on the asphalt, they began to play music. For most of the residents, it was the first music they had heard in two months, and they were so overcome with joy at the sound that they burst into uproarious shouting, clapping, laughter, and dancing.

Keith, Joe, Lynn, Faye, and Kent all helped themselves to more food and enjoyed the music. Malik and Jordan were dancing in the field and laughing at each other. They had never listened to bluegrass music before, much less danced to it, but they were so thrilled by the surprise that they had to join with the others, moving to the music under the clear, blue sky.

It was the first time since the blackout that the Rawlings family had left the house without someone inside. Faye continued to remind them periodically that someone could be walking around inside the house, looking through their things, or making off with their animals. Kent continued to tell her not to worry so much; they had locked the house, and they wouldn't be gone long enough for anyone to know the house was empty.

Across the bonfire, Keith could see Fred and Donna Packard sitting in lawn chairs and talking to the neighbors who lived next to them on Mount Sinai Road. Their neighbors were feminists—two middle-aged women who, from any distance beyond ten feet, looked like men—and lived in a picturesque, green house with their dogs. Before the blackout, they would have been the type to rant about how men had kept women barefoot and pregnant in the kitchen for thousands of years and how women needed men like fish need bicycles, but about three weeks after the blackout, they hired a man to help them with the manual labor required to survive in a world without electricity; they paid him with food, soap, and candles, and they never said a derogatory word about the fouler sex again. They would frequent the home of the Packards quite regularly before the blackout, and they continued the practice afterward, nearly every day crossing the boundary between their properties by the walking trail through the woods across the road from the Rawlings. Speaking quietly, Fred and Donna looked serious, as usual, seldom smiling or gesturing much. They nodded and blinked and shook their heads as their neighbors talked loudly and used all the gestures neglected by the Packards.

"Hey," Joe elbowed his brother.

"I see them," Keith responded.

"They look none the worse for wear. Let's go make sure they're alright." Joe led the way through the crowd of people sitting in lawn chairs and on logs, eating, talking, or clapping to the steady stream of upbeat bluegrass tunes.

As they came up behind the Packards, the two former feminists stopped and peered up at them. The brothers smiled as the Packards stopped and looked behind.

"You probably don't recognize us, but I'm Joe Rawlings, and this is my brother Keith. We've lived right across the road from you for the past twenty-two years or so." Joe reached out his hand with his most amiable smile.

"We know who you are," Fred replied, shaking his hand weakly.

"Oh, you do. Well, in any event, we just wanted to make sure y'all were doin' alright. We saw some guys shoot up your house pretty good, and we just wanted to check on you."

"We're fine, thanks."

"Well, I'm glad to hear it," Joe said. He stood quietly for a few seconds, waiting for the Packards to say something. They didn't.

Keith had already shaken hands with the Packards. He looked around, not knowing what to say or do next. He reached his hand out toward the two women, who were still watching them, and introduced himself. "Hi. Keith Rawlings. Good to meet you."

Joe followed. "Hey. Joe Rawlings. Nice to meet you."

The women shook their hands and replied the same: "Hi."

Joe turned to look at the Packards who had turned back around. He cleared his throat and said, "Well, I'd love to hang around and talk all day with you, but we gotta go work out some business with Jim Baker, so... You know how it is."

There was no response.

Joe elbowed Keith, turned around, and left. "That was weird," he said, making his way toward Jim Baker.

Keith shook his head. "Man, I'm sure glad I have such a socially adept brother to show me how to interact with people."

"Hey, man. It takes two to tango. The best talker in the world can't carry a conversation by himself."

"I can."

"Imaginary friends don't count."

Jim was talking to Jack Winters and Tim Faulkner. As the brothers approached, the men turned and nodded to them. "Fellers," Jim said. "How you doin'?"

"Doin' alright," Joe replied. "Tim, good to see you. Family doin' well?"

"Yeah, we're all well," Tim nodded.

"Jack." Keith looked into the man's dark eyes. "Doin' alright?"

Jack paused for a half a second. The men's eyes shifted to his face. He had to choose his response from the two options Keith's question laid before him. He could say with a display of anger, outrage, and indignation: *Well, Keith, two of my kids are still dead, but otherwise, just great. Thanks for asking.* But his kids were dead and buried. They weren't coming back. No amount of outrage would change that, and no one needed his self-pity. Instead, he chose the second option: "We're all good. Thanks." He didn't have the privilege of crying. He gave a half-grin in defiance of the pain, and they all nodded, breathed silently, and smiled with him.

"We were just talking about the communication plan." Tim scratched his patchy beard. "We think it needs some work."

Keith shrugged. "You'll get no argument from me. What do you have in mind?"

"We still don't have a way to know what's going on if someone invades from the woods," Jim said. "Sure, the property owner might start shooting, if he happens to be there when they come, if they don't take him out first, and if he happens to be armed while walking around on his own property at the time—all of which is in doubt, by the way—but how will we know he isn't just doing target practice or something? We won't know what's going on from the sound of shots."

Keith and Joe both nodded.

"We're too spread out to work together." Jim shook his head. "We don't have enough radios, boys."

"No. We don't. But each house is close enough to the next that people will be able to know if their neighbor is in a fight. The idea was that we would *not* work together as a cohesive unit. Every man defends his own."

"Right, but we can't afford to let people stand alone against groups of attackers. They'll be overwhelmed, and the invaders will get a foothold in the community. They could do a whole lot of damage before we stopped them—if we ever stop them. We need to communicate with each house."

"So, what did you come up with?"

"Well, we can't tell people around here not to hunt or shoot on their own land. That's not gonna fly, but Jack and his deputies will be able to ride to each house to investigate the sound of shots, and they can ride back to the barn to report so we can muster a response team."

"Okay."

"And we need runners. From each guard post. To run down the road, knocking up each house between the lookout and the barn to warn them."

"That's a lot of posts," Joe said. "How are we going to get that many volunteers?"

"I'll take care of that," Jack said. "I think it will be easier than you imagine. There are a lot of hunters on these roads. A lot of homesteaders, farmers, and gardeners. But there are a lot of people who don't have those skills, don't have the land to work with, and don't have the time to learn by experience. They need jobs."

Joe's eyebrows rose. "Are you suggesting we hire full time guards paid by the community?"

"It's not such a bad idea," Tim added. "They need food; the farmers need security. The planters can't be distracted by security concerns. The crops are going to require the full attention of the most experienced growers."

"You're talking about taxing people," Joe said, looking into the men's faces. "If there's one way to make people struggling to survive angry, it's to take what's theirs away from them and tell 'em it's for their own good."

"Go easy, Joe. It's not like that." Tim shook his head. "We're not trying to be the government. This is all voluntary. No one will be forced to do anything."

Joe shrugged. "Well, then, how are you going to get them to pay into a communal security fund?"

"We'll talk to them," Tim said.

Jack put his hand on Joe's shoulder. "Look. I understand where you're coming from. I hate taxes as much as the next guy, but it's not because I resent paying for services that I actually use. It's because I know that the government would always tax way too much, waste my money on stupid crap, and overpay themselves and their corrupt cronies for the job. That's not what we're doing. We're going to have complete transparency and have the guards and the residents come to an agreement on what will be paid for what services."

Jim jumped in. "I, for one, would be more than willing to pay for the security. And I bet most other farmers would think the same way I do. We all know what those marauders came for. We know who's most vulnerable." Jim nodded to Keith. "Keith, would you be willing to chip in a little meat and vegetables for professional security?"

Keith bobbed his head from side to side, as if weighing the options in his brain while staring at the ground. "Yeah, if we vet them. I don't want to be paying any drug-addled losers to take naps on duty."

"I don't think we have to worry about drug-addled losers anymore, but I'll vet 'em," Jack said.

The men looked at Joe for a second. He still looked uncomfortable with the idea.

Keith shrugged. "It might be the best way."

"As long as everyone agrees to it," Joe said. "In the meantime, now's as good a time as any to tell you about our own crazy idea."

"What's that?" Jim asked.

"You know that old truck we got back in the woods?"

"I think I saw a blue one back there when we got the water tank," Tim said.

"That's it. Well, we got it running."

"Great."

"And we're planning a trip to try to find Mom's family."

"Hmm." Tim looked seriously at the brothers with a frown; the others looked unhappy as well. "Where's this trip taking you?"

"Illinois."

"Holy…" Jim began to exclaim as Tim put a hand near his face to shush him. They didn't want to be overheard by the whole gathering. "You're right!" Jim resumed in a lower voice, half whispering, half shouting. "That is crazy!"

"Do you not remember how our trip into town went?" Tim prodded. "That was just to Bloomington. A few miles away. Only a week after this whole thing started. What do you think it's like out there now? And you want to drive out of state?"

"I know…" Joe was starting to say.

"No, you don't know," Jack interrupted. "You think you're the only ones missing family members right now? We've all got relatives living far away, and none of us knows if they're alive or dead. You know how many houses are empty now because people left to go find relatives and never came back? And now, you're going to leave when this community is depending on you? Have you thought about where that would leave the rest of us?"

Keith and Joe stood silent for several seconds. They hadn't thought of that. Neither of them had thought that they affected the community that much. They assumed that, if they had gone, people would go about their lives as if nothing had changed. The brothers glanced at one another. That seemed ridiculous now. Of course, they had an effect on the lives of their neighbors. Without them, it was far less likely that the community would survive.

"I hadn't considered that," Keith finally said.

"Look," Tim said, leaning in a bit and lowering his voice even more. "You're all free to make your own decisions. No one's going to hold you here against your will, but I'm telling you, this is a bad idea. Don't do it."

Jim and Jack both frowned at the brothers, shaking their heads.

Joe nodded, looked at Keith, and looked back at the three forbidding faces. "We thought you'd say that. We'll talk about it with the family. We were going to make a test run first anyway."

"You talk about it," said Jack. "And think about what we said. And don't take off without telling us first."

"We won't," Keith promised.

The group began to disperse. The crowd was gradually growing smaller as well. People trickled away from the gathering in pairs and small groups, walking down the road. The brothers turned to find the other family members. They found Kent, Faye, Malik, and Jordan sitting and talking with the Jorgensons. They looked around for Lynn but didn't see her.

Joe tapped on Kent's shoulder. "Where's Lynn?"

"I thought she was with you," he said. He didn't seem too concerned, but he also kept his voice low so Faye wouldn't overhear them; she was listening to Lydia tell a story.

Joe shook his head. "No."

"She's probably playing with her friends in the field. Go find her. If she's not there, check the outhouse."

They walked toward the field to see a couple dozen kids playing kickball and passing frisbees back and forth. They scanned the faces of the players. Lynn was not among them.

"I gotta take a leak anyway," Joe said.

They walked up to the barn which had been converted into a large outhouse with a row of stalls made from plywood, nails, and old door hinges dug out of toolboxes and coffee cans. There was a small line for the stalls, and after waiting for a couple of minutes, Keith and Joe took their turns urinating in five-gallon buckets housed in wooden boxes in the stalls. Ernie was not just getting rid of an old cow that was an unnecessary strain on his feed supply; he was collecting free fertilizer for his fields too. By the look of the full buckets, he was getting a sizeable return on his investment.

They didn't see Lynn in the line or anywhere around the outhouse. Keith called her name into the barn and listened for a response from one of the stalls. Nothing. They looked through the crowd again. The people were beginning to leave. Parents were calling kids in from the field. Ben Jameson was taking a load of passengers to the north end of the road. The sun was sinking. It was just touching the tops of the trees. The fire was dying down and the cooks were cleaning up.

The brothers walked down the sloping field toward the ravine. There were only a few kids left playing in the field now. The Faulkner kids were among them. Joe asked if they had seen Lynn. They said they weren't sure, but they saw some bigger kids go into the woods at the bottom of the hill. Keith and Joe continued down toward the tree line.

As they neared the woods, they saw a flash of blonde hair from behind a huge black oak tree. Lynn stepped backward for a second, unobstructed by the tree. She didn't notice them. She was looking at something behind the trunk of the black oak.

"There she is," Joe said to his brother.

Just then, they saw a hand spring out from behind the tree, grab her wrist, and yank her out of sight. Keith began stomping toward the black oak, his rifle slung over his shoulder, his right hand wrapping around the pistol at his thigh. Joe followed with clenched fists. As they approached, they saw Lynn reappear from behind the tree with her arms around a boy's neck, peeling her face away from his.

Keith and Joe stopped in their tracks. They were not prepared for that. Lynn separated from the boy and began walking up the hill toward them. They kept their eyes on the kid beside the tree as he watched their sister walk away. Then, his eyes met Keith's. His face went pale in an instant, and he disappeared behind the oak tree once again.

"I think that was Dan Tyler's kid," Joe said.

Keith relaxed his hand away from the pistol grip.

Lynn saw the brothers standing there. "What are you guys doing?" she said, continuing to walk past them.

"Looking for you. What were you doing? Who was that?" Keith pressed.

"Who?"

"What do you mean, who? The dude you were trying to resuscitate." They walked up the gentle rise toward the gathering.

Lynn continued in front of them toward the rest of the family. "Just a guy."

"Just a guy?"

"Unlike you two losers, I actually have a life."

"What's that supposed to mean?" Joe interrogated.

"You haven't been on a date in months. You're not getting any younger. And Keith hasn't dated anyone since he got back home. He's, like, middle-age now."

"Been a little preoccupied lately," Joe said.

"Yeah, well, if you stay preoccupied for too long, you're going to wake up one day and realize it's too late; you missed your chance at having something meaningful. It's not worth trying to survive if you forget to live."

Keith and Joe stood at the crest in the field. They looked at each other and back at Lynn as she continued to walk toward their parents who were packing their lawn chairs and waving at them to hurry up.

Chapter Thirteen

Day 61

S cott Adams looked around at his privacy hedge with a
suspicious eye. Was anyone watching him? He couldn't
be too careful. After buying a small rototiller and some seeds
with some of his batteries and MREs, he had decided to try
growing a garden to cover his bases. He tilled a small patch of
ground in his backyard and locked the tiller in the shed. He
went inside the house and lit a cigarette, watching through
the kitchen window to see if anyone peeked in through the
trees. Someone might have heard the sound of the rototiller
engine and thought about stealing it. Or they might come to
steal his plants. He needed more security, he told himself.

It looked like the coast was clear. Maybe they were afraid
to mess with him, he thought. Or maybe no one was around
to hear him. They were having an Easter celebration down
around Jim Baker's barn today. It was supposed to be a
Sunday service followed by an Easter egg hunt. It was a perfect day for it. Sunny with temperatures in the low sixties.
With the warmer weather over the past couple weeks, the
hens were laying again, and several of the homesteaders who
raised chickens were donating boiled eggs for the kids to
find. Jim Baker had invited him, but he declined. He didn't
want to be around all those people. He didn't want to be
away from the house for too long either. Plus, he had plans.
He was going to plant his garden today. He was getting tired

of MREs, and his supply of canned goods would only last so long. He figured he may as well try to grow some more food.

Scott stepped outside again, took one last drag on his cigarette, and pulled the plastic bags of seeds out of his pocket. He had never liked vegetables much, but he figured he could stand tomatoes, potatoes, and corn. He could eat corn on the cobb and dip French fries in his homemade ketchup. That didn't sound like too bad of a deal. He marked out some more or less straight lines in the dirt with a stick and began poking seeds down into the soil with his fingers. How far apart should he plant them? Oh, about six inches or so ought to be good, he reckoned. He used his hand as a measurement and brushed dirt over the seeds after poking them into the clay.

He looked up periodically to make sure no one was watching him, and when he finished, he stood back and admired his work. He had three rows about two feet apart from each other. He had seen some of his neighbors' gardens, so he knew he needed to be able to walk in between his plants to harvest his vegetables. "Oh!" he muttered to himself. He had almost forgotten. He went to his shed and got a bucket of water which he had collected from a rain barrel. Walking carefully between his rows, he poured water over the dirt where his seeds were buried. When he finished, he put the bucket away and took out another cigarette. "This is easier than I thought," he said to himself, and he went to putting up trip wires and alarms around the yard to warn him of thieves coming to steal his crops.

Day 62

The next day, Scott awoke to the sound of crows cawing outside his house. He thought nothing of it. He went to his pantry, retrieved a can of chili for breakfast, opened it, and turned on the kerosene camp stove to heat it up as he went to mix some instant coffee. He set the steel canteen cup on the camp stove beside his can of chili and took out a cigarette while he waited. The crows sure were noisy, he thought. Why were they annoying him today? "Why couldn't they go bother someone else?" he said to himself. Then, a thought came to his mind. "Scarecrows!" he yelled. He dropped his cigarette on the countertop and ran outside. As the screen door swung open, a mass of black feathers burst into the air and dissipated into the trees with a cacophony of discordant caws.

"Damn birds," he muttered.

After finishing his breakfast, he began working on building his own scarecrow. He drove a stick into the ground at one of the corners of his garden and took out some old clothes. He tied off the sleeves of the shirt and the cuffs of the pantlegs and stuffed them full of sticks. He wired the pants to the post, secured the shirt around the stick, made a head out of an MRE pouch stuffed with trash, fastened a hat on top, and tied it all up with paracord. Taking out a black permanent marker, he drew an angry face on the bag, complete with arched eyebrows and a crescent moon frown. "There," he said when he had finished. "That ought to keep them away."

He looked at the bare dirt of his garden. There were holes in the corn row where the soil had been scratched and dug through. "Dirty bastards probably stole some of my corn," Scott said to himself. "Ah well. Who needs corn, anyway? At least, they didn't get my French fries."

It was noon now. It was cooler today than yesterday. The thermometer on his back porch said fifty-four degrees. It was still a nice day, however, and as he sat on the porch with his shotgun, he watched the clouds roll past in the sky above his garden and lit another cigarette.

Day 65

Scott awoke in his chair in the basement as the radio crackled. He turned it off and went outside to take a leak. The cold air made him shiver, and he rubbed his arms against the chill. "Good grief," he muttered to himself. His breath poured out in a steaming fog.

He looked around the yard to see if anyone was watching him. He didn't see anyone. He unzipped his fly and began walking backward around the perimeter of his tiny garden, urinating on the ground as he did so. It might help to keep animals away. He was sure he had heard that somewhere. He almost made a complete circuit. Pretty good, he thought. He looked up at the treetops to see if there were any crows. He heard a caw and raised his shotgun. One of the black fiends flew overhead. He tried to draw a bead on the bird, but it was too quick and disappeared out of sight behind the roof of his house. "That's right, move along, buddy. You don't want any of this."

In the distance, he heard a clanging noise. He listened closely for a second. It sounded like a bell. Suddenly, he heard more noises mingling with the first, only fainter and coming from another direction. He heard some people shouting down the road, and he ran inside, down to the basement, and turned on his radio. He flipped it to the channel Jack Winters and the lookouts were using and listened as the voices reported over the radio.

"LP 1, radio check."

"Roger. Lima Charlie."

"LP 2, radio check."

"Roger. Lima Charlie."

"LP 3, radio check."

"Roger. Lima Charlie."

Scott keyed his radio. "Badger, this is Scorpion. I read you Lima Charlie. How me? Over."

Scott had insisted on the call signs. He said he wouldn't participate unless they used his call sign. The radio was quiet for a second. Scott repeated his transmission.

"Lima Charlie, Scorpion. Did everyone hear the signal okay?"

"Affirmative," Scott said.

"Good on LP 1."

"Good on LP 2."

"Good on LP 3."

"Roger. Solid. Turn off your radios. Thanks, guys."

Scott put down the receiver and turned his radio off again. He went upstairs to get something to eat, and as he pulled out a can of soup, he heard the cawing of crows in the backyard. He slammed the can on the countertop, grabbed his shotgun, and ran out the back door to see a crow perched on top of his scarecrow with a piece of a seed potato in its beak. The crow flew away as soon as the door swung shut, and it was followed by others taking wing from his patch of bare dirt. As the crows flew into the tree line, Scott fired toward them with a load of buckshot. He didn't hit anything. He cursed the crows and went to see what had become of his garden when he started to shiver and noticed his breath forming clouds in the air. He went back inside and shut the door behind him. He needed to build a fire.

Day 68

Scott hadn't seen crows in his backyard for a couple of days. Maybe he had scared them off for good with his shotgun. He walked out to the garden and looked closely at the soil, as he did every day, to see if any plants were coming up. He wasn't sure what a tomato plant looked like, but he did see several small, green leaves in his garden. They were all scattered throughout the dirt, though. Surely some of them had to be his plants, but the other ones must have been weeds, he thought. He hadn't planted that many seeds.

Crouching down and looking at the imaginary line between the stakes at either end of the rows, Scott thought there were a few leaves that looked different from the others, but he wasn't sure. They were still so small and indistinct he didn't dare try to pull any weeds. All the rows looked the same to him, so he went back inside to start making breakfast. He began cooking some eggs he bought from the general store and took out a can of spam from his pantry to go with it. On his little kerosene stove, he began heating water for some instant coffee as well.

Scott took his breakfast down to the basement and surfed through channels on his radio as he ate. Through the static, he heard something. It sounded like a voice. He adjusted the dials carefully, trying to get a clearer signal. The voice came in suddenly, and he removed his hand from the dial. It sounded like a man's voice. He was saying something about being in a building for six weeks working on a radio. Scott listened nonchalantly, shoveling spam and eggs into his mouth and savoring every bite as he chewed. Until now, the only eggs he had eaten since the blackout were rehydrated freeze-dried eggs which he covered with salsa to mask the dish soap flavor and rubbery texture. He wiped some egg yolk from his beard and licked it off his hand before taking a sip of coffee.

The voice on the radio continued in a tired, anxious tone. *"I'm still in the armory in Bloomington for now. The Indiana National Guard came here to facilitate the distribution of food and supplies from the food bank, but we could only find a few guardsmen who lived nearby."*

At the mention of Bloomington and Indiana National Guard, Scott froze and listened attentively, barely breathing. He set his coffee cup back down and turned up the volume. The man went on recounting his history of the past nine weeks. Scott shot up, knocked over his chair, and began searching around the room for a pen and paper. Looking on his shelves, he remembered that he had a notebook and pencils on his table, and he snatched them from on top of the ammo cans containing radios and backup batteries. He stood listening to the speaker and taking hurried notes in the dim light of a single lantern.

"I used their home of record addresses and found a total of eight. I told them we were acting under orders to secure the area until the army arrived. It worked for a while. I told them that it was just a local problem caused by a solar flare, but after a couple of days of driving around in my old pickup instead of a military vehicle and seeing that we never communicated with anyone else from the Army, they began to ask questions, and eventually, I had to tell them the truth. I took them to the armory and equipped them all. We tried to distribute food from the food bank, but that only lasted one day.

"On the second day, another crowd of people showed up, demanding food. We passed out all that was left, but it wasn't enough for everyone. The mob started accusing us of hoarding supplies for ourselves, and they began to get violent. We kept them back until we could get everyone out of there. It looked like some of the civilians were injured. They were mostly fighting each other over the food and supplies. The next day, we stayed at the armory, because the food bank was empty. We had boxes of MREs in the armory, but we needed to guard the weapons and government property from the rioters. It didn't take long for the mob to show up at the gates. They said we had stolen all the supplies and were keeping it for ourselves. They began throwing rocks and trash over the fence. I tried to tell them that we didn't have any more food, that the food bank had been depleted. But they would not accept it. The crowd was getting more and more violent. There were only eight of us and at least one-hundred of them. They demanded we bring them supplies. I wanted to pacify the situation as much as possible, so I had my men bring out boxes of MREs to distribute. We only had a couple of dozen, but we brought

out half of the boxes and began throwing individual MREs over the fence into the crowd. It wasn't enough though. The rioters started climbing the fences. Then, someone started shooting. It might have been firecrackers, but it sounded like gunshots. My guys panicked. They started firing into the crowd. I ordered them to cease fire, but they didn't hear me among all the shooting."

There was a break in the transmission for a few seconds. Then, the radio chirped, and the speaker continued his transmission.

"When the shooting stopped, there were something like fifty dead civilians, and dozens of wounded were dragged away or left to crawl. The soldiers retreated back into the armory, and we stayed the night there. The next day, all of my men deserted. I stayed.

"I've been walking around, trying to assess the situation. Every store has been looted. Most of the houses have been robbed or burglarized. Gangs rove the streets by day, raiding houses and threatening people. Mostly young people. I've seen hundreds of houses burnt to ashes. Some from arson. Most were probably accidents from makeshift woodstoves and fireplaces. Judging by the decrease in activity, the decrease in smoke from houses, and what I've seen in the nursing homes and hospitals, I would estimate civilian casualties around fifty percent. Exposure, hunger, sickness, violence. Bodies lay in streets and yards and hang from trees and rot in houses and stores. Packs of wild dogs dig through garbage and feed on the bodies. I've seen them attack people for food. I tried helping some before, but I saw so many people used as decoys or bait for traps. I almost got caught one time. A group of four people used a crying child to lure me in and rob me. I assume the child was one of theirs, but I don't know. I escaped. I killed three of them though. I'm sure I did.

"I went back to my apartment a couple days after I lost my men. The place had been ransacked. While I was there, someone stole my truck. I had to walk twenty-two miles

back to the armory. I've been huddled under blankets and sleeping bags, trying to fix this radio every night for the past seven weeks. I finally got it working. People tried to break into the armory again, a couple of times, but they weren't able to. If anyone is listening, do not come to Bloomington, Indiana. It's lost. There's nothing left to save. I'm on my last box of MREs. My batteries are nearly all dead, and I'm running out of fuel. I've been disinfecting ditch water with iodine tablets, but I'm running out of those as well. I'm going to head north tomorrow. I'll try to link up with another unit or something. Try to see how widespread the damage is. Hopefully, I can find another vehicle. I might have family up in Michigan still. I don't know. If Michigan is the same as this, maybe we can get asylum in Canada."

There was another pause.

"Is anyone listening? Can anybody hear me?"

Scott reached out for the radio but stayed his hand. What could he say? He couldn't tell the man about this place. Certainly not over the radio. It could be a trap. Anybody could be listening. How would he know? He retracted his hand and left the microphone in its place, and the exasperated voice returned.

"I'm going to try to find some more supplies, and then, I'm leaving first thing in the morning. I'll take the radio and keep trying to reach someone every day. If you do come through this area, whatever you do, stay away from campus. Lieutenant Morris over and out."

"Why?" Scott heard himself say. He almost grabbed the microphone again, but he stopped himself. He looked at the notes he had scribbled down.

Just then, there was a chirp, and another voice came over the radio. A deeper voice. Cruel and sinister. Scott's body tensed up when he heard it. *"What's wrong with campus?"* it said. There was no reply, but a hideous, shrill laugh followed. Scott stood out of his chair and shut the radio off. He shivered as he started up the stairs. He had to find Jack.

Kent eased the old, blue Ford between the barricades. At the gravel parking lot of the old church, he brought it to a stop and shut off the engine.

Tim Faulkner's green Chevy was parked directly in front of the church doors. Tim, Jack Winters, and Jim Baker all stood in the road beside the final barricades before the highway. They walked toward the parked truck as Keith, Joe, and Kent climbed out of the vehicle. The men all shook hands. "You sure we can't talk you out of this?"

"We're running dangerously low on supplies," Joe said. "If we don't go now, we'll lose our chance."

"We'll be alright," Kent smiled.

"I just want to make sure we have all our bases covered." Jim rubbed his nose with the back of his hand. "Tell us again where you're going."

Joe screwed the lid back onto his water bottle. "We're going straight to the bypass. And we're going to take it to Ellettsville and back."

"That road is blocked with traffic," Jim said, shaking his head. "Unless somebody moved those cars. And in that case, you might have even bigger problems."

Keith nodded. "If we hit an impasse, or something doesn't check out, we'll turn around and come right back."

"You take this." Jack handed Keith a radio. "It's already set to our channel. If you have any problems at all, call us. We're going to be waiting right here, if you need us."

"Actually," Jim put in. "Just keep your radio on and give us regular updates. I want to know what it looks like out there anyway."

"Yeah," Jack added. "We'll spare the fuel to recharge the batteries. Don't worry about that."

"And gentlemen," Kent said. "We're going to be back, but if something does happen, and you don't see us again, I'm leaving my house and all my property to my friends Malik and Jordan McCormick."

"Understood," Jack replied. "Good luck. Don't stop to smell the roses."

The men all shook hands again. Kent climbed back into the driver's seat, and Jack disengaged the parking brake of the car which acted as the gate for their blockade. The car was rolled out of the way, and the Rawlings brothers climbed into the back. Jack stood in the exit path as Kent pulled the truck forward. Holding his hand up, signaling Kent to wait a moment, Jack held his radio up to his mouth.

The radio in Keith's hand chirped. *"Blue Falcon, this is Winter. Radio check."*

Keith laughed and replied into the radio Jack had given him, "Loud and clear. How me?"

"Read you the same. Good luck." Jack stepped out of the way and waved them on through as Kent pressed down the accelerator.

Scott Adams knocked on the door to the Winters house. It was answered by a kid—Jack's youngest.

"Can I help you?" The boy asked.

"Hey, uh." Scott suddenly seemed to forget what he was going to say. "How are you doing? Oh, I'm Scott. Umm—" He looked around somewhat nervously. "Is Jack here? Your dad?"

"No, sir."

"Oh—uh—Where is he?"

"He said he was going up the road to the church," the boy responded.

"Thank you," Scott said as he turned to hike up the road. His plate carrier rubbed his collar bone beneath his jacket. He tried to ease the pressure a bit by lifting the front plate with his free hand as he walked. In his other, he carried his semi-automatic rifle. It was nearly a two mile walk to the church from his house, and it was more exercise than he had got in years. By the time he reached the church parking lot where Jack was standing with Jim Baker and Tim Faulkner, he was out of breath, sweating beneath his plate carrier, and cramping in his right calf.

The men stood beside the barricade and watched him struggle over the train tracks toward them, laughing quietly among themselves at how ridiculous he looked.

"Why is the gate open?" Scott panted, trying to catch his breath. He sat down on the concrete step at the front of the old church, rubbed his calf, and worked the lid off a canteen.

"What's got you so fired up? Take your time. Catch your breath." Jack grinned, amused at the man.

Scott began, "I..."

"Hang on." Jack stopped him and held up a radio so everyone could hear.

"Turning onto the bypass. It looks like most of the cars have been moved. There are barricades around parking lots. I'm seeing a lot of broken windows. A lot of burned down buildings. And Winter, we've got more bodies."

"Who is that?"

"Shush!" Jim held up his hand.

Tim was jotting down notes in a notebook.

"It looks like a warzone out here."

Jack brought the radio closer to his mouth and pressed the button. "Are there any threats? Anyone following you?"

"None so far. I've seen a few people walking around. Some were armed. They looked at us, but that was it. It looks like they've planted gardens in the golf course. Wait a minute. There are some people out there. Working in the fields with hand tools. They're digging up the golf course. Must be planting more crops. It looks like they've got armed guards watching them. Whoa. Somebody has painted a real masterpiece on the water tower."

"Who is that?" Scott repeated.

"Rawlings," Tim replied.

"They're going through campus?"

"Tried to stop 'em." Tim shrugged.

"No, you have to tell them..."

"Shush!" Jim hissed again as Jack held up his hand for silence.

"We might have a problem."

The men were visibly anxious. They looked like they were holding their breath as they waited silently to hear what new calamity had befallen them.

"It looks like there's an obstruction up ahead. The bypass is blocked. There are telephone poles lying across the road, just after the stoplight at Dunn Street. I guess we're going to turn on Dunn and take Seventeenth Street..."

"No!" Scott shouted. "Do not turn on Dunn! Tell them to turn around!"

Jack glanced at Scott out of the corner of his eye and brought the radio to his face once again. "Negative, Blue Falcon. Do not turn on Dunn. Turn around and come straight back. I say again: Turn around and come straight back. Get out of there."

There was a pause. Jack didn't dare try to transmit. He held the radio up and listened.

"Stand by."

The men waited, glancing at one another. Tim held his hand up over his mouth. Scott pulled out his notebook on which he had transcribed the details of the radio transmission he had heard about an hour ago. He handed the notes over to Jim Baker to read. Jim's eyes scanned over the notes quickly, and he handed the notebook to Tim who likewise examined the content. Tim passed the information off to Jack who nodded and frowned as he read.

"Winter. We're coming back now."

"Solid copy," Jack responded.

"But we picked up a tail."

Jack cursed and spat on the ground. "Alright. How many?"

"Two. They pulled out behind us when we passed Fee Lane."

"Are you taking fire?"

"No. They're just driving behind us like they just happen to be going the same way we are."

"Alright. Don't worry about it. Just come back like normal, and keep us updated on your progress."

"Will do."

"They're stalking," Jack said to the men standing with him. "They want to see where they go and what they have there."

The men nodded in agreement. Jack handed the notebook back to Scott.

"Turning off of the bypass now."

Jack raised the radio. "Roger. What are they driving?".

"Some old 1960s cars. Probably stolen," Came the response.

"Can you see the drivers? What do they look like?"

"I see two of them. They look pretty weird. They're definitely not from Mount Sinai. I don't want to fire on them unless they shoot first."

"Right."

"Just passed the post office."

"They're still following?"

"Yes."

"Okay. They're going to trail you until you stop. They want to see where you're going. You understand?"

"Solid."

"Here's what I want you to do. Drive straight past LP 1, and dog leg at LP 2. I'll take care of your tails."

"Understood. Passing the gas station now."

Scott looked around at the three men's faces. He wasn't sure what was happening. "What should we do, Jack?"

"Shut the gate," Jack responded. "Roll that car back into place."

Scott and the two others went to shove the car back into position in the barricade.

Jack addressed the lookout in the bell tower. "Lookout! Radio LP 2 and let them know that a blue truck is coming in. It's one of ours. Once you're done, take the rest of the day off. I'm relieving you."

The bell began to ring, Jack unslung his rifle and went inside the church. Up the road, they could hear the rumble of engines coming their way.

"Do not let them see you!" Jack shouted from the bell tower.

The men unslung their weapons and crouched down behind the barricade cars.

The blue truck smoked and growled as it crested the hill. It came roaring down the straight with the two cars following, drove right past the barricade blocking off Mount Sinai, crunched bones under its tires, and sped down the hill and around the bend. The lead car came abreast of the barricade, and there was a loud bang, the shattering of glass, and the revving of an engine as it veered off to the right, ran up onto the bank past the church, and flipped over onto its hood. Two seconds after the first, there was a second bang, and the rear car swerved into the barricade with a crash.

Scott remained crouching beside the other two men behind the cars until he saw the door of the old church swing open and Jack Winters walk out. He stood up and turned around to see a car crumpled against the barricade, its windshield spiderwebbed around a small hole on the driver's side. The windows and upholstery were splattered as if a gallon can of red paint had exploded inside the car. He stood, staring with his mouth agape, beginning to feel dizzy.

"You owe me two rounds of .308 Winchester," Jack said flatly as the brothers approached him.

"We're sorry, Jack," Keith began. "You were right. It was too dangerous. We shouldn't have gone. But it wasn't entirely up to us. It's Mom's family, you know? Anyway, we got a better idea of what's going on outside. That's got to count for something."

Jack was silent. He didn't look at them. His face didn't change. He merely continued tying the knots that secured the man's ankles to the legs of the chair.

Joe watched him awkwardly. "Thanks for helping us, Jack. Really."

Jack finished his knot, stood up, and glanced at the brothers. "You owe me two rounds of .308 Winchester."

"You'll get them," Keith replied.

They hadn't seen Jack look this way since the day of the hanging. He was somewhere else in his mind, it seemed. He had a job to do. A filthy job. A job that disgusted him. But there was no way around it; it had to be done, and he was the one who had to do it.

Keith knew the answer before he asked the question, but he asked anyway in an attempt to ease the tension in the room. "Who's this?"

"This is one of your tails," Jack replied, knowing they knew. "There were four all together. The drivers are both dead. The passenger in the first car was crushed when the vehicle rolled over on him. This guy was knocked out when his car ran into our barricade and his head bounced off the windshield. He's still alive for now."

"What are you going to do with him?" Joe asked. Once the words escaped his lips, he realized it was a stupid question.

Jack looked at him with a deadpan expression and let the question hang in the air. "Might as well try to get some information out of him. That's what he wanted out of you."

"Are you going to..." Joe began. "Shouldn't we take a vote or something to decide what to do with him?"

"There's nothing to vote on," Jack said. "We can't feed him. You let him go, he'll tell his friends about this place." Jack shook his head. "The fewer people who know about this, the better."

Keith and Joe didn't argue. They knew he was right. There weren't many options available. They looked at the kid tied to the chair. He was no more than Joe's age by the look of him. Long hair and a patchy beard matted with drying blood from his head and, presumably, that of his driver. He sat, slumped in the wooden chair, in an empty concrete pool at the front of the church.

"I'm going to ask him some questions," Jack said, scratching his beard. The light brown hair was quickly turning gray. "And then, we won't talk about this again. I'm on guard duty until tomorrow morning." He picked up a bucket of rainwater and looked at them. "You shouldn't be here."

Keith and Joe stepped back without saying a word. They walked out the door of the old church, and continued silently down the road, toward home.

Day 69

Scott sprinkled water over the rows in his tiny garden. He looked at the plants. He was beginning to see a difference in the leaves, he thought. Happy with himself, he stood up, looked around with a contented smile and pulled out a cigarette. He was reaching for his lighter when he heard the ringing of his bell. He had hung a small but loudly audible bell from the fence post near his mailbox for anyone who needed to get his attention. He didn't want anyone sneaking up on him or even stepping onto his property without his expressed permission, and it was mutually beneficial, since most of his neighbors expressed their desire to avoid encountering booby traps.

Scott made his way back into the house, peered through the boards he had nailed over his window frames, and saw Keith and Joe Rawlings standing at the end of his driveway. He stepped over a trip wire, unlocked the door, and went to greet his guests.

"Jim told us you had some information we needed to hear."

"That's right. Come on, we can talk inside. Just make sure you only step on the yellow rocks." He turned around and went back inside.

The brothers looked at each other. "Is he serious?" Joe asked.

"I'm not calling his bluff," Keith replied.

Keith kept his eyes on the colorful array of stepping-stones that made up the path to the front door. They were painted red, yellow, green, and blue.

Scott watched from the window to see if they would fall for it. He laughed as he watched them hopscotch over his walkway. There was nothing special about the yellow stones. When they reached the door, he opened it and waved them in.

"What would happen if you didn't step on the yellow stones?" Joe asked.

Scott smiled. "That's for me to know."

———————————

There was a knock on the door.

"That's him!" Lynn exclaimed. "I gotta go." She tucked her brother's holstered pistol in her waistband, grabbed a jacket and her picnic basket, and started for the door.

"Hold on," Kent said. "Do I know this guy?"

"Yeah, it's Matthew Tyler. Daniel and Susan Tyler's son. He lives at the top of the hill, in that white house with the horses, you know?" She reached for the doorknob.

"Alright, well, just don't..."

"I know," Lynn interjected.

"And don't let him..." Faye began.

"I know," Lynn rolled her eyes, grabbing the doorknob.

Faye grabbed her daughter and hugged her. "Make sure you..."

"Mom, I know! I'm not a child." Lynn wrenched away from her mother's grasp and opened the door.

Standing in the doorway, the young man stood smiling, hat in hand. "Good afternoon," he said with a false display of confidence.

Kent eyed the kid up and down. He was beardless, and it made him look very young compared to most other men—the beards now being what differentiated men from boys in the community. "Hello. Kent Rawlings." He shook the boy's hand.

"Matthew Tyler. It's good to meet you."

"Where are you guys going?"

"We were just planning to have a picnic down by the creek," the young man said, clearly nervous.

Kent nodded. "Well, you just make sure you bring my daughter back before dark."

"Yes, sir."

"And I mean well before dark," Kent added. "I know where you live."

"Alright, Dad. That's enough." Lynn poked her father in the gut with her index finger and took Matthew's hand. "Come on, let's go."

They stepped off the porch, walking hand in hand through the brown, fallen leaves and sprouting plants, and they carried their basket along with their guns down the hill among the chorus of birdsong.

Sitting on the bank of the creek, in a small field where wildflowers grew, they started a small fire to cook their squirrels, and they watched the gurgling creek running over green and brown sandstone as they waited and talked.

"What was it like out there?" Matthew asked, picking a wild tulip to keep from staring at her.

Lynn studied his face, his ears, the hair curling behind them. The blonde peach fuzz on his nineteen-year-old face was just beginning to resemble whiskers. He glanced back at her, and she looked away, trying to hide her smile. She sighed and said, "I was scared."

Matthew handed the tulip to her.

She took it with a smile and looked down at the small, delicate thing in her hand, the flames dancing and crackling behind it. "It's a ghost of what it was. It's hard to believe how different things are just outside of this tiny community— how bad it is out there. Who could have imagined that this would happen here?" She turned and looked deep into his eyes as he stared back at her. "Is there any future left for us?"

Day 70

Three weeks after the first day of spring, Scott woke up and immediately went outside to get wood for the stove. The thermometer said eighteen degrees. It was ten in the morning.

Sliding the logs onto the coals in the woodstove, he shut the door and opened the vents. As he stood beside the stove, looking out the window, he began to notice tiny, white specks drifting through the sky. He continued to stare as the specks grew larger and flew by his window at a higher velocity. The trees swayed in the wind. The sky looked dark and angry. Piling up on the rails of his porch, the roof of the shed, the grass in his lawn, and the bare dirt of his garden, was a fluffy, white snow.

The frozen precipitation accumulated for several hours, and when it stopped, Scott could no longer even tell where his garden was. Everything was buried beneath four inches of snow. Scott wasn't sure what he should do, so he lit a cigarette and began heating a can of soup on the stove.

CHAPTER THIRTEEN

Day 78

The temperature remained below freezing for seven straight days. By the eighth day, it was in the upper forties once again, and all the snow had vanished, leaving only puddles behind. Scott stepped outside in his rubber boots and trudged through the muddy slop to see what had become of his garden. The cold muck splashed up around his legs as he crouched down and shuffled between the rows to see nothing but a single dead tomato seed, fuzzy and swollen, with a tiny protrusion emerging from one end, lying in the mud among a stand of vibrant weeds.

Chapter Fourteen

Day 83

Women on Mount Sinai didn't wear flip flops or high heels. There were no sidewalks out here. There was mud, rock, thorns, poison ivy, poison oak, broken glass, rusty nails, yellow jackets, timber rattlers, and copperhead snakes. Impractical footwear, designed and marketed by women, bought and sold for ridiculous prices by women, and labeled by women as instruments of oppression attributed to "the patriarchy," was a product of the concrete deserts known as cities, where people were now raiding their neighbors' homes to survive, fleeing to the country, or dead. Here, on Mount Sinai, women, like men, wore running shoes for comfort and some form of boots for work as well as style.

Some of the hippies wore sandals, but they were odd that way, owing to a misguided delusion that they could live in harmony with nature, a fantasy afforded them by the technology and supply chains of yesterdays gone by. The medicine and medical procedures they used were tested on unwilling animals. The fruits, nuts, and vegetables they consumed were grown by farmers who cleared land of its natural inhabitants by poisoning and killing the flora, fauna, and insects that dwelt there. Their homes were built from the destroyed homes of animals on top of the destroyed homes of other animals. And they had felt good about themselves, because they wore t-shirts with peace signs on them, had bumper stickers that read "coexist" cleverly spelled out in religious symbols, refrained from eating meat or using too much of the water that fell from the sky, and charged their cell phones with solar panels—both of which were now fried. And now, they were all trading whatever soaps, candles, syrups, and honeys they could produce for pairs of used leather boots at the old man's general store.

It was planting season.

It was time to trudge shin-deep through wet, fecund humus mingled with rank rot and dung. Sandals were not the footwear of choice for this task. Getting a cut on a toe from a rock or piece of glass could mean a blood infection and almost certain death. They were not working with nature so much as trying to force nature to work with them, and they didn't have a lot of force to bring to bear in the enterprise. It would be difficult. Nature was working to kill them every second of every day, and nature had more power. But they had more intelligence. So long as they saw the world for how it truly was rather than how they wanted it to be, and so long as they acted accordingly, they could carve out a living against nature's will.

In the old world, men and women had become nearly interchangeable in the workplace, since most of the jobs no longer required strong backs at the acceptable expense of weak minds. The technology that automated manual labor sufficiently emasculated the society to allow for relative gender equality in all but sports and the most physically demanding jobs. Average testosterone levels in the former United States had steadily decreased over the past century as the world was made safer and easier, and the natural sexual dimorphism of the species began to recede to the mean. Instead of becoming first rate women, many women chose to act like second rate men, achieving most of the vices and few of the virtues of their male counterparts, and in the old world, they did not stand out, since the erosion of standards and the manipulation of nature had rendered most of the men second rate as well. Now, there were no climate-controlled office jobs. Like every generation prior to the twentieth century, they had to organize for maximum labor efficiency to stave off ever-present death at the hands of nature. Men and women no longer competed for status with one another by striving for the highest possible paycheck. There were no paychecks. The physically superior males worked the jobs outside the home which required physical prowess, such as cutting and splitting firewood, hunting and hauling wild game, and construction of the barricades, fences, and water catchment systems. The physically inferior females naturally performed the tasks to which they were best suited—tasks which required more patience, nurturing, and multitasking, rather than physical strength. Cooking, cleaning, and child rearing, along with foraging for wild edibles occupied most of their time. No one told them to do this; it simply had to be done to survive. If the labor was not divided in this way, most likely, all of them would die. After less than three months of living in the new world, they had all intuitively learned this lesson: that women prior to the twentieth century were not systematically oppressed by men, they were simply doing what they had to do to survive.

It was seventy-two degrees on this late April morning, and the workers stood ready in the fields with hand tools of all kinds: hoes, rakes, shovels, mattocks. They laced their boots up tight and stuffed handkerchiefs into the pockets of their bib overalls, jeans, or canvas pants. A few women stood alongside the men, ready to sling buckets of vile refuse and work it into the soil. Most, however, tended to the gardens or foraged for morel mushrooms and wild edibles such as dandelions, plantains, violets, smilax, and wood sorrel. The greens were a welcome addition to the meat, corn mush, and boiled acorns on which most had sustained themselves for the past month. And with these, some had returned to eating three small meals a day, mostly consisting of eggs and cooked greens.

They had divided into two teams. The first was the plowing and fertilizing team, which had consisted of about fifteen men, women, and adolescents filling the manure spreader with the composted excrement of the cattle, horses, pigs, and humans which they had been collecting over the past few weeks. Dan Tyler and his son Matthew pulled the spreader with their team of jackstock as some of the workers walked behind to break up any large clumps and spread them out more evenly. Behind them, the tractor came. It was a 1940s Farmall M pulling an old disc harrow that had sat at the edge of a hayfield, obscured by weeds and brush for two generations. The disc turned over the soil and crudely folded the manure in with it, as more workers followed behind, breaking up large clods of manure and sod. They had started at Bill Campbell's fields near the southern end of the road and were now working their way down Deer Creek to plow and fertilize the fields of all the farmers who had contracted their services.

The children gathered around to watch Dan Tyler's team of American Mammoth Jackstock lumbering toward the field, pulling the antique manure spreader behind them. The kids pointed and laughed and asked questions. It was quite clear that they would not be able to focus on their coursework with so much activity going on right outside the barn, and besides, this was an important part of a quality education—even here, on Mount Sinai, there were children who did not know where their food came from or how it got there. Emma Faulkner vowed that this failure of the education system in which those kids had been forced to participate would be corrected today. From now on, there would not be a one of them alive who wasn't intimately aware of just what it took to survive and where they stood in relation to nature.

Reunited with the reality of the world, no one could ignore just how fragile society was, nor how completely they were at the mercy of forces beyond their control. Should a pestilence of disease or fungus or vermin ravage the crops, should they suffer a severe drought or flash floods, or should an overwhelming force take the land away or steal the fruits of their labor, all of them would die a slow, painful death from starvation. With this renewed perspective of where they stood, came a religious revival that saw over one-hundred of the residents baptized in the creek within a few weeks. Every week, the barn was packed with gun-toting worshippers, and the numbers were steadily growing as more and more of the neighbors flocked to pray and sing and hear the word of God from the preacher. Some had never before heard or read a single verse in the society of the old world that pushed religion to the corner to be ignored or mocked. It was desperation that brought them now—desperation for life, for love, for community, for fellowship, for a moment of peace and contemplation, for a glimmer of hope in the struggle of life, for a sense of presence with the Divine.

Day 86

For the several fields they were planting, the discing and fertilizing took three days to complete. The majority of the ground could not be planted, since they did not have the seed, fertilizer, or fuel. Bill Campbell paid the workers with corn, but most of the farmers either promised a share of the harvest or rented out some of the ground to the workers to grow their own gardens.

The planters came with another tractor pulling an antique four row planter. The workers walked behind the planter, marking the rows and making sure each seed was buried with the soil. They couldn't afford to waste any seeds, since what they were planting was not truly seed corn. Even if they did everything right, most of it would not grow to produce a substantial crop for them. What was more, they would need to pull the weeds and remove the bugs by hand since chemical spraying no longer existed. So, Indiana's staple crop, which had formerly been grown with a highly efficient, precise industrial method, was now being grown like giant gardens. To maximize their yield, it would have to be.

Most of the cold-hardy crops such as lettuce, spinach, kale, beets, turnips, carrots, and radishes, had already been planted in gardens all along the road. There weren't many seeds left, however, especially since several of the residents had planted too early and had their plants killed by the hard frost as a result. Corporate marketing and kitsch home décor were partially responsible for the misconception that there were four seasons in the year. In reality, the traditional view of the seasons was more accurate; there were only two seasons: summer and winter. Any month in which the temperature of the air was low enough to turn water from a liquid into a solid was winter, and the months in which this did not occur were summer. Winter was the time of floods and freezes; summer was the time of floods and droughts, with the addition of bugs. People whose lapse in judgment allowed them to think that the word "spring" denoted anything more than a ploy to sell candy in stores, or that the word "fall" was significant of anything beyond pumpkin spice nonsense, paid for their folly with the loss of their crops. It wouldn't have been a major cause for concern in the past, when one could simply go to the store to pick up more seeds for a miniscule price, but now, it was a disaster. The waste of potential food strained the entire community by draining resources from the economy, and when the late frost had destroyed the blossoms on most of the fruit trees in the middle of April, morale in the community sank to new lows.

Any more loss could be catastrophic, so when Scott Adams came to the Rawlings family for help with his garden, he was told the best thing he could do to learn would be to help them with their garden and watch what they did. In this way, Keith Rawlings was able to get Scott to clean out his pig pens and chicken coop for him—a recompense for his trick with the yellow stones.

Day 88

Lynn poked the last seed into the soil and covered it with dirt. That did it for the beans. She took a stick, drove it into the ground at the end of the row, and impaled the paper seed packet on the stick to show what had been planted there. "Well, we said we wouldn't leave until the garden was planted. It's planted. Are we still going to Illinois?"

It was a subject that had been on everyone's mind for the past two weeks. No one had wanted to broach it though. Several times, they caught Faye choking back tears, and they knew what she was thinking of. They said that once the garden was planted, they would go. They wanted to make sure that the McCormicks were set up for success in the event that they did not come back. But now, they had done everything they said they were waiting for, Lynn had asked the question, and the family members looked around at one another, waiting for someone to speak.

"Well," Kent said. "That's up to your mom."

"Don't say that," Faye responded. "I'm not the only one making decisions here."

Kent shook his head. "I can't tell you which way to go. You know what it's like out there as much as any of us now. It's your family that's at risk either way."

"It's our family. Not just mine. Why do you have to twist things like that?"

"You bore them. You raised them. I just paid the bills. And my parents are dead. You know I love your dad, but he raised you. It's not the same for me as it is for you. This is something I can't help you with."

Faye looked at him, and her eyes began to well up again. "Don't put that on me. You want me to choose between two halves of my family?" Faye looked around at her children. "You guys are grown up now. You have to make your own decisions."

"I'll do whatever you want, Mom. I'm not splitting the family up now," Keith said. "It's up to you." The other two agreed.

Faye looked to the McCormicks who simply shook their heads and looked down.

"Jordan," Faye asked. "What would you do?"

"You know what I would do. It's what I'm doing now. What we're all doing. I have family too." Jordan shook her head. "You can't sacrifice your family's future for the past." Jordan looked into Faye's eyes with a show of resolve, but suddenly, her face turned a sickly color as the muscles in her jaw contracted. Her eyes rolled back, and she bent over and vomited onto the dirt.

The Rawlings stood frozen in place, not knowing what to do.

Malik placed his arms around her to support her as she wretched onto the ground. She struggled to steady herself with Malik's help and wiped the beads of sweat from her forehead as she regained her balance.

"Are you alright? What's wrong?" Lynn asked with concern.

"I'm okay," Jordan responded, wiping her mouth. Malik handed her a bottle of water, and she rinsed and spat before taking a couple slow sips. She looked at the family members who were still staring. "I didn't know how to tell you," she said, screwing the lid back on the bottle and glancing back at her husband. "I'm pregnant."

They were silent for several seconds. Faye stood with her mouth hanging open, her face still red and stained with tears. No one moved.

Finally, Lynn exclaimed, "Congratulations!" She looked around. "That's wonderful!" She went and hugged her as the others came forward to congratulate them. "How long have you known?" Lynn asked.

"About a month." Jordan wiped a tear from her eye.

Lynn smiled and laughed excitedly. "That's great!" She began talking about how they would have to build a crib and get some baby clothes, or better yet, make them, and she walked with Jordan back to the house to rest and eat.

The men shook hands with Malik and congratulated him. He smiled and nodded quietly and looked at Kent. "I know how tight supplies are right now. I want you to know, we're not going to need extra food. And I'll work twice as hard to make up for her, so you don't need to worry about that."

Kent shook his head and raised his hand to stop the man. "Don't worry about it. It's all fine. Everything will work out just fine."

Faye stood staring out into the woods.

Day 90

Kent climbed into the driver's seat of the old, blue Ford. Faye sat beside him in the passenger's seat, holding a jug of water, a small cooler, and a bag with flashlights, medicine, batteries, and other items. Keith, Joe, and Lynn settled into the bed beneath the camper shell, surrounded by cushions, boxes of tools, fuel and water jugs, blankets, and weapons. Keith opened the window between them and the cab. No one said a word as Kent looked in the bed to see that the tailgate was shut and everyone was ready to go.

As Kent turned the key in the ignition, he could see Faye shaking out of the corner of his eye. She tried to open a book and read, but her hands were trembling so badly that she lost the page. She shut the book and put it away before taking a drink of water. Kent put the truck in gear and rolled up the driveway as Malik and Jordan watched them from the front lawn. He glanced at them in the mirror. They stood still and somber, as if at a funeral.

This time, they planned to bypass the bypass. To take the backroads through Unionville and come out on Old 37, staying away from campus.

The light was just cresting the horizon. The sky was streaked with pink and purple, red and blue. Kent thought back to the test drive through town. He remembered what Jack Winters, Jim Baker, and Tim Faulkner had told them. He thought of what Malik and Jordan McCormick had said to him. Then, he thought of the child she was carrying.

The truck rolled up the hill to the top of the driveway. The gravel crackled underneath the tires. Up above, a vulture swooped overhead and perched on a tree branch in front of them. Kent pulled to the end of the driveway and paused. He looked at the mailbox, looked down the road to his right, at the houses, the smoke pouring out of chimneys in the twilight of the dawn. He put the truck in park and stared ahead blankly. "We can't do it."

"What?" Faye looked at him. Her lip quivered. Her cheeks flushed.

Keith, Joe, and Lynn said nothing, but watched their father.

"We can't do it," Kent repeated. He shook his head and clenched his teeth.

Faye began to cry. She buried her face in her hands and sobbed as Kent put the truck in reverse and looked into his mirror.

Day 92

Keith sat in the blind, looking out into the misty field beneath the trees. In the gray dawn, the dew drops sparkled like silver and gold tinsel on blue blades of grass, as streams of amber sunlight burned through the rustling leaves and shivering limbs. The scent of oak leaves and wildflowers and summer rain drifted through the air and mingled with the woodsmoke of the day's first cooking fires.

Keith scraped a slate puck with a carbon shaft, making a grating chirp sound, which he punctuated with clucking taps. Like a mannequin stone henge, the dark forms of the trash-begotten scarecrows surrounded the small field. They stood among the trees and brush, silently guarding the forest as dutifully as Easter Island megaliths. Sitting among them, Keith felt their ominous presence and reflexively glanced around at the imposters to see if they were looking at him and to be sure they didn't move. In a few of the trees, hung forms like piñatas swaying in the breeze. Windchimes made of pipes and sticks and bones clattered and moaned with every gust of wind. After a couple of weeks, the animals had grown accustomed to the changed environment, ignoring the movements and noises that were now a part of the landscape.

Keith clucked again and scraped out the sound of a purring turkey hen. Before he had finished, he received a thunderous gobble from the ridge just across the valley. The tom was coming in quickly, and he could hear the bird stomping its way through the dead leaves and foliage. He gave it another inviting call, and it bellowed out its reply. Keith clucked a couple more times and set the call down in the leaves. He picked up his bow and made sure the arrow was nocked and sitting properly in the rest. Attaching his release, he listened from behind his blind of brush as the tom crested the ridge and stepped out into the field. He watched it as it looked around for the hen and registered the sight of the scarecrows. The turkey looked right past Keith, as if he were just another lifeless form in the woods. It strutted with its shimmering plumage puffed out, dragging its wing feathers through the leaves and snorting. Not seeing the hen, it gobbled once more and turned away from Keith to look down the ridge. Keith drew back his bow and aligned his sight on the turkey's vent in the center of the radiating tail feathers. Silently letting out the last of the air in his lungs, he squeezed the trigger, releasing the arrow. The broadhead punched straight through the bird, exiting the chest and sticking into the trunk of the black oak tree behind it—Texas heart shot.

Day 95

At one of their weekly meetings, it had been agreed that the unoccupied houses should be taken possession of by the residents before they deteriorated to the point of becoming useless. It didn't take nature long to start reclaiming an empty house, especially when there was no climate control inside. Without someone continually cleaning and keeping up with repairs, the dust and humidity and fluctuating temperatures would first cause mold and rot, and within a year, the house would be full of insects, small animals, and vegetation growing on the walls and floors. Every homemaker and housekeeper was in a constant, monotonous war for territory with nature, though before the blackout, most did not properly appreciate the fact.

It was in the interest of the community to have every house occupied for several reasons. It was senseless to waste housing, especially when they had taken in so many from outside already. Many of the homes on Mount Sinai were packed with extended families of a dozen or more. They had disease to worry about; if people were too close together, disease would quickly spread, as it no doubt had in urban areas already. They wanted to house as many as possible because humans were the greatest resource in any economy—the more people they had, the more growers, builders, fighters, and innovators. So long as they were loyal to the community, everyone's security would be improved by the eyes and ears and guns spread out along the road.

There was disagreement over how they would decide who could take possession of houses. Real estate had always been the single most valuable investment and the thing over which more people had gone to war than anything else. Of course, there were multiple parties vying for ownership of each property, and while it was becoming clear that they would need to come up with a legal system to deal with the arbitration of each case, this case was relatively straight forward. The McCormicks had requested to take ownership of the little, purple house, not only for the raising of their imminent child, but to create a doctor's office as well. It was generally agreed that it would be beneficial to the community to have a doctor's office, and since no one else was ecstatic about the idea of moving into a building where three drug addicts had been found in a state of filth and decomposition, the McCormicks faced virtually no antagonism. They started thoroughly cleaning the house the next day, with the help of the Rawlings family, and now, they were ready to move in with the few belongings they had accrued since the blackout.

Jack Winters stepped down from his horse and tied the reins around a sapling growing up in the yard. The beast nibbled at the leaves of the bushes, sniffed the flowers growing in the ditch, and pulled at the grass in the yard, swishing its tail contentedly. Jack greeted the movers as they carried boxes and bags into the house.

"I'm glad to see someone respectable is going to be living here for a change," he said. "I don't remember the last time someone who wasn't a complete degenerate lived here." He looked at Joe Rawlings. "Do you?"

"Can't say that I do, unfortunately," Joe responded.

"Anything I can help with?" said Jack.

"I think we've just about got it," Jordan replied. "We didn't have a whole lot to move, you know?"

"Y'all ain't had any problems with neighbors, have you?"

"No, sir." Malik shook his head. "It's been quiet."

"Good. I know no one was really pushin' against you movin' into this place before, but you never know. It's not so nice with some of the other houses."

"What do you mean?" Joe asked. "What kind of problems have you been dealing with?"

"Well, so far, I've only had to really settle disputes over wages and stuff. I could handle that by myself, but the disputes over houses..." Jack shook his head. "It's on a whole different level. I'm afraid some of it is going to get pretty ugly."

"What, like feuds?"

"Maybe. There's already some bad blood. If people start fighting over this stuff, it could be a disaster. We're going to have to come up with a better system. You know, a legal system."

"Well, there sure aren't any lawyers out here." Joe laughed. "Unless they emigrated here and shacked up with a relative."

"I don't think we need any lawyers. We just need a few people with a head on their shoulders, some life experience, and some good moral sense."

Just then, Keith came walking up from the backyard, pulling what looked like a tiny house built on a huge wheelbarrow. It had a tin roof and chicken-wire-covered windows cut in the scrap plywood walls. It rolled on old bicycle wheels using a section of steel pipe for an axel. The handles were made of two-by-fours with another section of pipe fastened between them, which Keith used to lift and maneuver the contraption. Keith smiled as Malik and Jordan stepped around to see him. "I got you a little housewarming present." He set it down on the ground and opened a small square door on the side with the handlebars. Out of the door, came six hens. The hens began clucking and jumping out of the box to peck at bugs and grass in the yard.

"Oh, Keith, that's too much," Jordan protested. "We can't take these."

"Sure, you can. I've got fourteen more besides, and a couple broody hens are working on hatching another batch for me right now. This is no problem. It ought to be a good start for you though."

"I don't know what to say," Jordan began.

"You guys have helped us with plenty over the past couple months, and I want you to know we appreciate it. This ought to be enough for you to have breakfast every morning, at least."

Malik stepped forward and reached his hand out to Keith. "Thank you. It means a lot having friends as good as you." Keith nodded, and Malik shook Joe's hand as well.

"Don't hesitate to ask if you need help with them. I'm just right back there." He pointed back to the house down the long driveway, which could still be seen through the trees. "And don't forget, you still got plants in that garden."

Jordan dabbed her eyes and hugged Keith.

"That's alright," Keith said.

She let go of him and applied the same treatment to Joe. Keith looked at Jack. "How you doin', Jack?"

Jack nodded to him. "I was just telling them I think we need to come up with a better legal system. We need more than a sheriff and some deputies. We need laws and a judge."

Keith nodded and looked at the ground with pursed lips. "I've been thinking the same thing."

Day 100

The unmistakable sound of Lookout Post 3's alarm rang out through the hollow, reverberating off the hillsides which bordered the corn fields of Deer Creek Road. Jim Baker turned on his radio to hear the frantic sound of the lookout's shaky voice rapidly spitting into the radio.

"Break-Break-Break! LP3 to Barn owl, we have a group of walkers moving east toward LP3. Estimated fifty to sixty people traveling on foot. What should I do?"

Jim held up his radio, but Jack answered first. "LP3, do not engage. Try to stay out of sight. We are on our way with backup. Stay where you are unless they engage."

"They stopped when they heard the alarm. They're looking down the road at the houses now. They're getting

off the road and going down to the creek under the bridge. It looks like some of them have weapons."

"Alright. Hang on, we're coming."

Keith and Joe grabbed their bicycles and began pedaling down the road to the south with their backpacks on and their rifles slung across them. As they worked the pedals and panted, the clatter of hooves resounded over the asphalt, and Jack Winters rode past them at a swift gallop. Neighbors who had heard the alarm were outside their houses with rifles and shotguns, looking around for intruders or for someone to tell them what was going on. The Rawlings brothers waved to anyone they saw and shouted for them to follow up to the blockade at the highway.

Jack Winters brought his horse to a walking pace and radioed the lookout once again. "LP3, I'm going to approach the group. Keep an eye on them for me. If you see anyone raise a weapon in my direction, drop 'em." The lookout responded with an affirmation of his understanding, and Jack dismounted, tying the reins of the horse to a fence post before walking toward the barricade.

By the time the brothers caught up, the group was already huddled around the wall of cars at the end of the road, looking around and murmuring amongst themselves. Jack was approaching the crowd with his rifle slung over his left shoulder and his right hand near his pistol at his side. Keith and Joe ditched their bicycles on the side of the road, behind one of the baffle barricades, and quickly took their places on either side of Jack. As they walked forward, a couple of people in the crowd waved white pieces of cloth at him. They smiled weakly, raised their hands in a display of friendliness, and looked around to make sure no one was doing anything threatening.

The group in front of the barricade included several elderly people, as well as women and children, pushing carts, pulling wagons, walking bicycles and baby strollers. They were all pathetically thin, their faces gaunt and pale. Most of them looked filthy, with dirt and grime collecting in the creases of their skin and matted hair that came out in their fingernails when they scratched at the vermin in their scalps and clothes.

One of the men in the group looked around at the others, said something inaudible to them, and stepped forward to speak with the natives of this strange country behind the wall. He raised a hand and hailed the men walking toward them. "Hello, gentlemen. We're peaceful."

"Where are you coming from?" Jack inquired, looking around warily.

"Bloomington," the man said. "We're refugees. Our homes have been destroyed. We have no food, no shelter. We're seeking asylum."

Jack frowned but said nothing.

"My name is David." The man held his hand out over the hood of one of the cars in the barricade.

Jack looked at him straight-faced. "You'll understand if, under the circumstances, I don't shake hands with strangers. Where in Bloomington did you live?"

The man retracted his hand meekly and frowned. "No, of course." He wiped his nose and looked around. "Not too far from here. At least by driving standards. Over past the elementary school." The man pointed to the northwest. "We're all from those houses down there."

Keith remembered doing landscaping work in that area in a previous job. The houses there were all what the Rawlings family called mansions. That was where the doctors and lawyers and university administrators lived.

"What happened to your homes?" Jack probed.

"Gangs. Looters. I don't know what you call them, but they came through our neighborhoods and ransacked them. They burned down most of our houses, stole what they wanted, and destroyed the rest. Many of our neighbors were killed. We barely escaped with our lives." The man unscrewed the cap of a milk jug, struggled to lift it to his mouth with both hands, and took a drink of the yellowish water. "I hate to ask, but do you have any food?"

"No," Jack replied. "We've been eating grass and wild plants for the past month."

The man nodded, and like many of the others in the crowd, his eyes searched past the three men to the road behind them. "Same with us. Whatever we can find."

Keith turned his head to see what the man was looking at, and out of the corner of his eye, he could see some of the neighbors approaching and taking positions behind the vehicles in the baffles.

"What did these looters look like?" Jack prompted. "Do you know where they came from?"

"I don't know where they came from. They were mostly younger people, I think. They dressed like cartoon characters or something, really eccentric. They acted erratically— like they were on drugs—and they talked like cult members, about how we deserved what they were doing to us or something. I don't know, I didn't stick around to ask them questions after they started killing people."

"Did they drive any vehicles or have any police gear?"

"I'm not sure about police gear. They all had a hodge-podge of clothes and equipment, but I didn't see any vehicles. They came on foot. One day, some of them showed up and announced that we had to give them reparations; then, they left. We figured they were just some, you know, crazy, drunk people, but the next day, a large group of them came and started breaking in windows and doors. Some of my neighbors surrendered, and they took them as captives. They marched them off in chains."

Keith, Joe, and Jack all exchanged disturbed glances.

The man continued. "My wife and I escaped just before they got inside our house. We found some of our neighbors hiding in the woods surrounding the houses, and those of us that joined the group got out of the neighborhood before they found us. We thought we might as well go east after we saw what the town was like. We couldn't make it through town on foot with those people out there. It looked like east was the only way they hadn't already gone."

The people had given up hope of getting anything to eat here. They began to wander down the highway again, haggard and defeated. The man who did the talking looked behind him at his group as they limped on. He turned back to look at the men of Mount Sinai once again. "Thanks, anyway. We better get moving on. Good luck to you."

"Thanks. Same to you."

The refugees slowly meandered away, as if struggling to stay awake. They looked little more than skin stretched over skeletons. Some cried as they stumbled forward, footsore, into the awaiting day. The men continued to follow their progress with their eyes, and as they did so, some of the neighbors who had watched the exchange from behind the baffles joined them in watching the group stagger on down the road to where and what future God only knows.

"Harden your hearts, boys." Jack spat on the ground as he watched the pitiful march.

"Maybe we could help them," Joe said. "They might have some valuable skills."

"We can't," Jack said.

"I know we're stretched, but we haven't been starving. Look at them. You said we need to make laws. There are lawyers in that group. And we need doctors. There's bound to be some..."

"If we took one in, we'd have to take them all, and we don't have resources for sixty more people."

"We can make it work..."

Jack shook his head. "Look at them. They're sick. They're carrying disease. We can't risk it."

Joe turned to Keith with a look of disgust. "Keith—come on. Back me up."

"He's right," Keith said flatly.

As the last of the group disappeared behind the bend in the highway, Jack turned around and began walking back up the road to his horse. "We have to call another meeting."

Joe looked at his brother as if he didn't recognize him. "How can you?"

Keith turned and followed Jack. "If God can't help them, what are we supposed to do?"

Day 101

Keith and Joe watched as the cart rolled by, hauling the bloody remains of a dead man they didn't recognize. Jack Winters stepped up beside them and took a sip of hot blackberry leaf tea from his thermos.

"What happened to him?" Joe asked.

"Found a young woman foraging for mushrooms alone in the woods. Tried to rape her. Got six rounds of .38 Special for his trouble." Jack rubbed his nose and took another drink. "I just got done talking to her. She's with the preacher now." As the brothers shook their heads and watched the cart pass down the road toward the compost pile, Jack looked at them and cleared his throat. "You know, I understand how you felt back there at the barricade yesterday. I wanted to help them too." Jack spat on the ground and kicked some dirt over the damp patch where it landed. "I want you to know that I'm not just a heartless bastard. I didn't tell you. I didn't tell anyone, for that matter, because I didn't see what good would come of it. But you might as well know now. You know the preacher that lived on the north end of the road? Not Jorgenson, but the one that went to the church in Unionville?"

"Yeah," Joe responded.

"Well, there was a group of refugees came to the barricade up there. He said they were his family, and he was taking them in. So, the lookout let 'em come in, and he put them up in his house. He fed them from what little canned goods he still had, let 'em sleep in his bed, while he and his family slept on the floor in the living room. The next day, the preacher went to the general store to trade his last pair of boots for some food to feed the refugees. When he came back, he found his house had been ransacked, and his entire family had been butchered in the living room."

Joe said nothing. He stared, fixed in place with his mouth hanging open.

"Turns my stomach, remembering how I found those bodies." Jack spat on the ground again. "The sentry saw the group leaving the same way they came in. No one has seen them since." He took another drink from his thermos.

They were silent for a few seconds, looking into the woods.

The brothers both felt a hand alight on their shoulders and turned to see Malik standing behind them. The men all greeted each other and watched as people came walking and riding bicycles down the road, toward Jim Baker's barn. Off to the other side of the gravel driveway, Jordan was talking to Emma Faulkner and the Rawlings women. When Emma wasn't teaching classes to the kids, she was teaching classes to the adults about permaculture and wild edible and medicinal plants; no doubt, the women were asking her about different teas or things they could make.

"So, how are you doing, Jack?" Malik asked sincerely.

"I'm getting tired of dealing with a lot of this nonsense, but I'm alright."

"What kind of nonsense are you talking about?"

"Just personality clashes and all that. It's enough to have to worry about people outside without having neighbors trying to tear the community apart too, but that's one of the things we have to cover here today. We need to make some laws, and I can't be the one to do it. I'm not going to be a dictator."

"Good," Malik said.

"Yeah, I appreciate that," Joe added.

Jack smiled. "So, anyway, how's the healthcare business going?"

"Well, business is booming, as you can imagine."

"Yeah, I figured."

"We've lost someone over the age of sixty almost every other day," Malik said. "There aren't many left."

"Well, that's to be expected," Keith said, shrugging. "The average life expectancy in 1900 was 47. In 1750, it was 29."

Joe looked at his brother with a furrowed brow and shook his head.

"Well," Malik went on. "What we've lost in elders, we've made up for in new arrivals."

"You talking about people's relatives coming in from outside?" Jack nodded.

"I'm talking about pregnancies. No more birth control."

"Oh, I hadn't even thought of that." Jack put his hand on his head as if he'd been hit. "Damn. That's going to complicate things. We're going to need more food."

"We'll get it," Joe put in quickly. "Don't worry." He elbowed Jack in the arm and motioned toward Malik with his eyes when Jack looked at him.

Picking up on the hint, Jack added, "Oh yeah. No, I know we will. I'm not worried."

There was a slightly awkward pause in the conversation as Malik gave a weak smile with nervous eyes.

"How's your kid doing?" Keith asked, nodding to Malik.

"She's getting strong. I can already feel her kicking. And..."

"Her?" Joe interrupted. "You already know it's a girl?"

"No, but Jordan says it is. I don't know how, but she knows."

"Well, I don't believe I've congratulated you." Jack reached out to shake Malik's hand. "Congratulations. If I had a cigar, I'd give it to you."

Malik gave the hand a firm shake. "If I had a cigar, I'd give it to me too," he laughed.

From the north end of the road behind them, they heard the clopping of hooves coming their way. They turned to see Dan Tyler's team of jackstock pulling a wagon of passengers. After three months without being able to purchase fuel at a gas station, they had agreed to reserve fuel exclusively for essential needs such as chainsaws, tillers, tractors, and the generator which recharged their batteries and powered Jeremiah Davis's welder. No longer could they justify using fuel to transport people up and down the road to the meetings when horses or a team of jackstock could do the job for the price of grass and water. There was some protest of this policy, of course. Some of the residents said they would do what they wanted with their own gasoline, and to prove how independent they were, they burned the last of their supply, riding dirt bikes and ATVs up and down the road for fun. Afterward, when they tried to buy gasoline from their neighbors, however, no one would sell to them, so the fuel was conserved for work, while the dirt bikes and nonutility ATVs were left with all the other frivolous toys, never to be played with again.

Once the time for the meeting arrived and everyone gathered round, they held an election for a judge, settled disputes over unclaimed houses, and finally, discussed what they had learned from the wanderers about the gangs and the state of the town. It was agreed that they needed to improve their defenses, and people used the opportunity to volunteer all sorts of junk from their properties to contribute to the common defense.

Day 107

Among Kent's collection of junk, he had stacks upon stacks of plastic pallets from the factory in Columbus where he had worked. These pallets had been used to stack several layers of wheels. Why he had them on his property, no one knew. He had planned to build something with them, but now, he couldn't remember what it was. Under the circumstances, however, he was all too happy to sacrifice whatever that project had been and donate them to be used in the construction of a fence between the road and the highway.

CHAPTER FOURTEEN

Workers came and loaded them into wagons, and they were hauled off to be lined up, staked in place, and wired together alongside the ditches, where some of the gardeners transplanted the poison oak and poison ivy vines that enveloped their barns to climb and cover the black plastic pallets. By the beginning of summer, all that could be seen from the highway was a dense wall of green foliage, and Kent's property, while a bit overgrown with grass, was cleaner than he remembered seeing it.

PART IV
SUMMER

Chapter Fifteen

Day 138

K eith Rawlings had worked with a moving company for a few months in his past life, and in that job, he noticed that every customer he moved, no matter how wealthy, rural or urban, young or old—they all had something in common, something he had moved on every single job he had ever done—massive flat-screen televisions. Indeed, some of the customers had screens for every room in their house. Americans, on average, had invested more time and money in televisions than in their religious observances, their political processes, or being prepared for inevitable emergencies. As a result, the people no longer had much influence over their country's politics, their religion lost significance for them, they became addicted to entertainment, more dependent, and more easily manipulated. The intelligence of the nation's citizens had been on the decline for many years. Dogs could watch television. The investment of time and money into reclining chairs and sofas, surround sound systems, and screens the size of cars, was indicative of a special kind of planned sloth. They stuffed their bodies with cheap and abundant calories and vegetated in front of the screens for hours, not moving, not thinking, not producing anything or helping anyone—but not sleeping either, just killing time until time returned the favor. The sudden and striking change in their lifestyles brought about by the blackout, had far-reaching consequences that rippled throughout the society.

For one, obesity was no longer the leading cause of death. Those slothful and slovenly simpletons who had been addicted to a gluttonous indulgence in sugar and fat, as well as an avoidance of toil and sweat, were now either lean and active or dead. Their sustenance consisted of nothing but the most nutritious of diets which they took from the land. Popular means of recreation now included hiking in search of mushrooms and plants, archery, hunting, fishing, swimming in the farm ponds, and riding bicycles along the more than twelve miles of paved road in their village or on trails through the woods and fields. By June, the old man's general store had competitors on the north end of the road as well as to the south, on Deer Creek Road, and along with food, clothing, and tools, they traded board games, cards, and especially, books.

The demand for books and even old magazines had become so great that some of the ladies pooled their collections and started a specialized bookstore. They traded for all sorts of things, and often, books were traded for other books. This became so regular an occurrence, that the book shop became more of a library, where it was customary to take a book and leave a book. This renaissance of reading, both for entertainment and instruction, opened an entire world of literature previously unknown to most of the residents. In the pages of these literary works, were the combined experiences, knowledge, and wisdom of all mankind. They voraciously consumed them, and many of the women, though very few men, attended discussion groups where they would talk about the books they were reading. The irony of their situation was apparent to them; with the obliteration of the information-age and the credential-obsessed education system, they were better educated and more knowledgeable than they had ever been.

Kent sat in his chair, looking at the dead, black screen of his thirty-two-inch television—the largest he had ever had—the thing in front of which he had fallen asleep nearly every night for fifteen years. The television stayed where it had always been. He couldn't bring himself to part with it. It was, for so many years, his greatest comfort in the world, next to his overstuffed chair and the Bible he had never entirely learned to read, due to the apathetic teachers' unions which had monopolized public education at the expense of students, parents, and society. Now, to him, the television was like a photograph of a dead relative, being of no use and no comfort, merely a reminder of his loss which he felt obligated to view and endure. Sitting in his favorite, old recliner, he was finishing his breakfast of scrambled eggs and greens. He took a sip of sassafras tea and heard a sharp crack in the kitchen. "Got another one!" he announced, and he went to the kitchen, where he watched the dying mouse flop in the trap. He set his plate and mug down on the countertop, picked the pitiful thing off the floor, and took it outside, dropping the creature over the rail of the deck. Its convulsing body fell to the ground below and bounced off the pitiless clay, where the chickens swarmed and tore it to pieces.

As he listened to the birds singing, he breathed deeply of the sweet smell of pollen in the air, and he closed his eyes. The warm sun shone upon his face. Through the rustling of leaves in the breeze, he heard the blowing of the bugle signaling the call to meeting. The animal-drawn carts were rolling down the roads, picking up passengers to take to the barn. Kent stepped inside once more and announced, "Time for church! Hurry up or we're gonna miss the bus!"

Faye, Lynn, and Joe assembled in front of the door with their bags, water bottles, and Bibles. Joe tightened his belt and repositioned his holster.

Kent looked at his son, who stood with a Bible in one hand and a gun in the other, and he asked, "Do you still think you need to bring that to church?" He looked disapprovingly at his son's Sunday best.

Joe simply replied, "As soon as you tell me what Jesus really meant in Luke 22:36, I'll stop bringing it."

"Whatever." Kent shook his head. "Come on, or we're gonna be late."

Joe grabbed his shotgun as well, and they left.

Over the course of the past few weeks, Keith had collected all the old, damaged arrows he had lying around and repaired them. He had boxes of inserts, fletchings, and glue, as well as a collection of several kinds of arrow heads, from field points to small game points to broad heads of all kinds. Over the years of hunting, he had tried two blades, three blades, four blades, and expanding broadheads, but he never got rid of anything—much like his father. Now, he had two dozen good arrows, and he took his bow to do some practice and to keep the animals from destroying the garden.

Along with producing the fruits and vegetables they would rely upon for the foreseeable future, the gardens and corn fields were among their most reliable producers of meat. They tried to avoid killing the deer and turkeys outside of the natural seasons, but the animals came to ravage their crops daily. As much as they wanted to maintain a healthy wild game population for the fall, they could not afford to lose any more produce to animals. So, much like the security system of rotating lookouts to guard the roads from outsiders, they had an internal security system of rotating guards to watch over the crops not protected by proper fencing and shoot, or at least, drive away any animals that came to destroy them. These posts were often manned by the children and grandparents who would use bb guns and air rifles, slings or slingshots, or homemade bows and arrows to scare away the deer, rabbits, squirrels, crows, and raccoons that trespassed there. Keith and Joe had frequently taken their turns standing guard over the plants, and they used the opportunity to restock their canned meat supply. On two occasions since planting the crops, they had taken deer at night by shining a flashlight in its eyes and shooting it with a bow as it stood dazed.

Protecting the crops was the highest priority. They used sentries. They used guard dogs. But the second highest priority was building fences around the gardens. This was yet another design of the Faulkners. For every garden, they built two fenced in areas with one wall dividing them: on one side, the garden, and on the other, an empty pasture for animals. With this paddock system, they would rotate livestock and crops between the two fenced areas every six months. The animals, including chickens, pigs, and goats could all live together in a single paddock where they would eat the vegetation, leaf, stem, root, and seed. The pigs would till up the ground as they made wallows and dug up roots, and the chickens and other birds would even out the tilled soil as they scratched for bugs and seeds. All of them would fertilize the soil, and they could be easily fed unwanted weeds and spoiled produce from the garden in the adjacent paddock. Along with this diet, they would need plenty of grass, so a couple of the neighbors had taken up blacksmithing to create scythes and sickles along with many of the other traditional tools their new lifestyle would require. Once the last of the crops was harvested from the garden, the animals would be moved into the garden paddock to eat the remaining plants and rejuvenate the soil for the next planting, while the other paddock would be planted with fall crops such as garlic, cabbage, winter squashes, and turnips. This method was quickly gaining adherents, and livestock had become the most desirable form of currency, surpassing firewood, seeds, fuel, and even batteries, once the spring planting was completed. Many of the farmers, like Ernie Jacobs, gladly traded their animals for labor and goods, since they could no longer care for so many without supply chains.

Once again, canned goods were being traded, and the starving time was over. For the first month after the blackout, canned goods had been traded by the gardeners and home-steaders, like the Faulkners, who had collected a surplus. Some, including the Faulkners and the Jorgensons, even donated food to their neighbors for a while, but the supplies began to diminish quickly, and when their stockpiles dwindled to levels that would barely be sufficient to keep their families fed to the next harvest, they held on to what they had, while their less prepared neighbors resorted to buying or killing whatever meat they could find and going weeks, in some cases, without fruits or vegetables of any kind, save the feed corn from Bill Campbell's bins.

With the end of winter, came the abundance of eggs and the springing up of plants and mushrooms, and Keith and the Faulkners, along with a few others, taught their neighbors where to look and what to look for when foraging in the woods for sustenance. They were able to add a few morel and false morel mushrooms to their diet along with the greens from fern shoots and smilax and the leaves and flowers of several plants growing up in their yards. Now, however, with the summer in full swing, wild plants abounded. They taught the farmers and gardeners what weeds were good for food, and soon the growers were transplanting purslane and lamb's quarter, wood sorrel and peppergrass, docks, violets, dandelions, chicory, and many other wild edible plants, which they had formerly derided as weeds, into separate gardens. Walking through the rows of plants, growers would snack on the crisp, highly nutritious, sugar snap pea-flavored leaves of purslane, a favorite of Keith. They would even sell them in bags like chips. The peppergrass was valued for its use in place of peppercorns. The dandelion and chicory were used in teas and salads, but they were most valued for their use in making a substitute for coffee. Some growers volunteered their services to collect these so-called weeds from others' gardens and exclusively grew these plants rather than the expensive traditional fruit and vegetable seeds. They stood to make enormous profits at the harvest. One of the most valuable plants was also one of the most abundant. Lamb's quarter, or goosefoot, as it was also called, was one of the first plants to be domesticated by American Indians and one of the most nutritious plants in the area. It grew rapidly anywhere there was sunlight and disturbed dirt, and along with making an excellent substitute for spinach, it could be used to make flour. There was no wheat on Mount Sinai, no useable grains of any kind besides corn, so any sort of flour was highly valued. With the green lamb's quarter flour, they could make bread, pasta, biscuits, dumplings, pancakes, pies, and even cookies. Very few of the fruit trees could be saved from the late frost in April, but there were wild blackberries growing all over Mount Sinai, and many of the growers had managed to save their own berry crops from the frost by moving potted plants indoors or into heated greenhouses. With any luck, they would still have some fruit this year, and maybe Emma Faulkner would share some of her recipes.

The early crops were growing better than expected, and some had already gathered the year's first harvest of greens and root vegetables. The Rawlings family, along with the McCormicks, planned to glean some salad greens from their garden today, an occasion they had all eagerly awaited after the past months of almost nothing but roasted meat and stews.

Keith crept through the woods, treading softly over the leaves and undergrowth. Bow in hand, satchel slung over his shoulder, he searched the ground intently to see what he could find. From the time the first morels were found, until the snow began to fall, one could always find choice edible mushrooms growing in the woods if one knew where to look and what to see. While Keith never found more than a handful of morels in the spring, in the summer, these woods were overflowing with chanterelles—firm, orange and yellow mushrooms that looked almost like daylilies popping out of the forest floor. It was still a bit early for them, but he had already found a few. He kept his eyes open for the bright orange and yellow Chicken of the Woods—large, firm mushrooms which grew on oak trees and had a texture and flavor somewhat similar to its namesake. They could often grow up to forty pounds or more and could be found from May to November.

As Keith peered through the brush and brambles, he noticed an anomaly in the setting: A perfect, glassy circle hovering above the ground. He recognized it immediately and traced the outline of a rabbit, nearly invisible against the background of trees and brush. So close to the garden, this varmint most certainly had its own plans for their vegetables and would be ravaging the plants if left to its own devices. Keith drew back his bow, aiming his small game point just behind the rabbit's eye. Surprisingly, the animal remained frozen, not moving a muscle. Keith pulled the trigger on his release and sent the arrow flying toward its target. The animal ducked and sprinted off through the woods as the arrow bounced up into the air. Clean miss. Even with Keith's bowhunting experience, it was a lot more difficult than it looked on television. He retrieved his arrow which hung suspended in a briar thicket. None the worse for wear, he brushed off the dirt and put it back in the quiver.

There were fish in the stream and farm ponds around Mount Sinai Road. Deer Creek was treated as public property, where anyone could fish, swim, or collect water, and some of the pond owners allowed people to catch a limited number of fish for a small price. Kent's pond was probably the single best decision he had ever made regarding his property management. Long ago, he had traded a pontoon boat and some other things for an old bulldozer, and he decided he was going to build a pond so he could go fishing without ever leaving home. It took him over ten years to complete a functioning dam for the quarter-acre pond, but once he had it built, the rain filled it up, and they stocked it with fish from the hatchery. It was either a tiny pond or a huge mud puddle; no one would be fooled into thinking it was done by professionals, but it held water nearly ten feet deep, and for the past couple of years, it had provided them with more than a couple fried bluegill sandwiches.

When Malik and Jordan came down to the pond, they looked like two young kids excited to go fishing for the first time. It wasn't their first time; in fact, it wasn't even their first time this year. They had fished twice before in the Rawlings' pond with a couple of cheap, old rods with push button reels that Kent had fixed up for them. As friends of the family, they were granted the special privilege of fishing the little pond whenever they wanted, and when they got a break from the chores and tending to patients in the community, they gleefully walked hand in hand to the glittering, green water to turn over logs and rocks in search of worms for their hooks. This life was so much better than that in the crowded, polluted city—it was like a new world in which they now found themselves, and they wanted to experience every solitary pleasure of life out here, away from the noise and stress of the city. Even the ticks, chiggers, and mosquitos seemed to amuse them.

After Kent showed them how to fillet the fish, they invited the Rawlings family to join them around the campfire for fried fish and cooked greens. They couldn't get enough of it. Every time Keith saw them beaming over the new skill they had learned or the wild mushrooms they'd found, he smiled— he couldn't get enough of it either. He loved this land. This beauty. This life. This liberty. This was what he had signed up to defend. This, right here. This joy, this freedom, which would never be seen again for a thousand years if allowed to perish, for one moment, from the earth. It was worth it.

Malik and Jordan sat on a log beneath a hickory tree, watching their lines extending into the water. As Keith came over, he sat down and began pulling ticks off his body and flicking them into the pond. "How's it goin'?"

"Haven't caught any yet," Jordan said. "What's in the bag?"

Keith unslung the satchel and pulled out some of the chanterelles he had gathered. "Mushrooms."

"You can eat those?" Jordan looked incredulous.

"Yes, ma'am. They're good."

"I would have thought they were poisonous."

"I'll show you how to cook 'em later on if you want."

"I'll try anything, if I see you try it first," Malik laughed.

Keith retrieved a rod and cast it away from the others. "You know where everyone else is?"

"I think they went to have lunch with the preacher's family," Malik responded.

"They're meeting Joe's girlfriend," Jordan added.

"Girlfriend?" Keith looked at her.

"Yeah. I think they started talking at the Easter celebration."

"What?"

"You didn't know he had a girlfriend?"

"No."

"Maybe he didn't want to tell you because..." Jordan stopped and looked away at a fish jumping out of the water at the other end of the pond. "Look at that! That was a nice one! I'm gonna catch him."

"Why wouldn't he want to tell me?" Keith asked.

Jordan tugged on her rod. "I got one!" she exclaimed. She reeled the bluegill up onto the bank and carefully took hold of the fish, avoiding the spines on its back, as she had learned from experience. She removed the hook and ran a stringer through the fish's mouth and out its gills, tossing it back into the water once the stringer was secured.

Malik looked at Keith as Jordan was putting another worm on her hook. "We had a coyote get one of our chickens yesterday. Broad daylight too. By the time I got my rifle, it was already gone. What do you do about coyotes?"

Keith reeled in his line to cast again. "The only thing you can do. Catch 'em and kill 'em."

"Didn't you kill a bunch of predators in the winter? Why are there still so many?"

"In these parts, there are more predators than rabbits. You'll never get rid of them all. You have to be alert at all times and kill them whenever you see them. If you get complacent, they'll overrun you and kill everything."

Malik and Jordan stopped and looked at Keith who sat staring fixedly at his line. His hand methodically turned the crank in slow revolutions, reeling the line through the water. The line tightened, the rod tip bent, and he jerked back slightly, reeling a fat bluegill out of the pond. Smiling, he reached for the stringer.

While Kent, Joe, and Malik cleaned fish, Keith, Lynn, and Jordan picked greens from the garden. The rows of broad, green leaves almost glistened in the sun, still damp from the recent rain, with beads of water collecting in their creases. The rows of plants in the garden were now easily identifiable, but only a few plants were ready to harvest. With scissors and knives, they cut off the largest leaves from the plants and put them into their baskets. Along with the lettuce, spinach, and kale, they pulled a few of the largest radishes, beets, turnips, and carrots. The rows needed to be thinned, and they were craving vegetables. No part of these plants would be wasted. They would eat all the greens they could, and they would begin canning all the rest.

"Oh, man. I can't wait to taste this. It looks so good." Jordan grinned as she filled her basket.

"Why wait?" Keith said. He brushed off a beetle and a bit of dirt from a spinach leaf and ate it with a smile. "It doesn't get any fresher than this."

Jordan did the same with a piece of lettuce in her hand. She laughed. Lynn did likewise with a kale leaf. They began sampling the produce, passing pieces of plants to each other, brushing off dirt from carrots and radishes. Keith carved off chunks of turnips and passed them around to try.

"This is amazing," Jordan beamed, shaking her head.

Lynn picked off another leaf of lettuce. "So, when everything goes back to normal, are you going to move back to the city?" She continued filling her bucket. It was an innocent question, but it took several seconds for Lynn to realize that no one was answering her. There was an awkward quiet as she stood up and looked around.

Keith was silently looking at Lynn.

With pursed lips, Jordan put a hand on her bulging belly and stared at the dirt at her feet. "If everything went back to the way it was, I would much rather raise my children out here, where they could run through the woods, and find mushrooms, and play with animals, and grow their own food, and catch fish in the shade of a hickory tree. But I think that ship has sailed. Almost four months ago, I was running up and down this road, trying to help my husband save the lives of people, including little children, who had been shot by a gang of thieves. The thieves and killers weren't caught by police and taken to court and sentenced to prison. They were shot to death, and the survivors were hanged in front of the church at the end of the road, and their bodies were piled in front of a barricade of dead cars, and they were torn apart and eaten by buzzards and dogs, and their bones still lie unburied in the road." Jordan stopped. Tears ran down her cheeks.

Lynn and Keith were silent, and Jordan continued.

"And since then, I've helped Malik treat patients to the best of our ability without real equipment or medicine. And most of those we helped would have died if not for him. But do you know how many of your neighbors have died since we've been here? It's over a hundred and fifty, and by the end of the week, that number will be higher. There are no more seriously disabled people. Their families couldn't take care of them properly under these conditions, no matter how much they wanted to. There are no more diabetics. There are very few people with allergies now. You know why? Because if they come into contact with anything they're allergic to now, they just die, and there's nothing we can do about it. We've had over a dozen heart attacks from old people trying to cut and split firewood to keep from freezing to death. Twice that number died from running out of medicine for conditions they already had. We've had sixteen people die from parasites and bacteria because they drank contaminated water or ate undercooked meat, and there are a lot more soon to join them. Pneumonia and flu have taken at least thirty. There's no one with asthma or any respiratory problems after breathing nothing but smoke, dust, mold, pollen, and animal feces. Fourteen from axe and chainsaw injuries, six from fires, thirteen suicides, seven accidental poisonings from people eating the wrong mushrooms and plants. One guy died from a cavity he didn't tell us about until the infection had already worked its way to his heart. Infections from improper sanitation have been especially hard on women. Two have died in childbirth, and..." She trailed off. Tears were flowing from her eyes, and she wiped her face with her handkerchief.

Keith listened silently. As she started to cry, he didn't know what to do, so he ate another slice of turnip.

Lynn put a hand on Jordan's shoulder and hugged her.

Jordan wrapped her arms around Lynn and wiped her eyes again. "We're not going to get back to normal, Lynn." She coughed and blew her nose into the handkerchief. "Is it right to bring a child into this world?"

Lynn was crying too, now. "You can't think like that," she muttered, shaking her head. "Everyone dies. Is that a reason not to live?"

Jordan stopped crying. She breathed deeply and looked down at the bucket of greens in front of her. "How should we live at the end of the world?" She stared off into the burning horizon.

Keith picked up his bucket in his right hand and took Jordan's bucket in his left. "Let's fry some fish," he said. And without looking back or waiting for the others, he began walking toward the purple house.

Day 140

Dark clouds rolling across the sky. Wind in the trees. Leaves falling. Green to red to brown to gone. Keith, I love you. I want to marry you. I've already started making plans. We have to get a German shepherd. Sarah. Dogs barking. Night. Lights flashing. Pop-pop-pop. Crackling. Bang! Static. Screaming. Concertina wire. Drag your skull through the dirt! Boom! Flares. Fires. Smoke. Move! Kill! Kill! Kill! Dead cars. Garbage. Dogs chewing corpses. Dead man knifing dog. Child screaming. Stand up. Boom! Pink mist. Blood and bone and flopping arms. Kill, Kill, Kill 'em all! Dead faces. Sorry, Jack. Mound of bodies. Dogs barking. Howling. Screaming. Screaming!

Keith woke up with a start. The sound of shrieking chickens alerted his attention to the window. He looked outside before jumping out of bed and grabbing a 12-gauge shotgun which leaned against the wall, beside the door to his bedroom. He quickly reached the door to the back deck, opened it, and stepped out onto the porch. Lowering his muzzle over the rail, he brought the stock to his cheek, looked down the barrel, and aligned the silver bead on the neck of a large coyote trying to claw its way into the fence. The load of 00 buckshot dropped the predator in its tracks, and the explosion startled everyone in the house.

The coyote kicked in the dirt as small rivulets of blood pooled and ran down the slope, into the chicken run. Keith racked the slide, ejecting the spent shell. Dawn's cold, gray twilight was just conceding to the amber glow of the rising sun. The chickens clucked and screamed for a couple of minutes, but they soon calmed down once more, and huddling around the crimson flow, they dipped their beaks to drink from the river of blood.

After returning the shotgun to its place, Keith went downstairs with a hand on his pounding head as the other family members were coming out of their rooms, with guns, asking what he had shot.

Keith had cut up the coyote and put the meat into a stockpot to boil over the outdoor stove which they had built with the help of Tim Faulkner, for cooking and canning in the summer. It was poetic justice to feed the predator to the chickens. After breakfast, Keith asked Faye to keep the fire fed until they got back from the trial. Faye didn't want to go, so she agreed and said that she was going to make a big salad for everyone to eat when they got back. Faye had always loved salads and had been talking about how much she wanted a salad ever since the blackout. For the past few days, they had been eating salads with every meal, but after months without fresh fruits or vegetables, no one was complaining about that.

Kent and the three siblings walked along the road, looking at the various shops and gardens along the way. The ringing of steal resounded through the air as a blacksmith hammered out a newly forged froe, a precision wood splitting tool, on his anvil. Black smoke drifted from his forge as the hot embers of charcoal burned in the furnace. Honeybees buzzed around them, alighting on the clovers and wildflowers which grew abundantly around every house now. Outside one of the houses, a black cat prowled about the front porch and pounced upon a mouse. They strode down the hill, toward the barn, where a group was beginning to form.

The offender was a middle-aged man, around thirty years old, who had been accused of stealing crop from a farmer for whom he was working. During the starving time, the punishment for theft of food would have been death, no questions asked. Taking food from people was no different from murder. Now, however, no one was truly going hungry, and the community voted to enact new laws about matters such as this one. There were no lawyers or politicians on Mount Sinai, so they kept the laws simple. Feeding and sheltering criminals for free with their precious resources was out of the question, so prison was not an option. Therefore, the prescribed punishment for all violent crimes was still death, but for all nonviolent crimes, the punishment was indentured servitude, wherein the convict was to pay off the debt, plus interest, through manual labor for the victim under the supervision of one of the deputies. Once the debt was repaid, the criminal would apologize to the community and be forgiven and accepted as a neighbor in good standing once again. They had elected a judge who did his best to educate himself on legal philosophy with the books they had available, defendants and plaintiffs represented themselves, and the jury did not consist of twelve, but however many neighbors showed up to the trial. Votes were tallied by the raising of hands in the audience, and the judge pronounced the sentence.

In this case, the accused was found guilty after the evidence was presented and his story fell apart. Having not only stolen from his neighbor but lied about it as well, his sentence was especially hard. He would repay the debt to the farmer in firewood. The amount which he was convicted of stealing was estimated at a value of two-and-a-half rick of wood, and the interest made it three. Furthermore, for lying to the community about his crime, he was sentenced to cut two more rick of wood which would go to the barn. Under the watch of an armed deputy, he would spend the next few weeks sawing logs with a buck saw, splitting them with a froe, and hauling them with the use of either a wagon or a sled which he would pull by hand before stacking them. On top of this, he would have to work for his food and pay for the deputy's supervision during this time, so the sentence would likely drag out to well over a month, maybe two. It was harsh, but the residents almost unanimously agreed it was just. Theft and lying could not be tolerated, especially

CHAPTER FIFTEEN

when they counted on their supplies and crops for survival, and the truthful accounts of their neighbors for accurate information on which to base decisions.

When the sentence was passed, the convict lowered his head and accepted somberly. There was no point in trying to get out of it. If he refused to work, he would not be allowed to eat. If he fought against the deputies, he would be shot. If he ran away from the community, he would only find a harder world to try to survive in. There was nowhere to really hide on Mount Sinai either. While one could live in the woods without being seen for quite a while, he would immediately be recognized and apprehended as soon as he was discovered. The only thing for him to do was to accept his punishment, serve out his sentence, repay his debt to the society, and regain his honor. As the preacher said, once the debt was repaid and the offender had repented, he would be forgiven and welcomed back into the fold.

Out of the barn, the convict was led, to begin working on his sentence. The people of Mount Sinai filed out in pairs and groups, talking to one another about the trial, the crop, or what they were planning to do next. The sun was shining brightly, and the sky was clear and blue. Everyone seemed to be in good spirits. Justice was done, and order was restored.

As they were walking out of the barn, Kent and Lynn had stopped to talk with the Jorgensons. Keith and Joe drifted away from them and saw the Packards talking by themselves in the driveway.

Joe elbowed his brother. "It's pretty clear, they've never liked us. What I want to know is why. I'm going to find out." He started walking toward the Packards, and before Keith could stop him, they were already looking at him, as if to say: "What do you want?"

"Hello again. Joe Rawlings. How y'all doin'?" Joe held out his hand with a smile. Keith was now standing beside him, trying to look friendly as well.

Fred looked at his hand and back at his face. "Is there something we can do for you?"

379

Joe lowered his hand. "You don't like us, do you?"

"I never said that," Fred said with a deadpan expression.

"You didn't need to. It's pretty clear."

Neither of them responded.

"All I want to know is why. What did we ever do to you?"

"You want to know?" Fred said lowly. "I don't like your kind."

"What kind?"

"White trash hillbillies. Fat, lazy, stupid, apathetic, uneducated underachievers. I don't like your politics, your religion, your disgusting, thirty-year-old repo cars polluting my air. I can hear them rattling apart from five miles away. I don't like that you burn your trash because you're too cheap to pay for it to be removed. That you shoot off guns just outside your house. Your land looks like a dump. I can smell your garbage from my house. What do you do for me but pollute my environment and lower my property value?"

"Well, don't sugarcoat it," Joe said.

Fred frowned but kept his eyes on Joe. "Anything else?"

"Nope. That's what I wanted to know. Thank you." Joe turned around and walked toward Kent and Lynn who were strolling toward the road with the Jorgensons, still talking.

Keith followed, and the Packards watched them leave.

As they passed the intersection and started up the hill toward the Jorgensons' house, Kent asked them if they would like to come over for supper, maybe do a little fishing and share a campfire. "Keith makes a great bluegill chowder."

"Mmm. Sounds delicious," Lydia said.

"I don't believe I've ever had a bluegill chowder," said the preacher.

"Keith, would you cook us a bluegill chowder over the fire?"

Keith smiled. "Sure. If you clean 'em, I'll cook 'em."

"Deal." Kent grinned. He looked back at the preacher and his wife. "What do you say?"

"Should I invite Rachel and Abigail?" The preacher smiled.

"Well, of course. Bring 'em over!" Kent exclaimed. "I know Faye and Lynn would love to spend some time with 'em." He nodded toward Joe and laughed. "And I bet Joe wouldn't mind seein' Abigail either."

With the spring calving, came an abundance of milk, which was a most welcome addition to their diet. Farmers traded fresh quart jars of the stuff every day now as payment for labor or produce, and not only cow's milk; goat's milk was traded as well. They had so much that they could not begin to consume it all. Everyone could afford milk. Without refrigeration, the milk had to be consumed immediately, sold cheap, and restocked daily. Unfortunately, they couldn't make ice cream without ice, but several of the homesteaders had begun experimenting with making sour cream, butter, and cheese. Faye and Lynn went to the general store nearly every day now, to get out of the house and have something to do as much as anything, and they returned with a jar of milk every time.

Keith opened a jar of milk and poured it into his Dutch oven which hung over the fire, simmering. With corn, carrots, wild onions, garlic, fresh herbs and bacon, Keith tossed in the cubed bluegill fillets and gave it a stir. He put the lid back on and adjusted the tripod to raise it a little higher above the flames before returning to where Malik and Jordan stood waiting for him.

Jordan, still holding Kent's old compound bow, was trying to pull back the string, but couldn't get it to move more than a couple of inches. "Oh my goodness," she said. "How can anyone pull this?" She handed it back to Malik who wanted to try again.

"Yours is easier. Let me try yours," Jordan said.

"That's the lightest one we have," Keith said. "It's the minimum weight legal to hunt with." He picked up his bow which hung from a tree at the twenty-yard line of their practice range. "This one's about twenty pounds heavier."

"No way. Let me see." Jordan reached for the bow. When he handed it to her, she tried to pull the string, but it didn't budge. "Holy cow!" She handed the bow back to him.

Malik and Keith both laughed as Jordan shook her head. "So, anyway," she said. "What was Joe saying about your neighbors?"

Keith looked behind them to the pond where Joe was standing beside Abigail, fishing with the others. "Oh, he just wasn't too happy about what the Packards told him when he talked to them after the trial today."

"What did they say?"

Keith recounted the conversation and smiled. "He's kind of a social animal, so he cares about what people think about him. Lynn too."

"But not you?"

"Not me," Keith affirmed. "Most of the time, I'm trying to get people to leave me alone," Keith laughed.

"Well, some people just aren't going to like you," Malik said. "Nothing you can do about that. You can't expect everyone to like you."

"That's what I said," Keith responded.

"It's not as bad as the city, though." Jordan shook her head.

"No, that's true," Malik agreed.

When Keith asked what she meant, Jordan explained: "In the city, nobody likes you. You're just another obstacle taking up space. You're a type, a class, or a member of a group. Something to get money from, or something in the way of getting money from somewhere else. No one knows your name or cares to learn it. It's ironic. It's the places with the most people where you're the most alone. Everyone feels isolated. Most of them live alone in an apartment with a pet or maybe a roommate they don't talk to. A lot of them don't even talk to their parents or siblings. The closest relation-ship most people have is with the government. That's why they always vote for bigger government. It's like their daddy. It provides and protects. The more responsibility they give the government, the less they have to take for themselves."

"Yeah." Malik nodded, looking at the ground. "Most people don't really want to be free; they want to be taken care of."

"At least, that's how it used to be in the cities." Jordan shrugged. "I'm sure glad I'm not there now."

Malik clipped the release onto the string the way Keith had showed him. He made sure his finger was behind the trigger so there was no way it would fire accidentally. Pulling with all his might, he strained and clenched his teeth, trying to bring the string back to his ear. He stopped, took a breath, and watched as Keith pulled back his bow, aimed, and sent an arrow directly into the center of his target. Malik tried again. He still couldn't pull the string back. "I can't believe I'm this weak."

"It's not that you're weak. You just aren't used to using those muscles like that," Keith said. "Keep trying. You'll get it." He nocked another arrow, drew it back with ease, and fired, sticking the target about an inch away from the first arrow.

"You can do it, Babe," Jordan laughed. "I have faith in you."

"Thanks." Malik took a breath and tried again. His arms shook as the string moved back slowly. Finally, he managed to get the string back to his chest, and as he tried to breathe, the bow yanked his arm forward again.

"Ooh! You almost had it!" Jordan shouted. "Good job. That was very manly."

Malik laughed. "My back is cramping."

Jordan started rubbing his shoulder blades.

Keith sent another arrow into the target.

"Hey!" Kent shouted from the bank of the pond. "Is the soup ready?"

"Yeah!" Keith yelled back. "Let's eat!"

"Oh good." Kent started putting away his fishing gear. "My bellybutton's pushing so hard against my backbone..."

From the benches beside the pond, Eric and Lydia Jorgenson arose and followed Kent toward the campfire. Joe, Lynn, and Abigail reeled in their lines and followed behind them as Rachel and Faye came out of the house, carrying salad, bowls, spoons, forks, cups, and a large jug of sassafras tea.

They assembled around the campfire as the sun sank behind the trees, and after holding hands and giving thanks, they dipped up bowls and passed them around. Everyone commented on how good the food was, and they ate to their hearts' content, telling stories around the campfire and watching the mesmerizing flames dance into the night.

Chapter Sixteen

Day 151

There were, by now, American flags adorning every house and barn in the community. Over the past three months, the walls inside Jim Baker's barn had been covered with portraits of those neighbors slain by the marauders, hung to join the image of Jack Winters' children. From the rafters hung Gadson flags and flags for every military branch of the former United States. The outside of the barn was similarly arrayed. Tables were being set up outside the barn, food was being prepared, the bands were getting ready, and several reloaders were turning out ammunition for the day's target shooting competition. Shooting had become one of the most popular activities on Mount Sinai, and after months of practice, there were a lot of shooters who claimed to be the best. Today, as part of the celebration of Independence Day, they would get their chance to prove their skills.

Decorations were hung upon the barn and all around the field. On a huge, custom-made spit, three large hogs were being roasted over the fire. Several men were setting up the various shooting ranges—one for rifles, one for pistols and shotguns, and one for archery. There was a station for wood cutting competitions, wherein competitors would race to fell a tree with an axe, cut logs with a bucksaw, and split them with a maul. There was a baseball tournament and a bicycle race. Inside the barn, card tables were set up for various card games and chess matches. For the musicians, a stage was made from a tri-axle trailer. There was even going to be an artificial-lure-only, catch-and-release fishing competition at the pond just across the road.

For the kids and the young at heart, there were sack races, cornhole, horseshoes, and even baseball. Half of one of Jim Baker's corn fields had been converted into a baseball diamond late in the spring. They couldn't plant as much as they used to, so there were large amounts of open field left unplowed, and baseball was as good a use as any. The youths, as well as some of the adults, would frequently schedule games after the chores were done, and some of the residents would show up just to watch.

Everyone was required to pitch in something to the feast, and as the families arrived, they began talking with organizers and setting down large dishes of food on the tables. Everyone brought some contribution to the banquet, and soon, the long tables were spread with deviled eggs, mixed greens, salads, casseroles, cooked carrots, turnips, parsnips, beets, raw radishes, cornbread, baked and fried fish, whole smoked chickens, and a large pot of what looked like fat spaghetti noodles, but was in fact, cattail roots. At the end of the table were desserts, and indeed, there looked to be fruit pies, likely from the stores of preserves of one of the more prepared homesteaders. Beside the pies, there were bowls of fresh watermelon and cantaloupe.

The sight of the spread moved more than a few of the neighbors to tears. With the families all assembled, they looked at the food with anticipation. It was all the parents could do to keep their kids from sampling the desserts. Before they ate, they were asked to only take one scoop of every dish until everyone had eaten, and the preacher opened the ceremony with a prayer of thanksgiving. They formed a line with the women and children in front, and as they all got their plates filled, they sat down to eat in lawn chairs and on logs around handcrafted tables hewn from the timber. Once everyone had got a plate and had begun eating, the man elected as judge stood up and gained the attention of the gathering, and in honor of the day, he read them the Declaration of Independence. When he finished, a choir sang all four verses of "The Star-Spangled Banner."

At the conclusion of the singing, and once everyone had a chance to eat, the replacement guards went to relieve the ones on post, so they could come and get some food, and then, the games began. There were two bands. One of the bands began to play their number while the others ate and listened. After three songs, the bands would switch, allowing the others a chance to rest and get refreshments, and then, they would switch again. In this way, the concert would go almost uninterrupted for the next seven hours. Many of the older neighbors went directly to the card tables and chess boards. Some simply sat and listened to the music, talking amongst themselves. The call for the little league baseball game to begin brought the young children running to the ball field, their parents following behind them to watch.

For each event, there was a prize to be won by the champion. For the card games and chess tournament, the prizes mostly consisted of things like a jar of fruit preserves or a pie; however, some of the competitions, such as the wood cutting and shooting competitions, had prizes of livestock. The best fisherman would win a goat. The best shot with a rifle would win a pig. The best shot with a pistol would win a young cow. The winners of the baseball tournament would each win a chicken, as would the winner of the bicycle race.

Kent and Faye had gone to find a card table with Eric and Lydia Jorgenson. Keith had left, as soon as he finished eating, to monitor one of the shooting ranges. Lynn was with her boyfriend at one of the stations. Joe and Abigail sat across from one another, savoring pieces of cantaloupe and watermelon as they talked. Abigail stared into Joe's eyes and couldn't keep from smiling.

"What do you want to do first?" Abigail asked him.

"I thought we should do the shooting ranges first, so we're not tired from the other events when we go," Joe replied.

Abigail smiled again and nodded. "I like that plan. Let's go."

The two left their plates and walked hand in hand to the pistol range where Keith had lined up several shooters and was going through the rules and safety procedures. They watched as each shooter was directed to approach the firing line, one at a time, and fire three well-aimed shots from twenty-five yards once the command "targets" was given. Everyone used his own weapon and ammunition, regardless of caliber or other considerations. When the first group of shooters had gone through and had their scores recorded, Abigail and Joe got in line with the second group and took their turns. With her .22 revolver, Abigail put three holes in the paper, all within two inches of each other, and two of the three touching the center circle.

"That's some pretty good shooting," Keith said as he recorded the score. "It's gonna be hard to beat that."

Joe stepped up to the line and drew the .45 from his holster. At the word "target," he aimed and fired as carefully as he could. Two of his three shots were on paper, about eight inches apart, and nowhere near the center. He frowned as he looked at his results.

Keith shook his head as he wrote down the score. "Stick to bows and shotguns."

Abigail laughed at him as they walked away to the rifle range.

"It's not exactly fair, you using a .22 while I use a .45," Joe protested.

"I won fair and square by the rules of the competition," Abigail said.

"Where'd you learn to shoot like that?" Joe asked.

"Grandad taught me. He took me to hunt squirrels and rabbits a lot after my dad died. This was one of the guns he gave me to hunt with."

"Your grandpa taught you to shoot?" Joe said incredulously. "You mean on your dad's side?"

"No, my mom's dad. The preacher. Eric Jorgenson."

"I didn't think he ever touched a gun." Joe looked puzzled. "What made you think that?"

"I've never seen him carrying one. He's one of the only ones who doesn't, and since he's a preacher, I figured he didn't like guns or something."

"He doesn't carry a gun unless he's hunting, but he's a really good shot."

"Same as my dad. Except he's not a good shot because he's too cheap to spend the ammo on practice."

"I like your dad. I think he's funny."

"He's something."

"I like your sister too. She told me about her boyfriend. That's exciting."

"Exciting? Why?"

Abigail laughed. "I don't know! It's a girl thing! Guys get excited about bacon and tools; girls get excited about romance and gossip."

Joe laughed as well. "I do get excited about bacon."

Abigail stepped in line at the rifle range. "Well, what do you think about Matthew? Do you like him?"

Joe shrugged a bit. "Yeah. He seems alright."

"Just alright?" Abigail laughed again. "Well, I know something you won't like."

"What's that?"

"Losing to a girl twice in a row."

"Oh, okay. You're pretty sure of yourself, aren't you? Where's your rifle?"

"You have to let me borrow yours." Abigail looked into his eyes and smiled just as sweetly as she could, swishing her summer dress around as she did so.

Joe chuckled a bit and held up his AR-15, keeping the muzzle pointed at the dirt. "Well, this isn't exactly a .22."

"Can I see it?" Abigail took the rifle from him, slung it across her body, and ejected the magazine. She stripped one round off the top and held it up beside one of hers. "Actually, it is. See?"

Joe's eyes went wide. "Okay. Point taken."

Abigail smiled, pushed the round back into the magazine, and reinserted it.

Joe looked around and coughed slightly. "I think we might have to go to the wood cutting station next."

Abigail squeezed Joe's arm as she threw her head back and laughed.

————————————

The winners were announced, and once they had all collected their prizes, people began to pack up their things. It was getting dark, and there were almost no batteries left, other than the few rechargeable ones for the radios and power tools, which meant no one could afford to use flashlights to walk home in the dark anymore. As the sun touched the treetops, some of the kids lit firecrackers and roman candles, squealing with delight at the colorful flares and pops.

As some of the women began to pack up the leftover food, Jack Winters hailed them and asked if they could take some of the leftovers to the guards on post. It was only right, they concluded, since the guards had missed most of the celebration. The women agreed that taking them a plate of cold leftovers was the least they could do.

"Thank you, ladies," Jack said, as he and a deputy began filling containers with a scoop of everything left.

"We'll take some to post one," Keith volunteered.

"Thank you, fellas," Jack replied.

Scooping up enough to fill a Tupperware container, Keith and Joe began walking up the road. The rest of the Rawlings family, along with Malik and Jordan, had already left, as had most people. The sun was behind the hills now, and they only had about half an hour of daylight left.

As the remaining neighbors packed and drifted away, Jack nodded to the brothers from his horse. He turned and rode toward Post 3 at the end of Deer Creek Road while his deputy headed up to Post 2 on the north end of Mount Sinai Road.

"Alright. Let's hurry up." Keith turned to go. "It's going to be dark before we get back to the house."

The brothers walked swiftly up the hill, stretching their legs into long strides. The waning sunlight emanated through the trees and houses, casting long, blue shadows over the cracked asphalt. Near one of the houses, a black cat emerged from the tall grass, carrying a dead bird in its mouth. It silently darted across the road before them. Across the valley, to the right, an owl hooted into the coming night. Bats flitted overhead, snatching insects in their silent, erratic movements. At one of the houses, children continued to light bottle rockets and sparklers, giggling as they did so. Keith and Joe glanced at them a couple of times as they walked, not liking the idea of anyone shooting bottle rockets at night.

"You think we should stop them?" Joe asked. "It sounds like someone shooting a .22."

Keith wasn't comfortable with it either, but he hated to stop kids from having fun. He shrugged. "I think people understand that it's The Fourth, so it won't worry anyone."

Just then, a teenager came out of the house with a mortar tube and a bag of fireworks. Once the brothers had registered what he was doing, they both immediately started toward him.

"Whoa, whoa, whoa," Keith began. "What are you doing with that?"

The kid looked perturbed. "What does it look like I'm doing? It's the Fourth of July."

"Oh no," Joe put his hand up. "You can't be shooting that thing off right now."

"Why not?"

The screen door to the house opened with a creak, and a man in a tank top walked out onto the porch with another bag of fireworks. "What's going on?" he demanded when he saw the brothers in his yard. "Something we can do for you?"

"Yeah," Keith replied. "You can put the fireworks away. It's bad enough to be shooting bottle rockets at night, but you can't be shooting mortars up into the sky." He shook his head.

"Why the hell not?" the man said defiantly. "It's my property. I can do what I want with it. What gives you the right to tell me what to do?"

"Take it easy. No one's trying to take your property. But if you shoot that stuff off, it's not only going to scare your neighbors to death and make people think we're under attack; it'll be seen and heard from miles away, and there's probably a lot of people out there who'd be very interested in finding out who's got the resources and energy, not to mention the stupidity, to be shooting off fireworks for fun."

"Who are you calling stupid?"

"Do you think Jack Winters is going to be happy that someone's advertising our community's whereabouts to the world?"

"Oh, come on. It's just a couple of fireworks. Besides, you can't see them from the town. It's too far away."

"I'm asking you, please, don't do it. It's not worth the risk."

The man paused for a second. "Oh alright. Bring them back inside." He turned and opened the screen door once again.

The teenager hung his head and slumped his shoulders as he carried the bag and mortar back to the house. "Man, this is stupid," he mumbled.

"Thank you," Joe said. "We really do appreciate it."

"Whatever." The man turned back to the doorway. "Come on inside, kids."

The children groaned and complained as they dragged their feet.

The brothers moved on. Through the trees, they could hear roman candles shooting off, and they could smell the smoke of a bonfire. Voices carried through the hollows. There was laughter, and it sounded like someone was singing.

When they reached the old church, it was dark, and they called out to the sentry. "Hey, lookout," Joe said in a slightly raised voice. "It's Joe Rawlings. We brought you food."

"Oh, thanks," came a voice from the bell tower. "I'm coming down."

A few seconds later, the church door opened, and a young man stepped out. He took the container of food from Joe and thanked them before sitting down on the front step to eat. "Mmm. It's still good cold," he said as he chewed.

The faint moonlight reflected off the shattered windows of the barricade cars. It was just light enough that they could still see bats flying in haphazard circles through the air above.

"So, how was the celebration?" The lookout spoke between bites. "I could just faintly hear the music from here. Sounded good."

"Yeah, it was real good," Joe replied. "I think everyone had a good time."

"Did y'all win any of the competitions?"

"Nope." Joe laughed. "Came close on a couple, but..."

"Who won the fishing tournament?"

Joe was about to respond when they heard a whistling shriek come from the south. They looked to their left as an explosion of green and red stars burst high above the trees in the sky and was followed by a massive boom. All three of them jumped at the thunderous disturbance. A crackling shower of sparks rained down from the sky and disappeared into smoke. They heard laughter and shouting coming from down the road.

Keith cursed and took a drink of water. His heart was beating like a drum. The hair on his arms stood up, and his hands trembled from the sudden rush of adrenaline.

"Freaking idiots." Joe shook his head. "Couldn't let it go."

"You know who that was?" The sentry was still staring in the direction of the laughter.

"Yeah," Joe said. "We passed them on the way up here. Tried to stop them."

The sentry sat back down and resumed eating. "Well, hopefully, no one saw that."

Someone was yelling down the road. Then, there was another whistle, a flash of white light in the sky, and another window-rattling boom. A shower of flashing flames precipitated down below the trees. The air smelled of burnt black powder. Someone was shouting some colorful language. Probably a neighbor expressing his displeasure with the pyrotechnicians.

Suddenly, the horizon to the west lit up in a blast of yellow light. Like a clap of thunder, an explosion shook the ground. The sentry dropped the container of food, and all three of the men stood staring with open mouths as a roiling ball of fire rose into the sky a couple of miles away. It rose high above the treetops and lit up the sky in an orange glow until, high in the air, it burned out and faded from sight. The flickering orange light illuminated the clouds overhead. The sentry ran inside the church and up the stairs of the bell tower. The brothers followed closely behind him, and when they reached the top, they looked out to the west and saw a pillar of fire twisting and curling up into the sky. The orange light radiated out from the horizon, and in the glow, the black clouds rolling overhead looked like burning coals slowly dying as they were blown toward the east. Then, in the flickering luminescence and disconcerting calm, the disquieting rumble of beating drums echoed across the expanse and chilled the blood of everyone on Mount Sinai.

Day 152

"It was just a couple of firecrackers!" the man protested.

A small mob had formed outside the man's house. They had caught him in his outhouse without a weapon, and when he had opened the door and walked out, he saw the mob enveloping him, and he ran back into the outhouse, slamming the door behind him. They were shouting curses at him for shooting off fireworks while they were trying to sleep, for making them think someone was attacking, and for probably giving away their location to whoever had been playing the drums all night. Few of them had been able to sleep last night with the explosion to the west, the sky lit up by fire, and the ominous banging of the drums that didn't stop until just before dawn. Their eyes were red, swollen, and framed in dark circles. They were angry, and they had found the man to blame.

"Go away! Get off my property!" the man in the outhouse was yelling back at the mob.

A man with an axe approached the outhouse and swung the head over his shoulder, burying it in the boards of the outhouse door. There was a scream from inside as the axe was ripped back out, sending splinters flying all around.

"Alright! Stop it!" the man inside shouted. "I'll come out! Just put the axe away!"

The man lowered the axe and shouted for him to come out.

The door opened slightly and the man inside was yanked out into the crowd. His hands were up, and he tried to plead for his life. "Please, don't hurt me! I've got kids inside. They're scared to death right now."

A woman shouted back to him, "You weren't worried about anyone's kids when you told the whole county where we were last night!"

"My kids wanted to shoot fireworks," the man argued.

"You're the head of the household!" the woman shouted back. "You should know better! And I know you were warned beforehand, but you did it anyway! Don't use your kids as an excuse!"

There was more shouting from the crowd. People were grabbing and shoving the man as his kids watched through the window of the house. From the front door, came a shout from the teenager.

"You get away from him right now!" The teenager stood on the front porch, holding a shotgun pointed toward the crowd.

The mob stopped and looked at the kid.

"Put the gun away, son." From behind the trees, came a man riding a horse. It was Jack Winters. "Nobody's going to hurt your old man," he said.

The kid looked nervous. He hesitated.

"Let him go," Jack said to the crowd. "There ain't gonna be no damn lynch mob grabbing neighbors around here."

The kid lowered his shotgun as the crowd eased away from the man.

"But Jack," one of the neighbors started. "This clown was shooting off fireworks last night after multiple people told him not to. He sent a signal to those maniacs out there, letting them know we were here."

"I wasn't trying to..." the man protested.

Jack raised his hand for calm. "We don't know what that was about. We don't know why the gas station blew up, whether it was intentional or not, or if it had anything to do with the drumming, and we certainly don't know if it had anything to do with the fireworks. It was a stupid risk to take, shooting fireworks, but there's no sense in doing another stupid thing in response to it."

The mob had calmed down now. No one was going to push too hard against Jack. "Well, we can't just let people put the community in danger and get away with it."

The man looked around the crowd and pleaded. "Look, I'm sorry. I really am. I didn't mean any harm. I wasn't thinking, and..." he caught Jack's eye.

Jack stopped him. "We're not going to just let it go. That was a profoundly foolish act that could have cost the lives of your neighbors. Let's go." He looked down at the man and motioned up the road with his head. "Up to the old church. You're gonna get a reminder of what happened the last time someone told outsiders about this place."

The people parted and let the man pass, walking in front of Jack Winters' horse.

They passed the church cemetery, came to the end of the road and the final barricade, and stopped. The nooses still hung from the telephone poles. Jack dropped a spade down beside the man. The bones of the marauders were now bleached white from the sun, scattered about the road and the grassy field on the other side.

"Dig a hole," Jack said flatly. "These bones have been out here too long. They need to be buried."

———————————

Tim Faulkner knocked on the door to the Rawlings house. Faye answered.

"Hey, is Keith or Joe here?" he asked, looking slightly exasperated.

"Hi, Tim. Uh, they said they were going to Scott Adams' house. Is something wrong, or..."

"When did they leave?" Tim interrupted.

"About an hour ago. What's the matter?"

"Nothing. I just need to talk to them. Thank you. Have a nice day." He started off, back up toward the road.

When he crested the hill, he saw the brothers approaching the driveway with their bags and weapons and Keith carrying an axe. "Hey, Joe! Keith!" he waved as he jogged up to them.

The brothers waved back. "What's up, Tim? You alright?"

"Yeah, but I just saw a mob heading up the road. They looked angry. I think they're going to hang the guy who shot the fireworks last night. We have to stop them."

The brothers began jogging alongside Tim up the road. "Where's Jack?"

"I think he went with them. I saw him ride past with a rope and a shovel."

They picked up their pace.

"Ooh! I found one!" Lynn exclaimed as she bent down to pick a mushroom out of the leaves.

"Nice," Matthew said. "I think you're beating me. This bag is getting kind of heavy."

Lynn pulled the mushroom out of the dirt and turned to look at him with mock sympathy. "Oh, you poor thing. You need some help?"

"Yeah, I think I do."

Lynn leaned over and kissed him.

Matthew straightened up and smiled. "That's the ticket! I'm good for ten more pounds now."

Lynn grinned and shook her head. "Why do you have to be so cute?"

"Can't help it. Momma made me that way."

"Well, you're not getting any more kisses until you find some more mushrooms, so don't even ask." She kissed him again. "Starting now."

Matthew picked up his shotgun and adjusted the strap of his satchel a bit before taking her hand and starting to walk once more. They followed the creek bed through the valley, crossing moss-covered boulders and breathing deeply of every honeysuckle bush as they made their way toward the field of red needles beneath the massive pines.

They sat down at the base of an enormous pine tree and rested on the soft bed of needles. Lynn laid her head on Matthew's shoulder and closed her eyes. Butterflies and moths fluttered amidst the golden light streaming through the branches as it sparkled off geodes and bubbles of pine resin. The pine forest's aroma was enchanting, like escaping to another world where fairies and dwarves could appear from behind a tree at any moment. They listened to the rapturous singing of the birds and the soft, melodic gurgling of the stream bubbling over tiny waterfalls of mossy sandstone and fallen branches.

Looking out across the creek, Matthew saw a large fallen oak tree lying down with its branches extending into the creek. It stretched across the ravine from up on the side of the ridge where it had been uprooted by the erosion of the soil from a sequence of gulley washers and strong winds. On the trunk, near the roots, was a bright orange patch protruding from the charcoal bark.

"I think I found one!" Matthew proclaimed. He jumped up, and Lynn's head rolled off his shoulder as he grabbed his bag and shotgun.

They walked across the creek along a bridge made by another fallen tree, and reaching the other side, Lynn noticed a cave in the ridge, where water dripped over smooth, bare limestone before running down the slope into the stream.

"Isn't that a chicken mushroom?" Matthew asked, pointing to the orange fungus.

"Yeah, it looks like it," Lynn replied. "I've never found one, but my brother showed me what they look like."

"I'm gonna pick it." Matthew set down his bag and gun and pulled out his knife. As he leaned over the log to get his knife under the mushroom, he saw two brown eyes looking up at him from the ground. He froze, and the face looking up at him remained frozen as well, as if in shock. Then, it moved. Matthew jumped back, dropping his knife. He grabbed the shotgun leaning against the tree and swung the muzzle toward the log as a man sprung up from behind the tree, holding the knife he had dropped.

Lynn drew her pistol as soon as she saw Matthew reaching for his shotgun, and she aimed at the face of the man behind the tree.

"Who are you? What are you doing?" Matthew shouted. "Drop the knife!"

The man instantly dropped it and held his hands up in the air, shaking. "Please, don't shoot me." He was trembling all over. His emaciated form was pathetic. His withered face, shrunken arms, and tattered clothes were coated in dirt and grime to the point that he had nearly blended in with the forest floor. "I'm sorry." He looked as if he were about to cry.

"Who are you?"

"My—my name is—Noah Rosenbaum. I..."

"What are you doing?" Matthew shouted. He was so scared he had his finger on the trigger as he tried to hold the shotgun steady on the man's chest.

"I—I'm sorry. We thought this was a state forest. We're not trying to..."

"Who's we?" Lynn shouted.

The man looked around, not saying anything.

"Answer the question!" Matthew shouted, looking around.

"Please—don't hurt me," the man pleaded.

"Who's with you?"

"Don't shoot," came a woman's voice. "We're coming out."

From the mouth of the cave, appeared a group of more than a dozen filthy skeletons, dressed in rags. Women, children, an elderly man with a long, white beard. They carried bags and satchels slung over their shoulders, and most of them leaned on walking sticks.

Matthew and Lynn glanced at one another for half a second, keeping their weapons trained on the group.

"Please," said the woman. "We are unarmed."

"What's in the bags?" Matthew asked, lowering his voice to a normal volume.

"The last of our possessions," the first man said. "We are refugees."

"From Bloomington?" Lynn asked.

"Yes. I'm a doctor. I could offer my services to you in return for food, clothing, maybe shelter. Please..."

Matthew and Lynn looked at each other again, not knowing what to do. Matthew bit his lip and looked back at the man behind the fallen tree. "Give me back my knife. Slowly."

The man reached down and carefully picked up the knife by the blade, keeping his other hand raised above his head. He stood up again and held it out to Matthew.

"Lay it on the log."

The man set the knife on the log and raised his hands again.

"Back up." Matthew continued to hold his shotgun on the man's chest.

The man took three steps back.

Matthew lowered the shotgun, retrieved his knife, and put it back in its sheath.

The elderly man with the white beard let out a slight sighing sound and collapsed onto the ground.

"Rabbi," said the woman, kneeling down beside him. Two others helped her as she pulled him back to a sitting position with his back against a tree. "Here, drink." She held a bottle to his mouth and let him sip.

The man who called himself Noah Rosembaum looked back at the strangers from Mount Sinai. "Please, help us. You see the children. We have had nothing to eat in three days."

Matthew looked back at Lynn. Her face was red, and she had tears in her eyes.

Tim, Keith, and Joe crested the hill beside Bill Campbell's barn and saw the crowd standing around, talking to one another. Several of the neighbors were looking nervously down the road and train tracks. Once they saw that the situation was calm, the three men slowed their pace to a brisk walk until they encountered Jack Winters who stood watching a man digging a hole in the depression on the other side of the tracks. Jack's horse was tied to a post outside of the graveyard, eating the grass that grew along the edge of the road. The sheriff turned and looked at them as they approached. He nodded.

"Jack," Tim said, still breathing heavily. "What's going on?"

"We're burying the remains of those pirates," Jack replied. "They've sat here long enough."

"What's everyone else doing?"

Jack looked around at the neighbors talking and scanning the tree line. "They're providing security. Everyone's a little on edge after last night."

The man in the ditch continued to dig.

Jack pulled Tim closer, putting his hand on his shoulder and glancing at the brothers as he lowered his voice. "Did you see the fireworks last night?"

"Yeah," all of them responded in unison.

"I know you heard that drumming. And did you see the gas station blow up down the road?" When they affirmed that they had, he continued: "Well, so did everyone else. And they got the idea that the one caused the other. It looked like things were fixin' to get pretty ugly when I showed up. People are scared, and scared people do stupid things."

"Well, I'm glad to see you got it under control," Tim said. "We came up here to help."

Jack nodded. "Thanks. I think we should do some reconnaissance before long. See what caused that explosion. Try and figure out what's going on out there. I know I'd feel better if ..."

He was cut off by the sound of a horn blowing to the southeast. Jack grabbed his radio and turned it on. "Barn owl, this is Winter."

"Winter, I need you down here immediately. Get here as fast as you can. We've got a situation."

"I'm on my way. What's the problem?"

"We've got refugees. They're at the barn. Bring help if you can."

"Roger." Jack turned off his radio. "Damnit." He turned toward his horse. "Tim, can you come with me? I could use your help."

"Sure."

"Get to the barn as quick as you can." Jack looked at the brothers. "One of you guys, stay here and keep this situation under control."

"I can handle it," Keith said.

Jack mounted his horse. "Consider yourself deputized." He took off at a gallop.

"I'm going," said Joe as he followed behind Tim at a jog.

"We'll stop at my house and grab the truck," Tim panted. And they were gone.

Jim Baker watched the strangers with a wary eye. He didn't dare let them out of his sight. Could this be part of an attack? He wondered to himself. Sitting on the floor of the barn, the refugees looked pathetic. Exhausted, anemic, and dirty, they talked among themselves and helped each other sip the clean water Lynn and Matthew had given them while the couple went to get them some food. At the clatter of hooves outside, Jim started toward the barn door. Jack stepped in as he opened it.

Jack looked at the poor wretches huddled against the wall for a second and spoke to Jim in a low voice. "Where did they come from?"

"Two of the kids were out looking for mushrooms in the woods when they came across them," Jim replied. "They didn't know what to do, so they brought them up here."

"Where are they now?"

"They went to get 'em some food. What do you think we should do with 'em, Jack?"

Jack frowned and looked at them for another couple of seconds. "We need to try to get as much information out of them as we can before we decide. They've already seen your barn, the gardens around it, and some of the people here. They know we have resources."

Jim nodded and bit his lip. "Yeah. They could be scouts. Or infiltrators. Or just thieves. What do you think?"

"I don't know what I think yet. That's why I want to question them. See what I can learn about them. Joe Rawlings and Tim Faulkner are on their way now. They'll be here any minute. I can handle them in the meantime. Do me a favor and go get the doctor and the preacher. We might as well give them a meal, now that they know we have food. It might help us get more information out of them too. And we need to know if they have any diseases."

Jim nodded. "Alright. Where's Keith?"

"I left him at the old church. He's keeping the peace while the pyromaniac buries the bones of the thieves at the end of the road."

"If I don't come back right away, it'll be because I'm talking to Keith."

Jack gave him a thumbs up, and he stepped outside. Almost as soon as he stepped out of the driveway, Tim's green truck came around the bend and down the hill. Tim stopped at the intersection of Mount Sinai and Deer Creek Road as Jim approached the truck.

"Where are you heading?" Tim asked.

"I need to go get the preacher and the doctor."

Tim put the truck in park and got out. "Take my truck."

Joe climbed out and started walking toward the barn, and without a word, Tim followed him as Jim climbed into the truck and turned it around.

When he pulled up to the preacher's house, he found the Jorgensons already coming out of their house with baskets. Lynn and Matthew were helping them carry food down to the barn. He offered to give them a ride, but they said they would be there soon enough. He told them he was going to get the doctor and sped off toward the little, purple house up the road.

Pulling into the driveway, Jim climbed out of the truck and went to the door. When he knocked, Jordan answered and welcomed him in, where he found Malik prescribing a homemade drug to a patient. "Malik," Jim interrupted. "Sorry to interrupt, but we really need you down at the barn."

Malik looked up at him and asked Jordan to take over. He threw a backpack over his shoulder, grabbed his medical bag and his rifle, and followed Jim to the truck. On the ride to the barn, he asked Jim about the situation he would encounter, and as soon as Jim parked the truck, he was out, running to the doorway.

Jim stepped inside and saw Lynn and Matthew helping the refugees up and onto the cots Joe and Tim were setting up. Eric and Lydia Jorgenson were heating a kettle over a fire outside the barn and dumping in jars of soup. Jack Winters sat in a corner with one of the men, asking him questions. Malik had begun with the white-bearded old man who looked to be in the worst condition.

Seeing everyone busy with the facilitation of the refugees, Jim decided to stay out of the way and come back later. He stepped outside, climbed back into Tim's truck, and went to see what was going on at the old church.

The pyrotechnician finished digging his hole and sat down against a tree, sweat running down his face and soaking his shirt. He took a drink from his water bottle and spat onto the pile of dirt. Keith watched him and continued talking with one of the neighbors.

"Don't you think we should check it out?" the man said. "We need to know for sure what caused that explosion."

"Yeah, but I'm not ready to do anything crazy just yet," Keith replied. "We need to talk about it and get a plan together before we even think about going outside our borders again."

"Oh, it shouldn't be that big a deal. I can just take a couple of guys and walk down the tracks and check it out. Be back in an hour."

"Yeah. But that's a couple miles of walking on an easily identified trail through woods. It's a perfect place for an ambush."

"Hmm." The man nodded, considering.

"And if someone over there sees you, they could easily follow you back. You'd be doing more to lead people to us than this guy ever did." Keith motioned to the gravedigger with his head.

"You're right." The man shook his head. "I just wish we could find out what's going on out there."

The gravedigger got up and put his gloves back on. It was time to collect the bones of the twenty-six men strewn about the place. He picked up a bucket taken from the old church and made his way past the barricade.

Keith heard an engine humming from behind the hill, and he turned to see Tim Faulkner's green Chevy come over the rise and weave through the baffles along the road. The truck rolled across the train tracks and parked beside the graveyard. Jim Baker climbed out and raised a hand to Keith as he walked toward him. He looked around at the handful of neighbors standing around, and he glanced across the road at the man with the bucket picking up bones.

"Keith," Jim said, extending his hand. "How's everything going up here?"

Keith shook his hand and nodded. "As good as can be expected. What's going on at the barn?"

"Your sister and her boyfriend found some vagabonds down in the creek bed and brought them up to the barn. There's fifteen of them, and they look pretty rough. They're taking care of them right now. I don't know what we're going to do with 'em, but I expect we'll talk about that this evening."

The pyrotechnician came back from the field beside the highway with a bucket full of bones and dumped them into the hole. He turned around and went back to fill the bucket once again.

"Hmm." Keith stared blankly at the hole where the cracked and broken bones were tossed. He picked up a fallen branch from the ground and began to cut it into stakes with his axe.

Jim took off his hat and waved it in front of his face. "Man, it stinks up here." The sky was still hazy with smoke and fumes. "I heard about the explosion last night. Couldn't see it from down in the valley, but the smoke is starting to pool down there too, I think. It don't smell this strong though."

Keith lashed the two stakes he had cut into the shape of a cross and hammered the marker into the ground at one end of the hole. The man with the bucket dumped another load of bones into the pit. Keith and Jim followed him out past the barricade and stood among the litter of bones on the cracking asphalt.

As the hot sun began to sink toward the treetops, the yellow light filtered through the gray and black smoke which saturated the air. The entire landscape looked dirty. Buzzards perched atop the telephone poles lining the highway, basking in the heat and the stench and the hazy light the color of dark urine. From the west, a strong gust of wind blew the choking fumes toward them. Leaves and dust swirled about. A dead branch fell from a tree above the grave and crashed down onto the cross Keith had built, leaving the marker slumped to the side like an x. The old, worn-out flag over the graveyard tore at the eyelet and flapped erratically in the wind.

Keith held his hat on his head and looked up at the grease-stained nooses hanging from the cross members, spinning and flailing in the wind. Then, as suddenly as it came, the wind ceased, and the putrid, smoke-tinged air was still once more. There was a distant, low rumble of thunder far off in the distance. Two of the neighbors ran to the flag-pole to lower the colors and try to mend the fabric.

"Hey, look." Jim said, tapping Keith's arm. He pulled binoculars from his pack.

"What?" Keith turned around and looked in the direction Jim was indicating. He saw a black dot moving on the highway, far off in the distance. It was moving slowly, but gradually coming closer. Dark clouds rolled in, and the orange sun radiated through the haze as birds scattered from the trees around the approaching dark form.

Jim looked down the highway through his binoculars. "Something's coming."

Chapter Seventeen

"Lookout!" Jim shouted to the bell tower. "Sound the signal. Get a radio check."

The bell began ringing. The long tones rang through the hills and hollows.

"What am I supposed to do?" the gravedigger exclaimed. "I don't have a weapon!"

Keith motioned with his head back down Mount Sinai Road. "Go on. Get out of here."

"It's still coming, whatever it is," Jim said.

Neighbors began running out of their houses with rifles and shotguns. One woman approached Keith and Jim for word. "What is it?" she asked.

"Get some snipers in the ditch behind the tracks," Keith said. "Hold your fire unless I signal. Someone's coming."

"Okay." The woman took off toward the houses behind the tracks.

The encroaching black spot disappeared behind a rise in the highway.

"Let's get out of the open," Jim said, turning toward the church. He hailed the lookout once more as Keith followed him. "Let 'em know we've got visitors. Tell them to stand by."

"I did," the lookout responded. "No activity seen at the other posts."

"Alright."

Keith knelt down in the bushes and relieved himself. "You better piss now—just in case," he said, zipping up his fly. "I learned that the hard way."

Jim looked at him quizzically for a second and then took his advice. He kept his nervous gaze shifting around, up the highway, across the field to the west, down the highway's sloping bend to the north, and behind him, to the tree line surrounding the graveyard.

Vultures perched on the rooves of houses lining the highway. More circled high above in the sky, their shadows intermittently passing through the sunlight like a slow strobe effect. A murder of crows passed overhead with a single ominous caw. As Jim and Keith watched from behind the trees in the shadow of the church, the dark specter crested the horizon.

Jim looked through his binoculars. "What the hell is that?"

Keith took the binoculars from him and focused on the creatures approaching the barricade. What he saw appeared to be four naked men crawling on their hands and knees; naked, save for some sort of black leather underwear with tails protruding from the rear end of each. The tails even wagged as they crawled, probably through the use of springs. The men were skinny and pale and sunburnt. They had black kneepads and thick, black, padded gloves on their hands. Floppy dog ears sprouted from their heads by way of black leather or rubber masks which covered their entire heads apart from their eyes. They had black leather harnesses fastened around their bodies with silver rings at the intersection of belts between their shoulder blades. From the rings, ran black leather straps hooked to a wheelchair they pulled. In the wheelchair, beneath a rainbow umbrella, sat a man, or quite possibly a woman, dressed in what both Jim and Keith could only describe as a crazy, horror-movie clown costume. Its head was shaved except for tufts of long hair sprouting out sporadically—each one dyed a different color. Its face was painted with a thick coating of makeup, like a corpse at a viewing, only far less natural. Its green eye shadow, ridiculous overapplication of rouge, orange lipstick, and heavy, black eye liner were running down its face, like a melting candle, in the heat of the sun. Its face was littered with piercings of all kinds—gold and silver rings in its ears, nose, lips, and eyebrows. Gold and silver rings adorned every finger, bracelets covered the arms, and a multitude of necklaces hung from its neck. It wore a frilly, pink skirt and a blue, pinstriped vest from which its exposed arms displayed a myriad of tattooed images including a hammer and sickle, a red star, a portrait of Mao Zedong, and half a dozen cartoon characters. In its right hand, it held a black leather cat o' nine tails—in its left, a glass pipe from which it puffed clouds of smoke.

"The last generation," Keith muttered handing back the binoculars.

As they came to the barricade and the litter of bones strewn across the highway in front of it, the rider ordered a halt. The androgenous heathen master stood up, looked around, took a final puff of the pipe, and tapped out its ashes onto the back of one of the crawling catamites. The catamite winced, and the pagan clown flailed him with the whip three times, with all its might.

"Shut up, dog!" the clown screamed.

The catamite whimpered.

Jim handed the binoculars back to Keith. "Look at the wheelchair."

Keith looked. It was decorated with what looked like human bones. Skulls mounted on either handle in the rear, a string of severed hands draped over the back. Keith handed the binoculars back.

"What kind of monster is that?" Jim whispered.

"It looks like some of the kids I went to school with."

"Looks like they've run out of meds."

"Wag your tails!" The creature shouted.

The four catamites shook their rear ends back and forth, making panting noises as they did so. One of the dogs began to cry.

The clown kicked him in the stomach and shrieked, "Bark!"

After a second's pause, all four catamites were weakly imitating barking dogs, wagging their artificial tails.

The driver patted them on the head and said, "Good doggies."

The catamites stopped barking and took up their panting noises again, as the driver turned and looked around. The creature picked up a bone, studied it, and shoved it into the mouth of one of the catamites. It looked up at the nooses still hanging from the cross members of the telephone poles. Then, it looked at the church. "Come out, come out, wherever you are!" The fiend yelled. It banged on the hood of one of the cars in the barricade.

Keith motioned for Jim to follow him, and they crept back behind the old church, to the back door, before going inside. "I think I'd better go talk to him," Keith said as they walked to the staircase in the front of the building.

"What makes you think you can talk to that thing?" Jim asked.

"I have to try. It looks like he's unarmed..."

"Well, that don't mean you need to be."

"Certainly not. But if we can learn any information about what's going on outside, we need to do it." Keith took a few steps up the staircase and asked the lookout, "You see any snipers?"

"No. Looks like he's alone," the lookout replied.

"I'm gonna go talk to whoever this is. If you do see anyone out there besides us, don't let them shoot first."

Through the porthole in the tower, they could hear the voice outside. "I know you're in there! You rang your bells to greet me!" There was another banging on the car hood. "These cars didn't park themselves like this!"

Jim looked out the window. "Why don't we just shoot 'em?"

Keith turned to look at him with disgust. "They're unarmed, and they haven't crossed our boundary. Why would I shoot them?"

"It's what Jack would do," Jim shrugged. "You know he would."

"Jack's not here, and I'm not going to start murdering people for acting weird. We need to try and get some information out of them."

The voice outside announced in an authoritative tone, "We've been patient. But our patience is wearing thin."

"For the record, I advise against this," Jim said, shaking his head as he looked at the gorgon through a slit in one of the windows.

"Duly noted," Keith said. "We won't look any more vulnerable than we already do if somebody confronts them, anyway. Be ready." With that, he slung his rifle over his shoulder, gripped his axe in his right hand, and stepped out the door.

"There you are," the beast said. "Come out. I have something important to tell you." It reeked of some noxious chemicals.

"Who are you, and what do you want?" Keith demanded.

"Watch your tone, redneck," the heathen growled. "What's behind this barricade?"

"A whole lot of trouble."

"That's cute. Let's get to the point. We know you have stuff back there that you're, like, hoarding for yourselves. Bring it to us. All of it."

"And why would I do that?"

"Reparations. You're going to give us reparations for your rape of Gaia, your enslavement and oppression of minorities and indigenous peoples, and, like, to show atonement for your greed and bigotry. If you don't, we will decolonize your little settlement thing. And we will take it from you, like, on behalf of Gaia and all the disenfranchised you've hurt with your, like, hate and intolerance."

"Decolonize, huh?"

"And reappropriate—by any means necessary."

"I don't think I care for your offer."

"Shut up, you racist, inbred hilljack!" The clown spat. "You think your guns and religion will save you? You moron. You don't even have a college degree, do you?"

"What kind of degree do you have?"

"I have a master's in psychology."

"I see."

"No, you do not see. Because you are a not-see. Not-sees don't recognize their oppressive power structures. You're too stupid. And that's why you don't go to college. If you did, you would know your religion is stupid, your god's not real, and your guns are just, like, a projection of your toxic masculinity, or like, a compensation for your insecurity." The creature grinned. "You'd know that if you went to college."

"Is that right?"

"Yes. And you'd also know that you've been repressing your true identity your whole life. Perhaps you'd like to join them?" The clown motioned toward the catamites wagging their tails. "You can. They never have to worry about food or shelter. We take care of them."

"Perhaps you'd like to find out what those nooses are there for." Keith nodded to the ropes dangling above their heads.

"The sheer caucacity of you bigots! You deserve..." the creature was beginning to raise its hand with the cat o' nine tails.

"Or maybe you want to find out what this axe tastes like." Keith let the axe handle slide through his hand until the fawn's foot was near his wrist. The head hung at his side, unmoving, at the end of the stiffly held American hickory handle protruding from his white knuckles.

The clown lowered the flail slowly and produced a wry smile. "If you raise a weapon at me, you're dead."

"You'd need an army and a half to make that happen."

The creature growled with a sick, maniacal laugh. "You want to see an army? Careful what you wish for." It grinned, and saliva dripped from its stained teeth.

"That sounds like a threat."

The fiend shook its head. "We don't make threats."

Keith tilted his head to one side as if amused. "How many you got with you?"

The creature lowered its head with a sadistic smile, looking up at him from under its arched painted eyebrows. "The world. All the victims of your oppression. We're everywhere. All around. And we're not playing."

The creature turned and mounted the wheelchair. "If you bring us the reparations by this time tomorrow, you will be allowed to live. You will work for us and continue to pay off your debt. If you fail to comply, we will come back here, and we will redistribute your stolen wealth, abort your parasitic future bigots, and like, deconstruct your pathetic, little trailer park, or whatever you call this. And we will do to you what you did to, like, the indigenous peoples, and first nations when you came here." The clown laughed and fondled the glass pipe in its hand. "We're in the school building down the road. It's ours. Bring your reparations there." The clown flogged the catamites. "Turn around! Go back!"

Keith remained standing behind the barricade, watching them. As the wheelchair turned, Keith saw that the backside of the chair was covered with strings of severed hands, and strings of feet dragged behind the chair by a tether. Keith passed the axe to his left hand and touched his pistol grip with his right. He looked around at the tree line and the houses down the road and drew his hand back from the weapon.

The clown looked over its shoulder at Keith, "See you soon."

The barn was abuzz with activity. They had quadrupled the guards on each post and put everyone else on standby, ready to react at a moment's notice. When Keith and Jim Baker walked into the barn, the refugees were all sitting on cots, eating stew. Jack Winters met the two at the door and walked with them a little way from the barn to be sure the strangers inside could not overhear them. He was followed by Joe and Tim, who sat down on logs beside the three men and listened.

Jack looked around. "What happened?"

"I think we met one of the band members of last night's concert," Jim said.

"A messenger." Keith nodded. "Came to LP1. He was unarmed, and he knew we were there, so I talked to him. He didn't see anyone else."

"That thing did not look human." Jim shook his head. "Definitely mentally disturbed."

Beneath Jack's furrowed brow, his eyes squinted, and he frowned. "What did he say?"

"Said we had twenty-four hours to bring them everything we had and surrender."

"Or what?"

"Or they'd attack. Steal what they wanted. Kill everyone. Destroy the place."

"Did you kill him?"

"No."

"Why not?"

"That's what I said," Jim nodded. He looked at Keith. "Told you."

"He didn't have a weapon. He didn't attack us. He didn't even try to cross the barricade. And he made it sound like he had an army with him, which I'm guessin' is why he felt confident enough to come unarmed. I didn't want to risk it."

Jack shrugged slightly. "Well, no point second-guessing now. Any idea how many they have?"

"No. I only saw the one."

"Don't forget about the four dogs," Jim added. He shuddered slightly.

Jack looked puzzled. "Dogs?"

"Slaves." Keith shook his head. "He dressed them up as dogs. Had them crawling on all fours, pulling his wheelchair. It was sick."

"Was he disabled?"

"Mentally," Jim supplied. "Not physically."

"Rode it like a king or something," Keith continued.

"You should have seen how it treated those slaves." Jim shook his head, looking at the ground. "I don't think pulling wheelchairs is the only thing they use them for." Jim sunk down onto a log and began fumbling with the lid on a water bottle. His hands were trembling and sweat beaded on his forehead. "What are we gonna do, Jack? If we surrender, that's what they've got planned for us."

"We're not going to surrender." Keith looked at Jim who was sipping water. "We're not surrendering anything."

Jack looked him in the eye and nodded. "Of course, not. We'll defend what's ours."

All three of the men sat on logs now. They sat in silence for several seconds. They all knew what that decision meant. They didn't want another fight like they had experienced a few months ago. The wounds from that battle were still felt. They were sick of the death, of burying and composting their neighbors, of seeing vultures circle overhead and knowing what they were eating, of having no future to look forward to but the next meal, and the next.

"Damn it all," Jim finally said, staring blankly out at his cornfields.

"Yeah," Jack replied.

"What did you learn from the refugees?" Keith asked after another few seconds' pause.

"They're Orthodox Jews. Upper class. A doctor. A lawyer. A banker. Two professors. The rabbi. It sounds like they met the group that sent you the messenger. That's who they were running away from when your sister found them in the woods. They said they got the message too. Described the messenger pretty similarly." Jack looked at Jim. "Eccentric clothes, weird hair, makeup, tattoos, piercings, jewelry?"

"Yeah."

"Rode in a wheelchair pulled by naked men dressed as animals," Jack nodded. "They ignored it. Thought it was just some crazy people who were let out from an institution or something. The next day, they said, they were invaded by hundreds of the lunatics, their homes were destroyed, many of the elderly and children were beaten to death, and the men and women who didn't escape were taken as slaves. These people just managed to get out before they were caught, but the attackers hunted them. They hid in the day and only traveled at night, trying to get to the state forest where they thought they could try to build a campsite to wait it out. At least, that's their story. They say the group that attacked them has taken over the entire city. They call themselves the 'Servants of Gaia.' They're college students."

Everyone sat in silence, processing the information and looking around at one another.

"What are we going to do with the refugees?" Keith asked.

All eyes went to Jack as he answered. "They've seen too much of the community already, and with those psychopaths out there, we can't send them back out to get captured. They'll tell them what we have and how to get in, if they don't already know."

Keith saw Joe nodding out of the corner of his eye.

Jack went on. "Malik and the nurses checked them for diseases. They're good. They've got a doctor, so that might be helpful, but they've also got a lawyer and two professors with them. They could become a problem for our society here."

Joe began to interrupt, but Jack put a hand up to stop him.

"They're all urbanites," Jack continued. "And none of them knows how to survive in this world."

Tim interjected, "Neither did a lot of the people on this road before I taught them. They can learn."

"That's right," Joe seconded.

Jack pursed his lips and exhaled forcefully through his nose. His shoulders relaxed slightly, and he nodded. "Okay. We give them the option to stay here and learn how to provide for themselves as a part of our community. But they have to agree to accept our laws and our way of doing things and not try to change them. Otherwise, we'll hold them until we are no longer threatened by the students, and then, they'll have to leave. Agreed?"

The men all consented to the terms.

"One more thing," Jack said. "Regardless of what they say or anything else, I think we should all sleep in the barn tonight and take watch in shifts. We need to keep an eye on them, and we need to be ready for an invasion tonight."

They went back inside to present the terms to the refugees. Lynn and Matthew were collecting their bowls. The preacher had left with a list of sizes to get clothes for them. Malik and two nurses were cleaning cuts on some of the patients when Jack requested everyone else in the barn to leave. They looked at him and silently stepped out of the room without argument.

Jack pulled a chair in front of the cot in the middle of the barn, and sat down, looking at all the shriveled bodies and shrunken faces before him. "Alright. We just received a message from your friends, the students. So, you'll understand if we don't trust you too much at the moment, seeing how you show up in our community, uninvited, right before this group you know so much about comes to threaten us."

One of the refugees spoke up, "We're not affiliated with them! Please, don't send us to them! We swear..."

Jack held up his hand for silence. "You've seen too much of this place. We can't let you go right now. So, we have decided to give you a choice. We will allow you to stay here and join our community. We will set up a place for you, and we will show you how to work and gather food and survive out here. You can work until you're able to purchase a small plot of land to build on and farm and live as a member of the community. But you must accept our laws and our way of life around here. I don't know how you voted or what your politics were, and I don't want to know. I don't care. None of that matters now. You agree to our laws and our cultural norms if you want to be a part of this community. You do not get to try to change it into what you fled from. If you do, we will force you out of our community at gunpoint. Do you understand?"

They all nodded. "We understand," said the doctor. "But if we are not allowed to practice our religion here, then we will have to leave. We will not violate our conscience for the sake of a few more days of life on this rock."

"No one is asking you to violate your religion or your conscience, unless of course, your conscience has a problem with the ten commandments. I'm going to give you some time to think about your decision. If you refuse to assimilate, then you will be held here until we no longer feel threatened by the students, and then you will be sent on your way. Take some time to consider your options." Jack stood up and began to walk out of the room. The other men followed him.

There was some quick murmuring amongst the refugees, and as soon as Jack reached the doorway, the doctor stood up and announced: "Wait. We don't need to think about it any longer. We accept your conditions. We want to stay." All the refugees nodded in agreement.

Jack Winters and the men turned and smiled. "Well, that makes things simpler, then." Jack reached out and shook the man's hand. "Welcome to Mount Sinai."

The men laid blankets on the cots in the lantern light. The sun had sunk beneath the hills, and the light outside was almost gone. The men climbed into their cots, pulling blankets over themselves. With weapons at hand, they tried to go to sleep.

"It's just like old times, ain't it?" Jim grumbled. "Goodnight, Jack."

"Night, Jim-Bob," Jack replied.

Jim snickered and rolled over onto his side.

Keith had taken first watch and sat in the chair in the center of the barn, watching the refugees and glancing at the doorways periodically. After the day's events, they were all tired, but none of them was able to sleep. Every animal noise outside caused heads to jerk up from the pillows.

One of the refugees, an older woman who had identified herself as one of the professors, looked around the barn in the faint light. "Those are some beautiful paintings," she said. "Who are they?"

Keith glanced around at the images on the walls. "Those are paintings of neighbors who died defending this community from raiders."

"Oh," the professor said. "I'm sorry. They are beautiful. It seems so rare to see beautiful things nowadays." She looked at Keith. "You said your name was Keith?"

"Yes, ma'am."

"I'm Mary. It's good to meet you, Keith. Thank you for what you're doing for us. We had lost faith in humanity. It seemed like there was no good left in the world."

"I hear you." Keith nodded in understanding. "You said you were a professor?"

"That's right. I taught History at the University."

"Hmm. I don't suppose you had anything to do with the education of the Servants of Gaia?"

"Oh no. That wasn't me. I was one of the few heretics who slipped under the radar. In fact, I think I was the only one in my department who can say I didn't contribute to this."

"Well, that makes me feel better. You seem to know an awful lot about them though."

"I watched it happen. I recognized many of the students who burned down the synagogue. They were in my classes."

"Could you give me a lesson on the history of the Servants of Gaia?"

Lying in the cots spaced out along the walls of the barn, the residents of Mount Sinai—the natives and the refugees alike—turned toward the professor and listened in the flickering ambience of the lantern light.

The professor paused and nodded thoughtfully. "I could try. If you've got the time, I've got nothing better to do." She took a sip of water, screwed the lid back on her bottle, took a deep breath, and began.

"Diversity is synonymous with division, and division is the opposite of unity, so what is the opposite of diversity? If your answer is "university," you're right. The last study I saw showed that ninety-five percent of professors voted for the same party. That's across all schools and all fields. In many fields, and at many schools, there was not a single faculty member who didn't vote for the party. It had been getting more homogenous every year for more than a century. It wasn't because people who voted for that party were smarter, although that's what they said; it was because that party's worldview had become a religion, and the adherents to that religion hated infidels. They believed anyone who was not a true believer in the mission of the party was evil, so they discriminated against them. They wouldn't hire them. They wouldn't fund their research. They wouldn't peer review their papers. Denied them tenure. They blacklisted them, harassed them, brought allegations of crimes against them, got them fired or forced them to resign. And they made it clear to any non-believers that they were not welcome in the academy. They wanted to walk into a library with millions of books on the shelves—all different sizes, shapes, colors, and materials—and they wanted them all to say exactly the same thing. That was their idea of 'diversity.' The professor chuckled to herself and took another drink. "They called themselves progressive. Funny. My doctor said the same thing about my cancer." She paused for a couple of seconds and continued.

"They say communism is the god that failed, but they only tried it, and continue to try it, because it seems to them that all the other gods failed first. We are Jews, you see. Western Civilization began with our religion, and we've never been forgiven for it. Our moral law is displayed in the Supreme Court of the United States and most other court houses in the country—or at least, it used to be. But recently, nearly everything our God said is right, our modern American culture called wrong, and everything our God condemned as sin, our culture praised as virtue. The traditional standards and values of this country were chipped away over time, and we found ourselves in a world where everyone was afraid to speak the truth. Victimhood became social currency—which is exactly what you would expect in a post-Christian society. Christianity is a religion that values martyrdom above all else. Rather than trying to make good people and a good society like Judaism, Christianity's highest ideal was letting an evil society run by evil people victimize good people, so victimhood became synonymous with virtue—something we Jews see as a fatal flaw with Christianity—but anyway, when people stopped believing in the divinity of Christ, their moral sense was still informed by their Christian heritage. So, while they no longer believed in redemption, they continued to view victimhood as righteousness. That's how we got a society that divided itself into the oppressed and the oppressors. Everyone wanted to be seen as the oppressed, the virtuous, and collecting grievances became a competition to see who could show themselves the most victimized. But without a god to mete out justice in the afterlife, they had to take it upon themselves to punish the wicked. Instead of trying to stop the decline of society, Christians seemed to forfeit the world and all the converts they could have gained with it. Jews are more down to Earth; there's no talk of afterlife in our Bible. I don't mean to be too hard on Christians though; they did create the freest country in history after all, and it isn't as if Jews were trying to evangelize. But that was the old world. You couldn't afford to offend anyone in the old world. Every idea they came up with was essential to their individual concept of themselves, and who were you to tell them anything was wrong? 'Identity' was the word de-jour in the anti-theistic religion of the old world. As children grew up with more luxury, they were more coddled, and they became narcissistic. Their view of hardship and adversity was skewed. They didn't know what struggle meant, because they had no reference. Everything in life had been given to them without any effort on their part, so they came to believe they were owed everything they wanted. But it was never enough. They sought out imaginary challenges to overcome and causes for which to fight without ever sacrificing any of the luxuries they saw as rights and basic necessities. They thought of no one but themselves, and they each believed they were special, because that's what they had learned growing up. Because they were so special, they believed themselves smarter than all the generations who had come before them, so they rejected anything traditional. They subverted all natural and moral hierarchies, even blurring the distinction between humans and animals. They believed animals were part of nature, but humans were a plague on the earth that needed to be depopulated for the sake of nature. At the same time, it was crucial to them that they express their 'true selves,' so naturally, they did everything they could to disguise themselves and hide their natural appearance. If man was made in the image of God, it was their mission to distort, defile, degrade, and deface that image. They wanted God dead, and to keep Him dead forever, they would remove all traces of His work. They lacerated and obfuscated their bodies to the point that they hardly looked human at all. With eccentric haircuts dyed unnatural colors, tattooed skin, and pierced flesh protruding from decadent, impractical clothing designed to draw attention, the latest generation, heirs of the world, advertised their 'identity' which, indeed, appeared indistinguishable from that of their peers. It anxiously shouted, 'Look at me! Tell me I have worth! Tell me I have a purpose! Tell me the meaning to my existence!' For answers, they turned to their professors, the wise of this world, who circuitously explained that, indeed, they had none. Humans need religion to live, but they were taught that traditional religion belonged on the ash heap of history, so they turned to paganism, to spiritualism, to wicca, Zoroastrianism, and Eastern philosophy. They kept idols, read tarot cards, studied astrology, and claimed to worship deities they knew did not exist. They were allowed to believe anything they wanted, as long as it wasn't true. They showcased their virtue to everyone around them, shamed the heretics and apostates who did not sufficiently embody the prevailing dogma, and they spent their mental energy pretending to fight one half of a world war that everyone knew had ended long before their grandparents were born. They displayed their sensitivity to the plight of the oppressed by being offended by everything they encountered. They took offense to as much as possible, constantly trying to outdo one another in collecting grievances, and putting metaphorical notches in their belts every time they corrected someone's sacrilegious speech, every time they shouted down a speaker, every time they used real violence and intimidation in 'defense' against perceived 'emotional or verbal violence.' They sought to bludgeon the world with their superior virtue until it submitted. There, was meaning in life. No, the kids were not all right. But we refused to see it. Young women were trained to hate half the population, to shun family, and find purpose in eighty-hour work weeks, climbing corporate ladders, stamping out material for a system they claimed was oppressive and unjust, and to leave all their wealth to the government or party-affiliated corporate non-profits when they died alone in an apartment full of cats. Ethnic minorities were taught to hate the majority, to distrust anyone who looked different from themselves, and to judge people first on the basis of race in order to combat racial discrimination. Instead of embodying the teachings of Dr. King, they held exactly the same beliefs as the Klan. Workers of the world uniting didn't work for them; they had nothing but contempt for the workers of the world. Their call to action was more like 'Races of the world, divide!' That was their means of enacting cosmic justice. Otherwise-intelligent people with PhDs, accreditation, and accolades could claim to be fighting on behalf of the disenfranchised while simultaneously reducing them to nothing more than stereotypes devoid of agency and reaping all the praise and prestige of selfless heroism. The sexual liberation movement developed into a reality-denying cult that demanded absolute ideological conformity with the ever-changing standards in the name of Diversity, Inclusion, and Equity. Cognitive dissonance was the norm, but contradictory beliefs never phased them, because they believed logic itself was oppressive; therefore, they replaced objective reality with their own personal 'truths.' No one was allowed to disagree and remain secure from assault, let alone employed and welcome in society. Parents sent their children to schools, sponges ready to absorb the knowledge of the world; they came back brainwashed, angry, hating their own families, as well as their country, and ready to destroy the enemies of their new religion, by any means necessary, no matter who they were. They could not bear to hear the truth, so they gathered teachers to themselves to scratch their itching ears and teach them myths they wanted to hear. They called good evil and evil good. They became addicted to propaganda. They demanded all art be destroyed and forgotten and replaced with propaganda. All comedy, all science, all history, all religion, all language—everything was to be enrolled in the service of their religion. No one was allowed to laugh anymore. All joy was stamped out into dust. No one was allowed to be happy when oppression was everywhere. Degrees had become more common, more expensive, and worth less with each passing semester. The students grew less intelligent every year, but they believed themselves to be geniuses because, despite lower and lower test scores, the professors handed out A's, and the schools handed out degrees, like candy at parades. The only thing they cared about was getting rich and making radicals. And five generations of radical professors had warped the universities into propaganda mills churning out waves of depressed, resentful, hate-fueled, genocidal maniacs seeking revenge against existence, internally vowing to tear down the world and remake it in their corrupted image. It was all for one purpose: to build an army of revolutionaries that would tear God off his throne, so they could put themselves in His place. They were united by ignorance, hatred, and conceit. Without the technology on which the old society depended, civil order dissolved; the lunatics had nothing to lose and nothing to hold them back. All of them could be diagnosed with mental illness, but they're not merely mentally deranged; they're possessed. They cannot be reasoned with. Their beliefs cannot be refuted. They will never learn, listen, or respect. They've been infected with an ideological poison and are now rabid. They cannot be saved. They have no boundaries, no moral qualms, no forgiveness, and no mercy. In a world without barriers, the rule is established by whoever can bring the most force and violence to bear, and that means the most radical win."

"Well, the Servants of Gaia are the end result." The professor shrugged. "They are the most radical."

Day 153

At dawn, the fire-watch awakened the men of Mount Sinai. Roosters were crowing all around, and the sky grew pink as the sun shone on the horizon. The men rubbed their eyes and stretched, looking groggy and irritable. None of them had really fallen asleep until the early hours of the morning.

Jim Baker eased himself upright and put a hand on his back, wincing. "Oh, my back. Whose idea was this?"

No one answered him. Jack Winters got up, put on his boots, and slung his rifle over his shoulder. "Gentlemen, would you join me outside for a minute?" He looked around the barn and stepped out the door.

The refugees were still sleeping as the men of Mount Sinai got their boots on and met Jack in the steaming grass beside the barn.

"We need to make preparations," Jack began. "Get everyone ready to defend their homes. There's no telling when they'll come. Jim, I need you to stay here and watch the refugees. I still don't trust them. We need to keep eyes on them at all times, until we know they're not a threat. Don't let them take any weapons, and don't let any of them leave. We can't have them sending runners."

"Got it," said Jim.

"We'll send you some help." Jack looked at Joe. "Maybe your sister could help with escorting the ladies to the outhouse?"

"I'll send her." Joe nodded. "And we'll send Malik and Jordan McCormick to the barn as well."

"Good. And see if you can't get the preacher to come and bring more food and provisions. If I'm not back yet, get Scott Adams."

The brothers nodded in unison.

"You'll get some help as soon as we can send it," Jack said, nodding to Jim.

"Alright." Jim headed back into the barn.

"What can I do?" asked Tim.

"I could use a good talker like you to see if those guys got any fireworks we could use. They've already had a run-in with the rest of us, so they probably wouldn't cooperate well with us. But they might listen to you."

"I'll see what I can do."

"See if you can get your hands on some Tannerite while you're at it. It might come in handy. We'll see if we can't get Scott Adams and Jeremiah Davis to rig us up some gifts for our guests." Jack looked each of them in the eye and said, "We can't afford to call a meeting right now. We need everyone to stay near their houses. We'll have to run up and down the road and pass the word. Let's meet at my place, once we're done."

Tim and the brothers began to walk toward the hill when Jack stopped them. "And be sure to get something to eat first. But do it quick. We've got to be ready."

The brothers sent Lynn and Matthew to the barn along with the McCormicks and the Jorgensons. They walked to the fork with Jefferson Lane and parted ways with them, heading for Scott Adams' house. They had travelled less than half a mile when they saw the squat, balding man himself running toward them.

"Hey! Hey, guys!" he panted in his plate carrier. "I was just coming to tell you..." He slowed to a walk and caught his breath. "I was just coming to tell you I finally heard some news from outside. I don't know if it's legitimate information, but the word is that the Chinese are sending aid to us. I guess they're the only country with enough resources to help us rebuild, so they've taken control of the situation. They're apparently running a massive humanitarian mission to the United States."

"Whoa, whoa, whoa," Joe said, raising his hand. "Slow down. Did you write this stuff down?"

"Yeah."

"Well, hold onto it. We were just coming to tell you..."

"Hang on. There's more. The rest of the world has deferred to them, and other countries are beginning to accept Chinese Yuan as their currency. Mandarin is now the official business language of the world. They're requiring airport staff to be trained in Mandarin, and other countries are adopting Mandarin class requirements for their students."

"What?" Joe looked incredulous. "Did you say Mandarin is now the official business language of the world?"

"That's right."

"And other countries are using Chinese money?"

"Yeah, when the American military and economy disappeared, I would say our money became worthless, so the next most powerful country filled the void."

"Just like that, huh?"

"Well, I don't know if it was exactly a smooth and easy transition, but yeah, basically. Just like that. We've been replaced on the world stage. There's still no word on what happened or who caused it. I've been hearing people refer to it as "the American accident" or "the tragic events in America," but I can't seem to get any information on what it was. You don't think it was an inside job, do you?" Scott looked at Keith.

"What?" Keith shook his head. "No. That's crazy. No way."

"Do you believe China's sending help?" Joe asked.

"I never thought of the Chinese as allies," Keith said. "But they were always dependent on the American economy, especially agriculture."

"They say they're our closest ally, now," said Scott. "Maybe our government has made some kind of deal with them." He shrugged. "No one else is helping us."

"But the money?" Joe's eyebrows raised.

"Chinese currency is the most stable currency in the world now." Keith nodded. "Makes sense."

Scott jerked his hand up for them to listen. "There's more! I also heard…"

"I'm sorry, man, but you're going to have to hold that thought," Keith interrupted him. We've got bigger things to worry about at the moment."

The brothers gave Scott a rundown on the situation at hand. He continually interrupted with exclamations of "Are you serious?" and "Really?" and "What?" He was getting increasingly excited by the descriptions of the Servants of Gaia, and he let them know that he thought the refugees were probably spies or a Trojan Horse. When they reached the intersection with Mount Sinai Road, they found Jack Winters and Jeremiah Davis waiting for them. They were armed to the teeth and talking with grave expressions on their faces.

The men looked up at the three walking toward them, and Jack nodded. "Have you been brought up to speed on what's going on right now?" He focused on Scott's sweating face.

"Yes, sir."

"I've got a job that I think is right up your alley. Meet your business partner."

Jeremiah was looking into the man's eyes and rose to shake his hand. "Hey. Jeremiah Davis. How you doin'?"

Scott looked around. "Fine, but what are we working on?"

Jack turned to see the source of the sound coming down the road toward them. "Here it comes right now."

Tim Faulkner's truck rolled over the asphalt and came to a stop beside them with a pile of cargo sitting in the bed. The man who had been put to work digging a grave for the marauders' bones after his fireworks display of two nights ago climbed out of the passenger seat.

"I'm really sorry for the fireworks the other night," the man said. "I want to help."

"Good," Jack said with a slight smile. "We could use a pyromaniac."

The men stood and looked into the bed of the pickup truck, admiring the hundreds of pounds of fireworks, Tannerite, black powder, and various other explosives and incendiaries.

"I couldn't get much, but the neighbors let me borrow some of the stuff they weren't using." Tim grinned a bit. "I told them it was for a good cause."

"Alright," Jack began in his commanding voice. "They said we had until this afternoon to bend the knee. So, we expect they'll attack either this evening or tomorrow morning. We've got to get moving. I want you three to take this stuff, and whatever else you need, to Davis's garage and rig us up some surprises for them. We're gonna need all hands on deck to get our defenses as ready as we can make them."

As Lynn and Abigail served breakfast to the refugees, Matthew and the preacher worked to set up tents outside the barn. The refugees received their plates of eggs, greens, and venison, and sat down on the logs. When they had all taken their seats, the Rabbi said a prayer, thanking Divine Providence for the food, shelter, and community to which they had been led.

Jim Baker continued to watch them, never letting them out of his sight, continually counting heads to make sure none had slipped away. As he helped himself to some breakfast, he noticed Kent and Faye walking toward the group.

"Mom! Dad!" Lynn yelled as she approached them. "What are you doing here?"

"We came to help," Kent replied, grinning. "We brought food, and a couple of the old tents that's been buried in the garage. It took a while to find them."

"We just served breakfast, but you're more than welcome to help out with the tents," said Lynn. She took the container of food from Faye and looked inside. "What is this?"

"Pork sausage patties," Kent said proudly.

"Dad, they can't eat this."

"Why not?"

"They're all Jewish."

"So?"

Faye let out a truncated laugh and rolled her eyes. "Oh, come on, Kent. Don't play dumb."

"What?"

"They don't eat pork, Dad. Everyone knows that. They'd be insulted if you offered this to them," Lynn scolded.

Matthew bit his lip to suppress his laughter.

"I don't see why they should be insulted..."

"It's literally in the Bible, Dad."

"In the Old Testament, but..."

"But that's the only one they have," Lynn interrupted impatiently. "And since God's not here to clear up the confusion for us, you need to respect their views. Come on." She led them to the table where they put down the dish and met with the preacher.

Eric laid down his hammer, wiped his dirty palm on his pant leg and shook hands with Kent Rawlings. "Good to see you, Kent. You brought more tents? God bless you. We need all the help we can get."

"Yes, sir. I want to do my part, so let me know what you need."

"Well," the preacher said, looking around. "We could use some more clothing for our guests. I was going to go collect some. And we need more pillows, blankets, towels, soap, and toothpaste."

Faye began making a list on a small notepad.

The preacher continued. "We're trying to get them out of the barn as quickly as possible. Rachel and Lydia are in there with the doctor, getting it set up for a hospital once again.

"Hospital?" Faye's face went a shade paler. "Why? Did someone get hurt?"

"Not yet," the preacher said somberly. "You'll have to have Mr. Baker explain it to you."

Jim was standing near them now, having finished eating. He stepped closer and shook hands with Kent and Faye. "You two raised a fine young lady," he said, glancing at Lynn. "And two damn fine young men."

"Thank you," Kent replied.

"What are you setting up a hospital for? And where are my sons?" Faye pressed him.

Jim nodded and looked at the ground. He clenched his teeth. "How much do you know about what's going on outside?"

There was no garbage removal any longer, so most people filled trash cans, bags, boxes and pits with any trash which they could not find a use for or burn—everyone was a redneck now. That meant that the defenders of Mount Sinai had plenty of scrap materials to sort through, and they sent kids to go collect any dead batteries, broken nails, scrap pieces of metal, or broken glass they could find and bring them back to Jeremiah Davis's garage.

Jeremiah cut sections of rusted steel and corroded lead pipe with a hacksaw. He threaded the ends and screwed on threaded metal caps before passing them to the pyro-technician—he identified himself as Garret—who drilled a small hole through one cap, filled the cylinder with powder, screwed the other cap back on, and fed a small section of fuse through the hole. He placed the finished product in a crate with the others. Scott Adams lined up dead bat-teries on strips of duct tape before wrapping them around one-pound tubs of Tannerite. When he ran out of batteries, he switched to broken glass, metal, and shards of pottery. When the three men ran out of black powder and Tannerite, they began using duct tape to encase the mortars with glass, metal, and ceramic pieces. With dozens of these devices, they filled several boxes, and they loaded the bed of Tim Faulkner's pickup with the ordnance.

It was around noon when Tim Faulkner, Jack Winters, and the Rawlings brothers came back. They had split up to warn the neighbors and tell them the plan. They sent out patrols and sentries along the property lines to check the scarecrows and raise the alarm if intruders came in from the woods. Once they had done so, they took stock of the load in the truck, climbed in, and took it to the barricades.

Riding in the back of the truck, Keith watched as the neighbors went around their properties, feeding animals, putting things away, locking doors, filling water jugs, and taking down laundry from clothes lines. It was surreal, Keith thought. What were they doing? He had grown accustomed to the wrongness of the world, but now he was wondering if he would suddenly wake up and realize this was all a bizarre dream. Was this real life?

"What are you saying?" Joe asked.

"What?" Keith came back to himself and looked at his brother.

"You were looking at something and mumbling to yourself."

"Oh, I didn't notice," Keith answered. "I was just thinking how crazy this all is. I mean, we're about to go plant IEDs around the wall we built to keep out people from our hometown." Keith shook his head, smiling in a strange, absent-minded way.

Joe nodded and looked at the road behind them. "Yeah."

Day 154

Joe awoke with a sore neck and back. He had fallen asleep in one of the pews of the old church when he could no longer keep his eyes open, waiting for something to happen. Keith was sitting in a chair near the doorway, still looking out at the barricades and the road beyond. The red dawn was creeping over the horizon and streaming copper light through the windows of the church.

"You see anything?" Joe asked, rubbing his neck.

"No."

"Did Jack ever come back?"

"No."

Joe nodded, stretched, took a drink of water, and went to take a leak. He came back and stood in the doorway, rubbing his eyes and staring out the window with his brother. They stayed quiet for a couple of minutes, watching the birds and scanning the trees and houses. Nothing happened.

"Well, I'm gonna see what the lookouts are doing." Joe walked up the stairs and found two of the lookouts curled up under blankets on the floor and the other two playing cards.

The lookouts moved to cover the cards, but when they saw who it was, they relaxed once again and resumed playing. "Hey, Joe," said one.

"I guess you guys haven't seen or heard anything," Joe said.

"Nope. Nothing."

"Hmm." Joe looked at a scoped bolt action rifle sitting beside the shutters. "Mind if I look through your scope?"

"Go for it," said the lookout.

Joe picked up the weapon and pressed his cheek to the stock, peering through the glass. He scanned the horizon, looked into the windows of the houses he could see in the distance, searched around every tree, bush, and building. He saw a rabbit hop across one of the driveways. There were squirrels scurrying up and down tree trunks, and birds flitted about the scene, alighting on branches and power lines. But that was all; he saw nothing else. He put the rifle back as it was and went downstairs.

"There's nothing out there," Joe said.

Keith continued watching.

"Come on." Joe nudged him with his elbow. "Let's go get something to eat."

"They could show up any minute. This is the most crucial time to be alert. They're out there. I can feel it."

Joe looked out at the empty space beyond the barricade and back at his brother. "Yeah, but you could always feel weird stuff coming. You're paranoid. Not as bad as Scott, maybe, but you thought..." He trailed off when Keith turned and looked him in the eye.

Keith let the silence hang for about five seconds, allowing the realization of where they were to sink in. "I only had to be right once. You had to be right every day of your life. Mine was the safer bet. Every skill I tried to master, every tool I collected, every crazy thing I ever did has been vindicated a hundred-fold. My only regret is not preparing enough."

Joe frowned and took a seat in a chair beside his brother. "College students don't even wake up at dawn," he muttered.

"We're staying," Keith said with finality.

About an hour later, they heard the clopping of horse hooves outside the church and went outside to see Jack Winters escorting four more guards to replace the sentries.

The new lookouts nodded at the brothers as they passed them and entered the building.

"They say the best time to raid is at twilight. Dawn or dusk," Jack said, looking at the brothers.

"I don't think they know about that," Joe retorted with a smirk.

"If they're gonna come, let 'em. These guys will see anything coming down this road. There's no point in waitin' for 'em with an empty stomach. You don't want to faint when you see 'em."

Joe snorted and looked triumphantly at Keith who nodded his agreement.

"Come on. They got some breakfast down at the barn. A bunch of people pitched in to make it. Pretty good stuff." He turned the animal and rode back down the road.

The brothers climbed on their bicycles and followed.

The day went by uneventfully. People kept their weapons on them, and they talked among themselves, some wondering aloud whether the whole thing had been a hoax by the outsiders, if not by the neighbors themselves. Most agreed that the latter was unlikely, given how many neighbors had confirmed the encounter and the warning they had from the refugees. They discussed communications plans, worked to improve the scarecrows and booby traps, and voted to accept the refugees as citizens so long as they worked for their keep. Several citizens took quite a bit of persuasion to agree to the proposition, but after Jack Winters explained how the security concerns of letting them go outweighed those of letting them stay, they relented.

School was resumed, as usual, in the barn, but Malik and Jordan, along with the nurses and Emma Faulkner, made sure to stock the shelves inside with as much of the homemade medicines, dressings, and medical equipment as they could. Scott Adams even donated most of his medical gear. Some parents chose to keep their kids at home while the threat of invasion was looming over the community. Many of the parents were happy to send their children to school just for the security of a well-guarded, central building stocked with medical supplies. Some parents went to the barn with their children and stayed just outside for the entire day.

When evening came, there was a new, slightly diminished wave of anticipation. People scanned the trees, talked in low voices, and listened for movement or the raising of the alarm. But nothing happened, and as the sun sank behind the hills, people began taking their children back home. Jack Winters gathered several of the men to him outside the barn.

"Gentlemen, have you all gotten something to eat?" Jack looked around at the nodding faces. "Good. I don't know about you, but I want to know what's going on out there."

There were grunts and nods of agreement from the men.

"I think it's time we take a look at what's going on at the school," Jack continued. "I want a fireteam—four or five volunteers—to go with me and check it out. And I want to do it tonight." He scanned the men's faces. "Who's comin' with me?"

The men all looked around at one another. A few looked slightly queasy.

Joe looked at Keith. Keith nodded. "We'll go with you."

Jack nodded resolutely.

"Hell, there ain't nothin' good on TV tonight," Jim said. "I'll go."

The men looked around at each other until, finally, all eyes came to rest on Tim Faulkner.

Tim noticed everyone staring at him, and his shoulders slumped. "Fine. I don't know what I'm going to tell my wife, but..." He shook his head.

The men crept silently along the railroad tracks, stepping on the ties in the faint ambient light. They stopped several times at the sounds of animals rustling in the leaves and brush on either side. After about an hour of walking, they came to the road. The air was still, and the night was nearly silent. There were no lights anywhere. As they walked along the road, they stopped and looked at the charred rubble that was the gas station. They said nothing but kept moving to the highway.

Along the tree line, between the cul-de-sac and the elementary school, they crawled. The huge brick houses of the cul-de-sac were destroyed. Moonlight glistened off the shattered glass of the windows. The lifeless hulks of burnt-up cars sat in driveways and in the road. Doors were ripped off hinges, garbage was strewn about the overgrown grass, and graffiti covered nearly all the walls.

When they crested the hill behind the school, they crawled on their elbows to where they could see the entire building. There were no fires, no candles, no lights of any kind. They remained silent for several minutes, listening intently, straining their ears for the slightest sound. But there was nothing. Nothing but the chirping of crickets and the hooting of an owl somewhere off in the distance.

They got back to their feet and glided around the wooded bank overlooking the school parking lot until they reached the end of the tree line and encountered the road to which the parking lot connected. They neither heard nor saw anything moving anywhere.

Jack wormed his way to within inches of the others and whispered, "I'm going down for a closer look. Stay here and cover me. If something chases me, shoot it."

Keith nudged him and said, "I'll go with you."

Jack nodded. "Okay, let's go."

They ambled down into the parking lot and tiptoed around the scattered trash. The walls of the school were covered in graffiti, but nothing stirred. Piles of tin cans and plastic containers littered the blacktop. An enormous mound of ashes and charred objects rose from the center of the pavement. Jack and Keith both looked around and put a hand over the ash heap. It was cold.

Jack leaned over and whispered to Keith, "I'm going to turn on a light."

"Okay."

There was a click, and a soft beam of red light faintly illuminated the area. They could see the graffiti on the brick walls much more clearly now. The building was covered in an uninterrupted mural consisting of what looked like occult symbols and pictographs. Jack and Keith walked along the wall with the red glow passing over the images. There were depictions of what looked like ancient human sacrifice rituals, and directly behind the pile of ashes, a massive, crude painting of a naked hermaphrodite with spread legs, open arms, enormous flaming eyes and a grotesque, gaping mouth with dripping fangs.

"That's the same thing that was painted on the water tower," Keith whispered.

Beneath the image was what looked to be some sort of writing. After studying it for half a minute, they recognized it as English:

Gaia DEMandS rePeRAYshuns FOR 12,00o yeers of rape.

Gaia deMANdS BLOOD.

Jack switched off the light. "The building might be sabotaged. Let's get out of here."

The two men rejoined the others at the edge of the road.

"Did you see anything?" Tim whispered.

"No." Jack sounded nervous. "No one has been here for days."

Chapter Eighteen

Day 155

Most of the residents agreed that the "Servants of Gaia," or whatever they called themselves, were nothing more than a small group of petty criminals who used fear and intimidation to extort resources out of people. They were probably trying to scare the residents of Mount Sinai into dropping off a large supply of goods at the school where they would come by later to collect. They didn't have the weapons or the numbers to actually fight anyone; they were just bluffing to get a tribute from them. It was all a grift. This had been a common practice among tinpot dictators all over the world for decades. When the tribute didn't show up, they probably moved on to another community to try again. They were never going to try to take it by force.

When asked about the bones and the slaves, Fred Packard said they were part of the ruse. There was no shortage of bones or body parts to be picked up off the ground nowadays. They could have come from anywhere, and the slaves were probably in on the act, just playing a part. And of course, the graffiti and destruction of soft targets was just part of the hoax. Fred and Donna Packard said it was ridiculous to think that hundreds of college students would be taken in by an insane, violent cult. Ben Jameson and Ernie Jacobs agreed. The extortion idea was the most plausible.

"And what about the refugees' testimony?" Keith asked.

"They were probably lying, or at least, exaggerating what really happened to invoke our sympathy," Ernie said, shaking his head. "There's a lot of people looking for hand-outs nowadays," he added. "Looks like it worked too."

There were nods and murmurs from the crowd.

"What about the other group of refugees that came to LP3 a while back?" Keith looked around. His eyes came to rest on Jack who looked at the floor. "They said the same thing."

"Well, now, nobody's calling you a liar or anything," Ben explained. "But according to you, they said there were gangs running around, robbing people, and that's why they were fleeing the town. I don't think anyone here doubts that there are gangs—plural—small groups of people stealing stuff to survive. That's not the same thing."

More murmurs of agreement arose from the crowd. Keith turned to Tim, Jack, and Jim who stood together, listening to the discussion.

"You have to admit," Tim said with a slight shrug. "It sounds more likely than a group of hundreds of crazy students taking over the whole county." He cocked his head to one side a little with an almost apologetic expression.

"Jim, you saw the same thing I did..." Keith prompted.

"I don't know what I saw," Jim interrupted. "Everything's so crazy right now, I don't know what to think. What they're sayin' makes sense to me though."

Fred Packard was standing up in the center of the crowd now. "We don't need people spreading unfounded rumors around here. We have to live in reality, and pretending that our teachers brainwashed our students into becoming a bunch of violent lunatics is not reality. It's a dangerous conspiracy theory that could cause serious damage in this community. My wife was a teacher for thirty years. I watched her selflessly sacrifice her time and energy and health to teach her students seven hours a day, five days a week, eight months a year; it was nothing short of heroic, and I will not allow our brave and diligent educators to be slandered like this."

There was an awkward silence for a couple of seconds as some of the residents nodded; others looked confused, looking at one another.

Fred continued: "What's more, we didn't get a vote on the setting up of homemade bombs all over the road. I, for one, don't want to be riding my bicycle down the road and run into a trip wire from some Rambo wannabe's half-assed boobytrap. It's time to get rid of the ridiculous explosives that make our community unsafe."

Again, people nodded and mumbled their approval.

"Alright," Tim said. "Let's take a vote. Judge?"

The judge came to the center. "All in favor of removing the explosives, raise your hand."

A clear majority of the hands were raised.

"All opposed."

Keith raised his hand. A couple others put their hands up briefly but lowered them once again when they saw they were outvoted.

"The explosives will be removed," the judge pronounced.

Fred Packard looked contemptuously at Keith from among the crowd.

Keith said nothing but looked back at Jack.

Jack put a hand on his shoulder and looked him in the eye. "I'm just the sheriff, and you're just a deputy. The people have spoken. There's no point in trying to fight them on this."

Keith slumped his shoulders and exhaled, shaking his head.

Jack stooped down slightly closer and said in a low voice, "Stay vigilant."

Day 156

It hadn't rained in three weeks. Droughts were not unusual in the summer, but what used to be a great annoyance for gardeners in the past, now was a calamity. They no longer had the convenience of turning on the spicket and letting a sprinkler spray the plants with city water. Now, they had to find a way to collect it from a well, the creek, a pond, or the water tanks along the road, and transport it to the gardens. The water tanks were running low, the creek was barely flowing, and the ponds were down two feet, so Dan Tyler's team of jackstock hauled a 500-gallon tank of water from the creek to every garden that didn't have a well nearby, and it stopped at every well along the way to refill. The run was made twice every day—at dawn and at dusk. He would harness the team before sunrise, and starting at Jim Baker's barn at the intersection of Mount Sinai and Deer Creek, he would haul the freshly filled tank down one of the three stretches of road—a job which he could get done in about three hours when everyone along the way was ready and waiting to receive their water and help him refill the tank—then, he'd unhook from the tank, hook up to the wagon, pick up the school children, drop them off, unhook the animals, feed and water them, and conduct the whole process in reverse that evening.

The Rawlings family, however, chose not to take water from the delivery service. Instead, they had uncovered and renovated an old well which had been partially filled in and completely covered over with a mound of bricks on top of a mossy concrete slab. The well had supplied life-sustaining water to their ancestors who had settled the land in the early 1830s, and it had served as a place to hide contraband moonshine during prohibition. Now, the family's fortunes were tied to the old well once again. If the crops died from lack of water, it would be a hard winter indeed.

Scott tugged the cart from the well to the garden with the help of Keith and Joe, who steadied the fifty-five-gallon drum as they pushed. Kent had drilled a hole near the bottom of the barrel and had installed a spicket. Now, they simply filled the barrel with well water, pulled it to the garden on the cart, and filled buckets from the spicket to water the plants.

"So, how you likin' your new farming career?" Joe said, looking at Scott.

Scott wiped the sweat from his forehead. "To be honest, I prefer the old way of getting my groceries—going to the store where everything was just waiting for me on the shelves. All I had to do was find the right aisle."

Joe chuckled a little. "Those were the days," he smiled. "You know, the kids being born now, they'll never believe that there once was a time when you could go into a store and see food stacked on shelves for you to pick whatever you wanted."

"And how would anyone explain the internet to them?" Keith said. "It all sounds like a science fiction fantasy world."

"Yeah," Scott nodded. "Or if it all comes back, I guess we'll all be speaking Chinese by then. Speaking of which, I was going to tell you before, I've heard several guys on the coasts talking about fishing boats going out to sea and not coming back."

"Where do you think they went?" Joe continued pouring water on a row of tomato plants.

"Don't know. I suppose some of them were probably sunk in storms. No one can get any kind of weather predictions anymore, after all. But maybe some of them made it to another country and got asylum."

"Makes sense." Keith nodded. "I would think a lot of people would be trying that now if they had a boat."

"Some people think they're being sunk."

"That doesn't make sense. Why would anyone sink a fishing vessel?" Keith shook his head. "Who would do it?"

"I don't know, but no one's heard back from these boats, and you'd think at least a few of them would try to come back to rescue more people or something."

Joe stood up and looked at Scott, thinking. "No, Keith's right. It's hard to believe that." Joe frowned.

"It's hard to believe a lot of things right now," Scott replied, a strange tone to his voice.

Keith looked up at him.

"Hey, *I* believe you," Scott said defensively. "But you have to admit it sounds crazy."

"It *is* crazy," Joe said.

Keith turned his glare on Joe.

"*I* believe you too," Joe's eyebrows rose. "But that doesn't change the fact that it's crazy. It's a crazy thing to believe whether it's true or not."

Keith nodded. "The whole world's crazy right now."

"Well, that's for sure, but what are you going to do about it? Sometimes you just have to let nature take its course."

"Let nature take its course?" Keith's voice rose indignantly. "Nature is a series of colossal blunders. You know what happens if we let nature take its course?"

"Yes, I do," Joe said flatly. "The same thing that happens if we don't—everyone dies."

Just then, they heard laughter and turned to see Kent, Faye, Lynn, and Jordan coming toward them with hoes and buckets.

Keith deflated somewhat and turned back to Joe. "But they don't all have to die the same way." Keith tried to keep his voice low, but he had lost some of his hearing and hadn't been as quiet as he intended.

"Who's dying?" Faye interjected.

"Nobody," Joe said. "We're just talking about things."

"Well, you need to talk about other things. You shouldn't always be dwelling on negative stuff." Faye's brow furrowed, and she frowned.

Scott picked up his bucket of onions. "Well, I think I better get back. Thanks for the onions. I think I'll try to make onion rings." He walked toward the road.

"Mom..." Keith closed his eyes and shook his head as if trying to remain patient while explaining something for the thousandth time.

Faye put her hand up to stop him. "And Jim Baker told me what you've been up to lately. You told me you were helping the community. I thought you meant you were helping people take care of animals and haul firewood and stuff." Faye looked downright angry now. "I can't believe you've been making bombs!" Her face was reddening.

Jordan looked around awkwardly. She took her bucket to the garden and began picking beans. Kent seemed unable to decide which side to take.

"It's no wonder people don't believe you—making a fool of yourself, talking about hordes of lunatic college students coming to attack us. Keith, I love you, and that's why I don't want you doing anything stupid to get yourself or anyone else hurt. I really think you're starting to lose your mind."

Lynn joined Jordan, pulling weeds and filling her bucket with green beans.

Now, Keith's face was red. Anger boiled inside him. He couldn't believe what he was hearing. "Mom, I don't know what you've been hearing, but how you can say that after what you saw out there is beyond me..."

Faye cut him off again. "I saw graffiti and trash and people trying to grow gardens. And before that, I saw some misguided kids getting drunk around a bonfire. That's nothing new. You're getting too worked up about this stuff. You need to start going to church. And I don't want you walking around with guns anymore." Her voice quivered. "It just takes one mistake to ruin your life." Her eyes watered, and she turned to leave.

Keith was shaking. "This is the end of the world, Mom. You need to start acting like it."

Kent watched Faye walk away for a moment and turned to face Keith. "Your mom's right, Keith. Your mom and I care about you both. But you're too caught up in this world. If you ever get in a situation where it's your life or someone else's, I hope it's you that gets killed, so you don't take the life of another. There's no going back from that. Leave the guns for hunting." And with that, he left them and followed Faye.

Keith sat down on a tree stump and spat on the ground. The color had drained from his face. He stared blankly at the grass at his feet. "Can you imagine saying something like that to your son?"

Joe looked at him. "He means well. You know that. They both do."

Keith shook his head and took a drink from his water bottle.

"He's not educated like you and Lynn," Joe said. "He just didn't express it right."

Day 157

Keith sat on a stump to sharpen his axe while his squirrel and chanterelles cooked over the fire. The sky was overcast and gray. Squirrels barked in the trees, and woodpeckers drilled at rotting logs and standing dead sassafras trunks. Under the canopy of thick foliage, the forest at noon was dark as twilight. Keith had spent the past day cutting trails along the ridge and piling the beech saplings on the sides, creating walls of brush to funnel deer into his shooting lanes. The scarecrows stood, silently watching all around.

As Keith took his food off the fire, Joe came walking up the old logging trail, carrying his bow with him. "Looks like you've been busy," he said, looking around at the trails and brush funnels. He set his bow down and took a seat beside his brother.

"Squirrel?" Keith tore off a leg and handed it to Joe.

"Thanks."

The brothers sat and ate and talked about hunting, tossing the bones on the ashes as the fire died down to embers.

"That's been a good stand," Keith said, looking up at the tree stand above them.

"Yeah," Joe nodded. "I got my first buck out of that stand when you left. Somebody had to put meat in the freezer while you were gone. We were still eatin' good without you, but it wasn't the same."

Keith grunted and shrugged.

Joe stared at his brother. "I'm glad you came back. I missed you."

Keith was silent, watching the glowing coals smolder.

"It was hard when you weren't here. You've always been my best friend."

Keith turned to see his brother wipe his nose and grin.

Joe stood up with his bow in hand. "Well, let's see if you still got it."

Thirty yards from the stand, Keith had set his broadhead target. He grabbed his bow which hung from a tree branch nearby, and they took turns calling their shots and sending old broadheads streaking into the foam with gratifying thunks.

At the sound of crunching leaves and hard breathing, they turned and saw Faye stumbling toward them. She struggled to keep her feet under her, scrambling over sticks and rocks along the trail atop the ridge. Her hands were shaking, her face was red, and she wiped tears from her eyes.

Joe started toward her. "Mom, are you alright? What's wrong?"

Faye gasped and grabbed his shoulder. "A runner came to the house," she panted. "They found a girl's body in the creek down by the highway. She was—mutilated." Faye sobbed.

Keith stared at her as Joe glanced back at him, looking horrified.

"I don't know where Lynn is!" Faye was trembling violently. "Kent went to check at the Tylers' house, but I think they went down to the creek."

"We'll find her," Joe said. He took off behind his brother toward the ravine. "Get back to the house. We'll bring her back."

Keith grabbed his axe and held onto his bow as they hiked swiftly through the brush and briars down the hillside.

Faye's scream followed them through the valley. "Find her!"

Lynn sat on a mossy log, blending the graphite streaks that composed the shadows of her portrait. Matthew sat before her, looking into the water of the shallow stream and glancing toward the branches of surrounding bushes and trees, where birds alighted and sang.

"Hold still," Lynn said.

"I'm trying," said Matthew. "How much longer do I have to sit here?"

"I'm almost done." Lynn applied a few more strokes of the pencil. She rubbed the graphite in with a finger, touched up a few more lines, and examined the image. As she looked over the features of the face, the world seemed to drift away, and the sounds of the forest faded from her mind. "It's done," she said as she put away her things. She zipped up her bag, and realizing Matthew had said nothing in response, she looked up.

The air was still. The birds were gone. Matthew sat, frozen in place with his eyes fixed on something ahead. His arm extended slowly behind him, his fingers stretching toward the shotgun leaning against a log only a few inches from his reach.

"What is it?" Lynn asked quietly. Out of the corner of her eye, she caught a flash of pink and a shimmer of light.

Matthew snatched the shotgun quickly, and as he brought it to his shoulder, there was a loud thunk, and he instantly dropped it and slumped forward.

"Matthew," Lynn took a step toward him, not understanding what was going on. "Matthew, what's wrong?" she said in a low voice.

Matthew rolled backward off the log and hit the ground at her feet. His face was contorted in an expression of pain, his left hand grasping his right shoulder, from which a fletched carbon shaft protruded. Blood gushed from the wound.

Lynn's hand went to her mouth, and she remained fixed in place, unable to move or speak.

"Lynn," Matthew groaned. "Run." He pulled himself to his feet and grabbed her hand.

Lynn's mouth was dry, she felt dizzy and confused, and she couldn't feel her feet beneath her as Matthew half dragged her through the creek bed. As the blood pumped faster and faster through her veins, she began to regain the sensation in her limbs. As they ran, she glanced once more at the bolt sticking out of Matthew's shoulder and realized this was real. At a fallen tree lying across the ravine, they scrambled over just as another bolt struck the wood with a thud.

They splashed through the pools of water and ambled over and under logs and branches until they heard a snap like the breaking of a large stick and Matthew dropped to the ground. Lynn tripped and fell as she turned. She looked back at Matthew lying flat on his face, and saw not only the bloody, gritty head of the bolt in his shoulder, protruding a foot from his scapula, but a second bolt lodged in his spine just above his belt. She gasped.

Matthew's left arm curled under his chest. He forced his torso up enough to raise his head and look at her one last time. "Go, Lynn." Blood ran from his broken nose and a gash in his eyebrow.

"No." Lynn pulled her pistol out of her holster as she looked back at the group of attackers running toward them.

"Do it for me, Lynn," Matthew gasped.

Lynn reached out toward him. "Come on, get up." She pleaded through her tears.

Matthew drew in a breath, and with every molecule of air he could gather in his lungs, he roared. "Run!"

Kent wrapped his arms around Faye as she sobbed into his chest. "Don't worry. Everything will be alright."

She hated how calm he was. She was terrified of losing a child, and she didn't understand how anyone could possibly feel otherwise. She pulled herself away and looked angrily at him. "How can you not be worried about your daughter being alone in the woods with a killer?"

"I trust God to take care of us."

Faye's face was a deep red. She clenched her teeth as the tears streaked down her face. "God didn't take care of my sister. He didn't take care of your mom, and he isn't taking care of this country. How on Earth can you say something that stupid?"

"Faye, that's enough." Kent's face became stony and resolute. "You *say* you believe in God. Now, do it."

―――――――――――――

At Matthew's cry and the sudden realization of the assailants closing in, Lynn was so startled she jumped to her feet and took off sprinting.

With his eyes following her, Matthew collapsed back into the cool, wet sandstone, and the world faded away.

Lynn scrambled through the ravine past the spur of the ridge dividing the creek. Taking the right fork of the creek bed, she ran toward a draw cut deep in the ridge. As she pulled around a large sycamore tree, a hand shot out and wrested the pistol from her grip as another pulled her to the ground. She let out a cry before her mouth was covered, and she looked into the eyes of her brother.

"Shut up," Keith said flatly. He handed the pistol back to her. "Put that away and get back to the house."

Lynn looked at him, stunned. Tears were running down her face, and she struggled to bring her breathing under control. She grabbed his camouflage shirt and hugged him, shaking. As he patted her on the back, she saw Joe crouched nearby, silently looking at her and intermittently looking back into the valley behind her.

"Are you okay?" Joe whispered.

Lynn nodded and wiped the tears from her eyes. "But Matthew..." She stopped as she heard voices approaching.

"Hurry up. Get the other one. Go," a voice commanded from the ravine.

They could hear rapid footsteps crunching sandstone and splashing through puddles, coming toward them.

"Go, Lynn." Keith said. "Get to the house and lock the doors. Go. Now."

Lynn took off up the ridge along a deer trail, still clutching her portrait in her hand.

Joe knocked an arrow as Keith peered through the brush at the two pursuers running toward them.

"There it is!" one of them shouted, pointing to Lynn as she clambered up the deer trail.

The two sprinted toward the draw, and as the first came abreast of the sycamore, Keith's axe caught him in the solar plexus, sweeping him off his feet. His body was knocked back into the second, sending him sprawling down into the creek bed. Keith wrenched the axe head out of the fiend's shattered rib cage, ripping a piece of lung out with it. He swung the axe up over his head and buried it in the writhing villain's skull. As the second man pushed himself up to regain his feet, Joe released his arrow. The broadhead passed through his side, beneath his arm, through the heart and both lungs, exiting the other side and sticking in the dirt behind him. The man dropped facedown in a puddle and ceased to move.

"Up the ridge. Let's go," Keith said, picking up his bow.

Joe retrieved the arrow and followed his brother along the deer trail.

A stream of curses and shrieks followed the brothers up the ridge as the squad of students encountered the corpses of their fellows. Keith looked back to see a girl with blue hair raising a rifle toward him, but one with green hair stopped her.

"Not yet," said the green-haired one.

"Stop them!" ordered a pink-haired student.

Keith and Joe led the barbarians up to the top of the ridge, where they disappeared behind the brush funnels. The Servants of Gaia followed them into the corridors, looking around nervously. They searched through the brush and foliage, jumping at every scurrying chipmunk and at the sound of every woodpecker drilling a tree. They clustered together as they dragged their feet and stomped through the brush, kicking sticks and stumbling over roots and rocks. Keith counted twelve. They carried baseball bats, hammers, knives, and guns. The one with pink hair carried a crossbow. Most wore eccentric glasses and bizarre clothing. Nearly all had dyed hair, tattoos, and piercings.

When they came to the scarecrows, several of them jumped and raised their weapons, but they soon noticed that the scarecrows were nothing more than dummies made of trash. They shared puzzled looks, and the pink-haired commander motioned them to keep moving.

"Spread out, comrades," the leader said, staying in the rear as the others stepped forward into the clearing surrounded by a wall of brush.

They stepped on every stick they encountered and tripped over every rock in their path as they trod as quietly as they could over the forest floor.

Keith drew his bow, and once the bulk of the squad had passed, he took aim and released an arrow into the ear of the pink-haired one, nailing his head to a black oak tree beside him. Through the crunching of dry leaves and the breaking of sticks, the others didn't hear their commander die, and they kept walking. The pink-haired cadaver's knees buckled, and its weight hung on the arrow shaft until it snapped, allowing the body to crumple to the ground.

Joe took aim at the next to last, a yellow-haired one with a pickaxe. The arrow lodged in the barbarian's spine, and the androgenous creature fell to the ground. The green-haired girl turned and saw the two bodies just as Keith sent a broadhead into her chest. The arrow flew through the body and shot past the others into the woods. The carcass fell to the ground in the clearing, and the others turned as it thudded amongst the leaves. The nine remaining invaders cursed and asked what to do. They beat the brush with their weapons and shouted in frustration as Keith and Joe crept down the hillside to the north to get in front of them.

"Stay together, comrades!" the blue-haired student shouted.

In the distance, the pops and booms of gunfire erupted from down the road. After about a minute of the noise increasing in intensity, the ringing of bells joined in the clamor.

"They're behind us!" the blue-haired girl screamed.

The group looked around to see where the arrows had come from, and two more of their company were dropped from behind. They turned and fired guns at the scarecrows as the brothers moved around to the side. The group ran to the edge of the brush where the shots had been taken. Keith sent an arrow through the chest of one of the attackers and into another. For a second, the two were pinned together on the skewer, but when the first one fell, the arrow twisted and tore through the lungs of the one behind before snapping off. The blue-haired leader turned and fired her rifle from the hip, hitting nothing, before Joe sent an arrow through her mouth and out the back of her skull.

Keith sprinted around the wall of brush as bullets tore through the branches. One of the servants leapt onto the brush wall with a pistol drawn. He was tangled in the briars and saplings and accidentally discharged the weapon into his own knee. He screamed and dropped the pistol. A girl tried to pull him out as a student fired a shotgun at the brush where Joe was crouching. Another ran toward the opening in the wall ahead. Joe grunted as a load of shot hit him, and he pulled himself behind a large maple tree. The servant with the shotgun continued firing toward him. Keith drew his pistol and fired three shots into the man's back. Before the girl could bring up her rifle, Keith gunned her down with a torrent of bullets that tore through the face and chest of the man caught in the brush wall.

"Look out!" Joe shouted. He sent an arrow at the man running toward his brother with a baseball bat, but the arrow missed.

As Keith turned, the bat connected with his arm and sent the pistol out of his hand. The man swung the bat with reckless fury, trying to knock Keith's head off his shoulders. The bat just missed his temple but clipped the bridge of his nose with a blood-spurting crunch. Keith rolled backward down the slope of the ridge as the baseball bat swung and bounced off a tree. The man with the purple mullet was charging at Keith when an arrow struck him in the pelvis. He dropped the bat and screamed as he fell forward onto the arrow shaft, driving it through the bone and out his lower back. His face contorted in pain, and no sound emitted from his open mouth. Wide-eyed, he convulsed in the leaves, slowly sliding down the slope.

Keith pulled his hand away from his shattered nose and spat blood on the soil. His eyes were so full of water he could hardly see. Wiping the uncontrollable tears away, he breathed heavily from his mouth as the blood poured out of his face, drained into his throat, flowed down his chin, and spattered the leaves. He growled as he drew the knife from his sheath and crawled to the shaking man. The man looked into his eyes with rage and hatred as Keith shoved the blade up under his chin and into his skull. The man's eyes rolled back in his head, and a deluge of thick blood gushed down the hill as Keith withdrew the knife and spat another mouthful of blood.

There was a loud, frantic banging. Faye jumped and screamed. Kent put down his Bible and went to the door. Faye was trembling as she looked out the window.

"Mom! Dad! It's me! Let me in!" Lynn's voice screamed.

Kent opened the door, and Faye pulled her daughter inside, desperately grabbing her as she cried. Kent looked around the front yard and shut the door quickly, locking it once more.

Faye sobbed and struggled to breathe as she held her daughter in a tight embrace. She kissed her head as Kent hugged them both. Finally, noticing the blood covering Lynn's hands and clothing, Faye sputtered, "Lynn—what happened?"

"Are you hurt?" Kent asked, starting to tear up. "You're bleeding."

Lynn quivered as she choked out, "It's Matthew..." she cried. "They killed him." She clutched at her parents again.

Outside their windows, the sounds of gunfire and screams echoed throughout the hills and reverberated through the windows.

"Where are your brothers?" asked Kent.

Lynn's hand shook as she pointed toward the woods and wept.

"Are you good?" Keith asked his brother who winced as he stood.

"Yeah, I think I got hit with rubber shot. They must have just stolen police weapons and loaded whatever they found." Joe helped his brother to his feet. "Your face looks like roadkill."

"Thanks." Keith spat blood on the ground and wiped his beard with his sleeve. He grabbed his pistol and holstered it before picking up his bow. Joe handed his axe back to him, and they moved along the deer trail on the side of the ridge.

Down in the valley below, they could see more dyed hair and bejeweled servants running toward the houses. When they came to the edge of the woods, servants were climbing the ridge toward the field. One stopped and looked at a scarecrow, and from behind a huge oak tree, Joe sent an arrow through her stomach. She rolled back down the hill as another shot at the scarecrow. Keith put a broad-head through her throat, and she collapsed into the dirt and weeds. The servants pursued them into the tree line to the piles of junk scattered along the ridgetop.

Among the old lawnmowers and piles of rotting wood, the servants spread out, shrieking curses as they searched. Joe crouched behind an old tractor and readied his last arrow. A girl with a shaved head tattooed with party symbols ran at a scarecrow in the dark shadows of the forest. From behind the broken water tank, Keith caught her with a sweep of his axe, taking her legs out from under her. She sprawled on her face, in the leaf litter, and he planted the axe head between her shoulder blades, severing her spine. Another ran toward the water tank, and Joe put an arrow through his back, pinning him to a tree. The man writhed against the bark, gasping for help. Another ran to him, and Keith struck him in the back of the head with the hammer poll, separating his skull from his spine. The body fell into the man pinned to the tree, and the arrow snapped. Both corpses collapsed to the ground and lay still.

Joe drew his pistol and hid behind the massive steel tractor wheel as a servant fired at the tractor from a distance of fifteen yards. The student continued shooting until he had run out of ammunition, and as he tried to figure out how to reload, Joe peeked around the tire and shot him four times. A girl with a pink and green mohawk ran toward him with a crowbar, screaming. He fired, hitting her in the leg just as she reached the tractor, and she hurdled forward, bouncing her head off the front axle.

Keith retrieved his bow and quickly knocked an arrow. A man with pigtails, wearing nothing but women's under-wear, ran from the field into the woods, screaming wildly as he raised a machete. He charged at Keith who put an arrow through his chest. The drug-addled berserker con-tinued running as if he hadn't noticed he'd been shot. Keith dropped the bow and drew his pistol as the man slashed his arm with the machete. Keith fell onto his back and emptied the magazine into the barking maniac as the body fell onto him, slobbering and trying to bite him. Grabbing frantically at a piece of pipe lying beside him, Keith struck the man in the head, and as he rolled off of him, he grabbed the man's arm and snapped it over a broken chunk of cinderblock. The creature flailed and growled as Keith inserted another magazine, pinned the beast down with a knee on his sternum, racked the slide, pressed the muzzle into its eye, and squeezed the trigger.

At the sound of knocking on the door, Kent went to open it.

"Kent! Wait!" Faye shouted.

The window closest to the door shattered. Shards of glass scattered about the room as a brick skidded across the dining room tabletop and rolled onto the floor. Faye screamed as a kid with a black and purple mohawk and six nose rings thrust himself through the broken glass and climbed into the room.

"Capitalists!" the intruder shouted. He struck Kent in the face with brass knuckles and charged at the women as more came to the window.

Kent fell back into the wall behind him, knocking several pictures to the floor. Faye screamed and ran into the kitchen.

Lynn pulled out her brother's pistol as she scrambled around the dining table.

"No!" Kent shouted.

Lynn fired, missing the man with the first shot. He leapt over the table with a knife, and she shot again. The bullet went through the man's carotid artery and into his shoulder. He convulsed on top of the table as a geyser of blood sprayed over the room and ran like a waterfall off the edge of the wood, splattering the carpet beneath.

Kent crawled toward Joe's bedroom, seeing stars as blood ran down his face from the gash in his cheek.

Footsteps pounded on the deck as servants ran around the house. Lynn put a hand to her ear as she emptied the magazine at the female climbing through the window. With ears ringing, she stumbled onto the floor amid the noxious stench of sulfur as the window behind her was shattered.

Faye grasped a kitchen knife as she heard her daughter's cry. All the fear in her body was gone in that instant. All the world faded away, death was a nonentity, and nothing remained but her love for Lynn. Her blood boiled with fury as she strode into the dining room, clenching the knife with white knuckles.

The pink-haired man was on top of Lynn, pinning her to the ground with one hand on her pistol and the other on her face. He babbled about racists and justice as he struggled to pry the pistol from her fingers. His mouth opened, and his face contorted in shock and horror as Faye rammed the chef's knife into his kidney with a strength she never knew before. The body went rigid, and she yanked the blade free and plunged it into his back again. The man rolled onto the floor as Faye wrenched the blade loose and thrust it into his face where the blade snapped off in the bridge of his nose.

Kent grabbed his son's shotgun as the back door was smashed in. He heard the intruder snarling about vengeance amid the crashing of paintings and art supplies being cast to the floor. He followed the sound of the destruction and glimpsed a large man with a pickaxe stepping into the dining room where his wife and daughter lay crying for his help.

"Kent!" Faye screamed.

Kent bolted toward the doorway and leveled the shotgun at the man's head as he raised the pickaxe. "Stop!" Kent shouted.

The man looked at him, and his pierced lips curled into a wide, demonic grin showing teeth filed into fangs. He laughed as he swung the pickaxe over his head. Kent pulled the trigger and sent a rifled slug through the devil's head, blowing blood and brain and skull fragments all over the wall behind him. The pickaxe fell to the floor at the creature's heels and the cadaver toppled backward, bouncing off the woodstove.

Kent sunk to his knees and dropped the shotgun as tears streamed down his face. With his bloody face in his hands, he choked on the lump in his throat until he vomited.

When Keith and Joe reached the house, the servants had torn down the American flag and were ripping it to pieces, spitting on the tatters as they trampled it in the dust. Joe aimed his pistol and fired. The servants scattered, and as one ran behind a tree, the brothers saw him raise a shotgun in their direction. They dove behind a woodpile as a load of buckshot threw splitters and bark into the air.

"Pin him down!" Keith shouted.

They peeked out from either side of the stack of logs, throwing lead into the tree from which the shotgunner fired. Keith got up and bolted for the man with his pistol raised as Joe continued to fire every time the man exposed himself. As Keith came around the copse of trees, a loud crack sent him diving to the dirt. A purple-haired girl with a rifle shot at him from the driveway. He rolled over and raised his pistol, fired, reloaded his last magazine, and continued to fire. At the distance of thirty yards, he missed every time, and as he crawled behind the trees, a shotgun barrel pointed directly at his forehead. He grabbed the barrel and yanked it to the side just as the muzzle spat fire and thunder inches from his face. The shot went into the dirt and threw debris into the air. Keith's head felt like it was stuffed full of cotton. He couldn't hear anything. Not letting go of the hot barrel, he tried to pull the gun away from the man. The man pulled the shotgun back so hard that Keith was lifted off the ground. As his back hit the dirt, Keith chucked his empty pistol at the villain, and drew his sticky, red knife from the sheath. The servant kicked at him, and Keith planted the blade in his thigh. He felt the steel hit bone, and as the devil screamed, he took one hand off the shotgun. Keith yanked the knife back out and drove it through the man's foot, staking it to the ground. He pulled the shotgun free and slammed the butt into the man's crotch. As the gunman fell back to the ground, Joe put a bullet in his head. Keith racked the slide of the shotgun, rolled over, and sent a load of buckshot into the girl with the rifle. The nine pellets tore through her abdomen, and she crumpled to the ground, convulsing in a pool of blood, urine, bile, and the contents of her shredded intestines.

"Moon-wolf!" shouted a blue-haired female running to the twisted mass of flesh. "It's me. It's Starlight! Wake up!" She hyperventilated. "No!" She picked up the rifle, and Keith dropped her with another shot before ejecting the shell.

Joe was out of ammunition. He ran to the house to get a weapon. The front porch was on fire, and the flames were licking the siding as they slowly spread from the oil spilled on the deck. A man on the porch was battering the door with a sledgehammer while another was climbing through the broken window. Leaping over the steps, Joe grabbed the anchor chain of a foothold trap from one of Keith's buckets and swung the iron flail into the hammer wielding maniac's back. The servant bounced off the door, dropped the hammer, and stumbled backward, reaching for a shingling hatchet. Joe grabbed a leg of the man at the window and yanked him out onto the porch. The man's arms were lacerated on the broken glass, and he dropped his weapon inside the house. Shoving Joe back, he grabbed at the nearest weapon he could find and stood up with a splitting maul. Joe took hold of a chimney brush chain and swung the mass of steel wires into the assailant's face. The man fell into the fire and rolled on the deck. As the other attacker stood up with the hatchet, Joe took hold of a scythe leaning against the wall and swung the heavy hooked blade into the man's stomach. The rusty, curved edge tore through the man's intestines and spilled entrails all over the fire. Joe jerked the scythe back, dragging the writhing mess into the flames. Black sludge and thread-like worms spilled forth from the eviscerated bowels, and as Joe rolled the body over the flames, the fire was snuffed out.

Pulling his knife out of the dead man's foot, Keith got to his feet as another servant charged toward him with a bat. He raised the shotgun and pulled the trigger. Click. The man with the bat swung, missed, and Keith bent the shotgun barrel over the villain's collar bone, shattering it. The man fell to the ground, and Keith took hold of the shotgun by the barrel, swinging the stock into his chin, snapping his neck, and folding his head back under his motionless body.

Lightheaded and deafened, Keith scanned the area. Through the trees, he could see people running toward the road and houses. He turned and saw his brother on the porch, knocking on the door and shouting. A man with a chimney brush stuck in his face was crawling through smoking excrement down the front steps, dragging the chain behind him. Keith strode to the porch and stomped on the back of the man's neck, crushing his windpipe over the edge of the step.

Joe turned with a raised fist and met his brother's eye. "I'm going to check on Mom and Dad!" he shouted.

Through the broken window, Keith could just make out Lynn's voice yelling: "We're all okay!"

"Guard the house!" Keith shouted. He turned and found his axe lying in the yard.

"What are you doing!" Joe cried. "Come on!"

"I have to help!" Keith screamed back from the driveway. He took the rifle from the blue-haired corpse, checked to see that it was loaded, and began jogging up the driveway.

"You're hurt, Keith!" Joe shouted. "Keith, don't go!"

The front door opened, and Joe was pulled inside. Lynn and Faye wrapped their arms around Joe and squeezed him as he looked back over his shoulder to see Keith running up the driveway, disappearing behind the trees.

CHAPTER EIGHTEEN

Keith was utterly drenched in blood. A trail of crimson droplets fell from his clothes as he made his way through the trees to the purple house. His nose was shattered, and his mouth was full of thick blood that he could no longer spit. He gulped air through his dry, sticky mouth as he ran. His left arm was cut and bleeding, he was bruised all over, and he was beginning to feel a searing pain in his leg. It didn't matter to him now. His family had been saved, but Jordan was alone in that house.

Flags were being desecrated, houses were burning, and the sound of the McCormicks' front door being battered permeated the cacophony of screams, gunfire, and destruction. There were bodies lying about the grass all around the purple house, some moving, most not—all, it appeared, had sustained gunshot wounds. All the windows Keith could see were broken, and as one of the lunatics approached an entry point, he was smitten by a 5.56 mm rifle round from Jordan's AR-15. In the short amount of time she had spent training with Keith, she had mastered the weapon, and she was not going to allow anyone to take her freedom, her home, or a single piece of her family—not without a veritable bloodletting.

Through the window, Keith could see Jordan move to another part of the house and begin picking off assailants. A girl with bright red hair dressed in all black ran to a window with a beer bottle from which a burning rag protruded. Keith put a bullet through the girl's hip, and as she toppled over, the bottle turned upside down in her hand; the burning rag fell out, dumping the flaming liquid all over the arsonist, engulfing her in flames of her own making. Keith didn't waste a bullet as she shrieked and fizzled in the inferno.

As Keith moved toward the front of the house, he heard a loud snap near his face, as a bullet zipped past his head. Hitting the ground, he crawled behind a tree and saw a rifleman firing in his direction. The rounds threw clods of dirt into the air as they struck the ground around him. Keith could tell from the poor aim and fluorescent orange mohawk that the shooter was a servant. From behind him, a purple-haired girl charged at Keith with an axe and was struck in the knee by one of the rifleman's bullets. The knee exploded in a mist of blood, pulverized bone, and ligaments, and the girl's leg crumpled beneath her. The rifleman stopped shooting just long enough for Keith to align the sights and put three rounds into the shooter's body. As the purple-haired girl screamed and flailed, Keith put a bullet through her head.

The servants had stacked up around the front door where Jordan could not get a shot at them. Just as Keith was rounding the corner, the servant battering the door with a post driver smashed through the latch and knocked the door in. The servants rushed in as Keith poured fire into the group outside. Two of the bodies dropped in a heap of mangled flesh, and the bolt of the semiautomatic rifle in Keith's hands remained locked to the rear. There were shots from inside. Keith paused for a second, trying to think of what to do. If he ran inside the house, he might accidentally kill Jordan while fighting the servants, or she might accidentally kill him in the same way.

He hesitated, but just then, he heard a struggle and saw a pale man with red and green dreadlocks dragging Jordan out of the house by her hair. A girl with cartoonishly large glasses, multiple nose rings, face tattoos, and a white mullet was whipping Jordan with a rope that had been tied into a crude slipknot. The two servants shouted vile obscenities and racial slurs at Jordan as the girl with the white mullet flailed her with the rope. "Race traitor!" she spat.

The man with the dreadlocks looked up just as Keith dove into him, wrapping his arms around the heathen's waist and tackling him to the ground. The brute's head bounced off the hardpacked clay, and Keith struck him in the temple with the eye of his axe. The heathen swung a fist into Keith's ribs, and as Keith rolled backward, he drew his knife and slashed at him. The edge caught the villain's hand between the fingers and split his hand in half. Keith thrust the knife and punctured the man's upper arm as he tried to block his face. Wrenching the blade free, Keith plunged the knife into his side, splitting a rib, and twisting the blade in the fiend's deflated lung. The body lay gurgling in the grass as pink foam bubbled from his side and floated on the pool of dark blood.

Keith sheathed the knife and stood up with his axe as Jordan clawed at the white-haired girl's face. Clenching her fingers around the girl's ridiculous glasses and one of her massive nose rings, she ripped her hand back, taking the glasses and the nose ring with them. The neurotic shrieked and put a hand to the spurting shreds of flesh that were her nose as Keith stepped toward her with his axe raised. The maniac looked into Keith's eyes, pulled her hand away, and screeched, "Racist!" as the bit met her ear and hewed through the top of her skull, sending globs of creamy, pink sludge spraying through the air, and spattering the grass along with half of the white mullet. The corpse toppled over beside Jordan's feet.

Keith held out a hand to Jordan, and she scrambled away from him.

"Get back!" she shouted, feeling around for a weapon and keeping her furious eyes on the blood-drenched monster before her.

"Jordan, it's me. It's Keith."

Jordan stopped and stared at the entirely red form in front of her. With his mangled nose, and gore-coated body, he was unrecognizable. Blood dripped from his hands, beard, and saturated clothing. Jordan got to her feet, still keeping her distance from him.

"I got here as soon as I could," Keith said. He growled as he struggled to breath through the blood in his throat. "Get back to the house. It's safer there." With that, he staggered past her, limping as he tried to run toward the screams and tumult up the road.

With a hand on her bulging belly, Jordan stepped around the twisted piles of dead flesh on her doorstep, retrieved her rifle and magazines, and made her way through the trees to the Rawlings house.

"Privilege!" shrieked a skin-headed girl. She wailed and raved and cackled and barked, shooting holes in an American flag with a pistol. "Supremacists!" She jumped up and down, foaming at the mouth, half laughing, half screaming as she fired at the flag. "Down with the patriarchy! Redistribute! Abort! Deconstruct!" She continued pulling the trigger after the slide had locked back, and once she realized the pistol was empty, she fumbled around for another magazine, oblivious to the blood-covered man coming up behind her with an axe.

Keith swung the axe over his shoulder and clove the barbarian's head in two. The wasted skull split down the middle, and the axe head lodged so deep in the chest cavity beneath, not even the hammer poll was visible. Keith tried to pry the tool free but gave up after a couple of unsuccessful pulls. He took the pistol, dropped the empty magazine, and loaded the other after pulling it from the cadaver's hand. As he depressed the slide release, the slide sprang forward, chambering a round, and Keith took out his knife and limped toward the Packards' house.

Fred was standing on his front porch with his hands raised in the air, trying to talk with two of the servants. "Look, take whatever you want. You need it more than we do."

One of the servants began collecting the offerings from Donna, piling the canned goods and fresh vegetables into a wheelbarrow. The other man smiled, not hiding his enjoyment as he watched the grown man groveling before him.

"You need firewood? You need tools?" Fred pandered. "We can get you some trucks, and we can help you find supplies that the others are hoarding." Fred nodded excitedly. "You have a right to the things you need. We know that. We're not like these rednecks. We're on your side. We can help you." As Fred Packard smiled and looked into the man's eyes, a red hand appeared holding a pistol an inch away from the grinning servant's head. The pistol barked, and Fred Packard's face was spattered in blood and gore. He fell backward, wiping the residue from his eyes. With his hands on his ringing ears, he trembled as he looked up at the red man holding the pistol in front of him. After a couple of seconds, Fred recognized the eyes and the beard through all the blood.

Keith glared down at Fred Packard for several seconds until Fred turned away. He stepped over the carcass, and as a servant with half his head shaved appeared from the side of the house, pushing a wheelbarrow of loot, Keith shot him in the heart, dropping the man onto one of the Packards' rose bushes.

Servants were running through the Faulkners' yard, burning the American flag and trying to set the house on fire. Through the windows of the Faulkners' house, rifles barked and sent bodies to the ground amid bursts of pink mist. The servants were inside the barn now, and as the animals scattered in panic to the edges of the fence, the cultists smashed windows and scattered tools and supplies.

Tim Faulkner stepped out through the front door with a shotgun raised. As a servant stepped into the doorway of the barn, Tim sent a load of buckshot through his chest and racked the slide. He strode forward toward the barn as servants rushed him, and he mowed them down with a flurry of hot lead. Tim took shells out of his pocket as he moved to cover but didn't notice a servant sprinting toward him from behind. As he turned around to see the machete wielding attacker, Brad Nielson caught the man in the stomach with a butcher knife and tackled him to the ground. He plunged the knife into the man's chest as Tim noticed another running toward them. Tim fired over Brad's shoulder at the man running on the road. The shot struck the man in both legs, and he flew forward into the pavement, cracking his skull on the asphalt. Tim turned to see a blood-soaked form limping up the driveway. He drew a bead on the man but hesitated as he watched the man gun down a servant charging him from one of the baffle barricades.

Keith emptied the pistol into a green-haired servant as she aimed a rifle at Tim Faulkner from behind a dead car. Another reached for the rifle, and Keith hurled the empty pistol into the man's face, breaking his nose. The servant fell backward as Keith rushed him with the knife and plunged the blade into his neck.

Up ahead, Ernie Jacobs' house was burning. Plumes of smoke billowed into the sky as servants ran through the field. They slung accelerant onto the white barn and torched it as they cackled at the sight of the burning flags hanging over the doorway.

Keith's vision was blurring. His head was pounding. He could hardly feel his arms or legs as he struggled to keep his eyes open. He sheathed his knife, and picking up the rifle from the dead servant, he began firing into the crowd around Ernie's barn. Servants charged him. A rock bounced off a car hood and struck him in the jaw as they closed in. Behind him, he could faintly hear gunshots, and the bodies of servants fell among the tall grass of the field. A man in full police riot gear charged toward him. Keith fired just as his hand was struck with a baton. The rifle was knocked out of his hands, and the baton struck him in the head. Willing himself to stay conscious, Keith grabbed the man's riot shield and wrenched it away, slinging the aggressor into Ernie's cattle fence. The baton cracked him over the shoulder, and he lunged at the servant, grabbing his throat and ripping off his helmet. As Keith reached for his knife, the servant kicked him in the ribs, and Keith caught the man's leg. He twisted and sent the man falling to the ground. Keith stabbed at the slave's torso, and the point of his knife snapped off as it struck the armor plate. The servant swung at him with the baton and missed before Keith ripped the edge of his blade through the man's Achilles tendon. The lunatic screamed in pain and grabbed at the fence as Keith climbed on top of him, clenching the man's ponytail in his fist. With every ounce of strength he could muster, Keith jerked the villain's head up and slammed his hideous face into the cedar fence post. As the man's bleeding head fell back upon his limp body, Keith's failing eyes focused on three words tattooed across his throat. *"They/Them/There."* Keith was looking through a tunnel as the blackness closed in around him. He pressed the man's throat against the barbed wire fence and dragged the bleeding devil's neck over the rusted strands of twisted steel. Blood gushed from the ragged gash as Keith pulled the quivering carcass through the weeds, leaving shreds of skin and dripping flesh hanging from the barbs behind him.

Falling onto his knees, Keith let go of the corpse and collapsed into the hot grass. A wave of icy cold came over him. The light was fading from his sight, and the world appeared to drift away into the abyss. The last image he saw was the bodies of the Servants of Gaia falling on the road in showers of blood and flesh as a pickup truck full of armored men with rifles and shotguns rolled past over the blacktop, firing as the Hell-spawn fled. His head rested on the good earth, and he closed his eyes, drifting into the silent darkness.

Chapter Nineteen

Black. Blacker than pitch. The darkness was so thick, he could feel it. Like swimming through ink. There was no up or down. No sound. The silence was so complete, so absolute. Not even the deaf could experience silence like this. Nonexistence of vibration. Only cold, dark, and still. Pure serenity. Nothingness.

He had no name, no desires, no thought. There was no time, space, or matter. The absence of creation. Nonexistence. Eternity.

Such peace. Such Rest. Floating everywhere and nowhere. Endless millennia and not a second had passed.

But his mind, unbound, unhindered, unobstructed, limitless, remained. And the word. A thought. The word. What word? The word. The only word. I. A still, small voice, almost undetectable. But it was there. Where? Nowhere. And everywhere. Inside, outside, above, beneath, behind, beyond, throughout. And a second. Am. Two words, echoed like a heartbeat. The Logos. I am. Even here, in the absence of all else.

I AM.

Two words, three letters. All meaning.

He had fingers. He grabbed at the blackness and grasped something. He was somewhere. Rolling in the substance. He could feel and not feel. Clawing at the substance. Pushing away, he raised his head. Yes, raised. There was direction. And turning about him in the darkness, he strained to see anything. Something. There must be something. And through lightyears of darkness, haze, and shadow, blackness beyond description, he saw it. A speck. A dot. An infinitesimal glimmer. Something. A light.

For ten-thousand centuries, he crawled, dragging himself through cold and wet and silent, black friction. A hedge. A forest. Frigid, damp, and dark. Thick with nonmaterial nonlife. Over and over again, he lost sight of the light, but clawed through the obstruction, fought through the murky irrelevance, and found it again. Was it real? Was it there? Yes, it was.

The light was growing larger, clearer. The black trees were growing too, and the faint glow shone out through the darkness, its halo illuminating the dense, massive trunks. Heavy rain fell, stinging his eyes as he struggled toward the light, through black mud and brambles, over giant black roots, through tangled masses of tendrils.

A window up ahead. And the warm flicker of happy firelight radiated from the window in a cabin made of stone. He climbed to his feet, and he heard the sound of the rain falling all around him. Tears filled his eyes as he approached the oaken door, and he looked back at the black forest as he raised his hand to knock. So long had been the journey, so hard the path he trod. Cold and dark and lonely had been his struggle through the wood. But fear now filled his heart as he stood shivering in the cold. He took a deep breath and knocked three times upon the door.

The wooden door swung open, and his face was bathed in golden firelight. Holding the door, smiling, stood a man with golden hair. He was old. His face was wrinkled. He wore a sweater, shirt and tie, khaki trousers, and leather shoes, and with a look of exuberant joy, he raised a glass of dark red wine.

"Come in, Keith," said he. "And welcome. Please, have a seat beside the fire."

Keith was brought to a large leather chair beside the hearth, and he noticed the damp and cold had left him as soon as he stepped inside the cabin. As he looked around in wonder, he saw large wooden tables and chairs. Around the massive stone hearth where the warm and beautiful fire crackled, the walls were made of wooden shelves, completely filled with books, encapsulating the room. Above the shelves were many priceless paintings of the renaissance. Beautiful sculptures stood on the mantelpiece and in various places around the room. And upon the tables, among books and papers and writing materials, were musical instruments of all kinds. The cabin, which had looked small from the outside, seemed enormous now.

After shutting the door, the man returned from a table with another glass of wine and handed it to Keith.

Keith thought he recognized the man. He seemed to be someone he had known his whole life, but he was sure he had never met him before. "Sir?" Keith asked. "You seem to know me, but I don't recall who you are. And yet you seem familiar somehow."

"All in good time, sir," the man replied with a smile. "It's my place to know those who come to that door, and I do know you. I've been reading your story, and I know where you are."

Keith did not understand what he meant. "What do I call you?"

"My parents named me Roger. I am called by another name here, but that should suffice for now."

"Roger," Keith said, nodding. He recognized the man. "Am I dead?"

"Yes," laughed Roger, with a gleam in his friendly eyes. "But of course, I know what you mean. What you mean to ask is: are you alive?" He took a sip of the wine and smiled. "Perfectly reasonable question, sir. And the answer is: no. That is, not yet."

Keith still did not understand, but he took a drink of the wine as he looked into the cheerful fire. He had never liked the taste of wine before, but this was the most wonderful thing he had ever tasted. "What is this?" he asked, looking at the glass.

"Fruit of the vine," said Roger. "As it was meant to be." He savored another sip. "Excellent, isn't it?"

"It's unbelievable," Keith said, tasting it again.

"Ah, belief. Yes. That is the question."

"The question?" Keith asked. "Excuse me, sir. I don't follow you."

"Would you care for some food? I should fancy a bit of supper, myself."

Roger stepped out of the room, through a door at the other end of the fireplace, and through the open door, Keith could see a flood of light in colors he had never seen before. A dazzling brilliance of colors for which there were no names. From the doorway, there came the sounds of laughter and voices talking with one another amid the most beautiful music he had ever heard. His heart leapt for joy at the sound, and he set down his glass on the table beside him, rising out of his chair to see what was behind the door. Just then, Roger returned with a plate in each hand, and he set them down on the table before shutting the door behind him. The sounds of laughter and music faded away as the door latched and Roger looked into Keith's eyes with a sympathetic smile.

"What's back there?" Keith asked excitedly.

"I'm afraid you can't know that until your task is done."

"My task?"

"Indeed. Please," Roger motioned to him. "Have some food."

Keith sat down at the table and was overwhelmed by the most delicious aroma he had ever encountered.

"More wine?" Roger refilled his glass and poured for himself as well.

They ate in the light of the fire, and Keith had never tasted such amazing table fare. Between mouthfuls of the simple yet extravagant meal, Keith asked questions, overcome with curiosity and wonder.

"What is this place?" he asked.

"This place?" Roger smiled, looking around the room. "This is where my friends and I engage in argument," he laughed. "All the knowledge of mankind is contained in this room. All the great works of art and literature. They've been amassed over the lifetimes of the greatest thinkers ever to struggle through the land of the dead. Here, we meet and discuss the contents of those books, the ideas that created those works of art, and the eternal questions. It never gets old."

"These can't be all the books ever written," Keith said.

"All the books? No. All the good books. Which is far less than one one-hundredth of one percent of all the books. Most writers waste their time writing garbage. Most readers waste their time reading it. Of course, we have all the books, along with every work of art and artifice made by man, but we don't keep them all in this room."

"What are these books about?"

"Science, Mathematics, History, Philosophy, Art, Literature. All the subjects are the same subject. All questions are the same question, and they all lead to the same answer."

"What's that?"

"You know the question. The beginning and end of all questions. The beginning and end of all answers."

Keith nodded. He knew the question. He had fought with the question his entire life. "Can you tell me the answer?"

"It is not for me to tell you the answer. Part of me wishes I could, for I know the anguish of not knowing. But your journey is not complete, and if I told you the answer, it would alter your perception and remove your ability to choose freely. You have to find it alone, but you *can* find it. Or at least, you can find enough to get back here, where you will understand."

"What am I doing here?"

"Well, this is also where we welcome those who've helped to build this place through the works they've done on Earth. Every individual is endowed with inspiration—a small piece of the Spirit of God. But we also have free will. We can use that power to work toward Heaven, a union with the Spirit, through the pursuit of the True, the Good, and the Beautiful, or we can use that power to corrupt the Divine Image within us and create our own Hell. It is true—God does not create Hell for us; we create it for ourselves. Every choice has an effect that echoes through eternity, and through our choices, we can strive toward a unity with the Pure Love, the Pure Grace, and the Absolute Truth, or we can work against it and divorce ourselves from all that is good. You've been given a gift. A chance to see where you could go. Where you should go. What your decisions could lead you to. The potential end of all your labors. And let me assure you, Keith," Roger said with a glowing smile that seemed to radiate light and warmth. "It is really good."

"And we're not on Earth now?"

"Yes and no. I am there in the works I've left behind. You remain there in the works you have yet to do. And you'll have to return to complete them."

"I love this place. I don't want to go back."

"I understand you completely," Roger smiled. "But your task is not yet done. And you must find what you are looking for."

"What am I looking for?"

"What all men who come through that door are looking for. The Truth."

Keith shook his head, saddened. "I don't understand. How can I find it back there? It's so hard to know."

Roger nodded sympathetically. "Keep searching. Never give up."

Keith heard the laughter and music rising from outside the door, and he nearly leapt out of his chair to go and see.

Roger put a hand on his shoulder, and his smile turned to a resolute expression. "It's nearly time now."

"Please, I want to stay." Keith felt as if he was being pulled back toward the door to the black forest by some invisible force.

"I'm rooting for you, Keith. We're all waiting to welcome you home. It is my sincere hope that you will find your way back, so I can show you what's behind that door." Roger smiled. "Listen, Keith. Your brother has something you need to hear. Listen."

The door behind him was opening. Keith was moving backward out of the room as he struggled to stay.

"Fight the good fight," Roger said. "And never give up, Keith. Fight on."

The door closed, and the light faded away into the blackness once more.

Day 160

Noises. Murmurs. Voices. There was a bustling around the room as voices spoke in hushed whispers. Keith could feel the tingling in his limbs and felt the warmth on his face. Through his closed eyelids, he could sense a soft light. His head was pounding as his eyelids opened slightly. He could see the flickering flames of lanterns on the walls and the thick wooden rafters beneath a gray tin roof. He was in the barn. He had been somewhere else for a very long time, but he couldn't remember where it was. He shut his eyes again, willing himself to go back there. Where he wanted to go, he could no longer picture. The memory was quickly fading away, but he knew it was a good place. A place of comfort and unbridled joy. What was it? Tears leaked from the corners of his eyes. It was gone. Just a dream.

The sounds of footsteps and splashing water and voices grew louder and more distinct. Someone was talking nearby. He heard his father's voice.

"I killed a man," Kent said meekly. "How can I be forgiven? I can never forgive myself."

"You did no wrong," replied the preacher's voice.

"I took a life. It was not mine to take."

"You saved a life that was yours to save." The preacher's voice was calm and gentle. "And you stopped a murderer from carrying out an act of intolerable evil. How dare you be ashamed? You were put there by God to stop a violation of His will."

"I fear I sent a man's soul to Hell," Kent whimpered. "And maybe my own as well."

"It is not your place to decide what happens in the afterlife. Your job is to decide what happens here and now. If that man's soul is in Hell, it will be because he chose it, not you. You have no right to usurp the place of the Almighty and make yourself the judge of men's eternal souls."

"But I..." Kent sniffed.

"I too killed in defense of God's children," the preacher interrupted. "And not for one second do I regret my actions. Imagine what would have happened had you not acted as you did. Innocent blood would have been shed. That of your family, who it is your Divine-ordained duty to protect. Could you have lived with yourself if you had failed to defend them from such an atrocity?" The preacher's voice remained calm but strong. "You are acting as if allowing evil to triumph is a virtuous act of strength. I tell you, Kent, it is not strength but cowardice. And cowardice is sin."

"But we're supposed to love our enemies..."

"Yes, and pray for those that curse you. Pray for them, Kent, but stopping that man from staining his soul with the blood of innocents was the most loving and merciful act you could have performed in that moment—for your wife and children, for your community, for justice, for God's Holy Image, for His precious gift of life, *and* for the man you killed. Let God be the Judge, Kent, and let yourself fulfill your role as His instrument. You did what justice and the will of God demanded. It was no sin. Do not try to forgive yourself or excuse yourself. What you did was righteous, and as God is good, He will smile on your actions." The preacher paused, and there was the sound of a chair moving and footsteps. "Keep studying, Kent."

Keith's head was fuzzy and painful. As he opened his blackened eyes, he noticed an I.V. tube sticking out of his arm. The blood that had coated his entire body had been washed away, and he was wearing clean clothes—shorts and a t-shirt. Both his forearms were bandaged along with his right thigh. His face was swollen. There were plastic straws in his nostrils, he had knots on his head, and his body hurt all over, discolored with bruises and cuts.

"He's awake," said his brother.

Keith turned his head slowly and blinked a few times. His vision was still blurry, but he saw his brother sitting beside the cot along with Abigail, Lynn, and his mother. They all looked like they hadn't slept in days, and as they smiled, they wiped tears from their eyes and touched his hands with their fingertips.

"Wait, I'll go get Dad," Lynn said, getting up.

Joe breathed a sigh of relief as he stared at his brother with dark rings around his eyes.

From behind the preacher, Jordan appeared with a glass thermometer and put it under his tongue as she examined his dressings. She smiled as the preacher offered her his chair, and she sat down beside him with her hand on her belly. "Joe looked for you for hours," said Jordan. "He went to find you as soon as I got back to the house." Jordan looked to be holding back tears. "Thank you, Keith. You saved me." She wiped her eyes with a handkerchief and took the thermometer from his mouth. "Still a bit high," she said with a slight cough. "You need to rest." She got up and took the thermometer outside, wiping her eyes as she left.

"We found you unconscious in the grass beside a cattle fence," said Abigail. "You've been out for three days. Joe hasn't left your side since." She looked at Joe and took his hand with a tearful smile.

Lynn came back with Kent following behind her. They sat down in the vacated seats beside the cot.

Neither Kent nor Faye said anything as they hugged their children, patting Keith's unbandaged leg, and squeezing his swollen hand.

Beside another cot, Malik began performing CPR on a patient. Nurses rushed around the man as Malik called for them. After several minutes, he stood up and asked for the preacher.

The Rawlings family watched somberly as Eric attended to the man and consoled his family members. He read from his Bible and prayed with them as they cried, and Keith noticed that the preacher was also bandaged and bruised.

Eric Jorgenson placed his hand on the still body and closed his eyes. "Well done, thou good and faithful servant. Enter into the joy of thy Lord."

Malik scrubbed his hands with soap and hot water, and when he had dried them with a towel, he approached the cot where Keith lay. "It's good to see your eyes again, Keith. You saved my wife and child when I couldn't be there for them." With a look of profound respect and love, he took Keith's bruised and swollen hand and gently shook it. "Thank you, sir. It's good to have you back." And he turned away as a nurse called for him.

Joe sniffed and put a hand on Keith's shoulder. "When we got you to the barn, Malik performed CPR on you for half an hour," he said. "You were extremely dehydrated. You had a concussion, a huge cut on your arm that he sewed up, and you had been shot in the leg. He said it was a miracle after how much blood you lost." Joe looked wide-eyed into his brother's face. "Keith, you were dead."

Day 163

Keith lay on the cot for another two days, recovering. He was made to drink Emma Faulkner's medicinal teas, and Malik and Jordan changed the dressings on his wounds every day. They cleaned the cuts with boiled water and iodine tincture drawn from walnut hulls, smeared numbing cattail gel around the injuries, and applied plantain poultices to the wounds before wrapping them with sterilized strips of cloth. There were so many wounded in the raid that they could not all fit in the barn, and a secondary hospital, a large, aluminum-framed tent, was erected beside the barn to accommodate the others. Having run out of cots and spare mattresses, some lay on the ground as the men worked around the clock to build more beds for the wounded. Keith regained his strength, walking around the barn, favoring his right leg as he tried to keep from reopening the sewn-up gash where the bullet had torn through. Most of the neighbors he saw helping to supply the hospital and cleaning up the bodies were injured themselves. He was getting restless. He needed to get out and do something to help.

After Keith had awakened, his brother left him to get some rest, and after sleeping, he returned with food, water, clothes, and weapons for Keith. Keith gave up his cot and took himself to the tent to lie on the ground. The stench of blood and human waste was thick in the air, and he spent most of the time sitting outside in the shade, reading. The preacher, who spent most of the days and nights comforting the wounded and their family members with food and Bible readings, would frequently stop by and talk with him.

From inside the barn, came the screams of a man who was having his gangrenous leg removed. The preacher had stayed with the man and read to him as the rotting leg was rubbed with cattail gel—the best they could do for the pain. The man had been given willow bark tea with some of the last of the whiskey as the tourniquet was cinched down. The preacher left the doctors to do their work and joined Keith outside the barn.

"With all due respect, Mr. Jorgenson, I'm not in the mood for sermonizing right now," said Keith, setting down his book.

"Neither am I," replied the preacher. He looked tired.

Keith was somewhat taken off guard by this response and sat silently trying to block the painful cries from his mind. After several minutes of gasping and begging for the doctors to stop, the man inside was silent.

"It's a miracle you're here, Keith. I thank God for it."

Keith was growing hot, and his head was hurting again. "A miracle, huh? I guess it had nothing to do with the doctors then?" Keith's tone was sharp. "Well, I hope you'll excuse me if I don't sing hallelujah and express my amazement at the wonders of nature while that dying man's screams are echoing in my ears."

"No, I wouldn't expect that."

"I know you want me to come to church," Keith said. "I wish I could. But how am I supposed to believe in a merciful, loving God right now?"

"What do you believe?" the preacher asked.

"I believe the world has gone to Hell, and we've been left here to wallow in it."

"Hmm." The preacher nodded. "That's not far off."

Keith looked at him quizzically. He felt a rush of anger and resentment. He wanted to knock this holy roller off his pedestal and rub his nose in the dirt where the rest of us lived. "You know what else I believe? I believe there are more churches around here than hospitals, schools, banks, and grocery stores combined, and when the scientists and atheists told them their religion was bunk, none of them could come up with a response, so their parishes started leaving in droves. They started noticing their offering plates getting lighter, so they began conceding ground, parroting what the atheists said, preaching love and tolerance and people's feelings instead of morality. When the church let the world pull its teeth, it was forced to lap the spilled milk from the floor as it tried to avoid the boot. And as their congregations continued to empty, they joined the rest of the world in pushing radical politics, reducing their religion to being nice, turning worship services into music festivals and dinner parties, while their members acted the same as the non-believers and chalked it up to not judging. I didn't see churches offering much resistance to the insanity destroying us now. They either joined in or ignored it, thinking it was all a part of 'God's plan.'"

"You're an intelligent man, Keith. Are you surprised to learn that human beings are corrupt? The church has been teaching that for millennia. Christ was the flawless son of God, and He was tortured and crucified by the world for blasphemy. Believing in God is easier said than done."

"Well, you'll get no argument from me there. Can you blame them for not believing that some all-powerful being cares about them when everything is so bad in life? We deserve some sympathy for the struggle of wandering aimlessly through a life of suffering and death. But do we get it from God? No."

"How do you know that?"

"Look at the world! Why is it so bad?"

"It's not God's world. He gave it to us to take care of, and He gave us the free will to choose what we do with it. And people don't want the responsibility or the rules, so they make their own gods and their own religions that justify what they want to do but know to be wrong. And they teach those religions to others, so that they will not have to hear the truth and be convicted of their sin. Is it any surprise that thousands of false religions are taught by fools and liars? And is it any surprise that more fools and liars believe them? I've seen all the same churches you have. It doesn't surprise me. Yet God does not intervene, because this world is for us to shape, and we are free to decide what world we will create in this life. But actions have consequences, some far-reaching, affecting not only ourselves, but the lives of others around us and the world at large. These consequences echo throughout time and space, through eternity, and in the world beyond as well, and we are not free to escape them. You're right to say we have been left here to wallow in Hell, but it is a Hell that human beings created, not God. And it is we who must choose to change it back to the world God intended for us, if we have the courage and the strength to believe in spite of everything."

As Keith sat thinking about what Eric had said, Jordan stepped out of the door, covered in blood. She wiped her sweat-dripping nose on her shoulder and asked for the preacher.

Day 164

Kent had taken to harvesting cattails out of the small pond and delivering them to the barn when he wasn't working with some of the other men on building cots. He preferred to spend most of his time alone now. He no longer was the light-hearted truck driver telling jokes and quoting scripture. He kept to himself, speaking little, and when Faye saw him, he looked distraught and often rubbed his eyes.

Faye was numb to the world, feeling no more fear or sadness, but a sense of duty to clean. When Joe had dragged the bodies out of the house and away from the deck, Faye washed the table, walls, and floors until she had run out of soap and water, and seeing the stains still repugnantly visible in the carpet and on the wood of the deck, she used the last of Keith's supply of bleach to scrub them out, discoloring the floors in the process. Joe dragged the corpses from the house and the front yard, loaded them in the blue Ford, and hauled them back to the field where he dumped them over the far hillside, out of sight. When the house was cleaned up, and the windows were patched with sheets of clear plastic, Faye got the house key from Jordan and started cleaning the little, purple house as well. She looked determined to continue scrubbing the bloodstains until she could no longer see them. Lynn helped her mother, and the work helped her focus her thoughts on making the world a little better in the small but significant way that she could. When they had finished with the McCormicks' house, they offered their help to neighbors along the road, starting with the Jorgensons.

At the small, blue house, they found Lydia and Abigail scrubbing the scorched siding. When they asked where Rachel was, Lydia took them to a small grave in the backyard. Rachel Owens, Faye's closest friend on Mount Sinai Road, Lydia's daughter, Abigail's mother, had been killed.

Faye and Lynn sat in the long grass beside the garden, staring at the grave in sorrow and disbelief. In the shadow of the elms and the bullet-riddled house, they wept.

Joe came down the hill and walked around the barn, looking for Keith. He found his brother washing the tarp floor of the tent with lye soap and boiled water. "How you feelin'?"

"Useless," Keith responded. "I need to do something to help out."

Joe handed him his axe, a rifle and pistol, and a backpack full of water, first aid supplies, and ammunition. "I've been talking with Tim and Jack and the others. I'm afraid it's not over," Joe said solemnly. "Come on. We need to talk outside."

In the gravel driveway, near the road, a group of men stood, talking amongst themselves. Tim Faulkner, Jack Winters, Jim Baker, Scott Adams, and Brad Nielson were discussing their plans when they saw Joe emerge from the tent with Keith. Keith limped toward the assembly with his backpack and rifle slung over his shoulder. The men all had bandages and bruises showing.

"Still with us?" said Jim.

"I'm here," Keith nodded.

"It's good to see you on your feet, Keith." Tim patted him on the shoulder. "The last time I saw you, I think I nearly shot you. We didn't recognize you until we got you cleaned up."

"I saw Ernie's house burning. Is he alright?"

Jack looked down and spat. "Ernie didn't make it. We haven't found his wife either."

Keith grimaced and looked away. He shook his head and looked back at the men. "And are you guys—" His voice quivered a bit. "How are you? And your families?"

"We're whole, Keith," Jim assured him.

Keith nodded and breathed his relief.

"I didn't tell you," Joe said. "I didn't tell anyone else either, because I figure they didn't need to hear it right now, but Abigail's mother was killed. I helped Eric bury her."

Keith's heart sank. He thought of how he had talked to the preacher. What a callous fool he was. The preacher was not some sanctimonious hypocrite living in the safety provided by man's blood while attributing it to God's blessing. He was honest, practical, and down-to-earth. He had fought to defend his church as much as anyone. He had been wounded in the battle, and he had lost his only child too. Keith cursed himself for being so thoughtless.

"Keith," Tim said, interrupting his thoughts. "We've been cleaning up the bodies of the servants, trying to get the dead away from peoples' homes. It looks like most of them are diseased. We've had the doctors and nurses examine some of the bodies, and they're not sure what it is. They think it could be some strain of plague."

"We've counted over five-hundred bodies so far, Keith," Jack added. "And the others are still out there. They've set up camp in the field across from the church. We can see their fires at night, and we hear the drums. They're not done."

"We might have reduced their numbers by half," said Jim. "But they're emptying out the campus and staging for another attack."

Keith took a drink from his water bottle. "I'd like to see Fred Packard's face now," he spat.

"No one's seen the Packards since the day of the attack," Joe said. "We think they might have been taken."

Keith stared at the somber faces before him. "What do you want to do?"

Jack pulled out a map and drew their attention to it. "Last time, they surrounded us and hit us with a surprise attack from all sides. They weren't counting on meeting a bunch of hunters and woodsmen hitting back from the woods, and they weren't expecting to run into your scarecrows, Keith. That seems to have helped us out quite a bit. From what I can tell, they staged around the highways and took the creek beds to get inside the boundaries. Then, they climbed the ridges and assaulted targets of opportunity without much more of a plan than that. Their forces were untrained, unorganized, and unprepared for us. They were too divided to effectively coordinate. They won't be making that mistake again. I expect them to hit us with a full assault, concentrating all of their force at a single point where they can push through and take out every house along the road, one by one." Jack ran his finger over the map indicating the path he expected the army to take. "I've sent reconnaissance teams along the highways from LP2 and LP3. They haven't seen any activity there. The Servants will start with the church."

Keith nodded his agreement. "And you've reinforced the defenses?"

"We're concentrating our guards in the church, Bill Campbell's barn, and the cul-de-sac. We've reset the explosives and strengthened the barricades with fencing and barbed wire."

"Good," Keith nodded. "Good."

"I've been cooking up some more surprises for them too," Scott added with a nervous grin.

"We can't afford to wait for them to hit us. I want to get a closer look at what they're doing," Jack said. "Assess their numbers and weapons and try to get our people back if they have them. And I want to strike."

There was a pause as the men looked seriously at one another, and their eyes turned to Keith.

"I need men who can move quickly and quietly through the dark and shoot their way out of a bad spot if it comes to it. I know you're still recovering, Keith, but I could use your help on this one. We're going in tonight."

The stench of death hung heavy in the air. Fat blow flies and yellow jacket wasps buzzed about, swarming around the piles of bloated corpses decomposing in the sun. Many of the dead had been pushed into ditches with tractors or piled in fields; many had been left to rot where they fell. Nowhere on Mount Sinai could they escape the putrid reek.

In the field behind Jack Winters' house, the men rehearsed their plans. Ten men sat on logs beside the barn as Jack went over the map again.

"They burn huge bonfires every night. That's bad for them and good for us, because we'll be able to see them better in the light, and their night vision will be ruined. Our first priority is freeing the prisoners," Jack said. "As far as we know, the Packards are the only ones not accounted for, but keep an eye out for anyone who doesn't look like a lunatic. We'll cross the highway at dusk and reach the camp by dark. We use the tree line to get to their flank, and we low crawl through the grass." He ran his finger over the map. "If they have prisoners, and the prisoners are still alive, we try to get them back. For that, we'll need a distraction. That's where these come in." Jack held up a bag of fireworks, including smoke bombs, bottle rockets, and mortars. "We'll leave you four in the tree line to shoot the mortars and bottle rockets into the field behind them. Keith, Joe, and myself will approach the camp and try to get the prisoners while you three provide cover for us. We'll be carrying the pipe bombs. If you see explosions in the camp, you'll know that the plan has gone to hell and it's time to retreat back to the church. Dump any remaining mortars into the camp, and empty a magazine at them before you go. You're bound to hit something in a group that big. We need to cause maximum chaos to get out of there. They won't be able to see any of you, so just hightail it straight back through the field, and stay together. I've got snipers at LP1 ready to lay down fire if they pursue us. We've rigged flood lights on the church tower, so the snipers can see the field. When they come on, you won't be able to see where you're going. Just keep running toward the lights. Like I said, it's not much of a plan, but it's the best we can do right now."

"It sounds simple enough," said Scott. "When do we start shooting the mortars though?"

"I'll give you a countdown time based on how far of a crawl it is. We'll have to determine that once we get to the first objective point in the trees. Any other questions?"

The men were quiet, glancing around at one another.

"You know what our plans are," Jack said. "You don't need me to tell you how dangerous an operation this is. We may not all come back from this. If anyone wants out, say so now."

No one spoke for several seconds.

Joe spat on the ground. "If we don't win this fight, we'll all be destroyed. They'll have no mercy for anyone here. Our homes will be burned, the graves of our dead will be desecrated, and our families, down to the last child, will be murdered. All beauty, all freedom, and all justice will be eradicated. All that is good in the world will be gone forever. There is no turning away from this. We are the last hope." Joe looked around at the men's faces and nodded. "We're going."

The men nodded and voiced their agreement.

"Well said," Jack replied. He pulled out a box and opened it. "I was saving these for when the power came back on." He opened the box and revealed a row of cigars. "But I don't think I'm likely to see that now." He passed a cigar to each of the men. "It's an honor to be here with you all."

As the sun crept toward the trees, the men laughed and told stories amid the clouds of blue-gray tobacco smoke, frequently glancing at the setting sun and wondering if they would see it rise again. From Jack Winters' driveway, came a tall, darkly-tanned, old man in a straw hat and over-alls, walking slowly but upright with a rifle slung over his shoulder and a Bible in his hand.

Jack looked past the men at the preacher. "If the worst should happen, Eric Jorgenson will be leading the defense in my absence. He'll make sure that our families are provided for and protected. I've asked him to pray for us."

Eric stood before the group of men and read from the Psalms. The men listened attentively in the stillness, some wiping their eyes. When the preacher closed the Bible, he led them in a prayer.

"It's time," Jack said, after the prayer was done.

They stood and checked their gear, reciting the plan to one another. The preacher shook their hands.

Keith looked into the preacher's eyes as the man grasped his hand in a firm shake. "I'm sorry for what I said before," Keith said. "I didn't know. I'm so sorry for your loss."

The preacher patted his hand and said, "It's no loss. I'll see her again. Soon enough."

As they strode up the road toward the old church, Brad Nielson looked at the preacher who walked with them. "Are you coming with us, preacher?"

"I'll be manning my post at the church, awaiting your return. I'm a steward of the Lord's house, and I'll be damned if I allow it to be defiled by the Devil's spawn."

———

They peered out into the field beyond, through rifle scopes and binoculars. At this distance, they could just make out the mass of bodies pulsing and moving in the tall grass of the unmown field. The servants were moving large objects around, probably furniture from the houses to be piled and burned. As the light faded, Jack issued instructions to the guards at the old church. Keith left his axe inside the vestibule and returned to check gear with the men.

When everyone was clear on the order, Jack led the men behind the church, past the graveyard, and into the trees lining the highway. "Condition one," he ordered.

The men chambered rounds and checked their weapons.

Jack looked into each man's eyes in the twilight, and glancing at the horizon, he said, "Let's go."

With trembling hands and dry mouths, they crossed the highway and marched forward into the valley of the shadow of death.

Through the dark wood, they trod, swiftly and quietly, as the gray twilight faded into darkness. Through the trees, they saw the growing light of the fires, and as they approached their position, the thumping rumble of drums reverberated in their ears.

"They're not worried about being discovered," Jim whispered with a slight, nervous chuckle.

The group stalked around the field until they were slightly behind the encampment. They stopped about five-hundred yards away from the bonfires and set up their position.

"Remember, we're not meeting again until we get back to the church," Jack said. "Once we leave you, you're on your own. Aim the mortars behind them. Snipers, fire into the center of the group once you see the explosions. Same for the mortars. If they fire back at you, stay behind cover, dump all the mortars into them, and empty a magazine. Fire off the bottle rockets behind them. Then, get back to the church as quick as you can. Don't worry about us, we'll already be gone. We'll meet you there."

"Okay," Jim responded. "Got it. That's a long distance to crawl. How long do you need?"

They looked out across the field again, and Jack whispered to the Rawlings brothers. He looked at his watch and back at Jim. "What time you got?"

"9:50."

"Start firing at 10:30."

"10:30. Got it."

"Okay, let's go." Jack crawled forward into the clearing with Keith and Joe at his side.

The three men crawled on their hands and knees, each carrying explosives in their backpacks. Jack clenched his rifle in one hand and bolt cutters in the other. The pounding of the drums grew louder as they neared.

They crawled for what seemed like hours with the banging of the drums vibrating the ground beneath them. The smoke saturated the air and mixed with the noxious odor of sweat, excrement, and some unknown chemicals.

In the black shadows cast by the firelight on the mass of swaying bodies, the men crawled, periodically glancing at their watches and up ahead. They were within one hundred yards when the drumming ceased.

Keith's heart was pounding out of his chest. He clenched his rifle and tried to control his breathing as he listened and glanced at Joe and Jack. Had they been seen? He heard hysterical laughing and jeering coming from the servants. He looked up through the tops of the weeds. The Servants were all swaying and nodding. They passed around a basket, taking what appeared to be handfuls of mushrooms and stuffing them into their mouths before drinking from bowls of some liquid. Keith looked back at Jack who gave him a thumbs up. The servants had not noticed them.

The men crawled onward until they heard a deep, sinister voice which stopped them in their tracks and chilled their blood.

"For thousands of years, the white man has imposed his evil on the world. They are not humans. They are not even alive. The not-sees are nothing but a cancer. They do nothing but steal, kill, and destroy. They are the most violent and destructive force on the planet. Their existence is defined by the crimes they perpetrate. We stand on stolen land, stolen from the indigenous peoples and ravaged by the oppressors. Gaia is angry. She demands justice. She demands revenge."

The crowd of servants, draped in bones and jewelry, roared their approval with religious fervor. They were covered in piercings and tattoos, their faces and bodies painted, their hair dyed in various colors. Many were almost entirely naked, and their heads bobbed and rolled around atop their twitching bodies as foamy spit ran down their faces.

Keith looked for the Packards among the group, peering through the smoke and moving shadows, looking for a cage. He saw none. He glanced at his watch, shielding the light with his hand as he read the numbers. 2226.

"Our great comrades have sacrificed themselves in the pursuit of justice," the voice continued. "In their service to Gaia, they fought to show our truth to the not-sees. They were murdered by the supremacists, those oppressors, those rapists, the white-Christian scum!"

The mob shrieked and spat, clawing at themselves and gnashing their teeth in fury. "Down with the patriarchy! Kill the men! Fight the system! Eat the rich!" The mob shouted.

"But our comrades did not die in vain!" the voice shouted. "We showed the not-sees their place! The revolution continues! Hail, the glorious victims!"

Cheers erupted from the crowd.

"And tomorrow, we will dismantle their oppressive system of bigotry and hate, and we will liberate Gaia from the scourge of white filth!"

The heathen army roared and threw their arms in the air, jumping up and down.

"Bring the things to me!" the voice commanded. "It's time for blood! We start with the traitors! Let the oppressors see what happens to not-sees."

The mindless horde parted and formed a horseshoe around the fire with the opening toward the church on Mount Sinai Road. Keith could now see the speaker. The creature was nearly seven feet tall and painted with thick, clown-like makeup. It wore a horned headdress and a necklace of bones over a long, blood-stained wedding dress. Black mascara ran down its face toward the red lipstick smeared around its mouth.

Keith watched in horror as Fred and Donna Packard were dragged into the center and dropped at the feet of the monster. He pulled a pipe bomb from his bag and looked at Jack.

Jack put a hand on his arm to stop him. "We're too far away. We have to get closer." Jack left his bolt cutters in the grass and crawled forward with his bag of explosives in one hand and his rifle in the other.

Keith and Joe kept low to the ground, dragging themselves through the weeds and dirt. As they crawled, they heard the sobbing voice of Fred Packard pleading for his life.

"We came in peace. We tried to help you. We both want the same thing. We both want a fair and just world. We're not your enemy," Fred cried.

"Yes, you are, you stupid fool," the monster growled.

It was too late to save them. There was nothing they could do, Keith thought. They were thirty yards away from the mob, but if they started shooting, they would be overtaken in seconds.

Jack held out the pipe bomb in his hand so the brothers could see it. "We're going to plan-B."

"You're right," Fred sobbed. "We are privileged. We're sorry. Please, forgive us!"

The beast screamed, "There is no forgiveness!" The monster swung a pickaxe over its head and buried the point in Fred Packard's skull.

Donna screamed. Fred's body twitched and went limp, convulsing in the dirt.

Keith felt a wave of nausea overtake him, and he pressed his face into his shoulder as he gagged.

Jack flicked a cigarette lighter and held it out in front of them, immediately regaining their focus. Everything happened in seconds. Lighting the three short fuses, the three men hurled the bombs into the crowd. They heard a shriek from the woods behind the gathering, and as the gorgon in the center of the crowd raised the pickaxe, there was a deafening explosion of the mortar shell, and the blinding starburst of red, white, and blue sparks sent servants scrambling around in shock as the pipe bombs went off, blowing shrapnel throughout the mass of bodies. The monster with the pickaxe was thrown off its feet and sent sprawling into the fire. Donna was killed by the blast.

Jack, Keith, and Joe threw the smoke bombs into the crowd and opened up with their rifles, pouring fire indiscriminately into the scurrying servants as they tripped over corpses and climbed over writhing limbs and bodies spurting blood and fluids. The snipers in the tree line opened fire, and servants were struck down by the hail of lead as they scrambled around in confusion. The mortars began bursting all around and among the servants as the men in the tree line dumped the volley into them. The servants were so tightly clustered that nearly every bullet tore through three or four at a time. Bodies were ripped apart and set on fire as the mortars burst and scattered burning logs throughout the crowd.

As soon as they had emptied their magazines, the men reloaded and took off running through the field. Servants pursued them while others began firing into the trees behind them. The mortars stopped, and there was another burst of gunfire from the tree line. The rapid crackle of the bottle rockets popped off to the west and drew fire from the servants. Screams and chaos permeated the gunfire as they ran for the barricades through the long grass and shadow of night.

As they neared the road, a white light shone ahead and illuminated the field. Shielding their eyes, they kept moving as rifle fire cracked and muzzle flashes flickered from the church tower and the barricade. The bodies of their pursuers were dropped in their tracks as the snipers shot the illuminated enemy. Servants tried shooting at the light, but the bullets either missed or were deflected, and the shooters were quickly put down. Joe, Jack, and Keith ran up the bank of the ditch and crossed the highway, scrambling over the barricade as men pulled them across.

Rifles barked, and the running shadows dropped in the grass until one of the servants shouted to stop and go back. The others repeated the call, and the servants fled back to the camp as the snipers cut them down. The snipers picked off runners until they were out of range of the flood lights. For the rest of the night, the servants screamed curses and beat their drums and tried to put out the flames which spread through the dry field and enveloped several of their tents.

When the shooting had stopped, the seven other men came jogging up to the barricade in the beams of the flood-lights. They coughed and sucked in air as they filed in through the gate.

"I can't believe that worked," Jim said, trying to catch his breath.

"It didn't work that well," Jack said solemnly.

The preacher walked up to the group and slung his rifle over his shoulder.

"Thank you, Eric," Joe said. "That was some good shooting."

The preacher nodded and put a hand on his shoulder.

Jim looked around in the dim light. "Where's the Packards? Did you see them?"

"Yeah," Keith said. "They're dead."

In the darkness, amid the noise of shrieks and curses and the drumming of the Servants of Gaia, the preacher said a prayer for the souls of the Packards. Then, he prayed for the community, for protection, for strength and wisdom, and he thanked God for their success and for the people of Mount Sinai.

As one of the nurses applied fresh bandages to Keith's reopened wounds, Jack shook hands with the men and thanked them for their good work. "There's blankets and pillows for everyone in the church. Try to get some sleep, everybody. We'll need all our strength for what comes next."

In the field across the highway, the large houses went up in flames as the servants screamed and cursed them. The drums echoed off the hills as black smoke billowed out of the fires lighting up the sky.

"They won't come back tonight," Jack said. "They'll wait until daylight, and then, they'll come for retribution. It ends tomorrow."

PART V
THE FALL

Chapter Twenty

Day 165

The sun was just nearing the horizon when the guards roused the men sleeping in the church. A dirty, orange glow radiated from behind the hills, through a haze of black smoke and choking, gray vapors. The sky was empty of birds, and no life stirred in the trees and bushes surrounding Mount Sinai. In the eerie stillness of the smoky twilight, men appeared in the open doorways of barns and houses, and women peered through open windows, scanning the perimeter with rifles in hand.

Keith had hardly slept that night, unable to remove the image of Fred Packard's eyes rolling back in his head. He stepped out behind the barricade, watching the scene as neighbors scuttled about, delivering messages and supplies to the positions. His bandaged arm and leg were dripping blood once again, and he sat on the church steps to change out the dressings, cinching the new strips of cloth tight over the wounds. He took a drink from his water bottle as he watched a group of three armed women herding several small children and leading them down the road to the barn.

"Where are we going, Momma?" one of the children asked, rubbing his eyes.

"Shh. We're going to school, sweetheart," A woman replied, glancing over her shoulder.

"Are you going to school too?" the boy said in a loud whisper.

"Yes, baby. Come on. We have to hurry."

Keith watched as a bearded man approached the group. He could no longer hear them, but he saw the man hug and kiss one of the women as two little girls wrapped their arms around the man's knees. He picked them up and kissed them both as they patted him on the head and tugged on his beard. Setting them back down, he kissed his wife again and walked toward the barricade with his rifle, wiping tears from his eyes. The mother took the girls' hands and beckoned them on as one turned and yelled back to the man: "Have fun at work, Daddy!"

Keith heard the clopping of hooves on the pavement, and he watched as Dan Tyler's team of jackstock stopped just behind the rise. Only their long ears were visible over the edge of the barricade beside Bill Campbell's barn. The mothers loaded their children onto the wagon as Dan kissed his wife, handed off the reigns, and climbed down from the seat. Mrs. Tyler pulled the team around and drove the women and children back down the hill away from the front. Dan limped up the road toward the barricade, carrying a shotgun and a bandolier of shells. His face was hard-set, and beneath the stony expression, a cold fury resided in his eyes. Like his cousin, Jack Winters, he had buried two of his children in the last five months. He glanced at Keith and the others and said nothing as he took his place behind the barricade and adjusted his Kevlar vest.

The sun was creeping over the horizon now. All was quiet still. The defenders shifted the plate carriers and Kevlar vests around on their torsos, scratching their shoulders beneath the straps and placing tourniquets around their limbs in preparation. Men checked the defenses. Scott Adams and Jack Winters walked along the perimeter, looking at the explosives and quietly warning neighbors to avoid trip wires and pressure switches. Scott wore his plate carrier along with a ballistic helmet. Despite Jim Baker's prodding, Jack had refused to wear the armor taken from the marauders, instead giving it to one of the women. There wasn't enough for everyone. Tim, Joe, and the preacher moved supplies and provisions out of the church in wheelbarrows and wagons as a pickup truck rolled over the hill and pulled into the parking lot.

The green pickup parked beside the graveyard, and Lydia and Abigail climbed out of the passenger side while Emma opened the tailgate. Tim's seven children climbed out to hug their father. Tim tried to keep from crying as he hugged and kissed his wife and children. Eric approached the vehicle and embraced his wife and granddaughter while another truck crested the hill.

As Keith watched the rusty, blue truck pull in beside the green one, he felt his eyes water and a lump rise in his throat. The doors opened, and Kent, Faye, and Lynn climbed out. Keith and Joe met them beside the truck, and the family hugged one another.

Lydia, Abigail, Emma, and the kids began unloading casserole dishes from the trucks and lining them up on the rock wall beside the graveyard. Lynn and Faye began unloading food as well, and Jack and Eric called to the neighbors to join them around the truck. The neighbors lined up as paper plates were passed out, and they were served steak and eggs. As soon as the food was out of the two trucks, the sleeping bags and supplies from the church were loaded into the beds, and the women hugged their men once more. Abigail took Joe's face in her hands and kissed him before turning and wiping her eyes. They left the warrior's breakfast with the defenders and climbed back into the vehicles. Kent pulled his shotgun and a satchel from the cab of the old Ford, kissed his wife and daughter, and took his place beside his sons at the defense. Keith looked at his father quizzically as the trucks drove away. Kent said nothing as he looked at his sons and nodded.

Men and women sat on the stone wall and on the ground with plates of scrambled eggs and venison, eating quickly as the red sun shone out through the trees behind them. The orange beams of light filtered through the smoke and the green leaves on the trees of Mount Sinai. At eight o'clock, the defenders stood and watched as the flag was raised on the pole over the graveyard in the morning sun's brilliance. From the bell tower of the church, the preacher read Psalm 144 in a booming voice that carried over the blood-stained land and was heard by all—the servants of Gaia as well as the servants of the living God. The defenders watched through rifle scopes as the glittering mass of bodies in the field began to move.

As they took their positions in the houses and the church, behind the berm and along the barricades, a shrill, piercing scream erupted from the servants' camp in the field beyond, and the pounding of the drums thundered throughout the hills. The tormented shrieks and wailing of the heathens cut through the air, and the strident din of the grating voices pierced the ears of the neighbors who watched the barbaric horde in the distance, writhing and contorting themselves, throwing things in the air and making obscene gestures. They battered the drums with a savage, discordant rhythm of hate and discontent.

From behind one of the cars, a woman stood up in the middle of the road and began to sing. Over the noise of the servants, she could hardly be heard, but people near her began to join in, and as more and more began to sing with her, the song grew louder and clearer, clashing with the drums and screaming. Soon, all the residents of Mount Sinai were standing and singing at the top of their lungs, and in defiance of the terrible foe, they roared all four verses of the most beautiful song ever heard by the ears of man:

IN THE SHADOWS OF GODS

O say can you see by the dawn's early light,
What so proudly we hailed at the twilight's last gleaming,
Whose broad stripes and bright stars through the perilous fight,
O'er the ramparts we watched, were so gallantly streaming?
And the rockets' red glare, the bombs bursting in air,
Gave proof through the night that our flag was still there;
O say does that star-spangled banner yet wave,
O'er the land of the free and the home of the brave?

On the shore dimly seen through the mists of the deep,
Where the foe's haughty host in dread silence reposes,
What is that which the breeze, o'er the towering steep,
As it fitfully blows, half conceals, half discloses?
Now it catches the gleam of the morning's first beam,
In full glory reflected now shines in the stream:
'Tis the star-spangled banner, O! long may it wave
O'er the land of the free and the home of the brave.

And where is that band who so vauntingly swore
That the havoc of war and the battle's confusion,
A home and a country, should leave us no more?
Their blood has washed out their foul footsteps' pollution.
No refuge could save the hireling and slave
From the terror of flight, or the gloom of the grave:
And the star-spangled banner in triumph doth wave,
O'er the land of the free and the home of the brave.

O thus be it ever, when free men shall stand
Between their loved home and the war's desolation.
Blest with vict'ry and peace, may the Heav'n rescued land
Praise the Pow'r that hath made and preserved us a nation!
Then conquer we must, when our cause it is just,
And this be our motto: "In God is our trust."
And the star-spangled banner in triumph shall wave
O'er the land of the free and the home of the brave!

The rumble of drums reverberated off the hills amid the cacophony of high-pitched wailing. Sweating mothers and grievously wounded men stood, guarding the barn with fearful eyes and weapons in hand. They watched the roads and hillsides and creek beds in anticipation as the young children huddled inside the barn where fresh straw had been mounded over the bloodstained concrete.

Jordan McCormick's heart was pounding. Her hands were shaking. Cold sweat poured from her face and body as she tended to the wounded in the tent. She had hardly slept in the past week, and her entire body ached with the stress. Having barely survived the attack a week ago, she had begun experiencing contractions shortly afterward. She kept it to herself, however, only taking teas from Emma Faulkner, since she was only seven months pregnant and the doctors and nurses had more pressing matters to attend to. Now, her back was cramping, and she struggled to stand. The pain in her abdomen was so intense, tears leaked from her eyes as she clenched her teeth and tried to focus on helping the doctors. Eventually, she could no longer withstand it, and she collapsed to the floor with a cry.

"Jordan!" Malik shouted. He dropped what he was doing and lifted her body off the floor. Noah Rosenbaum helped him get her onto a cot and began checking her vitals. She groaned in pain and gasped for air.

Emma came running into the tent. After examining her, she looked up at the two doctors. "She's in labor. I can help her with the delivery. You should stay with the wounded."

"She's my wife," Malik said. "I need to help her."

"Malik, this man is dying," Noah said. "I need your help."

"I've midwifed for dozens of women. I can do this," Emma said firmly.

Malik looked to be in anguish, but he relinquished his wife's hand and turned to save the other patient.

Emma got her eldest daughter from the barn to bring her towels and her medical bag. They left the other children shut up in the barn with the dogs as the thunder of war drums echoed off the hills.

From the mass of bodies in the field, a strange, indistinct form made its way toward the highway. As it neared, Keith recognized the androgenous clown riding in a wheelchair pulled by leather-clad catamites. He whipped the slaves as they crawled through the burrs and nettles. Blood ran down their backs and seeped from the lacerations on their arms and legs.

The army of four-hundred strong moved forward toward the highway. The ranks parted, and toward the front, rolled several vans and trucks revving engines and spewing smoke as they pulled carts and wagons carrying crudely built guillotines and cages, racks and gibbets. The vehicles were painted with fists and rainbows, hammer-and-sickle flags, red stars, and slogans. One of the vans displayed an image of a black fist clenching a serpent and a slogan on the hood which read: "WE WILL TREAD." Another truck was adorned with a sign across the grill which read: "This machine kills fascists!" Flags flew from the vehicles and were waved in the hands of the servants. At a little more than two-hundred yards from the highway, they stopped and formed a solid line behind the vehicles. The calamitous noise of the drums and screaming ceased, and several servants pushed out a cart in front of the lines. Mounted on the cart, was an inverted cross whereon the naked body of Fred Packard was nailed. His hands and feet had been cut off, his eyes were gouged out, and his severed genitals were stuffed in his mouth. A jiggling stalactite of dark sludge ran from the hole in the top of his skull, and a sign hung on the bloody corpse with the words "Not-See" painted in blood. The servants laughed and jeered and slung bottles of urine and handfuls of excrement onto the desecrated remains.

Kent turned away from the sight and gagged.

As the clown was drawn nearer by the dehumanized slaves, Keith retrieved his axe from the church. The preacher met him at the front door.

"They're sending an emissary to talk," the preacher said. "We have to exhaust all options before we resort to war. If we can avoid any more bloodshed, we have to try. Let me talk to him."

Keith thought that ship had sailed, and any attempt at avoiding what was staring them down two-hundred yards away was futile, but he assented. No one wanted war, and it was only justified as an absolute last resort. "Alright," he said. "But don't expect much."

"I don't," the preacher replied. "Still, we have to try."

"Jack, cover us," Keith shouted. "We're going to see what this demon wants to say."

"I got you," Jack said, looking through the scope of his rifle. "Hold your fire until I signal!" he shouted to the line.

The preacher walked with Keith through the gate, and as the slave driver was pulled over the burnt house's driveway, they waited on the highway's asphalt. When the herald reached the highway, the drums and screaming subsided, and it was quiet once again.

The flail-wielding ghoul stepped off the bone-adorned wheelchair and shouted a string of profanities at the men. "Someone from your little—" the creature waived the flail around toward the road. "This, like, village attacked us last night. I know you know who it was. Bring them to us. Now!"

"Or what? You've made it quite clear what your intentions are whether anyone cooperates with you or not," Keith said.

The preacher put a hand on Keith's shoulder to stop him.

"Shut up, fascist!" the creature spat. "You know what we do to not-sees?" The creature raised its arm and threw something on the ground at Keith's feet.

The slimy orbs splatted on the blacktop and rolled down the slope. Keith glanced down at Fred Packard's eyes.

"Give us the not-sees that attacked us. Leave the tools, the food, and the animals, and clear out of this stolen land. If you do that, we'll let the rest of you live, even though you, like, don't deserve it."

The preacher gathered all his strength to remain calm in the face of the abject evil before him, and in a steady voice, he began to speak. "You have appointed yourselves to judge man and mete out vengeance, but it is not your place to judge. Even now, you can still turn back from your sin. Repent. Repent before it is too late."

"And who is this moron? Your idiot priest? I bet he's a rapist too. As well as an intolerant bigot not-see."

The preacher squeezed Keith's shoulder once more and steadied his voice as he continued. "Judge not, that ye be not judged. For with what judgment ye judge, ye shall be judged, and with what measure ye mete, it shall be measured to you again."

"What is that? Some old, dead, white man's propaganda? Shut up, fool!"

The preacher took a breath and shook his head. "Let go of this hate, son. Before it's too late."

"Son!" The ghoul spat in the preacher's face. "Did you just assume my gender? How dare you, you ignorant racist! You're going to die too!"

Keith's axe slid through his hand until the fawn's foot stopped at his palm.

The preacher pulled out a handkerchief and wiped the spit from his face. He raised his eyes to Heaven and said, "Lord knows we tried. Give not that which is holy unto the dogs, neither cast ye your pearls before swine." And he turned his back on the fiend and walked back toward the church.

The demon's bloodshot eyes bulged from its empty head as it shrieked "The Lord? Your god! You stupid rednecks! I AM GOD!"

In that instant, the creature's head snapped backward, and its mouth exploded in a geyser of blood and teeth as the hammer poll of Keith's axe struck it under the chin and shattered its jaws. The axe head arced up in the air as the clown's body fell backward, and Keith brought the blade down and buried it in the monster's chest. For a second, the wide-eyed savage hung in the air, suspended by its locked knees and the steel bit embedded in its sternum. Keith reached around with his left hand, grasped the shoulder of the axe handle, and wrenched the axe to the side, slinging the corpse onto the ground. The catamites yelled and barked as they scrambled toward him on their hands and knees, dragging the wheelchair behind them as they tried to bite and claw. Keith unholstered his pistol and gunned down the lot of them on the highway.

Immediately, the barbarian horde roared, and the drums thundered again as the engines revved and bullets cracked all around him. The army charged forward toward the highway. Keith leapt over the barricade as Jack raised his arm and swept it back down.

"Fire!"

Faye and Lynn helped prop Jordan up on a stack of pillows, and as Lynn wiped Jordan's forehead with a cool, damp rag, Faye continued sterilizing bandages and towels. Even with all the candles and cut flowers hanging around the tent, the stench was overwhelming. A curtain of bedsheets was set up around Jordan, partially for Jordan's privacy, but also to help Malik from being distracted and running to his wife. Jordan gasped and screamed in pain as blood and urine and translucent fluids spilled out onto the saturated towels covering the cot and dripped down on the towels beneath. Emma continually wiped the filth away from Jordan's legs, applied cattail gel, and changed out the towels as her daughter brought clean ones.

507

Malik struggled to focus on the wounded man whose sutured artery had reopened. He held the artery clamped shut as Noah Rosenbaum restitched it. One of the nurses was administering a direct blood transfusion from a woman who was struggling to keep her eyes open as she sat watching. At the sounds of Jordan's screams, Malik clearly wanted to go to her, but he resisted the urge and only allowed his head to turn away from his work momentarily.

"It's all perfectly normal," Noah said calmly, not taking his eyes off the needle and thread as he sewed. "She's fine. Don't worry." His soothing voice helped to ease Malik's mind, but only a little.

"Alright," the nurse said. "That's it. She can't give any more." The nurse put a wad of gauze on the woman's arm.

"No, he needs it," the woman said as if in a trance.

"You can't lose any more. You'll go into shock." The nurse continued to remove the needle. "You've done all you can do."

"Get her some honey water," Noah said. "Thank you, both. You've probably saved this man's life." He tied off the thread and snipped it. "Alright, Malik. Slowly."

Malik released the clamp gradually. When the artery did not spurt blood, the two doctors congratulated one another with weary, exhausted smiles.

"Let's get some antiseptic here," said Noah. "We're not out of the woods yet."

Jordan let out a wail. Her eyes bulged with the strain. Sweat streamed down her face, and spit ran from the corners of her mouth.

"You're almost there, honey," Emma said. "I can see the—" she stopped. Her face went pale. "Wait, Jordan. Hold on." She turned to her daughter. "Sterilize my knife over the fire."

The students were dressed in bizarre animal costumes and brightly colored outfits like deranged circus performers.

508

Their bodies fell to the ground as the snipers' bullets tore through them. Bullets riddled the thin metal of the barricade cars, but the vehicles, stuffed full of trash, stopped most of the projectiles from exiting. The servants shot while running, or from standing positions in the field, and at more than one-hundred yards, their shots went wild, hitting the walls of the church, the barricade, and the trees around the forty defenders. Charging forward, servants tripped over the fallen corpses of their comrades. The trucks and vans plowed toward the barricade.

"Take out the trucks! Take out the trucks!" Several voices shouted amidst the noise and confusion.

As the vehicles came within range, Kent Rawlings sent one-ounce rifled slugs from his shotgun through their radiators and into the engine blocks. Dan Tyler and a few of the hunters likewise used their rifled slug guns to disable vehicles. Smoke and oil and geysers of steam erupted from the machines as the slugs tore holes through the engines. The servants were within one-hundred yards now. The mass of bodies was being mown down by well-aimed rifle fire, but the army was soon to overrun them.

"Mortars!" Jack shouted.

As the horde closed in, now at seventy yards, the fireworks were trained on the swarm, and the explosions of dazzling colors blew holes in their ranks as glass and metal shards ripped through them. The attackers were momentarily blinded and deafened by the chaos, and fires engulfed the fuel-leaking vehicles and set the field ablaze. Flaming servants rolled and screamed in the fire and confusion.

Jack Winters shouted and waved his arms. "Fall back! Fall back! Get out of the church! Fall back to the second barricade!"

It was nearly impossible to hear the commands, but as the defenders saw their neighbors running back down the road, they passed along the message and poured out of their positions, sprinting to the second barricade, taking up cover in the trees on either side of the road.

"Bill! Get out! Fall back!" Jack yelled.

As the stragglers ran to their positions, Jack and the preacher aimed their rifles over the cars. A woman bolted out of one of the houses, making for the barricade as bullets cracked around her.

"Come on!" men shouted to her, waiving their hands.

She collapsed to the ground in a mist of blood as a bullet struck her in the spine.

Two of the remaining trucks, surrounded by servants, plowed into the barricade, and rolling directly over the pressure plates, they set off the explosives. With a ground-shaking explosion, the trucks were destroyed, and bodies were shredded by ball bearings, rusted bolts, and shards of glass.

Fireworks and Molotov cocktails were thrown into the church, and smoke billowed from the windows and doors. Bodies scrambled over the barricades, and the riflemen picked them off one by one, stacking the corpses around the wall. Finally, they overwhelmed the barrier, and landing on the road behind the cars, one of the slaves snagged a trip wire, and a series of zip guns was simultaneously triggered, firing loads of buckshot into the mass of bodies. They poured forth, charging the houses. Several of the lunatics ran into a strand of braided fishing line stretched across the entrance to the cul-de-sac. The line pulled a trigger which sent a firing pin into a shotgun primer set in a three-inch steel pipe full of black powder and packed ball bearings. They were instantly eviscerated.

The preacher took aim at a Tannerite bomb placed beside Bill Campbell's mailbox, and as the maniacs swarmed around it, he fired. In a cloud of smoke, the devils were lacerated and punctured by bent nails and pottery shards, and they fell to the ground, writhing in pain and pools of blood.

"Fall back!" Jack shouted.

The defenders ran through the trees toward Dan Tyler's driveway to take positions inside the woods at the ninety-degree bend in the road.

As the cul-de-sac burned, the brigands rushed down the road, screaming with fury. They threw rocks through Bill Campbell's windows and fired into the house. Jack Winters, Dan Tyler, and the preacher concentrated their fire on the servants trying to burn down the house. A pink-haired psychopath lit the rag extending from a beer bottle, and the preacher sent a bullet through the glass and into the neurotic behind it. The bottle exploded in a fireball and servants rolled on the ground, engulfed in flames. As the men continued firing into the crowd and picking off attackers, one of the beasts approached a broken window of the farmhouse with a pistol. Reaching into the window, his head was blown apart by a shotgun blast from inside the house, and his body toppled back off the porch. The villains rushed the house.

Keith and Joe picked off attackers as they climbed over the fence around Dan Tyler's horse pasture. The horses inside the barn were panicking and kicking against the walls. Keith aimed center mass at a blue-haired servant swinging its leg over the fence. He squeezed the trigger, and the 55-grain full metal jacketed bullet struck a rib at over three-thousand feet per second, deflected, and exited the top of the villain's skull, tumbling through the air in a shower of blood, pulverized bone, and liquified brain tissue. The servants poured over the fence and stumbled through the pitted clay and piles of horse manure. The defenders dropped them in the pasture as they neared, but they couldn't keep up with the wave of marauders pouring over the fence and running down the road.

Dan ran to the barn and opened the doors. "Stay back!" he shouted. The horses bolted out of the barn and down the road away from the gunfire. As Dan watched the horses running away, he was struck in the back of the head and fell forward on the ground, never to rise again.

Bill Campbell's house was on fire, and through the smoke, they saw Bill step out of his front door with a double-barreled shotgun. The servants had him surrounded, and as they closed in on him, the preacher fired at the savages, dropping bodies all around the porch until his bolt locked to the rear. He reached for another magazine as Jack Winters also ran dry.

"Bill!" Jack shouted, pulling out a fresh magazine.

Some of the other defenders directed fire toward the group surrounding Bill Campbell. Bill shot a servant in the chest as they swarmed him. He spun around and fired his last barrel into one's stomach. As he broke the shotgun open to reload, a large man with a ponytail grabbed it out of his hands and shoved him to the ground before beating him to death with the buttstock. The preacher sent a .308 under the man's arm as he raised the shotgun over his head. Shreds of heart and lung tissue burst out of the hole in his side with a spray of blood, and he took two steps backward before collapsing. The flames rose out of the upper windows and spread over the shingles.

"Back! Fall back!" Jack shouted. "Up the hill! Go! Preacher! Secure the hill! Keith, Joe, stay with me!" He quickly dragged Dan Tyler's body back behind the house and hid it beneath some brush while the brothers laid down cover fire.

The preacher led the defenders down the road, around the bend, and up the hill, to the barricade beside the burnt rubble of Ernie Jacobs' house and barn. Jack fired from behind the deck at the Tannerite explosive beside the mailbox fifty yards in front of the barricade, and shrapnel tore through the mass of bodies on the road. Keith and Joe followed Jack and retreated into the woods behind Dan Tyler's house with screaming servants pursuing them.

Kent had jogged alongside the group retreating to the hilltop, thinking his sons were with the group. In the confusion, he hadn't heard Jack's orders, and as he tried to catch his breath, he looked around for his sons, reloading his shotgun. "Keith! Joe!" he shouted when he didn't see them.

"Get down, Kent!" Scott yelled.

"Where's my boys?" Kent shouted.

"They're coming," said the preacher. "They'll be coming up from the valley over there! Now get down!"

Kent ambled around the line of defenders on the hilltop. He crawled to the left flank and sunk to his belly in the grass, watching the tree line. Black smoke rose above the treetops to the west as the houses along the road went up in flames.

The staccato of gunfire resonated in the valley. Screams and booms punctuated the cacophony while shaking men and women waited in terror for the battle to reach them. They watched the road and surrounding hills with the sounds of violence ringing in their ears and the smells of burning houses filling their nostrils as the smoke drifted through the hollows on the wind.

Those who could still walk, or at least hold a weapon, sat propped against tree trunks or lay in positions where they expected to die. They mumbled prayers as they prepared to give their lives defending the defenseless and the children in the barn. They checked and rechecked weapons, laid out magazines and loose shells in front of them, and took in what they expected to be their last glimpses of the beauty of the trees and fields. Each resigned himself to his fate in his own way. This was a good place to meet the end. It was a good fight. There was no better way to die. And through the pain of their injuries and the fear of what may come, they felt a strange sense of peace and even joy. Waiting for the forces of evil to pour over them, they smiled.

As servants tried setting Dan Tyler's barn on fire, Keith, Joe, and Jack picked them off, one by one, from the dark cover of the woods. Bodies fell in piles until the servants quit trying to burn the barn. The bulk of the army was moving along the ridge to the north of the road, working their way from house to house. Keith, Joe, and Jack moved around the barn and began taking out attackers from behind the fence posts. The fleeing servants staggered over the corpses of their fallen comrades as bullets dropped them in the road.

Jack and the brothers reloaded and moved back around the barn and behind the house once more. A group of half a dozen servants chased them into the trees, and as they scrambled over the uneven terrain, they sprayed bullets wildly into the woods. They looked for the three men, but it seemed they had disappeared. They screamed and shot at random trees, until one noticed the body of Dan Tyler beneath the brush and shot it several times. The servants gathered around the remains and began pulling the foliage off the body when a sudden burst of rifle fire dropped the six of them where they stood. They writhed and spat bloody bubbles as the life drained from the holes in their eviscerated flesh.

"Through the ravine, quickly!" Jack took off down the hillside with the brothers on his heels. They ran down the slope through the shadows of the trees, leapt over the creek bed and climbed the hill toward the line of defenders.

"Kill the not-sees! Kill the not-sees!" The barbarian horde stormed down the road and scurried over the hillside to the north like cockroaches from the light.

The preacher kissed his Bible and flipped off the safety on his rifle. "This is a good hill, friends! Defend this hill!" he shouted. He took aim at a servant running down the hillside, exhaled, and squeezed the trigger. The body rolled down the slope, leaving a trail of bloody leaves as it descended into the ditch one-hundred-forty yards away. The line of prone defenders opened fire, and corpses cascaded down the hillside and tripped up servants rounding the bend. With a hill on one side and a steep ditch on the other, the servants funneled into a choke point, and the mass of bodies was cut down by a hurricane of hot lead. A mound of cadavers was growing on the road. The preacher dropped snipers from the distant hillside as bullets kicked up clods of dirt and geysers of dust and grass all around the defenders.

Kent saw movement coming from the left flank, and he swung the barrel of his shotgun toward the threat. As the figures crested the hill, one was waving a hat at him, and he recognized Jack Winters and his two sons.

Glass shattered, and bullets tore through the thin steel of the barricade cars. Defenders cinched down tourniquets and continued to fight to their last breaths as their bodies were ripped and punctured.

"Kent, Tim, get a truck to evacuate the wounded!" Jack shouted. He began firing at the shooters on the hillside.

The two men crawled back over the crest and ran toward Tim's house.

The servants were charging up the hill, now within fifty yards. Jack knelt down behind the barricade and pulled a pipe bomb from his satchel. He lit the fuse and shouted, "Cover fire!" And as the rate of fire increased, he hurled the explosive onto the road among the servants.

Several servants tried grabbing the bomb to throw back but were struck down by bullets, and the bomb exploded, throwing bodies and pieces of flesh in all directions.

Tim's green pickup truck pulled up behind the barricade, and they began loading up the dead and wounded into the bed as Jack and the Rawlings brothers threw bombs into the mob of attackers. The truck drove away, the men threw the last of the pipe bombs at the horde, and Jack shouted, "Fall back!"

As bullets thumped against the cars and cracked overhead, the remaining defenders ran back down the road to the trees around Brad Nielson's house. Keith reached the woods and looked back to see Scott Adams caught on the barbed wire fence by his pant leg. Keith fired at the servants running toward them. Scott was trying to free himself from the fencing, bouncing on one leg as he pulled against the barbed wire. Suddenly, the thigh of his tangled leg burst in a mist of blood. He yelled, and his other leg was shot out from under him. Hanging upside down with his leg caught in the fence, he raised his rifle and fired at the servants until he was struck in the head, and his helmet popped off and rolled in a profusion of blood. His body went limp, and he hung on the fence as his blood ran into the grass.

There were fewer than one-hundred of the Servants of Gaia remaining, but they still outnumbered the defenders four to one. Tearing through the trees surrounding the field, the defenders encircled the marauders and cut down the screaming savages from the tree line. Keith loaded his last magazine and carefully aimed every shot; however, unless he managed to hit the heart, spine, or brain of his targets, the tiny .22 caliber bullets from his AR-15 barely phased the drug-addled assailants.

Keith fired the last rounds of his last magazine as one of the students charged into the trees with a pickaxe. The man swung at Keith and the pick lodged in the trunk near his head. Keith raised the rifle over his shoulder and slammed the butt into the man's face, knocking him to the ground. Pulling out his pistol, he fired a .45 into the man's chest and ducked back behind the tree, setting his empty rifle on the ground.

The servants ran through the field in no organized formation until their flanks were picked off as they neared the trees. Some of the leaders began shouting for the servants to get behind the cars, and they turned back to regroup at the top of the hill. The preacher continued to drop bodies as they exposed themselves, but he was quickly running out of ammunition.

"Winchester!" came shouts from defenders in the woods.

As the defenders fired the last of their rounds, the preacher called for the retreat.

The mob of students formed up behind a wall of servants covered in stolen police gear, holding ballistic shields and riot shields, and as they marched forward, they chanted. The drums started beating time again, and the servants chanted from behind the shield wall. "Death to America. Death to America. Down with the patriarchy. Down with the patriarchy. Liberate Gaia. Liberate Gaia. Kill all the not-sees. Kill all the not-sees. Property is racist. Property is racist. Christians are the enemy. Christians are the enemy. Silence is violence. Silence is violence. Freedom is slavery. Freedom is slavery."

The defenders regrouped at the barricade beside the Packards' house.

"I'm out," one woman said, panting.

"Me too," a man coughed. "We need more ammo."

"God will provide," said the preacher, holding a bandage over his bleeding shoulder.

"We've got weapons and ammo back at the house," Joe said.

Jack spat a stream of blood on the ground and struggled to breathe. "Alright—everyone who's out—run back—to the Rawlings house—with Joe—and get all the weapons and ammo you can—quickly."

Joe and five others took off down the long driveway and disappeared behind the ridge.

Jack took his last drink of water. Dark clouds gathered overhead. Blood, sweat, and urine dripped from the defenders and steamed as it hit the pavement.

Brad Nielson tied a bloody strip of cloth around his stomach where dark blood and green sludge was bubbling out from a hole in his shirt. He looked at the mess and sighed. "Jack," he said. "I've got a couple guns in the house. If I go through the woods, I can get around 'em. I can get my weapons and hit 'em from the rear. Draw 'em away for a little while."

Jack glanced at the gut-shot man's wound. He nodded.

"Somebody, tell my wife and kids. I love 'em. With all my heart."

"They know that, Brad," the preacher said. "But we'll tell them again."

Brad nodded and started walking into the woods behind the Packards' house.

"I'll go with him," another man said, following Brad into the trees.

Jack turned to look at Keith. "Keith, do you think—you can get around the woods—and hit them from the south—before they get here?"

"Yeah, I can do that."

Jack coughed as he sucked air through his mouth. "I want you—to meet up—with your brother—and the others—and take the ridge—through the trees—until you get—beside Tim's place. Then, open fire on 'em." He wiped the blood from his mouth. "We're gonna hit 'em—with a three-way ambush. Let loose as soon as you're ready—and keep your shots—between this house—and Nielson's. Go."

Keith took off toward the driveway.

The drumbeats and chanting were getting closer, but through the noise, they heard the low growl of engines. Two trucks drove up to the baffle barricade behind them, and Kent Rawlings opened the door of the blue Ford and scrambled around to the bed. He came back with rifles and magazines and began passing them out. Sitting in the bed were two wounded men holding shotguns. Behind the blue truck, Tim's green Chevy parked, and four men and two women climbed out with rifles.

"Where do you want us?" Kent asked.

"Behind cover and out of sight," said the preacher. "Hurry."

They took up positions with the defenders beside the Packards' house and behind the last barricade. A column of black smoke rose from the Nielson house.

Keith met Joe and the five other defenders beside the overgrown logging trail that ran from the driveway to the fence around Tim Faulkner's property. Joe handed him his .44 magnum levergun and followed him into the woods.

"Everyone loaded? Alright. We're going to hit them from the tree line beside Tim Faulkner's house. Let's go." He stepped quickly and quietly through the leaves and briars leading the group up to the crest of the ridge.

When they got in position, the mob was rounding the bend in the road.

"Keep your shots between the two houses," Keith commanded.

The riflemen lined up beside the trees and sighted in on the enemy. Just then, rapid shots were fired from Brad Nielson's house. The chanting and drumming stopped as bodies crumpled in the road at the rear of the column, and the screaming horde turned around.

"They're behind us!" shouted one of the servants.

The servants fired back toward the brown house and tried to get their shields to the other end of the mob to protect them.

Keith took aim at a rainbow-haired gorgon and squeezed the trigger. The six other shooters in the trees poured fire down on the clustered mass of bodies. Clouds of bloody mist exploded in the air, and shredded meat and bone fragments flew in all directions as the defenders at the last barricade opened up with enfilade fire. The servants had no cover. They screamed and fell over one another, trying to hide. They shot wildly in all directions, and several shot each other in the confusion. The defenders fired, reloaded, fired again, reloaded, and fired until the only movement seen on the road was mutilated carnage, corpses writhing and convulsing as they grabbed at nothing and bled out among the mound of wasted humanity.

When it was over, every one of the defenders reacted the same way. They said nothing but looked around and listened for others. No one dared step out from behind cover for several minutes. But all was silent, apart from the ringing in their ears. No more drums. No more chants. No more screaming or gunshots. Just the smoke of burnt houses and the stench of death. There were no cheers or celebrations when they realized they had prevailed. They checked themselves and each other for wounds and did their best to bandage their neighbors and load them onto the pickup trucks.

Keith limped over to the brown house as the flames spread over the roof, and he found a man sitting in the grass, staring down silently at a body lying next to him. When Keith looked down at the man, he saw a bloody hole in the man's stomach oozing greenish brown filth. He studied Brad Nielson's pale, lifeless face. His eyes were closed, and his mouth was curled in a slight smile. He was at peace. It looked as if he were sleeping and experiencing a very good dream.

When Keith walked around the pile of carcasses, he saw the ditch was full of blood running like a slow-moving river down the slope. It spilled over the road and ran down the hillside into the ravine. The dark clouds overhead blocked out the sun, and the light faded into dim gray. Thunder rumbled low in the distance, and as Keith stepped around the barricade, he saw the defenders gathered around a man sitting with his back against the car of the last barricade between the highway and the barn. Jack Winters sat struggling to breathe as pink, frothy blood bubbled out of a hole in his chest. His face was pale, and he looked calmly at the faces of his friends around him. Keith knelt down beside him and began digging through his bag for a chest seal to stop up the hole. He pulled it out and ripped open Jack's shirt, wiping the blood away with a piece of cloth. Jack's entire chest was a deep purple. His punctured lung was full of blood.

"Leave it," said Jack with a weary smile. His voice was faint, and his breath rattled in his throat. Blood ran from his mouth and dripped off his beard.

Keith took his hand and looked into the dying man's eyes already staring off into the distance, unable to focus.

"Bury me beside my children," Jack said just above a whisper. He wheezed.

"We will, Jack." Keith looked around at the faces of the neighbors, wiping tears from their eyes.

"I'm going to see them now." He drew in a raspy breath and gurgled, spitting a mouthful of blood. His lips were turning blue, and his eyes were red. His throat was bulging on the left side of his neck.

The neighbors knelt in closer to hear his final words. His voice was barely a whisper now. Keith put his ear closer to Jack's face.

Regaining his focus for a second, Jack looked into Keith's eyes. "Raise the flag," he rattled. His eyes wandered away again. "It's worth it." He exhaled his last words with his final breath, and he sat still, eyes staring ahead. Blood dripped from his mouth, and he sat silently, staring into the distance, the victorious warrior, while his soul drifted onward.

Keith closed his eyes, and tears ran down his face as the preacher prayed. Keith hugged his father and brother, and they drove the wounded back down the road to the barn. Raindrops fell.

In the barn, the doctors and nurses worked through their exhaustion, cleaning and bandaging wounds, administering intravenous fluids, and applying anesthetics as the barn was once again filled with patients. The children were cleared out and kept away from the wounded and sick. Jim Baker's wife invited them into her house where the teachers quickly came up with school lessons to keep the kids busy. The fighters washed away the blood and filth of battle with bars of lye soap in the pouring rain. Clothing was distributed to the defenders by family members and Lydia Jorgenson.

It took hours to attend to the patients and keep some from going into shock. In the light of the grease lamps and candles, the wounded defenders lay on their cots, holding pressure over wounds and waiting for attention. Keith had to have his cuts sewn up again, and he had acquired a new bullet hole in the fleshy part of his side, just above his hip. Joe had been shot through his right calf and hadn't noticed until the fight was over. The brothers lay beside one another with their father sitting on a chair between them. The old man fell asleep with his chin on his chest as Eric Jorgenson read from his Bible to the patients. Faye and Lynn met the Rawlings men at their cots, and seeing that they were all alive, they hugged them and went to get them some of the tea they had made for the patients. When the wounded had been stabilized, the doctors and nurses all cleaned themselves up and immediately went to sleep in tents set up outside the barn. All but one.

Malik went to the cot where Jordan lay. Emma pulled back the curtains, and he stepped in to see his wife.

Jordan lay propped on pillows, holding a tiny sleeping infant wrapped in a blanket. She looked up at Malik, with tears in her eyes, and smiled. "It's a girl. Malik McCormick, meet your daughter. Victoria."

Day 168

It took three days to clear away the dead. They used the last of the fuel to load tractor buckets full of corpses onto the trucks and haul them out to the field in front of the blackened rubble of the old church. The grass had been burned away by the wildfire, and in the scorched earth, they dug a pit the size of a football field with a bulldozer. As the trucks delivered their loads, they were scraped out by a backhoe, and the remains of the Servants of Gaia were shoved in and buried. Among the ruins of the servants' campsite, they found a large cauldron full of charred bones. The bones were small and bore the marks of cutting tools dragged across them; they lay piled in a pool of foamy, dark, gray-brown liquid. As Keith watched, the bulldozer pushed the cauldron into the pit with the corpses, and Keith saw a tiny human skull role out with the contents. He turned away in horror and limped toward the preacher amid the eye-watering stench, holding a cotton bandana to his mouth and nose. The preacher shook his head at the sight of the tiny, human bones that spilled from the cauldron. He closed his eyes and whispered something.

"Did you see that?" Keith said to no one in particular.

"I saw it," the preacher responded, his eyes still shut.

"What could possess someone to..." Keith's voice trailed away as he remembered what his professors had taught their classes.

"Do you not know?" the preacher said softly, looking into Keith's eyes.

"Know what?" Joe asked, wiping the sweat from his face and covering his nose.

"They only acted out what they were taught. It was science, they said. Humans are the same as any other animal, only more destructive. When the food ran out, they wouldn't kill other animals. Humans were the disease destroying nature. They reasoned that they were acting righteously by removing them from the top of the food chain. Putting them in their place."

"If there is no God, all things are permissible." The preacher nodded. "Dostoevsky."

"They relied on their feelings to determine morality," Keith said, staring off into the distance. "If they felt that two plus two made fifteen, who was to say otherwise? It was *their* truth. They felt that eating meat was immoral, but parasites—they had no rights."

"What are you talking about?" Joe looked quizzically. "You mean they ate..."

"Yes." Keith nodded solemnly.

"In my darker moments," the preacher sighed. "I sometimes think we deserved this." He looked around blankly and spoke as if to the ground. "We murdered a million innocent children a year, for decades. Over four times more than Hitler. The most innocent of us—we butchered them. We executed babies for the sins of their parents, and we all knew it was wrong. But we did it anyway. And for what? For our pleasure. Because we worshipped ourselves as gods, and every sacrifice to our own pleasure became a profane sacrament. Shame on us. If this world remains, future generations will curse us as monsters. And they'll be right to do it."

They were silent, the preacher's words echoed in their ears with the sound of the machines and the buzzing of flies.

Eric Jorgenson stood near the edge of the pit with the Rawlings brothers and several of the other workers, watching as the last truckload was emptied. The bloated corpses tumbled out onto the pile amid the cloud of flies and were buried with the machines and devices they had built. Eric Jorgenson read from his Bible and prayed as the remains were covered with the field's red clay. The preacher thanked God for the victory, prayed for the country's salvation, asked for comfort for those who had lost family, and pleaded for the strength to rebuild. When he had finished, one of the neighbors asked if he was going to say something for the souls of the students they were burying.

"I pray for the living," the preacher responded. "These vessels are dead, and their souls are already gone. Where they are now, it's not my place to say, but you can be sure that they have their reward, and it is just. They chose the path they followed, and they built their destination. It's too late for them. In life, they had no hope. They had no hope because they turned their backs on God. When you forsake God, you do not get rid of sin. The sin remains. The guilt and the shame and the anger, they remain, but the forgiveness is gone. Denying the Judge does not remove the judgment; it only removes the path to redemption."

Day 169

The bodies of the slain defenders had been washed, wrapped in sheets, and left in one of the barns until the road was cleared. Once they had collected the remains and identified them with name tags taped to the wrappings, they loaded the bodies onto Mrs. Tyler's wagon and hauled them to the graveyard. Holes had been dug in the requested spots, and as the wagon rolled slowly up the road, it was followed by all the residents of Mount Sinai. Even the badly wounded joined, being loaded onto a second wagon and pulled along in the procession. Of the more than five-hundred residents living on their two roads in February, fewer than two-hundred remained. Now, all of them were escorting the bodies of their fallen protectors to the grave.

The bodies were lowered into the earth, and the preacher delivered the funeral service. "Taps" was played. Everyone who was able helped to bury them, taking turns with the shovels, and all remained to place flowers over the graves. Simple, wooden crosses were hammered into the ground to mark each plot, and when the dirt was tamped down, they stopped and turned to look at the flagpole. A newly sewn flag was raised to the top of the staff, and it flew gallantly in the breeze. They wiped the tears from their eyes and smiled as they gazed on the glorious banner waving in the sun.

The preacher looked up and nodded before looking around at all the faces there. "We're here. We're still here. And with whatever time we have left on this earth, we're going to prove that these heroes did not die in vain. We're going to rebuild. We're going to keep the faith. We're going to hold on to each other, and we're going to shine the light out in the darkness. We'll strengthen our communities and extend the hand of friendship to everyone we can. We're going to rebuild this country. From the ground up. One step at a time." The preacher looked around and pointed at the blackened ruins of the old church behind him. "And we're going to start with that church."

The crowd nodded and clapped and shouted their approval. As Keith looked over his shoulder, he saw Malik and Jordan McCormick smiling as they held their baby girl. The infant was tiny, small enough to sit in one of Malik's large hands. Baby Victoria slept in her mother's arms with her tiny fingers wrapped around her thumb.

Chapter
Twenty-one

Day 180

He looked down at the woman in the casket. She was only sleeping. He was the one who died. All his plans were dead. How did it happen, an old woman asked. Drunk driver, a man whispered. And so young. She just turned nineteen. Sarah. They were going to get married, someone whispered. Poor young man. A hand on his shoulder. I know this is hard. I'll pray for you. To what? Don't go. Goodbye. 19,18! 17,16! 15,14,13,12! Get up! Go! Go! Go! Sergeant Rawlings! Down the murder hole. Smoke. Fire. Drums. Screaming. There is no forgiveness. Pickaxe. Eyeballs. Dan Tyler. Scott Adams. Brad Nielson. Jack Winters. Nooses hung above the road, and Rick Thompson's corpse dangled from them. Crows and vultures and dogs tearing human flesh. How many? He looked out over the horizon. The sky grew dark. A massive, black serpent encircled the landscape and twisted around the red sun. Tighter and tighter, the serpent coiled around the sphere. Blood bubbled up from the ground at his feet. The red sun burst, and a scarlet tidal wave swept over the hills. The trees were swept away in the deluge of blood. Blood rained from the sky, sprang from the earth, rushed over the hills and through the valleys, *until all the earth was covered and he was swept away. He flailed and struggled to keep his head above the surface. He was tossed around by the waves and desperately splashed in the blood which covered the earth as far as the eye could see. The torrent carried him away. He screamed for help, but no sound came out. Then, he struck his head against something hard, and he locked his arms around the thing, holding on with all his strength as the flood pulled on his body. He grasped the object and held on, every muscle in his body straining against the tide. He looked up through the downpour, and he saw the object he clenched was a cross atop a steeple, rising out of the blood, fixed in place against the current. Out of the sea of blood arose a figure coming toward him. Its head and shoulders emerged from the blood, and it looked at him with hollow, empty, lifeless, eyeless sockets. He recognized the face of Sarah, only dead and disfigured. Let go and be free, said the voice. He shook his head violently and held tighter. The thing reached out a hand to him, dead and rotting. Look what you've done. You killed me. There is no hope for you now. You're alone. Stop fighting. Let go. Tears ran down from his eyes as he opened his mouth and shouted. But no sound came out. The thing screamed and grabbed at him to pull him under, but he kicked at the specter and pushed it under the blood.*

Keith awoke with a jerk. He was soaked in sweat. He looked around and saw that he was back in his tent, and the soft light of dawn was streaming through the windows and glowing through the dirty, white canvas. His head was pounding, and he felt sick. He reached for the pills beside his cot and gulped them down with some water. His hands trembled, and his body shivered. Feeling a wave of nausea overtake him, Keith rolled out of the cot and crawled out of his tent. He vomited into the leaf litter.

I can't even keep the pills down to get rid of this headache, he thought.

Everyone was dying. The world had gone to Hell. How naïve, how stupid to think they could rebuild. There was nothing left to save. What was the point of going on? Keith's mind was spinning. He couldn't think. He collapsed onto the ground and began to cry. How could these fools continue to waste their time believing in a god who clearly didn't care about them even if He did exist? Who created these trees? he remembered his father asking him. The same thing that created the parasites that poisoned their water and the disease that was killing him, he thought. Some irrational, malevolent sadist, torturing people for fun and demanding they believe Him to be good and loving despite all the evidence. This was the god they had to worship? And if they didn't? What? He would condemn them to eternal torture? With a god like that, who needs a devil? Why would anyone want to live in a world like this? Better not to live at all. Keith vomited again. The wind changed directions and blew into his face. Something stank horribly.

Wiping the spit from his face, he crawled back to his tent to get a drink. The breeze carried the stench of death through the air, and Keith was overwhelmed by a need to investigate the source of the odor. He crawled on hands and knees until he came to a maggot-infested carcass lying in the brush on the side of the logging trail. This had been one of the students that he had killed. He could tell by the broken arrow shaft. As he neared it, something moved, and he watched a fat opossum crawl out of the filth, covered in grease and blood. It scurried away from him into the brush. The corpse was seething with flies, bees, ants, and beetles. Keith sat staring at the defiled remains.

He was so tired. He wanted it all to end. God, if you're out there. If you're listening, take this pain away. I can't do this. Help me. Keith closed his eyes and waited. For several minutes, he sat listening, waiting for something to happen. He opened his eyes and looked around. His head was pounding harder than ever, and the breeze shifted and blew the putrid miasma into his face. He gagged and vomited again. That's what I thought.

Keith crawled back to the tent and pulled his pistol out of the holster. He stared at it, then set it back on the ground. He took another mouthful of water and rinsed out the acrid taste of vomit. Then, he took a drink and picked up the pistol again. He checked to see that there was a round in the chamber, and he held it up in front of his face. Pressing the slide to his forehead, he felt the coolness of the steel. Then, he pulled it away again and studied the engraving. No, he wouldn't waste a bullet. He remembered Rick Thompson. He had been considerate enough to think of the community in his last moments. Keith could at least do that. He put the pistol on the cot and grabbed a coil of rope from inside his tent. Crawling outside once more, he climbed to his feet and looked for a branch to throw the rope over. He couldn't find one.

He staggered around, light-headed, and fought the urge to vomit. He stumbled into a tree and looked up. There was a branch. He untied the rope and tried to toss it over the branch but collapsed to the ground. He lay in the dust and leaves, defeated. He tried to catch his breath and suddenly, he felt a strange, irresistible urge to look at the corpse again.

He crawled along the ridgetop through the shadows of the trees, dragging the rope with him, back to the pile of rotting flesh. As he sat on the ground, staring at the grotesque body, he heard the crunching of leaves behind him and turned to see his brother.

"Here," Joe said. "I brought you some broth and some tea. It made me feel better." He handed a cup to Keith.

Keith looked down at the brown liquid, smelled it, and took a sip. Surprisingly, he didn't vomit. He took another. When he had finished the broth, Joe handed him a bottle of tea. Keith continued to stare at the corpse before him.

"God doesn't speak to me," Keith said flatly.

"Hmm." Joe sat down beside his brother and looked at the body in the leaves. "You're not special in that regard."

Through the leaves and torn bits of strange clothing, they could still see the lines of tattooed symbols grossly distorted beyond recognition now. Ants crawled over the hollow eye sockets and tarnished metal piercings.

Keith took a sip of the tea. "How does anyone still believe in God after all this?"

"Stubborn defiance, I guess," Joe shrugged. "Along with a good, hard look at the alternative."

Keith turned and looked at his brother. "You look at this kid, and you see a good God?"

"Of course."

"How?"

"The shadow."

Keith squinted and shook his head, trying to make sense of what he had heard.

"Look at him." Joe motioned toward the body with his head. "He came to a fork in the road at one point in his life, and he chose the wrong path. And he knew it was wrong, but he took it anyway. He may not have known right away, but he knew. And he had countless opportunities to correct his course and turn back, but he didn't. He continued to poison himself with hatred and resentment. He wanted nothing to do with God, so he ran as far away from Him as he could. Now, look at him. Look where all those choices got him. A mangled corpse lying in the dirt, distorted, disfigured, and hideous, getting eaten by crows and worms. In trying to destroy God's image, he destroyed himself. He wasted his one life running backward, and no one will ever care about what he thought he was going to accomplish. You ask me how I believe in God? I look at this thing before me, and I ask you, what choice do you have?"

Keith sat in silence.

"But what do I know? I'm just a dumb redneck who fixed air conditioners for a living." He got to his feet. "Well, I better get back. I'm helping them start work on the church." He looked at the rope on the ground beside Keith and picked it up. "Oh, good. I needed a rope, but I couldn't find any. Can I borrow this?" He took a couple steps and turned back to Keith. "You weren't using it, were you?"

CHAPTER TWENTY-ONE

Keith turned and looked at his brother. "No. No, I wasn't."

"Cool. Thanks. I'll bring you some more soup later today. Hopefully, you'll be feeling better by then."

He *was* feeling a little better. He was no longer nauseated, and the pain in his head was not quite as sharp. When Keith could no longer hear his brother's footsteps, he crawled back to his tent and dragged himself onto the cot. He looked around for a second as he set the bottle of tea on the ground beside him. His pistol was gone. The corner of his mouth twitched up in a slight smirk. He would go on, he thought. He would embrace a life of duty, to continue, suffering through whatever came, and living the best he could as he tried to help his neighbors and rebuild the world. He could do that. Death would come soon enough, and the rest was out of his hands. He rolled onto his back and drifted off to sleep, imagining a cabin full of books with a warm fire on the hearth.

Day 196

Since the day of the first battle with the Servants of Gaia, people began developing symptoms of some unknown disease. It spread throughout the community like wildfire. The doctors cleared out the barn and the tent, school lessons were suspended, and they quarantined themselves in tents and houses and drank teas of pine needles, mullein, comfrey, and plantain. They made broth from bones and turkey tail mushrooms, unable to keep down much else. Several of the older residents succumbed to the illness, but strangely, it seemed to have little effect on the children. The symptoms lasted for weeks in some cases, but once the afflicted recovered, they went to work caring for the sick. Most of the ones who were still recovering from wounds sustained in the battle were too weak to survive the new affliction, and by the middle of August, only one-hundred-forty-three residents remained, including the refugees and the infants born since the blackout.

The families who had lost their homes in the battle took up residence in the empty houses still standing, and some moved in with other families until new houses could be built. By the third week of August, necessity demanded that they prioritize the reconstruction of housing above the quarantining of the sick. The disease was a danger, but winter was certain. Anyone who was able to work was needed to help with the building. Having no more fuel, they couldn't even run the sawmill to cut lumber. The buildings would have to be constructed in the old way, with hewn logs and timber framing. To complete the church, they started cutting down the telephone poles along the road, and they dragged them to the site of the old church with the jackstock and draft horses.

As the fifty men and women labored in concert to complete the project, small teams of scavengers were sent out to find fuel and supplies. Keith and Joe led the expeditions. They took only the strongest young men, heavily armed, to go search for supplies or people to trade with. As it turned out, this precaution was no longer as necessary as they had expected.

In the cities, the only people who survived past the first two months were those who had turned to robbing their neighbors for provisions. Gangs were formed, and they fought one another for territory and supplies. Only the strongest and most ruthless survived the constant warfare. By the summer, the cities were completely depleted of food. Every store had been emptied, every stockpile ransacked, every cupboard raided. Those who had any ability to grow food were robbed by those who did not. The pets had all been eaten, and in desperation, some of the city-dwellers had turned to cannibalizing the dead. The gangs moved out of the desolate areas and began raiding the surrounding rural population. When they encountered communities of the more self-reliant hunters, homesteaders, and farmers, however, they were no match for the men and women who had relied on their weapons and skills their entire lives. The gangs wreaked havoc on the homesteaders, but eventually, they were destroyed. As it turned out, preying on one's betters was not a tenable plan for survival.

Few trees still stood in Bloomington. Many of the houses and buildings had been destroyed. Trash and rotting skeletons littered the ground. The cities, including this one, were barren wastelands, artificial deserts, now almost entirely uninhabited. Keith watched as a mangy dog trotted across the road with the gray-green carcass of a tiny baby in its mouth. The destruction had been almost total. Keith hardly saw a window that hadn't been broken, nearly half of the buildings had been burnt severely, if not completely, and what remained standing was vandalized with occult symbols, gang tags, and messages for help. The air stank. Areas of the sidewalks and streets were covered with dried feces and stained with blood and the residue of decomposed bodies. The scavengers, however, were able to find several vehicles which still had fuel in their tanks.

The next day, they returned with horse-drawn wagons and siphoned gasoline into fuel jugs. As they nervously looked around with their weapons ready, siphoning fuel from a car, they heard a squeal from behind a long-since overflowed dumpster. Out of the rubbish pile, a shopping cart emerged, pushed by a disheveled, old vagrant. His greasy hair fell halfway down his back, and his matted beard covered his chest. The light shone and sparkled off the millions of dollars' worth of gold and diamonds he was wearing and piling in his cart. The shopping cart was mounded with luxury suits and dresses, designer shoes and purses, and gold watches, diamond necklaces, rings, and bracelets. The vagrant stopped and looked at them, and across his grimy, emaciated face, spread a toothless, senseless smile. The man chuckled and continued on, pushing his cart God only knows where. Unmolested, they brought the fuel back to

Mount Sinai, and once again, they were able to operate their chainsaws, trucks, tractors, generators, and sawmill.

They returned two days later to get more, and as they pulled into the parking lot of the shopping mall, they found another group of people likewise filling gas cans and loading them into a truck. They kept behind a wall of parked vehicles one-hundred yards from the group and watched the scavengers who had clearly seen them. For a couple of minutes, the two groups stared at one another from behind cover, keeping their weapons at the ready. Then, Keith saw an American flag raised up on a pole above the other group's truck. He pulled out a folded, homemade flag from their own truck, tied it onto the handle of a shovel, and raised it high in the air in response.

"God bless America!" Keith shouted.

"Long live the republic!" a man shouted back. "Put your guns down, boys," the man said. "Those are Americans."

There was laughter from both sides as they walked out and met between the rows of dead cars.

"Y'all are a sight for sore eyes," said the man. "Weird, ain't it? We figured there would be more people like us around here, but for the last six months, we haven't seen anyone outside our community besides a gang of thieves. They didn't last too long in our neck of the woods. Name's Joshua. Joshua Jackson." The man put out his hand with a smile.

Keith shook it and replied. "Keith Rawlings. Good to meet you. Where you guys from?"

The man shook hands with Joe and the others standing with him. "Mount Hope. Over in Greene County." The man spat on the pavement. "You?"

"Mount Sinai. A few miles east of here."

"Not too far from town then," the man said with a nod. "You run into any thieves from the city? We heard about a big group that really terrorized the neighborhood for a while. Haven't seen any sign of them lately. Called themselves the Servants of Goya or some nonsense."

"Yeah. We ran into them. They're out of business now."

"I heard they had more than a thousand members," Joshua said. "Some people say a lot more. Wiped out every other gang in town and killed or enslaved most of the towns-folk that didn't run away."

"You heard right."

"You must have had some hell on your hands with them. How'd you stop 'em?"

"We had some damn good men," one of the young men said. "And maybe a little help from above."

"That's right," said Joe.

The man nodded. "Well, anybody that defends the republic is a friend to me. We ought to work together. Maybe we can start to clean up some of this mess."

"I agree," Keith said. "We'll talk it over with the community. Take a vote on forming an alliance."

"Maybe we can meet here again same time next week and do some trading too."

"We ought to do that." Keith took out a notebook and wrote it down.

"Call it a date then," said Joshua.

"Yeah," Joe added. "You say you're from Mount Hope. Do you know anybody by the name of Daniels out there?"

"Daniels?" The man scratched his head and turned to look over his shoulder at another man behind him. "We've got a Daniels family with us, don't we?"

"Yeah, I know 'em," the man said. "Dale and Beverly Daniels. They got a nice farm out there where we get beef. Big family living together. They're all doing good last I talked to 'em. See 'em at church every week."

"Those are our cousins," Joe said excitedly. "Beverly's our aunt."

"We ought to bring them with us, so you can meet up. Speaking of family, is there anybody by the name of Faulkner out by you?"

Day 199

When the scavengers returned, a meeting was called for all who could make it. Once again, they met in the barn, and Keith told the assembly about their meeting with the representatives from Mount Hope. The vote was taken, and it was decided that they would ally with the Mount Hope residents. Upon the decision, they decided it was time to elect a new sheriff. Five weeks had passed since Jack Winters had died, and in the dim light of the barn, surrounded by the paintings of the heroes of Mount Sinai, the neighbors pondered who was capable of filling the shoes of such a giant among men. After a moment of silence, it was proposed that Jim Baker should be the new sheriff. The vote was unanimous, and Jim Baker reluctantly accepted the position. They also needed a new judge after the previous judge had died from the plague. Baker nominated Eric Jorgenson. Tim Faulkner seconded the nomination, and the vote passed. No one was more qualified to judge cases than the preacher, who was well-versed in both Constitutional and Biblical law and had shown his character and leadership in battle. Upon his acceptance of the role, Eric proposed the election of a mayor, and he nominated Tim Faulkner for the position. Keith, Joe, and Jim all seconded the nomination, and when the vote was taken, Tim was appointed the new Mayor of Mount Sinai.

Jim Baker's first act as sheriff was to collect any usable supplies from Scott Adams' house and make sure that the house was not sabotaged. He left a deputy standing in the driveway as he approached the house. Walking up the path, he carefully looked around for trip wires or pipes like those he had seen used in the battle. He saw none. He walked around the house, examining anything that looked out of place. Satisfied that nothing was amiss, he took out the key-chain that he found on Scott's body after the battle.

Stepping inside, Jim lit a candle and gingerly stepped over the vinyl floor of the hallway. He went around the house, looking at the rooms. Everything was fairly neat and clean, certainly by Mount Sinai standards. He opened the drapes over the windows, letting light into the house. The cupboard was still stocked with cans and dried foods. He would take those to the church to be donated to those who had lost their homes, he decided. Looking out the kitchen window at the overgrown, failed garden patch, Jim smiled to himself. There were no booby traps. Scott was crazy, but not that crazy.

Beside the kitchen counter, there was a door. Jim opened it and walked to the basement. The familiar shelves were still stacked with supplies, but they were far less crowded than they had been the last time he had seen the room. The table stood against the far wall, beneath the maps and charts and diagrams. Jim looked at the radio among the ammo cans and batteries, and reaching to flip a switch, he stopped himself and thought for a second. He had no idea how to use this high-tech equipment, and if he pushed the wrong button or something, he might mess it up and make it more difficult for them to use. They needed information, but he would have to find someone who could operate the radio. Maybe Tim could figure it out, he thought. Looking down at the notebook on the table, Jim opened it and flipped through some of the pages. He shut it and took it with him as he left the house.

Day 202

With the rafters in place, workers took up froes and shingling hatchets to cut the cedar shakes for the roof as the split timber decking was nailed to the beams. There were a few neighbors who still had large quantities of nails which they donated to the project, and any nails that could be salvaged from scrap lumber piles or ash pits or coffee cans in garages were collected and reused if possible. For the framing, they had used wooden dowels to secure the joints, so that only the roofing would require the precious nails. Even with this frugality, they would need to acquire more nails from scavenging or trading to rebuild the destroyed houses. They would cross that bridge when they reached it. For now, no one on Mount Sinai was without a roof over his head. Some had moved in with friends and family in the community, and others were able to occupy the houses vacated by the deceased. Winter would be upon them soon enough, and after what the community had gone through over the past six months, no one was denying shelter to the neighbors they had left. They had come to regard one another as family.

As the work on the new church building slowly progressed, Tim Faulkner worked with Jim Baker to figure out how to use the radio. All of Scott's batteries were dead, and Scott had given the last of his supply of gasoline to fuel the trucks that were needed to evacuate the wounded in the battle, so the first thing they had to do was get fuel for the generator. After recharging the batteries, Tim began flipping switches, pressing buttons, and turning dials. He was able to get the screen to light up, but not much else was happening. There were no instruction manuals, and they hadn't found any notebooks with information on how to operate the radio.

"This might take me some time," Tim said. He got on his hands and knees and began tracing the cables and wires beneath the table with his fingers in the dark and quiet basement.

Jim squinted at the hastily scrawled chicken scratches on the notebook in his hands. Some of the notes were unintelligible. There were abbreviations he couldn't interpret, one word bullet points, and illegible handwriting. As he studied the last page carefully, his eyes opened wide, and he jumped out of his chair. "Tim!" he shouted.

Tim jumped and banged his head on the bottom of the table. "Damn it! What?" He put a hand on the top of his head and crawled out from under the table.

"They're running a blockade around the country! They're cutting us off!"

"What? Who?"

"The Chinese! That's why the world is switching to Chinese currency! That's why there's been no government response! They must have done this to us!"

Tim frowned. "Or if they didn't, they certainly weren't going to let a crisis go to waste."

"No one is going to tangle with the Chinese Navy. I bet they're planning to invade!"

"Keep your voice down, would you?"

"What are we going to do?" Jim paced around the room, shaking his head. "I mean, we got to... There must be... We need..." his voiced trailed off.

Tim sat quietly for several moments. "What do you think we *can* do? If that's true, we don't have a chance."

"But we have to... There's got to be something—someone who can help us."

"Do me a favor, Jim. Let's keep this to ourselves. We don't need to cause a panic right now. And we don't need people to despair going into winter. We're barely hanging on as it is."

"You want to just ignore this?" Jim looked disbelievingly at Tim, his fists clenched.

"No." Tim shook his head. "We'll talk to Eric, and maybe with some of the guys from Mount Hope when we meet with them, but there's no point in spreading rumors around. We don't even know if that's legitimate. It might just be some theory he heard from somebody, or one he came up with himself. He was kind of crazy, after all."

"People have a right to know, Tim."

"We'll tell them. But we need more information first. Let me get this thing working and see if we can corroborate it before we give people another reason to kill themselves."

"Alright, Tim. I'll keep my mouth shut, but we better figure this out. Fast."

As the workers nailed down the decking, a man looked up from the rooftop to the highway beyond. "Someone's coming," he called down to the preacher below.

The preacher laid down his froe and the wood he was splitting into shakes before looking up at the man. "How many?"

"A large group. They've got trucks. And trailers. There's people riding in the beds."

"Are they armed?"

"I can't tell."

"Alright. Get off the roof. Everyone, get to cover. Do not fire unless they attack first."

A wave of fear and excitement swept over the workers as they took up their weapons and got into defensive positions behind the berm of the railroad and the walls of burnt-out cars and logs.

The preacher looked at the Rawlings men, "You guys, stay with me, please."

Keith, Joe, and Kent stood beside the preacher with their weapons at the ready, looking toward the horizon.

The preacher took his rifle and peered through his scope at the group coming over the rise. "One, two, three, four, five trucks with trailers." The convoy passed over the rise and out of view behind the crest of the ridge.

They waited, but the convoy did not appear. Then, a figure emerged on the horizon, walking along the highway. He held up a staff with an American flag waving in the wind above his head, and he waved it back and forth as he walked toward the barricade.

"It's Davis," the preacher said, looking through his scope. "He found his family."

"That's quite a large family," Joe commented.

The man strode forward, keeping the flag raised over his head as he closed the distance. Behind him, the trucks followed in a slow procession. When they were within fifty yards of the barricade, the preacher and the Rawlings men met Jeremiah Davis on the highway.

"I found them hiding out in the woods," said Jeremiah. "They had been attacked by a gang from Indianapolis. They fought them off, but their homes were all destroyed. This is what remains of their church congregation."

"Did you inform them of our laws?" The preacher inquired.

"I did. They've all agreed."

"Ask them to come out and talk with us."

The refugees dismounted from the vehicles and assembled in front of the barricades. People of every walk of life gathered to join the community—a family of Indian-American gas station owners, a family of Chinese-American restaurant owners, a Brazilian-American truck driver and his Irish-American wife, a Mexican-American math teacher and her Puerto Rican-American husband, a Nigerian-American welder and his Italian-American wife, German-American farmers, a Tanzanian-American roofer, a Filipino-American family of factory workers, a Cuban-American carpenter, a Venezuelan-American electrician, a Swedish-American plumber, a Japanese-American chef, and a French-American banker. They had children of all ages with them and two elderly people who walked with canes.

"This is my family," Jeremiah said. "And they're here to join our community and help rebuild."

The preacher looked over his shoulder and called out to the residents of Mount Sinai, "Come out and witness this, friends."

Neighbors arose from their covered positions and slung their weapons as they congregated behind the barricade to look at the newcomers.

The preacher waited for everyone to assemble and glanced around at all their faces before speaking. "We've made a commitment to rebuild the country and the lives we once had, and we've agreed to take in any refugees who would choose to live by our rules, work to provide for themselves and their families, and be loyal to the community. If these people agree to share in our labor, defend the community, and live in accordance with our laws, will you accept them as your neighbors, to live and work and raise their children alongside you?" The preacher paused and waited for their answer.

"Yes, we will," a woman said. Several voices agreed.

"If anyone objects, let him speak now."

There were no objectors.

"Very well." The preacher turned his attention to the group of refugees. "Here, in the community of Mount Sinai, we live and govern ourselves by the principles set forth in the founding documents of the United States and the laws of the God of the Bible. If you wish to be a part of this community, you will respect and adhere to those laws, and you will not try to change them. The penalty for crimes against the property of your fellow citizens will be debt-slavery. You will be forced to repay the victim of your crime with your labor, and you will labor to repay the community for your violation of its trust. Lying and stealing will not be tolerated. Murder, rape, abuse of children, the destruction of another's house, or any such crime will be punished by death. Slander of our God, our country, or the legitimacy of our founding principles will be treated as a renunciation of citizenship and of one's rights. If you do these things or try to discredit our institutions or spread antithetical views to your fellow citizens, you will be forced out of our community at gunpoint. Whatever your lifestyle, religion, or political views were in the past is irrelevant; if you choose to join this community, you are swearing an oath to support and live by our laws and to defend our values with your lives if necessary. This was a nation built, not on blood and soil, but on ideas.

Therefore, to be a citizen of such a country means to adopt and believe and live by those unchanging principles. Those are the conditions for membership. Carefully consider these terms before making your decision. Each of you must agree to the terms if you want to live here."

The refugees looked around at one another and talked amongst themselves.

"We accept your terms," one said, after a couple of minutes.

"We need all of you to agree," the preacher replied. "If you agree to the terms, raise your hand."

All of the refugees raised their hands.

"Anyone who does not agree, raise your hand now."

No hands were raised.

The preacher nodded and looked back at the residents of Mount Sinai. "You are all witnesses to the oath taken by these people. Open the gate." He turned back to the refugees and smiled. "Welcome to Mount Sinai. Meet your neighbors."

Day 206

A week after their meeting with the residents of Mount Hope, they loaded up three trucks full of people and the items they were bringing to trade. Driving through the ruins of town, they saw signs of life returning to the desolate landscape. Small saplings were pushing through the unmown grass. Birds flitted about the air. Squirrels barked from rooftops and ran over the sidewalks. Rabbits munched on clover in front of abandoned houses. Two deer ran across the highway in front of them just as they were turning onto the road to the mall.

When they pulled into the parking lot, they found the residents of Mount Hope awaiting them with four vehicles laden with items for barter. The trucks were surrounded by armed security who watched the approaching vehicles intently. When Joe parked the truck on the other side of a row of cars, Keith got out and raised the flag. They watched as the other group raised their own flag in response before calling out to their passengers to meet their new friends. Weapons were slung, and the groups met between the rows of dust-covered vehicles.

When the Rawlings family recognized their cousins, Faye nearly burst into tears. It seemed like years had passed since they had last seen them. The whole family turned out to meet them. They hugged one another, and then, Beverly pulled away to look at them all again.

"We didn't recognize you guys with the beards. And Kent, you've lost so much weight!"

"Me? I've always been in shape. Look at Dale!"

His brother-in-law's baggy pants were being held up by suspenders and a belt with a dozen new holes drilled in the leather.

Beverly laughed at the sight of her shrunken husband. "He hasn't been this size since high school," she said, wiping her eyes.

Beside them, Josh was picking up his nieces and nephews, hugging them and patting them on the heads. "Oh, I missed you guys."

"Look at my puppy!" shouted the youngest Faulkner, holding the beagle in his stubby arms.

Josh scratched the creature's ears as it licked the child's face and wagged its tail.

Everyone shook hands with their new acquaintances and made introductions. Then, the trading began. Like generations before them, going to town was now an exciting event, and the traders gleefully went around to see what there was to buy, talking and joking with one another.

Tim pulled Josh aside to talk with Jim away from the crowd.

The residents of Mount Sinai had been without salt for weeks now. The Faulkners, and a few others with sizeable stockpiles, generously traded within the community, but after months away from supply chains, eventually, the community had run out, and it was one more item they had to learn to live without. The Mount Hope community was made up of mostly sheep, cattle, and pig farmers, and they kept massive quantities of mineral salt for the livestock. After a bit of haggling, the residents of Mount Sinai were able to trade a couple of radios, rechargeable batteries, and some weapons taken off their enemies for five-hundred pounds of the stuff. They traded soap, candles, clothing, homemade toothpaste, maple syrup, ammunition, tools, honey, canned goods, and even some grain alcohol. After several hours of laughing and arguing over prices, everyone left, feeling happy with the trades. They agreed to meet up again the following week, and before they parted ways, they gathered around, holding hands as a preacher from Mount Hope said a prayer for them.

Driving back through the dead cars pushed to the sides of the roads, they passed a man and woman walking into town with backpacks. The couple got away from the road when they saw the trucks coming, but when Joe waved at them, Keith saw a hand wave back in his rearview mirror.

Day 231

With the refugees came many skilled workers who helped to accelerate the construction of the church. They not only brought a diligent workforce with them, they brought a large supply of tools and building materials as well. Among their supplies, was an immense quantity of nails. While the shakes were being nailed down on the roof, the added laborers were able to construct an outhouse behind the church, several benches, and a pulpit. When the benches were completed and the roof finished, all the neighbors assembled to watch the completion of the project with the final piece put in place.

On the morning of the first day of autumn, the old bell was cleaned off and polished and hoisted up to the bell tower with a block and tackle. When it was mounted on the yoke in the tower, the laborers fastened the rope and rang the bell. The crowd erupted in cheers and applause, and the preacher stepped in front of the doorway to address the crowd.

"Friends, we've been through a lot in the past few months, but with the help of the Lord, we have come together as a community and accomplished something amazing. We have completed the first step in rebuilding a nation that was founded on Biblical principles but had been torn down a piece at a time over many decades. We have seen what a world without hope in God looks like, and we have turned away from that path. Our work is not finished. We have much more to do. The road ahead will be hard, but with God, all things are possible. We must never lose hope. We must never lose faith. We will love our neighbors as ourselves, and we will not give up on God or on each other. Today is the first day of fall. Let us consecrate this day with prayer and singing. The door of the church stands open."

The preacher opened the door as the people cheered. A few tears were shed as the neighbors walked past the grave-yard and looked over the rows of markers beneath the flag. They filed in through the door, carrying Bibles with them, shaking hands with the preacher, and hugging one another.

The Rawlings family stood outside as the last of the group entered the doorway. They looked solemnly at Keith and said nothing as the sound of cheerful voices emanated from the church.

"Come on, Keith," Joe said. "Come sit with us."

Keith looked at them but said nothing. His face turned toward the graves, and his jaw clenched. Faye's eyes began to water as Kent turned and went inside. Lynn took her mother's hand and followed Kent into the church. The preacher shook their hands and walked in with them. Joe stayed behind with his brother.

Joe shook his head and spat on the road. "Keith, I know it's hard, but just try. Let it go. Let *her* go."

Keith's fists tightened as he looked into his brother's eyes.

"Step out of the shadow. There's light out here. Just waiting for you." Joe took a step toward the church and turned around again. "Do you have somewhere better to be?"

Keith watched his brother walk through the door of the church, and he turned to the graveyard. Walking through the rows of stones, he read the names of the dead. Tyler, Jacobs, Campbell, Adams, Nielson, Winters. He lost count of how many they had lost. He sank to his knees among the graves and wept for his country, for his life, and for the lives of those he loved. The flag flapped in the breeze above, and Keith looked up. A warm, golden beam of sunlight shone out from behind the church and glowed upon the banner. It glinted off the staff and shimmered on his face. The sound of joyous singing poured out from the church, and Keith rose to his feet. The sunlight shone around the church in a radiant halo, and Keith wiped the tears from his face as he stepped out of the shadow. The brilliant, golden glow washed over him, and warmth flowed through his body as he strode forward, forward through the open door.

Epilogue

Day 399

Malik and Jordan hugged each of the Rawlings family members.

"Be careful out there," Jordan said, squeezing Lynn's arm.

Malik patted Kent on the back as he embraced him. "Y'all hurry back now, you hear me?"

"Yes, sir," Kent said.

Faye squeezed the baby's hand and smiled as the girl stuck out her tongue.

"You Ready?" Kent asked, looking at his wife.

"Yeah." Faye looked nervous.

Keith, Joe, and Lynn piled into the bed and shut the tailgate as Kent and Faye shut the doors of the cab.

"Don't worry," Jordan said through the open window. "We'll take good care of everything while you're gone."

"I know you will. I'm just nervous about the trip. Thank you, guys, again. We'll be back as soon as we can. Hopefully tonight."

"Don't do anything I wouldn't do," Malik said.

"I make no promises," Kent replied.

The McCormicks waved as the truck rolled up the long, muddy driveway. Jordan smiled at the baby in her arms and held the child's little hand up. Little Victoria's tiny fingers moved up and down as she giggled.

When they reached the top of the driveway, Kent pulled onto the road and wove through the cars. He stopped at the broken stop sign at the end of Mount Sinai Road and looked at the church standing prominently above the landscape and the flag flying in the graveyard beside.

They no longer kept a solid barricade at the end of Mount Sinai Road. The cars had been rolled into two columns, forming a funnel through which traffic could pass unhindered until the alarm was sounded. The community had expanded to nearly double its size after the residents of Mount Sinai had allied with a group from Unionville and had reappropriated the vacated houses along the highway for miles in both directions. Now, the first blockade was positioned on the highway, at the edge of town, near the ruins of the old gas station, but the alarm had not been sounded for an attack for several months.

They sat for a few seconds, looking at the church.

"Do you think it's safe?" Faye asked.

"You know the answer to that. Of course, it's not safe. The question is: Is it worth it?"

Faye nodded. "It is."

"Alright then." Kent turned onto the highway and started for the west.

Neighbors were working on repairs to houses, and they waved as the Rawlings family passed by. At the blockade, they stopped and waited for the car to be rolled out of the way. The young guards waved at them and told them to be careful and hurry back, and the old, blue Ford rolled on. The roads around Bloomington were clear of obstructions now. The dead cars on the roads had been pushed to the sides to allow traffic to pass, and Kent Rawlings eased the truck along, passing under lifeless stoplights as he drove.

Keith, Joe, and Lynn sat in the bed of the truck on cushions beneath the camper shell, staring out the windows, looking for signs of trouble. In the past year, the farthest they had driven was to their aunt and uncle's house in the

Mount Hope community, and now, they were finally going to cross the state line.

Over the past few months, several families had ventured outside the community to find relatives and friends. With every new group of immigrants being brought into the community, Faye looked at Kent with anxiety and longing in her eyes. Kent knew what she was thinking—what she had thought about every day since the blackout—he simply nodded every time and went to make improvements to the truck or take stock of their preparations. Throughout the fall, they had to prioritize preparing for winter. Harvesting and canning food, cutting firewood, and building or repairing shelter for their neighbors were the highest priorities. The months of December, January, and February were out of the question. There was ice on the roads, and the truck was far less reliable in the cold. In March, they had a break in the weather. The temperature hovered between the mid fifties and low seventies for two weeks. The roads were clear, the skies were clear, the gangs were gone, and their supplies were renewed. After talking with the community leaders, they decided now was the time to go. Faye hadn't had a peaceful night's sleep in over a year, and they couldn't continue living with the guilt of not doing all they could to find her family. Thirteen months after the blackout, they were all internally bracing themselves for what they might find, but they were going.

Just as they had seen on their previous trips through town, every church in Bloomington had been destroyed. Weeds grew up through the cracks in the sidewalks and asphalt. Massive ash heaps were all that remained of many of the houses in town. Others were scorched or severely damaged in various ways, but as they traveled farther away from the city, the landscape looked more like how they remembered in a past life. There were fewer cows in the pastures, the vast corn and soybean fields were overgrown with weeds, but the farms remained, functioning as they had for generations before, sustenance farming done the old way.

When they came to roadblocks along the way, they got nervous but explained where they were going and why. Keith, Joe, and Lynn sat in the back, with weapons ready in case of an ambush, but they found no cause to use them. Along their path, were mostly friendly communities who would let them pass through or tell them how to go around. The highways were still cluttered with dead cars, but they had little trouble with maneuvering through the lines of lifeless, rusting metal and fading, dusty plastic.

The interstate was even less of a hindrance, since the majority of personal vehicles were parked in business parking lots. Most of what sat stationary on the interstates were delivery trucks and semis.

"Man," Kent said, shaking his head. "I can't imagine what it was like for these truckers being stranded hundreds of miles from home."

When they came to a construction site, Kent pulled off the road, drove across the median and passed by the obstruction on the other side.

Finally, the truck passed the sign reading: "Welcome to Illinois: The Land of Lincoln." It had taken them nearly three hours to reach the border with all the obstructions and roadblocks they had to bypass. Now, on I-74, they would head straight into Champaign, where Faye's father and aunt had lived in a small townhouse.

They encountered no roadblocks on the way into town, but as they drove through Champaign, they could see that the college town had been ravaged nearly as badly as Bloomington had. The churches were destroyed, and many of the buildings were reduced to rubble. Scattered bones and trash littered the roads, broken glass glittered in the sun, and graffiti covered the walls of banks and businesses. Kent took a detour, keeping away from the campus. Like in Bloomington, many of the houses showed signs of extensive fire damage, either from makeshift woodstoves or from arson. Faye chewed her bottom lip as she took in the sight of the destruction.

When they turned into the cul-de-sac, the place was empty. Squirrels, rabbits, and birds hopped through the road and long, dead grass of the yards, but they saw no people. All the trees had been cut down, and one lay across the crushed roof of a house. Two other houses had been burned, and cars sat in the entrances of driveways with trash piled inside the vehicles and around mailboxes. When they came to the house, they found that it was still intact. Some of the windows were broken, and garbage was strewn about the driveway and front lawn, but the house still stood. Kent turned the truck around in the circle and parked in front of the driveway.

Kent placed a hand on Faye's arm as she opened the door. "Maybe I should go in alone."

Faye looked at him with a furrowed brow. "No, I'm going in."

"Faye..." Kent tilted his head and kept his voice low and calm. "You might not want to..."

"I know what you're saying, Kent. But I'm going in." She climbed out of the truck and made her way to the front door.

Lynn and Joe climbed out of the bed.

"Somebody needs to stay with the truck," Kent said.

"I got it," Keith replied, standing beside the tailgate, holding his rifle against his chest.

Joe and Lynn followed Kent to the front door as Faye began to open it.

"Slow down, Faye," Kent cautioned. "We're coming."

Faye ignored him and pushed the door open. The lock had been broken off, and the frame was splintered. The resistance she felt came from a dented microwave sitting against the door. As they stepped inside, they found the house had been ransacked. Broken glass and empty tin cans covered the floor.

"Dad!" Faye called.

"Faye," Kent began, keeping his voice low. "Careful."

Something stirred from behind one of the walls.

"Dad, it's Faye!"

The sound of bottles skidding across the floor echoed through the house, and they heard rapid footsteps running toward them. Joe pulled out his pistol as a dirty figure ran out from the hallway and bolted out the back door. Faye jumped as the man scrambled past them and stumbled down the steps of the porch before sprinting through the backyard and out of sight. As they watched him go, they noticed that the wooden privacy fence was gone, probably burned for heat in the first winter.

They searched around the house, finding nothing but trash, empty pill bottles, and smashed picture glass. Everything useful had been taken. Every tool, every blanket, every cushion, the knives and forks and spoons, along with every piece of wood or flammable material, was gone. There was no one there.

"My sister probably took them to her house," Faye said. "We have to go there."

Kent pursed his lips in a sympathetic smile. "Of course, we will." He followed Faye back out to the truck. "We need to refuel first."

They pulled gas cans out of the bed and topped off the fuel tank before loading up and heading out once more, traveling west on I-72.

It took almost two hours to get to Springfield. They saw more packs of feral dogs than people. Two old cars passed them on the highway, and an Amish man drove a horse and buggy down the road with a shotgun in his lap, but the rest of the drive through the state was eerily uneventful.

The big city of Springfield was a disaster. As soon as they came within two miles of the city, the stench became overpowering. Before the blackout, Springfield, Illinois had a population roughly fifty percent larger than Bloomington, Indiana's. Like Bloomington, it was surrounded by farmland, but its people were densely packed in high-rise buildings, entirely dependent on supply chains for their existence. While not as condensed as cities like New York, it was still a large city where virtually no one knew how to provide for himself. Everyone who didn't immediately move out and find a relative in the country with whom to live, either turned to raiding their neighbors or died. After a couple of months, there was nothing left to steal, and the gangs moved out of the city or killed each other for the last scraps of sustenance. The city was so saturated with death, that even after the bones of the dead had been picked clean by scavengers, the odor of rotten flesh lingered. The removal of America's technology had amounted to the deadliest genocide in human history.

The Rawlings family moved through the city as quickly as possible, taking I-55 until they reconnected with I-72. Around Lake Springfield, they saw people camping and fishing on the shore. Scores of boats dotted the water. Kent kept driving, hoping to not be noticed by desperate city-dwellers. Faye's sister had lived just outside of Springfield, on the western edge of the city. Seeing the results of the blackout in Springfield, Kent doubted they would have survived here, but they had come this far, and he wouldn't dissuade Faye from doing all she could to find her family.

Faye reminded Kent where to turn, and he pulled into the subdivision, parking the truck in front of the house. The door had been forced open and was unlatched. Kent followed Faye into the house, glancing at the graffiti on the siding. The house was less cluttered than the other, but it too was empty of useful items, and once again, they found no one present. A thick layer of dust covered everything in the house.

"Hello!" Faye called, moving quickly from room to room. "Is anyone here? It's Faye!" Her pace quickened as she frantically searched.

Kent stood, quietly leaning against the refrigerator, waiting for Faye to finish. Joe and Lynn left the house to help Keith refuel.

"They're not here," said Faye. "They must be at Kevin's parents' house. Or maybe they're with my cousin Janine." Faye paced around the room, staring ahead, focused on something abstract, searching her memory for all the possible places her family could be. "They could be with Greg Williams down by the old farm, or..."

"Or a hundred other places," Kent interrupted.

Faye stopped and looked at him, red in the face.

"Faye, we tried. We're running low on gas, and the sun's going down. We don't want to spend the night out here. We've got a six-hour drive back home as it is."

"But if we just check," Faye began. "I'm sure we can..." Tears began running down her face. "They're out there! Somewhere!" she screamed. "I have to find them!"

Kent stepped toward her, reaching out to pull her close to him. She backed away and smacked his arms away from her. "No!" she screamed. And she threw her fists at her husband's face and chest and shoulders. "No! No! No! No! No!"

Kent squeezed her to his chest as she struggled to breathe. She trembled in his arms, sobbing. They stood there for several minutes, locked together in her sister's kitchen, saying nothing as the noonday sun began its descent into the west.

Faye was silent on the ride back. She stared ahead with a blank expression on her face. No one spoke. As the family drove east, around the edge of the city, they noticed a change in the atmosphere. It was hard to say what it was, exactly, but everything seemed even quieter than before. Keith and Joe had a bad feeling and looked nervously out the windows. Kent slowed the truck. He could sense it too. With the windows rolled down, he tried to listen for strange noises, but over the sound of the truck's engine, they heard nothing.

"Do you smell that?" Joe said through the cab's rear window.

"I smell it." Kent pulled over beside a stalled semi-truck just before the bridge over I-55. He shut off the engine.

"What is it?" Lynn asked. "Is something wrong with the truck?"

"No, I don't think so," Kent said quietly. He looked around. "It smells like diesel."

"Get down," Keith whispered. "Someone's coming."

Kent slumped in his seat as the muffled thumping of hooves sounded off the ground beside them. A big man on a horse rode past with a rifle in one hand and a pump-action slug gun slung across his back.

Keith flipped the safety off of his rifle and pointed his barrel toward the windshield as the man stopped in front of the truck and looked out over the Interstate. The man wore hunting camouflage with no hat or sunglasses, and as Keith studied his face, he thought he recognized the man. The big man looked through the scope of his rifle along the interstate, and a black Labrador retriever sniffed around the blue truck before putting its paws up on the door and growling. The man on the horse lowered his rifle and turned the horse to the north.

"Let's go, Mickey," said the man.

Keith recognized the voice, and after hearing the name of the dog, he was certain that the man was one of the members of his old platoon, Michael Sherman.

The dog followed the rider off the interstate and down the hillside into a brush thicket growing beside the overpass. As the man rode toward a stand of trees, he motioned to someone with his arms, and Keith saw movement in the thickets as several camouflaged forms moved through the brush. They disappeared from sight, and the smell of diesel, blown through the open windows by the southern breeze, grew stronger in the air.

"What do you think that guy was doing?" Lynn whispered.

"Be quiet," Kent warned.

A humming noise reverberated off the buildings as a miniature aircraft buzzed overhead, traveling in a straight line above the interstate. As it passed out of sight, the humming faded into the distance.

"What was that?" Joe whispered. "Did you see it?"

"A drone," Keith replied.

From the south, came the growl of engines rumbling toward them. Kent and Faye sat up in their seats, and Keith, Joe, and Lynn squeezed forward to look out the windshield. A convoy of machines streamed up from the south in a single file line, driving forward through the halted traffic, with a lead vehicle shoving cars out of the way.

"Do you think the government is finally bringing aid?" Lynn asked hopefully.

"Those aren't American," Keith said somberly.

Passing under the overpass, a massive column of military tanks rolled north along the interstate. Behind them, a line of dozens of six-wheeled trucks followed—all the machines bore a single red star on the side. When they passed out of sight, the Rawlings family sat in silence, listening to the rumbling and the screeching of cars being crushed and shoved aside.

"What just happened?" Joe said flatly. "Did they win?"

"They didn't beat us," Kent said. "We beat ourselves." The old man shook his head as he reached for the key in the ignition. "We forfeited our own country." Tears welled in his eyes, and his voice quivered. "It's going to be a hard road ahead. Kids, I'm sorry this is the world you inherited."

Keith nodded. "It was a great country."

Kent started the truck and put it into gear. The fumes of death and diesel lingered in the air, and as the sun went down on the West, they drove along the roads less traveled, back to the beautiful country.

Second Epilogue

They didn't learn until much later what had happened to their country. It was pieced together from information gathered by various groups they connected with. The news acquired over the radios was difficult to ascertain. Theorists in other countries shared their opinions until they were shut down, and their information was hardly reliable. Most of what they heard from radio operators discussing news was the product of censorship and propaganda. On the coasts, operators told of fishing boats that went out to sea and never returned. It wasn't clear what had happened to them. Some said they died in storms. Some said they fled to find refuge in areas that may not have been affected. Still, others believed they had run into a naval blockade of a foreign military and had been apprehended or sunk.

As time went on, talk of a military blockade continued, but very little from the outside world corroborated this information. Official news said that the Chinese were sending aid to their allies in America, and the Chinese navy had been deployed to deliver medical supplies, food, clean water, and infrastructure, along with doctors, administrators, advisors, and security to help the United States get back on its feet after a coronal mass ejection had destroyed America's infrastructure. These reports were even confirmed by some American government officials and multi-billion and trillion-dollar business CEOs who repeatedly thanked the Chinese government for their help in the matter. Despite the reassurances that help was on the way, no one in the States had seen the first sign of disaster relief from any government, not until a year after the blackout.

What, in fact, had happened was rather different from what official news reported.

America had become a plutocracy. It was run by a group of corrupt oligarchs who cared nothing for rights or representative government, and they controlled every aspect of American policy. Regardless of what the people voted for, the machine kept moving in its predetermined trajectory, which was designed to dismantle America one step at a time. Nearly one-hundred-fifty years of radical activists infiltrating the universities and cultural institutions had turned them into pure anti-American propaganda mills stamping out true believers in their global utopian vision of the future. To succeed in academia, one had to show true faith and allegiance to the vision. As a result, almost every graduate was a member of the party that sought the destruction of Western Civilization. The credentials obtained from these institutions, however, were still considered the best measurement of qualification for a career in fields such as entertainment, journalism, law, military leadership, and government. The radicals rapidly overwhelmed and transformed every sector they entered to benefit themselves and their agenda, and they weaponized the institutions to punish those stupid, evil, backward, unwashed masses who did not wholeheartedly support their anointed vision. They knew they were smarter and more virtuous than everyone else, and they wanted unchallenged power to force their will on the world and get rich doing it. They blatantly flouted their own rules, but rules were for little people; they were above such things.

They considered themselves citizens of the world. As such, they had no loyalty to any particular country, least of all to the United States, which they saw as uniquely evil. On the contrary, they envisioned a world in which there were no sovereign nations, no borders, no rights, no representation, no checks on their decrees, only a global market that funneled money to them and a meek and compliant global underclass for them to rule in perpetuity. Patriotism was an outdated form of intolerance that got in the way of their vision, so they ran massive propaganda campaigns to discredit their opposition, equate patriotism with bigotry, and silence the dissidents. They made deals with other nations, giving away tax money to foreign adversaries, exporting American jobs to countries that employed slave labor to produce artificially cheap products.

The elites paid off politicians and judges, bought government bureaucrats, and kept the government's policies directed toward a globalist vision wherein they would get richer at the expense of everyone else. They imposed higher taxes on American businesses than any other country, and they imposed crippling regulations that made it increasingly impossible to do business in the United States. The taxes were not to provide revenue for the government, nor were the regulations intended to protect the environment or the safety of workers and customers, only to keep American businesses from being competitive. They sponsored radical activist groups to intimidate and harass their opponents, and the activists made their role into a religion, thinking they were fighting the system on behalf of the disenfranchised, never realizing the fact that they were nothing more than puppets for the powerful. They drove up the national debt with out-of-control spending and printed valueless currency to hand out to their constituents, keeping them dependent on the establishment. Unemployment went up as workers chose welfare over wages and businesses moved to other countries. It had no negative impact on the ruling class—their jobs were secure. They had tenure, tax-payer funding, tax law loopholes they designed themselves, and global markets for their products made outside of the country. Only their competition would suffer from their actions, and gradually, they would all go out of business, leaving the anointed oligarchs with untouchable monopolies. When the United

States collapsed, they would simply pick up and move. They wanted to be rich and powerful; they didn't care which part of the world they did it in.

Meanwhile, no one employed slave labor like the Chinese Communist Party. China had been an empire of slaves for thousands of years. They controlled every aspect of their society with an iron fist, spying on their citizens, and disposing of dissidents as soon as they exposed themselves. Within a few short years of being brought into the global market, they deployed their massive population to take over manufacturing of the world's products. Apart from food production, manufacturing was, and always would be, the most consequential aspect of any economy, and a decade into the twenty-first century, China owned the world's manufacturing. Along with their slave labor working for next to nothing, they maintained lower taxes than Western nations and almost no environmental regulations at all, making it nearly impossible to produce products anywhere else. But if they wanted to rule over a global empire, they would have to become completely self-sufficient.

China had a fifth of the world's population, and feeding such a population required enormous quantities of grains, vegetables, and meat, which in turn, required vast tracts of farmland—something China did not have. There were pockets of good farm ground all over the world—Africa, South America, the Middle East, the Asian Steppe, etcetera—and China gradually expanded their influence into these regions to gain the territory, but none was big enough to supply the needs of the Chinese empire. Ukraine, the breadbasket of Europe, was out of the question, as they had learned enough from history to know they had no desire to get into a conflict with Russia. For such a task, they would have to look at North America, and specifically, the United States, which had the highest quality, and greatest quantity, of farmland on the planet, not to mention some of the largest deposits of coal, oil, natural gas, timber, rivers, lakes, minerals, and metals anywhere in the world. There was no choice but to take it.

Since the collapse of the Soviet Union, America had been in an increasingly rapid decline—culturally, militarily, economically. Even their average intelligence levels were dropping along with their below-replacement birthrate. They had to import low-wage workers from Central America, not only to provide cheap labor and captive voters for the oligarchs, but also to keep their population afloat. The largest migration of people in human history moved unchecked over their southern border and increasingly flooded the country with drugs, gangs, and human traffickers smuggling child prostitutes and labor slaves to send money out of the country. The oligarchs knew that America could not be invaded by a military force, but in their weakness, Americans would do nothing to stop an invasion of unarmed civilians. So, to conquer the nation, they would send their forces with women and children, armed not with weapons, but with cameras and pitiful looks of desperation. All the weapons in the world were worthless without the will to use them, and Americans would never intentionally use force against what appeared to be unarmed civilian migrants.

More and more people were becoming addicted to drugs, dependent on welfare, and beholden to the government and corporate supply chains for their existence. The American concept of "human rights" grew to include getting everything they wanted for free. The Chinese laughed at the reports from their spies describing the culture of victimhood and hurt feelings in the richest country in history. When Yamamoto attacked Pearl Harbor, he had awakened a sleeping giant, but that was a different country then. That giant was dead now, the Chinese reasoned. All that stood in the way of their conquest of this docile dwarf was the highly advanced technological defense system, but the Chinese had been preparing to deal with that for decades.

Practically everything in the modern age was controlled by computers, and practically every computer was made in

China. Few technologies in the world remained secure from the reach of Chinese spies, and absolutely nothing made in China did. Party members were assigned to every factory in the empire, and they collected the plans and data for the party. While most technologies were invented in America, they were quickly stolen and replicated by the Chinese, so that while America relied on China for its manufacturing, China bought nothing from the Americans except for the agricultural products which they could not produce themselves.

They stockpiled grain for twenty years in preparation for the collapse of their supplier. They made sure that all of the technology the American government relied on was able to be hacked into by party members. They kept track of every American military installation, every carrier group, every submarine, and every satellite. They had spies in every branch of the American government, working as staffers, analysts, and advisors. And they produced hundreds of nuclear weapons fine-tuned for high-altitude burst. Then, they coordinated a full-scale assault on every piece of the American defense system. To pull off the greatest attack in history, they would have to take out everything, their entire defense system, all in a matter of hours.

The American government had known about the threat of electromagnetic pulse since the 1960s, but they did nothing about it because they got paid to take their information from lobbyists pretending to be experts. The lobbyists fed them bogus reports and paid them to keep the issue quiet. The lobbyists were paid by the unions who didn't want an electric grid to be durable enough to withstand a pulse, since that would make it less vulnerable to storm damage, which meant less work fixing the grid, and thus, less money. Everything in America was designed to fail so that someone could make money repairing or replacing it.

Nor was American intelligence oblivious to the Chinese ramping up production of warships or their fast-paced launching of satellites and space missions. Many officials were concerned about the threat of war, but they were assured by the top brass that China was not an enemy. Several of the generals, along with the agency bureaucrats, worked for the communists, being devout believers in the vision. They explained that America needed China, and they couldn't risk provoking war with the largest military on Earth, or the largest economy for that matter. Still, rich donors were fearful of a disruption in the market, so in a meeting with Chinese officials, diplomats expressed their concern and asked what the Chinese were doing. The Chinese, having studied American politics more closely than the Americans did, accused them of being racist. The Americans apologized, begged for forgiveness, and whimpered away from the meeting, having gained no concessions from the Chinese. The Chinese barely tried to keep a straight face as they left the meeting.

Finally, when everything was ready, and when they were sure that the U.S. would not retaliate, they launched a full-scale invasion of Taiwan. The Taiwanese had defied the party for too long, and it was time to bring them to heel. One-million men invaded the island and crushed the rebels in a week. The leaders of their government were publicly executed. The people of Taiwan gathered in the streets to protest, waving American flags and singing the American National Anthem as they took videos on cellphones and streamed them on social media. The social media companies all worked together to block the videos and remove them from their sites, the American media labeled anyone who shared the videos or commented as "racist conspiracy theorists," and all the dissidents of Taiwan were gunned down in the streets. Two million people were murdered, and the rest were rounded up and sent to reeducation camps. The U.S. responded by putting a five percent tariff on soybeans. This was less than twenty percent of the tariffs the Chinese put on all American goods, but the Chinese accused the Americans of starving their people and perpetrating genocide. The tariff was lifted the next day.

When intelligence reports showed that the Chinese were planning a massive attack on the United States, the ultra-wealthy oligarchs and government officials moved whatever money they had in the States and boarded planes to other countries for business trips and world leadership summits. On February Fifth, the Chinese took out the American satellites, hacked into the government computer systems, disabled the nuclear weapons, shut down communication between the fleets and military bases, and from strategically positioned merchant freighters, they launched seven nuclear missiles into the atmosphere over North America. One over Alaska. One over Hawaii. One over Saskatchewan. One over Quebec. One over Ohio. One over Colorado. And one over Mexico City. The warheads all detonated within two seconds of one another, and just like that, all of the United States, and nearly all of North America was without electricity. Five minutes later, three smaller weapons were detonated above South Korea, Japan, and Okinawa. The entire Pacific fleet was offline, and they had got revenge against the Koreans and Japanese in the process.

As soon as the success of their operation was confirmed, they moved to set up blockades around the Japanese islands and the Korean peninsula. Three days later, they had their warships in place, and no one would dare to challenge the Chinese Navy. Upon the completion of phase two, they deployed three quarters of their naval ships to blockade the United States. In two weeks, the North Koreans had taken Seoul, and the Chinese had successfully cut off any movement into or out of North America. They controlled everything from the Panama Canal to the Bering Strait and the Davis Strait. Then, they waited.

The American military deserted in droves. With no communication, they couldn't get orders, and the stockpiles of food quickly ran out. The service members began leaving the bases within the first few days. By the end of the first month, only the married military members who lived in base housing remained. A month later, most of them had left in search of their families. Rather than run humanitarian missions to try to supply their fellow Americans, most of the commanding generals hoarded the food, water, and medical supplies, justifying their decisions by categorizing the military as a high-priority, essential service that would be needed to reestablish order when the country came back online.

Within two months, the Japanese islands, which relied entirely on imported food to feed their population, suffered more than fifty percent casualties from starvation. Within three months, South Korea was under North Korean control, the dissidents had been executed or sent to reeducation camps, and the death rate in Japan was over eighty percent. By May, more than half of all people living above the 45th parallel in North America had died from exposure, hypothermia, and frostbite, and another twenty percent had succumbed to hunger, sickness, and violence. Seeing that the United States was no longer a concern, Iran detonated a nuclear warhead forty miles above Israel, taking out their infrastructure. They invaded a week later.

The elite members of the United States government, who had turned a blind eye to the imperialist expansion of China for the sake of increasing profits, saw the Chinese ascendency as inevitable, so they reasoned that, since they could not beat them, and didn't want to, it was better to join with the Chinese Communist Party and retain their wealth and position. From day one, they worked with the Communist Party to promote the humanitarian efforts of the Chinese on the world stage, pushing to silence dissidents, and advocating for the adoption of the Chinese currency as the official currency of the world. They were rewarded with billion-dollar contracts and positions within the Chinese empire, and they enjoyed their mansions, thousand-dollar meals, yachts, and private jets.

In June, the Russians invaded Ukraine, and the U.S. military commanders in Europe, having no orders from their government, erred on the side of caution, refusing to be the cause of World War III, and they surrendered their positions, abandoned their posts, and left the bases along with all their equipment in the hands of the Russians. The Russians launched a full assault on Eastern Europe, and by the end of June, Russia had taken Ukraine. By September, they had conquered Estonia, Latvia, Belarus, Moldova, and Georgia. Russia was welcomed into the European Union, and the headquarters was immediately moved to Moscow. Since the collapse of the American Empire, the European countries had lost nearly all of their defense funding and economic subsidies. They printed fiat currency to fund their social welfare programs, causing hyperinflation. When their economies collapsed, they became entirely dependent on Russia for their economic sustainment. The European Union turned into a conglomeration of vassal states for Russia in a matter of weeks.

Countries which had relied on the United States' foreign aid now lined up to beg China for subsidies, and they signed over the rights to their natural resources to get them. China had embassies in every country on Earth, and most of those countries were on the Chinese dole. Mandarin became the official business language of the world when it was mandated for airports. The countries scrambled to impose mandatory Mandarin language courses and conform to the new standards.

One year after the high-altitude electromagnetic pulse over North America, casualties in the United States were estimated to be over ninety percent. After fifty-three weeks of maintaining the blockade around North America, the Chinese military launched their invasion of the United States. Four-million men, ten-thousand tanks, fifty-thousand armored vehicles, one-hundred-thousand trucks, five-hundred unmanned aerial vehicles, one-thousand helicopters, and three-hundred jets were deployed from a fleet of five-hundred military transport ships. With precise communication and coordinated timelines, they simultaneously landed forces in Boston, New York, Annapolis, Norfolk, Charleston, Savannah, Jacksonville, Miami, and New

Orleans as well as several port cities on the West Coast from Vancouver and Seattle down to San Francisco and San Diego. It was the largest amphibious invasion in history. They slowly worked their way inland from the coasts as transport ships moved up the Mississippi River toward St. Louis, where they unloaded two-million troops and accompanying equipment to divide the country in two. They assembled their forces in massive multi-division lines on either side of the river and pushed in both directions, creating two simultaneous subcontinental double envelopments.

Learning from the Americans' experience in Vietnam and Afghanistan, the military was ordered to clear the land of inhabitants, leaving nothing alive except the livestock and wildlife. They had no use for the people, only the natural resources. Even with such a massive force, it would take years to completely secure the vast expanse of the former United States, a land area roughly twice the size of the Roman Empire. Once the task was completed, however, they planned to import almost half of their population to North America to farm the land and supply the empire. Seven-hundred-million Chinese subjects would be shipped to North America to replace the erased population, and absolutely nothing but an act of Almighty God would stop the Chinese Communist Party's empire of slaves from establishing unchallenged hegemony over the entire world until the end of time.

CPSIA information can be obtained
at www.ICGtesting.com
Printed in the USA
BVHW081933100122
625917BV00005B/229